1814

1814

BY

CRAIG GODFREY

When True Love Triumphs in the End

www.penmorepress.com

Address all correspondence to:
Penmore Press LLC
920 N Javelina Pl
Tucson AZ 85748

DEDICATION

For Libby
Love triumphs.

ACKNOWLEDGEMENTS

Tales of Tasmania by Coultman Smith, *Corruption and Skulduggery* by Alison Alexander, *Victims of Tyranny* by Brendan Whiting, *1788* by David Hill, *The Bay Whalers* by Michael Nash, *Sea Wolves and Bandits* by L. Norman, *Joshua Barney* by Louis Arthur Norton, *The Burning of Washington* by Anthony S. Pitch, *Floating Brothel* by Sian Rees, *Australia's Birth Stain* by Babette Smith, *The Rocks* by Grace Karskens and *Launceston* by John Reynolds.

Prologue

1812-1814.

The Colonial Americans and England—under the reign of King George the Third and his son the Prince Regent—had been at loggerheads since the American Revolutionary War, when the Colonials won their Independence, in 1783.

The new, young country planned expansion but had border disputes with the British colony of Canada. The British objected to any expansion. They fought back by restricting the United States' trade by blockading shipping— especially as America was trading with Britain's enemy, France—and also encouraging Canada and the indigenous peoples to wage war against the colonies wherever possible.

But Britain was locked in a long and bitter conflict with France under Napoleon Bonaparte. Britain had neither the ships nor the men to take on the Americans in a full-scale war—not yet, anyhow. They seized American merchant ships, taking the vessels as prizes and confiscating the cargo. The sailors on board were pressed into the Royal Navy and forced to fight for Britain while Britain built up its strength in the area, including the building of a British base on Tangier Island, in the middle of Chesapeake Bay.

Now pressured, the Americans fought back, taking on the most powerful navy in the world. They issued Letters of Marque, which made it legal for American privateers to capture British merchant vessels. There was a fine line between privateering and piracy. War was imminent.

President Madison established a patriot army of two thousand army regulars and ten thousand reserves: militiamen. These men were ill trained. Indeed many in the senate thought the British would not attack Washington anyhow. But then, on June 18th, 1812, President Madison signed a declaration of war against Britain, as voted by Congress; however, the House and Senate were angrily divided on the issue. The divide fell between the Western and Southern congressmen who supported the war and the Federalists—New Englanders who relied heavily on trade with Britain.

At first the Americans dragged their feet. They were complacent—until the Royal Navy's Admiral George Cockburn arrived from Bermuda in the spring, following North America's bitter winter, with the Washington capitol in his sights.

However, the British were unfamiliar with the territory, and struggled with the adversarial tides and winds in the Patuxent wetlands. But, as the summer advanced, so did the British, although the heat unsettled them, especially as they were ill-prepared for it in their redcoat uniforms of thick wool.

By late August, they had managed to land five thousand troops at Benedict, in Maryland. Here, they encountered an American warrior, Commander Joshua Barney, a well-known, yet and respected enemy of Britain. At his side, Barney had a true friend in ship's surgeon Rowan Craige, himself a reluctant hero. Unfortunately, these two men— — their bravery in the face of death unquestionable— - were overpowered by sheer numbers. The red coats finally marched on Washington.

Poorly defended, Washington soon fell to the British, who torched the public buildings, including the president's home, The White House.

The war culminated with the signing of a treaty in the neutral country of Belgium, at Ghent, on September 11th, 1814. Lands conquered on both sides were to be returned and boundaries between Canada and the United States were settled.

But before then...

PART ONE
DOWNHILL PATH
ELIZABETH EVELEIGH

CHAPTER ONE

February 1814.
England. Bristol to Newgate.

It was a typically cold February evening in Bristol. The misted River Avon cast a drizzling sleet on the slate grey cobbles of Fishponds Road, making them shiny as glass and perilous for any careless horseman.

Sixteen-year-old Elizabeth Eveleigh was nervous. She feared for her wellbeing, pressured into a life of crime she wanted no part of, forging the King's coin—the lower denomination sixpence. This, in the eyes of the laws of England, amounted to treason. The punishment for such a crime was death.

Elizabeth stared at the kitchen table. They had completed eight coins, shiny from the mould, all copied from the same master coin featuring old King George's profile gazing off into the future, complete with a laurel wreath upon his head and his extra chins and jowls.

Theophilus Brand stepped out from behind undergarments drying on a line near the cottage fire. He shoved Elizabeth in the back.

'Wake up girl,' he grumbled. Theophilus was the mastermind of this dangerous pursuit. A vulgar man, he was thin as a lash, six foot, bony and gaunt with an aquiline nose, hollow eyes and jaws like a rabbit trap. When he was not plagued by arthritis he found entertainment in lascivious pursuits. He was in his late fifties.

'Sixty even,' Elizabeth thought. 'Who knew? Who cared?

'Get yer ear to the door like I told yer.' The second shove saw Elizabeth to the cottage's front door. She listened. There was not much activity in Fishponds Road this night. The rain had stopped but the streets were icing over and, if it wasn't for the smelting on the fire, the cottage would be icy too.

They worked by the light of one lantern and the illumination of the open-hearth fire, where the crucibles filled with melted tin smoked in a melding stink of nauseous smoke. Elizabeth felt her head ache from the pungent fumes trapped beneath the low beamed ceiling in the confined space and from the tense moods of her company. Little was said, as the adjoining walls of cottages and dwellings of the Bristol slum were infested, not only by rats, disease and cockroaches, but with the ears and eyes of the curious, who would fetch the night watchman at the drop of a hat— anything to gain a few shillings reward and put bread on their table.

Theophilus returned to the kitchen bench, where Tempess Green, his bed companion and partner in crime, mulched a piece of bread dunked in ale, along with a lump of melted cheddar, from one gum to the other. The fifty-year-old woman had lost most of her teeth to decay, and eating was not the pleasure it had been ten years earlier.

Together they waited for the crucible of tin to liquefy. Tempess meanwhile rubbed a forged coin between forefinger and thumb with cork wrapped in smooth scouring paper. It was best that Tempess manage this chore, as Theophilus had the hands of a cobbler. His hands were leathery and scarred from needlework, but making and mending shoes was nowhere near as lucrative as forgery. Theophilus's experienced eye gauged the malleable and ductile contents of the crude pottery cauldrons of crystalline, silvery-white metal. Elizabeth watched the fire from the cottage door. She had learned that tin melted at lower temperatures than other metals, like bronze.

Elizabeth smacked her cracked lips; her mouth was parched from the metallic acridity of the fire with its smoking crucibles. Theophilus sensed Elizabeth's eye and turned slowly to acknowledge her innocent attentions with a salacious smile. He wet his own cracked lips with his lizard-like tongue and shot a snake eye to Tempess, to confirm that his lecherous thoughts had gone unnoticed by his mistress. Elizabeth looked away, only to profile her petite young body in Lucifer's light. The glowing coals accentuated her pert, upturned breasts, further arousing the forger. Tempess remained oblivious.

''Tis almost done.' Theophilus's voice rasped as he regarded the smoking pot. He coughed and cleared his throat, but it was too dry to spit.

'Pass me ale,' he demanded, his voice low and croaky. Elizabeth filled his stone mug with ale from a half-gallon pitcher. It was hot, thirsty work; they were running low on ale and the excuse to fetch a refill from the nearby inn cheered her. She stepped up with the two-handled mug and her uncle received her hospitality by taking both Elizabeth's hands in his own mitten scratchers, allowing his fingers to tinkle Elizabeth's in the playful manner of a serial libertine. Elizabeth caught the fetor from his unwashed body. The man always stank, but tonight's efforts over the fire made the stench intolerable. With one eye on Tempess and one eye sparkling with lewd thoughts, the man took the refreshment and drank greedily, as Elizabeth pulled away abruptly and returned to listen at the door.

1814

Echoed hooves of a passing horse put the three on guard. They waited in stony silence. The cause for alarm finally passed and Theophilus lifted the metallic liquid from the coals with long iron tongs borrowed from Benjamin Undercliff, the blacksmith, a fortnight earlier. Tempess stood well clear as the crucible was swung with care to the kitchen table, where a mould had been prepared in a pottery pipkin. The pipkin held the wet, coarse sand that was used to make an impression of the real sixpence, first one side and then the other. When this was done, the pores of the coarse sand were filled with finer sand, which was dried over the fire. When set, the casts were filled with melted tin. Aqua fortis, a highly corrosive mineral acid, was added to bring the silver to the surface. The two halves were then joined together. When the coin was hardened, Tempess would file the edges and polish the surface with smoothing paper and cork. It was a laborious yet profitable business, but the threat of capital punishment hung like a mortician's pall about the smoky room.

Elizabeth wiped her sweating brow and refilled their three stone mugs. Outside might be chilly, but the locked cottage was becoming claustrophobic and oppressive. Tempess fanned the freshly poured coin with a wooden paddle and snatched the mug from Elizabeth with an ungrateful scowl. She swallowed the contents with a voracious thirst, wiped her mouth on her sleeve and belched a grunt at Elizabeth for a refill.

Elizabeth could barely conceal her contempt for the old crone. 'It's all gone.'

What Theophilus saw in the woman Elizabeth could only guess, but the baying and snorts from their shared cot at night left little to the imagination. Tempess glared at Elizabeth with her cold, black and always angry eyes. 'All gone? Then go fill the bloody thing.'

'I need sixpence.'

Tempess spat on a recently completed coin, clasped in her grubby fingers; the dirt under her nails was filthy and as black as the coals in the hearth scuttle. She rubbed the sixpence clean on her smock and handed it to Elizabeth. Theophilus hissed in a silent rage, 'Are you mad, woman?' He snatched the coin.

'Wha'?'

'Ya don't shit in ya own bed. Satan's blood, yer a bigger fool than I thought.'

Tempess withdrew like a slug back into a shell and Elizabeth did little to disguise her smile.

'Bah!' The hag's face reddened.

Theophilus fished in a leather pouch plucking a real sixpence, minted at the Tower Mint, and handed it to Elizabeth. 'Here. And talk to no one, ya hear?'

Tempess craned an ear. 'Wait!' The three listened.

Somewhere in the distance a dog barked, followed by the strains of a poorly played fiddle. The faint sound of merriment continued. The door at the nearby Pig and Wheel Inn opened and closed and a knot of loud, inebriated voices could be heard down the street, coming towards them. It was late, and drunks with emptied purses stumbled by. Suddenly, there was a bang against the cottage door. The three counterfeiters froze. It was a definite thump, not a knock. Theophilus, his face masked with firelight, held a finger to his lips, but there was no need. Tempess and Elizabeth dared not move a limb.

They waited.

Laughter followed the sound of trickling urine against their door. Elizabeth cast an eye over the kitchen table. If the constables came knocking now, she would be a dead woman, for the complete forger's tool kit lay before her—moulds, cork, pliers, crucibles, phial of aqua fortis, crude lumps of tin, brass scales, a pottery jar of white arsenic and a small pile of freshly minted sixpences.

The pissing stopped; there was more laughter. Then silence returned, as the men moved on. Theophilus took the key from his pocket and carefully, measuredly, opened the door. He stepped over a puddle and into the chill. The road to the inn was clear. Theophilus peered back up the street towards the medieval market hall at the crossroads a hundred yards in the opposite direction. There was no one about—no one foolhardy enough to remain outdoors on such a frosty night. Only the muffled gaiety of the fiddler and the cloaked laughter of revellers in the taproom disturbed the darkness.

'Go!' Theophilus jerked his head towards the inn. Elizabeth threw her shawl over her shoulders and hurried towards the Pig and Wheel with the empty pitcher slung from her hand. The cottage door locked behind her. If she had money, Elizabeth would have kept walking—walking through the city gates and away from Bristol. But Elizabeth had nothing but the clothes on her back, an empty pitcher and a sixpence. Elizabeth walked close to the planked wooden cottages on the opposite side of the street, careful to keep under the eaves, in case someone emptied their night bucket out the window. But most occupants of this neighbourhood, factory workers from the cotton mill or dockside labourers, retired early, unable to afford to burn their few candles. Besides, burying oneself deep beneath the blankets on cold nights took one's mind off hunger.

Elizabeth wondered briefly if she might scrounge a lardon or a slice of cold meat from the inn. Sometimes the innkeeper's kindly wife would spare her a titbit when she fetched her guardian's beer. Elizabeth felt her stomach rumble at the thought. It had been eight hours since she'd shared a bowl of pudding Tempess had boiled on the fire; the pudding had been tasty enough, made from flour, water and fat, rolled into balls and dropped into boiling water with some herbs and salt. There was never enough. The chill air cleared her head. When, somewhere, a baby cried, Elizabeth's thoughts went to her mother.

Elizabeth's mother, Charlotte Compton, had told her daughter, on occasion, how she had moved from Barnsley, in Yorkshire, to Bristol, where she'd hoped to better her life, as a seamstress. But good fortune had deserted her. She met a swank young man, Edward Eveleigh, at the Sword and Flag Inn. The rakish fast-talker told Charlotte he was a professional gambler. They married three months later. Within a week of their wedding, Charlotte was summoned to Bristol Watch House, where she was to farewell her husband: 'Caught with a gentleman's watch up his sleeve.' Charlotte learnt her gambler was really a pickpocket. Edward was taken to London and sentenced to hang, but this was later commuted to fourteen years of Transportation to Port Jackson, on the other side of the world.

Elizabeth was born eight months later.

The year was 1798. Charlotte had good intensions of bringing Elizabeth up as a lady. At the very least, Charlotte taught Elizabeth the manners of a lady and insisted that she *talk proper*. Charlotte struggled to survive, but she was a resilient woman, resisting the temptations to prostitute her body or drown her woes in gin. She found employment at a Bristol pottery factory, where she was exposed to lead glazing, year after year. She died of lead poisoning at the age of thirty, when Elizabeth was ten.

After two years in an orphanage, Elizabeth had been employed as a maidservant in the home of a watchmaker, Isaiah Moses. At first, her new home was a happy one. The family of six accepted Elizabeth, and Mrs. Moses taught

Elizabeth the ways of a lady. Only the cook, Mrs. Mattey, made life difficult for her. Then, two years later, in 1812, Mrs. Moses died from lung fever. The household fell into disarray. Isaiah Moses became more and more dependent on the bottle. The two oldest children left home—Sarah married a soldier and Rodney left for a position in a law firm in Plymouth. The fourteen-year-old twins were left to their own devices mostly, as Moses fell into the dark world of Madam Gin.

Mrs. Mattey had had enough. She walked out, leaving fifteen-year-old Elizabeth to run the household.

Elizabeth had grown to trust the father figure in her lonely life, so Isaiah Moses's advances had been as unexpected as they were savage. The incident took place in the early evening. Elizabeth was in the kitchen. Moses grabbed her from behind, his lust fuelled by loneliness, a sense of ownership and Dutch Geneva. Elizabeth had heard tales of men's inveterate desires, but was ill equipped to handle the situation. Isaiah's manhood protruded from his loosened britches, pink and red, threatening.

''Mr. Moses...' she pleaded. But his arousal was beyond retreat, his cheeks bloated and red, his face sweaty from carnal expectations. Isaiah hoisted Elizabeth's skirts, groping her breasts from behind, his firmness hard against her body.

'No!'

What happened next was born of pure instinct for survival. But in the eyes of the law, Elizabeth was nothing more than a wanton whore. She snatched a cleaver from the bench, swinging it behind her. The blade missed her attacker's manhood by less than an inch, but the blade buried deep in Moses's thigh. He cried out. He wailed in pain. Elizabeth had never seen so much blood. Terrified at what she had done, Elizabeth dropped the clever and ran from the house as the twins rushed towards their father's pleas for help.

Elizabeth spent the night on the streets. She knew no one, had no money and was now a felon. She walked to the docks, where she met twelve-year-old Jimmy Tegg, a streetwise tyke she came to trust, because of his youth. Jimmy tried to convince Elizabeth that whoring was good and easy money. He knew of a pimp who would take her under his wing. Elizabeth, however, knew better. She would rather beg... or steal if she had to.

'Then steal we will,' said Jimmy Tegg, clearly a young hand at an ancient profession.

Virginia Street was a street of small shops and cheap lodgings. 'Easy pickin's if'n we're careful, like.' Following Jimmy's brazen example, Elizabeth accompanied her new acquaintance into a lodging house. On the first floor Elizabeth found a bedroom door ajar, and, against her better judgement, she entered the empty room, snatching a pair of women's shoes and a silver-and-tortoise-shell comb from a chest of drawers. Meanwhile, downstairs, Elizabeth heard shouting. Jimmy was being pursued, escaping the building with an apple cake from the kitchen. Elizabeth, however, was trapped—caught red-handed. She was locked under the stairs and Constable Stanford Myers was summoned.

Good fortune, however, played one last card for Elizabeth. Constable Myers was a Jew who saw the good side of Elizabeth. For one thing, *she spoke proper.* As she was young, she was taken to his parish and presented before Mabel Myers, the constable's older sister, who ran a parish orphanage for older girls. Within a year, Elizabeth had been taken into the household in Fishpond Road, where she now lived with Theophilus Brand and Tempess Green.

It was not long before the more sinister side of her benefactors'—or malefactors'?—character reared its ugly head and, with nowhere to go, Elizabeth had no choice but to become party to Theophilus and Tempess's nefarious activities.

A year later...
Elizabeth crossed Fishponds Road to the Pig and Wheel Inn. Frost had settled on the thatch and icicles adhered to the vertical black and white boards like melted candle wax. The solid oak door was hefty, more a fortification than a portal. Elizabeth hoed her shoulder into the door and entered. The tobacco-stained walls of the taproom complimented the spectre of pipe smoke and the airless fug trapped in a room of imbibers, who were happy to share the windowless room, away from Jack Frost. With the door open, fustiness escaped, and the nearest patrons turned their heads to a portrait of sweet innocence. Elizabeth kept focussed. Head down, she shoved past the lascivious smirks and wanton crude comments fuelled by cheap gin, and made the counter in quick, measured steps. Elizabeth had learnt to ignore the groping. She ignored the gnarly hands of wishful suitors, most with the intention of a three-penny hump against the alleyway wall. Innkeeper Lurlie Pepper was no different. He ran a canny eye over the empty pitcher in Elizabeth's hand.

''Aving a few late ones with Theo tonight, huh?' The innkeeper was sweaty and portly from triple helpings of his own inn fare, usually stewed fatty mutton, the fattier the better, and potatoes. Elizabeth said nothing. She pushed the sixpence through a pool of stale ale and wiped her hand on her smock. The fat man took the pitcher. He pumped vigorously and the half-gallon jug filled smartly from a lead pipe leading up from the cellar.

'Well?' the innkeeper said over his shoulder, 'The cat got ya tongue?'

'He's working late on a pair of boots for Captain Treadway,' Elizabeth lied.

'Oh is 'e now?' Pepper drew the ale short, at an inch from the lip. Elizabeth's fabrication was a gamble, as Captain Treadway, a retired soldier, lived only a mile away, and it was a risk that he might visit the Pig and Wheel this night, but it was all Elizabeth had, at short notice.

'A nice pair o' boots, eh? For our Cap'n Treadway?' The innkeeper placed the pitcher before Elizabeth and took her hand before she had a chance to draw it away. 'Ya know ya can always come 'ere an work for me, lovey, eh?'

He ran his tongue across his bottom lip. Elizabeth tried to pull her hand free but the innkeeper's grip was strong. 'You could earn half a guinea 'ere every night.' Pepper treated himself to an eyeful of breast. 'Or does yer think yer too good for the Wheel, huh?' Mrs. Pepper appeared from the scullery and Elizabeth tore her hand free.

'Would be easy, lovey.' These words of wisdom came along with a roaming hand behind Elizabeth. The assailant groped her buttock. Doing it tough on the streets of Bristol had taught Elizabeth one thing: act fast. She turned on her assailant. Her right leg swung back, bent at the joint and she slammed her knee into the man's crotch. His cry silenced the taproom. Heads turned.

'You would do well to keep your filthy scratchers to yourself,' she said, fetching up the pitcher.

'Ya bitch.' The assailant's hand swung in a closed fist. Elizabeth jerked her head sideways and felt the knuckles breeze by her cheek. She had stepped backwards to defend herself when the crowd parted, and a uniform of the guard stepped in to face the brute. The scuffle was short. The assailant's arm was thrust up his back and the guard held the aggressor against the wall.

'What's it to be, Jeffrey? Night in the cells?' Clearly, the two were acquainted.

'Go bugger yourself, Marcus.'

'I don't think so. I've warned you before about touchin' the ladies.'

'Ladies!' Jeffrey spat on the floor. 'Thuy's nothin' but whores in 'ere and you know it.'

'Apologise.'

'Apologise fa what? Fa touchin' a whore?' He seemed to consider taking on the soldier, but there were other uniforms in the room. The guard wrenched the man's arm by the wrist to his shoulder blade. He cried out in pain.

'Yer a tough bastard when yer got yer mates with yer, eh?'

'Apologise.'

'Alright, alright. Jesus Lord. I apologise.'

'Louder. Say it louder.' This humiliation was almost as painful as the hold on his arm.

'Firk! Aye. I apologise!' the man wheezed loudly.

Elizabeth said nothing. She collected the jug and, focussing on the front door, she walked through an aisle of sniggering drinkers. The guard followed her onto the cobbles, pulling the red military coat of a British soldier over his shoulders. He caught up with Elizabeth under a lone street lamp and Elizabeth had a moment to study the sturdy sergeant—recognisable by the three stripes sewn to his red coat, which was festooned with aiguillettes, white leather braid and polished brass buttons. He pulled a feathered shako onto his head and straightened the sword at his side. The clean-shaven, redheaded man was baby-faced, making him appear younger than he was.

'Here.' He made to take the pitcher. 'Let me carry that for you... You can't be going far, I would assume.' Elizabeth stared into his sharp green eyes. She felt as if he could read her mind. He was certainly tall and handsome, with a toned body, to boot.

Elizabeth pulled the jug out of his reach. 'I can look after myself, you know.'

'Oh, I don't doubt that for a moment.' He stepped in front of her. Elizabeth made to step aside but, annoyingly, he stepped once again into her path. 'Marcus Marriot at yer service, miss.'

'Fine,' Elizabeth said, exasperated. 'Now, if you do not mind...'

But the guard did mind. 'And you are?' he asked.

Elizabeth had a flash thought that the man's advances might signify he was flexing his authority and not the playful courting she had first imagined. 'Elizabeth,' she answered, grudgingly. 'Elizabeth Eveleigh.'

'Elizabeth Eveleigh... What a beautiful name.'

Elizabeth allowed the slightest hint of a smile.

'Let me carry that pitcher for you. I do believe I heard you tell the fat innkeeper that you were fetching for the cobbler. We can't be too far now, can we? It would be my pleasure.' He reached once more for the pottery jug.

'No!' Elizabeth said, louder than she'd intended.

Marcus Marriot feigned dismay. 'Why? Do you have something to hide?'

'No... No, I don't. It's... it's just that the cobbler is my guardian and he instructed me to fetch this from the inn and to speak to no one.'

'Then he must care for yer welfare.'

Elizabeth wanted to scream 'He is a monster!' but only said, 'He does.'

'Why, you must be a woman unto yer own. A real lady, no less, by the sound o' yer.' The soldier stepped back a moment, taking in an eyeful of the beauty before him. There was no arguing, this Elizabeth Eveleigh was, indeed, a most beautiful young woman, with her long, hazel hair dropping to her lower back, her clear blue eyes and the long, thin legs he imagined to be hidden under her skirt. 'You said you could look after yourself. How old are you anyway...? Seventeen?'

'Sixteen.'

'Sixteen. Well, then, there you go, Elizabeth. This cobbler, Theophilus, this guardian of yours, has no restraint over you. At least let me see you to your door.'

'"Theophilus," you said. Do you know him?'

'No.'

'But you called him by name.'

The guard's face appeared unguarded. 'I must have heard the innkeeper mention it.'

'Look,' Elizabeth said, 'I do not understand your intentions, sir...'

'Marcus Esquire, at yer service.'

'I do not know your intentions, sir,' Elizabeth persisted, 'but if it is to acquaint yourself with me, I must tell you, here and now, that I am not interested in your advances.'

'My, my, you *are* forward.'

'Me? Forward? You, sir, are the one confronting me.'

'Call me Marcus, please.'

Elizabeth was tempted to become acquainted. The man was keen and that was flattering enough. 'Besides, Marcus,' she said cheekily, 'you are too advanced in years. How old are you, anyway? Thirty?'

'Now *you* are too bold, young lady. I celebrated me twenty-fifth birthday two weeks prior.'

'Twenty-five! There, then—you are an old man.' But Elizabeth knew she was flirting with danger, and if this playful insult didn't work, Elizabeth now worried, how *would* she lose this persistent suitor and make for the safe haven of her cottage?

'Old man, indeed.' Marcus Marriot's tone stiffened. He was not a man used to rejection. 'Very well then, Elizabeth Eveleigh, carry your own jug of ale. You can break a leg, for all I should care.' Elizabeth's face bore a hint of rejection.

'I jest, Elizabeth. I think you are the prettiest lass in the village. Will I see you tomorrow? At the market maybe?'

'Maybe.' Elizabeth felt a flutter in her belly, a flutter she had not felt before.

The soldier then played the oldest ruse in the book by feigning disinterest, for the moment. 'Then it's at the market I shall see yer." He turned sharply on the heels of his polished boots and strode, with a cheerful whistle, back towards the inn.

'What took so long?' Tempess Green stabbed a bony finger into the tenderness of Elizabeth's shoulder blade. Elizabeth planted the jug on the table as Theophilus locked the door with the only key. It turned noisily in the lock and Elizabeth was once again confined in the metallic sour fug. Her claustrophobia returned.

'Well?' Tempess persevered, hammering Elizabeth's skull with two clenched knuckles. Elizabeth winced from the pain but refused to acknowledge any suffering. 'What took ya so long, then? Didn't hike up ya skirt for a quick threepence, did ya?' The hag coughed out a laugh at her own warped humour.

'I was accosted by Jeffrey Smith.'

Theophilus knew the village cooper well. 'So what? You can 'andle yaself.'

Now that Elizabeth was back under Theophilus' roof and felt the weight of responsibility crush her shoulders once more, she contemplated her situation, consorting with forgers. 'There was a soldier of the guard in the taproom, a

Marcus Marriot. He gave Jeffrey a what-for and followed me outside....'

Tempess's eyes narrowed. 'Marcus Marriot! Ya got 'is name then.' She slurped freshly poured ale. ''Ow did ya manage that? Sluttin' about like a trollop?'

'He followed me outside. He tried to make my acquaintance.'

'And?'

'And I told him I was not interested.'

'That's my little Bessie.' Theophilus took the opportunity to hook an arm around Elizabeth's shoulder. 'Ya done good, girl.' The hand slid to Elizabeth's waist before she was able to pull free.

'He knows your name... Theophilus. Are you certain you do not know him, this Marcus Marriot?'

'How does he know me name?'

'He mentioned you—"the cobbler Theophilus." He said he heard Mr. Pepper say your name, but I know he was not in earshot just then. He knew Jeffrey's name also.'

Theophilus's red face whitened. Seriousness washed across him like a sudden fog appearing on the moors. 'Quickly—we need to tidy up. Quick, now.'

Against the north wall of the cottage Theophilus stored his cobblers' collection of shoe lasts—the foot surrogates over which the leather shoes were formed. He snatched up the last for a large man's boot. He twisted the veneered layers of wood at the heel and a hollowed section revealed itself. While he scooped the handful of shiny new sixpences into their hiding place, Tempess slipped the phial of nitric acid into a larger preserving jar and poured a stone crock of pickled onions over the top. The phial vanished. As rehearsed, Elizabeth drew nails from floorboards in the bedroom with a claw hammer and dropped the smoking crucibles, the moulds, various pipkins, jars of sand, cork, paper, and crude tin into a ready-dug pit beneath the cottage foundation. Tempess stoked the fire; the coals flared and crackled as evidence of tin slag disappeared into the ashes. Elizabeth replaced the boards and nails and unrolled her mattress of blankets across the floor where she slept in front of the fire each night. Theophilus positioned the boot last on the kitchen table, which doubled as his workbench. He spread out his materials—heels, soles, tongues, and leather shanks—and gathered about him the awls, hammers, scissors, needles and threads of the cobbler. He pulled his stool close to the table and took in a deep breath. He flipped the lid of his fob watch. It was after nine in the evening. The counterfeiting had been in process since two o'clock in the afternoon. It was time for them to eat supper and relax. *Yes, we should try and relax. It is probably nothing,* he thought to himself, *but we have made preparations for the worst.*

'So, he called me by name... He said "Theophilus"?' the cobbler asked Elizabeth to confirm.

'Yes.'

'Then let's eat some bread, drink our beer and retire for the night.'

Tempess fetched the remains of a bread loaf. Like all residents of Fishponds Road, they purchased bread from the village baker, as only wealthy households could afford an oven and the fuel required to bake their own bread. Elizabeth fetched a jar of pickled vegetables, a lump of cheddar, plates and a knife, placing them on the end of the table. She charged all the mugs with ale, and together they ate in silence, with a nervous eye on the door and an ear to the street.

There was no warning. No polite knock. The cottage door splintered around the lock, shattering on impact; rammed by the breech of a hundred-pound swivel cannon wielded by two soldiers, each gripping a mullion. The noise, the shouting and the sight of redcoats sent fear coursing through the three occupants.

'Up, up! All of you, up.' Marcus Marriot, the sergeant of the First Foot Guards, followed his men into the cottage. He had no qualms about eyeballing Elizabeth. 'The cobbler's niece, huh?' he scowled. 'This cottage stinks like a smelter's shed.'

Elizabeth felt betrayed—violated. She saw, in the lantern light of the cottage, that the man's eyes were evil black orbs, not the green eyes of the handsome redheaded soldier with whom she had flirted earlier. The cold eyes darted about, surveying the room. Instantly a misplaced sixpence, freshly minted, caught Elizabeth's eye. The coin sat, mislaid, on the table, half covered by a lump of cheddar. Tempess saw the angst on Elizabeth's face. She followed her eye, saw the coin and sucked in a gasp of chilly air.

Sergeant Marriot's head snapped about. 'Do we have a problem?'

Tempess shook her head vigorously. 'Problem? Why, nay. Nay, sar.'

Sergeant Marriot stalked the room and, taking a bone and ebony swagger stick from under one arm as if he were a king's officer, he proceeded to jab, trash and defile any object that took his fancy.

'May I ask ya, good sar,' Theophilus asked in a shaking voice that would best have been left to silence, 'wha' exactly you are lookin' for?'

'Don't try me as a fool, Theophilus Brand. You know only too well what I seek, and find it I shall.' He speared one end of the swagger into the cobbler's throat, connecting with the man's goitre. Theophilus gargled a guttural sound. 'I can smell your nefarious activity, cobbler. So, where have you hidden the treacherous evidence?'

'I know nothin' of what ya speak.'

Marriot raised the swagger high above his head and brought the weapon down with a sickening thud against Theophilus's skull. Theophilus wailed. 'No, sar,' he cried in pain, 'please!'

Marriot didn't hesitate. He raised his arm again, as the four soldiers laughed. 'Well?' he screamed in the old man's face.

Elizabeth saw her chance. She stepped aside to avoid the sergeant, pretended to stumble, and her hand darted forward to block her fall. She snatched the sixpence, squeezing it into a lump of cheddar as the swagger struck Theophilus's shoulder. The cobbler screamed again. Elizabeth feigned a cough and threw her hand over her mouth, swallowing the sixpence as she did, but her actions were clumsy.

'Sergeant!' Elizabeth's efforts had been in vain. Marriot poised for another strike. 'Sergeant!'

'What?'

'This one 'ere.' The soldier known as Norton grew bold. He snatched Elizabeth by the collar. 'I seen 'er swallow somethin'.'

'Oh, did you, now?' Marriot rounded on Elizabeth. His eyes narrowed as he stared into her angry blue eyes.

'I ate a piece of cheese,' Elizabeth said defiantly.

'Oh, "I ate a piece of cheese,"' the sergeant mimicked, his face darkening. 'Now, of all the times to be eatin' cheese... or is it me what makes yer hungry, eh?'

Elizabeth felt her chalky white face redden. The sergeant caressed her cheek with the tip of his swagger. Gently at first, but menacing, drawing himself close. Elizabeth smelt his sweat but there was something else—an animal musk she sensed occasionally, about men... men who were aroused.

The swagger stroked Elizabeth's cheek, dropped to her shoulder and rested on her arm while Marriot ran his eyes over her breasts. The room had filled with the night's chill. In the deadly quiet, Elizabeth could hear the heavy breathing of the soldiers.

Marriot's attention was drawn to her slim waist before fixing on Elizabeth's face once more. She held his gaze. 'Yer like cheese?' he finally said, barely in a whisper. 'Is that it? Yer like eatin' cheese?' Teasing. Relishing his authority.

Norton cleared his throat. 'I seen 'er swallow a piece o' cheese sergeant, an' there was somethin' else with it, cos she swallowed 'ard.'

'Hard?'

'Like it were stuck in 'er throat.'

'A coin maybe? A threepence?' Marcus Marriot stepped back and stabbed the point of the swagger into Elizabeth's chest. 'Or a sixpence,' he said angrily, 'like the ones that 'ave been turning up at the markets round Bristol of late?'

'I am an honest cobbler, sir,' Theophilus started. 'I...'

'Shut it!' Marriot commanded.

'It is true, sir,' Tempess pleaded. 'We barely make a livin' 'ere, sir, as yer can see by our 'umble cottage.'

Marriot's eyes were locked on Elizabeth's. 'Ruthers, Jones...' he said, without looking away from her.

'Sergeant.'

'Take the pathetic cobbler and 'is dog to the Watch House,' he ordered. 'Norton and McMillan, search this hovel.'

Elizabeth held the pugnacious soldier's gaze. She knew she had the one asset the man craved—the one asset all men desired—but her mother had taught her virtue, and to be honest to herself.

'Well, Miss Elizabeth Eveleigh,' he said in a softer voice, 'open your mouth.'

'Pardon?'

Behind them, the two remaining redcoats rummaged through the cottage noisily.

'I said, open your mouth... if you please.' Elizabeth obeyed, rewarding Marriot with a tongue scattered with cheesy mulch. 'It appears you *have* partaken of a piece of cheddar.' Elizabeth remained silent. The answer to his question was clearly evident. 'Why, I beseech you, would you decide to embark on a morsel of cheddar when you were about to be interrogated by the King's men?'

'I told yer, Sergeant,' Norton said, 'she swallowed 'ard, she did.'

Sergeant Marriot rounded on the soldier, fixing the man with his venomous black eyes. 'Did I ask you to interfere?' Norton faltered. 'Well? Did I?'

'I... ah... I was only tryin' to 'elp, Sergeant.'

Marriot chewed his tongue a moment. Both soldiers looked to their superior in anticipation. 'Leave us,' Marriot said sullenly.

'Sergeant?'

'Are you deaf? Both o' yer. Leave us. I want answers an' you two ain't 'elpin' none. Leave us. Come back in ten minutes. Go smoke a pipe.'

'Aye, Sarge.'

Norton and McMillan repositioned the damaged front door as best they could and departed, not arguing with the chance to take tobacco.

'Elizabeth,'—Marriot's voice was high now—'tell me the truth and I will see yer not harmed.' He pushed Elizabeth gently towards Theophilus and Tempess's bedchamber, where a soiled, tattered cloth served as a partition.

'Wh-what are you doing?' Elizabeth felt her heart quicken.

'I just told yer, yer won't be harmed, not if'n yer behave yerself and lie with me.' Elizabeth stood firm, but the soldier pushed her through the curtain.

'No!' Elizabeth cried out. 'No, I say... What...?'

'Keep yer mouth shut.' Marriot shoved Elizabeth backwards and she tripped, falling onto the bed. The soldier threw his coat aside and started unbuttoning his britches.

'No!' Elizabeth kicked out.

Marriot jumped onto her writhing body, cupping a hand over her mouth. 'Do yer wanna hang fer treason, huh? Cos that's what forgery o' the king's coin 'll get yer—hanged!'

'Please,' Elizabeth mumbled, through Marriot's fingers tightly clamped over her mouth, 'I beseech you, sir, do not do this.'

But the pleas only aroused the soldier further. With his spare hand, he hoisted Elizabeth skirts and groped about for her womanhood. Elizabeth struggled, but the man was considerably heavier than she and twice as strong. She felt his firmness poking about her undergarments. The musk was overpowering. His face was red and beads of sweat pooled on his forehead. He leaned in to smother her lips with his.

'No!' Elizabeth wailed.

Marriot lifted his arm and slapped Elizabeth hard with an open hand. 'Shut it, yer bitch!'

'No! No!' Elizabeth wrestled beneath his weight. He was breathing heavily, consumed by his lust.

'Keep quiet, yer whore. Who knows, yer may even enjoy it.'

'Get off me!' Elizabeth managed to raise one knee, but that only served for her assailant to part her legs further. He tore her bloomers free and thrust himself into position. 'Sergeant!' Norton's voice travelled in from the street. 'Sergeant?' The damaged door was shoved aside, falling noisily against the inside wall.

'Not now, Norton!' Marriot shouted back from the bedchamber.

'Sergeant Marriot...'

'Jesus Christ!' Marriot rolled off the bed, redressing, incensed at the interruption. 'What the firk?' he raged at Norton.

'Captain Fairbairn wants to see you immediately.'

'Captain Fairbairn? Now?'

'Yes.' Norton snapped to attention as the army captain pushed by him and into the cottage.

'Yes, *now*, Sergeant Marriot,' the captain called back. Forty-four-year-old Fairbairn stood taller than Marriot. On his neck he sported a gnarly scar from the Peninsular Wars, which was further irritated by the brass gorget of authority hanging about his neck.

Marriot revealed himself. Fairbairn stood by the fire, legs apart, with one hand on his sword hilt and the other raising his coattail to warm his backside. 'Do we have a difficult situation here, Sergeant?'

'Situation?' Marriot replied sheepishly. 'Why no, Captain.'

Captain Fairbairn heard a whimper from the bedchamber as Elizabeth tidied her clothing.

'I trust you have been no more than interrogating the prisoner, Sergeant?'

'Sir, I have reason to believe the girl swallowed the evidence.'

'Swallowed the evidence... Interesting. Come out, girl.'

Elizabeth threw the curtain aside. 'This man was assaulting me, sir.'

Marriot turned on Elizabeth. 'I was not.' It would be his word against hers. 'This bitch tried to seduce me...'

'Liar!' Elizabeth screamed.

'She tried to corrupt me—to keep me mouth shut.'

'Lies, all lies. This man was forcing himself upon me.'

'Why, you trouble makin' whore...'

'Enough!' Fairbairn ordered. 'Both of you.'

'Sir,' Elizabeth started, her eyes welling with tears.

'Be quiet,' the captain said sourly. 'Do you think I give a rat's arse about a trollop like yourself?' Fairbairn looked to a smirking Sergeant Marriot and asked, 'She swallowed the evidence, you say?'

'Aye, sir, a sixpence, I'm thinkin'.'

'Then arrest her...'

'No, sir,' Elizabeth pleaded. 'I am innocent. You must believe me. I...'

'Norton and McMillan, are you not?' the officer said to the two soldiers, who were now back in the cottage. 'Take her away to the cells. See that she is not left alone until she passes the coin.'

'Sir?'

'You understand?'

'Aye sir... Until she passes... Sir... ah... it could be some time.'

'Then feed her a laxative. I don't care what you do, but see that she is not left alone until that coin passes. It is King's evidence.

CHAPTER TWO

Over six weeks later. November 1814.
Newgate Prison.

Newgate Prison—a solid stone and brick edifice of austere bleak appearance, challenging those tempting to commit crime, designed to incite fear, in those inside *and* out. The entrance was commanding, as it was tall—the height of three men, Elizabeth thought—and narrow, to prevent rioters passing through from inside or out. The wooden door was a foot thick and plated with iron sheets bolted to the wood with large rounded nuts, not unlike the studded leather collar of a pit-bull.

'Welcome to ya new 'ome ladies.' The hairless gatekeeper was uncommonly jovial for a man suffering from inflamed gums. Most of his yellow ivories appeared loose and the scent of his breath was familiar, like the effluvium rising from a cesspit. He allowed his eyes a generous perusal of the newly arrived prisoners before scrawling a signature on the parchment proffered by the head guard at the prison gate, the very same man who had delivered the prisoners from Bristol, relieving himself of the responsibility. The gatekeeper slammed the door with an ominous echo behind the Bristol guards who were now standing out on Newgate Street.

'Now, you lot,' the gatekeeper said, speaking to the four new prisoners listed on the vellum covered prison register, 'place ya marks 'ere.' Elizabeth took the goose quill, dripping ink, and made her mark—'E. E.'—the way she had been taught by her mother. The gatekeeper dusted the initials dry with chalk dust as Edgar Drake, the turnkey, stepped out with a limp from the prison shadows to inspect his new charge.

'Aye, this is yer new 'ome.' The insidious turnkey salivated involuntarily. Drake had recently enjoyed his fortieth birthday, and by all appearances, he had overindulged every one of them. 'Built thirty year ago, thereabouts, on the site of its 700-year-old predecessor.' The short and bloated guard caught a breath, arched his back with hands on hips and admired the stonework as he rattled on like some guide at the British Museum. 'I 'ope ya got some silver, me lovelies, cos any extras will cost yer.'

The turnkey hustled the small group along a cold, ill-lit passageway to their lodgings, the Felon Women's Quadrangle. 'The Felon Men's Quadrangle is at the rear of the prison.' Drake continued his tour as they walked along. 'An' the Debtor's Quadrangle's on the opposite side of the building. There's no less than four heavily guarded entrances and...'—he made certain he had their attention—'there ain't no chance of escape.'

They arrived at the prison proper, where a stench hung heavily in the air. One of the prison warders unlocked the barred door built into the floor-to-ceiling bars. ''Ere we are, ladies,' the gatekeeper said. 'The Felon Women's Quadrangle.'

Here one hundred fifty women were packed into three cells built to accommodate seventy. And seventy prisoners were all that were rationed for. Any prisoner with hidden coin sewn into the hem of her dress could purchase food, a blanket, maybe, or other types of favours. Others starved. It was truly the abode of the damned, without the fire and brimstone. The fetid putridity of unwashed bodies, the miasma of overfilled waste buckets, the reek of unattended menstrual rags, the abhorrent stink of festering wounds and the odour of the sick and dying made Newgate Prison the most dreaded address in London. And if the fetor was not bad enough, the groans of those so pained or the cries of the indisposed was a constant reminder of man's inhumanity to his fellow human. If ever there was damnation on earth, Newgate Prison was it.

Each of the three cells had a window opening onto an interior wall. There were no beds or bedding, only straw on a flagstone floor. But a ramp at one end of the cell was furnished with a wooden beam fixed to its rise, which functioned as a pillow. Only the strongest and fittest enjoyed this privilege. Elizabeth scanned the sea of misery staring back at her—faces of wretchedness studying her like she was a piece of meat. She felt the lump rise in her throat but fought back the tears and had only one thought... Survival.

Months passed.

Elizabeth had had a lot of time to think. If there was one thing she had plenty of, it was time. She sat squat with her back to the bars, her arms hugging her knees to her chin, and surveyed the dark, miserable corners of her dungeon; for that is what it was, a dungeon shared by hundreds of others.

Elizabeth's thoughts returned to the night of her arrest. The humiliation in the cell at the Fishponds Road Watch House, being forced to drink an *opening medicine* and being constantly under guard until the coin had done the laxative's bidding. When she'd passed the forged sixpence she'd been obliged to fish it from the bucket herself.

King's evidence. Evidence of Treason!

Six weeks had passed without correspondence from the courts. No legal advice, certainly not for an ignorant Bristol girl foolish enough to forge the coin of England—six weeks alone in a tiny cell, with a tiny, barred, unglazed window. She was allowed out one hour a day for exercise and fed on bread and water only, with fatty meat one day of the week. Now Elizabeth had been sentenced by the circuit magistrate to be transferred to London for trial. She recalled the four-day journey, shackled in irons, together with three other women in a cramped prison carriage, forced to sit on the floor amongst the excrement and piss of the other terrified prisoners. Now, three and a half months later in Newgate, she awaited her fate. Her nightmares continued, waking her in a cold sweat in the middle of the night, her screams ignored by those around her. Nightmare visions recurred, of the pious judge with his square of black cloth resting on his wig, staring down grimly from the bench and sentencing her to death by hanging, or, worse still, to be burnt alive at the stake. But at least, these *were* only nightmares...

Elizabeth waited. The weeks turned to months and autumn turned to winter.

Chapter Three

June 1st 1814. Maryland. Chesapeake Bay. Patuxent River.

An attack was imminent, but the patriots under the command of fifty-six-year-old Commander Joshua Barney were prepared with their flotilla: thirteen armed barges, their five-gun cutter flagship *Scorpion*, two gunboats and a galley. With the British advancing, Barney had ordered his flotilla into the shallow waters two miles distant, on Saint Leonard's Creek, off the Patuxent River. Now the enemy had blocked the entrance to the river.

And they waited.

Twenty-eight-year-old ship's surgeon Rowan Craige took up his spyglass. He studied the menacing Union Jacks atop their mastheads, where they barely showed over the treetops of the marshland, drooping like washing in the still air and the oppressive heat. These were anxious times.

And all they could do was wait.

Commander Barney watched his friend a moment. Finally, he interrupted the racket of the cicadas, which was amplified over the still water. 'That's the seventy-four-gun HMS *Dragon*—and two other warships,' he said of the distant ships.

The surgeon lowered the glass and sighed.

'They also have fifteen barges, one a rocket barge.'

'What is your plan?' Rowan asked out of the crew's earshot.

'For the moment, we wait on the tide.'

Rowan was familiar with warfare. He had spent some time at sea with Commander Barney; the two men, despite their age difference, had become close friends. With the tide in their favour, Rowan had time for more pleasant thoughts. For one, his wife of three years, Jessica, was finally with child.

Forever the romantic, Rowan treasured Jessica's presence and valued their time together more than time itself. Twenty-three-year-old Jessica York—whose large topaz blue eyes never ceased to enchant the ship's surgeon—was blessed with smooth, pale skin and a petite slender figure. Rowan adored the woman, from her cascading long blonde curls to her tireless good humour and generosity. And pregnancy suited Rowan's wife. She was radiant and happy and in great health -- she was perfect. There was not a man in Baltimore who would not wish to court her. The two were in love, hopeless captives of Cupid's arrow.

Jessica, for her part, was stimulated by their conversations, over the dinner table or across the pillow. They shared a passion for politics and were both staunch patriots. And Jessica praised Rowan for his professional dedication, which showed in his constant study of the latest medical journals and tireless compassion towards his fellow man. Rowan's good looks—with his fair-hair, green eyes and athletic six-foot figure—was but a bonus. And although Rowan Craige's career as a ship's surgeon saw him at sea for months at a time, they were fiercely faithful, dedicated to one another like doves—mates for life.

Rowan and Jessica had married three years earlier, once Rowan had completed his medical studies at Pennsylvania Hospital, America's first hospital. Jessica's father, a fur trader, spent much of his time away, buying skins in Fort Astoria, Oregon. This absence had accustomed the women of Jessica's family to the continuing absence of their men. Her eleven-year-old brother James and a black servant, Charry, were the only males in a household of nine.

Jessica's siblings and her mother, Sophia, adored the doctor in their lives. He was a father figure to them. However Jessica's father, Silas York, was pig-headed and fervidly protective of his daughters. He was a powerfully built man and dangerous to cross, drunk or sober. Rowan's memories of meeting the man for the first time would never fade.

It was the spring of 1810 when Silas York returned from Oregon to the Baltimore docks with his season's merchandise of over five thousand skins—beaver, bear and sea otter. Although the skins were cured, there was still a stink of death permeating the waterfront.

Rowan was summoned—not asked, but summoned—to meet the fur trader in the taproom of the Bull's Head Tavern. The waterfront inn boasted an oak bar parallel to the full length of the taproom. Shelves, running the length of the bar, were groaning under the weight of bottles and barrels. Kegs of house-brewed ale, porter and German hop beer were jammed under the counter. The floor was made from packed earth scattered with sawdust collected from a nearby sawmill, and the horizontal timber walls, floor to ceiling, were held up with untreated oak beams. It was everything the waterfront patrons of Baltimore could wish for.

Rowan stepped into a fug of stale grog and bodies, closing the inn door on the chill of Baltimore in February. Here the language was as colourful as the whores' petticoats and bloomers. The characters were eclectic, from drunken navvies to whiskey-pressed Indians, and Rowan soon realised it was not a room within which to stare wantonly.

Silas York clenched a long clay pipe between healthy white teeth in his vice like jaw. Rowan recognised the man immediately from Jessica's description. Dressed in a long-sleeved, cowhide jacket with calico britches and knee-high boots, he leant with one elbow on the bar, his back to Rowan. Pushing six foot two, York had the shoulders of a lumberjack and a short ponytail, tied off beneath a bald, weathered scalp. A full and wild beard lent the distinction an observer would expect of a well-travelled merchant in his mid-fifties. His tricorn hat sat on the bar, next to a quart tankard of dark beer and a bottle of Irish whiskey. He drank alone, although Rowan noted two pewter spirit measures before him.

Rowan removed his own hat, fiddling with the brim while he rehearsed his greeting. He had heard stories about the fur trader and knew the man did not suffer fools lightly. Now, Rowan's intention was to ask this man for his daughter's hand in marriage—the hand of the daughter of a stranger, a man he knew little about, except for those *damned* stories.

A drunkard ploughed into Rowan. Rowan ignored the clumsy drunk, but the commotion was enough to turn wary heads. Silas wheeled about. He eyeballed Rowan, who stepped forward.

'Mr. York?'

'Aye.' Silas York had a deep, resonant voice—the voice of an orator or narrator at a public gathering. A voice that commanded attention. 'You must be the sawbones... Craige, huh?'

'Aye... I mean yes, sir.' Rowan presented a hand in greeting and Silas clamped his own giant fist about Rowan's wrist, gripping flesh tightly in a display of testosterone masculinity. Rowan held the man's scrutinising gaze, returning the competitive grip, until, without warning, he was pulled to Silas's bosom in a manly embrace. For a moment, the two were cheek to cheek, and Rowan smelt the bitter but not unpleasant aroma of fermented hops on the older man's breath.

'You look after my little princess, Sawbones,' he said in a deep whisper, 'or I'll skin you alive.'

If Rowan had been uncomfortable upon entering the Bull's Head Tavern, he was certainly feeling awkward at this moment. Jessica, however, had warned him. Rowan returned the vice-like grip on the man's own wrist. 'I can assure you, sir, that I have the most honourable intentions. Your daughter and I are in love, and we intend to spend the rest of our lives together.'

'Love!' Silas blew out his cheeks, mocking the word. 'Live together, huh?' Silas York broke off the greeting and stepped back to focus on this man of medicine. 'How old are you?'

'Twenty-eight.'

'Twenty-eight... Aye, a man should be with wife at twenty-eight. I trust you will marry my Jessica before you bed her.'

'Sir, I beg you not to speak of Jessica that way.'

'Oh do ya, now?' Silas scooped up his quart and Rowan could see that it was still full. 'Bring the whiskey and them two measures; we'll take a pew in a corner some-a-wheres and you, Sawbones, can try to convince me you are the right man to wed my little princess.'

Rowan stood a moment staring at the full bottle of whiskey. York turned and pointed to the bottle with his tankard. 'Yer a drinkin' man are yer not, Sawbones?'

'Occasionally.'

'Good,' York said with a wry grin, 'cos a bird can't fly on one wing alone, eh?'

A lone drunk slept, his head nestled on crossed arms, upon the only available bench. His gin mug was empty and he snored, spittle bubbling from the corner of his mouth with each breath.

'Move it, yer drunken sod.' Silas hefted his foot and shoved the man off the end of the bench with his boot; he fell heavily to the floor.

'Jayshus.' The drunk made to stand, but swayed unsteadily.

'Go and sleep it off in an alley somewhere, Hatch.'

'Silas?' The drunk's eyes crossed over and he looked dangerously like he was about to jettison his last meal.

Silas York took the man by his collar and ushered him through the door.

'You know that man?' Rowan asked the obvious.

'Aye. He's my packer and camp cook, Matt Hatch. Can't hold his liquor.' Silas nodded to the vacant bench, where no other man dared sit. 'But he's a good lad, really, salt o' the earth. It's just that he's got more sail than ballast. Now sit.'

Silas poured the whiskeys. 'Well, Sawbones, a drink to the Union of America.'

Rowan accepted the salute proudly and drank half the measure, while Silas downed his in one gulp and took a long draw on his tankard, finally wiping the discarded froth on his sleeve. 'Do yer want a chaser with that?'

'Chaser?'

'Aye, the landlord here brews a perfect German beer.'

'Ah... no. The whiskey's fine, thank you.'

'Maggie!' Silas called to a passing wench within earshot, a rounded woman of mature years and an appetite to match, with whom he was clearly familiar. 'Get this man one of Robert's hop beers, if'n yer please.'

Rowan dared not protest, and the wench shoved through the rowdy crowd like a sow to the trough.

'So, Sawbones, have yer seen men at their worst, fightin' these silly wars?'

'Please, call me Rowan.'

'Rowan, then.'

'If you mean the British blockades, then yes, I have been involved in one or two skirmishes at sea.'

'As a sawbones.'

'Ship's surgeon. Yes.'

'And you've lopped off a limb or two, I take it.'

'Yes, sir... I have.'

'Call me "Mr. York,"' he said bluntly. 'I ain't that fond of bein' called "sir."'

'Mr. York.' *Mr. York!* Rowan had a distinct feeling the meeting was not going as well as he would have liked.

Maggie plonked a quart tankard in front of Rowan. 'Being the surgeon on board a ship at war is not for the weak-hearted,' Rowan said.

'Aye—I'll drink to that. Are you a religious man, Sawbones?'

Rowan did not disguise a sigh of exasperation. 'If you mean, do I believe in god, I am not all that certain.' York sat on the bench with his back hard against the wall, fixing Rowan with a scrutinising stare. 'You see, sir... ah, Mr. York,' he continued, 'I was raised a Quaker and had religious instruction forced upon me, so I struggle to believe in the scriptures. Having said that, I am a moral man who can be trusted, and I abide by the Ten Commandments, for what they are.'

'Ten Commandments, huh? So yer *are* a religious man.'

Rowan shrugged, noticing that Jessica's father had a star tattooed between finger and thumb. Rowan knew this to be a talisman to bring a man home safely. A superstition. 'Are you a superstitious man, Mr. York?' Rowan's words were wily, like the move of a chess player.

'Aye. You saw me star, huh? Do yer know its significance?'

'Yes, to guide you home safely. And does your religion sit well with superstition?'

Touché.

Rowan had spiked a nerve. York's left eye twitched slightly; his gaze narrowed and he studied Rowan even more carefully. 'And *you* are not superstitious or religious, Sawbones? Saving men's lives surely must levitate you closer to the Almighty.'

Rowan was growing irritable. He would marry Jessica regardless of this man's ignorant beliefs. 'I fear that I see life differently than you.'

York's other eye twitched. 'Oh, do yer, now?' York filled his own measure, shot it back in one gulp and slammed the pewter cup on the table before filling it again and topping up Rowan's, as if in a challenge.

'Jessica's had many suitors, yer know. Weaklings all of them. Shipping clerks, a baker, a fruit merchant... One was even a clergyman—a Protestant pastor, for Jesus sake. So why should a sawbones be any different? You've seen battle, certainly, but have yer ever killed a man? No.'

Rowan saw red. 'Look ,York...'

'Don't get me wrong. I don't condone killin' and I wouldn't allow Jessica to marry a soldier, either. 'Less he be an officer. But...'

'I agreed to meet you because I love your daughter.' Rowan cut to the bone. 'She loves me, and to speak frankly, *sir*, we intend to marry with or without your blessing.'

'Oh, do yer, now?'

'Yes. She is not sixteen anymore.' Rowan stood, planting his legs apart with his hands on his hips. Eyes and ears nearby pricked with tattle. 'In the eyes of the law....'

'Sit down,' York interrupted, in a surprisingly low but demanding voice. 'Keep yer shirt on. Sit... Rowan.' Rowan felt his face flush. 'There's no need to be makin' a scene in the Bull's Head like some fishwife. Now sit.'

Rowan obeyed the command and sat, grinding his teeth.

'I've already made my mind up.' York sipped his beer.

'Oh?'

'Aye, Rowan. You have my blessings to marry Jessica.'

Rowan's face brightened. 'I do?'

'Aye. Well, yer already had Mrs. York's blessin' and, God only knows, that woman is never wrong. What did yer think? I was some old grizzly bear? I know what love is too, yer know. I was young once.'

'That is music to my ears, Mr. York.'

'"Silas," Rowan—call me "Silas."'

It was now clear to Rowan that he had passed a strange test.

Silas York hefted his tankard and clunked it against Rowan's. 'Here's to Jessica's and your union.' Both men drank heartily, as Rowan suddenly realised how thirsty he was.

'That scar, lad?' Silas finally asked. He had eyed a small wound on Rowan's neck the moment they'd met. Now it was time for answers. 'That a fightin' scar?'

'I am a doctor, a ship's surgeon. I do not fight battles.'

'Yes, but you've been in a few scraps, have yer not?'

'Ye... yes, I have. I've seen my fair share.'

'Then, the scar? Were it durin' one of those scraps?'

'In a sense, I guess you are right, Silas. I was cut by one of my patients.'

'Huh!' Silas laughed. 'Now, why would the beggar do that?'

'I took his leg,' Rowan explained. 'If I had not, the man would surely have died. Blown asunder by powder and ball, he was. I amputated his leg and months later I met the man in an inn and he took unkindly to me. He thought I could have saved it.'

'He stabbed yer?'

'Yes. He was drunk.'

'Too drunk to kill yer, no doubt.' Silas smacked his lips and placed his tankard on the table. 'I'll tell yer something else, Rowan.' Silas leant forward conspiratorially. Rowan met him half way. 'I've got a caul sewn into me trousers.'

The caul, Rowan knew, was the holy hood, or foetal membrane, which sometimes covered the face of a newborn at birth. Medical studies had taught Rowan that this caul was to prevent the baby from drowning in the womb. Superstition held that if a man were to end up in the sea during a shipwreck while he had the caul on his person, it would save him from drowning. Rowan smiled at the macabre thought.

'I'm a good judge of character, Rowan,' Silas said, grinning, 'and I think there is more to you than meets the eye —just quietly.'

'Then that, Silas, is something we have in common.'

Memories of his Baltimore wedding regularly filled Rowan's thoughts. It had been a moderate affair, as the fur trade had been slow, in Silas York's disfavour, that past year. The guest list was short, for Rowan was an only child and his parents had both died of yellow fever during the Philadelphia epidemic of 1793. Rowan had been seven years old when he was adopted by a Quaker family from whom, through faults of their own, he was now estranged.

Rowan had, himself, shot the wild boar for the wedding feast, but it was prepared by Jessica's mother, Henrietta York, and her sisters. Henrietta was a fine and attractive woman and it was clear Jessica had inherited her mother's good looks. Silas, for his part, managed to secure French champagne, although, recently, an embargo had been put on French merchandise.

Now three years had passed since the wedding, America had declared war on Britain and Jessica was with child. Rowan was to be a father in a matter of days. But for now, Rowan was a battlefield surgeon and...

An attack was imminent.

Chapter Four

London. Newgate Prison.

Elizabeth was beyond crying. Her tears had dried months before. There was no pity in Newgate Prison and Elizabeth was astounded at her own resilience. She had hardened, these past months, into a she-wolf with honed survival skills as sharp as her fingernails—a she-wolf who could stand face to fist with the toughest bitch in the prison. The months passed by, each day with new challenges.

Betty Bryant was a whore. She had been whoring since she was thirteen. Betty had turned twenty-seven one week earlier, but was still a most attractive woman with long, soot black hair and slim legs. She now awaited transportation to the colonies. Like Elizabeth, Betty had only heard rumours—Sydney Cove at Port Jackson on the other side of the world was now twenty-six years old, but it sounded like paradise compared to Newgate. Betty's crime was stealing the clothes of a sailor she had bedded. She had shared a meal of oysters, mutton and gin with the man at a Southwark inn. Later, after the sailor had had his way and fallen into a deep sleep, Betty stole the man's clothing and purse. But an astute night watchman, always on the alert for the reward, and familiar with Betty Bryant the whore, stopped her on Fleet Street, where she'd intended selling the clothes to a pawnbroker.

Seven years' transportation to Sydney Cove.

'Seven years,' she spat at those who would listen, 'for a lousy pair of britches and a frock coat. I even left 'im 'is boots, fa Christ's sake. Oright... so, there was five shillin's in the purse. But seven years, for firk sake.' Betty hitched up her skirts and discharged her business into the prison soil bucket. She caught Elizabeth watching her, and scowled. Elizabeth held her eye and Betty dropped her subterfuge, she had learnt in the past weeks not to challenge Elizabeth friggin' Eveleigh, the counterfeiter.

Finally word arrived from Bristol. A distant cousin of Theophilus, Jonathon Brand, had bribed his way into Newgate. Elizabeth barely knew the man, a scrawny, narrow-faced lad a year or two older than she was. The young man's eyes were cold and dark, darting about with nervous apprehension.

'I come from Theophilus,' he mumbled through the iron bars, a scented cloth over his nose to filter the stench.

'What news do you have?' Elizabeth gullibly expected good news, a reprieve, maybe. 'Theophilus and Tempess have pleaded guilty have they?'

'Not likely, girl. Jayzus.' The dark, beady eyes shifted endlessly like those of a lizard stalking an insect. 'Them soldiers never found nuthin'.'

'So they are free, then.' Elizabeth's voice was still strong with hope.

'Aye, an' I'm 'ere to advise you to plead guilty.'

'Guilty!'

'Keep ya firkin' voice down.' Jonathon Brand licked his parched lips, staring down those prisoners who had crept forward to eavesdrop. Elizabeth turned and scowled at the intruders. They shied away. The cousin was impressed. 'Theophilus always said yer could look after yerself, Bess, eh?'

Elizabeth ignored the compliment. 'What do you mean, "plead guilty"?' she snapped. 'I'm no more guilty than Theophilus and Tempess.'

'Well 'ere's the thing, see. As they found no evidence in the cottage, exceptin' fa that sixpence what ya shat in the bucket, if'n you plead guilty ya only get sentenced fa bein' in possession of a forged coin. If'n you open ya gob to what they was really doin', then surely you'll all hang—savvy?'

An obtrusive and repetitive clanging drew closer as the turnkey dragged a metal baton across the iron bars. 'Ya time's up, lad,' he called ahead to Jonathon Brand on his approach.

''Ere.' Jonathon Brand exposed a cheesecloth parcel from under his coat.

'What is it?'

'Two quid an' some cold meat and cheese. Somethin' to soften the deal, like.'

'"The deal"?' Elizabeth questioned in disgust.

'You stay mum about the little enterprise in Fishponds Road. Plead guilty to possession and sail the blue seas...'

'Sail?'

'Transportation, luv. To Sydney Cove... It's gotta be better than doin' the devil's dance at the end o' a rope.'

The clanging baton grew louder. 'You 'ear me boy?' The turnkey grew irritable. 'I said times up.'

'Are you agreed?' Jonathon Brand hissed at Elizabeth.

It was better than nothing. It was something. 'Agreed.' Elizabeth snatched the bundle and slipped it under her skirt. Jonathon looked briefly into Elizabeth's eyes for a sign of betrayal. Theophilus had invested three guineas in his quest for Elizabeth's silence, but the lizard boy had seen fit to keep one of them. *Hell, she'll probably cark it from the pestilence in this place any'ow,* Jonathon thought, justifying his theft. He covered his nose with his handkerchief once more and walked away, his own filthy, unkempt coat dissolving into the leaden shadows of the cold, dank corridor, and then stepped out into the dull light of late afternoon London and freedom.

September 1814

It would be another month before Elizabeth's case was brought up before an Old Bailey judge. Herded through Dead Man's Walk—an underground passageway from the prison to the Old Bailey courthouse—Elizabeth was presented before the Judge, Sir Skelton Buckley Harridan. The man sat reverently beneath the Ionic order façade with its raking cornice and triangular pediment. A petit jury of twelve men had been sworn in for the day's cases. They waited, seated, between the judge and the defendant's dock. Off to one side, the public gallery was filled to capacity—including the standing room—with family and friends of the defendants, along with sightseers and hecklers. Standing in the dock with Elizabeth were nine other desperate women, all guilty of their crimes, from larceny to common prostitution. Elizabeth cast a defiant eye over the gallery. They were all strangers; there were no familiar or friendly faces.

Judgement day had arrived.

Judge Harridan was only too familiar with the overcrowded prison and the endless parade of the miserable, wretched and anguished members of the lowest classes. He had daughters at home in Mayfair who were similar in age to these women. He had learnt to brush aside their pleas, ignore their pathetic excuses and don the black cap of death, if necessary, with indifference to their suffering.

Elizabeth's keen young eye watched the judge fidget; he was a neat and well-groomed man of large proportions, with the jowls of an overfed hound. His wig had been freshly dusted with chalk and a fine peppering of the powder had settled on his shoulders like dead skin from his scalp. Judge Harridan slid the inkwell to his right and nestled the goose feather quill at a parallel to his fat belly, pushed up against his podium. He arranged his gavel in such a position so it could be readily slammed against its dented wooden top, demanding attention to his authority. His nose twitched and the attention of the nearest guard was summoned. He muttered something in the guard's ear and the man in the blue uniform, nodding profusely, delegated the judge's orders to his peers. Windows were hastily opened, even though a chilly autumn wind blew along Newgate Street. Elizabeth, of course, was oblivious to the stink that had followed her and the prisoners from the cells.

The court clerk, Mr. Banton, a rather insipid, thin and effeminate man with ridiculously hirsute side burns, called out the name of the first defendant across the courtroom. 'Mary Mortimer.' The prisoner stepped forward. 'How will you be tried?'

'By God and my country,' Mary Mortimer answered as she had been instructed, and in a soft trembling voice. The woman, who was not much older than Elizabeth, pleaded not guilty to larceny. She was accused of removing children's clothing from Mathew and Mathew, Drapers, Knightsbridge. The woman pleaded not guilty but a witness stated otherwise. The gavel slammed the podium. Seven years transportation.

Sandra Billings of Saint Giles pleaded guilty to the theft of stealing five yards of silk cloth and two gentlemen's frock coats—value, forty pounds—from Humphrey and Sons, the men's clothing parlour in Soho. This was a capital offence and the sentence would be death. Judge Harridan showed no emotion in the face of her pleas. His stomach growled and his thoughts drifted to the roast pheasant lunch he had been promised, with his colleagues, at the nearby Cow and Saddle. He looked to his gold turnip, placed open on the desk before him; the time was only eleven. He had an hour to wait.

Sarah Melody pleaded guilty to stealing a silk handkerchief from the pocket of a gentleman in Covent Garden. Molly Goodman pleaded not guilty to pickpocketing the fob watch and chain belonging to Winston Davies, also in Covent Garden and on and on the list went. Elizabeth was last.

'Elizabeth Eveleigh of Fishponds Road, Bristol, how will you be tried?'

Elizabeth gripped the iron rail of the docks. She dared bypass the court clerk and stared the judge in the eye. 'By God and my country,' she said calmly and clearly.

'You have been charged with being in the possession of a counterfeit coin, namely a sixpence.' The clerk nodded to an assistant and the coin was presented to Judge Harridan on a small tray. 'The said coin, Your Honour,' the clerk informed His Honour. The judge eyed the tarnished specie with some curiosity. This was a crime out of the normal run of things. 'A forgery, you say?'

'Yes, Your Honour.'

Judge Harridan plucked the sixpence up from the tray and studied its detail. He sighed. 'I am hesitant to admit that this specimen is very like the real thing, not that I handle too many sixpences.'

'Of course, Your Honour,' the clerk agreed, knowing the judge's keen eye to be more experienced at handling guineas and guineas.

'And this coin was found in the prisoner's possession?'

'Yes, Your Honour. The prisoner had actually swallowed the evidence, so there was no denying her guilt.'

'Swallowed it?'

'Yes, Your Honour.'

Judge Harridan's face screwed into a knot of inquisitiveness. 'If she swallowed it, Mr. Banton, how, pray tell, did the said coin re-appear?'

'Ah... She was given an opening medicine, Your Honour...'

'An opening medicine! You mean a...'

'A laxative, yes.'

The judge threw the sixpence onto the tray, from whence it bounced to the floor, chased by the clerk's assistant.

'Fetch me water, soap and a towel,' he growled. 'Immediately.'

Judge Harridan listened intently to the evidence before him. John Bishop, moneyer of the mint, stated categorically that the sixpence in question was forged. 'Thar be no doubt in me mind, Yer Honour.'

The judge's voice boomed across the courtroom. 'Elizabeth Eveleigh of Fishponds Road, Bristol. You have been found guilty of coining. That is, being in the possession of one piece of counterfeit coin to the exactness of one English sixpence, the which, falsely and traitorously, you did copy and counterfeit, for which the punishment is death.'

The public gallery murmured restlessly.

'However, taking into consideration your age and the fact that you were coerced by others yet to be arrested, I commute your punishment to fourteen years' transportation. You will be sent from this place to the hulks, where you shall await your fate: to be taken aboard one of His Majesty's ships to the colony of New South Wales.'

The gavel slammed onto the podium. The decision was final. There would be no appeal. Elizabeth's fate was sealed and she was escorted, once more, back through Dead Man's Walk.

Chapter Five

August 1814. Maryland. The Chesapeake Flotilla
defending Baltimore. Saint Leonard's Creek.

Only the choking smoke concealed the scene of devastation. Ship's surgeon Rowan Craige knelt by the dying man. Ned Woodward had been hit by shrapnel from canister shot, or possibly a sniper's musket ball. Rowan could never be certain which. He *was* certain however, that there was nothing he could do to save the man, and he had neither laudanum nor whisky to dull the man's brain. Rowan held Ned's head but there was no stopping the blood pouring like warm molasses from the gouged wound in his neck.

'My wife E... Elvira, sir—there is a letter in my pocket... You'll see she gets it...? Please... Promise me... '

Another artillery black powder rocket, fired from one of the fifteen advancing British barges, exploded only feet from the barge's gunwale. Their anchorage was shallow and Rowan was drenched in churned mud and spray from the resulting geyser. Rowan crouched below the gunwale, fearing he could be the next sniper's target. He looked Ned in the eye, the man's eyelids heavy as death surely claimed another brave fighter.

'S... sir. My wife...' the dying man pleaded.

'Of course.' Rowan took the neat, pre-addressed envelope from the man's coat pocket, checked the Baltimore dockside address, and pocketed the letter at the moment the man expelled his last breath.

Rowan was aboard one of thirteen barges, fixed side-by-side with kedge anchors from their sterns. They were fitted with 12-pounder cannon and a number of swivel guns capable of spitting shot and shrapnel. Under the captaincy of Commander Joshua Barney, they crossed the mouth of the Patuxent River—running parallel to the waters of Chesapeake Bay—in the shallow waters of Saint Leonard's Creek. Barney was a respected commander, a vigorous, handsome man, five feet eight inches tall with black hair, dark complexion, ambitious eyes, the tenacity of a pit-bull terrier and a way with the ladies.

Here they defended Baltimore from attack by the British forces. Barney also had charge of two gunboats, one galley, one lookout boat and their flagship, the cutter *Scorpion*. By all accounts they *should be* able to fight off the advancing British.

Should be!

The barges—rapidly built floating fortresses with a shallow draft for the wetland creeks and rivers of Chesapeake Bay—were each manned by up to twenty able and well-armed seamen. These men were not experienced soldiers but dedicated Americans, determined to fight the repressive British. They had, however, been trained by none other than the unstoppable, courageous and fiercely patriotic Commander Joshua Barney.

Barney stood with legs fixed apart, looking every inch the experienced sea captain, while all about him projectiles sent up spray. He ran an experienced eye through the lifting smoke. 'Those damned rockets!' he yelled over the din.

'At least they're imprecise,' Rowan said.

'Yes. But they are finding their range.'

And now, the barge's twelve-pound shot were having little effect on the British blockade ships further east. They were simply too far away.

'We'll take the offensive.' Barney passed his pistols to an aide to reload. He called to his second in command, Lieutenant William Devon, a battle-scarred Marylander with more than a natural hatred for the British, who had taken the life of his younger brother.

'Devon.'

'Sar.'

'Dismantle all masts,' the commander ordered regarding the single-masted barges. 'Stow the sails.'

'Sar?' Devon instinctively questioned his commander's wisdom. It had been a knee-jerk reaction that he hastily regretted. 'The masts, sar? Sails?'

'Yes. The bastards are using our sails to range their shots.' He nodded to one barge already lost and sitting on the shallow riverbed. It had been hit by a lucky rocket. 'Dismantle them now, stow them with the sails, and weigh anchor. Have the rowers take positions. Load all cannon. We'll take the fight to the bastards ourselves.'

'Yessar.' Devon, a hard-headed, no-nonsense man with years of experience at sea, curled the corners of his mouth in a gnarly grin. Devon had served under Barney on a number of occasions and was a loyal follower and admirer. Barney watched Devon delegate and then he looked across at his men on the other barges. They were all volunteers, proud patriots from Maryland. Each man looked striking in his blue-striped white britches, brass-buttoned blue waistcoat crossover white canvas shoulder belts, felt top hat, and a cotton sweat cloth tied about his neck. And every man was armed with a Brown Bess musket, a bayonet and all the accoutrements required to enable him to be an efficient killer. The officers wore the full dress of a continental army lieutenant: blue coat with brass buttons, red lapels and waistcoat, blue britches, and a cockade with a knot of ribbon as a badge of rank.

The commander's eyes dropped to the casualty resting at his surgeon's feet. 'Passed?'

'Yes.'

Barney snapped about to the nearest two seamen. 'Get him ashore. Hurry, now.' The sailors took the man by his feet and shoulders and dragged the dead weight into the tall duck grass at the river's edge where they covered his body with sailcloth. They would have to fetch him later.

As the flotilla drifted silently towards the enemy, Barney took a final glance over his shoulder at his flagship, the *Scorpion*. The eighty-ton, five-gun, two-masted cutter would remain moored where it was. The *Scorpion* was far too valuable to risk against the seventy-four-gun, third-rate ship of the line, HMS *Dragon*.

The morning sky streaked with the spitting flames of yet another rocket. 'Jesus!' Commander Barney watched the rocket peak at two hundred yards, and then commence its descent. 'Stupid bastards couldn't hit a mountain.' And there was truth in that. The Cosgreve rockets—so named after a Royal Arsenal engineer, William Cosgreve, who had *perfected* the idea stolen from the Moghuls in India—were notoriously inaccurate. However an accidental direct hit on a barge and its arsenal was still a possibility. The order was passed from barge to barge and the coxswains on board could be heard crying their orders. Without sails, the barges had to be rowed.

'Heave!'

1814

Barney took up his spyglass and focussed through the lingering smoke. The humid morning air coming from the wetlands was overwhelming. 'We're in for another hot day, Rowan,' Barney told his old friend from the corner of his mouth. 'And I feel our enemy is rugged up for the Arctic. Fools.' Barney knew that the British, of course, with all their regimental pomp and ceremony, dressed their fighters in thick, woollen red coats, while the mercury in the thermometer was already lifting above eighty degrees.

With the warmer months had come the enemy, arriving from across the Atlantic. Barney also had intelligence that other British warships were rendezvousing in Chesapeake Bay and blockading all trade. It was time to roll up their sleeves or surrender.

Surrender!

The very thought of the word sent a shiver down Barney's spine. Craige knew his friend's strategies well and prayed that the man's bravado would bear fruit, without too many casualties dropping from the perch.

'Are they moving?' he asked the commander.

Barney had his eye wedged fixedly into his spyglass. 'No, they're not moving yet, but they will.' The top of the masts of the HMS *Dragon* and those of an unidentified but well-armed schooner projected above the forest of pin oaks and elms surrounded by black mulberry bushes that separated the opposing foes. Barney's biggest fear was that the ships were almost within range of Annapolis, once the temporary capitol of Maryland. The patriots advanced slowly, rowing with the outgoing tide. The enemy kept their distance, withdrawing their barges, back towards the safety of the warships. It was a game of cat and mouse as the sun continued its eternal arc in the clear blue sky of Maryland's summer.

'They're trying to draw us in, Rowan,' Joshua Barney muttered so softly he could hardly be heard above the racket made by crickets at the riverbank. He slid the brass sheaths of his spyglass together. 'But we are no fools—eh, my friend?' Barney said, slapping Rowan Craige on the back.

'Indeed, Commander.' Rowan maintained the formality of his friend's title in front of the men. 'Indeed. They don't have a clue whom they are up against.'

Without question both men were confident. Rowan had nothing but respect for his captain. The two men had served in several battles together and had grown to be good friends. Rowan knew the commander as a genius tactician who had outsmarted the enemy on many occasions. Only recently, when Barney had been enlisted to take two ships to France with dispatches from the American Congress, he'd met a British blockade on Chesapeake Bay that was keen to take him prisoner, along with his ships, as prizes of war. But Barney ordered a small pilot boat to lead the two ships through shallow coastal waters in early evening and within sight of the British blockade. As the moonless night approached and darkness fell, they doused all lanterns and doubled back towards shore and safety. The British, certain their enemy had sailed out onto the Atlantic, had followed. By morning the British ships were at sea, but there was no sign of the Americans. The British assumed they had slipped away, and abandoned the chase. Then, with the coast clear, Barney had sailed out of Chesapeake Bay and across the Atlantic for Calais. Brilliant.

'So, Captain, what's the plan? Should I sharpen the teeth on my saw?'

'Devil's blood, Rowan, you young sawbones, I would not give the English dogs such satisfaction. Unless you want to jump ship and saw the bloodied limbs of the British casualties I forecast, you can keep your bloody saw in its case. Now, Devon...'

'Sar.'

'Are the guns armed?'

'Yessar.'

Gunners stood by, wielding smouldering matchlocks ready to kiss the powder in the touchholes. The head gunner on Rowan's barge, Henry Malloy, rubbed his open palm on the iron barrel of the cannon as a countercharm, to scare away the devil. Another man took a dried twig from his pocket and snapped it loudly for good luck, another superstition passed on from father to son. He caught Rowan watching. 'For a lucky break, sar,' he said nervously.

Christ, Rowan thought, *if that's what you're thinking, you'll need more than a stick.*

Powder monkeys, some as young as fourteen, stood by to assist the six-man gun crews in the reloading. Others stood by with damp fleeces on the ends of worm hooks to swab the barrel clean of stray sparks before the next charge could be rammed down to the breach.

Barney watched as they approached the bend in the river. 'Keep a sharp eye out for shooters, lads.' He alluded to the shoreline, only yards away, where long grass could hide even a redcoat. 'Gunners, stand by. Rowers, ship oars. The tide's with us. Save your strength for our retreat.'

The first barges drifted around the point in the river. Immediately, they were met with enemy musket fire. The enemy barges, including a rocket barge armed also with swivel guns that fired half-pound shot and destructive thirty-two-pound carronades, were dead ahead. Barney thanked his lucky stars they weren't the ship's sixty-eight-pounders with their range of two thousand yards.

'Their ships are putting on sail, sar!' Devon cheered.

'So they are.'

The two warships were retreating into deeper water. The Royal Navy were taking no risks. Instantly, hissing smoke, followed by balls and flame, were chased by the sound of artillery.

'Take cover!'

Only a yard from Rowan, a flotilla man collapsed under a pink mist. A musket ball had entered through his right cheek and made an exit through the left temple, shattering teeth and sinuses. Rowan dropped to his knees at the man's side, but there was nothing he could do about the tooth fragments embedded in his airway.

The rowers were stooped below the gunwale, but the gunners were exposed. 'Devon.'

'Sar.'

'Rapid fire, if you please. Pass it on down the line. Fire at will.'

'You heard the commander,' Devon screamed the order. 'Fire at will!'

The leading barge's twelve-pounders exploded, blasting at the British barges, now only three hundred yards ahead. Within seconds, the smoke of battle had totally masked the American barges and Rowan watched in awe as blackened streaks pierced the smoke, accentuating the passage of enemy cannon fire. Cannon balls flew dangerously close by...

And life or death was nothing less than a lottery.

'The ships are firing their Long Toms!' Barney yelled over the cacophony of firepower, Long Toms being long-barrelled six-pounders, used for long-distance shots. They packed a nasty punch, but at a mile distant their accuracy was limited and they were more a harassment than a threat. 'Maintain rapid fire. Give the bastards what-for, lads.' An iron ball sizzled close by boring a hole in the smoke. The patriots fought back harder. The enemy rocket barge took a direct hit on its magazine—the explosion was devastating. Rowan watched victims wheeling through the air, their screams reaching out to him over the pandemonium of warfare. During the skirmish the unnamed eighteen-gun schooner sailed close to shore to pick up survivors, only to become a statistic herself. The American firepower was just too much.

'*Huzzah!*' Barney's flotilla men cried.

'Aim low, men!' the commander shouted to all gunners within earshot. 'Aim low at her waterline!' The schooner took several more hits below the water line. She listed to port and the screams of men were heard as loose cannon crashed across the deck, crushing any man in their path. Then, the final strike: The patriots' twelve-pound shot severed the main mast of the schooner as it beat out, attempting to catch a fresh wind and retreat. Fearing to lose his ship, her captain ran her ashore.

'*Huzzah!*' Barney's flotilla men roared, and their cheer echoed across the water. '*Huzzah!*'

The Americans had lost one barge, back at their blockade, but the sight of the abandoned schooner spurred them on. Their twelve remaining barges drifted on the tide towards the enemy, endlessly blasting with cannon, swivels and musket fire. The British attackers had become defenders. Furious at the British losses, the Royal Navy commander, Admiral Cockburn, ordered the British barges to return. But he was not prepared to engage his flagship—the seventy-four-gun ship of the line HMS *Dragon*—in a troop landing just yet. He awaited backup, and the British had no choice but to retreat, to fight another day.

Barney knew of Admiral George Cockburn. He knew him to be a tall, slender and proud man in his forty-eighth year, a man of impeccable manner and dress. His commission had been purchased by his father, Sir James Cockburn, 8th Baronet, when George had been a young man. Educated at the Royal Navy School, George became Captain's servant in the sixth-rate HMS *Resource* in 1781. He'd come up through the ranks smartly: midshipman, 1791; acting lieutenant, 1792; lieutenant, 1793; commander, 1793; and acting captain, 1794. Then, two years earlier, in 1812, he'd been promoted to rear admiral...

And he was now a tenacious foe.

Hours had passed. The sun slipped away over Virginia to set in the west. With darkness, peace returned. Barney knew it would have been a folly to chase the retreating barges further. This would only bring them into the range of the HMS *Dragon's* cannons. It would be suicide.

With the Patuxent River cleared to the mouth, Commander Barney ordered piles driven into the riverbed and a chain boom dragged between them. This would slow another advance by the enemy barges on the morrow.

With luck.

All the same, an attack *was* imminent.

On board the patriot ship *Scorpion*.

'Some say *I* am the cause of the mischief the British have done to our United States,' Commander Barney told Rowan. 'Fools.' Barney tipped back his head, pouring the cognac down his throat like medicine. *But cognac was medicine, was it not?* He had grown fond of the delectable French spirit while wining and dining with the revolutionaries in Paris. Barney turned away from the stern window of the captain's cabin, where he watched an overcrowded wherry drop officers aboard the American gunboat moored to starboard.

'I have been a prisoner of the British,' he went on passionately. 'In Plymouth. Imprisoned in The Old Mill Military Prison for revolutionary prisoners.'

'Yes,' Rowan said. 'And you escaped.'

'Damned right I escaped. And it was a clever ruse, too.'

Rowan Craige had heard the story several times, of course. It was 1780 and a young Lieutenant Joshua Barney was the temporary master of a prize ship captured from the British, a merchant ship named the *Charming Molly* bound from Jamaica to New York. But they were themselves captured by the British blockade ships of the line, the HMS *Intrepid* and HMS *Raleigh*. Barney and his small crew didn't stand a chance. They were taken prisoner and transported to Plymouth. But the wily Barney escaped with the help of a mocked-up British guard's uniform and much courage, eventually escaping back to Chesapeake Bay.

'Bastards,' Barney said sourly. 'Bastards, the lot of them.'

'They are not all bad, Joshua,' Rowan said of the English. 'I was on board the *Pelican*, a privateer under command of Captain Henty Patterson, when he captured a British merchant barquentine *The Rosemary,* heading to Bermuda. The English fought well and there were many wounded and I was party to saving many lives, I must say, with some modesty.'

'You mean you separated a few men from their arms and legs?'

'Something like that. Anyhow it turned out that Captain Patterson was a sympathiser with the American cause. He had even had dealings with the French.'

'So, he was a traitor to Britain.'

'Not exactly. Anyhow, he knew of my address in Baltimore and sent me a letter of thanks for saving his men, and he sent a lovely wheel of English cheese along with it. Turns out, one of them was his nephew.'

'A prized delicacy, I must say. That was jolly decent of him.'

'That is what I thought.'

The cabin steward poured the commander a refill from a crystal decanter. 'I've appealed to Washington,' Barney said when the steward departed. 'But I'm afraid my fears fall on deaf ears. President Madison, it seems, listens to others who are closer to him. This is Federalist country here, Rowan. Many here in Maryland are old-fashioned Tories—they side with the British. I am convinced, my friend, that many landowners about these parts pass on information to the British warships. Traitors, every single one of them.'

'Deep breath in, Joshua,' Rowan advised his confidant. 'You will do yourself an injury. We'll win this war, you will see.' Rowan emptied his own glass and together they watched in silence as the *Scorpion's* battle-scarred cook entered the cabin with a pewter charger of roasted wild ducks for the table. 'Now eat,' the surgeon ordered his friend. 'It will build your strength, body and soul.'

'Eat?' Joshua Barney looked a moment at the brown glistening birds smoking from the galley fire, their juicy yellow breast meat sliced and ready. The cook had excelled himself this evening. He had seen fit to send his young assistants, dressed as local tykes, to fetch the ducks, murdered by stray shrapnel, from the riverbank where the main fighting had taken place.

'Eat?' Barney questioned his appetite.

'Aye, eat.' Rowan stabbed a stiletto into a half bird, letting it slide from the blade onto his plate. 'But I advise you to chew well and carefully, or you may chip a tooth on shot.'

Lieutenant Devon entered the cabin unannounced. Such petty etiquette was for the pompous enemy. He, however, had risen through the ranks from a commoner by showing leadership skills. There'd been no paid commission from *his* family. 'You'll be glad to know, sar, thart the militiamen are positioned along the banks o' the creek.'

'How many?'

'Six hundred, thereabouts.'

'Good.' Barney felt at ease. That was six hundred troops protecting the high banks of Saint Leonard's Creek against an enemy ambush. No one liked surprises, especially not during warfare.

'And Captain Miller?'

'He stationed one hundred of your flotilla-men alongside 'em, sar. Like you ordered.'

'Thank you, Devon. Now pull up a pew and partake of cook's fine repast.'

'Don't mind if'n I do, sar. I'm so 'ungry I could eat the crotch out of a low flyin' duck.'

'Well you are welcome to the crotch of all the ducks on that platter Devon. I am a breast man, myself. But I must warn you, our good surgeon here tells me we may encounter a bullet or two.'

The steward pulled the cork from a red Bordeaux wine and left the men to their meal.

'We have unrest down the ranks Devon, ever since Carberry deserted his post.' Barney spoke of Colonel Henry Carberry, who had deserted with his troops, only days earlier. He'd even taken supply wagons with him. 'Many American colonists think the British should be left alone and then, maybe, they would leave us alone,' Barney said, disgusted. 'And that the United States should never have sided with Napoleon Bonaparte. Bah, I say!' Now, Joshua Barney questioned the loyalty of some of the Maryland militiamen, particularly the ones living in the wetlands of the Chesapeake.

'I hear talk, sar.' Devon ate so fast Rowan feared the man would choke.

'And?' Rowan prompted.

Devon greedily slurped his goblet, spilling wine down his blouse. 'Colonel Carberry, for one...'

'Talk!' Barney reddened. 'From that traitor!'

'Aye.' Devon speared a boiled potato, holding the starchy bulb on the point of his knife and waving it about as he spoke. 'He was tellin' all 'em what would listen that Admiral Warren had sailed from Bermuda with his troops.'

'Yes, I heard that rumour. Maybe that Carberry is a coward as well as a traitor.'

'Bastard... Excuse me cussin', Commander. Trouble monger, that's what Carberry is.'

'I'm glad you agree, sir. Colonel Carberry should be shot as a deserter.'

Devon took too large a bite from the steaming potato and rolled it from one side of his mouth to the other in a vain attempt to cool the vegetable. Finally he managed a mumble. 'The enemy's amassing its troops in the bay, sar. What now?'

Barney pushed his half-eaten duck breast aside. He had lost his appetite. 'Maybe a wedge of cheese?' he asked the steward, a dedicated servant, always at hand. The commander took up his goblet of red wine. 'We've been ordered to sink our barges where they are,' he said matter-of-factly.

'Sink our barges. In God's name, why?' asked Rowan.

'The Navy Department fear the British will capture them and use them against us... to attack Washington.'

'Surely not.'

'Surely so, dear Rowan. The powers that be have little faith in us, as they feel we are outnumbered by overwhelming forces. We are to fall back to the Washington Navy Yard,' Barney spoke of the navy shipyards and ordinance stores on the Anacostia River, in East Washington, Maryland's Plymouth.

'What will you do?'

'Obey orders, of course, but I won't leave without a fight.'

'Oh?'

'Look—the men's morale is low. Are we fighting for a *United* States, or not? The men are confused.'

Rowan had seen the temerity in his friend's eye before. Trouble brewed. 'But you are not?'

'What?'

'Confused.'

'Lord, no!' Barney slapped the table once again demonstrating his impatience. 'We will attack *them*.'

Devon jolted upright with a spontaneous grin. 'Aye!' he repeated, joyously spitting potato flakes across the table. '*We'll* attack *them*.'

Two days later. Stern cabin. *Scorpion*. Patuxent River.

The day started on the right foot for both Joshua Barney and Rowan Craige: roasted ham hocks, okra stew and red beans. The ship's cook, Buller, Jamaican-born of English parents and nut brown after thirty years at sea, was generous with spices. He had learnt many recipes from African slaves in Spanish Town. In fact the entire ship's compliment was well fed; as they were in home waters, Buller had managed to source fresh supplies daily.

With full belly, the commander addressed the gathering of colonels, lieutenants and marine captains gathered in his cramped cabin. Before them, spread across the table, was a large hand-inked vellum map of Maryland and the wetlands, each corner weighted down with smooth river rocks kept for that very purpose. All heads gathered about, their eyes floating over major landmarks from Washington to

Baltimore or the Potomac to Chesapeake Bay itself, and from Delaware to Virginia at the map's periphery.

'Intelligence just received, gentlemen, confirms that the two enemy ships recently moored at the mouth of the creek are the frigate *Loire*, thirty-eight guns under command of Thomas Brown and the frigate *Narcissus*, thirty-two guns under Captain John Lumly. Anyone familiar with either of these ships, or their captains?' Barney was answered with the silent, collective shaking of heads.

'Colonel Wadsworth,'—Barney singled out the militiaman and Chief of Ordinance, Decius Wadsworth—'You will set up an artillery battery here.' Barney stabbed a finger at a spot representing the high banks of Saint Leonard Creek. The veteran soldier nodded sagely. Barney faced Marine Captain Samuel Miller.

'Captain Miller.'

'Sir.'

'You are to select twenty of your best sailors and join the militiamen. See that they are well armed. You will also instruct your sailing master, John Geoghegan, to do likewise.'

'Yes, Commander.'

'The remainder of us will attack the two ships, cause as much damage as possible, preferably sink the bastards, then withdraw to the flotilla, where I am under orders to destroy the barges. But I have a surprise under my hat for the redcoats who pursue us.'

'Surprise, sir?'

'Yes. We'll destroy the barges with powder charges, but not until the last minute. With good fortune we will destroy many of the enemy at the same time.'

Over shoulders, Rowan watched the *Scorpion's* third mate, Ryan McCray, enter the cabin, nearly unnoticed. He was a short man, as were most of the crew. McCray caught the surgeon's eye and jerked his head, indicating he requested a private ear. Rowan excused himself and met the man at the bottom of the companionway.

'Here, sar.' McCray handed Rowan a sealed envelope addressed to him personally. Rowan recognised the untidy scrawl as the hand of Silas York, Jessica's father.

''Twas just delivered by a young farm hand who rode from Baltimore. Said it's urgent, sar.' The mate looked embarrassed for a moment and shuffled his feet awkwardly.

'What is it?' Rowan asked.

'Ah... sar... I ah... 'ad ta give the messenger a dollar, like.'

'Thank you, Mr. McCray.' Rowan passed the mate a silver dollar and read the note in silence.

The news was bad.

Baltimore was a cheerful home for patriot Rowan. It was a prosperous port at the head of the Patapsco River, high up on the Chesapeake Bay, and the third largest settlement in the United States. But it was now a prime target, despised by the British, as Baltimore had been the home port to many an American privateer sailing out to capture British merchant ships as prizes. Baltimore was also populated by large numbers of Irish, German and French immigrants, who made life unpleasant for the Federalists, the Tory supporters who resisted war with England. In fact, for the Federalists, Baltimore had become downright inhospitable. The Royal Navy retaliated by blockading shipping and halting trade.

Fed up with the Royal Navy blockades, President Madison had made a declaration of war on England two years earlier. The federalist newspaper *Federal Republican* publicly condemned Madison's cause—which was supported by the majority of Baltimoreans. Rowan had witnessed the so-called Baltimore War of 1812, in June of that year, when the streets of Baltimore turned ugly. The newspaper publisher, Alexander Contee, had been forced to flee and his printing press had been destroyed by an angry mob. City officials were reluctant to intervene. Many Republicans justified the violence, arguing that the Federalists protesting against the war threatened American freedom.

Now, two years later, Baltimore was a prime target for the British. For the sake of their unborn child, Jessica had thought it prudent to escape to Georgetown near Washington, where her uncle, Silas York's brother, owned a warehouse. But Washington, Rowan now dreaded, was the bigger target.

With the cabin finally vacant, Joshua Barney glanced at the words scrawled on Rowan's single-paged letter, but he did not need to read it. The look on his friend's face was enough. 'You must go to her at once, Rowan.'

With the British threatening to sack Baltimore, Jessica had been loaned a carriage and had ridden to Georgetown, three miles northwest of Washington's Capitol Hill. She was chaperoned by Charry, their servant, to take refuge with Jessica's aunt and uncle.

'Georgetown will be a greater target than Baltimore,' Rowan said of the affluent merchant port town on the Potomac River. 'And Washington is surely a greater prize than Baltimore, also,' Joshua paced the cabin with his hands behind his back. 'If they seize Washington—and it does not look good, Rowan—they will cause havoc. No one will be safe there.'

'Jesus Lord.' Rowan's handsome features looked weary, his eyes dark and sunken. 'Who in the devil's name suggested Washington?'

'Your baby is due any day now,' Barney said. 'You have no choice but to go to her.'

'But I'm needed here. God only knows, my work is needed here at this moment.'

'Go, man. You must go to your wife.'

'But I'm needed... '

'Leave. Go. Do you think you are the only sawbones around who can remove limbs from dying men? No! Now, go.'

Chapter Six

London. Newgate Prison.

Betty Bryant grew up on the wrong side of Southwark. Through no fault of her own, as she told those who would listen, she took up whoring.

'Don't bother me none, doing tricks for them lonely sailors. Besides,' she started to chuckle loudly, 'I enjoy the sex.' And now the whoring had led to larceny and seven years transportation to New South Wales.

Betty had watched the lizard-like Jonathon Brand from Bristol with a keen prisoner's eye when he had paid Elizabeth Eveleigh a visit at Newgate, some weeks earlier. She was certain she'd seen a glint of gold exchange hands between the two, and was even more certain when, hours later, Elizabeth casually borrowed a needle and thread from Mary Taggert, the seamstress. *She's squirrellin' them coins into her hem,* the whore told herself.

And she bided her time.

Betty guessed it was somewhere between three and four in the morning. She returned from the quarters of Gilbert Cramme, the turnkey, after exchanging sex for gin. Middle-aged Cramme was an unfortunate specimen of the human race -- a short man, less than five feet tall yet stocky, with a bulbous belly from excess. To add to his woes, he had putrid breathe, the consequence of tonsil infection. Betty's mind was befuddled on the cheap spirit, but she was not incapable, and it was only her maudlin ramblings to the turnkey that forced her from his bed earlier than usual. He led Betty by the meagre light of a candle stub, one hand cupped before its flame. They walked silently - except for the turnkey's occasional slurp of pooled saliva - along the stone passageway leading from the keeper's house back to the Felon Women's Quarters, where he unlocked the bar cage door and let her into the wards. Here seventy women snored or cried out in their sleep, struggling with the demons of their nightmares. Betty hoisted her skirts and relieved herself in the night bucket, then found a vacant site and lay on the putrid straw. But as her eyelids grew heavy, Betty noticed Elizabeth Eveleigh in the faint light. Betty edged closer and listened. She waited. Elizabeth slept soundly, her head on a wooden pillow, pouting rhythmically. Betty ran experienced thieving fingers along the hem of Elizabeth's brown serge smock, until her calloused forefinger and thumb felt the unmistakable. It had to be guineas. Two of them. Betty slipped the blade of a broken razor from a hidden pocket and went to work. But she was remiss with gin, and Elizabeth was a light sleeper. Elizabeth felt a gentle tug.

'What in the Devil's name... '

Betty expelled a foul breath of gut-rot. 'Shut yer gob!'

Elizabeth suddenly realised the thief's progress. 'You thieving bitch!' Elizabeth struck out, catching the older, stronger woman in the face with a closed fist.

'Give me them coins or I'll slit yer throat.' Betty slashed out with the razor's blade pinched between her fingers. Elizabeth felt the sharpened steel slice her smock. She punched back, two successive swipes to the whore's face and neck. Elizabeth heard the tinkle of the blade scatter on the flagstones. Betty jumped to her feet, leaping for Elizabeth. She dropped on top of her, one knee on either side, pinning her seventeen-year-old adversary to the prison floor as she lashed back at Elizabeth's face.

Someone screamed out in the dark.

'Fight!'

Seventy women stirred. Then the next ward, and the third. Soon the whole female prison was cheering. Elizabeth took a beating about the chest and head. Her immediate reaction was to protect her face from the fierce, relentless blows, but Elizabeth had also learnt to fight back. She jerked her knee upwards, punching her kneecap into the other woman's crotch. Betty sucked in an angry breath, as pain shot through her body. 'Firkin' bitch!' she screamed, kicking back. But the kick threw Betty off balance and the gin made her acumen sloppy. Elizabeth stepped aside but lost her footing and fell. Betty pounced, pinning Elizabeth to the flagstones, while swinging a balled fist down hard. Elizabeth jerked her head aside. The fist pounded the stone floor. Betty cried out in pain, retracting bloodied knuckles, ready for a second punch, but Elizabeth managed to break free. She body-rolled aside and the whore rolled off her, onto the floor.

'Fight!'

Light from several lanterns oscillated shadows along the passage walls. The guards approached, infuriated that their sleep should be disturbed by brawling women.

'Stop this!' Gilbert Cramme was unsteady on his feet. 'Stop at once.'

'What the bloody hell's going on?' another guard yelled. But his words fell on deaf ears, amongst the shouts and jeering of nearly two hundred women, starved of entertainment.

Elizabeth and Betty stood hunched, shoulders raised, facing off. Both were panting and grinding their teeth, their eyes wide and angry. The whore let out a roar. She rushed forward to execute a body tackle. Elizabeth waited...

And stood her ground.

Betty ploughed into Elizabeth at full momentum, just as Elizabeth snatched Betty's shoulders with both hands. She wrenched her forward, sidestepped, and launched her attacker against the iron bars. The spectators let out a collective groan. Betty crumbled to the floor, half unconscious.

The guards forced a path through the tight gathering, beating the women closest into submission with lead-weighted batons; foul language was rife, and the hissing and booing was that of a cock-fighting pit.

Elizabeth stood over Betty, straddling her, one leg either side. Betty's brow was cut deeply from the impact against the iron bars.

'Apologise!' Elizabeth shouted so all could hear. The last thing Elizabeth wanted was to accuse Betty of trying to steal from her as it would only draw attention to her guineas. Betty whispered something.

'I can't hear you,' Elizabeth persisted, relishing victory. 'Do you apologise?'

'I... I apologise.'

'I still can't hear you.'

Betty raised her voice. 'I apologise.' Elizabeth offered the whore a hand. Betty took it and rose to her feet. At that moment the guards broke into the inner circle. Elizabeth turned to face the first guard, who stood with baton raised.

'Back away,' he ordered.

Without warning, Betty threw a crushing blow. A windmill motion—an extended arm with a closed fist. It slammed the side of Elizabeth's head. Elizabeth felt faint.

She felt her knees weaken, then blacked out, briefly, dropping to the floor.

Betty's rage had flared.

Gilbert Cramme rushed forward, but several women tripped him. He tumbled to the cell floor. Elizabeth lay dazed, her vision burry. She snatched short, sharp breaths. Betty saw her chance. She raised her foot to stamp on Elizabeth, but Elizabeth clamped her hands either side of Betty's foot...

And twisted.

Those closest heard an unnatural sound of muscle tearing. Betty screamed out in sudden agony. Still clamped on Betty's boot, Elizabeth knelt groggily. The circle cheered. Betty hopped, one-legged, backwards before Elizabeth threw her aside. Betty crashed heavily to the floor. Elizabeth dived forward, took her opponent by the hair and twisted her head, plunging it into the night-soil bucket. She held Betty's face in the putrid bucket of human waste as the crowd pushed away, gagging, for fear of being soiled themselves. Even the guards were hesitant. But, when it appeared that Elizabeth would drown the woman in her own muck, one of them hefted his boot into Elizabeth, kicking her aside.

'Fetch water,' the guard ordered those nearest. 'Now!'

Seven days' solitary confinement trifles with a prisoner's sanity. Total darkness. Absolute silence. Complete loneliness. In a stone-walled cell, eight foot by four and fed with a daily ration of bread and water. It was the middle of winter and Elizabeth sat huddled in a corner without a blanket, and for the first time in months, Elizabeth cried.

She sobbed.

She fought claustrophobia and panic attacks, and had difficulty thinking straight. *What if there was a fire and she was trapped? What if a rampant disease attacked the prison and she was the only survivor, trapped in this tiny, dark cell? What if...?*

Elizabeth admonished herself. *You're tougher than that. You're tougher than all of them.* She had spent six weeks in a tiny cell in Bristol, of course, but had been allowed out daily to exercise in the yard. Also, that cell had had a window.

Elizabeth told herself she was lucky... lucky it was not a month's sentence. She thought herself fortunate that she was not in solitary on Norfolk Island, for an old lag had told her how men were lowered into a pit in the centre of the courtyard within Norfolk Island's penitentiary walls. 'The pit 'o despair it were called,' the woman told Elizabeth. The pit was ten feet deep with a tiny trapdoor at the top. 'Like them bottle neck dungeons in them castles back 'ome,' the lag cackled, for Elizabeth's amusement. 'Like bein' buried alive, they say. One offender got a year in that 'ole—a firkin' year— and fer what? Talkin' back to the guard. Bastards. 'E was let out in the middle o' the day in bright sunlight, after a firkin' year! Went blind, 'e did. Blind and mad.'

But I'm tougher than most, Elizabeth repeated to herself over and over. *I'm tougher than all of them.*

The days dragged on. Elizabeth lost all sense of time. She resigned herself to her fate, lay on the lice-infested straw scattered across the stone floor, curled into a foetal position and shivered herself to sleep.

CHAPTER SEVEN

August 1814. America. Maryland.

Commander Barney's army captain, Captain Samuel Miller, spat fury. 'That stupid bastard!' Miller's men were positioned to the left of Wadsworth's battery while Sailing Master Geoghegan positioned his forces to the right of the promontory, at the western entrance to Saint Leonard's Creek. They were within firing range of the enemy ships. Now Wadsworth had disobeyed orders.

'The stupid bastard!' Miller fumed. 'Commander Barney distinctly ordered the man to place his guns on higher, firmer ground.' The sound of more cannon fire drowned his anger. 'There—see?' He elbowed his field sergeant, who was shaking his head vehemently. As they watched, Colonel Wadsworth's cannons—positioned below the brow of a distant hill—recoiled violently on the soft, sandy soil, and the shot sailed harmlessly over the spars of the British ships. 'Fool!'

While they watched, the enemy's thirty-eight-gun frigate *Loire* and the thirty-two-gun frigate *Narcissus* returned fire, four times to Wadsworth's one.

Meanwhile, several miles distant, Barney commanded his barges. They drifted, again, on an outgoing tide, but where Saint Leonard's Creek narrowed Barney was forced to reduce the number of vessels to eight abreast. Ahead awaited the British frigates and two new arrivals, well-armed schooners. Alongside the British ships were the Royal Navy's shallow depth barges, while along the shoreline several thousand soldiers assembled.

A commotion on shore drew the commander's attention; a militia runner appeared, relaying barge to barge along the riverbank.

'Dispatch, sir.' The runner handed Barney a leather satchel with intelligence from Wadsworth—the British were landing troops upriver.

'Where?'

'Northeast, sir.'

'How many?'

'The colonel thinks at least a hundred or so, with light arms.'

'They'll be skirmishers.'

'Aye, sar, thart's what the colonel said.

'Devon.'

'Sar.'

'Get word to Miller and Geoghegan immediately. They must, at all costs, counter the landing.'

Devon sent his own runner forward.

Moments later, the British ships came into view, only four hundred yards away. Barney didn't hesitate. The bombardment commenced with a pounding volley of twelve and eighteen-pounders, handled by his experienced gunners. The *Loire* alone received fifteen hits from the American barges. They penetrated her hull and caused considerable damage topside, with bar shot tearing through the sails and rigging. However, there was no loss of life. The *Narcissus* was also damaged, but less so. The ships returned gunfire, but now, with the British successfully landing their redcoats on the shore, the Royal Navy played it cautious, added sail and withdrew their ships out of range.

Barney yelled to his first mate, Benjamin Smith, a tough seaman with the unfortunate profile of a sloping forehead and aligned nose. 'Damage report?' he ordered.

'Two of our barges sunk and eleven men killed or wounded.'

'Devil's blood!' Barney balled his fists. 'God rest their souls.'

'Amen to thart, sar.'

Late that afternoon Commander Barney ordered a long and narrow gig to be rigged as a six-oar scout. At first light the next morning the small jury-rigged craft sailed silently up the Patuxent returning shortly thereafter.

'Well?'

'It's not good, sar. The HMS *Albion* has entered the mouth of the Patuxent,' the scout said of Admiral Cockburn's flagship, and we counted no less than twenty-three warships.'

'Oh, Christ!' Devon's shoulders sagged in defeat.

'And?' Commander Barney prompted.

'They are landing troops south of Benedict, sar.'

'Benedict!' The men looked at the dog-eared map before them. Benedict was just south-east of Washington.

'That was their crucial first step toward taking Washington. Jesus Lord, we have to stop them. How many troops?'

'I estimated five thousand.'

'F-five thousand!' Barney repeated, louder than he intended. The number was not a surprise but hearing it spoken aloud was still a shock. 'They will outflank us in no time. We must move fast and take the defensive. I want four hundred flotilla men taken off the barges immediately. We'll march them to Marlboro -- here.' Barney ran a finger from Benedict to Marlboro, where the British would have to march overland across unfamiliar territory to take Washington. 'That will leave one hundred and twenty men with the barges. Lieutenant Frazier.'

'Sir.'

'You will remain in charge of the flotilla.'

'Yes, sir.'

'You are to destroy them before Cockburn gets his hands on them.' Barney was shaking his head at the map. He looked up at the lieutenant. 'Do you understand?'

'Yes sir.'

'Then we will rendezvous at Upper Marlboro.'

Within two hours, Admiral Cockburn had taken his shallow draft barges to engage the Americans. The patriots were outnumbered and were prepared to desert their own barges, but not before Frazier and his men set charges on every craft in the flotilla. The redcoats could not believe their luck and stormed the abandoned vessels, which exploded spectacularly in the faces of the advancing soldiers. The barges sank into the shallow mud of the river, effectively blocking it, forcing the British troops to unload their own barges and march overland. Admiral Cockburn was furious.

Lieutenant Frazier had, however, managed to save five cannon from destruction—two eighteen pounders and three twelve-pounders—along with shot and powder. Without horsepower, the flotilla men had to drag the guns on their carriages with sheer manpower. It was exhausting in the heat, but they were accustomed to the Maryland summer and the steamy tidal water countryside and the British were not.

Marching for hours on end, dressed in their thick woollen coats and britches with each man carrying seventy-pound kit —a pack, haversack, pouches of ammunition, lead and powder, canteens, billhook, muskets and bayonets—they forged ahead. The redcoats were already weary, but they stubbornly persevered, for Commander Barney had stirred a hornet's nest.

As the enemy advanced towards Washington, Barney re-assembled his troops at the village of Upper Marlboro. Frazier's one hundred and twenty flotilla men were unavoidably delayed, steadfastly dragging the five rescued cannon overland, towards the patriot army. They were days behind, but catch up they would.

Orders for Commander Barney soon arrived from Washington. The five thousand British troops under the command of Major-General Robert Ross were advancing on Bladensburg, northeast of Washington. Barney was now ordered to move southwest from Upper Marlboro to intercept them, post-haste.

On arrival, Barney's small army found that other Americans had already set up defensive lines on a hill commanding a view of a shallow valley which overlooked a creek crossed by Turncliff's Bridge, only miles from Washington. But misfortune stalked ahead of them...

They heard that Bladensburg had fallen.

Barney reported immediately to General Winder, who ordered him and his men to set up their defensive artillery position where they stood, at Turncliff's Bridge.

...

Rowan was drained by fatigue—exhausted—after days of hiking, playing cat and mouse, avoiding the advance parties of the enemy. General Ross's redcoats, whom Rowan had been told had just taken Bladensburg, were now marching towards Washington, six miles to the southwest. But Rowan knew they would have to cross at Turncliff's Bridge, and that, thankfully, was well behind him.

Rowan knew the roads well and travelled at night, lest he meet British reconnaissance parties. It was cooler and safer. He travelled west along gravelled roads, through tobacco plantations and cornfields surrounded by thick woodlands. Armed with a dirk and a small purse of silver, Rowan hiked on foot, wary, trusting no one, least of all the black slaves who worked the plantations and had gained sympathy from the British. He travelled on foot to avoid attention, managing rare meals in roadside inns. He avoided unnecessary conversations, for he was in Federalist country and the humidity of anarchy hung heavily in the air.

...

The British army were close, but Barney and his compatriots, guarding Turncliff's Bridge, stood between them and Washington. Makeshift cannon batteries were erected by the Americans, while all the supply wagons carrying spare wheels, gun carriages, axles and the necessities of warfare were positioned on each flank for cover, little cover though it was. Barney's extra flotilla-men, now acting as infantry, were positioned in front of the cannon, but well down a hill slope, out of the firing line. Captain Miller's marines guarded Barney's battery flanks, while further back the Maryland militia—made up mainly of Maryland citizens—gathered in unknown numbers.

Next to each cannon canvas sail sheets lay on the damp grass, stacked with ammunition—round shot strapped onto wooden sabots ready to be loaded with a charge of gunpowder, each portioned carefully into fabric bags or loaded as canister shot. These deadly cylindrical tins were loaded with musket balls, some with nails, bolts, chain, or scrap iron. When fired, the thin tin tore apart and the shot spread, peppering the enemy with deadly shrapnel. It was hard to miss—and, understandably, it was not deemed sportsmanlike.

But this was war.

Each artilleryman checked the tools of his trade. Besides ammunition, artillerymen required ramrods, worm-hooks, drag chains, sponges and water buckets. They were prepared to defend their country.

They chatted uneasily by their cannon. They smoked their pipes, talked of family and politics, wrote letters to loved ones and drank brewed tea laced heavily with rum...

They waited anxiously.

As darkness claimed the night, Commander Barney and Lieutenants William Devon and Jesse Huffington looked from their campsite across at the distant hills where glowing fires from the British bivouacs spoke of their numbers...

It was daunting.

'God Almighty, we are outnumbered by thousands.' Devon pushed back in a folding campaign chair, keen to remove his boots but worried that his feet would swell and he'd never be able to pull them back on.

'General Winder says they'll march at first light,' Lieutenant Huffington said, a hint of apprehension in his voice.

'I tend to agree,' Barney said. 'So we must be ready to defend that bridge.'

Dawn.

The advance happened as the Americans had predicted. The overwhelming number of the British soon outflanked them on all sides, but the bridge separated them. The red coats had the advantage in numbers, but as the day warmed it was clear that they had not acclimatised, marching rapidly through unknown territory in Maryland's summer heat. Again, the humidity was high. For a moment the Marylanders had the advantage. The redcoats were fatigued and their determination foundered when they realised that the only way across the river was over Turncliff's Bridge. The small bridge was heavily guarded by the tenacious Commander Barney and his men, armed with the five cannon dragged cross-country from Saint Leonard's Creek.

As the sun rose higher to the east five thousand enemy soldiers, unfamiliar with the territory, were bottlenecked at the bridge. They had no choice but to spread out along the opposite river banks, on each side of the bridge. It was a terrifying sight for the Americans: row after row of red-coated soldiers in white britches and tall black shakos, all gathering with determination and fixed bayonets. As the patriots watched on—waiting for the inevitable—the British army reassembled into their respective units.

Commander Barney was restless. He drew his straight edged sabre and spurred his horse into a trot before galloping along his battery line.

'Fire at will!' he roared at his men.

The first volley shattered the silence. Iron balls chased fire and smoke from the barrels of his cannon.

The enemy scattered, but fifty men stormed the bridge.

Barney's sea-trained artillerymen could reload in minutes. They crammed fabric bags of gunpowder down the barrels, followed by iron shot. A grommet wad held the ball in place. Then the gunners spiked goose quills filled with powder into the touchholes. On the gunner's order...

'Fire!'

The powder ignited. Fire and smoke trailed the explosion and recoil. Instantly, the crew repositioned the gun...

'Reload!'

A wet fleece on a ramrod swabbed the barrels, dousing any sparks. The next bag of gunpowder was rammed home. After the first few volleys had descended on the enemy, the canisters were crammed down the barrel. Detonated, the canisters would fragment, shredding the advancing enemy with scrap iron and glass.

It was devastating. The screams of the dying and wounded at the bridge echoed out from the ravine, and the river below ran red with British blood.

It was a massacre.

But the redcoats along the river's bank were well trained, determined, and angry as disturbed hornets. Barney's battery took a volley of wild musket fire. Although the enemy was several hundred yards away and their fire inaccurate, some of his men fell. Through the smoke Barney could hear the enemy ramrods. They clattered into the long barrels of the British muskets...

Powder, ball and wad.

Another volley ripped through the artillerymen. At the bridge, a trumpeter called the enemy to arms. Another troop of British soldiers advanced onto the bridge.

'Fire!'

The American shot churned the paddocks. The artillery splintered the bridge, but, more importantly, it decimated those crossing.

Still more redcoats advanced. British troops along the opposite river bank returned volley after volley. Musket flashes pierced the smoke. Whistling musket balls pricked the air. The sound of musketry grew louder, incessant. The enemy fell...but more made it across the river -- there was no stopping them. The British marched forward; six hundred men had crossed by the third attempt. It was a courageous display of pigheaded determination.

1814

Barney ordered Captain Miller's contingent to meet them head on.

'Remember men,' Barney shouted at the soldiers, 'shoot the infantry in the belly and shoot the horses out from under the officers.'

Miller's seventy-eight marines fixed bayonets and charged the bridge, screaming hell-fire as they raced across an open field to meet the red coats. Barney's artillery fired shot after shot at the opposite side of the bridge, preventing backup forces from joining the six hundred already across. The American defensive was so brutal, so single-minded, that they caused many British casualties and forced the enemy down the ravine, back into the river.

Word came to Barney that Miller's attack had wounded the British commander of the advancing infantry regiment, Colonel William Thornton *and* his second and third-ranking officers, Lieutenant Colonel William Wood and Major George Brown. Fate had favoured the Americans—their assault had been a success. Now, an immediate counterattack was imperative. But as the smoke of battle dissipated, it became clear to Commander Barney that his men and Captain Miller's were the only soldiers remaining on the battlefield. Commander Barney had been deserted.

In the panic created by the British crossing the bridge, the Maryland militia to the rear had abandoned their ground, leaving Barney, to his horror, with only his own marines, his sailors and two small militia detachments. He was hopelessly outnumbered.

Thousands of red coats swarmed across Turncliff's Bridge... The march on Washington had begun.

The Americans' bravery and their short-lived triumph now haunted them, as they were surrounded by the British.

'Save the cannon,' Barney screamed at his retreating men as they fell back in order to make a last stand to save Washington.

'We've been deserted, sar!' Lieutenant Huffington spat.

'Damned cowards!' Barney roared after the deserting Maryland militia. 'We could have had them on a counter-attack. Cowards!'

'They took our munitions wagon with them!' Lieutenant Devon was disgusted. 'What are your orders, sar?'

'We have no choice but to evacuate.'

'Yessar.'

Barney mounted a horse to lead an evacuation. Somewhere on higher ground, Barney wound up in the sights of a sharpshooter. He never heard the random shot but his horse fell. The animal crumbled beneath him, braying in pain. Barney regained his feet, looked about for cover, but it was too late. The next musket ball slammed into his thigh. He, too, collapsed. The pain was excruciating. With the cannon depleted of ammunition it was time to retreat. 'Shoot the horse,' he ordered Huffington, through a fog of pain. The horse jerked and twitched in lathering death throws.

'Sir?'

'Shoot the damn horse, man.'

Huffington planted his musket against the forehead of the thrashing beast and pulled the trigger in a merciful explosion. The horse died instantly. Barney was losing too much blood. He grew weak and his mind and vision blurred. 'Leave me! Go!,' he ordered. 'Call the retreat. Fall back and defend Washington.'

The lieutenants wanted to stand and fight, but with their commander wounded the men had lost their will to fight—it *was* time for retreat...

Fall back and defend Washington.

1814

Lieutenant Jesse Huffington insisted on remaining with his commander. 'Respectfully, sir, I'm not going anywhere. I'm remaining with you.'

'Are you insane, man? You will be taken prisoner.'

'Then so be it. You need assistance, otherwise you will surely die.' Huffington called for a stretcher.

Ten minutes later, surrounded by the detritus of war, including Barney's precious cannons, Barney and Huffington surrendered to the redcoats.

Chapter Eight

August 24th 1814. Washington burns.

It was late evening, five miles southeast of Washington. Rowan had smelt the smoke for hours now and he feared the worst. Washington was burning. The capitol, although it was more a large township of eight thousand people than a true city, glowed tragically through the night. From the hills he had a view of the terrain along the Potomac River. Rowan saw the Capitol building ablaze. Many other public buildings surrounding the Capitol also burned.

'Jessica,' he sighed anxiously. 'Please, Lord, give her strength.'

Rowan had no way to know it, but the panicked and inexperienced American militiamen had set fire to their own munitions, arms and ships—the warships *Argus, Lynx* and *Columbia*—at the Washington Navy Yards, to prevent them falling into enemy hands. It was a lost cause. Rowan felt ill, useless. 'Jessica,' he heard himself whisper over and over. Then he took in a deep breath and made his way along the riverbank.

The streets were deserted. Admiral Cockburn's sailors and Major General Ross's troops had stormed the capitol.

Some residents barricaded themselves inside their homes but nine-tenths of the population had fled, to hide in the dense woodlands surrounding the capitol. Rowan had missed the panic of earlier that day, with wagons and carriages loaded with furniture and private possessions trundling away from the invaders. The city was near anarchy. There was no law and order. Slaves cut loose to steal and loot and genteel folk were robbed of their possessions, while fighting broke out over carts and horses or any other sort of transport.

Amongst Ross's men were non-British foreign legion soldiers—the Chasseurs Britanniques—and Spanish mercenaries. There was little resistance. Immediately the invaders went about, burning the government buildings. However, Admiral Cockburn ordered private dwellings to be left in peace, unless they were the homes of citizens aiding the militia.

Under the cover of night Rowan paid a ferryman five silver dollars to row him across the river, dropping him half a mile east of the blazing naval yard. 'As yer can see, Admiral Cockburn and General Ross are already on Capitol Hill, sar.' The ferryman dipped the oars with powerful arms in an effortless crossing. 'It was under their orders what started them fires.'

Rowan stared at the flames over the oarsman's shoulders. They spilled down to the shoreline and their reflection on the water made it look like the river, too, was burning. 'Bastards!'

'Aye. I hear 'em say it's retaliation for us Americans destroyin' the British capitol o' York in Canada last year.'

'It's bad,' Rowan muttered softly, his eyes focussed on the flames.

'Aye. They tell me one wealthy merchant put a bounty on Cockburn's 'ead, sar. A thousand dollars on his 'ead and five hundred dollars on each ear.' The man coughed a laugh between strokes. 'Aye. It's as bad as it can get.'

'Where is the militia, for God's sake?'

'Evacuated, sar...'

'What!'

'After Bladensburg fell, I'm told, them troops re-grouped at the turnpike gate a mile and half from the Capitol, along with Colonel Minor's 60th Regiment from Virginia, but when General Winder saw the pathetic condition of the men,' the ferryman said of Brigadier General William Winder, "E ordered 'em ta retreat. Said 'e'd rather save the lives of 'is men than save Washington.'

'And Madison?' Rowan asked of the President of the United States of America.

'Took off to the country, sar.'

'Then Washington is doomed.'

Had Rowan known the stark reality, General Winder had no choice. His undisciplined ranks had thinned, exhausted from battles elsewhere, like Bladensburg. Many militias returned to save their own families across the countryside as far away as Baltimore. Had the General stayed, the British would have trapped the Americans and starved them into submission while still occupying the city.

The sight of the retreating army—footsore and uncoordinated, slogging west along Pennsylvania Avenue and out of town across the bridge at Georgetown—angered the few residents holed up in their homes.

For another five dollars, Rowan exchanged his clothes with those of the ferryman whom, fortunately, was of a similar build. Rowan thought the transaction should have been the other way around, given the number of patches and tears and the insidious odours the garments bore; however, he was now dressed as a pauper and had more chance of negotiating the occupied capitol.

A quarter of a mile east Rowan watched the naval yards burn. It was sickening. Under orders of the Naval Secretary, William Jones, a close friend of President Madison, Naval Yard Clerk Mordecai Booth and Army Captain John Creighton had set alight fuses leading to the ordinance stores and naval shipbuilding warehouses. With such great stores of tar, paint, canvas and cordage for fuel, the fire spread rapidly to the mast and timber sheds, the joiners' and boat builders' workshops, mold lofts, block makers and blacksmith shops and finally, the administration buildings. They then torched the navy ships in dock. It was a maelstrom of fire.

On Capitol Hill the ten-year-old, three-storey Capitol building was also well ablaze. The British invaders had managed this by piling furniture into the centre of the Chamber of Representatives, an oblong, octagon-shaped room, sixty by eighty-five feet. They ignited the bonfire by emptying the powder from their Congreve rockets amongst the mahogany desks, chairs and tables. The flames caught on the green-lined, crimson silk curtains and made short work of the public galleries and wooden platforms with yellow-pine floorboards elevated seven feet. On the ground floor the soldiers had a more difficult task, there being more marble and masonry and less timber. However, once again, the furniture combined with the highly combustible rocket powder made a fierce bonfire.

With the destruction and vandalism came looting. Not even Admiral Cockburn was immune from souvenir hunting. It transpired later, Rowan heard, that the Admiral himself took President Madison's financial ledger as a memento of his triumph. In the Senate Chamber the blue mantra curtains lined with buff silk, their colours inspired by the Revolutionary War uniforms, went up like newspaper, along with elegant drapery, hangings and luxurious carpets. Here, the intense heat cracked the freestone and the marble columns crumbled like plaster.

Rowan crept through the woods below Capitol Hill. He could see redcoats gathering around the flames, yahooing, enjoying the destruction and setting alight anything that represented the government of America. The fire spread rapidly, taking hold of the heavily timbered Library of Congress with its thirty-six-foot ceiling. Its wooden shingled roof caved in, destroying the three thousand books stored on the wooden shelves. The Supreme Court was next. From where Rowan watched, the roar of the flames and exploding buildings sounded like thunder—his heart sank.

He had to find Jessica, and fast, but Georgetown was to the west...

...and the soldiers also marched west.

Hurrying amongst patches of darkness, while flames danced across open spaces, Rowan made his way to the outskirts of the township. Here, he was relieved to see the citizens' homes were mostly unscathed. Neat rows of two-storey, horizontal timber residences with their attics and bay windows, vegetable gardens and white picket fences were unmolested. Some lights flickered through closed shutters, but most properties had been deserted. Rowan kept to the shadows along Pennsylvania Avenue, Washington's main thoroughfare. The avenue was a hundred and sixty feet wide, a gravel roadway flanked on both sides with Lombardy poplar trees. Pennsylvania Avenue also led to Georgetown, where Jessica's uncle and aunt lived at their merchandise warehouse.

As Rowan made his way west, he encountered British soldiers marching in an orderly column, two abreast, along the avenue. He discovered later that they'd been headed to the arsenal at Greenleaf's Point but, fortunately, Colonel Wadsworth of the militia had spirited much of the arsenal out into the surrounding woods only the day before.

Skulking from building to building along the exposed avenue, Rowan made painfully slow's progress was painfully slow. He was contemplating his next move when a group of one hundred or more of Ross's soldiers and Cockburn's sailors marched, in two orderly columns, down off Capitol Hill and onto the avenue. the flaming backlight of the blazing Capitol building behind them silhouetted the men. They had been ordered to keep silent and, for a large group, they were eerily quiet. Many carried torches on long sticks and Rowan guessed, correctly, that they were headed towards the president's house, a mile and a half distant. Four officers on horseback with their chapeaux-bras high on their heads followed the foot soldiers, while excited freed slaves ran ahead of the invaders. Rowan sank into the shadows. The private homes on both sides of the avenue were deserted; only a lamp flickered in the odd window.

Suddenly, the window on the second floor above Rowan rattled open. The resident, an old man, waved a white flag at the approaching soldiers. Rowan backed smartly into the dark alleyway between the houses. Afraid to breath, he caught a glimpse of the older officer approaching on his black stallion. It was then that Rowan recognised the tall, slim officer as Admiral Cockburn himself. Cockburn steered his horse by the alley to beneath the window.

'What ails you, sir?' Cockburn called up to the old man, who could quite easily have been a veteran of the Revolutionary War. Rowan's nose caught the sweat of the horse. He sensed the admiral's testosterone, sweating with success.

'I plead with you, sir,'—the old timer's voice was frail —'Do not burn my home.'

Rowan heard the admiral comfort the old man with a pledge that no private property would be damaged. Little comfort, Rowan thought, when behind them the invaders left a trail of destruction.

'Be under no apprehension, sir,' Cockburn told the resident as he trotted away. 'My advice to you is to remain at home. Tell your neighbours—do not quit your houses.'

Rowan watched the troops march away and cursed under his breath. Now he had Cockburn, of all enemies, between him and Jessica in Georgetown. The chance of being shot on sight was a reality. But, should they head for the president's house, which Rowan imagined was a prized target, he might have a chance to escape past them while they were preoccupied.

All looked promising until the troops, seemingly unrushed, gathered outside the Washington Hotel on the corner of 14th and 15th Streets. Here they rendezvoused with the companies from the 21st and 85th Foot Regiments. Diagonally opposite the hotel was a long, low brick building that Rowan knew as Mrs. Barbara Suter's boarding house. He had taken lodgings there, on occasion. It was a prime location, being the closest building to the president's house and other important government departments.

It was an hour before midnight. Rowan heard General Ross order Mrs. Suter to kill some chickens in her backyard and cook his dinner. He would be back later, he said. All this destruction had given the man a healthy appetite. Ross then dismounted and walked the two hundred yards to President Madison's residence. Rowan's heart sank. From where he'd positioned himself, he watched as British troops entered the president's residence unchallenged.

Even the Madison's servants had vacated the building. Surprisingly, the president's wife, Dolly Madison, and her entourage, had left in such haste that the dining table was laden with food, set for a party of forty, along with coolers of wine and ale. The redcoats, who had marched into Bladensburg and defeated *that* city before midday and then marched another six miles to Washington, now enjoyed a midnight feast in style.

Mrs. Suter's chickens would have to wait.

By all later accounts the tired, hungry and thirsty soldiers gorged themselves like Viking raiders, quaffing Madeira from crystal goblets while greedily devouring the banquet. And no one enjoyed the celebrations more than Admiral Cockburn. The invaders toasted their Prince Regent, while the admiral insisted that a local man, Roger Weighman, be dragged into the elegant home and ordered to feast with them. *To be a witness.* The admiral then commanded Weighman to take a souvenir. Bewildered, the local faltered until Admiral Cockburn scooped up several ornaments from the mantelpiece and pressed them into the anxious man's hands.

'These will answer as a memento,' Cockburn declared, charged on success and wine. The admiral then cast an eye about the dining hall and announced, 'I must take something, too.' He souvenired the president's old hat and a cushion.

The soldiers then went on a looting spree. The president's ceremonial dress sword and personal medicine chest would be two souvenirs returning to England.

It was time to burn the White House.

And nothing gave Admiral Cockburn more pleasure than destroying the American president's property. Four years earlier, President Thomas Jefferson had vacated the twenty-three-room house, leaving it tastefully furnished for the new president. Now mahogany writing tables, desks, crimson sofas, commodes, four-poster beds, dining tables, chaise lounges, chests of drawers, dressing tables and much more was about to be used as kindling. Some pieces, Rowan was told later, had belonged to George Washington himself.

While a bonfire was being set in the ground floor foyer, Cockburn's sailors, who were masters of destruction, rushed up the grand U-shaped staircase, setting fire to curtains, bedding, and other flammable fixtures in the rooms and bedrooms off the hallway. Many personal items belonging to the president and his wife—dinner and dessert chinaware, silverware, personal furniture and artifacts of Madison's presidency—were lost to the insatiable flames. The president's home burnt freely. While windows exploded and mirrors shattered from their frames, the yellow damask curtains and draperies turned to cinders in minutes. In the oval drawing room, sailors danced a jig in merriment watching the cherry-yellow satin upholstery of mahogany sofas combust. Matching high-backed chairs along with a majestic carved sideboard large enough to furnish the largest of parlours turned to charcoal in minutes.

At the corner of 14th Street and Pennsylvania Avenue, Rowan joined a dozen elderly residents, their faces reflecting the horror and the flames engulfing President Madison's once magnificent home. One witness wrote later in his diary, 'The spectators stood in awful silence, the city was light and the heavens reddened with the blaze.'

In nearby woods north of Washington, a small group of American militia also watched the flames in silence. There was nothing they could do. Armed but helpless against such a force, the raw recruits could only cower and gaze in pain at the destruction of one grand structure after another.

No one took a second glance at the pauper in the ferryman's stinking clothes. Disgusted at what he was witnessing, Rowan slipped away from the crowd and hurried on towards Georgetown unmolested.

94

CHAPTER NINE

SERGEANT MARCUS MARRIOT

August 1814. London. Whitechapel.

Disgraced sergeant Marcus Marriot sat alone at a corner table in the taproom of the Black Bull in Whitechapel. He sulked into his penny gin, drawn from a hogshead branded Old Tom, alone with his black-hearted thoughts. Recently demoted back to a private in the King's Army on suspicion of raping the fourteen-year-old daughter of a poor Bristol weaver, Marriot had been transferred to London. But making an honest soldier of himself eluded the man. Certainly, he was fit and mostly healthy, but being a creature of lazy habits, he was more drawn to a life of crime. Marriot swallowed his gin and bought another. He was angry. He felt hard done by.

Sure, he was guilty of lying with that weaver's little bitch, but the tart had asked for it. His thoughts went to the cobbler's cottage in Bristol where he had caught that other bitch, Elizabeth Eveleigh, conspiring to counterfeit the king's coin. Did he get credit for that? *No. Captain Bloody Fairbairn took all the credit.*

1814

Marriot suddenly caught sight of pretty young Melody Clarke. She walked past the taproom door, on her way to the inn's parlour, where she, too, bought herself a penny gin. The attractive lass had not gone unnoticed by other rakes in the inn, so the disgraced soldier moved fast.

'Hello, beautiful.' Marriot said, and then gestured to the vacant chair at her table. 'Drinkin' on yer lonesome, eh? Mind if'n I join yer?' The slightest hint of a smile invited his company. Marriot bought the next two gins and, slowly, Melody Clarke warmed to this handsome acquaintance. She was a servant at the residence of Lord Richard Thomas, Esquire, of Saint James Square, she told Marriot. She was in Whitechapel visiting her sickly mother. Melody Clarke told Marriot that she was unhappy with her employment; she was underpaid and over worked. Marriot told Melody he was a sergeant in the King's Army, on leave from Bristol.

The other rakes began to circle.

'You 'ungry?' Marriot asked Melody.

'Starvin'.'

'Come on, then, I'll buy yer a pie.'

Violet's Cream Bakery on Whitechapel Road four blocks away boasted the best pork pies in London, Marriot told Melody. 'Usually they serve 'em cold but I likes 'em jus' after they come outta the oven.' Marriot purchased two pies wrapped in paper and they sat together on someone's doorstep. 'Now be careful, like,' he said. 'Yer gotta lean over to take yer first bite or else the warm juice'll run down yer chin and neck.'

Marriot knew better than to appear too keen. He took Melody to the Goose and Quill, where they had two more gins each. By the time Marriot walked Melody the three miles to Saint James Square, he had won over her confidence and convinced her that souveniring some of the tyrant lord's silver was her God-given right.

Washington

The acrid smoke of destruction clung in the night air. Rowan left the open road occasionally for the cover of the woods, but in the darkness he was aware of being observed by shadowed faces. Silent movements or the snapping of twigs divulged the locations where refugees from Washington were hiding from the invaders: deserting militia, absconded slaves, looters, young men, old men, women and children. The stench of anarchy lingered. Half a mile out of Georgetown Rowan met a delegation of eight panicked businessmen carrying white flags and heading towards the flames. Rowan recognised one man, Benjamin Jones, who had a warehouse for cotton and tobacco three doors from Jessica's uncle and aunt's warehouse.

'Rowan? Is that really you?'

'Yes, Benjamin. What are you doing?'

'We hope to arrange an audience with General Ross and Admiral Cockburn.' Benjamin's face was tight with worry. 'The flames, Rowan... Is the whole city ablaze?'

'They burn the public buildings only. Any private residences ablaze are collateral damage or belong to citizens they see as aiding the militia.'

'Damn their eyes, Rowan. Damn them to hell.'

'Why do you seek Ross and Cockburn?'

'To parley. To plead with them not to destroy our town. We will offer no resistance in exchange.'

'Then good luck to you. Do you have any news of Owen and Eugene York?'

' 'Tis sad news, Rowan.'

'What?'

'Their warehouse was ransacked. The troops took everything of value for the army and navy—flour, wheat, salted meats, wine, beer ... everything. As I deal in tobacco and cotton they let me be for now, but I know they will return.'

'And Jessica, Benjamin—have you news of my wife?'

'No, sorry, lad. Is she not in Baltimore?'

'No. She thought Georgetown would be safer, but now...' Rowan's voice trailed off.

'Come, Benjamin!' one of the merchants yelled back. 'This is no time for gossip.'

Benjamin Jones bowed slightly and hurried after his friends. 'I must go, Rowan. Godspeed.'

Back under the low smoke canopy of conflagration the raiders continued their destruction. They moved to the Treasury Building on the eastern flank of the president's house, as well as government offices to the west, before returning towards Capitol Hill to retire for the night. For the British torchbearers it had been a most successful and rewarding, yet exhausting twenty-four hours.

Sometime in the early morning, President Madison and his entourage were milling about the countryside of Virginia, west of the Potomac, watching the distant flames; they were at a loss as to what to do. Finally they spent the night at Salona, a 466-acre estate at Little Falls owned by Reverend William Maffitt. The reverend's brick mansion lay just four miles from Washington on the road leading from the bridge over the Potomac River. Had Admiral Cockburn known, he would have sent men to capture President Madison.

Towards Georgetown Rowan encountered carts and barrows clattering noisily over the rough gravelled avenue. Here, knots of redcoat soldiers verbally harassed the fleeing inhabitants who had left late and decided to escape their homes in the dark.

Rowan knew the town well, with its streets named alphabetically one way and numerically the other. He also knew the nuances, as many smaller streets and alleys repeated the names of the larger avenues and boulevards, confusing visitors. And it was fortunate that he did, as marauders were lurking in the sultry darkness -- soldiers of fortune with bellies full of grog, looting in the name of recompense.

With the flames behind him, Rowan walked smartly across fields at the river's edge. He entered Georgetown on the Potomac to the northwest of Washington. Keeping to the shadows, he avoided the chilling menace of the horse patrols passing frequently. Rowan finally made the waterfront, negotiating a narrow alley between a tannery and a walled canal.

'You there. Halt.' The sergeant's voice came from behind. 'Halt, I say, in the name of King George.' Rowan was dressed in the clothes of a poor man, clothes that smelt as foul as they looked, but Rowan suspected once the soldier held a lantern to his face, he would be recognized. Rowan heard the clatter of several nail-tipped boots as other redcoats joined their comrade. Rowan continued on.

'Are you deaf, man? I know you speak the King's language, you traitorous American scum.'

Rowan fled.

'Bastard!' The soldier screamed after him. Shots rang out.

Hot lead sizzled by Rowan's ear. Another musket ball tugged at his coattail. The third shot shattered a brick wall, spitting debris in the instant Rowan disappeared around the corner.

'After him—now!'

The corner turned onto a short footbridge that crossed the canal. Beyond, in the moonlight, Rowan saw an open field. He would be an easy target, even at night. But on the other side a narrow cobbled path ran parallel to the canal and led through an arch, into what appeared to be another alleyway. Rowan heard the rattle of ramrods. Powder, ball and gauze were jammed down the barrels of muskets. He rushed the bridge and sprinted along the path towards the arch.

'There!' Rowan heard someone yell. He had been seen. He twisted on the run. Out of the corner of his eye, Rowan saw four men. One held a lantern.

'For Christ's sake, shoot!'

Rowan rushed under the arch, down the ill-lit alley and

into a dead end. He was fifty yards back from the arch. The soldiers rounded the corner. They stared into the blackness, immediately pushing their backs against the wall, where their eyes adjusted.

'There!'

'We got 'im,' one gloated.

With Rowan going nowhere, they approached cautiously. Rowan fumbled under his rags and unsheathed his dagger, commending himself for having had the blacksmith grind and polish a razor's edge on the blade...

But he was a doctor, not a killer. He questioned his courage. *Jessica* he said silently to himself, over and over, *Jessica*.

'Don't waste powder, lads,' Rowan heard the sergeant say. 'Ned, fix ya bayonet.'

'With pleasure, Sarge.'

In the gloom of the semi-covered alleyway Rowan had not noticed a wooden doorway to his left. Now, as the lantern light crept ever closer, distorting shadows along the wall as it approached, Rowan glimpsed the outline of a portal. He heard the subtlest creaking of rusty metal, followed by a faint voice.

'Psst! Sir. Come.' The door opened a few more inches. 'Make haste now.'

Rowan dived for the opening. He was swallowed into pitch darkness. The door slammed shut and he heard the sound of a bolt driven home. Instantly a warm hand took his. Outside he heard muffled curses. Rowan allowed himself to be ushered through the dark. He could see nothing before him, but fear began turning to trust. Behind him, the butts of muskets crashed against the alley door. He heard more curses, shouting.

At the end of the passage, his saviour, nothing but a dark shape, opened another door leading to an attic stair. Soft moonlight washed across the treads.

'Go,' the woman's voice whispered. Rowan could just make out her face. She was a good ten years older than him, with a kindly face. A gold crucifix rested on her bosom. 'Go onto the roof,' she whispered. 'Climb roof to roof and be off with you.'

'But what about yourself?' As Rowan spoke, he noticed the finest string of light, accentuating a doorway in the passage. It was clearly the woman's lodgings. A lone candle burnt within.

The pounding on the door grew louder. The sound of splintering wood.

'Go now. Hurry... please.'

Rowan took the woman's hand, cupping it in his. 'Thank you,' he said, his words barely audible.

'God be with you.'

Rowan slipped onto the stairway. Again, the door closed behind him. Escaping onto the roof did not seem the smartest idea, but it was all Rowan had.

The alley door crashed open, followed by angry shouting.

Rowan mounted the stairs, tripping onto a small platform on the roof. A widow's tower. Rowan could see the harbour.

1814

Behind him, Washington blazed. Instantly flashes of lightning lit the darkened horizon to the east. A thunderstorm approached from the Atlantic. Rowan felt the wind picking up. The destruction of Washington had drawn a gale towards the capitol—an invisible ghoul to fan the fires. Beyond the widow's tower was the shingled roof of a three-storey terraced home. He was not an enthusiast of heights. Without looking down, Rowan climbed the rail. He balanced precariously on the steep apex of the gabled roof and crept forward.

Sounds of rushing boots on the stairs pushed Rowan forward. There was no way to escape from here but to go down. The steps grew louder. Men shouting, cussing. Rowan reached a four-pot chimney. It was not wide, but maybe...

Just maybe.

'Can ya see 'im?' A second soldier pushed past the first onto the platform.

'Nuthin'. Not a bloody thing.'

'Do ya reckon he escaped across the roof?'

Both men stepped forward to the edge and looked down. 'I don't like 'is chances. Hurry. 'E musta doubled back somewheres.'

Rowan waited for minutes that seemed hours. He heard the echo of soldiers' boots clattering noisily along the cobbles below. Then all was quiet, except for the wind and the approaching storm.

The rain finally hit, in plump, warm globules, like a tropical downpour. It came in at an angle, drenching everything, and Rowan prayed it would douse the fires, but the squalls came in short bursts. Rowan negotiated the roofs of five dwellings. They were terraced, joining at roof level; the going was not too difficult. The first sign of trouble came when shingle turned to slate—wet, slippery slate. Rowan had no warning. His feet slipped out from under him and he crashed heavily onto the seat of his britches, descending down the high-angled roof. He closed his eyes as his body launched from the edge and his life flashed before him. Rowan plunged. His mind went blank.

'Wake, wake!' The young woman's voice was urgent. She shook Rowan's arm and saw his eyes flicker. 'You *are* alive.' The woman's voice was troubled.

Rowan sat upright with a jolt. 'Where...? What...? Where am I?' His voice was croaky and he was aware of a thumping pain in his head.

'You're in my barn—you fell through the roof. Lord only knows what you were up to, but my guess is you were up to mischief.'

'No... No... I was...' Rowan's voice trailed off as he scrutinised the woman, for she could easily be a Federalist. The woman returned an inquisitive expression.

'You don't sound like a looter. You sound like a gentleman.' Her eyes studied his rags by the little moonlight that filtered through the hole he had just made in her barn roof.

Suddenly, the memory of the fall flooded back. Rowan looked up at the damage. Somehow, by sheer good fortune, he had plunged between beams as the slate had given way. He lay where he had fallen, on the hay.

'I'm surprised you live to tell the tale.'

'How long have I been here?'

The woman studied Rowan a moment longer, comfortable now that he was not a threat. 'Quarter of the hour,' she answered. 'No more, I'm thinking.'

Rowan groaned and held his head.

'Here.' The woman placed a knitted woollen cap on his head that smelled pleasantly fragrant. It was soggy and he felt something trickle over his forehead.

'What's this?' he asked, fearing the something was blood.

'A cucupha, sir. You have a lump on your head and I prepared this immediately when I saw you lying there, to alleviate any pain.'

Rowan knew the peasant remedy for a sore head was a cucupha of knitted wool infused with herbs and lavender, and he had to admit that it had a soothing influence on his pain.

'What's your name?' Rowan asked as colour returned to his cheeks.

'Mary, sir.'

'Well, thank you, Mary, but I must leave… '

'It's you they were looking for, isn't it?'

'Who?'

'The redcoats—sods… Please excuse my language, but they *are* sods, no better than Indian savages, all of them. Well?'

'Well, what?'

'You're the man the redcoats are after, aren't you?'

'Yes.'

'They came to this house, searching. Said they were looking for a spy… a traitor.'

'I must leave,' Rowan said. 'Immediately. If the soldiers return and see me here, you will be arrested, and God only knows what would happen to you then.'

'Why do you… ah…'

'Ah what, Mary?'

'Well excuse me for asking sir, but why are you dressed in those clothes? I mean, since you are a gentleman… and I must be honest and tell you, they… well, they…'

'Smell dreadful?'

'Yes, sir.'

'I can assure you, these are not my normal clothes. It's a long story.'

'Where are you from?'

'Baltimore.' Rowan stood groggily and immediately groaned with pain. He could hardly stand.

'Are you alright, sir?'

'I've twisted a muscle in my ankle. Damn it... Now *I* must ask *you* to excuse my cussing, Mary.'

'That's all right, sir, my father cussed all the time.'

'Where is your father?'

'Dead, sir. He's been dead a year now. Caught the fever and died suddenly.'

'Oh, I'm sorry to hear that. Then why did you not flee with the rest of the population?'

'I have a sick mother, sir. She dies of a lump in her bosom and refuses to be moved. I swear, the sickness was brought on by father's death.'

'How advanced is this lump?'

'It is like a boiled fowl egg under her left armpit.'

'Take me to her.'

'Sir?'

'I am a surgeon. I may be able to help.'

'You're a surgeon?' Mary was amazed.

'Yes, a ship's doctor, actually. Can you find me a stick with which to aid my walking?'

'I can do better than that, sir. My granddaddy was an amputee, lost a leg in the wars. His crutch is still in the house; I'll fetch it.'

Outside, the smoke thickened. The storm's preliminary winds had spread the fire. Rowan hopped, one-legged, to the barn door and peered out. He heard distant shooting and muffled screams, and nearby a dog barked incessantly. Mary returned with a crutch.

'Mother wants to know your name, good sir.'

'My apologies—I did not introduce myself. I'm Rowan Craige.' He added, 'Doctor Rowan Craige.'

Mrs. Nellie Bachelor, Mary's ill mother, was at first wary. The woman lay on her bed on the first floor. She was pale with worry, pale with the sickness and now pale with the angst all about her, as the city burned. Her brow glistened with sweat—she had a fever. Rowan spent a moment building the woman's confidence. She was an attractive woman for her advanced years and Rowan imagined she would have been beautiful in her youth. But he saw determination in her eyes. She knew she would die soon if the sickness was left untreated, and she was aware of the procedure, having a neighbour who had had her own demon cut from her breast. She had lived another ten years. Showing regard for the woman's modesty, Rowan unbuttoned her nightgown, exposing her sick breast. The lump was, indeed, the size of a chook's egg. He felt confident and told her so.

'Have you done this before?' she asked Rowan.

'Yes, Mrs. Bachelor,' Rowan lied. He had seen the procedure done twice on patients in Baltimore when he was studying, but he he had certainly never carried out the operation before. His talents had predominantly been employed at sea, and upon men.

Sheet lightning illuminated the room briefly, but the gloom instantly returned.

Mary was nervous. She was certainly more nervous than the patient. 'What do you need?' she asked.

Rowan limped over to Mary, taking her by the elbow and ushering her into the passageway. A low rumble of thunder followed the lightning.

'Do you have a roasting fork?' he asked in a whisper.

Mary's bottom jaw dropped, but she reigned in the burning questions. 'Y-yes sir.'

'Then fetch it please. I also need boiling water and soap, and do you by chance have any bandages?'

'No, sir.'

'Then I'll need towels. As many as you can spare.' He looked over his shoulder at the patient. 'And I'll need more light. I'll need leather straps, belts or rope... '

'Rope?'

'Your mother will have to be restrained. I'm sorry.' Rowan thought a moment. 'And please bring me a needle and thread?'

Mary nodded anxiously.

'One last thing.'

'Yes?'

'I will need a small brazier, or, if not, a pot with red hot coals and a smoothing iron or a spatula, maybe.'

Nellie Bachelor lay on her bed, stoic and resigned to the pain. She asked that the wooden crucifix on the wall be taken down. She wished to hold it during the operation.

Mary returned with the items required. She placed them on a bedside table and returned with the family's iron cooking pot, full of red-hot coals. This she carefully placed on a broken flagstone on the landing outside the room. The coals taken from the oven glowed red in the night, fanned by a draught from the floor below. An extra lantern of clear-burning whale oil was pegged on a beam over the bed, lighting the subject. Mary held up a wooden-handled baking spatula. 'Will this suffice, sir?'

'Perfect. Now place it in the coals.'

Mrs. Bachelor's head turned towards the glowing coals and she muttered a silent prayer. Rowan discarded the ferryman's coat and rolled up the sleeves of his shirt. Although it was not a part of his training, Rowan always regarded washing his hands a necessity, as a defence against later infection. Pouring some of the boiling water into a dish he scrubbed his hands with brush and soap. Together he and Mary strapped the patient tightly to the bed with her left arm secured above her head, so that the pectorals muscles would push the breast upwards.

Rowan looked the woman in the eye. She was certainly brave and phlegmatic, trusting in her faith as she squeezed the crucifix.

'Do you have any spirits?' he asked Mary.

'Only a little of father's rum. We don't imbibe sir.'

'Fetch it, please.'

'I don't need rum, Mr. Craige,' Mrs. Bachelor said adamantly. 'I have the Lord to curb my pain.'

'You may have the Lord, Mrs. Bachelor, but I have conducted many operations, and believe me when I say comfort from rum or whiskey is beneficial.'

While Mary helped her mother with a cup of dark Jamaican rum, Rowan took his dirk from its sheath. Until now he had kept it hidden. 'Are you ready, ma'am?'

'As ready as I'll ever be.' The patient started reciting the Lord's Prayer and Rowan thought silently that she would need more than faith.

Outside the rain thickened, large drops spattering the windowpanes only to stream down the walls to flood the alleyway below.

As ordered by Rowan, Mary held her mother down by the shoulders. 'Here, Mother, bite down on this.' Mary placed a wooden spoon in the woman's mouth and Mrs. Bachelor's prayers continued in a muffled mumble. Rowan took the carving fork in his hand; its prongs recently sharpened, and he pushed them deep into the breast. The patient screamed in agony, and, mercifully, fainted. Rowan worked quickly, lifting the gland from the breast wall with his left hand while he sliced the base of the bosom with his dirk. Rowan removed the breast completely, but the disease had spread further than he had suspected during the examination. Knots of tumour could also be felt in the lymph nodes under her arm. The patient groaned, drifting in and out of consciousness, while Rowan removed the extra tumours in a mess of blood. All the while Mary's attention was fastened on the wall to one side.

'Are you all right?' he asked Mary, who had turned white from the sight of blood and the cloying smell of sickness. 'Mary. Are you alright?'

'Y-yes,' she answered, her head remaining turned.

'Then pass me the spatula, smartly now.'

Mary gladly left the bedside. She returned with the red-hot spatula and passed it, wooden handle first, to Rowan. The stench of burning flesh permeated the room as he cauterised the worst areas of bleeding. With needle and thread at the ready, Rowan sutured the open wound as best he could. He felt that the operation had been a success, but the woman's left side would remain an ugly sight. Rowan felt a wave of triumph. The whole affair had taken less than half of an hour.

'Will she live?' Mary asked weakly.

'She'll live. But there is going to be a long recovery. Months, even. But I am confident she will live to a ripe old age.'

Mary was overwhelmed. She threw her arms around Rowan, hugging the man, oblivious to the state of his blouse and trousers, which were saturated with blood. 'How can I ever thank you? What you have done, sir, is no less than a miracle.'

'I've done what I was trained to do, Mary, nothing more, nothing less. What I would ask of you, however, is, do you still have any of your father's clothes I could change into?' Rowan knew he was a marked man wearing the ferryman's clothes.

'Yes, of course. All of father's clothes are still in his trunk. Come to the attic and you can choose whatever you need.'

The attic was steeply gabled and Rowan could only stand his full length under the apex beam. He kept balance on the crutch while Mary fossicked through the trunk. 'Here, this should fit.' Mary held up a dark blue swallowtail coat with striped britches to match.

'Perfect. What was your fathers industry, if I may ask?'

'Ah…' Mary returned a cheeky smile. 'Father was…'

The pounding on the front door silenced them. 'Surely it is not the soldiers. They have been here already.'

Rowan cuffed a hand over Mary's mouth and pressed hard against the window. Peering down into the street, he recognised the shadows thrown by the street lamp. Redcoats' shadows.

'Devil's blood—it's soldiers.'

The pounding grew louder. 'Open in the name of King George!'

'Get in here.' Mary pushed the trunk aside to reveal a small secret cupboard. Rowan climbed inside. 'I was about to say father was a smuggler,' Mary said. 'This is one of his hiding places for contraband.' Mary pushed Rowan's head into the narrow space and closed the hatch. Rowan heard the trunk slide back into place and Mary's footsteps descend the stairs. *Jesus Lord!* he suddenly thought, *how will Mary explain Mrs. Bachelor lying in her bloodied bed?*

The rain now pounded on the slate roof overhead, cascading off the sides and pouring into the streets, forming muddy puddles below. Although Rowan was in complete darkness, he caught flashes of the electrical storm over Washington. Suddenly he heard voices that seemed to be at the attic doorway. He heard a slap and a whimper.

'Mary?'

Silence.

The wait was unbearable.

The soldiers' voices dissipated and claustrophobia stalked Rowan in the darkness. After what he felt was ample time, he felt about the edges of the hatch cover for a handle, but the hatch was flush with the wall. It had never been intended to be opened from the inside. Rowan felt anxiety rise in his throat. He felt parched. His headache returned.

Then, over the tempest, he heard a scream—a muffled woman's scream.

Mary!

Rowan dug his fingernails into the joins of the hatchway. Nothing. It was jammed fast. Then he remembered his dirk, sheathed at his bloodied hip. Blindly, he felt for the widest gap. He poked the knife tip into the joint, and twisted, and the point dug into the wood. Rowan levered the knife blade and a halo of lantern light appeared around the edges. He wriggled his fingers into the gap and clawed the hatch open, pushing the trunk aside. Rowan crawled free, taking his crutch. Changing clothes with haste, he hobbled silently to the stairwell and listened. He heard voices on the ground floor.

In the kitchen?

With his ankle twisted, Rowan descended the stairs on the seat of his pants, one at a time. On the first landing he peered in at his patient. Mary had covered her mother with blankets and she was sleeping groggily from the rum and the pain. Rowan crawled down to the flagstones of the ground floor, where he could move in silence, but only with the aid of the crutch.

Yes. They are in the kitchen.

The front door was wide open and the rain outside was now torrential. Damaged guttering caused a waterfall from off the neighbouring roofs. The noise of the storm masked Rowan's movements, but he was exposed in the passageway.

He had no illusions as to what would happen to him if he were caught. Cursing his twisted ankle, he manoeuvred towards the kitchen doorway. The voices sounded affected by drink, lascivious in tone. Rowan heard a slap and then a short cry.

Mary?

The door was ajar. He passed the entrance and entered the darkened scullery adjoining the kitchen... and listened.

The soldiers were clearly oiled on rum. They teased Mary, intimidated her. Rowan peered through the gap between jamb and door. There were three of the bastards, drinking what must have been her father's rum from a stone bottle. Mary was slumped in a chair. Her eyes were swollen and red, and the skin on her face was raw. The man nearest her struck her again. 'We can do this all night you colonial whore. Where is he?'

'I told you," Mary's words came slurred from her tumescent lips. 'He escaped when he heard you knocking.'

'Well who is 'e any'ow? Yer husband?'

'Brave bastard, eh?' another soldier sneered. 'To run off an' leave a little treasure like you behind.' His hand caressed Mary's exposed leg.

The first soldier raised his fist again. 'I said who is 'e?' Rowan ground his teeth. His gut knotted. He wanted to burst into the room and take on all three of them. He felt his headache thump. 'Well? Is 'e yer husband? Father?'

'He was a stranger in passing,' Mary managed through tears. 'A doctor.'

'Oh, a doctor, eh?'

'Yes, and a good man,' Mary spat. 'Not a sodding British soldier.'

The balled fist slammed into Mary's face and she slumped forward in her chair. Rowan could take this no longer. He unsheathed his dirk. Suddenly, wet hob-nailed boots crashed through the front door and along the passageway towards the kitchen, followed by shouting. 'Corporal? Sam? Jack? You still 'ere?'

'Aye.'

'Cap'n Fothering'am's lookin' for yer all.'

'Jesus! Where is 'e?'

'Three doors back. We're movin' to the docks. Hurry.'

Mary's tormentor drained his teacup of rum. 'It's yer lucky day,' he snarled at her, as his mates gathered their weapons and kit. The man leant in to kiss Mary but she turned her head, and he ran his rum-soaked tongue up her cheek. Certain that the men had departed, Rowan pushed the scullery door open.

'Are you all right?'

'Mother,' Mary cried, 'how is she?'

'Fear not. She sleeps.'

Mary was bruised but in good spirits. 'Thank the lord.' She wiped blood from her lips. 'Sods. All of them.'

'I'm so sorry... I ...'

'Do not apologise, sir. You have no cause to apologise.'

'I heard everything. You are a brave woman, Mary.' Rowan made certain they were alone and then hurried to the open front door, where rainwater had already flooded the floorboards. He bolted the door shut. He returned to the kitchen. Mary was washing her bruised face before dabbing snake oil from a brown bottle to the affected areas.

'You can stay here with us,' Mary offered.

'Thank you, but I have urgent business in Georgetown.'

'Oh?'

'Yes, I must find my wife.'

'You *are* married. Then she is a lucky woman.'

'My wife is with child. She only has days to go and she has chosen, rather unwisely, to journey here, to Georgetown, from Baltimore.'

'Then you must go to her immediately.' Mary placed a hand on Rowan's arm. 'Please,'—she looked him in the eye —'If you need a roof over your head or a place to hide, both you and your wife, you are always welcome here.'

Chapter Ten

London. Whitechapel.

Sergeant Marcus Marriot stepped from the Goose and Quill into the dense, misted haze of a foggy February night. It was difficult to see the features of people on the street until they came fairly close. It was the perfect night for crime.

Marcus Marriot felt on top of the world. He was drunk on cheap gin. Familiar sounds ahead caused Marcus to feel some wariness. He stopped to listen. Then a faint yellow flame exposed the position of the local lamplighter across the street. Marcus lurched towards the man.

'Bloody lot o' good that'll do,' he muttered at the lamplighter.

'Aye. All the same, I am enlisted to do me duty.'

Marcus could barely make out the spectral shape of the old lamplighter teetering at the top of his ladder. 'Aye... yer duty,' Marcus mocked. But at one shilling and sixpence remuneration a day when he had been a sergeant, Marcus could hardly crow. Marcus patted his pocket. His purse might be empty but the silver spoon he had bought with his last crown was worth two pounds from any pawnbroker, if only he could find one open at this hour. Marcus smiled at the memory of seventeen-year-old Melody Clarke. She was a pretty little thing and the thought of lying with her stirred his desires. He had listened to her sob story when they'd first met at the Black Bull. Her master, Lord Richard Thomas, Esquire, an industrialist, was moving to his country estate for the remainder of the winter and no longer required her services.

"'I no longer require yer services," 'e said,' Melody Clarke told Marcus. ''E got the footman to let me go, an' all. Wouldn't face me 'imself, gutless bastard. So I nicked this spoon out o' the scullery after supper. Before it all got locked away, like. Just like yer told me to do.'

'How much do yer want for it?' Marcus asked.

'You told me you reckoned ten bob for a servin' spoon.'

'Aye. But this 'un's worn, like. It's old, luv. I can give yer a crown.'

'A crown? Yer know it's worth five quid, easy.'

'A crown. It's all I got.'

Melody Clarke took the crown. Marcus snatched the spoon, hiding it in his coat folds, and left the foolish girl to her own means. Now Marriot needed to find a pawnbroker to pawn the silverware, and then find a bottle of gin.

Marcus continued along Butcher's Row to Temple Bar at the beginning of Fleet Street. He knew the area well and imagined Logan Wellington, the pawnbroker, would still be trading. Wellington never asked questions and gave fair prices... Well, almost. Marcus kept one foot against the curb, judging his distances. Footsteps passed in the night, coughs signalled others in transit. Cab drivers walked their horses, too fearful to mount up in the hopeless gloom. Marcus ambled through the fog. He moved from lamplight to lamplight and finally stood in front of Logan Wellington's shop. *Closed*.

He turned on the spot. Marcus knew of several pawnbrokers in the area. He noticed, nestled between lamps across Fleet Street, that Nicolas Coote seemed to be open. The brass bell jerked on its coiled iron spring, warning the shopkeeper that someone had entered, and Nicholas Coote's older son, Anthony Coote, stepped down from the living quarters at the rear of the shop.

'Yes?'

'I've a silver spoon to pawn.'

Anthony carried a small lantern with him to compliment the lone candle burning on its candlestick in the shop window. The shopkeeper was about the same age as Marcus, and he thought he knew the man's face, but could not place it.

Coote took the large silver-serving spoon and rolled it in his hand. 'Where did you get this?'

'It's me ma's,' Marcus lied. 'The rent for our lodgin' is overdue and she told me to pawn it.'

'Ah-huh.' Coote feigned interest. 'How much are you wanting for it?'

Marcus did not hesitate. 'Three pounds.'

If Anthony Coote thought the price too much, his expression gave nothing away. 'Let me show it to Mr. Coote.' He disappeared back through the curtain and Marcus heard soft voices. Marcus felt an unease that was hard to explain. Finally, Mr. Nicolas Coote, a sickly old man with jaundiced skin, not unlike the skin of a ripe quince, stepped into the shop from the back rooms. He wore a smoking jacket and silk slippers. The pawnbroker made idle conversation. Irritated, Marcus interrupted. 'Look are you interested in the spoon or not? I haven't got all night.'

Suddenly the doorbell rang, loud and clear once more, and Marcus turned to face a night watchman. Anthony Coote was right on his heels. 'This 'im?' The watchman held a cosh at the ready.

'Yes.'

'What's this all about?' Marcus shifted anxiously.

'I'm sick and tired of thieves, Mr.... whatever your name is.'

'What are you talkin' about?'

'This!' The pawnbroker pointed to the crest on the silver handle—a unicorn's head in a wreath, something that had not caught Marcus's attention. 'That is the family crest of Lord Thomas; I know all the family crests in London. It is something I have proudly memorised, being a pawnbroker, to catch thieving scoundrels like you.'

Marcus turned to tackle the watchman, but the man was at the ready. Anthony Coote twisted the key in the door lock.

'You're under arrest.'

Dawn. Washington. Georgetown.

Admiral Cockburn and General Ross were rested. They had managed four hours of sleep in comfortable beds at Mrs. Barbara Suter's Boarding House. They enjoyed a dawn breakfast in the dining room while two hundred yards away the embers of President Madison's house hissed and sizzled in the rain. All about them, their nine hundred troops sheltered under roofs, wherever possible.

It was 6 am. The bugles called the troops to assembly. Once the men were grouped for action, the destruction of Washington resumed.

The State and War Department buildings were first. Once again, furniture kindled the blaze. In the Patent Office thousands of files fuelled the fires. Fortunately the most prized trophies in the War Department—the standards and colours snatched from the British during the Revolutionary War over three decades earlier—had been taken away and hidden.

Only hours earlier, Rowan had hitched up his collar against the driving storm and, keeping to the edge of the alleyways and unlit streets, had hurried as best he could with his damaged ankle, north to Jessica's aunt and uncle on the Potomac waterfront, a mile distant. Silas's brother Owen York, Jessica's uncle, and Eugenie York, her aunt, were merchants of moderate means, trading amenities to the many ships that anchored on the waterfront. Their premises were one of many handsome three-storey warehouses, neatly built side by side. Earlier, from Mary's rooftop, Rowan had observed that the Potomac waterfront appeared untouched by the fires. But he noted in the moonlight the mastheads of what he was certain were Royal Navy ships moored mid-river, nearby. Getting past them would be a challenge.

Dawn approached, bringing with it a ferocious storm. The rain and thunder rolled over the capitol, menacing a city already brought to its knees by war. Although the deluge had doused the fires, strong winds persisted and fierce, almost hurricane-force winds were chopping up the river and threatening ships. Roofs lifted off nearby buildings and Rowan was in danger of being hit by falling slate. The soldiers and remaining citizens took refuge in the buildings, as the winds, like an omen of doom, threatened to destroy what remained of Washington.

With head and shoulders stooped, Rowan hurried by the Golden Eagle Tavern, where light came from the taproom windows and he was certain British soldiers would be present. Near the warehouses Rowan backed into a doorway. A hundred yards away he recognised the sign -- *York Merchants*.

'Jessica,' he said, under his breath.

Debris raced by along the dock, like tumbleweed in the desert, and water sprayed the buildings in random geysers as the chaotic winds pounded the harbour. The enemy ships moored on the river had battened down hatches and bore their bows into the wind. Rowan was guarded. The storm was ravaging the streets and turning the alleys into wind tunnels of airborne refuse, but at least there were no soldiers.

Stooping low, Rowan limped to the warehouse. He was certain he saw the light of a lantern at a second floor window where Owen and Eugene had lodgings.

Rowan pounded on the door with his fist, but could barely hear his own actions over the howling winds. He stepped back, briefly peering up at the second-floor window. There was definitely a hint of lantern light. Rowan wanted to call out but feared he might attract the soldiers. He bashed on the door again. Nothing. Rowan was aware of a back entrance at the end of a narrow and tapering laneway, between "York Merchants» and "Selfridge, Chandler." He squeezed through missing palings at the rear of the warehouse. Here, at least, he was out of sight and had some protection from the worsening wind. The rear door was bolted.

Rowan cupped his hands, peering through a window into the gloom of the ground floor. In the dimness of a murky dawn the warehouse looked to be in disarray -- barrels broken open and their contents discarded, merchandise scattered. He bashed hard on the window and called out. There was no response.

With the aid of a loose stave Rowan smashed the glass window and, laying his coat over the jagged edges, snaked his way over the sill, falling clumsily onto the warehouse floor. Limping with the aid of the crutch, Rowan negotiated the disorder all about him.

The damned soldiers have looted the place.

Many barrels had been trashed and left on their sides. Some were still full of salted pork or beef, others held ship's biscuit and others contained apples or potatoes. Rowan was limping across a flagstone floor awash with spilt wine and ales when he caught a shard of light escaping down the stairs. He mounted the treads, hopping awkwardly on each step.

Instantly, he was accosted. 'Take one more step and you are a dead man.'

Rowan stood motionless. He focussed on the silhouetted figure of an older woman at the top of the stairs. She was aiming a musket directly at him. 'Eugenie?'

'Who's that?' the woman called down, straining to see into the shadows.

'Rowan, ma'am... Eugenie, it's Jessica's Rowan.'

'Oh, dear Lord.' Her voice softened. 'Rowan. I thought you were a soldier come back to steal some more from us.'

'No. Please point that gun away.'

Shapes and distorted shadows jounced and danced as Owen York approached the top of the landing with a lantern.

'Rowan.'

Owen, too, stood at the top of the stairwell. He raised the lantern high, trusting its light did not betray him. 'Rowan?'

Rowan now recognised them both—Silas's older brother, Owen, and his wife, Eugenie. Life until this day had been good to them. Both were portly and well dressed, but their usually cheerful faces were lined with fear.

'Rowan, is that really you?'

'Yes. I've come for Jessica.'

Jessica's aunt and uncle stared back, their faces solemn and miserable. Rowan noticed that Owen's right eye was closed shut—it looked like he had been pounded in the face with the butt of a soldier's musket.

'Jesus, Owen, what happened...?' But Rowan knew the answer before he asked. 'Where's Jessica?'

Owen sighed heavily and his shoulders drooped like those of an old man. Eugenie took her husband's hand and squeezed hard.

'Jessica? Where is she?'

Eugenie could contain her emotions no longer. She broke into tears and sobbed.

'Jessica?' Rowan felt his heart hasten its beat. 'Speak to me!' His face reddened and he was losing his breath, fearing the worst.

'Jessica!' Rowan screamed.

The wind howled, buffeting the window shutters.

'Jessica!'

Rowan mounted the next treads but his ankle slowed him. Owen met Rowan half way. He took hold of Rowan's arm. 'She... she has passed on, Rowan.'

'W-what? What do you mean?'

'She's passed, Rowan. Jessica is...'

'No! No! You must be mistaken. No, Owen.' Rowan looked past Owen to Eugenie, now slumped on the top step, sobbing.

Passed on.

The words plunged Rowan into morbid darkness. It had to be a dream—a nightmare. Rowan's voice was suddenly hoarse. 'What do you mean "passed on"?' Rowan's face was contorted, pained beyond recognition. 'Owen? What do you mean?'

'She's dead, son.'

'No! No!'

Owen took Rowan in his arms, the old man's own tears now flowing uninhibitedly.

'How can it be?'

'The soldiers...' Owen's voice trailed off. He found it hard to talk, choked on his own words. Rowan looked up at Jessica's aunt. The look on her face confirmed that this was the reality. He slid from Owen's grasp and knelt on the stair, the crutch clattering back down the stairs. Rowan felt like someone had ripped his guts out.

'She was with child...' Rowan's words were whispered. In his shocked state he had a sudden hint of hope. 'The baby?' But the look on Owen's face confirmed the worst. Rowan's jaw hung open and he, too, began to sob.

London

Marcus Marriot was escorted by soldiers back to his barracks. He was vilified, tormented and shamed as a thief. He had let the brigade down. He was stripped naked and imprisoned in the garrison stocks—a pillory where his head, hands and feet were trapped in place—and then he was given fifty lashes.

The military lash, known as the cat o' nine tails, consisted of a two-foot wooden handle with nine whipcord lashes attached, each knotted seven times. Marcus Marriot was told, that on Norfolk Island, some of these lashes were knotted with tiny lead balls and applied while the victim was bound to a triangle, an easel-like frame. Often, if the sentence was for a high number of lashings, perhaps three hundred, two flagellators were used, one on each side, a left-hander and a right-hander. Usually, blood flowed after the first one or two strikes. With flecks of bloodied flesh threatening to tangle the cat into one tail, Marriot's flagellator was forced to run his fingers between the individual lashes to separate them. Marriot screamed out after the second strike, which tore his skin mercilessly. His blood flowed freely, but this was only the beginning.

Marriot was made to wear a suit of yellow cloth and was then put in irons. First, a collar was fastened around his neck and chains were fastened to the collar, which attached to the leg irons at a length that prevented him standing erect and straightening his back. Marcus was then shamed and drummed out of the regiment, in front of his assembled peers, to the rogue's march played by drummers and fifers. He was marched to the barrack's gate where his gaoler and two constables met him. He was then taken to Newgate Prison.

Marriot had no relatives in London and he certainly didn't have any friends. He was also aware that Newgate was privately run. If a prisoner had money, they could buy food. They could order in ale, gin or rum. Some were known to accommodate whores in their cells. But Marriot had nothing. He would be fed bread and water or, if his luck ran, he might receive a bowl of gruel made from oats, water and salt.

Marriot was thrown to the floor of a punishment cell. Here he would wallow in his irons and filth for weeks, lying on soiled straw, unable to stretch at full length to sleep. His neck was already swollen from chafing. His ankles chafed as well. His back was caked with dry blood, and his future looked bleak. Marcus wept. But self-pity turned to determination and hatred.

Washington. Georgetown.

Owen and Eugenie York sat with Rowan at the bottom of the stairs and wept. The three sobbed for what seemed an eternity. Finally Rowan cleared his throat. He wanted answers. 'What happened to her... to Jessica?'

'The soldiers, they ransacked our warehouse...'

'You can see the damage,' Owen cut in.

'Jessica would have none of it. She went to confront them...'

'We tried to stop her.'

'The soldiers were drunk...'

'Drunk on our brandy.'

'Then Owen went to drag her back upstairs, back to safety, when two of the soldiers beat him—savages they were. They just kept punching and kicking...'

'That is when Jessica flew into a rage. I have never seen her so angry.'

'She started hitting back, and from nowhere a soldier appeared and stabbed her in the belly with his bayonet.'

'No. Oh god, no.'

'It was not just any soldier, Eugenie,' Owen specified. 'It was a sergeant, a mean devil, if'n I've ever seen one. Devil incarnate he were. He had a fully shaved head with the tattoo of a fouled anchor on the back of his neck.'

'For good luck.'

'Aye.'

Rowan stood over his wife's body, stretchered out on a workbench in the warehouse and sewn into canvas by Eugenie. Thankfully, her wound was obscured. Jessica faced towards the heavens, her face angelic in death, although a waxy whitish grey. Rowan laid a hand on the bump of her belly. He would never know whether a baby girl or a baby boy lay within. Fresh tears welled and Rowan wept for the woman he loved—his first love, the love of his life—and for his child.

'It was quick, Rowan,' Owen said, as if it made all the difference. 'She died in my arms. I am so sorry.'

Overcome with grief, Rowan felt a dark cloud descend upon him. Grief turned to hatred and this hatred became an overpowering urge to kill. Revenge seethed through his veins like acid. His mind fogged with the vision of his soulmate, Jessica, the lunging soldier, the blood, her cries of pain, the death of his unborn. Rowan's guts snagged and his fists clenched. 'A sergeant, you said? Shaved head. Anchor tattoo.'

Owen had no doubts. 'He was one of Admiral Cockburn's marines. A sailor.'

'They are marshalled at the Golden Eagle, yonder, across the street,' Eugenie said.

'Are you certain?'

'Yes. I heard them talking about it. After they looted our warehouse they were ordered to take supplies to the docks and rendezvous at the Golden Eagle. Then this storm came racing in and I heard, as they couldn't row back to their ship, they took over the inn.'

An upright clock in the Owens' lodgings struck 6 am. The winds were deserting the city, leaving a fine mist of rain. Rowan walked to the window and looked out. The sun struggled to appear in the east. Suddenly, activity on the docks below caught his attention. The enemy was wasting no time. Wagons with looted provisions were being unloaded and the supply barges and ferries were pressed back into action.

Owen joined Rowan at the window. 'They've done their worst in Washington and the word is that Baltimore is next.'

'Folks were saying they wouldn't stay long,' Eugene said. 'They got what they wanted—burnt Washington in retaliation for Americans destroying Port Dover in Upper Canada. Now they retreat.'

'I heard rumours they set fire to Congress and the Treasury,' —Owen looked at Rowan—'Is that true?'

Rowan heard nothing but his own fury. His voice was calculated and cold. 'Do you have a gun?'

'There's naught you can do, lad. You'd never get near the mongrel.'

'Do you have a gun?'

'Jesus Lord,'—Owen shook his head—'yes... I have a gun.'

'Then kindly fetch it for me. Bring powder and shot and change the flint.'

Owen wandered off reluctantly. The wind had died considerably now and the gilded rays of an early morning sun edged over the sills.

'Are you certain you want to do this?' Eugenie could relate to revenge, but questioned the wisdom of walking into a tavern full of enemy soldiers. 'I plead with you to think this through.'

Rowan was incapable of answering. His heart was a furnace of hatred and this was the only chance for retribution. Owen returned with a blunderbuss. Rowan looked at the tapered barrel with its wide muzzle, designed to spit shrapnel rather than fire a single musket ball.

'It's all I've got,' Owen said, avoiding his wife's anxious stare. 'I changed the flint like yer asked and she's loaded...' He paused a moment. 'Loaded with scrap iron, glass and buckshot.'

Rowan took the blunderbuss in his right hand and held it at his side while he steadied himself with the crutch. The gun was heavy in one arm, but the vision of Jessica lying dead on the bench gave him strength. It gave him power and determination.

'Please think this through, Rowan,' Eugenie pleaded once more. 'Please... They will kill you.'

1814

Rowan's answer was as cold as the Arctic. 'Do you think I care?' He turned to Owen. 'Would you be so kind as to fetch my coat from the rear window?'

Rowan took one last look at Jessica. He studied her innocent face. His tears had been replaced with an obsession for revenge. Rowan leant in and kissed his wife on the lips. 'Goodbye my love,' he barely whispered. There was a brief silence. Owen and Eugenie knew there was no stopping Rowan. Owen returned with Rowan's coat and helped him into the long swallow-tailed jacket. Rowan buttoned the front with the blunderbuss hidden from sight. 'There's fresh powder in the pan, Rowan. All you've got to do lad, is aim and fire.'

The Golden Eagle Tavern had taken its share of abuse. Rain might have washed the vomit from the cobbles outside, but the stink of human abuse hit Rowan like a fusty miasma as he entered. The taproom was a sauna. Wet uniforms hung about on hooks and lines, drying near the huge open fireplace. Logs blazed, even though the day was shaping up to be pleasantly warm. Rowan kept the blunderbuss strapped to his right leg with a short belt, well hidden under his coat. He limped through the door and in between an aisle of kit bags and haversacks. The soldiers had slept wherever possible—in the rooms above, on the stairs, on the taproom floor. There was no sign of the innkeeper, who had deserted his business the day before. The bar was depleted, looted, vandalised. Most of the soldiers were still sleeping off their debauchery as dawn encroached on the gloom, but small groups of men in dark corners watched the man with the crutch make his way to the bar. The chatter hushed.

'Inn's closed,' someone bothered to say.

Rowan ignored the man.

'I said, the inn's closed.'

Rowan reached the bar and turned to face the taproom. Dozens of curious faces now stared back. He leant against the counter for support, one elbow on the bar, and deftly loosened the belt restraining the blunderbuss. The hammer was already cocked. He said nothing, but his eyes searched the room. There must have been thirty men before him.

Rowan saw no sign of the bald-headed sergeant.

The man who had spoken grew angry. *Was this lame Yankee challenging him?* 'You hear me, cripple?'

The raised voice woke those who were asleep. Some laughed at the sport; some were wary. The taproom fell deadly silent. Rowan remained aloof. He ignored his tormentor.

'Jesus Christ, I'm talkin' to you, yankee.' Feeling threatened, the speaker determined he was not to be made a fool of. He stood, unsheathing his bayonet, but Rowan had a plan and he didn't want this loose cannon to spoil it.

Rowan finally addressed the room, his voice resolved. 'I am looking for a sergeant.' He now had everyone's attention. 'A tall man with a shaved head.' Murmurings within the taproom confirmed that he was in the right place. 'And he has a tattoo of a fouled anchor on the back of his neck.'

The hollow sound of boots on floorboards had heads turning toward a doorway to the side. 'You lookin' for me, cripple?'

Rowan turned suddenly. The man's appearance was now unnerving. Rowan held the sergeant's gaze. He was a solid man, well over six feet tall, in his forties, clearly a veteran of many battles. Rowan felt his gut pinch. For the briefest of moments, he questioned his actions, but images of Jessica flashed before him.

'Well, cripple? Cat got ya tongue?'

The room laughed.

1814

'I guess you are the man I am looking for,' Rowan finally said softly and slowly, and the room fell into hushed silence once more.

'So,' the sergeant untucked a napkin from his collar and wiped grease from his mouth. He threw the napkin to the floor. Soldiers stepped aside. And he walked slowly towards Rowan. 'So, what can I do for you... Yankee?'

'You murdered my wife.'

'Huh!' The sergeant puffed out his cheeks, almost as if the comment were a relief. He looked about the room at his comrades. 'Is that all?' he said, throwing the palms of his hands out like an actor, to beg applause from his audience. But this sergeant's audience *wasn't* applauding. There was something strangely disarming about a man with the courage to walk into this bar with that accusation.

Is that all?

Rowan felt his eye twitch. He had lost the love of his life; he would have done anything for her. He would now die for her, but he would take this bastard with him.

So help me God, I will take this bastard with me.

The sergeant walked forward slowly, calculating his adversary. He, too, had pride. Half of his command was watching. 'So, which bitch was yours, cripple? I've had my way with so many.'

Nervous laughs from a minority.

'My wife had a name – Jessica Craige.' The sergeant was two yards away now. 'She was with child. You stabbed her in the stomach for trying to save her uncle from a cowardly beating.'

'Oh, I remember the feisty whore.' The sergeant's face twisted with anger. He pulled a knife from his belt and marched towards to Rowan. 'She was begging for it...'

The blunderbuss rose with astonishing speed and accuracy. The sergeant was literally looking down the barrel when Rowan pulled back the trigger. He was inches away. The explosion shook the room. A shockwave of detonating black powder chased by broken glass, nails, iron and buckshot. The sergeant's head exploded, leaving a severed body, which stood momentarily as if nothing had happened, before crumbling to the floor, a headless corpse. Those closest were peppered with splintered bone and shrapnel.

It took seconds for the men to realise what exactly had happened. Muskets were immediately raised and Rowan was looking at a firing squad. That no one fired was a miracle, for if someone had, the whole command would have emptied their musket barrels into Rowan. Rowan remained unemotional, resigned to his fate.

Without warning, the tavern door was kicked open and two armed redcoats entered, followed closely by a lieutenant. 'Arms down!' the lieutenant yelled at the marines. 'That's an order! Arms down!' Rowan stared beyond a crowd of seething, angry faces. He expected to be peppered with lead any moment. Reluctantly the marines downed muskets. The room filled with hushed silence. Rowan dropped the blunderbuss, his blood-splattered face expressionless. The lieutenant, a tall slender man with a scar over one eye, read the scene immediately. He knew the dead sergeant as a loose cannon and was not surprised it had come to this. Two men grabbed Rowan by the arms, pinning them behind his back.

The lieutenant looked at Rowan a long moment. 'I know you,' he said, with assurance.

Rowan was in shock. He felt no emotions.

'You're one of Commander Barney's men, are you not?' the lieutenant asked. Rowan said nothing. 'Yes, yes. I recognise you from the flotilla. You were on Barney's barge. I saw you through my eyeglass from the rocket barge. You were constantly by his side. I'm good with faces. You are a surgeon—well?' Rowan remained silent. He was drained.

1814

'Very well, then'—the lieutenant's face darkened—'put that Yankee murderer in irons.'

Heavily guarded and restrained, Rowan was taken out to the frigate *Seahorse,* where he was hauled aboard, like so much plunder stolen from the warehouses. 'Throw him in the brig,' the lieutenant ordered. 'The Admiral will want to talk to this man, I am certain.'

Rowan said nothing. The chains, the degradation, the misery and the pain were nothing compared to the loss of Jessica and his unborn child. He sat in silence, numb, hunched, chained to the hull wall in a narrow, dark cell, alone with his thoughts. Alone, in the blackness of the ship's prison.

Rowan lost all sense of time. Exhausted both mentally and physically, he drifted into a comatose sleep. He had no idea how long he'd been out, but when he awoke in complete darkness, he realized that the ship was under sail. The creaking of the timbers was almost soothing. His mouth and throat were parched, his head throbbed and his twisted ankle ached. Immediately he became aware of what had woken him—voices outside his cell. The sound of a key twisting in the lock echoed, and the door swung open wide enough for a Jack Tar holding a lantern to warily peer into the cell.

'You alive?'

Rowan said nothing. The lantern flame made him blink and he bowed his head.

'I said, are you alive?'

'How long have I been here?'

'Oh, 'e speaks. You are alive, then. Good. Yer wanted up top.'

With the aid of two seamen Rowan was dragged on deck and presented before the captain of the guard. The arresting lieutenant stood next to him, a man Rowan now heard addressed as Lieutenant Gregor Warburton. The lieutenant was vindictive by nature and hardened by war, and more than anything he hated Yankees. On shore, a mile distant, Rowan recognised the port settlement of Alexandria on the Potomac River. Rowan could make out several ships of the line taking position in the port. Although the settlement had surrendered, the ships nevertheless positioned themselves with their portside cannons rolled out, ready to annihilate the township, should the circumstances change.

Lieutenant Warburton studied Rowan's reaction. 'Yes, Alexandria surrendered without a fight,' he said with an air of stubborn self-esteem. 'What is it with you people—no pride? Washington wasn't much better.'

Rowan remained silent. He felt dispirited and alone. With the smoke smouldering upriver from the pillaged capitol of Washington, and now news that Alexandria had surrendered without a fight, Rowan was totally demoralised.

'Alexandria, I do believe, offers fair maidens,' Warburton went on. 'Yes, whores at least. We will find out shortly, when we sail into harbour.' Rowan ignored the man. 'Baltimore is next,' the lieutenant took great pleasure in reporting. 'And I imagine that she, too, will wave the white flag with her tail between her legs.'

'Baltimore has backbone,' Rowan heard himself mutter under his breath.

'Baltimore has backbone, says he!' the officer chided. The marines and seamen standing about laughed. 'Bah! Baltimore will cower like the rest of this godforsaken country.' The lieutenant circled Rowan, finally whipping his back with a swagger stick nestled under his arm. Rowan groaned at the unexpected assault. 'You're an associate of Commander Barney, are you not?'

No answer.

'He is our prisoner, too, Doctor Craige.' Rowan flinched at his own name. 'Oh, yes, we know all about you. Your uncle Owen York told us everything before we hanged him. Him and his mouthy wife, Eugenie York.'

Rowan stiffened. 'What are you talking about?'

'Your uncle and auntie. They were both hung as conspirators, yesterday afternoon.'

'Jesus Lord... You bastard!' Rowan tried to struggle free but the marines restrained him.

'And not before they sang your praises, Rowan Craige... Told us all about you.'

Rowan's eyes were red with fury, and he was grinding his teeth while spittle dribbled down his chin.

'And as I said, your mate, Joshua Barney, is our prisoner, too. He and his lieutenant... What's his name? Huffington...? Yes, that's him. Lieutenant Huffington.'

Rowan's face dropped to the deck. It was highly possible.

The wounded Captain Barney and Lieutenant Huffington had been taken prisoner at Turncliff's Bridge and removed to Admiral Cockburn's flagship, HMS *Albion,* where Captain Wainwright was captain and commander of the redcoats. The admiral's senior surgeon had attended to Barney's wound, a nasty musket ball wound to the thigh, at the order of the admiral, who had great respect for Barney, the commander. Knew him as a hero. Barney then met the Admiral and General Ross, who commended his bravery. When he was able, Barney had been removed to an inn in Bladensburg, now under British control. But he was a prisoner, nonetheless.

'But our Admiral,' Lieutenant Warburton went on, 'Admiral Cockburn, in all his wisdom, has chosen to honour this Barney man later, aboard his flagship. But I dare say, one day this commander of yours will get his comeuppance.'

Rowan refused to be riled. Lieutenant Warburton rounded on Rowan, his face inches from the surgeon's. 'But not you, you murderer. You are an insult to your profession, a disgrace to your Hippocratic oath. You killed a man in cold blood.'

'That man murdered my innocent wife. He killed my unborn child.'

'That man was doing his job as a soldier. Your whore wife got in the way.'

Incensed, Rowan found new strength; he twisted one shoulder free and then the other and leapt forward on his good foot, catching the lieutenant with both hands about the throat. Both men fell to the deck. Rowan managed one punch, a second punch. The lieutenant screamed out for help and Rowan succeeded in a final blow that loosened one of the man's teeth. Instantly, three marines lifted Rowan from the fray and another pressed a bayonet point to his chest.

'Stop!' Warburton staggered to his feet, spitting his words through splatters of blood. 'Stop! I want that man alive. I want him to suffer. I want him to hang in Baltimore's Market Square, where all his filthy brethren can watch him do the devil's dance at the end of a rope.' The lieutenant pulled a handkerchief from his britches pocket and wiped the blood from his face. He ran his tongue over a chipped tooth, cursed and spat a bloodied glob onto the deck. He stared Rowan in the eye and, when he was satisfied that Rowan was pinioned with both hands behind his back, Warburton launched a wild blow with his swagger across Rowans cheek. 'Bastard,' he spat again. 'Take him below.'

Rowan was manhandled down the companionway by two marines; they descended to the bowels of the ship once more, past the bilge pumps, between the water casks, by the magazine and, finally, back into the brig, where Rowan knew from experience he was only inches from the rudder. Here, he was shackled with irons attached to iron rings in the hull, and left in total darkness once more – alone with the rats and his miserable thoughts.

It was Thursday, August 25th, and Rowan thought he could not sink any lower.

CHAPTER ELEVEN

London. Newgate Prison.

Newgate Prison turnkey Gilbert Cramme was a miserable sod. At least that is what those who had the misfortune to cross his path thought. He was even known to the beggars around West London, who turned the other way as he passed, for should they dare catch Cramme's eye or rattle their cup before him, they knew they would be rewarded with a sharp kick. He was a despicable soul, disdained by his colleagues *and* his family, a man of lower intellect with a mean disposition, hailed by his superiors at the prison for his tough stance on the unfortunate sad scum festering within. A man without pity, he was also a stranger to soap -- an odious human with an offensive odour. The only time Cramme shared a vague smile was during personal gratification with a prison doxy desperate for gin.

Elizabeth awoke to the sound of the key clinking in the lock. She had not the remotest notion of the time of day, but guessed it was night as Gilbert Cramme let himself into her solitary confinement cell, holding a candle stub twinkling in a pewter candleholder. The door opened enough for the short gnome-like man to present himself.

1814

'Happy birthdee to yer, luvey,' he said with a lascivious grin, made even more sinister by the dancing flame.

'Birthday?' Elizabeth was taken aback.

'Yes, dear girl.'

Elizabeth wanted to believe the man's kindly tone was genuine. She had not heard another voice in the past seven days. Elizabeth craved contact, for not a word had been exchanged, even when her bread and water was pushed through the slot in the door.

'It is not my birthday.'

'Oh, ain't it? I rather thought it were.'

'What time is it?' Elizabeth asked.

'Time fer a birthdee gift.' If it was not for the stench of rotting teeth, Elizabeth might have identified the gin on his breath.

'I said, it is not my birthday. What do you want?' Elizabeth felt undecidedly uncomfortable once more. She pushed back into the corner of her cell.

'What do I want?' he almost giggled. 'What do I want?' he reiterated. 'Now, let me see.' The turnkey plucked a small parcel from his pocket. 'Ah... Happy birthdee from Uncle Gilbert.' He presented a package from his frock coat pocket. 'Now what 'ave we 'ere?' he said, thoroughly enjoying his entertainment. He opened the packet and sniffed. 'Cheese!'

Elizabeth's acute sense of smell identified the fatty West Country cheddar. She salivated and her stomach rumbled involuntarily. The gnome read the want in her face. 'It's all yours, luvey... '

Elizabeth almost believed him. She *wanted* to believe him.

'All yours as long as yer spread them lovely thighs for Uncle Gilbert.'

'Get out.'

'Why, you ungrateful sod.' The odious little man stepped forward.

'Get out, I said.'

'Oh, yer wanna play hard ter get, do yer?' The turnkey pulled the door shut. He unbuckled his britches. Unhitched, they fell to the floor and Elizabeth caught a glimpse of the man's twitching arousal in the light of the dancing flame. He threw the candle aside. The cell went black. Elizabeth heard the turnkey shuffle forward. Elizabeth kicked out the moment she felt a sharp slap across her face. 'Lay still, yer bitch.' Cramme shoved Elizabeth to the floor and fell upon her, trying to force himself within. Elizabeth wretched at the vile smell of his unwashed crevices, the fetor of his breath. He struggled to place his face close to Elizabeth's. When she felt his fat tongue lick her neck, she reached out, scratching the man's face with a downward stroke of her untrimmed nails.

'Firk!' he screamed out, slapping Elizabeth. 'Firk!' He touched his face and felt his own warm blood. The turnkey's second strike was a closed fist. Elizabeth threw wild punches in the blackness. 'Damned bitch!' he cried out. Elizabeth heard the man's laboured breathing as he determined that she was not worth the effort -- he would seek gratification elsewhere. 'You'll pay fer this. You'll pay... Yer hear me?'

Elizabeth backed hard against the rear wall and remained silent. The door slammed shut. The key rattled in the lock. Elizabeth sniffed the dank darkness. Besides the lingering odour of unkempt body, there was the sweet aroma of cheese. Elizabeth crawled about in the Stygian blackness, searching the flagstones until she felt the package. She threw aside the cloth and attacked the cheddar with a ravenous appetite. Nothing had ever tasted so fine.

Hours later, the head of the guard stood outside her cell door and read out the latest charge: attacking a representative of the law and stealing a wedge of cheese. Another seven days in solitary. Elizabeth listened in silence. And then she wept once more.

August 29th, 1814. Alexandria Harbour, south of Washington.

Five days of surviving on one small bowl of gruel per day had taken its toll on Rowan, but it was sustenance, nonetheless. He had lost track of time and even the hour of day. He was, however, aware that the ship was now at anchor. The loud echo of the key twisting inside the door lock broke Rowan's dire reflections. The door creaked open, more slowly than usual, and the welcome light of a lantern flooded his cramped space. Along with the blinding light came a sharp odor and Rowan recognised the salty aroma of boiled pickled pork.

'Doctor Craige, sar.' The voice was soft, almost a whisper. Rowan blinked a dozen times, frowning, trying to focus beyond the lantern flame.

'Y-yes.' Rowan's voice was croaky. He hardly recognised himself and, for the briefest of moments, he wanted to say, "Of course it's Doctor Craige. Who the hell do you think it is?"

'"Tis Henry Barker, sar, cook's assistant.'

Rowan reached out with his shackled hands to take the bowl, but the lad, maybe nineteen, scrawny and clean-shaven on account of being unable to grow facial hair, slipped silently into the cell. He handed Rowan the wooden bowl before once more checking the passageway outside. The lad closed the door behind him. 'I must be hasty, sar, I will be flogged if'n they find out I was talkin' to yer.'

'Then why risk it, Henry Baker?'

'Jayzus... Dear Lord, tell me I've not gone crazy,' the lad said, talking more to himself than to Rowan.

'What?'

Henry Baker took a deep breath. 'I want to be helpin' yer, sar.'

'Help me?'

'Aye. Escape.'

Rowan instantly felt uneasy. Was this some sick trick? A trap, so they could shoot him in the back as he tried to escape? 'Why?' he asked.

'Look, I gotta be real quick, sar, or the marines'll come lookin'. I was press-ganged in Portsmouth, two year ago, press-ganged from the streets, on me way to me ma's. Bastards chained me, dragged me aboard this 'ere *Seahorse* and sailed me to the Americas. I help you, sar, and you 'elp me.'

'How can I help you?' Rowan lifted his irons and rattled them as if to make a point.

'Hush, sar. Keep the noise down. I will help you break free from this 'ere ship and together we escape through the countryside. You *do* know the countryside, do yer not?'

'Yes, and extremely well.'

'Good. Then we's partners—all right?'

Rowan had nothing to lose. 'Yes. Partners.'

Henry Baker spat on his palm and offered Rowan his hand. They shook.

'Now I gotta go, sar, Rowan... Can I call yer "Rowan", sar?'

'Of course.'

'Good. I must leave, and I will tell yer more, same hour tomorra.'

Henry slipped silently back through the door. 'Oh!' he turned back and took a small parcel from his pocket. 'Near forgot. Got yer a juicy piece o' pork. 'ere.' Rowan snatched the parcel mid-air. 'Thank you… thank you so much.' The door swung. 'Wait!'

'What, sar?'

'Where are we?'

'Alexandria harbour.'

The door closed, the pitch darkness enveloped Rowan once more and the key spun in the lock, but for the first time in a nearly a week, Rowan felt a flicker of hope.

Under the leadership of Commander Gordon, Alexandria was occupied for three days. The settlement was largely unmolested by cannon fire as a truce had been struck between the mayor, Charles Simms, and the British commander. However, the price Alexandria paid for peace was high. The warehouses were looted and twenty-one captured American ships were loaded with sixteen thousand barrels of flour, one thousand hogshead of tobacco, one hundred and fifty bales of cotton and five thousand dollars' worth of wine, sugar and household items.

September 4th, 1814.

Piece by piece Henry Baker extracted information, relaying it to Rowan. 'Tis true, your commander Joshua Barney convalesces at an inn in Bladensburg,' Henry said.

'When was he captured?'

'On the 21st August. But Admiral Cockburn has given strict instruction he is to be treated like a gentlemen, an' when 'e is able to travel 'e will be allowed to travel to 'is home in the country, back to 'is wife.' Rowan felt a measure of relief. 'Do yer know a Cap'n Miller, sar?' Henry asked.

'Yes.'

'Well, 'e were also wounded an' captured and convalesces at the same inn as yer commander.' Henry Baker considered his next words carefully. 'I don't know whether yer want ta hear this, Rowan...'

'What? Speak up, lad.'

'Well, Admiral Cockburn conceded that you Americans could have beaten the redcoats at Turncliff's Bridge on account o' them bein' exhausted from hikin' overland in that awful heat, but the Yankees retreated.'

Rowan felt more frustration.

'Sixty-four British soldiers were killed at the bridge skirmish compared to Miller's eleven. What 'appened?'

'I don't know, Henry. I really don't know. What's happening ashore here in Alexandria?'

'Word is Admiral Cochrane 'as ordered Commander Gordon's ships to re-join the British fleet in the Chesapeake,' Henry confided to Rowan. Rowan knew this Admiral Cochrane, a fifty-six-year-old veteran of the Napoleonic Wars, to be the British commander in chief of the North American war.

'Where's Admiral Cockburn, then?' Rowan asked the lad.

'After 'is success in Washington, Admiral Cockburn's preparing to sail for Bermuda. Cochrane's in charge now.'

'Oh.'

'So we's withdrawing from Alexandria and sailin' for Baltimore.'

'God, no. When?'

'Today. I thought you'd be 'appy about it, sar.'

'I have many friends in Baltimore, Henry.'

'Well I'm thinkin' this'll be our chance to escape, during the mayhem of battle.' Henry thought a moment. 'But, for now, you Yankees have defences at White House Point, and they reckon they'll put up a fight. Commander Gordon 'as sent ships ahead—a recon, they say.'

1814

For three days and nights the British ships bombed White House Point Fort with cannon balls and rockets. Then, on the 6th of September, the frigates pounded broadside after broadside into Brigadier-General John Hungerford's troops of the Virginia Militia, who were skirmishing along the riverbanks among the pine forests. The attack was so incessant that Hungerford could not deploy his artillery to retaliate. This allowed the British ships to slip closer to Baltimore. Further downriver Commander Gordon came under heavy artillery fire, but suddenly the commander could not believe his luck. The American heavy artillery guns fell silent and the British invaders escaped unscathed into the greater bay. It would transpire later that the militia had run out of heavy artillery ammunition.

As the ship sailed into deeper waters and Rowan remained imprisoned in the brig, he recognised the sound of the pintle and gudgeon bolts directly behind him manipulating the *Seahorse's* stern-mounted rudder.

'Where are we?' Rowan asked Henry Baker between mouthfuls of boiled salt pork and a generous crust of bread that the lad had managed to smuggle down to him.

'On the Patuxent River. We're 'eaded to Baltimore.'

Rowan had mixed feelings, and one of the strongest was the fear of hanging, should he not manage to escape.

'But I have some good news for you, Rowan.'

'Oh?'

'Lieutenant Gregor Warburton is no longer on board.'

As far as the vengeful lieutenant was bothered, his Yankee prisoner was festering in the brig. He had not shown interest in Rowan since the altercation on deck, but keenly awaited the Rowan's humiliation and public hanging in Baltimore Market Place. Besides, the army veteran had been busy ashore, commanding his marines as they escaped the fresh assaults, after their success at Alexandria.

'And why is he not on board?' Rowan asked Henry.

'He has been transferred to the frigate *Menelaus,* under Captain Parker. They preparing to place troops on the ground, to land at North Point.

Rowan sighed. He knew North Point to be south-east of Baltimore. Just two hours' walk from the settlement.

But the Royal Navy was in no rush. The ships sailed slowly for Chesapeake Bay, giving the foot soldiers time for much needed rest, after their hundred mile trek overland to Washington, and then their further hike to Alexandria.

Rowan was finally allowed on deck, his twisted ankle having healed somewhat. His first visit aloft was at night, the evening light being more obliging to his weakened eyesight after a fortnight of darkness. The summer air was sweet and balmy and Rowan found himself largely ignored by most of the crew and marines. He was no longer a curiosity. He was accompanied to the gunwale, where the water looked inviting and Rowan could see that the shore was only a mile distant; but his shackled wrists and ankles would see Rowan drown in minutes, should he try and jump overboard.

Newgate Prison. London.

It was a month since Elizabeth Eveleigh had been freed from the solitary cell. She'd spent two weeks in that loathsome, stonewalled black hole through no fault of her own, barely surviving. Now she languished once again in the overcrowded Felon Women's Quarters, with hundreds of lost souls.

1814

Others came and went. Some were reprieved, some freed on a bribe. Others simply died from gaol fever, or a broken heart. But there was no possibility for a reprieve for Elizabeth. Forging the king's coin was treason and she was lucky she would not hang.

Prison time had hardened Elizabeth. She had no time for the weak. She despised the swindlers and the pilferers and would stand firm in the face of adversity. The other women steered clear, as no one dared tackle her. Betty, the whore, had a renewed respect for her since their brawl. They tolerated each other, watched each other's backs. Some even thought them to have become friends, and together they were a force to be reckoned with.

Weeks had turned to months and Elizabeth was beyond her seventeenth birthday when news came that they were to be ferried down the Thames to the prison hulks at Gallion's Reach. Something was better than nothing, and now they were one step further towards transportation to New South Wales.

On board the *Seahorse*, near Baltimore.

Rowan's life was filled with joy. Jessica lay naked across the bed; her head on his shoulder with her long blonde curls tickling his face. She took his hand and together with hers, she placed it on her bulbous, chalk-white belly. 'Feel that?' The baby kicked a third time. 'He's a healthy little man.'

'He?' Rowan propped up on one elbow, his eyes bright with contentment. 'You think it is a boy, then?'

'I'm certain of it.'

'Then we should name him Rowan,' Rowan jested.

'I think he should be called Silas,' Jessica shot back, her large topaz eyes full of happiness. 'Yes, "Silas,"—my father would love that.' Jessica giggled and leant in, kissing Rowan fully on the lips. Her lips were soft and moist, warm and sweet...

'Wake up, yer murderin' bastard...' Rowan was hauled from his dream into a reality of dank darkness and hatred. The marine kicked Rowan a second time. 'I said, wake up. Here's yer food, and God only knows yer don't deserve it. I'd see yer starve if'n yer were my prisoner.' In the lantern light Rowan caught the silhouette of the square-jawed redcoat with the piercing, small black eyes. The man slopped the wooden bowl of gruel at Rowan's feet and threw the wooden spoon to the floor.

'Where's Henry?' Rowan heard himself ask, without thinking.

'That traitorous dog's scrubbin' the 'eads. You won't be getting' all chatty with 'im no more. Now eat, cos yer not gettin' nuthin' more for a while.' The soldier caught Rowan's questioning eyes and couldn't keep from spilling the news. 'Cos we're goin' into Baltimore this day. Burn the firker to the ground and give all yer women folk a good time.'

'Baltimore? We are in Baltimore?'

'Close enough. The soldiers are landin' at North Point, as we speak. You Yankees are firked, good n' proper. Now shut yer trap.' The soldier slammed the door and Rowan dissolved back into darkness with a thousand questions.

Sunday, 11th September. The invading fleet of forty-seven ships anchored at the mouth of the Patapsco River, fourteen miles southeast of Baltimore. Between Baltimore and North Point, six miles distant, was Fort McHenry, a coastal pentagon-shaped bastion. As the British were unfamiliar with the river's depths and hidden shoals, they were unable to take the heavily armed ships further, for they could easily be grounded. The risk was too great, and with the army troops trapped on these ships they would be in easy range for the militia cannon.

That night was still, and the ships were anchored under the canopy of a clear sky and the light of a full moon. All sounds travelled clearly across the water. At 2 am, the Royal Navy gun brigs moved closer to shore, to cover the mass movement of troops, and steadily, professionally, the men were rowed from ship to shore in the landing boats.

With Washington fallen, Baltimore was dispirited, the population agitated. Many were frightened. Morale was low and many were too disheartened to fight. The Federalists, naturally, gloated.

By first light on Monday morning of the 12th Baltimoreans had gathered on Federal Hill high above Baltimore to view the awesome spectacle. By 7 am, the last of five thousand enemy soldiers had landed with knapsacks, muskets and ammunition at North Point, as they watched. The British landed with their horses pulling six field cannon and two howitzers. The assault on Baltimore was to be executed under the command of Admiral Cochrane himself. But Cochrane impulsively recalled Cockburn before he sailed for Bermuda, deciding he needed the man on the ground, in charge of the marines.

At 9:30 am Admiral Cochrane transferred from his flagship, HMS *Tonnant*, to HMS *Surprize*, a lighter ship, capable of taking him further up the shallow river towards Baltimore. Meanwhile, Major General Ross and Cockburn went ashore with the army of redcoats and marines.

Waiting in defence, three thousand American militiamen prepared themselves in forward positions, seven miles southeast of Baltimore. They were under General Samuel

Smith, who had taken command of Baltimore on August 25th. He was highly qualified for the appointment; he had been a Revolutionary War officer and a leader in the U.S. Senate. He was now a successful and wealthy merchant, with a lot at stake.

Under Smith's command were the Maryland rifleman, wearing black shakos with green ribbon, green uniforms with red trim, cow horn powder flasks, daggers on belts and over-shoulder satchels of ammunition for their muskets. Backing them were the Volunteer Militia, wearing blue and white coats over white britches, black shakos with a wide blue puggery and black boots. These men were experienced with small arms only.

They had camped Saturday night, the 10th, at the head of Bear Creek, whose waters ran into the Patapsco River near Baltimore. At 7 am the Americans were ready. Reconnaissance horsemen reported the enemy landings at North Point, and the militia spread out amongst the forest trees, as ambushing snipers.

General Ross, British hero of the Washington assault, had led an advance party to high ground in flat and heavy woodland. The day was hot and once again, the redcoats, wearing their woollen uniforms and lacking exercise from idling on the ships since Washington, sweltered and tired early. For this reason Ross chose to camp his troops for the night on high ground, before attacking Baltimore on Tuesday.

But Ross's luck had run dry. While riding back along the line, a sharp shooter shot Ross through his arm and the musket ball lodged in his breast. He bled profusely. As he had only hours to live, Colonel Arthur Brooke assumed command. While many skirmishes continued between the advancing troops and the patriots that day, the Americans finally fell back, to join their fortifications.

1814

Tuesday, the 13th,the weather proved hot and hazy with a soft breeze blowing from the south and east off Chesapeake Bay. This aided the British squadron of seventeen frigates, sloops, schooners, bomb boats and a single rocket ship, *Erebus*, in their effort to sail up the thirty-nine-mile-long Patapsco River, of which the tidal portion forms Baltimore's harbour. It was a slow advance, as rowboats ahead of the ships took depth soundings so as not to ground the warships on hidden shoals. Should this happen anyhow, each ship was armed with kedge and stream anchors with coiled cable to pull them free. They also had scale ladders at the ready for carrying ashore, to storm the fortifications. Now they took their positions in a line nearly three miles from Fort McHenry.

The frigates moved half a mile closer to make their cannon range. From the fort's parapets Major Armistead of the 3rd Artillery Regiment, the youthful American leader in command of Fort McHenry, observed the British advance and immediately ordered a massive retaliation. First, a battery of 24-pounders returned fire to the ships, followed smartly by the fort's long-range 42-pounders. It was a brutal response and tons of metal and explosives fell about the enemy ships, striking them in several places.

The artillerymen cheered and their musicians piped "Yankee Doodle."

The frigates pulled back out of range, only to be replaced by the five bomb ships. The fort tried their mortars, but these ships were too far away and the massive mortar balls plunged into the river. The bomb ships replied with shells, weighing in at two hundred pounds each, and many hit the fort.

It was now 2 pm and raining heavily. The bomb ships moved in and bombarded the fort relentlessly. Many of the shells were fused to explode overhead, showering the hapless defenders with red-hot shrapnel and shot. The fort cowered. Then, during a lull in the fire, when the British had trained their spyglasses on the target and noted the militia clambering to help their wounded, they decided to sail closer and finish them off. It was a bad move, which gave the fort a chance to retaliate. The ships had to back away once more.

Six miles distant, Rowan crouched in involuntary silence —alone in a black hole. His ship was one of the vessels left behind. But even from here he could smell the black powder and hear the muffled roars of the cannon. Night fell.

In Baltimore darkness draped the city, but the sky was lit up with bursting shells, burning gunpowder and rockets. The Americans had scuttled ships at the mouth of the harbour as a fortification, with their gunboats drawn up behind them. This made a sea invasion impossible for the enemy and a land invasion very awkward, especially as British intelligence was receiving reports that militia re-enforcements were pouring in daily from Washington and other areas. Estimates that there could be as many as twenty thousand American soldiers in the streets of Baltimore had reached Cochrane. Yet he was confident of success.

Capturing Baltimore would not compensate for the loss of British life in the process. Cochrane looked to the future, where a major assault was planned for New Orleans from the Gulf of Mexico, and he could not afford to lose men here in Baltimore. Also, Admiral Cockburn and Colonel Brooke, who took command of the army troops, were under no illusion; they could not take Baltimore without the naval big guns. The two men agreed—it would be suicide.

However, many skirmishes continued around the coast, including a disastrous barge attack that was attempted at Fort Covington. By morning several British corpses littered the shoreline, their horrendous open wounds washed clean by the waters. It was rapidly turning into a defeat for the invaders. The last shots were fired at 7 am. Beaten and with low morale, the British troops marched back to North Point.

By 9:30 am on Wednesday, the 14th, the British had commenced their withdrawal, and the stars and stripes remained flying above all the forts and battlements. The British finally ordered a full retreat on Friday the 16th.

The injuries of the wounded stretchered back to the *Seahorse* were horrendous, from torn, shredded limbs to exposed innards from cannon, bullet and shrapnel. The stench of death cloyed the below decks. Rowan's expertise was needed desperately, and he was soon dragged from the brig and pressed into service. The dying and wounded lay on stretchers in the converted surgery of the *Seahorse's* orlop deck, between the pump room and the steward's cabin in the stern. Rowan barely recognised himself in a mirror. His beard was full, his hair matted and wiry.

'Doctor Byron,' the head surgeon introduced himself to Rowan, head tipped back and peering at Rowan guardedly, over the blood-splattered pince-nez resting on the bridge of his nose. Rowan nodded, acutely aware of his own appearance.

'Rowan Craige, sir.'

'Yes, I know who you are,' the man said bluntly, his nose purple and face red from too much wine. He was totally bald except for tufts of grey, curly hair on each side of his head. Bushy mutton chops cascaded down his cheeks, meeting under a clean-shaven chin. 'You studied at Philadelphia, did you not?'

'Yes...'

'And you sailed under Commander Barney, I am told?'

'That is correct.'

'Then wash smartly in that bucket.' Doctor Byron wiped blood from an amputation saw onto a rag. 'And take this. You can manage the amputations while I see to the officers.'

The cries and groans were incessant. Young sailors screamed for their mothers; other men, in too much agony to even whimper, faded in and out of consciousness or simply died from their horrific afflictions.

Rowan was no stranger to the urgency, and with the assistance of Walter—a young surgeon's assistant who was under no illusions about becoming a surgeon himself—Rowan threw himself into the work. Selecting the sharpest knife offered, Rowan attended his first patient, a marine corporal whose leg dangled from shattered bone where he had been clipped by a cannon ball, just below the knee. Rowan clamped his left hand on the man's exposed thigh, swiftly slicing the leg to the bone, just above the knee. Thankfully, the patient fainted. Walter knew his business. He, too, worked hastily, tying a tourniquet to stem the blood. Rowan took up the serrated instrument, and as Walter pulled the flesh apart at the incision, Rowan proceeded to saw through the bone. Having been severed, the limb dropped unceremoniously into a well-placed basket of straw. The severed end connected to the unconscious patient was then cauterised with boiling hot tar. Mortality rate? Rowan expected four in ten would die.

Rowan turned to the next patient lying on a stretcher on the deck. The man was terrified and totally speechless. 'Help me get this man onto the bench.' The probing for possible shrapnel buried in the man's flesh was more than the patient could bear. His blood-curdling screams echoed off the bay. There seemed no end to the mutilation, and whilst the *Seahorse* was still anchored Rowan's thoughts centred on his escape.

The musket ball lodged in one man's lower arm came free with forceps. Rowan poured rum on the wound. The man screeched. 'Bandage it,' Rowan ordered his overwhelmed assistant. Walter uncoiled a soiled bandage from a basket; saved from the corpse of a marine no longer requiring the dressing.

It was early evening. Although Rowan was weakened by the incarceration, he had worked tirelessly on the wounded for five hours. But now he saw light at the end of the tunnel. He excused himself to take some fresh air. Rowan climbed the companionway amidships, where his attention was drawn to the yardarm. Suddenly he was sickened. Young Henry Baker hung by the neck from the yardarm. The body of the lad who had tried to help him twisted sluggishly in the breeze, dangling from a rope. A passing sailor saw Rowan staring. 'Traitor, sar.'

'Traitor?'

'Aye. Deserter, 'e was. Tried to change sides. Admiral Cochrane don't take too kind to deserters... No, sar.'

This incident hastened Rowan's decision. He estimated that the *Seahorse*, one of a dozen ships anchored there, was about four hundred yards from shore, where dozens of bivouac campfires from retreating soldiers still smouldered. They awaited evacuation. All about him, the ship was in frantic activity in preparation for sail. Rowan noted that American civilian prisoners were amongst the deck crew, stowing looted produce that had been ferried from the shore. The British were retreating from Baltimore and the mood was bleak.

Immediately, out of the dark, Rowan's attention was drawn to one particular navy launch approaching. Rowan sensed danger. A resonant voice was recognized, from across the waters: Lieutenant Gregor Warburton was returning to the *Seahorse*. Rowan slipped discreetly from sight and waited. The tender struck heavily alongside; the oars were stowed and the officers climbed on board. Directly behind them, another officer, badly wounded, was hoisted on board on a makeshift stretcher. A midshipman hurried to meet the lieutenant. 'Welcome back on board, sir,' he saluted Warburton.

'Get me surgeon Bates.'

'Begging your pardon, sir, but the surgeon is extremely busy and asked not to be disturbed.'

'Then get me the surgeon's mate,' Warburton snapped, shooting the lad a humiliating glance.

'Sir... ah...'

'What?'

'Begging your pardon again, sir. He, too, is busy. We have many wounded below.' The sixteen-year-old midshipman looked at the wounded officer drifting in and out of consciousness. 'Maybe you wish me to fetch the prisoner doctor, sir.'

'Prisoner?'

'Doctor Craige. He has been assisting. He has been seeing to the amputations, and what a fine job he has done too, sir...'

'He what?'

'He's been...'

'Guard!' Warburton summoned two marines and disappeared with the men down the main hatch companionway. Rowan's hand was forced. Dodging lantern light, Rowan climbed unnoticed to the quarterdeck. This was no place for a common seaman, let alone a man who looked more like a vagrant, but the industry of preparing to depart whilst in enemy territory was in Rowan's favour. From the quarterdeck, the poop deck was in complete darkness. Rowan climbed the companionway to the upper stern deck, hurried to the gunwales and climbed over onto the mizzen chains. If he dived in from here he would be heard. Rowan looked down to the river; black and uninviting with unpredictable currents. It was forty feet to the water, but the starboard gun ports were open, facing the shoreline, and the guns were rolled out, with gun crews at the ready in case of attack. Rowan climbed down the side, cannon muzzle to muzzle. The gun deck crew stirred.

'What's afoot...?'

'What is *your* business?' another shouted after him.

Rowan made the lower gun deck.

'It's a Yankee!' someone screamed out.

Rowan didn't hesitate. He took a deep breath and dived. Although the evening was balmy warm, the water was freezing. Rowan felt his body sink deep. The water was cold, yes, yet refreshing on his grimy body. He levelled out and kicked for the shoreline, aware of flaming lights on the surface. Overhead, another tender rowed for the ship. As silently as possible, Rowan surfaced at the stern of the row boat. He briefly held onto the dinghy, but would soon be back alongside the frigate.

'You there!' Warburton's voice boomed across at the approaching tender. 'Did you see a man there in the water? An escapee?'

'No, sir.'

'Look carefully, man, he must be right under you.'

Rowan dived back under. The men in the stern sheets peered over the sides. Nothing. Rowan trod water beneath the craft, aware that the launch Warburton had arrived on was being occupied once more. Clearly, a search party was going after him. He surfaced between the port side of the launch and the starboard side of the frigate. Rowan restrained his breaths, barely daring to breath. He floated in the dark recesses offered by the stationary vessels, waiting for the soldiers on the launch to alight and for Warburton's men to depart. He took another great breath and, slipping beneath the ship, made his way to the dark port side and then to the stern, where he surfaced next to the anchor cable and waited again.

Ten minutes passed and Rowan shivered uncontrollably. He felt the high tide returning. His energy was drained. He would have to make it to shore before exposure paralysed him. In the darkness of a clouded moon he kicked away from the ship's hull and instantly felt himself tugged upriver by the tide. The waters here in the Patapsco River were shallow and the tide hastened. Rowan took short strokes to maintain direction and shortly felt the muddy sludge of the riverbed beneath his feet. He dragged himself amongst the reeds, through a cacophony of noisy frogs, and collapsed into an exhausted sleep.

Chapter Twelve

England. The Thames Hulks.

Shackled in leg irons Elizabeth and the other women shuffled awkwardly to carts in the prison yard, where they were transferred to Blackfriars Bridge. Here, they were ordered onto lighters and ferried down the Thames to the prison hulks moored at Gallion's Reach, a stretch of water between Woolwich and Thameshead.

Months had passed since Elizabeth's arrest and imprisonment, months festering at Newgate Prison. So for Elizabeth the chilling air of the Thames was refreshing. But all hope faded as the hulks appeared through the morning fog. These had once been imposing ships of the line. Now their rigging had been removed, their masts cut down to stumps, their gunports nailed shut and the hulks anchored mid-stream. As the prisoners were rowed closer, the smell of Newgate returned. The stink of human waste thrown overboard from dozens of ships, meandered on the tide. Elizabeth gaped up at their new place of confinement as they approached and her heart sank once more. There would be no escape.

The weeks passed, sleeping on benches and fettered to the ship at night. The women were kept busy with the laundry during daylight hours. This included the laundry for the male prison ships moored nearby, where Elizabeth watched the men being ferried ashore each day to work the chain gangs, only the Sabbath excluded. The women also laundered the soldiers' uniforms, including those of the men of the Royal Artillery Barracks at nearby Woolwich.

As the monotonous months passed by, Elizabeth witnessed desperate scenes.   She watched on as loving parents, husbands or brothers pleaded with the authorities to have their loved one's case reprieved. They pleaded their innocence, appealing on grounds of bad judgment due to youth or poverty. They appealed for an early release or, at the least, that they should be treated with leniency once in the colonies. Poor families were made even poorer, pawning their possessions to use as bribes, but very few achieved success.

Near Baltimore

Something woke Rowan—a metallic sound—and close by. He opened his eyes, blinking uncontrollably in the bright dawn sun. He had slept for hours. Six? Eight, even. He lay face down in the mud of the shoreline amongst the reeds and was comfortable enough, shaded from the day's early heat.

But the incessant sound ground on, nearby. Rowan waited. When the sound appeared to have moved away, he knelt awkwardly, finally peering over the reeds. He could now hear voices. After weeks of listening to his captors' accent he finally heard fellow Americans. He stood, his head at the height of the reeds. As he watched, two bullock carts trundled on the road towards North Point. They were scavengers. Baltimorean scavengers would come to salvage equipment or anything of value abandoned by the retreating invaders. Rowan staggered along the path after them.

The last dray driver reined in his bullock. The old man looked over his shoulder as Rowan caught up to his cart and noticed Rowan's chaffing ankles and wrists, red and raw from irons. 'You escape?'

Rowan nodded.

'Good for you, lad. Climb on, matey.' Rowan felt such relief that all his strength seemed to desert him. The old man helped him alongside, onto his seat. The young man with him, possibly his son, seemed disinterested in Rowan. He had seen it all. He walked alongside the wagon, more interested in looking for salvage.

'The pickin's are lean,' he muttered to no one in particular. He kicked an empty rum keg and a rat flew out of one end. 'Bastard! I'll bet it's a British rat... bah!'

The old bullock driver caught Rowan scouring the horizon upriver. 'Them sails are long gone... but there's talk o' them returning.'

The wagon up ahead had stopped and its driver studied the escaped prisoner behind him.

'Rowan!' the man called out. 'Is that you? Rowan Craige?'

'Max?' Rowan recognised the man - about his own age and of similar height - as one of Silas' storemen from his Baltimore warehouse.

'Devil's blood, man, what 'appened to yer?'

'Where is Silas?'

''E were volunteer at Fort McHenry, Rowan, last I 'eard. 'E should be safe, I'm thinkin'.'

'Then you must take me to him. I have grave news.'

Silas was war weary, exhausted, nevertheless he managed a smile at the sight of Rowan who caught up with him outside the fort. But any cheer was destroyed at the news of his family.

Silas sat on the rear of Max's dray, his legs dangling over the end of the tray. He stared off into nowhere. Rowan sat in silence next to him while Max drove the bullocks back to Baltimore, sparse of many spoils. The joyous victory over the British was now a blurred memory as Silas absorbed the fate of his daughter, grandchild, brother and sister-in-law. The six-mile journey seemed a lifetime, and not a word was exchanged until the travellers rolled down the slopes with the port of Baltimore in sight.

Rowan had told Silas most of what he had seen and done, even regarding the lives of the British wounded he had saved.

'Yer did good, lad,' the tired old man finally spoke. 'Yer did what yer were trained to do. God help me, I would've strangled the bastards with me bare hands, but yer a doctor. Yer signed the hypercritic oath. Yer did the right thing and God'll thank yer for it one day.'

Rowan was silent a long moment, then suddenly confessed. 'I killed him.'

'W-who?'

'I killed him, Silas.' Rowan felt his eyes welling with tears.

'You killed who, lad?'

'I shot the man who... who murdered Jessica.'

'You did?' Silas was incredulous. He turned to look Rowan in the eye and saw the raw pain torturing his son-in-law.

'Yet, I feel no remorse, Silas.'

But Silas read the strain etched across Rowan's face.

'You found her killer?'

'Yes. I found the man and I shot him.'

'Jayzus Lord. There is a God after all. That is justice Rowan... true justice.'

'Now they hunt me,' Rowan said.

1814

'The British? They run with their tails between their legs, lad. Worry not.'

Silas insisted on hearing the entire story. He listened in respectful silence. Finally Rowan asked, 'What will *you* do now?'

'Do? I'll be going to Washington and bringing back their bodies, that's what I'll do. Give 'em a proper burial.'

Rowan thought of Jessica sewn up in the canvas sheet. 'Then I must join you.'

Baltimore was a community in celebration. The residents had defended their town and were mighty proud of the fact. Washington's citizens, in contrast, moped in disgrace and sorrow.

Silas hired a four-wheeled horse-drawn carriage and prepared for a two-week return journey to Washington. At Silas's suggestion, Rowan maintained his generous growth of beard for anonymity He caught up with his father-in-law in the courtyard, behind his warehouse. He was loading supplies and stowing empty barrels and salt, for he knew the bodies, if he found them, would be in poor condition. Rowan suspected Silas was about to leave without him. 'You're leaving now?'

'Aye.'

'I'll just fetch my kit.'

'No, lad, I'll be goin' alone.'

'No, Silas, I...'

'Listen, lad,' Silas rounded on Rowan with that fearful face he remembered from the time they'd first met, in the waterfront tavern.—'I've made preparations for yer. I bought yer a horse, a black stallion, and 'e's in the stables, waitin' for yer.'

'What?'

Silas sighed heavily and looked about him to ensure that they were not being watched. 'Come.' Silas put a hand on Rowan's shoulder and led him past empty corrals, into the stables. A black stallion in the furthest corral whinnied as they entered. 'Barney, I called 'im, after yer mate, Joshua Barney.' For the first time in days, Silas allowed himself the slightest smile. ' 'E be a gooden, a fast horse what'll take yer to New Bedford in no time.'

'New Bedford! No Silas, I will accompany you to Washington.'

'Listen, lad'—and Silas checked over his shoulder once more before dropping his voice—'There's mongrels afoot... mongrels what want ta see yer dead...'

'In Baltimore?'

'Aye. In Baltimore. Federalist mongrels what plans to kidnap you and use you as a hostage exchange for American prisoners. They have already been negotiatin'. You have quite the price on yer head. That bastard Warburton is pullin' out all stops to have yer captured.'

'How do you know this?'

'I have friends, matey, spies—real friends what watch me back and me kin. They know the truth. But like I said, there are those what call 'emselves Americans what will do anything to appease the British.'

'But Warburton has sailed.'

'Aye. But there is talk the ships will return. Besides, they still anchor in the Chesapeake, undergoing repairs and preparin' to attack New Orleans.' Rowan rubbed his forehead. This turn of events was totally unexpected. 'There's naught yer can do in Washington. If'n they catch yer, you'll hang, lad, an' I can't have that on my conscience. Here....' Silas handed Rowan a purse. 'Take this. It'll see yer safe passage, away from America awhiles.'

'Silas! I can't...'

'"Can't"! There ain't such a word as "can't," lad. So go, make a fortune, return it to me if'n yer must, some day when America is safe once more. You'll also find a letter of introduction. An acquaintance of mine in Boston owes me a favour—a big favour. Make yerself known to 'im and he will see yer set sail on a merchant.'

'A merchant. I know nothing of the business.'

'Yer don't need to. You'll sign on as a surgeon.'

Barney whinnied once more. The young stallion looked eager for the journey. 'Barney's papers are in there. Sell 'im in New Bedford; yer should get another three hundred for 'im. Now go, before I rat on yer meself.'

Newgate Prison. London.

For three weeks Marcus Marriot was left to fester in his cell. For three weeks he remained stooped by chains two short to allow him to stretch to his full height. He had no idea when he would be shackle-free. It seemed that being a shamed soldier was a reason for extra punishment. Finally, his cell door opened for the prison blacksmith, who threw an anvil on the floor next to Marriot and began pounding the rivets from his shackles. Marriot had a hundred questions, but the man was a mute, and, besides, he showed no empathy. He completed his duty and returned to his own dark space somewhere in this hellhole. The turnkey prodded Marriot with a baton toward a latrine where there were water troughs.

'Yer stink. Wash.' He threw Marriot a square of calico. After ablutions, Marriot was led to the men's cell, where fifty or more prisoners watched on without interest. Marriot was weak, his back still stooped. He shuffled to a corner in the shadows and squatted, hugging his knees.

After months languishing in Newgate Prison, Marriot was ushered along Dead Man's Walk beneath the street, to the Old Bailey, where he was presented to the judge and sentenced to seven years transportation to New South Wales. At 4 am, a week later, Marriot and a dozen others were chained together in double irons and taken by enclosed cart to Woolwich, where they were rowed out to the hulk *Birmingham*.

Marcus Marriot was fortunate, in the sense that he would only spend one month imprisoned on board the hulk *Birmingham*. In late spring he and seventy-nine others were taken aboard the 964-ton barque *Indefatigable* under the captaincy of Captain Alex Jack. As the weather was stormy the prisoners were kept below decks. Three days passed and the *Indefatigable* sailed to Norfleet, taking on another fifty prisoners at Nore. Another thirty transportees were boarded at Sheerness three days later, and even more were loaded at Portsmouth. Finally, with two other transports and a frigate escort—as these were times of war—it was time to sail for the colonies. On board the *Indefatigable,* in cramped conditions, were 367 people. One man, however, had managed to escape. The unaccounted prisoner had slipped his leg irons and dived overboard. It was presumed he had swum the two miles to the Isle of Wight. A boat was sent to look for him, but returned in the dark, unsuccessful. And this gave the others hope.

Ships pass in the night. The *Indefatigable* and its convoy sailed past other transports preparing to leave. Some of these would languish for months before sailing. One of these was moored off the coast. She was a female transport, and her name was *Magdalena*.

Boston

1814

Lucius Brown had celebrated his sixtieth year in the Albatross Tavern, two days before Rowan rode into town. The semi-retired merchant was still suffering from the sore head that had greeted him the morning before. Lucius was corpulent but showed all the jovial signs of an overweight, over-indulged and happy soul. Rowan arrived at lunchtime, where Lucius had what the French would call a pique- nique —a spread of leftovers laid out on a blanket—on his office desk before him. There was partridge pie beneath a suet crust, buffalo sausage served cold with currant sauce and johnnycake bread made from corn. A rich, yellow cheese in the shape of a ball—minus several large wedges—sat to one side. There was no sign of any vegetables or fruit, unless one claimed the mustard pickles as vegetables.

'My clerk tells me you are Silas York's son-in-law.' Lucius studied Rowan only briefly before he returned his wandering eye to the feast before him. His eyes were small and round, dark orbs lost amongst the fat and jowls of his huge head.

'Yes, sir, I was married to Silas's daughter, Jessica.' Rowan's voice broke at the memory. It had been some time since he had mentioned Jessica's name.

'*Was* married, Mr. Craige?'

'She died, sir, murdered by a British marine.'

'Oh, dear Lord. I had not heard.' Lucius scratched his beard a moment; it was a wiry affair of mutton chops joined under his chin—the beard of a Quaker, Rowan surmised. 'Please accept my deepest sympathy... Dear me, I've known Jessica since she was but a wee child.' Suddenly Lucius checked his manners. 'Please sit, Mr. Craige...'

'Call me Rowan, please, sir.'

'And you may address me as Lucius, Rowan. Now please, sit.' He pointed to a spare chair, nursing leather-bound accounting tomes. 'Put the books on the floor. Now, you must eat...'

'Oh, I... ah...'

'Nonsense, I insist. I have food enough here for an army.' Lucius looked at the repast a moment before re-evaluating his comment. 'Well, a small army, anyhow.' He looked about inquisitively, tore a sheet of paper from a blank notebook and passed it to Rowan to use as a plate. 'Here.'

'Actually, I have not eaten since last evening.' Rowan sensed he was salivating.

'Good'—Lucius passed a serving knife to Rowan, whalebone handle first—'Start with the partridge pie—my housekeeper makes it, a black woman who's been with me more than twenty years.' The merchant went on to sing the woman's praises in many ways beyond her cooking, and he hinted more than once that the woman shared his bed.

'Wine?' Lucius held up a half empty bottle of French red wine from the province of Burgundy.

'Thank you.'

After lunch, Lucius Brown re-read Silas's introductory letter and agreed wholeheartedly to help Rowan find passage on a merchant ship. 'Damned English. Damn the bastards to hell.' Lucius drained the remains of a second bottle of wine into their goblets. 'Silas told you I owe him, did he not?'

'He did mention it, yes.' Rowan looked at Lucius with an inquisitive eye.

'Well, enquire all you want, lad, but I will not be telling you why. Let us just say the time has come for me to honour my debt. How soon can you leave?'

'I am ready now.'

'Good. Because you'll leave on the tide, tomorrow morning.'

'Tomorrow!'

'Is there a problem?'

'No, Mr. Brown... Lucius. No problem at all.'

'Good. Now, come with me. I'll introduce you to Captain Nathaniel A. W. Moss.'

Autumn was only days away. A stimulating breeze greeted them as the two men left the warehouse. They headed down an alley leading from North Street to Ship Street and west towards Long Wharf, a particularly long pier, reaching out into Boston Harbour.

'Watch the cobbles, Rowan,' Lucius warned of the shiny rounded rocks underfoot. 'A man could twist his ankle easily, I fear. They are new. There is much progress occurring in Boston at this moment, much reclamation of land from the sea.'

'Progress is good, is it not?'

'Aye, lad. Mill Pond just northeast half a mile is the next great project.'

'Mill Pond?'

'Aye. It is a huge pond created by a milldam, providing power to nearby gristmills and sawmills, but it is to be landfilled to create commercial real estate. I am thinking of speculating, but it will more than likely be occupied by industry, like the Boston Manufacturing Company.'

'Oh.'

'Did you know they now have machines to covert raw cotton into cloth?'

'These are fascinating times in which we live, Lucius.'

'Indeed... Ah, there we are—the *Suffolk*.'

They stopped a moment at the waterfront between Clark's Wharf and Lee's Shipyard. Rowan followed Lucius's chubby finger pointing out across the bay to a small fleet of ships at the far end of the long quay. The three-masted, 240-ton barque was the last ship berthed at the pier. To Rowan, she looked a grand enough vessel with her freshly painted black hull and fore and mainmasts rigged square, with the mizzen rigged fore-and-aft and her sails furled and neat.

They started along the pier and, for a fat man, Lucius kept a steady pace. 'She was built in New Bedford, intended as a whaler,' Lucius said, snatching breaths. 'But the ship builder went broke and Captain Nathanial A. W. Moss and three other investors bought her for a song. Good luck to them, I say.'

'Where's she sailing?'

'She's taking a speculative cargo down to the West Indies and then on down the east coast of South America, loaded with tobacco, household fittings, cotton cloth, confectionary, salted fish. Crazy, isn't it?'

'What is crazy?'

'That refined sugar from the West Indies is traded in Boston, turned into sweetmeats and sent all the way back. Would one not think some entrepreneur would build a confectionary enterprise in the West Indies?'

Rowan smiled at the logic.

'Oh, yes, and he carries a cargo of five thousand *Books of Common Prayer* and Bibles. I know this because I sold them to him.' Lucius noted the curious expression on Rowan's face. 'They are for the missionaries in Guyana, to convert the slaves, sad heathens that they are. The books are printed here, in Boston.'

'So, is South America the final destination?' Rowan worried.

'Oh dear me, no. In the West Indies the *Suffolk* will take aboard molasses and rum and, along with three hundred barrels of household fittings, those will be traded in Rio de Janeiro for coffee. The coffee will then be taken to Manila and sold for Spanish gold, which in turn will be exchanged for tea and porcelain in Guangzhou...'

'China?'

'Aye. We Bostonians do a great trade with the Chinese.' Lucius' attention was distracted a moment. He stopped on the wharf, looking out across Boston Harbour. 'Did you know my daddy, Samuel Brown, was one of the founding members of the Sons of Liberty, and a leading protester in the so-called Boston Tea Party back in '73?'

'Really?'

'Yes, really.' The jolly merchant broke from his reverie. 'Anyhow, Rowan, you will be able to lose yourself in any of those ports you may wish. I will furnish you with letters of introduction to the most agreeable and lucrative merchants in each port and, God willing, you will make your fortune and return in years to come, a wealthy man.'

Captain Nathanial A. W. Moss knew Silas well—they had conducted many deals between them over the years, mainly in furs—and he greeted Rowan with a munificent smile. The man was short and stocky and Rowan thought he looked as strong as an ox. His grey hair was as generous as his welcome, blowing in unruly disarray as a stiffened breeze swept in off the Atlantic. The three men retired to the captain's cabin, where Lucius explained Rowan's dilemma over porcelain teacups filled with steaming black China tea.

'Then I suggest yer settle yerself aboard now, lad,' Captain Moss finally said. 'I see yer got yer kit with yer. Keep a low profile until we're at sea tomorra.' The man became serious. 'I hate ta say this about me fella Americans, but there's spies about in Boston. Bastard Federalists givin' information to the enemy.'

Rowan took Lucius Brown's large hand in his and thanked him for all he had done. 'You mentioned earlier that you wish to dispose of your mount, now resting in my stable —a stallion?' Lucius asked. Rowan nodded. 'And I believe the price suggested by Silas was three hundred dollars?'

'Yes.'

'If Silas says the animal is worth three hundred, then three hundred it is worth.' Lucius passed Captain Moss a pre-written advance note. 'Here, Nathanial, kindly honour our friend this credit, and I will settle with you next time we meet.' Lucius Brown pinched his lips and gave Rowan a sentimental nod. In the short time he had known Rowan, Lucius had grown to like him. 'And besides, I will be curious to hear of your final destination.'

172

PART TWO
TO PARTS BEYOND THE SEAS

Chapter Thirteen

Mother Bank outside Portsmouth

With the warmer weather of an English summer came the news at last. The convict transport ship *Magdalena* was finally preparing for the voyage to Sydney Town, Port Jackson, in the colony of New South Wales.

'On the morrow,' they were informed, 'you will be ferried to the Mother Bank outside Portsmouth 'arbour, where yer ship awaits.' Mother Bank, Elizabeth would discover, was the point from which all the transport ships departed.

The women were transferred, back in irons, on board the *Magdalena;* their meagre belongings, should they have any, were stowed in allocated small lead chests in the hold, to be returned to them in the colony.

The three-masted, 110-foot barque *Magdalena*, under the captaincy of Captain Winston Cholmondeley, was thirty feet wide at her widest. Built in 1798 to service the London to Jamaica run, she had seen better days. But her dimensions and the height between decks at six foot, three inches made her suitable for conversion to a five-to-a-berth transport ship.

Cholmondeley was paid just over six pounds for each prisoner transported by the Admiralty. The ship's surgeon Phineas Beckwith would receive his bonus of five shillings for each prisoner delivered to the colonies, if in fair health.

The *Magdalena's* foremast, mainmast and mizzen were rigged to carry three square sails. The 25-foot bowsprit supported three foresails. The raised quarterdeck was for officers only, whereas their quarters were below the quarterdeck. The one hundred and fifty transportees were quartered on the lower middle section of the orlop deck. Here, the deck had been especially converted by the carpenters to accommodate the prisoners; shelves sleeping five prisoners each were fastened to each side of the hull. Stores were kept on the same deck, forward and aft. The forecastle, the deck between the main mast and the bow, accommodated the seamen and one hundred new marines for the colony, all in hammocks.

Once the prisoners, crew, marines and officers were all aboard, the *Magdalena* weighed anchor and sailed for Plymouth. From there the ship was piloted around the Isle of Wight's shoals west, for Cawsand Bay in Plymouth Sound, where dozens of ships—merchants, navy or East Indiamen— took on provisions. It was here that preparations for the months at sea were made in earnest.

Business ashore boomed. First, the hold was filled with water barrels. For a week, the women prisoners watched as supplies were ferried out to the ship in hired lighters. Harold Ryther, the ship's cooper and the man responsible for all the barrels, checked every keg, barrel and hogshead minutely. If any food spoiled, he would be to blame. He worked closely with Philip Paxton, the purser, and together they visited the Plymouth abattoirs and market gardens to secure meat and fresh produce. Live sheep, goats, hogs and chickens were also brought on board and stowed in special pens on the foredeck.

Another fifty women, with five infants, were brought on board in Plymouth. As the prisoners' accommodations were fought over on the cramped orlop deck, it soon became clear that the sailors, marines and officers expected female company in their hammocks or bunks. Many women were prepared for the situation. A partner for the five-month voyage would mean extra rations, *and* for what? Some lovin', some carousin'—and why not?

The real art was not to become pregnant for, without doubt, the child would be taken from the mother to an orphanage, after she gave birth in the colony. For seventeen-year-old Elizabeth, avoiding the advances of so many aroused men would be a challenge.

Once the women were on board, the ship's carpenter was ordered to strike off the leg irons, and the women were allowed on deck for fresh air in groups of fifty. They took in the crisp fresh air in silence, each prisoner lost in her own thoughts, wondering if she would ever see her mother England again.

On board the *Suffolk*. Atlantic Ocean.

For Rowan, it was something to feel the undulating Atlantic rolling beneath his feet, bow to stern, once again. And the *Suffolk* proved a sturdy vessel well ballasted with a rich cargo. Sailing south, Captain Nathanial A. W. Moss was confident they would not encounter any Royal Navy ships, for it was now common knowledge that the British fleet had no intention of returning to take Baltimore. New Orleans was in their sights. It was also for this reason that Captain Moss insisted on sailing south to the equator in October, as it was hurricane season and the Royal Navy were inclined to delay sailing south, most likely docking for the season in the British Territory of Bermuda.

In Fort-de-France on Martinique fifty barrels of household utensils and a thousand yards of cotton cloth were traded for sugar, rum and cocoa. Throughout these weeks, dark clouds maintained their distance. Sailing conditions were near perfect. On Saint Martin, tobacco proved more popular than the cotton cloth, but trade goods were in short supply and Captain Moss accepted gold and silver, instead.

It was mid-November when their luck ran dry. The squall gave little warning and had battered the *Suffolk* into submission before the hurricane hit. It rolled west across the Caribbean Sea, an avalanche of disaster. For three days, the storm pounded the ship. Rowan had rarely seen such weather. Three men were lost overboard while the helmsman, roped to the wheel, battled to keep their heading into the wind and waves. Occasionally, the lower yards dipped in the ocean and Rowan was amazed that they stayed afloat. Then, on the night of the third day, misfortune struck. Under strain, the main mast splintered, twenty feet above the deck. It appeared they were doomed, destined for the bottom of the ocean, when, almost as fast as it had approached, the hurricane had petered out.

At first light, Captain Moss made his reading and was certain they were off the coast of Venezuela. But since the wars with Napoleon, Spain had been having financial problems with its colonies in Venezuela, with several provinces declaring themselves independent.

'There is much civil unrest there,' Captain Moss warned Rowan. 'We have little choice but to sail to French Guiana.'

Three weeks passed. Three weeks limping across the ocean to French Guiana under the canvas of two masts instead of three; the mosquito-infested town of Cayenne, the capitol, had never looked so inviting.

'Cayenne was captured by a Portuguese-English squadron in '09,' Captain Moss informed Rowan, 'but the signing of the Treaty of Paris two months since has seen it returned to the French. Therefore, we will be welcome.'

Rowan accompanied captain Moss to the shipyards of Cayenne, where a suitable mast, salvaged from a ship that had been wrecked some months before, was secured. However, the *Suffolk* was not the only casualty of the recent hurricane and they were obliged to wait, as the shipyards were overworked and labour was in short supply.

Rowan's foot had finally healed, and he took short excursions into the interior of French Guiana, where the deafening sound of the jungle insects and the animal kingdom took his mind from the stifling humidity and his own uncertain future.

The weeks dragged by. It was December before the *Suffolk* sailed back onto the Atlantic. Cape Horn at the southernmost tip of South America tested Captain Moss's skills, as the ship ploughed through massive waves that had swept four thousand miles across the Pacific. Here, at the Horn, the waves channelled through the narrow Patagonian Cape, and the ice shelves of the Antarctic created unpredictable seas. These conditions were made even more dangerous by the 100-mile-per-hour winds howling down from the Andes, which could turn into a massive storm, throwing up fifty-foot waves with little warning and burying the *Suffolk's* deck beneath icy green water.

So, it was with some relief, ten weeks after sailing from Cayenne, that they sailed northwest and across the vast blue of the Pacific Ocean.

1814

Atlantic Ocean south-west of England, on board the convict transport *Indefatigable.*

There were 367 people on board Marcus Marriot's transport ship: 179 prisoners, 90 crew, 65 marines—a detachment of the 46th regiment of Foot—and 33 passengers, including twelve men, nine women and twelve children. Anxiety, fear, anger, uncertainty and rationed cheer convened between the decks like an invisible haze. Below the main deck it was cramped and oppressive. For the prisoners, it was impossible to lie straight to sleep. From the moment each man sought a berth, brutal fights broke out. It was dog eat dog, but Marcus fared better than most, for if there was one thing the miscreant had learned in the army, it was to fight dirty—the dirtier, the better. Tiers of bunk benches were to be shared, with a minimal partition between each man. The lower benches were used for dining tables, where the men grouped in messes of eight to eat. The younger men slept in hammocks amidships, slung at night only. Each man was issued a one-pint mug and a knife and fork, to be returned after each meal.

The monotonous voyage had begun. Marcus Marriot knew he would have to survive this horror for over four months. The tedious diet of boiled salted meat, wormy biscuit and rancid water took its toll, and six weeks after sailing from Cape Town the first men fell ill from scurvy. The ship surgeon knew the symptoms immediately: anaemia, the loosening or loss of teeth and small red dots appearing under the skin.

Marriot had heard the rumours, of course—the stories that their ship surgeon superintendent, Mr. Hugh Llewellyn, and Captain Alex Jack had sailed together before, on slavers. They had delivered African slaves to the West Indies and held little sympathy for the well-being of the thieves and felons of His Majesty's prisons. The surgeon was also a drunkard and addicted to laudanum, of which he cheated prisoners who needed the medicinal juice of the poppy to relieve pain.

'Then what is your incentive to see these animals delivered to the colony in good health?' Marcus overheard an officer of the guard ask the surgeon one morning.

'As surgeon superintendent,' Hugh Llewellyn answered, 'I am entitled to five shillings for each prisoner delivered safe and sound. And I will receive a certificate from the governor on arrival in Hobart Town verifying that my conduct merits such a gratuity.'

Entitled. Gratuity. Marriot spat on the deck.

All the same, the surgeon condoned the frequent lashings on board for what appeared to be minor misdemeanours. He even appeared to enjoy watching, supervising the punishment. Marcus would feel the cat o' nine tails across his back twice during the voyage. Neither time did he feel he had deserved it. Once was for complaining about the food. The purser, it seemed, had purchased several barrels of salted pork and beef, leftovers from other voyages and already several years old, at a cheaper rate, and he had pocketed the difference. The meat was rancid and its boiling alone stank out the galley, permeating the below decks. Seven prisoners would die on the voyage, three of scurvy, the others of typhoid or cholera, through the failure of the surgeon. Marcus had witnessed the surgeon's blatant neglect and made a promise to himself, that if the opportunity for anonymity should arise, he would give the man a beating.

Atlantic Ocean, on board the *Magdalena*

Although winter approached, the autumn months still offered fine weather, and Elizabeth's transport ship was ready to depart. The *Magdalena* caught the wind in her topsails and, leaving Plymouth Sound, she cleared Rame Head sailing west and well south off Cornwall's rocky coast. They were headed for the open Atlantic at last.

Elizabeth had never felt so ill. Seasickness struck most of the women in the first days at sea. Confined below deck, all Elizabeth could do was lie on the bench bed and feel miserably sorry for herself. Most of the women were so indisposed that they could not even make it to the night buckets, for the hatches were bolted from dusk until dawn. They simply vomited where they lay. To add to their woes, the fumes of effluvium from the bilges cast a nasty miasma—an invisible vapour from human waste—which had seeped into the bowels of the ship, an accumulation of years and years that was impossible to clean from the ballast of gravelly pebbles used to correct the ship's buoyancy. The scene was nothing less than a nightmare.

The weeks passed and, thankfully, so did the malady. Elizabeth settled into a routine of shipboard life, aware that the ship was at the mercy of the wind and currents, skilfully operated by men, ropes and canvas, divided into three daily watches of eight hours each, heralded by the ship's bell. During the day, if the weather permitted, the prisoners were allowed on deck in groups, to take in the fresh air deemed by the ship's surgeon to be beneficial to their health. It was during these most pleasurable moments that Elizabeth had the opportunity to observe the running of a ship, something she would never have thought possible back in Bristol. Elizabeth observed the mate of the watch on the quarterdeck as he studied the wind direction and the configuration of sail and then barked his command to the boatswain, who would pipe orders to the seamen, who understood the coded whistles clearly. They would scamper up the ratlines and out onto the yards, some fifty or sixty feet above the deck, where they *trimmed* the sails for the best manoeuvrability.

Part of Elizabeth's routine was to scrub the deck with holystone and seawater—a backbreaking chore, but one that Elizabeth enjoyed for the exercise and fresh air.

Captain Cholmondeley, although a God-fearing man, quickly showed his intolerance, should discipline be abused. He had the authority to order the cat-o'-nine-tails, the dreaded whip, and was generous in its application. Cholmondeley also insisted prayers be read on the main deck for crew and prisoners alike, weather permitting. For most, it was a chance for the women of the *Magdalena* to fraternise, albeit discreetly, with the crew. Liaisons were inevitable with so many men and women at sea on a ship for months. The captain was aware of this and turned a blind eye for the sake of a contented ship. But woe betide any who flaunted their indiscretions. The captain himself had a wife and five children in Cornwall and was a chaste man.

Master's Mate Edmund Browning, a rather naïve twenty-one-year-old from Liverpool, finally found himself within earshot of Elizabeth. He was slim, muscular and of average height. He was not particularly handsome, but had an agreeable guilelessness about him. Together with the prisoners, the crew stood on the main deck for the Sunday sermon. Priggishly erect on the quarterdeck alongside the captain, Chaplain Knockley read his own handwritten sermon, pinioned in the pages of a rather large family Bible to prevent it from blowing in the breeze. Edmund Browning shuffled closer to Elizabeth, pushing the nearest seaman aside.

'You're Elizabeth, ain't yer? Elizabeth Eveleigh.' Elizabeth ignored the man. 'Wha'...? Not talkin'?' Elizabeth tried to step aside unnoticed, but Betty Bryant, standing on

Elizabeth's other side, would have none of it. She blocked Elizabeth in. 'Well?' the master's mate persisted.

'Yes, she is,' Betty answered for her friend. 'An' I'm Betty,' she added.

'Yeh. I know you an' all—Betty Bryant, ain't it? But it's this 'ere Elizabeth wha' I was hoping to make my acquaintance.'

Betty elbowed her friend. 'It's a long voyage, girl,' she said under her breath. 'You'll be wantin' all the friends yer can get.'

' 'Ere.' The master's mate slipped Elizabeth a small package and her sharpened nose identified pickled onion and... *was that cheddar*? 'Put it away in yer skirt 'fore anyone sees it,' he whispered conspiratorially.

Betty saw the exchange. 'See, I told yer.'

'Keep it!' Elizabeth pushed the parcel aside. 'I don't want your charity. Leave me be.'

'Oh!' Browning hissed back. 'Like that, is it?'

'I'll 'ave it,' Betty interjected, and snatched the package from her friend. The movement caught the attention of a guard. Betty smiled at the man and lifted her skirt artfully to flash off her ankles. The guard returned a lascivious smile and the parcel disappeared into Betty's slip.

'You're incorrigible,' Elizabeth told Betty back at their cot later.

'An' yer a fool,' Betty retorted. 'Take a lover and this voyage will be a lot more comfortable.'

'I don't want a lover.'

'Then yer won't be wantin' to share this, then,' Betty said angrily and unfolded the generous hunk of dry cheddar cheese, while the pickled onion escaped, rolling across the cot. Betty sank her teeth into the cheese, looked at Elizabeth red-faced, and capitulated. 'Bugger it,' Betty muttered, feeling guilty, and broke the lump in half, passing Elizabeth the smaller piece. Elizabeth said nothing, but was not stubborn enough to refuse. She bit into the cheddar and felt its sharpness tingle the sides of her tongue. Betty collected the onion, bit it in half and passed Elizabeth the other half. After boiled salted pork and gruel day after day, the cheese was an unimaginable luxury. Betty noted her friend's pleasure. 'There—better than sex, huh?... Well, almost.'

Elizabeth giggled for the first time, it seemed, in months.

'All yer gotta do, girl, is hitch up them skirts and let lover boy do 'is business. Think about cheese while 'e's ploughin' away.'

Pacific Ocean, on board the *Suffolk.*
3,000 nautical miles off the coast of Chile

'Ahoy, on deck! Sail! Port bow!' Andrew Talbot, the young lookout in the crow's nest high up on the *Suffolk's* main mast, called down to the quarter deck through the hazy light, sometime between early morning and dawn. First Mate William Pickering planted the eyeglass firmly to one eye, closed the other and aimed the piece across the ocean. Gradually the bow lanterns of the other ship, two miles distant, drifted into focus.

'What is it, William?' Jim Harman the helmsman asked, glad of the diversion to the monotony of his watch. 'A whaler?'

'Maybe'—the mate clenched his teeth, concentrating through the lens—'Maybe.' Although the pirates of old were disappearing into the history books and the scribblings of fictional fancy, William Pickering was primarily a wary man. There were, after all, privateers still sailing the oceans, unaware of the recent developments between Britain and America, and he wanted no mishaps during his watch. Not while Captain Nathanial A. W. Moss slept in his cot at this early hour. For ships to pass on vast oceans was a rarity; especially as the other vessel was heading east and the *Suffolk* west, he knew his captain would want to haul to, catch up on news from across the Pacific and exchange letters for loved ones back home. All the same, he must be wary.

'Steer to starboard, Tom,' Pickering told the helmsman. 'We'll see if they, too, change course.'

An hour later it was clear—the other ship had closed the distance between them. The two ships eventually exchanged signals with bunting, a semaphore of messages. 'Like us, she craves gossip,' Captain Moss said, now standing refreshed on the quarterdeck with legs apart, hands locked behind his back, staring across the sea at the approaching sail. He had eaten a hearty breakfast of boiled egg, oatmeal with molasses and hard rind cheese, along with three mugs of hot black coffee. Despite suffering from constipation, he was enthusiastic to rendezvous on the high seas and exchange news.

'She flies the American flag, sar,' the first mate told his captain. 'A whaler, I'm thinkin'.'

'To be sure, William. These waters are rich with the monsters.'

Another hour passed and the two ships shortened sail as they approached hailing distance. The whaler, a three-masted barque square-rigged on the fore and main masts and fore-and-aft-rigged on the mizzenmast, dropped a sea anchor.

'What ship are you?' the stranger called across the ocean through a speaking trumpet.

'*Suffolk*, Boston. Under the command of Captain Nathanial A. W. Moss. And you, sir?'

'The *Essex,* out of Massachusetts,' came the reply. 'Captain Fry. You head for Sydney Cove, do you not?'

'Aye. With a cargo of sugar, tobacco, coffee and cotton.'

'Permission to come aboard, Captain Moss? I have letters; I imagine you, too, Captain, have exchange for Boston.'

'Aye. Come aboard.'

Captain Fry was in his sixties. He was a tall man, made taller by his beaver skin pipestack topper, propped proudly on his head, shiny in the morning sun, as his crew rowed him the fifty yards between ships. He sat bolt upright in the sheets and Captain Moss suspected he had changed into his Sunday best for the occasion, as he dressed in a dark blue, double-breasted seafarer's jacket with wide lapels and brass buttons polished like gold. He had a fashionable beard under a clean-shaven chin, deep-set eyes with a large nose accentuating furrows in his face that betrayed his age.

'Top o' the mornin' to yer, Captain Moss.'

'Aye. An' ter you, too, Cap'n Fry.'

The two captains shook hands firmly. In Moss's stern cabin the *Suffolk's* steward brought coffee and Madeira. Captain Fry sat where he could keep an eye on the *Essex* out of the stern window.

'I'm guessin' yer a Quaker, sir,' Captain Moss said, still standing, and oscillating the decanter of Madeira as if the ship was in a heavy swell. 'Is it too early for yer to imbibe a refreshment?'

'Aye. Just coffee, thankin' yee.' The *Essex* captain's eyes wandered about his peer's cabin whilst Moss poured himself a glass of wine. He noticed there were not too many home comforts. A portrait of an attractive, dark-haired woman was fastened to the wall next to the other captain's cot. 'Your wife, Captain?'

'Aye. Melanie. You married, Captain Fry?'

'I were, sir, but she died eight year ago now—sickness of the stomach.'

'Oh, I am sorry to hear that.'

Fry hefted a bundle of scrolled documents tied in blue ribbon onto the captain's table, where they gathered against the fiddle rope tacked around the edges, a necessity aboard any ship, to prevent dinnerware sliding off the table in rough weather.

'These here are all my crew's letters. We've been at sea fifteen months and three weeks already and the hull's only one quarter full of oil. I am thinking this voyage will be another two years at the current rate. So, if you will be so kind as to get these on board a ship to London out of Sydney Cove and hence across the Atlantic, then I would be much obliged to you sir. It'll boost morale on board the *Essex*.'

'Be my pleasure.' Captain Moss sipped his Madeira and nodded toward his own ship's exchange, wrapped neatly in cloth.

'You will more than likely be back in Boston before me, Captain Moss, but I will take the letters, all the same. Tell me, sir—you loaded coffee on board in Rio?'

'Aye.'

'And chose to sail around the horn and across the Pacific?'

'Aye. I've made the voyage before, Captain. I prefer the Pacific to the Indian Ocean.'

'You were delayed in the West Indies, were you not?'

'Aye, damaged keel and broken forward mast... nasty squall in the Caribbean Sea.'

'I see. Because I sailed out of Boston only a week after you sailed, sir.'

'Is that so?'

'Yes. So, the *Essex* gained two months on the *Suffolk* and here we are, meeting in the middle of the Pacific. A rare coincidence, sir.'

'Aye, that it is.'

'Tell me, do you perchance have a surgeon on board, a gentleman named Rowan Craige.'

'Why?' Captain Moss was immediately alert. 'Do you need medical assistance?'

'No, sir, on the contrary, I am fortunate to have a crew member who was surgeon's mate on board the USS *Chesapeake* back in '06, '07. He is proficient enough to administer to all our humours.

'Most fortunate.'

'Yes. He is conversant in the art of surgery, has amputated only once, I will confess, but the operation was a success. One of my men fell from the yards and pulverised his leg.'

'Unfortunate business, Captain Fry, but why do you ask of Mr. Craige?'

Captain Fry leant forward, as if avoiding prying ears and eyes lurking behind the timbers. 'He is a wanted felon.'

'Then I cannot help you, sir; I have no one on board of that name.'

'Then maybe he has adopted another name.'

'I know all of my crew, sir—know 'em well, and the man of whom yer speak is not on my ship.'

'I just thought I should mention it, Captain, because the Royal Navy has a warrant out for him—a warrant for murder. And they were informed that he had set sail from Boston on board this ship, the *Suffolk*, presumably bound for Sydney Cove. My ship was searched before I was permitted to leave.'

'Well... I don't know what to say. I don't know where they would derive such intelligence.'

'The Royal Navy are not to be trifled with. Do not misunderstand me, sir. I despise the British as much as any American. I simply wish to make it known that every Royal Navy frigate, transport, ship of the line, seeks this man, and they intend to hang him—make an example of him, I was told. So beware, sir. I would hate to see you lose your ship. Whether the man is innocent or guilty, he will hang.'

'Well, thank you for your advice, sir. I will be vigilant, thart's to be sure.'

Captain Moss watched in silence as Captain Fry was rowed back to the *Essex*. As the older captain was hauled on board his own ship, Moss turned to his first mate, who was preparing to order the boatswain to give the order for full sail. 'William,' he called out.

'Sir?'

'Fetch the surgeon.'

Atlantic Ocean. On board the *Magdalena*

After weeks at sea, a hierarchy had been formed amongst the prisoners. It had been inevitable; even the officers knew that. Sally Fetter had taken it upon herself to lead the pack. Sally was from York, a common prostitute charged with assault after bashing a patron who was foolish enough to short change her a shilling, after services rendered. Three new silk handkerchiefs valued at fourteen shillings, stolen prior and in her possession upon her arrest had fetched her the seven years' transportation. Sally was five-foot-eight and masculine, broad-shouldered, sharp-witted and sharp-eyed, with a shaved head due to lice. She wore a longhaired, curled wig of human hair—expensive and stolen—although she swore she'd paid four guineas for it at a wigmaker in Drilfield.

Sally coerced the younger, prettier prisoners into doing favours in return for her protection. Once the voyage settled into its monotonous routine, the seamen had more time on their hands—more time for lustful pursuits—and Sally seized her opportunity. *Woe betide any bitch who questioned her authority.*

Seventeen-year-old Elizabeth Eveleigh, with her innocent looks, would have been the cherry on Sally Fetter's salver of sweet delights. However, Sally knew better. Like most of the women, she had seen the scrap with Elizabeth and Betty Bryant at Newgate Prison. Sally knew Elizabeth would be nothing but trouble and for this reason she kept her communication respectful.

The *Magdalena* lurched over the crest of another bow wave crashing into its trough with a hiss of spray across the forecastle. So far, life at sea had been bearable, and the crew had told the women they were making good progress. They should see the Canary Islands on the horizon in a day or two.

Betty elbowed Elizabeth in the darkness as they lay on their shared bunk. It was late in the night and Elizabeth groaned awake, annoyed. She had fallen into a deep sleep, but now Betty's face was so close that Elizabeth caught the exhalation of her tart breath. 'Elizabeth. Wake up.' Elizabeth squinted in the faint light cast from a night lantern oscillating rhythmically to the ocean's swell.

'Elizabeth.'

'What?'

'Sally's sellin' tricks to the lads,' Betty whispered. 'I firkin' knew it.'

'So? Go to sleep.'

'Sleep? Firk. I hear that bitch's sellin' them girls for a florin a go an' keepin' half for herself while she keeps her own legs shut.'

'You said yourself, no man would want to lie with her.' Elizabeth said. She leant on one elbow, staring off into the shadows, focusing on a blackened gap in the bulkhead, where loosened planks had been removed. Apparently, Betty had witnessed the last whore squeeze her body through to a storage hold situated between the women's and the seamen's quarters. 'Why should you care, anyway?'

'It's easy money, I tell yer,' Betty fidgeted. 'That's why I care.'

Four weeks had passed by the time the *Magdalena* sailed into Santa Cruz de Tenerife in the Canary Islands. Once the Spanish Governor had granted permission, the purser took a crew ashore to re-supply the ship with fresh vegetables and fresh meat. This would be a pleasant change from the monotonous salted meat in the barrels, which required soaking for hours to rid the tight grey pickled flesh of salt, before it could be cooked slowly, for hours, in boiling water. At Santa Cruz, fresh water from a river flowing into the settlement from inland mountains would also be supplied.

While moored in the harbour, Captain Cholmondeley ordered that the *Magdalena*'s decks be scrubbed and the below decks aired. Soiled clothing was finally boiled in fresh water rather than seawater. The women then beat the laundry with rattan beaters and it was hung to dry in the rigging.

It was mid-November when the *Magdalena* finally sailed south from the Canaries, restocked with fresh produce, livestock and water. To make the most of the Atlantic Ocean's currents and the November winds the ship sailed south-west to the Portuguese islands of Cabo Verde, before sailing well out onto the Atlantic and sailing south-east once again, then towards the equator.

Here, the imaginary line equidistant from the North and South Poles divided the two hemispheres. The act of crossing the equator was also steeped in tradition for those who had sailed previously across *the line*. They called themselves Shellbacks. These men and women played shenanigans on the Pollywogs—those who were about to cross the line for the first time. For a brief period and beyond the captain's jurisdiction, ship protocol was abandoned. The Shellbacks dressed as sea creatures; even King Neptune himself—dressed in the skin of a dolphin—inflicted atrocities on the Pollywogs, atrocities like dunking them in a barrel of bilge slops before tying them to the end of a rope and throwing them overboard, to trail behind the ship for a half-mile or so. For many it was a relief from the boredom, but for the victims, it could be terrifying.

Shenanigans over, and with the wind in their port beam, the *Magdalena* left the equator astern, now sailing the Atlantic's Southern Hemisphere for Cape Town on the southwest tip of Africa.

They were one week south of the equator when Seaman Brinley Thurston's courage and good fortune brought him face to face with Elizabeth. The young seaman was smitten. He had also observed how Elizabeth had remained aloof from the liaisons between the female prisoners and the seamen. Elizabeth, in the company of five other women on their hands and knees, was scrubbing the orlop deck with honing stones and seawater. Brinley slopped a bucket of water next to Elizabeth and fetched up the empty bucket beside her. Elizabeth continued scrubbing, but shortly became aware that the bare feet beside her were not retreating. She looked up at the water carrier, who beamed back cheekily.

'Mornin',' Brinley called, grinning, his face silhouetted by the sunlight shining down the companionway. His sun-bleached hair was unruly and barely held behind him in an untidy ponytail. Elizabeth maintained a sour face and simply grunted. 'Yer Elizabeth, ain't yer?' Still Elizabeth remained silent, more concerned about being punished for stopping work. 'Me name's Brinley… Brinley Thurston.' Elizabeth chanced a peek over her shoulder. The guard stared back at her, also grinning. It appeared the overseer was in cahoots with this contravention. 'Well?' Brinley persisted.

'Well, what?'

'Ah… it don't matter none. I know yer name's Elizabeth.'

'What do you want?' Elizabeth scowled.

'Jus' tryin' ter be friendly.'

'Well, don't.' Elizabeth stopped briefly, grateful for the respite. The sailor shifted slightly and the light caught his face. He was young and handsome and now Elizabeth sensed that she had taken the wind from his sails. He looked away, biting his lip, losing nerve before his peers. 'How old are you?' Elizabeth asked.

Brinley's face brightened at the interest, if it could be construed as interest. 'Fifteen,' he answered brightly.

Molly Cummins, at Elizabeth's side, twisted her face to Brinley. 'Bit young ter be chattin' up yer elders, ain't ya? Now, sod off.'

'You mind yer mouth, woman, or I'll see yer flogged.' Molly Cummins gasped a brittle laugh at the lad's insolence but thought it best to let dead dogs lie. Both women knew this to be an idle threat. Elizabeth noticed the seaman checking with the overseer, as if requesting permission.

He took a small parcel from his pocket, drawing Elizabeth's attention to it before whispering in her ear, 'I want to talk, nuthin' else, like. Just talk. Come 'ere a moment.' Elizabeth caught a sweet aroma. Her stomach rumbled. She looked back at the guard, who feigned to be looking elsewhere.

They stepped aside, into the shadows behind the cots. 'What is it you want?' Elizabeth asked the young sailor.

Brinley answered with an action. He pressed the fist-sized parcel into Elizabeth's palm. 'Spotted Dick,' he said under his breath, speaking of the suet pudding with currants and sugar, saved from the previous evening's ration.

'I don't want your charity,' Elizabeth pushed the parcel back.

'Oh! Please don't misunderstand. I jus' wanna be friends.'

'Friends? Why?'

'It seems to me in your position you'd be wantin' all the friends yer can get.'

'Not at your price.'

'My price?'

'You just want me for the same reason all the other sailors want the women.' Brinley's face reddened. He looked genuinely upset. 'Sorry,' Elizabeth sighed heavily. 'Look, you're probably a nice person, Brinley Thurston. But the truth is, I cannot give you what you want.'

'I've been watchin' yer since the day you first come aboard'—Brinley bowed his head—'I... I'm really fond o' yer, Miss Elizabeth.'

'Thank you for the compliment, but one of the other prisoners will make you happy, I am certain.'

'I don't want no whore!' Brinley said louder than he should have, raising heads from the scrubbers on the deck. An officer's boots appeared on the top tread of the companionway. A subtle whistle came from the overseer. 'Here.' Brinley closed Elizabeth's hand around the pudding once more. 'Please keep it.' And the besotted sailor hurried away.

1814

On board the *Suffolk*. Pacific Ocean.

'Land Ho!' The cry from the crow's nest swept the deck below bringing with it relief. Relief that only the safe haven of land in the middle of an ocean as vast as the Pacific could bring to weary sailors.

'Land ho! Starboard bow!'

Captain Nathaniel Moss raised his spyglass and brought the distant island into focus—it looked green and lush. The man smiled proudly at those around him. 'Friendly Islands, excellent,' he said, thankful his navigational skills *and* dead reckoning had paid off.

The *Suffolk*, desperate for fresh water and vegetables, sailed into a bay on Lifuka, one of the Friendly Islands, an archipelago of one hundred and seventy islands east of Fiji and south of Samoa. Rowan joined Captain Moss on the quarterdeck while William Pickering, the first mate, levelled his eyeglass at fires smoking on the nearest beach.

'Friendly Islands,' Rowan remarked. 'I take it the natives are hospitable, then?'

'According to Captain James Cook, they are.' The captain squinted into the tropical sun reflecting off the silvery bay. 'He was supposedly the first European here some forty years past.'

'Aye,' the mate said from the corner of his mouth, searching the shoreline for any sign of trouble, 'but we have two Hawaiians on board who warn us otherwise.' Pickering spoke of two Hawaiian seamen who had been a part of the *Suffolk's* company over the past three years. 'So I advise caution.'

'Here they come now.' The helmsman was the first to spot the flotilla of native outriggers with their lateen sails pushing into the surf. Rowan guessed there must have been a hundred or more warriors, with each canoe skippered by a chieftain. Captain Moss turned to his first mate and said quietly, 'I don't want the crew alarmed, but break out small arms and have them at the ready, discretely now.'

'Aye, sar.'

'Friendly Islands!' Moss muttered to Rowan. 'I hope Cook was right.' The outriggers glided by, surrounding the *Suffolk*, which had yet to drop anchor, although the sails had been reefed. 'Depth?' Moss called to the second mate.

'Six fathoms, sar. I can see the bottom clearly.'

Immediately, dozens of natives climbed aboard with the agility of acrobats. They were animated but smiling openly, touching the lapels of clothing, admiring the ship, its ropes and canvas. One chief, who commanded more respect than the others, stood before Captain Moss whom, with past experience of visiting ships, he had singled out as the ship's chief. He stepped forward and hugged the wary Bostonian, finally rubbing his nose against Moss's. This brought spontaneous, albeit nervous laughter from the crew.

But William Pickering was less trusting and ordered his men to prevent more boarders from joining those already on the deck.

'Gently, gently, Mr. Pickering,' the captain said in a soft voice.

'These natives are armed, Captain,' he said of the spears and lethal clubs in their possession.

'I can see that, but so are we.' Moss smiled, showing off white teeth to the chief, who by now was studying a leather fire bucket strapped to a mast step. Small gifts such as nails, trinket mirrors and baubles, carried just for such occasions, were handed to the natives, while token baskets of yams and coconuts were hefted on board. It was time to trade.

Kaliko, one of the *Suffolk's* Hawaiian seamen, approached the mate. 'I speak some of this language.'

'Really?'

'Aye. I would also like to warn you these people show happy face but cannot be trusted.' Pickering had grown fond of the two Hawaiians, Kaliko and his cousin Tua. They were giants of men, great seamen, and warlike themselves, and their tattooed bodies bore the strength of four men. Pickering heeded their advice.

With the bartering complete, the men of the *Suffolk* spent the entire day filling water barrels from a freshwater brook flowing off the island's one mountain. Livestock such as pigs and chickens were taken on board and extra pens built. The cook and his assistant stacked crates of vegetables and fruits. Meanwhile, the women of the village prepared a feast of wild hogs cooked in fire pits at the edge of the beach. With Kaliko interpreting, the head chieftain, Finau Ulukalala, entertained Captain Moss, his mates and Rowan with coconut shells filled with kava, a potent alcohol made from the fermented kava plant.

'Warn your men to keep their wits about them, Mr. Pickering, if you please,' the captain said, whilst wearing a wide, innocent grin for the benefit of the chief. As the kava flowed, Chief Finau Ulukalala showed all signs of being the perfect host. But he soon tired of interpreted politeness and the chief began to question the Hawaiian seaman Kaliko about the *Suffolk*. Kaliko was no fool and lied about the cargo on board the *Suffolk*, the quantity of arms on board, the number of crew and other impertinent questions. Then, quite casually, Ulukalala mentioned there was another white man ship anchored in the next bay.

'What?' Captain Moss was astounded. 'What ship?'

'He say the ship have allegiance to another white-man chief. No King George. A man they call Napoleon...'

'The French! Here?' Moss glanced warily at the chief, who was now supervising the excavation of the roasted hogs. The kava had taken effect and the chief was clearly hungry, barking instructions to the women with the looseness and hooded eyes of an inebriate.

'Send Rayden and Bortwick,' Captain Moss said of the second mate and the boatswain. 'See that the men are cautious. They are to sail the pinnace to the bay north and make contact with a French ship anchored there. I wish to know her business. Maybe we could rendezvous in the morning.'

'Aye, sar.'

Seaman Kaliko watched Finau Ulukalala waving his hands about and nagging the women. While the chief was preoccupied, he approached his captain and Rowan. 'Captain Moss, sar.'

'Kaliko.' Moss looked up at the Hawaiian from where he sat on a flat rock, a little more relaxed than he cared to be. 'You've done good, lad, with the translatin'. Lucky we had you on board.'

'Ah... Captain.'

'Got somethin' on yer mind?'

'Aye.'

'Then speak up, lad.'

'This man, Finau Ulukalala -- he have bad plan for *Suffolk*. Bad plan for our men, I am thinking.'

'Oh?'

'I hear other chief say they want ship cannon.'

'Cannon? What would these savages know about cannon?'

'People of Lifuka fight people of other islands. Chief Finau Ulukalala, he say another chief, Taku-aho, rule other islands but Finau Ulukalala want to rule. He need cannon and he will take *Suffolk* to do these things. He make *Suffolk* men use cannon and the rest of crew -- he kill, I'm thinkin'.'

Rowan shifted unsteadily, casting an eye over the feast preparations. 'You heard all this from the chief?'

'I hear from warriors. They drink kava and speak. They not realise Kaliko smart native.'

'Then we should leave.' Pickering had returned from the beach and heard everything.

'It's not as easy as that. They are preparin' a feast in our honour.'

'Last supper, you mean!'

'If we up and leave now, we'll cause a fracas,' Moss said quietly, forcing a smile. 'They'll get suspicious. No, we must enjoy the celebrations first and then make a polite retreat to the ship for the night... Satisfy 'em that we will return in the morning with more gifts.'

On board the *Magdalena*. Atlantic Ocean.

Elizabeth stepped to the gunwale amidships and sucked in the sea breeze. The weather of late had been moderate and the seas a pleasant undulation of rhythmic consistency. The ship's surgeon had been recommending that the prisoners take the fresh air, and the latest prediction put arrival in Cape Town at one week. Elizabeth and Bindley had managed several meetings, albeit brief. Romances on board the female transport were quite acceptable—encouraged, even—as the captain knew it led to a contented crew... in general. Even the officers had taken *wives* for the duration, and who knew what relationships would blossom into marriage once they arrived at their destination?

For Bindley, he knew where he stood with Elizabeth. The friendship of the fifteen-year-old seaman and the seventeen-year-old prisoner was recognised by the others on board for what it was, a platonic relationship. Bindley, for his half, settled for the company of this intelligent transportee, and although he clearly wanted more, he respected Elizabeth's restraint.

'I'm from Yarmouth in Norfo'k,' Brinley had told Elizabeth. 'Me pa was a fisherman... herrin's, yer see... an' he wanted me to do the same.'

'So' why didn't you?'

'I wanna see the world, not the Channel. Besides, me pa was killed at sea.'

'Fishing?'

'Nay. Me pa was press-ganged in Yarmouth in '08 when the Navy fleet sailed to Copenhagen to fight Bony. He ended up bein' killed—fell from the mainsail in bad weather—fell overboard.'

'Oh, I am sorry.'

Bindley fidgeted anxiously. 'This year, I turned fifteen and joined the *Magdalena* crew, voluntary, like. I'm the third oldest out of seven—five boys, two girls. I jus' wanna make me ma proud. I'm savin' all me earnin's fa her.'

Chapter Fourteen

Pacific Ocean. Friendly Islands.

The sun peeled away from the horizon, a grand golden orb casting its wealth of treasured sunlight over the lush tropical jungles of the Pacific islands. The *Suffolk*, anchored one mile off shore, with the French whaler *L'Archimède* close by, made a most attractive sight to Chief Ulukalala, but he was furious that he had let his guard down, furious that his visitors had slipped through the net. He had hosted them with admirable friendship but somehow, he was certain, they had seen through his plan, and now the connivers rendezvoused in the bay... *King George and Napoleon must pay.*

'It must have been that Hawaiian traitor, Kaliko,' Finau Ulukalala reasoned with his war chiefs; he swore to kill the Hawaiian himself.

Captain Moss and Capitaine Jean-Francois Langlois from Normandy sat in Moss's stern cabin, sharing a breakfast of eggs from the ship's cooks and slices of jambon de Bayonne that the French captain had brought to the table. The capitaine's English was reasonable, but Moss's French very basic.

'Forty-five of the whale I catch last sea-son,' the Frenchman boasted to Moss. 'From Twofold Bay to the shores of New Zealand.'

'Then I commend you, sir, you appear to be making more of the industry than many of my acquaintances out of Nantucket.'

'*Oui*. Yes. I 'ave been fort-unate. Many a lamp I aluminate in the *rues de Paris*.'

'When do you ascertain, sir, that you will be returning to Le Havre?' Moss asked, standing to stretch his legs and open the stern windows to allow a better view of the beach. So *far so good*, he thought. There seemed to be little activity ashore and, although he was tempted to weigh anchor, he did not believe the islanders would be so adventurous as to attack. Besides, his larder was only half full.

'My plan ees to be 'ome in *cinq mois*... ah... five months— *oui*,' the Frenchman said, as a stiff breeze crossed the bay, flushing stale air from the cabin.

'I have a favour to ask of you, Captain Langlois.'

'Fa voir?'

'A courtesy, yes... ah... I would like you to do something for me if you can.'

'Then I am your guest, Captain, please ask.' The Frenchman listened with some interest to Rowan describe his dire circumstances.

'And the *Suffolk* is sailing into Port Jackson, where the British Navy will be waiting to board and search her,' Moss said. 'The *L'Archimède*, you said, is destined for Batavia, to trade oil for spices before returning to France, is it not?'

'*Oui*. A surgeon, you say?'

'Aye, sir, and a caring one at that. You can be assured your men will endure good treatment between here and Batavia. Craige would remain aboard your ship, sir, until you reached Batavia, where he would disembark and go his own way. I believe he has ambitions to join traders in the Orient.'

Langlois leant forward in his chair with a scheming smile. He twisted the ends of his generous moustache between forefinger and thumb. 'You ask me to, ah... how you said... stick it in the Anglais.'

'In a sense, yes.'

'*Très bien*, I will do thees thing.'

Someone gave a quick knock at the cabin door and, not waiting to be answered, swung the door open in a panic. 'Captain,' Second Mate Tom Rayden blurted without apology, 'Mr. Pickering said to come quick, sar.'

'What?'

'The natives have launched their canoes. They look awful warlike, sar.'

It was then that the two captains heard the approaching drums—single, rhythmic beats synchronizing the oarsmen—over the sound of the distant surf.

'Devils blood!' Captain Moss and Capitaine Langlois watched horrified as canoe after canoe pushed into the surf a mile off. 'They mean business, do they not?'

'It don't look too friendly, sar,' the helmsman muttered nervously.

'"*Friendly Islands*" Cook named 'em.'

'"Friendly," my arse,' Pickering spat. 'I fancied that Finau Ulukalala was up to somethin'.'

'Mr. Bortwick,' Moss said to the boatswain standing at his side.

'Captain.'

'Weigh anchor and set all sails, if you please. Mr. Pickering.'

'Captain.'

'See *Capitaine* Langlois safely to his ship. Smartly, now.' Moss turned to the Frenchman. 'Do you have any cannon, *Capitaine?*'

'I 'ave... ah... *deux* cannon,' he said, wide-eyed, transfixed by the attackers. 'Ah... same as your 4-pounder.'

'Then may I suggest that your arm them, sir?'

'Do you really theenk this natives is hostile, Captain Moss?'

'Aye, I do now.'

'I've heard of similar situations in these parts,' the helmsman said. 'These people won't stop until they have looted everything off these ships and removed every iron bolt and nail.'

'I'm afraid it's more than nails and bolts these savages are after, Mr. Harman.'

Rowan watched Langlois drop into his pinnace, where his crew pushed away urgently towards the *L'Archimède,* a hundred yards to port. Rowan twisted back to see the canoes. He guessed at about twenty men to each craft. As he watched, once they had cleared the breakers they spread out in a semicircle. The war drums sounded frighteningly close when their worst fears were realised; warriors at the bow of the canoes were taking position to heave spears.

Captain Moss hurried up the companionway to the quarterdeck. 'Jesus Christ will yer look at 'em? There must be three hundred o' the buggers—more!'

'I've ordered the swivels loaded with shrapnel!' William Pickering yelled from the foredeck, where both gunwale-mounted poop deck guns were loaded with broken glass, pebbles and smelter slag. At the same moment the men on the capstan weighed anchor. Immediately, wind billowed out, unfurling the mainsail, and the jib stiffened with a loud crack. Moss gripped the rail and bawled at the boatswain. 'See that every able-bodied man is armed!'

'Aye, sar.' The armoury chest of small arms was dragged onto the deck. 'You heard the man!' he roared at the nervous crew. 'Arm yourselves!' The boatswain helped himself to a brace of loaded flintlock pistols, securing them behind the belt that held up his britches.

'Fire a warning shot over their heads, Mr. Pickering.'

'Aye, sar.' The mate turned to the seaman levelling the port gun over the canoes. 'You heard the captain. Over their heads. Fire!' The seaman lowered the smouldering linstock to the powdered touchhole. The ignition was instant, the exploding cannon deafening. Shrapnel whizzed over the closest canoes, peppering the water about the craft behind them, but the islanders persisted.

The sounds of urgent French voices and *L'Archimède's* snapping canvas joined the commotion on the *Suffolk* from across the bay. *L'Archimède* had the advantage of deeper water, but, as Rowan watched, six canoes broke away from the flotilla in pursuit of the French ship. Crewmen reloaded the swivel. The gun on the port gunwale was dismounted and secured next to its twin on the starboard side.

Chief Ulukalala was in the leading canoe, his body adorned with war paint complimenting his tatatau tattoos. He was bare-chested and wore armbands of seaweed, as well as a shark tooth necklace and an expression of hostility. The 25-foot outrigger sliced through the swell rolling in off the Pacific. While the chief's outrigger came along on the port side, reefing in the sail, another war rigger approached on the starboard.

Warriors scrambled on board.

William Pickering didn't hesitate.

He swung the swivel to starboard and fired.

Jagged wedges of slag and glass shards whipped along the gunwale, tearing human flesh like parchment. Warriors screamed in agony. Many fell into the bay where, earlier, Rowan had seen tiger sharks, attracted to the ship's waste.

The second canoe rammed alongside.

'Fire!' Pickering screamed. But the seaman froze. Terrified. 'Fire, damn you.' Rowan snatched the linstock. *God forgive me.* Lifting its iron tail, Rowan swivelled the gun, aimed, and sparked the powder.

The gun jerked violently and the shrapnel caused sickening carnage at such close quarters. The two closest outriggers backed away. 'Here!' Pickering threw Rowan a cutlass as warriors from Ulukalala's rigger stormed the quarterdeck. A spear pierced the helmsman's throat and he slumped over the wheel. Captain Moss drew his pistols, cocked both hammers and fired at his attackers. The first ball ripped half the face from one and drilled a hole in the next attacker's chest.

'Bastards!'

Moss drew his sword, hacking into the oncoming fray. A strong current caught the rudder. Without a helmsman, the wheel spun out of control, threatening to shift the *Suffolk* and lose the wind in her sails. The ship would slow and the deck would swarm with attackers.

Captain Moss was quickly outnumbered. Rowan, Pickering and four others charged amidships, leaping decks. With their spears spent, the warriors fell upon the seamen with clubs, gnarly spiked tree roots of hard wood. Kaliko, the Hawaiian, rushed back to the foredeck swivel. He remembered the drill....

Load the gun... He knew how, but had never put his knowledge into practise.... *Powder first. Ram home the shrapnel.*

Chief Ulukalala saw his adversary. He was an old man, but agile. Screaming a war cry, the chief climbed aboard. This fellow islander, this Hawaiian devil traitor, must die.

The chief leapt along the deck towards Kaliko with agility, wielding a spiked club as long as his arm. Kaliko scooped up the smouldering linstock. He aimed the swivel...

Rowan took *Suffolk's* wheel in both hands. It spun loose on the spindle, but then he felt the tiller ropes tighten. The wheel stiffened and the sails filled. The nearest warrior lunged with his club. Rowan ducked and the vicious weapon pounded the wheel. The native realigned his weapon. He swung for Rowan's head. Instantly the assailant's head exploded in a mist of brain and blood. Pickering had fired just in time. 'Keep 'er steady, Mr. Craige!' the mate shouted. He drew his sword and swung back into the fray.

On the foredeck, Kaliko swung the swivel directly at Ulukalala. The agile chief ducked to his knees and swung his club, crushing the Hawaiian's shinbones. Kaliko's screams of pain reached cousin Tua in the rigging. He dropped to the deck as Ulukalala made his escape. The chief mounted the gunwale, starting up the ratline, but Tua had the linstock. He aimed the swivel and fired. The shrapnel shredded flesh from the chief's arms. He lost his grip, and, as his warriors looked on, Ulukalala spiralled from the rigging into the bay.

Three hundred yards away, the French opened fire. They had loaded their 4-pounders with canister shot and the results were devastating. Three outriggers were immobilised while another began to sink.

Immediately war cries turned to mournful calls to retreat. The nearest outrigger sailed past the chief's lifeless body and he was dragged into the canoe. Other outriggers appeared, sailing alongside the *Suffolk* as the warriors made their hasty escape, carrying their injured and dead with them.

Pickering stepped over the dead helmsman and made to stab an escaping native.

'Leave 'em be, Mr. Pickering...'

'Bastards,' he cursed.

'Leave 'em be, I said. They'll not be givin' us grief now. Rowan.'

'Captain.'

'See to our wounded, if'n yer please.'

Hours later, Rowan changed ships at sea. It was an apprehensive and solemn moment for Rowan. He had grown fond of the *Suffolk* crew. He had felt himself a part of a family, but now, not knowing what his future held, a pall of loneliness shrouded him. But he knew it must be. He would certainly be the cause of Captain Moss's arrest and would probably bring about the confiscation of the captain's ship, should he be discovered aboard the *Suffolk* in Sydney Cove.

The thought of swinging at the end of a rope darkened Rowan's thoughts further, but Captain Langlois was a most obliging man and Rowan thanked his good fortune.

'I bid you farewell and good fortune, Rowan.' Captain Moss passed Rowan ninety pounds in Bank of England ten-pound notes and a few gold guineas. 'And here is a receipt for the two hundred and ten pounds remaining. I will notify Lucius Brown when I return to Boston. He will hold your credit. I am sorry, Rowan, but that is all the currency I can spare at this moment.' Rowan appreciated the gesture. Moss was under no obligation to honour the payment for the stallion, unless he ran into Rowan in the Orient.

'Thank you for all you have done, Captain.' Rowan shook Moss's hand. 'Maybe we will meet again one day, under better circumstances.'

Rowan boarded the *L'Archimède*. The cabin boy stowed his swag below as a stiff breeze stirred, but Rowan remained on deck as the two ships continued on their set courses, and he waved his farewells as the *Suffolk* sailed away.

On board the Convict Transport Ship
***Indefatigable*. Indian Ocean.**

1814

Marcus Marriot could take the taunting no longer. The man next to him on their sleeping bench, Samuel Morgan, was forty pounds heavier than Marriot, although he had lost twenty pounds on the voyage so far. *He's still a fat bastard,* Marriot thought, and he would've liked to have told him so. But he was a tough *fat bastard* who had repeatedly attempted to steal Marriot's rations; he abused his position, hogging the bench to such an extent that Marriot felt he would drop to the deck. Marriot struggled to sleep. He could hear the whimpering man on the other side of Morgan pleading, as he was repeatedly raped. But the men were shackled together. There was no escape and no escaping the threats of the prisoner by your side.

Marriot's misery and hatred festered. After some consideration, he cared no longer for life or death. He fashioned an eight-inch splinter of wood from deck timber, honed the point with a shard of glass, and waited. Days and nights passed. Marriot was finally blessed with a gale-force wind—the tempest howled on deck, the *Indefatigable* pitched and rolled in heavy seas, and, while the fat bastard Morgan slept, Marriot cozied up to the man, spooning him from behind. Before Morgan was aware of Marriot's intentions, Marriot had thrust the splinter into Morgan's throat, piercing his trachea and driving it into his spine. Samuel Morgan thrashed, choking in his own blood. He gargled, spluttered a plea, and died horribly. Marriot was amazed at the amount of blood. If any other prisoners heard the commotion over the storm they did not let on. The blood pooled about them as the man who had been abused by Morgan turned to the commotion in the darkness of their confinement. Marriot immediately forced the murder weapon upon the innocent accomplice and screamed for the guard.

Anthony Tallow was hung from the yardarm the following morning. The sickly clerk, who had stolen from his employer and was being transported for seven years, did little to defend himself.

Marcus Marriot watched him hang.

On board the *L'Archimède*. Pacific Ocean.

Rowan knew little of the French language, but with the tutoring of the patient Captain Langlois, Rowan honed his language skills admirably. The month sailing towards the east coast of Australia was uneventful. One could describe the voyage as comfortable yet unprofitable, as they had not sighted one whale. However, *Capitaine* Langlois was confident they would fill their barrels once they reached the Tasman Sea, and then, only then, they would sail for Batavia. Rowan resigned himself to the fact that he would be with the French whaler for six months or more.

Captain Langlois studied Rowan a moment. He had enjoyed the American's company over the past weeks, especially their intellectual debates at the dinner table concerning the volatile politics of their respective countries. He had also taught the American wine etiquette to accompany the appreciation of French red wines, of which he had a well-stocked cellar in his cabin. The food however, was less palatable. As the supply of *jambon* and livestock was depleted *L'Archimède*'s cook was compelled to boil the mariners staple—barrelled salt pork—but Rowan was pleased to acknowledge that at least the cook had added onions, garlic and herbs.

Capitaine Langlois macerated the chewy meat on one side of his mouth and then the other, gave up, and washed the lump down his throat with wine. 'Jules makes a wonderful fritter when we have made a kill,' Langlois said of the ship's cook, Jules Clément.

'Fritters?'

'*Oui.* Fritters made from the brain of the whale, mixed with egg, flour and tarragon and fried in whale oil. *Magnifique*, Row-an.' Rowan thought of the delicacy and had to agree he would try anything at the moment. 'I tell you something else: the whales are a grand source of barnacles. The men pluck them from the whales' backs, Jules drops them into boiling water, and we eat them with vinegar. Delicious, *non*? And the best barnacles come from inside the whales' noses.' Rowan reminisced about a plate of oysters or muscles from the Chesapeake, and the two chewed in silence a moment.

'You asked me earlier where we are.' The Frenchman contemplated the last morsel of meat on his plate and decided to leave it.

'Yes.'

'Well, by my dead reckoning we are 'alfway between Norfolk Island and Cape Reinga, the northernmost tip of New Zealand.'

'Halfway?'

'*Oui*, about a week's sail in either direction, north or south...'

There was no warning.

The two men were jolted by a hollow thud, followed instantly by a juddering throughout the cabin. '*Sacre bleu!*'

Rowan jumped to his feet. 'What was that?' Rowan followed the *capitaine* to the stern window and together they stared out at a black sea on a dark night. A fist thumped the door and First Mate François Reyer threw the door open.

'*Avez-vous entendu cela, Capitaine?*'

'*Oui. Qu'est-ce que c'etait?*'

CRAIG GODFREY

On board the *Magdalena*. Atlantic Ocean.

It started with whispers. Elizabeth lay awake on her shared bunk on the orlop deck in the unbearable heat of the doldrums, that unique windless, breezeless ocean over the equator where prevailing winds abandon sailing ships, becalming them on a vast silvery ocean of unpredictability. From what Elizabeth could ascertain from seeing the full moon in a clear sky entering the open port windows, it was early morning. She lay deadly still, feigning sleep, while beads of sweat pooled about her near-naked body onto the hard planks of her shared cot. She listened to the whispers.

A conspiracy was afoot. Sally Fetter lay with two others on the adjoining bench. The air was stifling, still, and the effluent fumes rising from the bilge were thick with putridity and sickness. Some women were succumbing to scurvy for lack of fresh vegetables—Margaret Sampson, for one, with blackened gums and loose teeth, lying nearby in the darkness in a semi-conscious state, struggling to breath. There was little Elizabeth could do to help the woman. She lay in silence, alone, listening.

Betty Bryant had earlier slipped through the secret opening in the bulkhead. The opening led through the stores to the seamen's quarters, and it was Betty's nocturnal activities, rewarded with luxury items like pickled sauerkraut, that Elizabeth knew had saved them both from the dreaded scurvy.

The words were barely discernible, but Elizabeth recognised the voice of Fawn Lytle, lying with Sally. 'Why wait till Cape Town?'

'Cos that's when Garre says 'ell have the numbers.' Sally Fetter's whisper was so low she could hardly be heard. *Magdalena's* oak bones groaned weakly as the meanest of swells rolled beneath her keel. For three nights now

Elizabeth had caught scraps of the plot and what she'd heard terrified her. Garre Skelton was the ship's third mate. Half Scott, half French, the wild redhead made up for his moderate height with a robust physique and broad shoulders. Skelton was also, unfortunately, burdened with short outbursts of rage, triggered by what would appear to most to be minor discrepancies. He was priggish, intolerant and, all in all, not an easy man to befriend. And tonight Elizabeth was fitting the keystone pieces of the puzzle together.

'Like I told yer,' Sally Fetter whispered, 'Garre's become matey with Samuel French, the armourer, what's got the keys to the ship's armoury. French loves a Geneva, so, sometime soon 'e'll get the mongrel drunk in his cabin, nick the keys long enough to make a mould, return 'em, then visit the locksmith when we're in Cape Town, to get copies made.'

'What's it like in Madagascar?' Eleanor Green's northern accent was strong, and with her mumbling whisper she was difficult to understand. But the word Madagascar struck Elizabeth like a sledgehammer. 'There be bands o' lawless ruffians there, I'm told.'

'Bah,' Fawn Lytle scoffed, 'we can 'andle a few ruffians, eh, Sally?'

'Aye.'

But Eleanor Green was not convinced. 'I'm talkin' pirates.'

'Pirates be buggered. Lawless ruffians, yes.' Sally Fetter's dark cold eyes sparkled at the thought of freedom. 'Garre tells me there are still some villains what live in small communities on the east coast. They leave the Madagascar natives be and the natives leave them be. 'E has acquaintances there what's established. 'E says we will be welcomed like kings and queens when we turn up with this ship and a load o' lovelies.'

'Tell us about them Arabs again.'

'Garre told me those bastards have riches beyond your imagination, Fawn Lytle. They trade in the north around Arabia... Trade in jewels an' gemstones an' gold. We'll live like firkin' queens... all o' us.'

'Wha' about them wha' don't wanna join us?'

'Well, now'—Sally Fetter clearly enjoyed the power she lauded over the other two—'as I told yer, we take the ship a week out from leavin' the cape, then sail north, and them what are unwilling will be put ashore on the African coast. Then it's Madagascar.'

Betty was astounded. Elizabeth had waited until deck muster the following morning to convey the plot to her friend.

'What will we do, yer ask?' Betty answered, biting down hard on her fingernail. 'We do nuthin', girl. That's wha' we do.'

'Do you want to end up a castaway on the coast of Africa?' Elizabeth argued. 'Do you? Why, there's cannibals and man-eating lions, and...'

'Then go to the captain. Do yer really think he'll believe yer?'

On board *L'Archimède*. Tasman Sea.

First Mate François Reyer stood in the stern cabin doorway, his bulky frame filling the entrance, his face grey with worry.

'I don't know what we have struck, *Capitaine*—a whale, maybe. But Raphael and Louis have gone to inspect the hull.' He spoke of the carpenter and carpenter's assistant. Rowan followed *Capitaine* Langlois and the mate amidships and down the companionway to the lower deck towards the bow.

'Christ!'

'It does not look good, *Capitaine.*' The carpenter was ankle-deep in water. As Rowan watched, the Pacific Ocean poured through a damaged plank. 'Can you stop it?' the captain asked, doing his best to filter fear from his voice.

'Yes. Luckily the damage is at the waterline, but I need men on the pumps, sir—and will someone fetch the sailmaker? I need canvas and pitch, fast.'

On the evening watch, Pierre Paquet hailed the captain from the main deck. 'It was a palm tree, *Capitaine*—big bastard, half submerged. It must have hit us head-on, dislodging the planking. What are the chances, eh?'

'What are the chances?' *Capitaine* Langlois shook his head. He looked at Rowan. 'It is unfortunate and incredibly rare to hit such a threatening object in the middle of an ocean.'

All sails were reefed with only the topgallants catching the night's breeze, reducing speed while the carpenter and his mate did what they did best. Enough cargo was shipped to port side to list the ship slightly, lifting the damaged hull above the waterline. Soon the smoke of melting tar permeated every corner of the ship, as did the news of the damage. The carpenter rubbed melted tar generously over squares of canvas and patched the hole, which was about the size of a man's head. Nails were hammered around the four edges, hemming the patch in place, and then short wooden planks were nailed over the patch.

Capitaine Langlois's eyes watered from the tar smoke lingering heavily in the hold. He looked at the repair. François Reyer had done well—the cold ocean water hardened the tar almost immediately. Both men listened a moment to the gentle slapping of waves on the exterior and the constant chug nearby as men manned the pumps. Both men knew that if the ship were hit by a storm the patch would not hold. Langlois held his lantern high to catch the carpenter's eye. 'Is that going to do?'

'Only temporary, *Capitaine*. We need to make repairs at the earliest opportunity.'

'And the earliest opportunity,' Langlois told Rowan in his cabin ten minutes later, 'is, I am afraid to say, New South Wales.' Rowan sank back in his chair and took in a deep breath. '*L'Archimède* needs to be repaired on dry land, Rowan.'

'Are we talking Sydney Cove?'

'*Non, non.* I do not think the Frenchmans would be too popular in Sydney Cove. *Non*, Rowan.' Langlois tapped a pair of dividers on a chart headed 'New Holland'. 'Here. Twofold Bay. Many whalers, they use this bay. We will have to careen the ship as well, and pray the Royal Navy do not visit us while we are vulnerable, yes?'

Rowan sighed.

'Who knows, we may even catch a whale or two.'

Rowan had little to say. He bid the *capitaine 'bonne nuit'* and retired to his cramped cabin with his own dark thoughts.

1814

On board the *Magdalena*. Atlantic Ocean.

Anxious days drifted with the *Magdalena*, her sails set, yet sagging. Elizabeth had assembled on the main deck with the other women in reverent silence as Margaret Sampson's canvas-shrouded body slid overboard into the dead calm of the eternal sea. Scurvy had finally taken her to a better place. There was not a breath of wind as the ship's chaplain, Reverend Knockley, muttered a few words of prayer from his good book before the body splashed into the ocean.

Barely had the order been given for the women to return to their berths when the assembly were startled by snapping canvas. It was like an omen from the afterlife. The stiffened sails billowed out and a soft breeze swept the deck, followed by an instantaneous cheer from crew and prisoners together. They had passed out of the doldrums. But two thousand miles still stood between the transportees and Cape Town. Three weeks' hard sailing. Elizabeth struggled with her conscience. *Should she report the conversation she had heard between Sally Fetter and Garre Skelton to the officers?*

Based on Betty's reckoning, they both agreed it would be wise to wait until the ship moored off the cape. At least there they would be able to monitor the mutineers' progress. Besides if Elizabeth were to go to the officers without proof it could well mean her death sentence at the hands of Sally Fetter.

Twofold Bay. New South Wales.

It took the damaged *L'Archimède* two weeks to reach Twofold Bay. The bay was a millpond—not a ripple broke the surface. The air was still, the atmosphere oppressive and the wildlife sounds coming from this distant and foreign land could be clearly heard across the water.

'Hot, *non?*' *Capitaine* Langlois stood with Rowan at the gunwale, wiping a trickle of sweat from his brow. He stared off into the crystal clear water. 'I would like to cool off in the water.' Almost immediately a school of salmon swam toward them in a disturbed circle. A predator was nearby.

'I would not think it wise to swim in these waters, my friend,' Rowan told the French captain. A tall dorsal fin cut the surface, diving under the ship and chasing the salmon.

'*Sacre bleu!* That ees a big fish!'

Immediately their attention was drawn to the fishing boat *Flying Fish*, the only other craft in the bay this day. Rowan had had the good fortune to encounter the one-masted sloop in the bay and had negotiated a three-day sail to Sydney Town for three pounds. One of the sloop's crew grapple-hooked *L'Archimède's* starboard and the two vessels rode at anchor together.

'Your swag's aboard the sloop,' the cabin boy told Rowan in French.

'*Merci*, Jacques.' Rowan flipped the lad a florin.

'*Au revoir*, my friend.' *Capitaine* Jean-François Langlois threw an arm about Rowan's shoulders. 'I do wish you would reconsider your decision, wait for repairs to be completed and journey on to Batavia with us.'

'Thank you, Jean, but, as you may have noticed, my friend, I am not cut out for the whaling industry, and, besides, it might be a year before you fill your hold with oil and sail to Batavia.'

'This is true.'

'I wish to act sooner than later with my letters of recommendation from Boston. The letters of introduction should see me well positioned in the Orient, and I believe many ships leave for northern waters from Sydney Cove.'

'Then *bonne chance*, Rowan Craige, and take care.'

CHAPTER FIFTEEN

1815. Sydney Town.

Population—more than 12,000 (of those, approximately 4,400 convicts). Twenty-seven years since Settlement.

The one-masted sloop *Flying Fish* cleared the headlands —the North and South Heads—at the gateway to Port Jackson, and sailed into the calm blue of Sydney Cove. To starboard, the rolling swell of the Pacific Ocean terminated against the vertical cliffs in their explosive finale. In the distance, smoke from Sydney Town's fires of industry hung over the landscape, and as they approached Rowan felt an acute awareness.

Thankfully, the fishing boat attracted little attention. They docked alongside the fish market, amongst half a dozen similar craft, and were absorbed into the hustle and bustle of a busy marketplace. Rowan hefted his swag over his shoulder, pulled his collar high and angled his tarred boater well over his forehead. With the hot New South Wales sun directly overhead, this action would not look untoward and he stepped ashore at Sydney Town, resigning himself to his fate... or good fortune.

He would have to be vigilant.

The sight of the first British soldiers in their red coats with their white britches and tall black shakos brought instant memories of home, none of them pleasant.

Rowan walked the foreshore in search of an area named The Rocks, on the rocky outcrop west, where the *Flying Fish* skipper had recommended cheap lodgings overlooking the water. At first glance, Sydney Town appeared to be the quintessential colonial settlement, where the most important buildings dominated the landscape. Rowan passed the hospital wharf stretching out across the cove. Nearby stood the General Hospital, along with the merchant warehouses, dominated by that of Robert Campbell and Wharf House. Between the hospital and the water's edge were busy shipbuilding yards. To his left, Rowan observed a prison hulk moored offshore, near a ship-careening beach. Close by was the Italianate Government House, with its handsome gravel carriage loop and the lush vegetable gardens between it and the waterfront. Here, on the governor's lawn, Rowan saw his first native kangaroo grazing contentedly, apparently a tamed pet. In front of Government House and extending across the water was the Government House wharf, leading to the official Dry Stores, The Naval Investment Stores. More warehouses led down to a rivulet named Tank Stream, named so after four large sandstone tanks, which were cut into the creek bed to filter the town's water. Here tall pine trees lined the stream's banks. A stone bridge crossed the creek on Bridge Street. Sydney Town was only in its twenty-seventh–year, but Rowan noted that poverty amongst the stinking tanneries and slaughter yards already lined the rivulet's banks.

Rowan walked along a wide, dusty road sign-posted 'Sergeant Major's Row,' which ran parallel with the south shore of Sydney Cove. Here a chain gang of fifty or more shackled felons laboured on the road works with sledgehammers and picks. It was gruelling work, overseen by guards with fixed bayonet muskets and whips. Rowan diverted his path. Further on were government offices within a neat, straight row of cottages built parallel with Bridge Street. This connected with Market Place. The town pillory stood at the market square and already a cussing woman was anchored by hands and feet in the stocks, surrounded by discarded rotting vegetables that had been used as projectiles. Across the road from where Rowan stood was the Orphan's School. *Were the stocks a lesson for the orphans, maybe?* Looking over his shoulder, Rowan observed the Bonded Stores, including those for salt provisions and liquor. The jail was uncomfortably close. From this position Rowan watched the fluttering flags of the well-armed fort at Dawes Point guarding the cove before making himself inconspicuous on the stone steps behind the General Hospital and ascending to the higher ground of an area known as The Rocks.

The view from The Rocks was spectacular. Here, the emancipated convicts themselves had been settling the steep craggy outcrops since the 1790s. Hundreds of one- or two-roomed thatched huts—hipped roofs with a centre timber post and wattle-and-daub walls—perched in random rows along the rocky ridgelines. At the southern end of The Rocks a windmill gave the main *street* its name -- Windmill Row. But Rowan was informed that the governor, Major General Lachlan Macquarie, was in the process of replacing the unofficial titles of these disorderly streets with viceregal names. Windmill Row was to become Prince Street, for example. But the residents insisted on using the one address... The Rocks.

Up here Rowan had a fine perch from which to study the settlement. He noted that Sydney Town spread well off into the surrounding hills, where clusters of residences and industries appeared to thrive.

On The Rocks each shanty sported its own small garden amidst the trunks of tall gum trees, some thriving, some dying. The area was only accessible to those on foot, which gave Rowan some comfort, seeing as there were so many redcoats about the harbour itself. For the most part, the inhabitants of The Rocks were maritime workers, emancipists, navvies who now tendered the jolly boats, warehousemen, shipwrights, wharf watchmen, seamen or waterside workers. Others worked the quarries or public buildings. But along with the bonds of the small and like-minded community at The Rocks came also the thieves and cutthroats. With twenty or more drinking houses, mostly small dwellings, came drunkenness, prostitution, gambling and rats—four- and two-legged.

All was not sinful, however. Rowan was aware of a positive side to the inns. They met the social need for locales where drinking, dancing and conversation could take place, meetings could be held, travellers could catch up on the news, and locals could court.

The day was sweltering hot, the air still. Rowan rested on his kit for a moment. Looking across the cove at the hills to the south, Rowan saw several windmills for grinding grain, their sails turning lazily in the breeze off the Pacific Ocean. He counted nine ships in the harbour, including one Royal Navy frigate. The harbour was also busy with light craft, wherries and ferries and single-sailed clinkers. Rowan even saw his first Australian natives, naked as the day they were born. The small group camped on a rise near where he rested, their shelter being mere sheets of bark leaning against the trees. The aborigines fossicked through discarded rubbish, collecting shards of blue and white crockery or black glass, which they fashioned, by knapping, into spearheads and other flint-like tools. Rowan wondered about their relationship with the whitefella.

Out at sea, faint lightning on the horizon caught Rowan's attention. As he watched, the windmill sails picked up momentum and the skies darkened. A tropical storm approached. Pleased to be ashore and free of the approaching weather, Rowan was directed to The Three Jolly Settlers, where he headed for shelter.

The taproom was busy. It seemed everyone had the same idea. Although the doors and shutters of the horizontal timber, shingle-roofed inn were all propped open, the atmosphere was dank with burning tobacco, stale grog and stinking bodies. The room was packed with well-oiled seafarers, ticket-of-leave convicts and filles de joie conversing in half a dozen languages with a dozen accents. It was not an inn for the genteel, but for Rowan it was a place of refuge until he could find a berth on a ship.

'You look all lonesome,' the voice over his shoulder purred. Rowan had had no conversation with a woman since the Friendly Islands and the tone was a pleasant change from the coarse badinage of seafarers. 'Why so serious?' the woman asked. She looked to be near forty. Her face was red from toil and exposure and Rowan could see that she had once been a most attractive woman, now blossoming in maturity. She wore a clean but stained apron over an ankle-length skirt with a cream cotton blouse loosely laced at her bosom, which was generously proportioned, and which she was not so prudish as to conceal—not completely, anyhow. Upon her head she wore a maid's mop hat cap, and she carried a dozen or more empty pewter tankards with ease.

'Seriously?' Rowan asked over the din of the rabble.

'Aye, sar. Yer look worried.'

'Oh, do I?' Rowan answered vaguely. At first he thought he was being spoken to by a scarlet woman of Sydney Cove. Suddenly he felt clumsy. 'I just have a lot on my mind.'

'What can I fetch ya?'

'Oh... a quart of that porter, I should imagine.' Rowan nodded toward the swaying man next to him, who held a large dark brew and leaned heavily against the bar ,which appeared to be built from ship decking.

'Fine, sar, I'll just drop these to the scullery.' The barkeep disappeared with the tankards, returning shortly after with a tall porter, its caramel head frothing down the sides. 'There, sar.' Rowan passed the woman a florin and was given a shilling in change. 'Sarah Fox, sar,' she said. 'Innkeeper.'

'Innkeeper!' Rowan smiled, surprised.

'Aye. Near five year now—got me licence back in '10.'

'Then I must congratulate you on your success, madam.'

'Call me "Sarah"... if'n it pleases ya.' The sound of low, rumbling thunder approached. 'We're in fa a good dousin'.' The innkeeper scanned an eye about the room—all was well. 'An' what name do you go by, sar, if'n ya don't mind me askin', like.'

'Oh... ah, Samuel,' Rowan lied.

'Samuel, aye, yer look like a Samuel.'

The inn darkened considerably from the approaching storm and other wenches busied themselves striking up lanterns.

'Tell me, Sarah, do you have rooms here at the inn?'

'Aye, I have two, but they's paid for this night.' The woman thought a moment. 'I tell ya what, ya can share a bed with Billy—'e won't mind, sar. Nice lad. He's a bit simple, like, but I know 'e won't mind sharin', as long as *you* don't, sar. An' It'll only cost ya half a crown.'

Rowan saw two redcoats push into the crowd. They made their way to the bar. He had few options, and sharing a cheap room would be good cover. 'Billy, you say?'

'Aye. 'E's offa that sealer in the cove, the *Sea Rat*. Billy's the cook.'

'Oh—you said he was a little simple?'

'Aye, sar, simple and harmless with a 'eart o' gold.'

'And he won't mind, you say?'

''E won't mind, sar, but you might, if'n 'e farts and snores.' Sarah's laugh was infectious.

The rain pummelled the inn's shingles in a tropical downpour. The thunder rolled low overhead and the colony was treated to Mother Natures wrath in a show of lightning and gale-force winds. Soon the packed earth floor of The Three Jolly Settlers was a quagmire of mud. It was all over in ten minutes. The storm passed and the sun returned, creating puddles of steam. The taproom emptied slightly as patrons took advantage of the ensuing sea breeze. Sarah Fox made the most of the situation to collect up more deserted tankards and glassware before returning to her gentleman guest. 'Would yer be wantin' to eat, sar?'

Rowan had eaten a hearty breakfast before disembarking. For now all he wanted was to quench his thirst. 'Oh... ah... no, thank you.'

'Pity, sar, cos cook's got fresh trevallys.'

'You talk of a fish, I take it?'

'Aye. Twenty of 'em she purchased from Mary, the fishmonger. Caught in the cove, they was. She has three left, sar. Cooks 'em whole with flour and salt and serves 'em with boiled tatties.'

'Thank you, but I have eaten...'

The sound of a panicked man choking hushed the taproom. Rowan wheeled about to see a large man, mouth wide open and eyes bulging, with his hands clutching at his throat. Instantly Rowan thought the man had had his throat cut. The man dropped to his knees and a pewter plate of fish and potatoes scattered across the floor about him. His mates stood by helplessly. Rowan rushed to the mayhem. 'What's happened?'

'Dunno, squire,' one said. ''E be eaten' fish, then...'

'Is 'e poisoned?' the other asked, taking anxious glances at his mate's plate of fish. The choking man knelt on the ground, unable to speak, his eyes terrified.

'Have you swallowed a fish bone?' Rowan pressed. The man nodded. 'Stand back,' Rowan ordered the onlookers. Rowan took the man from behind, locked his arms beneath his rib cage and jerked him roughly. Twice. Three times. Nothing. The man's face went from red to purple—his airway was blocked. He panicked. 'Get me a knife,' Rowan called out. The closest man slipped a dagger from the sheath on his belt. 'No! A dining knife! Sarah!'

'Aye.'

'Do you have tweezers?'

'Yes. Yes... I'll find something,' she said, running off.

'Help me get this man on his back,' Rowan said urgently, calmly. His mates lowered their friend to the dirt floor. Someone thrust a dining knife into Rowan's hand. He used the flat of the blade to press the man's tongue. An onlooker blocked his light. 'Move it! Out of the light, man!' The fellow stepped aside. Rowan peered down the victim's throat. Nothing. Rowan lifted the tongue against the roof of the man's mouth. 'There!' he said more to himself than to anyone else. The patient was terrified. Gagging. Wheezing. Choking. Rowan kept the flat side of the knife blade against the tongue to keep it retracted.

'Here.' Sarah pressed a long pair of tweezers into Rowan's open palm. Rowan fished for the wider end of the bone. The hysterical man started shaking his head. 'Hold him steady someone, for Christ's sake.' A mate locked an arm about the man's head. The bone was an inch and a half long, with the sharper end piercing the palatine tonsil. When Rowan was satisfied he had the bone in his grip he slid the needle end from the flesh, then pulled it free. He held the tweezers high for all to see.

The patient coughed, gasped and sat up with the help of his friends. Tears ran down his cheeks. Rowan stood and wiped his brow. He was saturated with sweat. Suddenly the taproom was too oppressive, and he took his porter outside. Sarah joined him.

'Yer a sawbones, ain't yer?'

Rowan did not have to answer. 'You was so calm, sar, calm under pressure an'... an' yer knew what to do. You can stay 'ere tonight on me, sar. Forget the 'alf crown. I'd like to find ya somewhere more befittin' of a gentleman sawbones, but, truth is, with all them ships in the cove there ain't no lodgin's anywheres close.'

Rowan retired early and prayed he had not drawn too much attention to himself. There were, after all, soldiers in the taproom. He dragged the double cot bed across the room to the attic window, where a slight breeze through the shutters kept the mosquitos at bay. After stowing his kit beneath the bed, Rowan stripped down to his long-tailed shirt tied back and front beneath him. The room was a steam bath but, exhausted, Rowan lay on top of the straw mattress and drifted into a dark and heavy slumber.

Sometime later—Rowan hadn't a clue how long—the door slammed open against the wall and the light of an exceptionally bright oil lamp filled the room. Rowan woke, disorientated, and stared at the shadow of a portly man was cast against the wall like some sinister stage illusion. Billy, his roommate, had arrived.

'Sawbones Samuel, Sawbones Samuel,' the simpleton sang in a high-pitched voice, followed by an imitation of a cat meowing. Rowan recognised the characteristics that were familiar to the surgeon: upward slanting and hooded eyes, flattening of the back of the head and uncontrolled dialogue. Rowan had heard these characteristics referred to in Philadelphian medical circles as Mongolian. His jolly shaped body bespoke a man who enjoyed eating, even to excess, a common trait of Mongoloids. Billy slammed the door shut. 'Sawbones Samuel, aye. I'm Billy... Billy Cake. Sarah tol' me ya'd be here...'

'Then, I shall thank you to douse the lamp, Billy,' Rowan said 'and kindly go to sleep.' At first Rowan thought the man had been drinking, but in fact he was sober. 'Want to see a magic trick, Sawbones Samuel?'

Rowan straightened and propped himself on one elbow. He sighed. If he wanted peace and quiet, he thought, he had better humour the man. 'Make it quick, then.'

Billy's large mouth curved into a huge smile. He placed the lamp on the washstand and produced a copper penny, holding it up in front of him in his right hand between forefinger and thumb.

'I make this disappear,' Billy said proudly. He placed the penny in the left palm and closed his fist. 'Abracadabra,' he said in a theatrical flourish and opened his left fist. No coin. 'Gone. Magic, see!' Billy concentrated intently on making the coin reappear. His tongue protruded from the corner of his mouth and his eyes were wide with infant excitement. He floated his right hand back over the *empty* hand, twinkling fingers like a magician might do, and finally opened them to show the coin had reappeared. He looked at Rowan like a pet dog expecting a treat.

'That is very clever,' Rowan humoured the man. 'Now, please, will you douse the lamp and come to sleep?'

But Billy was not easily swayed this night. 'I seen you downstairs today,' Billy said. 'You saved Thomas Redfern's life. You done good, Sawbones.'

'It was nothing. It is my situation.'

'Billy Cake is cook on *Sea Rat* with Captain Leblanc,' Billy persisted. 'We's sealers in Bass Strait. Live on island. Island called Bull Seal. Captain Leblanc, he look for sawbones for island. Keep 'em all good, captain say. Sometimes fix 'em wounded, like when Harry got leg crushed by bull seal, he died of leg rot.'

Rowan's interest peaked. 'What do you mean, Billy?'

Billy sighed as if he hadn't made himself clear. 'Captain Leblanc, he want sawbones to come live on island. Make people better.'

'How many people live on this island?'

'Thirty six, if'n ya count the little bastards.'

'You mean children?'

'Aye. Little bastards... That's what Captain Leblanc calls 'em.' Billy suddenly remembered he was wearing new boots, of which he was proud. 'Billy's got new boots.' He stood to attention and looked over his belly and down at his feet. Rowan leant across the bed. The boots didn't look too new, but he guessed that for the simpleton they were. 'Nice, Billy. Tell me, when could I meet this Captain Leblanc?'

Billy's face lit up. 'When the sparrow farts, Sawbones Samuel. Billy take ya to him then. He'll be mighty pleased ta make ya acquaintance.'

'Then douse that lamp, Billy, and let us catch some sleep.' Rowan turned his back and curled into a foetal position. He listened to Billy disrobe, then the light was extinguished and the bed creaked in its frame as the rather fat ship's cook sank onto the straw mattress. Billy immediately cuddled up to Rowan, who realized that the man was naked. Rowan shifted. 'Ah Billy, kindly put your britches back on and leave some space between us, man—it is hot enough this night without sharing body heat.'

'Sorry, Sawbones Samuel. Billy like company. Billy make animal noises, Samuel Sawbones.' And he proceeded to crow like a rooster. Rowan closed his eyes and prayed for peace.

'Goodnight, Billy.'

......

Captain Amos Leblanc was in his mid-fifties, but his tanned and weathered seafarer's face made him look older. He was well presented in his frock coat, worn over a leather waistcoat along with a chequered scarf. He had a serious but wise face with tired eyes. His hair was neat, white as breaking surf and combed close to his scalp with perfumed bear's grease. Rowan guessed it was to comb over the encroaching baldness. He wore a full beard, ashen grey, extending from his luxuriant side burns, but it was the earrings that caught Rowan's attention most -- gold guineas. One George the Third guinea hung from each ear, as a not so subtle show of wealth. He was a big and solid man with a demeanour that commanded discipline in others. In contrast to the earrings was a beaded rosary, carved from black lava, wrapped about Leblanc's wrist. Billy had told Rowan that the captain had a passion for books and reading, with a leaning towards the scriptures, and had Rowan looked carefully, he would have recognised that the book on the table in front of the sea captain was a Bible.

Billy ushered Rowan by the arm onto a flagstone balcony that ran the full length of The Three Jolly Settlers. Leblanc sat at a table in the shade, overlooking Sydney Cove.

Billy balanced on one foot and then the other, making his enthusiastic introduction: 'Sawbones Samuel, Cap'n.'

'Samuel,'—Leblanc nodded to a spare chair at the table—'sit.' Billy stood by, admiring his new boots. 'Hey, Billy.'

Billy snapped to attention. 'Yes, sar, Cap'n.'

'Go tell Sarah to set two breakfasts.'

'Aye.'

'He's a good lad, is our Billy Cake,' Leblanc said as Billy sauntered off in the direction of the kitchen.

'Is that his real name? Cake, I mean?'

'No. As I am certain yer have figured fa yourself, Billy is kinda particular.'

'You mean a Mongol?'

'Aye. The Lord works in mysterious ways. He's a simpleton what so 'appens to be a good cook. 'E got the name Cake from his love of the sweet treat. Being a simpleton, he doesn't know when to stop eatin'. We gotta watch 'im; otherwise 'e'd be the size o' a whale.'

'It is a trait,' Rowan agreed. 'Overeating... with Mongoloids, that is.'

'Aye. So... yer American, huh?'

'Is it that obvious?'

'Yer accent is.'

'Well, yes, I'm from Maryland.' Rowan was keen to steer the conversation away from his own past. 'So, you are familiar with this inn, with the cove?'

'Aye. I always lodge at The Rocks when I come to Sydney Town. I take lodgin's next door to this inn. And I can keep a sharp eye on the *Sea Rat* from here.' The captain gestured toward the sweeping view of the harbour.

'The *Sea Rat*,' Rowan acknowledged. 'Rather an unusual name for a ship, sir.'

'Aye. But we are sealers, and the Sydney Town Gazette—prudes that they are—wrote of us once in their rag as sea rats, so I thought, "There's an idea..."'

'Billy says you are in the need of a surgeon.'

'Aye. Straight to the point,' Leblanc said. 'I like thart. He is correct. I be needin' a surgeon, at sea and on land.'

'And by land you mean Bull Seal Island?'

The captain's eyes narrowed and he studied Rowan carefully. 'What did Billy tell yer about Bull Seal Island?'

'Nothing,' Rowan answered warily. 'Nothing at all, in fact.'

Leblanc leant across the table and lowered his voice. 'I'm a very private man, Samuel, very private indeed. I have built Bull Seal into a community over the past decade. No one rightly knows about it 'ere in Sydney Town. But now that they's settled a colony down in 'Obart Town, in Van Diemen's Land, since '04, it'll only be a matter o' time. So here's the deal. My little family needs a surgeon and I'd be correct in sayin' you could use the gold, so I'll cut ya in on a percentage of the skins. It's lucrative, but it won't last for ever.'

'I don't know, Captain. I...'

Captain Leblanc sat back and played his trump card. 'From whom do ya hide anyways, Rowan Craige, Esquire?'

'R-Rowan... Rowan Craige? Of whom do you speak, sir? My name is Samuel...'

'Don't waste me time with ya fabrication, Rowan. Billy rifled yer kit when ya was asleep, man. 'E read yer papers.'

Rowan stood up, pushing his chair back angrily. 'He what?'

'Keep yer shirt on. Billy was jus' doin' wha' I ordered 'im to do... Sit yerself back down and talk man ta man. I don't give a rat's arse what ya gone an' done, but as yer runnin' from the redcoats, I reckon it's political. Is that correct?'

'In a fashion.'

'In a fashion, huh?'

It was time for Rowan to ask questions. 'Leblanc is a French name, is it not? But your accent is almost Gaelic.'

'Aye. Scottish Gaelic—me pa was from Antwerp and me ma from Aberdeen in Scotland, where I grew up.' Leblanc caught Rowan reading the spine of the book before him, a rather thick leather-bound book with a brass clip to keep the Holy Bible's pages in order.

'Are yer a religious man, Rowan?' Leblanc asked, remembering his rosary, which he fingered reverently.

'God deserted me long ago.'

'Then maybe he delivered yer to me, to rekindle yer faith.'

After a breakfast of blood pudding, damper and hot sweet tea, the two men spent the best part of the morning in parley, exchanging histories. Rowan, for his part, liked the captain. He was straightforward and told Rowan about Bull Seal Island—everything, that is, except its exact location. The name, he himself had bestowed upon the island, which had not been chartered by explorers Bass and Flinders when they'd mapped the strait sixteen years earlier. But the man was no fool. The future of sealing in the strait was coming to an end. Why, there were whispers out of Government House here in Sydney Cove saying that Governor Lachlan Macquarie was concerned that the seals in the area would be depleted and that the kill would have to be outlawed.

'Then we will hunt whale,' Leblanc told Rowan matter-of-factly when Rowan asked what he would do if that were to be the case.

Sarah Fox brought a stone pitcher of sweetened ginger beer to their table and Rowan noticed the captain and the innkeeper's hand connect in familiarity; discrete smiles were exchanged, and it occurred to Rowan that the captain might have shared her lodgings last night.

'When I was seventeen,' Leblanc said, 'I joined crew on a lumber ship takin' oak down the coast from the Isle o' Mull to Liverpool. Then I worked fishin' boats on Saint George's Channel out o' Fishguard, before endin' up at Falmouth in Cornwall. I were there in Falmouth nigh on fifteen years before signin' on as second mate on a mail packet, what took mail round the Empire. After my second trip, when I was nearly drowned, I chose to stay in Bombay. Then, in 1804, famine struck Bombay. It was awful—children dyin' in the streets. I managed a passage south to Goa on an East Indiaman. I should mention 'ere, lad, that I had good fortune in India. I had savings in gemstones, rubies an' the like, so in Goa I invested in tea and rum and sailed fa Sydney Cove, arrivin' at the end o' '04. I sold me rum and tea fa four times wha' I paid for it and bought a half share in the barquentine *Saviour,* which we now know as *Sea Rat.*

'So you have a business partner?'

'Did 'ave.' The captain shooed flies from the rim of his ginger beer. 'Frank Stevenson, a merchant. But 'e were killed in '09 out on the 'arbour here, drowned, and I bought his widow out o' the business.'

'Were you ever married?'

'Aye, to a Cornish lass in Falmouth. She died in childbirth.'

'I'm sorry to hear that. Did your child survive?'

'Nay.' The memory was clearly still painful and Leblanc cast an eye over Sydney Cove. ''Twas God's will. The child was missin' a wing.'

'But surely you do not think it God's will to take your wife.'

Leblanc looked at Rowan stubbornly. 'She bled to death.'

Rowan was about to criticise the man's religious ignorance, but chose to refrain. There was activity on board the Royal Navy frigate anchored in the harbour and the captain's eyes narrowed while he studied the ship carefully. 'And you, Rowan,' Leblanc finally asked, 'do you have any children?'

Rowan's own memories were raw and painful. He was silent a moment and the captain sensed the pain. 'My wife died at the hands of a British soldier,' Rowan finally managed.

'Lord, no! How terrible! May I enquire how?'

Rowan looked up from the Bible and into the eyes of this stranger, a stranger in whom he felt he could confide. From past experience, Rowan considered religiously minded people shallow, but this seafarer was different. In personality he was not unlike Rowan's old friend Joshua Barney back in Maryland. Rowan felt he could trust Leblanc, who so openly despised the British *tyranny* in the colonies. 'You've seen the convicted felons, the men chained together and used like carthorses,' Leblanc had said earlier of the transportees. Rowan took a moment to compose his thoughts and then told Leblanc of his own recent past and finally of his wife's death.

The captain read the pain in Rowan's heart and asked out of nowhere, 'You killed him, did yer not?'

'Excuse me! Captain?'

Captain Leblanc shuffled his chair closer to Rowan. He spoke softly, with conviction. 'The man who murdered yer wife. Thart soldier. Yer killed him, eye for an eye. That's why the Royal Navy hunt yer. Am I not correct, Rowan Craige?'

Rowan lifted his head and looked directly at Leblanc, who watched a single tear escape Rowan's eye and trickle down his cheek and knew he had struck the truth.

'Yes, I killed him. He bayonetted my wife in the belly and she was with child.'

'Dear Lord, no!'

'I shot the man in front of his regiment,' Rowan confessed. 'And there are thirty or more witnesses.'

'Is there anything else I should know about yer?' Leblanc asked. 'Like that scar on yer neck?' Leblanc nodded to Rowan's old wound. 'Is that from a fight? It looks like a knife cut.'

'It is.' Rowan told Leblanc the story of the disgruntled amputee whose leg he'd removed.

'Ungrateful bugger, huh?'

'Something like that.'

Innkeeper Sarah Fox appeared from the taproom, wiping wet hands down the sides of her apron. She stood back a moment when she sensed her gentlemen guests were deep in parley. She cleared her throat.

'Aye... Sarah.' The captain leant back in his chair, greeting the woman warmly.

'I don't know if'n this is any o' my business, Cap'n Leblanc, but there's been an officer in the taproom askin' 'bout Samuel 'ere.'

'Oh! When?'

Rowan reddened.

'Half the hour earlier.'

'And what exactly did this officer want to know?'

''E heard there was a Yankee in the taproom last night what saved Thomas Redfern's life. A doctor, says 'e.'

'And what did yer tell 'im?'

'I says I know nuthin' about 'im, but I says the Yankee was makin' enquiries last night about hirin' a ferryman to get him to Parramatta.'

'Parramatta. Good lass.'

'Aye. I thought that'd throw 'im off the scent, like. Anythin' else I can be gettin' yer, Cap'n Leblanc?'

'No, thankin' yer kindly.' The two men watched Sarah walk back into the taproom. 'She's a good woman, thart Sarah,' Leblanc told Rowan. 'Hates the constabulary—who don't?'

If Rowan had been a little more alert, he might have noticed the innkeeper and the captain exchanging knowing glances.

'Then you have no choice, Sawbones,' Leblanc said. 'The *Sea Rat* sails with the tide tomorrow morning. We will have to disguise yer as crew, rough yer up somewhat, cos the Row

Guard are watchin'. They be watchin' for absconders and smugglers from daylight to nine of the clock at night. So we'll slip yer on board before sunup and keep yer belowdecks, for as sure as there's hell fire, the bastards'll follow us until we clear the heads.'

On board the *Magdalena*. Atlantic Ocean

Betty Bryant finally caught the pox. And she was spreading it. Confiding in Elizabeth, she had no qualms about allowing Elizabeth to examine her body; modesty, after all, was not an issue. Elizabeth was none the wiser but confirmed that small-ulcerated pimples—of a brownish colour with a callous hardness surrounding them—appeared on Betty's vulva.

About the same time, the ship's surgeon, Phineas Beckwith, recognised Second Mate Jack Phillips' signs immediately. Besides agonising burning pains when relieving himself, the mate had sensitive tell-tale ulcers on his genitals. Using steel tongs, surgeon Beckwith released the sickly member drooping from the man's britches.

'I've seen enough,' the surgeon commented, reeling back from the sickly odour. The second mate buttoned up his trousers. 'You know what you've got, I take it?' Beckwith asked.

'Is it the pox?'

'Aye.'

Jack Phillips felt even more poorly than he looked. 'Jayzus, what will I do?'

'The only treatment is with iodine therapy: potassium iodide with small doses of mercury.'

'Will that rid me of the... the damned pox?'

'That and the hand of God.' The surgeon knew the dangers of mercury, especially ingested, but there were no options, and the treatment needed to be continued until the patient was cured or died.

Within days, another five sailors ventured to the surgeon's cabin aft. All, it transpired, had had liaisons with Betty Bryant.

Captain Cholmondeley stood next to the helmsman—legs apart, buckled boots planted firmly on the quarterdeck, balancing himself against a rolling swell—and listened to the news in brewing anger.

'Heaven forbid, Mr. Beckwith,' he spat at the surgeon. 'If we are not careful, this pox will spread about the ship like a raging fire. I need not remind you, sir, that each man aboard a sailing vessel the likes of the *Magdalena* is needed to operate the ship. Should men suddenly be confined to their hammocks, ill with the pox, this ship could become incapacitated.' It was a very serious problem.

'If the captain will forgive me, sir, you have condoned these relationships.'

'Condoned?' The captain's eyes narrowed. 'I condoned relationships, yes. Relationships, one on one. Lord only knows, it helps run a smooth ship. But rampant prostitution'—the captain's eyes darkened and his voice became resonant—'I never condoned that, sir. This... this'— the captain waved a hand about—'this pox, as I said, could cripple a ship. How, in the Lord's name, did this Betty Bryant manage to inflict her filth on so many men in such a short time?'

'It appears a portion of the orlop bulkhead was removed, with the aid of the men and... '

'But there are stores betwixt them.'

'Aye. But the stores between the crew quarters and the bulkhead were shifted sufficiently to allow the women to squeeze through.'

'Women? You mean, there is more than one whore?'

'Aye, sir.'

'How many, pray tell?'

'From what I can ascertain, twelve, maybe thirteen.'

'God, no! And do these other women have the pox?'

'It appears not, sir. Some, I believe, have been using protection to prevent such conditions.' Captain Cholmondeley knew that the surgeon spoke of the intestines of the pig.

'Then they are to be commended.' The captain had a thought. 'I met the eminent botanist Sir Joseph Banks in London some years back and he told me the South Seas islanders insert seaweed into the vagina.'

'Fascinating, sir.'

'Indeed. However, we must make an example of this Betty Bryant. Have the guard bring her on deck and rope her to the foremast. I want the other prisoners brought on deck to witness ten lashes of the cat.'

'Yes, sir.'

'That should put an end to it.'

Betty was dragged to the foredeck shouting curses. She was fastened with leather straps to a wooden triangle against the foremast; her blouse lowered to expose her back but hooked over her breasts to allow some modesty. Crew and prisoners were made to watch. Will Thackeray was her flagellator, having drawn the short straw. He had been one of Betty's luckier customers and was sickened by what he had to administer.

'Put your back into it, man,' first mate Robert Knight warned Thackeray, 'or you'll be feeling the cat on yer own back.'

'Give it yer best, Will,' Betty uttered through clenched teeth. 'Get it over with. I'll not let these bastards beat me.'

'Here,'—Will Thackeray placed a length of thick folded leather in Betty's mouth—'bite down on this.'

The first lick of the cat drew blood and Betty let out a guttural roar through her gag. The second strike with the nine eighteen-inch lengths of knotted thread tore the skin. Betty's eyes filled with tears—tears of pain, not self-pity. On the third lash Thackeray withdrew the lash, speckling spots of blood across his own weathered face.

'Don't hold back Thackeray,' Knight cautioned the flagellator once more, 'or yer know the consequences.' The onlookers remained completely quiet, many silently querying the captain's justice. Then, after the sixth lashing, Betty's muted screams went silent. Her head tipped forward loosely, like that of a rag doll. Betty Bryant had slipped from consciousness.

Betty came to face down on her cot. Elizabeth, Flo Bell and some others had placed blankets beneath her and now washed her wounds with salt water.

'Jayzus Christ, what are yer doin' to me?' Betty screamed at her carers.

'Quiet, Betty,' Elizabeth said. 'Surgeon Beckwith told us to wash your back with salt.'

'Aye,' Flo Bell added, 'it will hasten yer recovery.'

'A pox on all o' them,' Betty cursed, 'includin' that firkin' captain. Pox to all, I say!'

Flo Bell stifled a laugh. '"Pox" yer say, Betty—yer gone an' give half the ship pox anyways.'

CHAPTER SIXTEEN

Bull Seal Island

The aft hatch of the barquentine *Sea Rat* banged open. Rowan blinked, bathed in sunlight. Bright, welcome sunlight. He threw up his hand to shield himself from the blinding light, for he had been trapped in darkness for two days. Harpooner Uriah Coffin gaped down at him, the brilliant sun silhouetting his face into a dark, unrecognisable orb. Uriah Coffin was a New Zealander—a Maori. He was well beyond his fortieth year, with a chiselled face and large flat nose on a large, round head. His wiry, thick hair was cropped short and high off the brow to show off his geometric tattoos. Tattooed palm fronds and concentric circles covered his entire face, and continued down his neck and body. Even at five foot five, he looked the fearsome warrior, with intense deep brown eyes that Rowan imagined had witnessed many a battle.

'Bull Seal Island, Sawbones.' The Maori's voice was deep but friendly enough. Rowan had been locked belowdecks, for the sealers wanted him disorientated with regard to the location of their unchartered island. They were somewhere in a turbulent sea of water named Bass Strait, off the south coast of Australia, the strait being named after naval surgeon

George Bass, Rowan was told, who discovered the sea passage with navy captain Mathew Flinders. That had transpired sixteen years earlier.

Rowan accepted this treatment with understanding, even though he'd had no prior warning when Captain Amos Leblanc ordered that he be locked below. But for Rowan's part, as a felon wanted to stand trial for murder by King George, being able to hide from a determined Royal Navy with these men, and on one of the world's most isolated oceans, was a godsend.

'We're here, then?' Rowan asked with a croaky voice.

'Aye, Come on up.'

Rowan's eyes quickly adjusted. He climbed the companionway to be greeted by salty air on a stiff wind with a rhythmic swell rolling under the keel. The sky was scattered with cloud but none masked the welcome sun. Rowan gasped in deep breaths of crisp, fresh air and held the ratline for balance, tipping back his head to look at the sky. His hair had grown long and it whipped loosely about his face.

Leblanc, standing by the helmsman Cornelius Riddell, addressed Rowan with an expressionless nod. He was more focussed on the approach to the island. The captain ordered the sail shortened, and the helmsman guided the *Sea Rat* masterfully through the narrow but deep channel leading between two headlands into Seal Bay. The bay was shaped like a giant fishhook, Rowan had been told, and the unique layout of the geology concealed the bay to passing vessels, should a ship ever venture into the unknown. From offshore the island looked most inhospitable.

The *Sea Rat* glided between the headlands—so tight was the opening that Rowan felt he could reach out and touch the cliffs. Certainly, no ship of a larger draught could make the manoeuvre. The vertical cliffs soared fifty or sixty feet up from the bay's bedrock, and sparse trees lined the shore, all listing east from the wild winds off the sea. Rowan snatched one last look over his shoulder—all he could see in their wake was a vast empty ocean before the *Sea Rat* nosed into the sheltered bay itself, hidden from any passing vessel out at sea.

Both port and starboard bow anchors shattered the serenity, plunging to the seabed in three fathoms of crystal clear water, where Rowan watched startled fish scatter from the anchors' landing sites. Orders passed down the line and the *Sea Rat* was secured. Clearly the crew were thankful to be home and their excited voices reverberated off the cliffs, mingling with the screeches and squawks of the abundant seabirds spiralling in tightening circles overhead, expecting food. The island appeared deserted and Rowan suddenly felt a hint of anxiety. Yet he was revered as the settlement's new surgeon for he had the medical expertise these men depended upon.

'Don't look so serious, man!' Captain Leblanc slapped Rowan on the back. 'Fetch yer kit, we're goin' ashore.'

Instantly figures arrived, clambering over the rocks of the northern side of the bay some hundred yards distant. Cheerful faces called out, whistling, yodelling.   Rowan guessed there to be two dozen at least—a ragtag assortment of men, women and some little ones. All the women were black skinned and naked from the waist up. The indigenous people of Van Diemen's Land, Rowan assumed. Charcoal black, they were nothing like the American Indians in appearance. Rowan watched men drag two clinker dinghies onto a beach of round pebbles, where the boats were immediately launched and rowed out to meet them.

'Ahoy!' The rowers laughed in greeting the barquentine's crew as if they were strangers.

'Ahoy back, yer bastards!'

'Did ya get me nails?' one rower, a ship's carpenter, yelled. 'I ain't takin' yer ashore if'n ya don't 'ave me nails, Edward Caleb.'

'Aye, I got ya firkin' nails – an' ya rum.'

The other rower, Ned Talbot, caught the captain's eye. 'I trust ya got plenty o' salt, Cap'n, huh?'

'Aye. Twenty barrels.'

'Good, cos we run out while ya was away. We got skins stinkin' the place out.'

'You'll be goin' easy on it, Ned, on account its price advanced five shillings a barrel.'

'I hear they found salt pans on Bruny Island in the south, Cap'n, an' they's been sellin' it in George Town.'

'I'll look into it.'

Rowan watched the industry with interest, and Billy Cake studied Rowan's face intently as they were rowed ashore. The simpleton was thrilled to be home. 'Whatdya think?' he asked with boyish excitement.

'Well... I...'

'This 'ere's Seal Bay.' Billy caught Rowan's hesitation. 'Seal Bay on Bull Seal Island. An' them heads we sailed through are called Forget Me Not Heads, an' this 'ere beach, where we're goin' to, is called Billy Cake's Beach.' This he said with a contagious grin. 'Ain't it, Cap'n? Billy Cake's Beach.'

'Well,'—the captain sat next to Rowan on the forward thwarts—'I guess it is now, Billy,' Leblanc said, humouring the man. 'It is now, lad.'

'You named these landmarks yourselves, then?' Rowan asked Billy Cake.

'No, sar, not me, no, no,'—the simpleton cook shook his head vehemently—'never. It was Uriah and Cap'n Amos, sar... an', an' Gabrielle an' Scully what named 'em.'

'Yes,' Rowan reiterated 'that's what I meant to say—you sealers named them yourselves?'

'Yes, Rowan,' the captain answered. 'No other beggar has dared venture 'ere before us, 'ceptin' fer some o' those natives yer see on the beach.'

On shore the rocks were nearly impossible to traverse barefoot; the awkwardly round, goose egg-sized rocks had been smoothed by millennia of the ocean's abrasive action. The natives and their offspring, however, walked upon them as if on a cobbled street.

Once Rowan and the captain were ashore, a small landing party joined the tenders and along with Uriah Coffin and the crew they began the chore of rowing supplies ashore. There, the heavier items, like barrels of salt and nails, were loaded onto sleds pulled by two donkeys.

'Ah, if'n it's not Elihu Smyth,' Captain Leblanc greeted a lanky man with greying hair, who, Rowan suspected, was suffering from consumption. He wore the tarred oilskin boater hat of a sailor. The man's pigtail was also tarred for safety aboard ship, this custom giving seamen the nickname of 'Jack Tar'. Elihu clamped hard on a clay pipe wedged through a gap in yellowing teeth as he leered at Rowan with uncertainty.

'This be Rowan Craige Esquire, Elihu.' Captain Leblanc smiled at his friend, but the smile was not returned. 'He's a sawbones.'

'Sawbones, huh? Can we trust him?' the man asked Leblanc without taking his eyes off Rowan.

'Aye. He knows what'll happen to him if he crosses us, Elihu—now greet the man proper like.'

'I'll be greetin' no stranger...' —Elihu spat a brown glob of spit onto the rocks—'...sawbones or not... 'til I'm satisfied.'

'Suit yer self, ya cantankerous bugger. But there'll be no fightin', ya hear me?' Elihu Smyth walked ahead in a huff.

'Take no notice of 'im, Rowan. The man's got aches an' pains what need fixin'. That's what makes him snake-like, but 'es a good man, when he pays attention to the scriptures. And 'e's me first mate, so 'e's in charge when I'm not 'ere.'

A catlike sound made Rowan turn. It was Billy Cake. He scuttled up behind Rowan panting. 'Sawbones Rowan, Sawbones Rowan,' he chanted. 'Ya still don't know where ya goin'... do yer, Rowan? Ro-wan don't know where he's go-in.' Billy Cake chuckled at his rhyme. He followed the others up a well worn path of crumbling gravel to where it levelled to a horizontal landing, at least twenty feet above sea level. Off to one side the narrow ledge dropped into the bay. The ledge followed the curvature of the land and Rowan now noted a natural low arch ahead. At first he thought it led to a dead end, but soon realised it was a cave disappearing into the cliff face, a natural passageway leading on for fifty feet or more. And beyond was light.

Rowan was the centre of attraction. Everyone watched for his reaction upon going through this passageway. They were not disappointed. Rowan stood fast and gaped, open-mouthed. Before him, laid out in a neat crescent, was a small shantytown, a gathering of makeshift dwellings sitting snugly on a wide, quarter moon-shaped ledge. Huts that appeared to be made from driftwood and the timbers of a wrecked ship were all built against a vertical 20-foot cliff wall at their rear. They were built one against the other, side by side, for support and strength. Lanterns hung from davits. Fishing nets were slung like hammocks and pegged washing shivered in a fresh sea breeze. It was like a tiny village built in a crater.

'Welcome to Mast Head Bluff.'

Each shanty faced north, to make use of the sun's path, and barrels were positioned to collect rainwater from their sloping roofs. In front of the dwellings, the crescent-shaped ledge dropped away sharply to a steep, sloping pebble beach that led out to sea, but only through a large natural arch that had caved in long ago, leaving just enough headroom at low tide for a tender to row out to the open sea. Behind the small community, above the crater rim, a barren, treeless mountain rose four hundred feet to a craggy, windswept summit.

'Paradise,' Leblanc said proudly, placing a reverent hand on Rowan's shoulder.

'Amazing, Captain. It is a credit to you... a credit to you all.'

'Aye, thart it is, lad. There musta been a mammoth landslide 'ere eons ago, before the natives even, I'm thinkin'. An' it slid into the sea, leavin' this 'ere nice sheltered cove.'

'Most fortuitous.'

'Fortuitous. Aye. Now there's a word, and make no mistake.'

'How many did you say live here?'

'There's thirty-eight of us livin' on the island,' Uriah Coffin told Rowan. 'Eighteen women, twelve men and eight bairns.'

'An' Kalanga 'as one in the oven,' Billy Cake hooted. 'One in the oven. One in the oven...'

'All right, Billy.' Leblanc grew impatient—he motioned for Rowan to walk on. 'Billy's excited to be home—aren't yer, Billy?'

'Aye, Cap'n... Uh, Cap'n?'

'What, Billy?'

'Has Cap'n Leblanc got a woman for Sawbones?'

'Now don't spoil the surprise, Billy.'

Helmsman Cornelius Riddell watched Rowan crane his head to the mountaintop. 'That's Eagle's Nest,' Riddell said, choosing to avoid eye contact, 'our lookout.' This was the first time he had spoken to Rowan directly. Rowan found the man to be insecure. He had a long, narrow face with sunken eyes and deep cheek creases. His huge hands were calloused. His hair was greasy and matted, for personal hygiene was not a priority. All in all, a rather unlikely choice for a helmsman Rowan thought. However, Leblanc swore Riddell had an uncanny sense of navigation and could read the stars as well as any sea captain.

Rowan caught movement halfway up the steep slope. 'Are there goats?'

'Aye,'—Captain Leblanc nodded approvingly—'we set eight o' the beggars free, half a dozen years ago, a coupla bucks an' six nannies, an' they breed like rabbits.'

'But when we want one for dinner, tha bastards hide.' Riddell grinned. 'So now what do yer think, Sawbones?'

'I am... ah... amazed. Simply amazed.' Rowan stood, legs planted apart, hands on hips and gaped. 'How long did you say you have you been here?'

'Ten year, more or less.'

Out of nowhere two huge hounds came bounding along the water's edge. 'Hamish, Bones, me little lovelies.' The dogs jumped up on Leblanc, barking, licking his face, clearly delighted. 'Good hunters, these two,' Leblanc said as the dogs turned on Rowan sniffing and panting. 'Go ahead, give 'em a pat an' a rub, they won't bite.'

Suddenly a roar caught Rowan's attention, a throaty roar of seawater racing through a blowhole fifty yards away. Immediately the blowhole expelled in a geyser of water some twenty feet into the air, the water landing in a showery hiss as it splashed across the rocks and streamed back into the sea.

'Whoosh!' Billy Cake imitated the sound and performed a jig on the spot.

'We have two blow'oles here, Doctor Craige,' Leblanc said. 'The other one's smaller and it's called Satan's Pit.'

'Satan's Pit, Satan's Pit,' Billy giggled like a schoolboy.

'Satan's Pit is our latrine,' the captain told Rowan, matter-of-factly. 'We do our daily business in a rock pool next to the geyser and it gets washed out to sea. Ya wouldn't get sanitation like that in Washington or Baltimore.'

'An if'n ya standing right...'—Billy's face contorted mischievously—'...ya get ya arse washed at the same time.'

'Come.' Amos Leblanc led Rowan down steps chiselled into an embankment. He turned to two young half-caste boys, maybe ten or eleven years old, who struggled after them, carrying Rowan's kit, including the medicine chest Leblanc had purchased in Sydney Cove. 'You put those in Pollyanna's hut,' Leblanc ordered the boys, 'Smartly now.'

'Pollyanna?' Rowan asked.

'Aye. Pollyanna's a Van Diemen native. She's your woman now, to do what you want with her.'

'Can I not live alone?'

'No, yer can't. Pollyanna's a good cook—she'll fatten you up and give yer lovin' if'n that's yer medicine. She ain't the Venus de Milo, but a man has his needs.'

With a change in the afternoon sea breeze came the stench of rotting seal meat. 'Smell that? I need to tend to the tannery,' Leblanc said. 'Follow them lads; yer in the hut third on the left, where I can keep an eye on yer, not that ya goin' anywhere a whiles now, lad.'

Gossip swept through Mast Head Bluff along with the stench of curing sealskins. Pollyanna, whose aboriginal name Rowan thought sounded something like Gununa, was thrilled to have a new guest. She fussed about from the moment Rowan stooped beneath the low doorframe. Rowan waited for his eyes to adjust to the gloom. The hut had one window, covered with a kangaroo skin. A double cot took up one quarter of the space and a low table with rudimentary utensils stood alone, with two chairs beside it. All cooking was done over a rock hearth outside the door, where a tripod held a pot of water steaming over dying coals. The two young boys dropped Rowan's kit and chest on the floor.

'Careful!' he yelled at them, more loudly than he'd intended. 'Medicine, yes? You must be careful.' The lads gaped about the hut until Pollyanna shooed them away.

'Me Pollyanna.' Pollyanna smiled shyly at Rowan. Her skin was blacker than that of any slave Rowan had ever seen. She was pleasantly proportioned in figure. Her matted hair was cut short and had recently been scented with perfumed oil. She was barefoot and wore an ankle-length skirt that had seen better days. She was naked from the waist up. Rowan could not help stare at her firm, unrestrained breasts. 'You like 'em native girl?' She smiled, showing off perfect white teeth.

'Pollyanna... My name is Mr. Craige,' Rowan said awkwardly. He wished he had had more to do with the indigenous people, back in North America. 'Ah... I guess you can call me Rowan.'

'Ro-waan.'

'Yes... ah... do you have a shirt?'

'Shirt?'

'Blouse. Or a shawl, maybe? Something to cover yourself?' Rowan mimed the donning of apparel. 'To cover your bosom.'

'Bosom?'

Rowan imagined she had never heard the word. He pointed to her chest.

'Ah, me titties. Rowan no like Pollyanna's titties?'

'That's not what I said, Pollyanna. I just asked... Oh, never mind.'

CHAPTER SEVENTEEN

They gathered after dusk: native women, bastard children, seafarers, sealers and harpooners. A gang of misfits, all harbouring their own dark secrets. They assembled for the one thing all humanity had in common, the evening meal—eating, drinking and merrymaking, the vital requisite that has bonded mankind since the beginning of time. Rowan stepped from his shanty to face a world he could never have imagined a year earlier.

He struggled with mounting anxiety. The spontaneity of his decision now threatened to crush him. He was trapped on an unchartered island with an assortment of scoundrels—deserters, sealers, escaped convicts, kidnapped aboriginal women and their half-caste offspring, along with mongrel hounds stalking the shantytown perimeter, awaiting scraps.

On an overhanging ledge the communal fire beckoned. Flames from the log fire reached into the enveloping darkness, challenging the night, peppering the blackness with a billion sparks. The heat drew Rowan forward; he was never shy, but was now apprehensive. But his trepidation dissolved when a pewter mug was pressed into his hand. 'This'll warm yer,' his benefactor said cheerfully. 'Henry Tuckerman, yer humble servant, squire.'

Rowan could smell the rum immediately. It was not his normal tipple by any means, especially not neat by the half pint. However, Rowan was grateful for the offer of camaraderie. 'Thank you.'

'It be my pleasure, matey. Here's mud in yer eye.' Henry took a generous tug at his own rum, smacked his lips and sighed appreciatively. He stood expectantly before Rowa waiting for the ship surgeon to do likewise. Rowan took a mouthful and made to cough, but caught his breath in time. He swallowed and the effect was instant. His throat burnt as the spirit pooled in his empty belly.

Rowan and Henry joined the others at the bonfire, where they watched Leblanc, at the water's edge, butcher a goat by slitting its throat through the jugular, to thoroughly bleed it. He separated the skin from the meat with experienced slashes of his well-honed dagger. The carcass was hung by the hind legs on a drift wood triangle and beheaded; then the dressing began. Leblanc sensed Rowan watching. The captain twisted about and looked up from the pebbled shoreline to his audience. He wore a wide grin and a leather apron bespattered with glossy, fresh blood from chest to ankles; Rowan had the impression that the man enjoyed his toil.

'Yer hungry?'

Rowan nodded. As he looked on he could not help wonder if this God-fearing captain had slaughtered a fellow man at some stage. It didn't bear thinking about. The chilling memory of the soldier Rowan had killed put a stop to his considerations and he returned soberly to the fire.

Although most meals were cooked independently, outside the individual huts, at least one evening meal each week was a social affair. Tonight's festivity, Rowan was informed, was in his honour. Billy Cake already had two kangaroos roasting on retired harpoons converted into a spit. They sizzled at the fire's edges, along with several small birds the aboriginal women had caught in their burrows and salted. The natives called them *yolla*. The men called these grey-feathered birds 'mutton-birds' because of their generous fat. Rowan heard their diet occasionally varied, and included porcupines and wombats.

Billy Cake tended the whole kangaroos, basting them with salted lard mixed with bush herbs. He raked the coals to even out the heat and finally, after several hours' roasting, the meat fell apart onto the hearth. Suddenly Rowan realised how hungry he was.

The rum made Rowan complacent. While he stared vaguely into the flames, Henry Tuckerman tipped the keg to fill a silver ewer with the syrupy, dark brown rum. If anything was out of place, it was the helmet-shaped ewer raised on an oval foot with repoussé shell and floral decoration. It was the kind of tableware made for nobility, and Rowan knew enough about silver to, on closer inspection, discreetly note a silversmith's hallmark for Birmingham—a rampant lion, a ship's anchor, King George's profile and the letter O, all within individual cartouches. The ewer was new and worth several years' wages for a seaman. Rowan's interest in it did not go unnoticed.

'We like to enjoy the good things o' life 'round 'ere,' a good-looking cove three or four years younger than Rowan said. He had tightly curled, short blonde hair and was, of lean build; his square jaw was almost lost behind a goatee beard and long, thin sideburns.

'"The good things,"' Rowan repeated. 'But where...?'

'Ask no questions, hear no lies,' the man answered with a rakish wink. He reached out with his right hand. 'Edward Caleb.' The two men shook hands vigorously. 'Are yer really a surgeon?'

'Yes.'

'Cap'n tells me yer American. I thought yer accent were Irish.'

'No, American, from Maryland.'

'I'm from Gravesend.'

Rowan knew Gravesend to be on the Thames River, east of London. 'You are a long way from home.'

'Aye.' Edward Caleb looked solemn a moment. 'Transported, wasn't I,' he said sourly. Rowan thought it not his business to ask why, but Caleb offered. 'Got fourteen years for being acquainted with a highwayman, namely The Major.'

'"The Major"? Was that his real name?'

'Nar. 'Twas on account o' his regimental appearance. Jayzus, I only met the cove once but some villagers seen me exchanging conversation with the man at Blackheath, like, an' next thing yer know I'm up before the magistrate. Fourteen years, the bastard gave me, and for what? For naught.'

'Sorry to hear that.'

'Yer, well, I escaped didn't I? Escaped from a chain gang, where we was reclaiming land on 'Unter Island.'

'Hunter Island?'

'Aye. In 'Obart Town. They be buildin' a wharf there, with plans for ware'ouses an' all. Cartin' rocks dawn ter dusk be the devils errand, squire. I escaped along with five others but them others was caught. I were lucky. Hid 'til nightfall and walked all night towards whaler's fires down the coast—south, like—where I met up with John there.'

John Stuart Radge heard his name mentioned. He looked across at the two men from where he sat on the trunk of a felled tree, dressed for the very purpose. Rowan had caught Radge's eye earlier that afternoon but the man had showed no desire to make his acquaintance. Radge shot Rowan an aloof glance before dismissing the chance of any introduction by slapping a young native woman on the backside and pulling her roughly onto his knee. She giggled and sat shamelessly.

' 'E's a blacksmith,' Edward Caleb told Rowan. 'And an absconder, like me. 'E forced 'imself upon a woman back in Southwark in London, got sentenced to hang, what got commuted to fourteen years' transportation, like me. We's mates on account we escaped together, but yer wanna watch 'im.'

Rowan studied Radge discreetly, with an intelligent eye. The man was older than Caleb and was powerfully built, with the broad shoulders expected of a blacksmith. Radge had been a handsome man once, but a gnarly scar disfigured his right cheek and continued down his neck. Caleb leant in closer to Rowan on the lee side of the blacksmith. 'The scar's a keepsake from a knife fight, 'e once told me, a fight over a woman on the Thames docks. Now 'e's blind in the right eye. 'E's all right once yer gain 'is trust, like. But I warn yer, Sawbones, 'e's hard work.'

The tattooed face of the Maori harpooner Uriah Coffin materialised from a spiral of smoke. He handed Rowan a pewter plate of steaming meat. 'Here. Eat.' A bone-handled fork projected from the shredded, slow-roasted meat and Rowan was bathed in the aroma of the lean marsupial. A fat wedge of baked damper balanced at the plate's edge, soaking up any stray meat juices. The harpooner rolled an empty keg alongside Rowan and sat next to him with his own plate piled high.

'Kan-gar-oo.' Uriah Coffin articulated the word as he forked a large portion of the animal's meat into his mouth and watched Rowan take his first bite. 'Bloody good sar, eh?'

Rowan readily agreed. He was ravenously hungry and found himself eating faster than he was accustomed to. Between mouthfuls, the harpooner willingly told Rowan how he had learnt sealing and whaling back in New Zealand, at Kororareka at the Bay of Islands. He'd taken his name, Uriah Coffin, from the missionary who'd converted him to Christianity. But the Maori saw the hypocrisy of the missionaries—to them he would always be a tattooed savage. Kororareka became an important whaling port and Uriah recognized a need in the sailors who had been at sea, some of them for a year or more. He procured native women, whom he took to the ships to exchange *short-term marriages* for muskets, blankets, gowns, boots and utensils. The sailors paid Uriah a small commission, mostly in commodities, but also in silver. Then the missionaries found out.

'"Sodom and Gomorrah!" they screamed.' Uriah, a natural thespian, re-enacted the moment. His eyes grew wide with mock anger and he barred his teeth, while the campfire flames transformed his tattooed face into a demonic mask. Three half-caste toddlers approached warily from the peripheral darkness of the night to listen to Uriah Coffin's pantomime. The Maori spun to face the children, puffed out his chest and threw his arms up like a grizzly bear. 'Sodom and Gomorrah!' he roared and they ran away, squealing with delight.

Uriah Coffin slurped at his rum, ran an arm across his chin, and leant close to Rowan. '"You have turned Kororareka into Sodom and Gomorrah," the bastards whined at me. "The scourge of the Pacific, which should be struck down by the ravages of disease and depravity," they said.' The harpooner's eyes lit with anger once more. 'They try put a stop to Uriah's venture, but I'll have none of it. We argue. The missionary calls me "black devil". I had enough and hit the bastard with my *wahiaka*, almost killing him when I smash his collar-bone.'

'What's a *wahiaka*?'

'War club. He report me to a visiting Navy frigate, but I escape on whaler. Later I meet Captain Amos Leblanc in a Sydney Town waterfront inn...'

'The Three Jolly Settlers?'

'Aye. That be eight year ago now.'

Captain Amos Leblanc, surrounded by squealing, excited children, made a grand exit from his shanty where he had changed into fresh clothes. He took a moment to survey the gathering around the campfire. All eyes fell upon the man, and there was a lull in conversation. Leblanc stretched his arms, arching his back, and stepped first before Uriah Coffin. He looked down at the Maori's nearly empty plate.

'I trust that you've said grace?' he enquired of Uriah Coffin, knowing of the man's distaste for the church. The Maori refused to be drawn into a debate on the merits of religion. He had been there before with the captain, who made no bones about the fact that he was a God-fearing man.

'Yer a heathen, Uriah Coffin,' Leblanc said with a wry smile. 'But it don't necessarily make yer a bad man, huh?'

'We was talkin' of them bastard missionaries, Cap'n,' Uriah said, tipping a nod to Rowan.

'Aye. An' Sodom an' Gomorrah.' Leblanc winked at Rowan. 'Yer know them scriptures or-right.'

Uriah Coffin wiped the remaining chunk of damper across his plate sponging the juices, and filled his mouth, before he expelled demeaning words concerning the Christian god. Leblanc was also in no mood to antagonise his best harpooner. He twisted and looked at Rowan. 'So, Sawbones, you like them vittles?'

'Very much.'

'Kangaroo. You'll be seein' plenty o' them hoppin' about on Bull Seal tomorra. We nearly wiped 'em out a few years back, but now we bring 'em back live from Van Diemen an' let 'em run wild here. Keep stocks up, like them goats.' The captain ran a hand through his hair, patting a waxy tuft over a bald patch. He motioned Billy Cake to bring the ewer and a mug. Leblanc topped Rowan's tankard, then his own. 'Stand up, lad.'

Rowan stood unsteadily. The overproof rum was strong. 'Quiet, the lot o' yer!' Leblanc bawled out over the returning chatter. 'Quiet, I say. You,' he yelled at the circle of native women, 'cut yer chin waggin' a moment!'

There was silence, except for the crackle of a roaring fire, the timeless gushing of the blowholes and the melody of eternal waves pounding ashore.

'For those o' yer who haven't met our newcomer, this 'ere is Rowan, our new sawbones. He brung with 'im a chest o' medicines, what we purchased in Sydney Town, so see him for yer humours an' ailments. He is also experienced in sealskins, a practice what 'e learned in America, from where 'e escaped the tyranny o' England. In other words 'e will occasionally be coming along on our sorties. Savvy?'

'You sayin' he gets an equal share?' First Mate Elihu Smyth's voice resonated over the murmurings. His face was sour and his downturned horseshoe moustache gave him a permanent scowl.

'Aye'—Leblanc looked squarely at his first mate—'He'll be toilin' just as hard as any o' us. What with the duties o' his chosen profession as well. Yer all aware that we lost little Daniel to the tremors last winter.' Communal utterings of remembrance rose from the fire lit faces. 'Well, if'n we 'ad a sawbones 'ere on the island then Danny might still walk amongst us.'

Smyth cleared his throat and spat into the fire before running a defiling hand up the skirts of his woman.

'Now, Sawbones,'—Leblanc threw a comforting arm about Rowan's shoulders—'I ain't gonna introduce everyone, as yer wouldn't remember 'em name fer name any'ow. So *you* get to know 'em one by one. We're a good team.' Leblanc chinked his tankard against Rowan's. Both men drank. Leblanc ran his coat cuff across his rum-stained lips before subtly drawing Rowan's attention back to Elihu Smyth, now preoccupied with his amorous intentions. 'Aye,' he said softly to Rowan, 'we're a good team, as long as yer don't cross no one.'

'I'm sure I'll be fine, Captain.' The rum gave Rowan confidence and the chatter grew in volume once more. 'Ah, Captain...' Rowan clearly had a request.

'What's botherin' yer, lad?'

'I'd prefer to be called Rowan, not "Sawbones", if you don't mind.'

'Mind? Mind? Why should I mind? Rowan it is.' Leblanc silenced the gathering once more. 'Hear that, one an' all? Sawbones wants to be called Rowan... an' Rowan only.' He raised his tankard. 'I give yer Rowan—huzzah!'

'Huzzah! Huzzah!' The extraordinary assembly cheered and drank to Rowan's health. Everyone, that is, except for Elihu Smyth.

Night over Bull Seal Island turned coal black. The sky was cloudless while lucent stars winked in varied degrees of brightness and a quarter moon was setting lazily on the western horizon like a rind of lemon. The sea air, the roaring log fire and the laughter put Rowan at ease. Billy Cake was the village jester, enjoying the limelight with his animal impressions, everything from a crowing cock to a howling hound to a bellowing bull. And while Rowan experienced mood swings, from a sense of camaraderie to moments of loneliness, the rum helped circumvent his fears. Finally, strains of old shanties like 'Leave her, Jack' or 'Sea Sally's Petticoats' played by Billy Cake on a fiddle mellowed the exhausted surgeon's humour.

As everyone overindulged in the rum - including the older children - Rowan cast a subtle eye over his adopted 'family'. Clearly, first mate Elihu Smyth had taken a disliking to him. Rowan suspected the man saw him as a financial threat. Smyth and his native woman were the first to retire. Arm in arm, they staggered unsteadily towards their cabin. As a medical man, Rowan reflected again that the first mate was probably suffering from consumption. He was thin and gaunt in the face with yellow teeth and pallid eyes, and Rowan was certain he had seen blood on at least one occasion when the man coughed and spat.

Looking about the collective of seafarers, absconders, native women and their brats, Rowan felt optimistic about gaining their trust. The only other rival appeared to be the blacksmith, John Stuart Radge, who also maintained an unfriendly disposition towards Rowan. He was an angry man harbouring dark secrets, and Rowan had become aware that Radge enjoyed tormenting the native women, treating them like dogs. He was handsome enough, thirty-one or −two years of age, with curly blonde hair and sideburns growing down to a shaved chin. His leathery-soled feet were bare and a sealskin jacket hung off his shoulders where the stained ribbon around his boater hat dropped to his back like a serpent's tongue.

Leaning with rakish arrogance against the nearest hut, feet and arms crossed and enjoying a pipe, was Ned Talbot. He was about the same age as Radge and they appeared to be good mates. He mirrored Radge's arrogance, but Rowan assessed the man to be just that, a mirror. Uriah Coffin told Rowan that Talbot was an experienced artillery gunner who had been with the British, fighting Napoleon in Spain in '08 and '10, in what was called the Peninsular Wars, but a brush with death had led him to desert.

Ned Talbot—if that were the name his parents *had* bestowed upon him—was thewy tough, yes, but rake skinny. He had a thin face with a pointed nose and alert, beady eyes under raised eyebrows. His sideburns were thin, running down the sides of his face and meeting under the chin. He had no moustache. Like Radge, he wore a sealskin jacket over calico blouse and britches tied with a cord.

Edward Caleb once more joined Rowan, who was seated on a log. Youth was Caleb's friend. He wore the tight-fitting garments of a well-muscled lad in fine fettle—white breeches, an open-necked calico shirt tucked under a brass-buckled belt, and a sweat cloth flapping in the breeze. He looked smart, suited in his navy blue waist cut jacket with cream lining and brass buttons, a boater hat and clay pipe clenched between porcelain white teeth.

'Captain Leblanc is a fiercely religious man, I notice,' Rowan said to Caleb. 'Are you a religious person, Edward?'

'Some say I am.'

'You believe in heaven, then?'

'Oh, aye. Where a sailor goes to paradise—there's endless grog and baccy, with inns on every corner serving roast beef every night, and beautiful women to sit on ya lap, keepin' ya glass full and ya pipe lit.'

Rowan took a shine to Edward, and Edward to him. The lad had a sense of humour and there was no malice about him. In fact, Rowan wondered why such a man would end up with a gang the likes of this lot, known to the authorities as sealers.

'I was a clerk in a counting house in Liverpool,' he told Rowan. 'A quantity of tobacco went missing and I got blamed for adjusting the record books.'

'Oh, and did you?'

'Aye, I done it, all right. The navy pressed me pa into service, left Ma with four youngens to feed. I seen the discrepancy as a way out of hell for me ma. But I gone and got caught.' Edward Caleb's eyes watered and Rowan wondered if it was from the painful memory of his mother or the campfire smoke. 'Firk 'em,' the clerk stiffened defiantly. 'I'd do it all over again.'

Rowan's contemplation was interrupted by the approach of a powerfully built black man, his dark skin silhouetted by the flames behind him as he approached.

'How to do, mon?' he said in greeting.

Rowan found himself looking up at this giant of a man; he was six feet six at least. 'Gabriel, is it not?' Rowan remembered Uriah Coffin pointing out his fellow harpooner earlier in the evening.

'Aye, mon. Gab-riel... American Ne-gro slave, escaped from Mississippi. You, too, Ameri-can, huh? From Washing-ton?'

'Baltimore, actually.'

'Mary-land?'

'Yes.'

Rowan soon recognized the powerfully built Negro, a favourite of the native women, as an intelligent man. He was in his early thirties, a fierce-faced man with ineradicable scars from smallpox covering his face, and the unmistakable sign of a previously broken nose. Gabriel told Rowan he'd escaped when disruptions broke out between the British and Americans. He'd found a working passage on a Spanish ship fleeing New Orleans to the West Indies. He'd been accepted on board a New Bedford whaler as a free man, the captain being a staunch abolitionist. Gabriel discovered he had natural skill as a harpooner and cemented a good relationship with all in the crew, except one, Adam Skye, with whom he'd fought. Skye had fallen, crushing his skull on the deck, and died. The captain had had no choice but to put Gabriel ashore in Sydney Cove. Rowan listened to the man's story, noting his huge muscled arms and legs and imagined him capable of tackling several men at the same time. *A man to keep on his side.*

When Billy Cake, Captain Leblanc, his two aboriginal wives and most of the other women retired for the night, Rowan was keen to withdraw himself, but there were three Bull Seal Islanders he had not acquainted himself with, and he thought it diplomatic to, at the least, acknowledge the men. As Rowan circled the dwindling campfire, he noticed that Cornelius Riddell, the helmsman he had met aboard the *Sea Rat*, was asleep. His head was stooped forward, facing an empty pewter mug at his feet which he had kicked over. Sitting along a log in a tight knot, laughing drunkenly at one crudity after another, were Skeffington Lutwidge, a seaman, and Henry Tuckerman, the ship's carpenter, whom he had met earlier, and Joseph Scully. Scully, an absconder, was barely coherent, drunk on rum and nodding himself asleep. Skeffington Lutwidge stood groggily at Rowan's approach. 'Shorebones,' he slurred, and thrust his hand forward in greeting. Rowan took the hand proffered and shook heartily before releasing his grip, but the seaman would have none of it. He held firm, whether in friendship or to support himself, Rowan was not certain.

'Jayzus,' Lutwidge admitted, 'I'm merry weather.'

Henry Tuckerman maintained the safer position by remaining seated. He looked up at Rowan with heavy eyelids. ' 'E ain't had rum fer a week,' he excused his inebriated friend. 'We run out, see, and tonight's the first tipple we's had in all that time.'

'I see,' Rowan said awkwardly. 'I just wanted to introduce myself before I retire.'

Joseph Scully snorted awake at the sound of a strange voice. 'Shu ... Shully,' he garbled.

''E means "Scully",' Henry Tuckerman said.

'I... I can fight, yer know,' Scully managed to say before sliding from his perch onto the ground.

''E's an absconder,' Tuckerman said, 'and quite proud of the fact that he bashed his overseer for givin' him the cat.' The carpenter spoke of the lash. Joseph Scully, Rowan discovered, was a biscuit maker from Seven Oaks in Kent who had stolen two pounds, five shillings from his employer. 'Seven years, 'e got. The judge told 'im if'n he'd been caught ten year earlier, 'e would 'ave swung by the neck.' The law had been stricter then.

'So, how did he escape?' Rowan asked more from politeness than interest, as he, too, was fighting fatigue. 'I mean, did he abscond after his altercation with this overseer?'

'Nay, 'e got thirty days' solitary confinement and more o' the cat. That be back in '09, like.'

'In Sydney Town?

'No, Van Diemen's Land. Then, only weeks later, 'Obart Town were short o' supplies... meat, like... and Scully, amongst others, were trusted with muskets and dogs and sent into the bushland to shoot kangaroos fer the barracks.'

'Then he escaped?'

'Kept on walkin', 'e did. Straight through the middle o' the island. It were months before Cap'n Leblanc found Scully 'ere, wanderin' blindly in rags on the northern coast near Port Dalrymple. The cap'n, yer see, were there tradin' with the natives. Tradin' huntin' dogs for young women.'

Rowan bid his company farewell and retired to his cot where, as exhausted as he was, he could not sleep. His first challenge was to overcome the claustrophobia brought on by thoughts of his isolation on a small island on a deserted sea where few men had travelled. He had fears that he had been too impulsive when he'd accepted Captain Amos Leblanc's offer at Sydney Town, ten days earlier. But then he reminded himself of his options.

He would work the sealing with these men, earn their trust and accumulate enough wealth to sail on to the Orient. Rowan lay beneath kangaroo skins, trying to push images of Jessica's fate from his thoughts, listening to the hypnotic waves tumbling smooth stones back and forth along the shoreline in an eternal symphony. He finally dozed off into sleep. He woke briefly, rolled over and succumbed to his dreams once more. Jessica was forever on his mind - in his dreams and occasionally in his nightmares. He saw her assassin... the bayonet... heard her screams...

Rowan was aware that dawn approached. The morning was cold and he was pulling the skins to his chin when he felt the gentle hand of a woman on his manhood. Rowan gasped, almost crying out. He sat bolt upright. Somehow, Pollyanna had climbed beneath the skins without disturbing him and lay with him, naked, her hirsute mound of tight black curls inviting him inside. Earlier, at his insistence, she had gone to sleep in the single women's hut for the night. Now, she fondled him in his sleep. He threw back the skins and leapt from the cot. 'P-Pollyanna!'

'Row-an no like Pollyanna?' She was clearly upset. Although it was dark, he could see the pearls of her teeth and the whites of her eyes accentuated against her black skin. Her eyes filled with tears. She sobbed softly.

'It is not that I do not like you, Pollyanna... but... I am a married man.'

'Married man?' Pollyanna repeated the words but did not comprehend.

'I have a wife, Pollyanna.' Rowan sighed. 'I have woman. Well, she has passed, but....'

'Pollyanna know this. She gone to stars, whitefella tell me before.'

'Yes, Pollyanna, and I stay true to her.'

Pollyanna climbed from the cot and stood in the filtered dawn light. As primitive as her culture was, Rowan guessed her to be an intelligent woman who would understand his position and respect it. She stood silent a moment, in contemplation.

Maybe this whitefella would have a change of heart.

Rowan noticed that Pollyanna had a firm and moulded body, quite perfect, really. Suddenly he realised that he, too, was naked and he tore his eyes away, cupping his hands over his manhood. Pollyanna giggled in a suggestion that crossed all cultures.

Rowan's first breakfast on the island was invigorating—damper bread and native red flowers boiled in water and drunk like one would drink China tea. It was also the perfect laxative and Rowan found himself completing his ablutions at the rock pool of the geyser. Satan's Hole was a narrow funnel in the ledge. Over the millennia erosion had created a rock pool, and ankle-deep water flushed into the pool and swept out again, providing a most hygienic latrine. Rowan was impressed. Privacy, however, was something else altogether as the place was communal, without the luxury of partitions. Nonetheless, as Captain Leblanc would say laughingly, 'The view out to sea could not be finer.'

Climbing back down the path to the camp ledge, something in a small jagged rock ravine at high water mark caught Rowan's attention. It took a moment for him to realise it was a cage, no larger than a cubic yard. But what was more disturbing was the native woman imprisoned within, naked to the elements.

No! Surely it cannot be!

Rowan rushed to the cage, a crude, rusting iron bar enclosure. The woman saw Rowan approach and backed away, terrified, but there was nowhere to escape. Rowan knew the tide was coming in and would leave the prisoner in several feet of freezing water. 'Dear God!' He lifted the external catch and threw the door open. 'Come,' Rowan offered his hand. The frightened woman made to crawl free, but stopped as footsteps on the pebbles approached behind Rowan. It was Billy Cake, who ran off, returning immediately with an angry Elihu Riddell.

'What d'ya think yer doin', Sawbones?'

'What on earth is this woman doing in this... in this contraption?'

'That's the trap.' Riddell planted his hands on his hips with undisguised contempt. 'Fa anyone what wrangles the Cap'n.'

'What?'

'You deaf? I said... the trap. Daisy there, well she go an' punch Radge. Punched him good an' proper, she did. Cut 'is lip an' all.'

'Get out,' Rowan told the woman. The aboriginal cowered. He softened his tone. 'Daisy. Come.' He offered his hand once more.

'And what makes yer think yer got the authority to do thart?'

'She's not an animal.'

'Oh, yer think so?' Riddell circled in a wide arc, not too certain how far he should take this confrontation. Daisy stood stooped, as it now pained her to stand upright. She offered Rowan a tense smile, hissed at Riddell and hurried away.

'Firkin' dog!' Riddell spat after the native and turned back to Rowan. 'We'll see what the cap'n's got to say about this.'

'Fine. I'll be telling him personally.'

Captain Amos Leblanc's shanty was deceptive. With two thirds of the structure built under the natural rocky overhang, it was an underground chamber fronted by a wooden façade with a door and a glazed, lead-lined window. Rowan thumped on the door.

'Come,' the captain called.

Rowan stooped beneath the arched entrance, a ship's quarterdeck door, hinged to jams crafted from yardarms. In fact, Rowan was becoming aware that all the structures of Mast Head Bluff were made from salvaged ship timbers, and their variety hinted at more than one vessel. As Rowan's eyes adjusted to the gloom, he was astounded at the ostentatious clutter within the oak-panelled walls. A large dining table made from ship decking took centre stage, but what captured Rowan's attention immediately were the pair of candelabras upon it—solid silver flamingos, Spanish treasures by all appearances. The three-foot-high candleholders were rich in silver plumage, holding half a dozen sconces apiece, their shafts dripping in solidified wax. Even more flambouyant were the tall-backed carved oak chairs each end of the table. But the most astounding piece of furniture was the mahogany four-poster bed Rowan noted in the darkness behind ruby velvet curtains hanging from a brass pelmet.

It was all so surreal.

'Ah, Rowan,' Leblanc greeted Rowan as he stepped bare-chested from behind the curtain, wearing only three-quarter britches. 'How was yer first night's kip on Bull Seal Island?'

'Fine,' Rowan said curtly.

The captain sensed a problem. 'Fine, eh... but?'

'I just released a native woman from a cage, down near the water.'

'You what?' The captain's mood darkened.

'I think you call the medieval contraption "the trap".'

'Aye, and what business is it o' yours to go meddlin'?'

'She is not an animal.'

'I beg ta differ. She's a feisty one, thart Daisy, an needs restrainin' from time to time.'

'You cannot be serious. I forbid you to treat the natives like that.'

'Forbid!' The captain raised his voice. '*You*, forbid *me*! By Jove, man, you have some nerve.'

'She could die of exposure, contract pneumonia...'

'She's a savage, man. She attacked Mr. Radge...'

'For what, may I ask? I dare say the man was mistreating her.'

Leblanc lowered his voice. 'Look, Sawbones.'

'It is Rowan, remember?'

'Rowan.' Leblanc stepped close to Rowan. The two men stood face to face, only inches apart. 'You will do better in my books if'n ya keep ya sanctimonious opinions ta yerself. Yer a hypocrite, man. I'm bettin' yer had a slave or two workin' yer tobacco farms or cotton or whatever yer family done back in America.'

'No, sir. I am all for the abolition of slavery, Captain Leblanc.'

'Abolition—huh! Maybe yer are. All the same, I'm warnin' yer now. Stay outa me affairs an' we'll get along jus' fine. Savvy?'

Rowan did not answer. Obstinately, he held the man's gaze. When two native women stepped from behind the drapes, Leblanc's mood mellowed. They were younger than most of the women in the camp, sixteen or seventeen, Rowan guessed, with supple bodies in good health and with cheerful, carefree giggles. Unlike the other women, these two wore blouses covering their breasts. Leblanc watched Rowan a moment. 'You like native women, Rowan?'

'Ah...' Rowan shifted uncomfortably. 'I would not know. I have had no experience with them.'

'What? Did you not lie with Pollyanna last night?'

Rowan wanted to repeat that he was in love with Jessica and how much he missed his wife, but thought it best left alone at this moment.

Leblanc read his mind. 'I know about your murdered wife. You acquainted me with yer history, don't yer recall? She's a ghost, man.' Rowan flinched at the insensitivity. 'If yer'll take my advice yer'll lay with these native women. They'll help alleviate the pain in that damned heart o' yours.' The captain thought a moment. 'Although, I gotta admit, we are a bit short o' women at the moment.'

'Short!'

'Aye. I hear o' some sealers, them ones near the Tasman Sea around the Furneaux Islands, take up to five wives each.'

'Five.'

'Aye. These women make perfect sealers, so the lads have a code, see, 'an five is the most, so not any one man can 'ave a monopoly on catchin' the skins.' Leblanc outstretched both arms and the older of the two native girls eased a shirt onto his back.

'That is an appalling abuse of the natives. Those men are no better than pirates.'

'Pirates. Aye. Thart they are, lad. An' they swap women like possessions, trade 'em for huntin' dogs or rum.' Leblanc eyed Rowan, waiting for his reaction. He wanted to tell this naïve medicine man that it was he, Captain Amos Leblanc, who personally selected many of the women. They would sail to the north coast of Van Diemen's Land watching for native fires and wait off shore until nightfall. Then they would raid the camps—hit and run—take the young, nubile women and escape, all at gunpoint. If any native tried to stop them, he was shot dead. *Hell!*—Leblanc smiled at his own cunning— *I've even been known to take one of the two- or three-year-old toddlers with me from Bull Seal Island, to use as bait.*

Rowan knew his place, for the moment.

'So, I suggest yer lay with Pollyanna, lad. She be a good wife to yer.' The captain grabbed one of the women by her buttock and pulled her close kissing her on the neck. 'This is my little sweetmeat,' he said, rubbing his body against hers. I named 'er Beatrice, or Queen B fer short.' The other girl flirted shamelessly with Rowan. 'An this'n is Myunga.' Rowan sighed in distaste. 'I find the native women more submissive than their whitefella brethren,' Leblanc said. They're uninhibited by the restraints taught to the whitefella women in the scriptures.'

'For a God-fearing man, you have a double standard, sir,' Rowan said curtly before he had thought it through.

'They're savages. So don't preach to me about God-fearin' ways.'

'They are fellow humans, Captain.'

Leblanc pushed Queen B aside. He stood his ground and snorted. 'Fix some vittles,' he finally ordered the native, 'there's a good lass.' The captain leant toward Rowan once more, fixing an eye on him. 'Look, man,' he said softly, 'I like yer... I liked yer the day I met yer. Yer an honest, hard workin' cove who's been done wrong by the bastard British, but I'm tellin' yer now: stay out o' me firkin' business. I run this 'ere island—me, Captain Amos Leblanc. Do as yer told an' we'll get along jus' fine. Savvy?' Rowan took in a deep breath and nodded ever so slightly. 'Good.' Leblanc slapped Rowan on the back and dragged him close. 'I can see we'll get along.'

With Rowan's anger temporarily subdued, he observed the misplaced luxury all about him. In one corner sat a walnut writing bureau and in another, a stern cabin chart table was stacked with leather-bound books. More newspapers and books sat neatly on a shelf next to the table. Rowan's attention was drawn to one new edition.

'"Swiss Family Robinson",' he read aloud. 'I have heard of this.' Rowan read the inside cover. 'Johann David Wyss. 1812. Have you read this, Captain?'

'Aye, of course. It's a great adventure about a family, the Swiss family called Robinson, who were wrecked aboard an East Indiaman on their voyage to Port Jackson. Yer welcome to read it, Rowan, bein' a learned man an' all.'

Rowan capitulated. 'I would appreciate that. I would also like to use these books to educate the older children, if you will indulge me.'

'Indulge yer? Why o' course, lad. Fill yer boots. The little bastards could use some learnin'.'

'Tell me,'—Rowan placed a hand on a deed box—'was this washed up? I mean, it is in very good condition, if it did.'

'No, lad, I traded that recent like, with another captain in Sydney Cove,' Leblanc answered. But his shifting eyes told another story.

About the room, stacked untidily, were several trunks full of quality clothing, silks, and rugs. Crates of expensive wines in black glass bottles were stacked against one wall. There were barrels of household items, including more crates of bottled pickles recently grown in English gardens, and other preserves, such as jams and jars of potted meats, potted shrimp, bloater and anchovy pastes in attractive china pots advertising the manufacturer on the lids. Hanging from the spar beams holding up the roof were cured hams from Portugal and French cheeses with thick wax skins. Rowan was bewildered. Captain Amos was about to speak when Rowan's attention was drawn to a piano in the shadows, to one side of one room.

'A piano?' Rowan said in a respectful tone.

'Aye. Yer command o' instruments o' leisure astounds me Rowan,' Leblanc said with humour. 'Yes, it's a piano.'

'But here?'

'Why not? And it ain't no ordinary piano one would find in a whorehouse, tis a Stoddard square piano. Best money can buy.'

Rowan admired the rosewood veneer, the ivory and ebony key tops, six delicate reeded legs and matching damper pedal with an engraved silver nameplate on the fallboard. But the instrument was desperately in need of a polish. 'It is beautiful. I was not expecting to see a piano here. Or any of this, for that matter.'

'Six octaves,' Leblanc thought to mention.

'If you do not mind me asking, Captain, where did you come by such magnificent furniture? And... and the... wine and...'—Rowan picked up a porcelain jar with the label *Parfum de Paris*—'and this. It is expensive French perfume.'

'Let's just say it was washed up.'

'Washed up?'

'Aye.' Captain Amos' eye twitched. He scrutinised Rowan. 'You're a naïve lad, ain't yer?'

'Naïve?'

'Aye. We leave for Blubber Beach as soon as I eat some vittles. Grab a flask o' water and yer hat and meet me near Satan's Hole.'

Rowan stepped from Leblanc's well-stocked cabin with a thousand questions. He looked to the seascape once more. The vista was extraordinary, beautiful and untamed. He sucked in a lungful of sea air and looked to the blue sky, which was clear, as the breeze was crisp. Rowan fetched a leather water sack and his tarred boater and sheathed his knife at his hip before walking to Satan's Hole. Uriah Coffin was already waiting, admiring the blades on the new flensing tools made by a blacksmith in Sydney Town.

'Mornin', Sawbones,' Uriah greeted Rowan with a warm smile.

'And a good morning to you, Uriah. It is to be a fine day, I hope.'

'Yer can never predict the weather 'ere on Bass Strait. So how was yer first night on this 'ere rock?'

'Strange, to say the least, but I will adapt.'

'Aye, thart yer will.' The giant Maori looked back towards the dwellings. There was no sign of the captain so he thought this an opportune moment. 'Ah, Sawbones...'

'Please Uriah, it's Rowan. I'm not some ship's barber, you know. I studied medicine at Pennsylvania Hospital.'

'"Rowan", then. I... ah...' he started, but stopped and mulled on his words. 'Look, I like yer, Rowan. I can see yer a good man. Christ knows what yer doin' with all us felons.'

'You know my story. The captain's told you. I am a felon also, although what I did was an eye for an eye.'

'Yer, well, thart's another reason I like yer... you look as though yer can look after yerself.'

'I have seen my share of battles, Uriah,' Rowan answered, not overjoyed by the memories.

'I just wanna say, watch the cap'n. He ain't the preacher kind 'e makes out to be.'

'Oh?'

'Aye. Look, don't get me wrong, like. 'E's a good cap'n, a good man to serve under... jus' don't cross 'im, all's I'm sayin'.' Uriah made certain no one was watching. 'Only a month ago 'e murdered Clive Carter.'

'Murdered!'

'Aye. Clive was a bit of a mouth. Always arguing. I got on all right with 'im, but 'e an' the cap'n fought all the time. Then one mornin' when we was on the water, near Guinea Rock, an argument broke out betwixt the cap'n 'an Clive. Clive pulled a knife on the cap'n an'... well, the cap'n forced the poor bastard onto a rock a yard square, no more. Waves were washin' over it and it was only low tide. Clive couldn't swim, neither, not thart it would'a been any 'elp.'

'Didn't someone intervene?'

'No. 'E kept a brace o' pistols on us. Said 'e'd shoot any man what tried. Mad as a sack o' ferrets, 'e were.'

Rowan had not thought his benefactor capable of such callousness.

'An' if'n yer still not certain, look to Beatrice and Myunga's bare backs. They've tasted the cat, both o' them.'

'You speak of the lash.'

'Aye. 'E keeps a cat made o' the sinews of kangaroo gut. Nasty piece o' work, thart is.'

'That's why those two wear blouses.'

'Yessar.'

'And to think, I thought it was for modesty.'

A disturbance back at the dwellings had both men turn. Leblanc was strapping native women into harnesses in preparation for carting supplies along the cliff edge to Blubber Beach.

'One last word o' Maori wisdom, Rowan.' Uriah dropped his voice.

'Oh?'

'Elihu Smyth an' John Stuart Radge… Neither will ever be yer friend.'

Climbing from Mast Head Bluff, Rowan followed Leblanc along a crumbling path held together by deep-rooted pigface, tussock and ice plant. They marched east for a quarter of a mile, followed by Billy Cake, Gabriel and Uriah Coffin carrying the tools. Eight of the aboriginal women struggled after them, each carrying coils of rope. Others walked with kegs of salt stretchered between them, while still others supervised the hauling of giant glass carboys of vinegar, tethered to the donkey sleds.

'We have four donkeys on the island,' Uriah informed Rowan. 'They're an Irish breed. We had a time of it, gettin' 'em ashore, an' thart's no lie. Kickin' and hee-hawin' like fishwives at the market, they was.'

To their right, the slope climbed steeply four hundred feet to the summit, where a single dead gum tree caught Rowan's attention. He was certain he saw movement at the top of the tree, where a small man-made platform had been built. 'Eagle's Nest, thart be called,' Uriah told Rowan. 'Thart's where we post our lookout.'

'What for? Seals?'

'Not fa seals, man—fa ships.'

'But I thought ships rarely sailed these waters.'

'That's true. But occasionally we see one off in the distance an'...'

'An' we don't encourage visitors.' Leblanc had overheard the conversation. 'But it'll only be a matter of time before this island is on the Admiralty charts.'

Leblanc was first over the rise, where the steep embankment ran down to the sea. 'Ah... there she be,' he said, 'Blubber Beach.' The captain nodded at a cove far below. Rowan stood a moment. The scenery was magnificent, picture perfect, reminding Rowan of the Cornish coast. But Rowan sensed malice about the rugged shoreline.

The group negotiated a goat path down a steep cliff to the working end of the beach, a gloomy pebbled foreshore that rarely attracted sunlight. Here, the stench was nauseating and the cries of circling gulls deafening.

Four women and two men were already at the beach, preparing sealskins. Rowan watched the skilled women remove the larger pieces of fat from inside the hide and wash them in seawater while the others rubbed the salt generously into the skin. The skins were then folded, flesh against flesh and fur against fur, and left at the mouth of a cave where a natural sloping ledge acted as a draining board. Rowan knew from his time with Jessica's father, Silas, that the skins would be left for two days, shaken out, re-salted and then left another five days. Two huge rendering cauldrons boiled on the beach.

'The blubber is rendered,' Leblanc told Rowan, 'in them cauldrons, to get the oil, and then stored in barrels in the cave. Bull seals, mostly, for the oil, and fur seals for their skins. Thirty-five to forty two pound a ton it sells for in London.'

'And the skins?'

'Six and up to fourteen shillin' each.'

'But we trade some, also,' Uriah Coffin said. 'Twelve skins'll get yer a gallon o' rum.'

'Now Sydney Cove's been declared a free port and them East India Company bastards no longer 'ave a monopoly, we trade there every few months,' Leblanc said. 'Before, commodities had a price fixed by the governor; now it's free trade an' 'bout bloody time. We used to trade in Port Dalrymple on Van Diemen, but them bastards were cutthroats—rob yer blind. Aye, Sydney Town be best prices now. You'll be a rich man in a few years, Rowan. Come.' Leblanc walked up the beach. 'See the pickling process. We pickle 'em in the cave yonder.'

While the others joined in the labour, Rowan followed Leblanc into the steeply inclining cave. Once inside, he saw that it opened into a larger cavern. With the recent warmer weather the humidity here was oppressive and the odour worse. 'Here the skins are placed in barrels of vinegar.'

'You are well placed here, Amos.' Rowan was impressed with the industry. It was a well organised enterprise. After a week's pickling, the milky white skins were then shaved of hair, washed in a bath of water and bicarbonate of soda and drained well. Dried, the skins were then oiled on the flesh side, folded once more and left to sweat. Once this process was completed, the hides were worked by hand to stretch them. The completed hides were roped in bundles of ten and transported back to Mast Head Bluff. From there they would to be taken to Sydney Cove for sale.

'And the seals?' Rowan asked. 'Where do you kill your seals?'

'There *were* thousands upon thousands of 'em around the shores o' Bull Seal Island,' Leblanc said. 'Weren't there, Gabriel?'

'Aye. But we killed 'em all and scared off any survivors,' Gabriel said in passing. 'That fact puts off any other wanderin' sealers what may pass by 'ere.'

'Aye. Thar be no doubtin' the pickin's are dwindlin',' Uriah Coffin said. 'Why, you told us yerself, Cap'n, about the Yankee ship what killed fifty sea elephants in one day, what yielded six thousand gallons o' oil.'

'Aye. In '14,' Leblanc confirmed. 'But yer'll never see thart again. So now we take the sloops to the outer islands.'

'Sloops?' Rowan asked.

'Aye, *Queen B* and *Jolly Mary*.'

Rowan had not noticed any other vessels.

'They're kept safe in a bay on the other side of the island, in a cozy cove away from sight of any passin' ship.' Captain Leblanc stood silently a moment as the two men watched the picklers pressing hides into large barrels of acidic brine, using branches of driftwood.

Suddenly the aboriginal women grew excited. They downed tools and gathered together on the beach. Flying low across the ocean towards the island from a northerly direction was the most amazing sight Rowan had ever seen.

'Ha! Well will yer be lookin' at thart?' Leblanc's manner enlivened. 'Mutton birds... millions o' the tasty devils.'

'*Yolla! Yolla!*' the women shouted. As Rowan stood captivated by this natural migration, the first birds flew directly overhead. They were a blunt-tailed bird with a long wingspan and black bills. The stream of birds was fifty yards in depth and three hundred yards or more in breadth. They flew in a tight formation, as close to each other as possible, and Rowan could see no end to the flock. 'That is the most amazing sight...' Rowan muttered, his mouth agape.

'Aye, lad. Amazing. An' I'll tell yer somethin' else. There are so many of 'em it will take an hour or more for them to pass over.'

'No!'

'Oh, yes, Rowan. An' it'll be roasted mutton birds for supper tonight.'

'An' the next night, an' the next,' Uriah Coffin said with a laugh.

'Aye. Now Rowan,' Leblanc started, turning back towards the path, 'I'll take yer to see what I know you're really desirous to be acquainted with.'

The hike to the next headland took the two men nearly an hour. There Rowan took in the breathtaking view as the last of the birds passed over. For as far back as the eye could see, was dark green ocean. Amos Leblanc pointed out a group of lonely islands, specks on the horizon. 'That be where we fetch most of our seals of late -- them tiny islands -- but they're more rocks in the ocean, really. There's colonies of the beggars waitin' for the club or Uriah's harpoon.'

To the south, grey clouds gathered on the horizon. 'Looks like we're in fer some nasty weather, wouldn't yer be agreeing, Rowan?'

'It looks that way.'

'Alrighty, then, follow me.'

They walked in silence another twenty minutes, down through a gully and up over another headland, where below, a quarter of a mile distant, another beach faced west.

'Bone Beach,' Leblanc said, with some satisfaction.

The sandy beach was half a mile long, bleached white from the sun and wind. Here, a malevolent surf thundered ashore, off the open sea.

'Is that what I think it is?' Rowan made out traces of a shipwreck, well up at high-tide level, on the rocks directly below.

'Aye, lad. That's all what remains o' the *Globe*, a merchant out o' Cape o' Good Hope, what run aground 'ere a few years back. An' them ship's bones is why we call this 'ere beach Bone Beach.'

Rowan gazed at the remaining timbers, reminiscent of the skeletal left overs of a beached sperm whale.

'Are you saying that is where your piano came from?'

'Aye, lad. Me piano an' all them other luxurious items what ya seen back at Mast 'Ead.'

'Why, that is incredible.'

'Aye, thart it is. Chock-a-block full o' luxury items what make life a pleasure. What do yer say, Rowan Craige?'

'What happened to the passengers... and the crew?'

'Dead, lad,' Amos said in the blink of an eye. 'All of 'em. Not one survived. The ship wrecked on thart reef yonder.' Amos flicked a casual finger at submerged rocks that jutted out from the shoreline and into deep water. 'Razor sharp, them rocks, an' hidden just below the surface. They all drowned. Terrible sight it were... bodies washed up on the beach. Thirty-two o' them. There would 'ave been more, but thart's all we found. We buried 'em, of course.' Leblanc looked suitably contemplative. 'There, see, above the high-tide mark. Yer can see the cairns we piled up where we buried 'em in groups o' four or five. God rest their souls.'

Rowan's sharp eye made out several rock cairns along the beach. 'Not one survivor?'

'No, lad.'

Rowan was tormented by the thought. So many dead, right here on this beach. He could not help think of the mooncussers in America, or the wreckers, as they were called in Cornwall. Rowan had read reports in English newspapers and even in the *The Gentleman's Magazine* from London—available at book merchants in Baltimore—about coastal communities building bonfires during storms or setting lanterns ashore near headlands, to lure distressed ships onto the reefs. The ships would tear apart on the rocks, spilling cargo and passengers into the turbulent waters. Then the wreckers stormed the beaches, armed with pick axes, crowbars, hatchets and ropes. Survivors who managed to struggle ashore were deliberately drowned in the shallows or bludgeoned to death. Bodies were then stripped naked for their clothes and rifled for valuables.

The horizon appeared closer as the dark clouds rolled with menace towards Bull Seal Island. 'I'm thinkin' we should return to Mast 'Ead an' batten down hatches. That's a big storm brewin'. Captain Amos Leblanc turned to make his way back down into the gully, the way they had come, when a speck of white caught his eye well out at sea.

'Jesus Lord! Is thart what I think it is? Is thart a sail or is it the devil playin' tricks with me tired old eyes?'

Rowan followed the captain's eye. There was no mistaking it—across the white water of breaking waves, well on the horizon, he could make out the faint sails of what seemed a large ship.

'I didn't bring me spyglass, God damn it,' Leblanc cursed, 'but it's a ship, all right, and it looks like she's chasing the winds before that storm.'

The two men hurried back along the ocean track as the winds picked up and the air dampened with a fine spray from the ten-foot waves now exploding on the rocks a hundred feet below. 'See how the weather turns, Rowan,' Amos yelled over the wind. 'This is the Bass Strait yer will get to know lad, one moment a trusting friend and the next moment a spawned lover.' Leblanc took a final glance at the ship before pushing on along the cliff edge. 'Mariners call passing through the Strait "threadin' the needle",' he said. 'Now yer can see why.'

Dark-skinned, eight-year-old Tommy ran to meet the two men as they passed level with the Eagle's Nest. 'Sail ahoy, Cap'n.'

'Yes, Tommy, we seen the sail. There's a squall up 'er arse as well, boy.'

'Aye, Cap'n'—the tyke wiped snot onto his dark, weathered arm and his keen eyes dashed once more to the horizon—'there's a squall up 'er arse, all right,' Tommy repeated with an infectious grin. 'An' I'm thinkin' it'll blow the bastard to New Zealand... or maybe she'll run aground 'ere, sar.'

'Now I'll 'ave none o' thart talk, young Tommy.' Leblanc frowned at the lad, but the captain's sly wink did not go unnoticed by Rowan. 'Now get your arse back up in the nest.' Amos watched Tommy run back up the mountain slope, running barefoot on gravel and prickly weeds as if they were polished floor boards. 'His daddy is Gabriel, the Negro. Gabriel is a well-travelled harpooner and teaches the boy good... geography and the like. The little bugger can read, too.'

'And his mother?'

'Napangka. She's a fiery bitch what looks after the hounds. They're a good match, them two, her and Gabriel.'

The squall washed over the white sail on the horizon and swept by Bull Seal Island, dumping fresh water on the roofs of the huts at Mast Head Bluff. By the time they returned to the campsite the weather had cleared, but the water barrels were overflowing. Amos fetched his spyglass and searched the horizon. Nothing. The ship was nowhere to be seen. Rowan watched Amos study the skyline. There was something disturbing about the man that Rowan could not figure. And Bone Beach? The laden wreck with no survivors seemed a little too convenient, and Rowan made a decision—at the first opportunity he would investigate the beach unescorted.

Rowan left Amos alone with his thoughts and returned to his hut, only to find the simpleton, Billy Cake, rummaging through his medical chest.

'Billy! What, may I ask, are you up to?'

Billy flipped his head about looking as guilty as a scullery maid with her purse full of the family crested silver. 'Rowan, sar,'—his usually cheeky face was guilty and flushed—'you back early.'

'Yes, well, there is a squall coming.'

'A squall!' Billy said excitedly. 'Billy must go.' Billy made to push by Rowan.

'Not so quickly, Billy. What were you doing in my medicine chest?'

'I wasn't... was I? Oh, aye... I... ah... have a toothache Rowan, sar, an' thought you might have a medicine for it.'

'Fine, but do not touch anything in that chest. Do you understand?' Billy stood, head bowed and his bottom lip curled. 'Do you understand, Billy?' Billy's eyes filled with tears. 'Lord save us, man, do not get upset.'

'Billy have tooth ache. Billy want medicine.'

'Which tooth?'

Billy opened his mouth and Rowan could see the culprit immediately. A right molar was yellow and rotting and Billy's foul breath hit the surgeon in a miasmic mist. Pollyanna heard voices and entered the hut.

'Good timing, Pollyanna. I will need your assistance.'

Pollyanna grinned happily, keen to assist.

'This tooth will have to come out.'

'No, Doctor! Billy seen William French get tooth pulled. He scream like madman.'

'It is all right, Billy. I am trained in modern practises and have clove oil to numb the area first.'

Billy shook his head violently. 'No. No!'

'Then go about your business with an aching tooth.'

Billy looked petrified, thought a moment, and capitulated.

'Good. Now lie on my bed.' Billy did as he was ordered. Rowan first poured clove oil onto the corner of a handkerchief and rubbed the gum area around the tooth.

'Pain gone, Rowan, sar.' Billy smiled nervously and sat up. 'Billy go now.'

'No, Billy. That is temporary. The tooth must come out.' Rowan looked at Pollyanna. 'Hold his shoulders, please, firmly, now.'

The dental key was a fine and modern dental tool made of polished steel. It had an adjustable claw at one end of its shaft, designed to grasp the diseased tooth. As the instrument was rotated, the tooth loosened from the jaw. Occasionally Rowan had broken a tooth, fractured a jaw or damaged bone and gums, but this fact was best kept to himself.

Billy looked terrified, and the fact that he was a mongoloid made Rowan anxious. 'Think of nice things, Billy.' Rowan knelt on the bed, one knee either side of his patient. 'Open wide—wide, Billy—really wide.' Billy's lips trembled.

Slowly his mouth opened. 'Wider, man. That's better.' Rowan adjusted the clamp head around the tooth to be extracted. Billy's mouth pooled with saliva and the simpleton rambled incoherently. 'Nice things, Billy, think of nice things.' Rowan nodded to Pollyanna and she pinned Billy's shoulders firmly. Rowan twisted the clamp, pulled hard and the tooth came free from the swollen gum in a gush of blood. 'All done. Pollyanna, fetch Billy some rum. Billy, go spit. Rinse your mouth in sea water then drink a cup of rum.'

'Billy good now?' Billy sat upright, bloodied drool dribbling down his shirtfront.

'You'll be fine. Here, take this handkerchief and rub your gum with more clove oil until the hurt goes away. You will have some discomfort for the next day or so.'

'Billy good now.'

'And Billy...'

'Aye, Rowan, sar.'

'If the pain is too much I can give you some laudanum.'

'Billy like laudanum. Billy had laudanum before.'

Rowan's dreams of Jessica persisted. Often they were of an intimate nature, dreams of making love by a lonely river off Chesapeake Bay in midsummer or love snatched between snug woollen blankets in their Baltimore lodgings as snow gathered by the window panes—but each dream always ended in agony. The colour would drain from Rowan's visions and an evil darkness would envelop him, waking him in a lather of sweat and gasping for air.

Days turned to weeks and the weeks soon tallied a month. Indeed the red thick meat of the mutton-bird—named so for they were fatty like mutton—were a frequent staple on the menu. But Pollyanna knew of Rowan's love for foods from the sea and managed to vary his diet with oysters and other shellfish he had never seen before, like a large, black lipped mollusc she tenderised with a rock, and another clawed species similar to the American lobster.

Rowan spent as much time as he could muster reading books with the older children. Gabriel and Napangka's eight-year-old Tommy and nine-year-old Luuk were the fastest learners. Luuk was a Dutch sailor's contribution to the population, before he had jumped the *Sea Rat* in Sydney Town. Two other boys, Koa, five, and seven-year-old Jiemba, enjoyed arithmetic and geography, and the little girls, Kirra, Merri and Lenah, were eager to learn reading and writing.

But it was Rowan's skills as a medical man that were sorely needed and most appreciated. His knowledge was put to the test daily, from treating sufferers of effluvium to the flux—an inflammation of the intestines—and pleurisy and fever. Rowan's first challenge was a bout of influenza. He immediately isolated his patients—two aboriginal women, Lowanna and Myunga, along with Myunga's four-year-old son Herman and Leblanc's second mate, Skeffington Lutwidge. Rowan prepared a mixture of liquor of acetate of ammonia, sweet spirits of nitre, sugar, vinegar of squills—an extract from a lily bulb—and, finally, syrup of poppies and water. The strict isolation kept the fever from spreading and by all accounts, the four grew healthy once more.

Pollyanna showed more and more interest in whitefella magic and she proved herself a fast learner. Rowan explained the contents of his medicine chest. 'This one is meadowsweet.'

Pollyanna held the fine glass jar with its glass stopper and paper label. 'Meadow... sweet,' she recited.

'Very good. For reducing fever. This one here...'—he exchanged jars—'this one is like a tea drink, made from motherwort, for calming nerves.' Rowan explained that baking soda was for digestion, honey for insect bites, apple pectin mixed with its juice for arthritis, and a tablet to cure headaches was made from the bark of the willow tree.'

Kolangka, the native woman shared by Ned Talbot and John Stuart Radge, came to Rowan for whitefella magic. She suffered from irritability, insomnia, fainting and fluid retention. Rowan diagnosed 'female hysteria' or the vapours.

'The cause is unknown,' Rowan told Pollyanna who translated to Kolangka for him. 'Although academics in Philadelphia have suggested it is caused by the retention of female semen, which they believe mingles with male semen during intercourse.'

'You make Kolangka more better?'

'Explain to her that she needs a water massage of the genitalia.' Pollyanna looked none the wiser. 'Her woman's parts, Pollyanna.' And Rowan pointed to his own business. 'And make her drink some motherwort tea.'

But Rowan was no fool. He had no doubts about his position on Bull Seal Island. He was their medical saviour, yes, but a prisoner nonetheless, an outsider. Captain Amos Leblanc had given him sanctuary from the law, but at what cost? His own freedom?

Each morning, Rowan watched the men sail on the sloops *Jolly Mary* and *Queen B,* to the many tiny islands that dotted the strait. There they clubbed and harpooned the seals in their ocean colonies, finally returning to Blubber Beach, where the pelts were prepared. They worked hard and drank harder, and for this reason the treatment of the native women was abominable. The women were no better off than the Negro slaves back in America. Captain Amos Leblanc, however, treated Queen B with some civility. Rowan sensed he even had affection for the attractive aboriginal; he had, after all, name her Queen B and named a sloop after her.

Myunga, who at sixteen was younger than Queen B, seemed content to live with Captain Leblanc as wife number two. Captain Leblanc informed Rowan that the two were both from the same tribe, the Van Diemen's Land North-east Tribe. They had been traded for hunting dogs. Most of the others had been kidnapped from the Northern tribe and the North-western tribe—some had been as young as ten years of age when captured—and had grown to womanhood accepting the ways of the whitefella.

Rowan tackled Leblanc on the subject of polygamy. "You say you believe in the scriptures, yet you live with two women.'

'Rowan, Rowan,' Leblanc answered, feigning shock, 'have you not read the Bible?'

'No, but I am familiar with its message.'

'Then you must understand that in the Old Testament God encouraged man to take more than one wife.'

'How is that?'

'Women who could not find a husband became concubines. It was God's will.'

Rowan wanted to tell the man that it was now the 19th century and these were modern times, not ancient.

Aside from treating ailments, Rowan found he had plenty of time to enjoy reading Leblanc's books, as well as teaching the children. He was desperate for any distraction, for as each day passed he felt more alone, a prisoner on Bull Seal Island, surrounded by an unpredictable ocean, like the Swiss family Robinson in Johann Wyss's book.

Chapter Eighteen

Cape Town. On board the *Magdalena*,
Moored in Table Bay

Once a Dutch colony, Cape Town was now in the possession of the British due to the Anglo-Dutch Treaty of 1814.

The turgescent clouds over the Cape reflected the warm colours of a dying afternoon sun as Elizabeth, enjoying a certain freedom on the *Magdalena*'s main deck, watched the ship's longboat return. On board was Third Mate Garre Skelton, returning to the ship after his sojourn ashore. Elizabeth stole a glance at conspirators Sally Fetter, Fawn Lytle and Eleanor Green, whose attentions were also drawn to the longboat. The three women huddled together unpegging dry bedding from the rigging. The female prisoners had been fortunate enough to wash their laundry in fresh water for the first time in over a month, and now the balmy breezes had dried the clothing in a short time. Garre Skelton, carrying his swag, scaled the rope ladder and climbed on deck through the port gate amongst a dozen other sailors.

Elizabeth's gaze remained subtly fixed on the ship's mate. In passing, Garre Skelton gave a sly nod to Sally Fetter. Sally acknowledged it with the hint of a smile. Elizabeth understood clearly that the copying of the ship's armoury key had been a success.

Late that evening, possibly after midnight, Elizabeth watched and waited, feigning sleep amongst the many cots of snoring women. The prisoners slept comfortably for a change, their bellies content from gorging on fresh fruit and vegetables, with rations of fresh meat. After hours of fighting fatigue, Elizabeth was finally rewarded with movement nearby. Sally Fetter's dark shape, barely distinguishable except for her silhouetted feminine form, felt its way to the bulkhead, lost in blackness. There followed the faintest knocking—three short and sharp, two slow. The loosened planks were removed and a smear of light from a black, cloth-covered lantern framed the entrance. An exchange was made, soft whispers traded and then the two conspirators returned to their respective quarters, where Elizabeth immediately recognised Eleanor Green's northern accent.

'Got it?' Eleanor whispered, too clearly for Sally Fetter's liking. An unintelligible curse was exchanged.

Fawn Lytle, lying on the other side of Eleanor Green, stirred awake. 'What did he give it to *you* for, any'ow?'

'Cos 'e fears 'e might be double-crossed. Tis safer with me.'

'But if'n you get caught with it, you'll swing from the yard arm, Sally Fetter.'

'Shut it,' Elizabeth heard Sally Fetter spit in a low voice. 'Shut it, both o' yer. Now go ta firkin' sleep.'

Elizabeth dared not move. Of those in her cot of six, she was the closest to the conspirators' bed. She would wait for first light—wait for the first chance she had to confirm the key and report to the ship's captain.

It proved to be three anxious days before Elizabeth had the opportunity to rifle through Sally Fetter's bedding. Nothing. Her small wooden box of personal belongings was near empty: a love token on a leather strap, a small tortoiseshell locket with a hinged lid and a lock of brown hair, three well-used clay pipes and an empty tobacco pouch, but no key.

Each day, the urgency to set sail for the eight-week journey from the cape to Port Jackson grew stronger. A distance of six thousand miles, Elizabeth had heard the sailors say. It was the last and longest leg of the voyage across the Indian Ocean, and the captain was keen to catch the trade winds known as the Roaring Forties, which blew between latitudes forty and fifty degrees.

But the weeks dragged by. Table Mountain, Devil's Peak and Lion's Head all became familiar landmarks, as did the Castle of Good Hope, a pentagon-shaped fortress built by the Dutch East India Company to protect Cape Town, with its symmetrical streets of neat, flat-roofed dwellings all in good order. Eventually, the worst of the scurvy victims, convalescing in the township, were brought back on board. Shore parties, under the watchful eye of Stanley Ruthers, the purser, scoured the markets for livestock such as hogs and chickens, while the ship's carpenter and his mates built extra pens on deck. Finally, the water barrels were refreshed and fresh fruit and vegetables shipped on board.

It was time to sail.

Bull Seal Island

It was a dull afternoon and rain threatened. Rowan guessed it was about mid-week, but he wasn't quite certain why. Usually, the only way to gauge the day of the week was when the Sabbath occurred; however, Captain Leblanc had a tendency to preach whenever he felt the *family* needed scriptures.

On this day the camp was nearly empty. Two native women tended to their young and Billy Cake was about somewhere, preparing the evening's communal meal. The two hounds watched Rowan with some interest, but soon tired and remained curled, half asleep, under the bark roof of their shelter. Rowan found Myunga squatting outside the captain's shanty repairing nets. Myunga looked up at Rowan blankly. She had given up flirting with the newcomer some time ago.

'I—come—for—books,' Rowan articulated, before he remembered that the woman could not speak his language. 'Captain—say—borrow—books.' Rowan mimed the opening of a book with the palms of his hands hinged. Nothing. Myunga pursed her lips and continued with her needlework. Rowan pointed to the door of Leblanc's shanty, opened it a bit and made a sign that he wished to enter the captain's hut, where he knew Myunga also resided.

'Queen B?' he asked, pointing at the door.

'Queen B,' Myunga repeated, and then shook her head. This she understood. Queen B was clearly at sea, sealing with the others.

'Book.' Myunga appeared to finally recognise the word.

'Yes, book.'

Myunga waved her hand at the door and nodded, muttering in her native tongue, and continued with the nets. Feeling uncomfortable, Rowan entered, but Leblanc had given him permission to borrow books whenever it took his fancy. He found *Gulliver's Travels* neatly wedged between the works of Shakespeare and other leather-bound novels. Thinking that the children would love this story, he slipped Jonathon Swift's novel free by its spine, causing a bundle of

Sydney Town Gazette newspapers to fall to the floor. He was about to replace them on the shelf when a shipping article caught his attention.

'Missing, assumed lost at sea. *The Globe*, merchant out of Cape Town with thirty-eight crew and ten passengers with all their worldly possessions and a cargo of flour, cotton, livestock and household amenities, bound for the merchant stores of Sydney Cove. Believed lost in Bass Strait.'

Rowan read the date: 'March, 1811.' The article had been circled in graphite pencil. He unfolded others and felt numb...

'The barque *La Marianne* from Marseilles, headed for Sydney Cove with twelve passengers, eighteen crew and a cargo of tar, potash, deerskins, cotton, liquorice-ball and Florence oil. It was also thought to be carrying two thousand pounds in gold, twenty-franc coins.' This article was also circled. Rowan knew that *The Globe* had wrecked on this island, and that Leblanc had never notified the authorities when in Sydney Town. Rowan felt sickened. Suddenly he feared for his life. He filed the gazettes vertically back in position, praying they were exactly as he'd found them, and left smartly with *Gulliver's Travels* tucked under his arm.

The following morning the skies were clear and peacock blue. Rowan watched from Satan's Hole as a healthy breeze billowed the mainsails of the *Jolly Mary* and *Queen B*, and the sloops left the sanctuary of their hidden cove for the open sea. The sealers were sailing early this day and had left in good spirits.

Rowan wasted not a moment. He hiked off along the cliff path. Knowing Eagle's Nest was not manned when the sloops were on the hunt, Rowan headed north-west, hurrying by Blubber Beach, down through the gorge and along the cliff edges overlooking Bone Beach. There he scaled the dangerous, crumbling gravel slopes that would take him to the summit and then down to the southern coast. From the mountaintop, Rowan saw the entire island for the first time. He guessed he was three or four hundred feet above sea level. The view was spectacular, but his mood darkened.

Was he ever to be free of this godforsaken island?

As he descended the southern slopes, the wind picked up. Overhead, Pacific gulls mewled and swooped, following the intruder in never-ending circles. Since much of the island's coastland was comprised of rocky vertical cliffs, it was a slow trek. Rowan had made out three other bays with crescent-shaped beaches, all smaller, to the north and west. The first was pristine, barren and bleak in the shade. Rowan hefted his collar up against the chill in the wind and crossed several acres of barren mountainside, so steep in places Rowan feared that if he should slip on the pebbly surface, he would continue sliding on his britches until he vanished over the precipice to the sea, a hundred feet below.

By mid-afternoon Rowan had managed to descend to the cliff's edges by bay number three. He imagined he was some three miles from completing his coastal excursion. Having no way of ascertaining the safety of the ground beneath him, he lay on his belly and crawled to the cliff's edge. He peered over the precipice, sucking in a sharp breath. There, at the base of this vertical drop, were the remains of a ship destroyed by fire. Little remained except charred timbers, but there was no mistaking the two-masted skeleton of a barque.

'*La Marianne*,' Rowan expelled in a whisper, 'it has to be *La Marianne*.'

It was getting late. There would be no time to confirm his suspicions. The sloops would be well and truly returning to Blubber Beach by now. Rowan had successfully hiked the entire coastline and was approaching Mast Head Bluff from the northeast when he made his final discovery: the mooring place of the sloops *Jolly Mary* and *Queen B.* The natural cove was horseshoe-shaped and had a narrow entrance, narrower than that of the Seal Bay's headland, and would be impossible to see from out on the ocean. To confirm his discovery, Rowan noted two empty barrels floating mid-bay —the sloops' moorings. And tied to one of the moorings was a small tender.

Indian Ocean. One week's sail from Cape Town.

Ten days had passed since leaving Cape Town. The *Magdalena* sailed further and deeper into the Indian Ocean, deeper into the unknown waters of one of the planet's vastest seas. Dusk loomed early this day. Dark clouds on the eastern horizon challenged the mettle of the lonely ship, its anxious passengers and crew. There was no turning back.

Captain Winston Cholmondeley did not need to study the barometer in his cabin for long. The three-foot-long mahogany instrument swayed on its wall-mounted gimbal. The mercury was low. Very low. A storm was imminent.

Cholmondeley took solace in the fact he had God on his side. He tapped the prayer book in the pocket of his oilskins and felt courage in its company. The Book of Common Prayer gave him confidence. He stepped out onto the quarterdeck where his first mate, Robert Knight, stood by the helmsman. The two men were trying to share a pipe, but increasing winds prevented them from maintaining a spark. The captain raised his voice in greeting, over the wind. 'Mr. Knight.'

'Afternoon, Cap'n.'

'Bowen,' the captain acknowledged the helmsman, his voice drowned by the boom of a wave detonating beneath the hull. The helmsman, known only as Bowen, stood with feet planted firmly, wide apart. He returned the acknowledgement with the pinched brow of a nervous sailor.

'It don't look good, Cap'n,' Knight said. Instantly, like a salute from old Neptune himself, sheet lightning flashed the full length of the black curtain prowling along the horizon.

'Jayzu....' The helmsman made to curse in the Lord's name but checked his blaspheming before his God-fearing captain. 'Devil's blood, Cap'n, we're sailing right into 'er an' night's on its way.'

'That we are, Bowen, that we are.' Cholmondeley faced the first mate. 'Mr. Knight.'

'Sar.'

'My guess is we have two hours. Make preparations, if you please. See that the prisoners are fed and locked below. See that the crew eat a hearty meal before the galley fires are doused. Keep an eye on that storm and reduce sail as you see fit, fore and main top gallants only.'

'Aye, sar.'

Captain Cholmondeley had great faith in his first mate. He locked eyes with the man and leant closer. 'It is going to be a long night, Robert,' he said solemnly.

The captain had once, in his early twenties, been a junior officer aboard an East Indiaman, and he'd made three voyages from England to Madras. It was on an August night in 1782, a night not dissimilar to this night, that his ship, the *Grosvenor*, wrecked on the South African coast, north of the Umzimvubu River, only a few days' sail from the *Magdalena's* present position. Captain Cholmondeley's older brother, also on board, had drowned that night. Out of one hundred and fifty souls on board, only eighteen had survived; they'd walked to Cape Town, 400 miles south. Now Robert Knight watched the captain bow low under the lintel leading back to his stern cabin and considered the man's parting words.

Bull Seal Island

As the weeks passed, Pollyanna's behavior toward Rowan became motherly rather than desirous. She devoted herself to him, understanding his pain and accepting his celibacy, as it had become clear that they would never be intimate. Daily, Pollyanna and Rowan grew closer. Despite their cultural differences, Rowan found Pollyanna to be an intelligent soul with a hunger to learn, especially to understand the ways of the whitefella outside the mentality of a sealer's camp. Under Leblanc's orders a separate cot was built by carpenter Henry Tuckerman for Pollyanna. She was to remain with Rowan—essentially as a spy. But Rowan was no fool, and, besides, he enjoyed the native's company. She was a good cook, and he taught her about his medicines. When surgery was required, on fine days it was conducted on his porch, and in bad weather he tended to his patients in his humble shanty, under the light of seal-oil lamps, which burnt brightly and were, thankfully, smokeless.

All in all, the small community was a healthy one. Lean kangaroo and goat were the staples, but there were other game meats and barrels of salted pork and salted beef as back-ups. When the short-tailed mutton-birds flew to their burrows around March, they were caught by hand, preserved with smoke, and hung in a special cage, making a pleasant alternative. The aboriginal women also gathered plants and succulents that Rowan realised held the precious vitamins needed to combat scurvy. But what Rowan loved to eat most were the fish and shellfish the women collected from off the rocks. He watched them tirelessly, fascinated. The women created tightly woven baskets from island plant fibres and wore them around their necks as they dived for oysters and mussels. The men folk, for their part, taught the women how to fish with line, musket ball sinkers and hooks, using shreds of cloth to attract the fish to the bait.

Rowan had remained aloof from the beatings the men gave to the native women. It was a common occurrence, as if it were a right for the men to take such liberties. Usually it was no more than a slap. The women never complained. Besides, he had his own safety to consider. But when Myaree came to him with a deep stab wound in her right arm, Rowan could turn a blind eye no more.

Her man, John Stuart Radge, was a Jack Tar, a veteran of the Royal Navy who had been press-ganged in a Plymouth waterside inn when he was nineteen. He'd survived Trafalgar in '05 as a gunner on board the 98-gun ship of the line *Neptune*. Wounded by splintered timber, he'd been put ashore at Gibraltar, where he'd convalesced and then deserted. He had witnessed a gun deck awash with blood. He had seen good mates blown asunder by cannon balls. And for what? The glory of England, a country that had turned its back on him. John Stuart Radge was a stubborn bastard. He would not take no for an answer. He was determined, ambitious and ruthless, and at six feet tall he was lean and toughened—a hard fighting man.

'What did Myaree do to deserve this?' Rowan asked Pollyanna, who stood by translating, curious as to why Rowan cared about the daily abuses the women suffered.

'Myaree, she say no to Radge. The man rough. He want to sex her like dog. Bad man.'

As the sun dipped towards the ocean in the west Rowan waited on the shore of Blubber Beach for the sloops to return. They were late this day. But the sloops arrived soon enough, sailing with a good tail wind. They rode the surf and sailed up onto the beach, reminding Rowan of pictures of Viking raiders he had seen in schoolbooks. The women joined the men, unloading the gutted seals and carting them above the high-tide mark.

Rowan called John Stuart Radge aside. 'Radge, we need to talk.'

'About what?' Radge was instantly defensive, guessing what the sawbones wanted.

'Myaree. You took a knife to the woman, and she is cut deep.'

'So?'

'So I cannot... I will not stand by and watch these native women be abused so.'

'Firk you, Sawbones. The bitch deserved it.'

'Because you tried to rape her?'

'Get outta my face.'

'No man has the right to stab a woman.'

'Why? Do you want her?' the thug crowed loudly for all his mates to hear. 'Is that what this is all about?' Radge made to walk away but Rowan would have none of it. He grabbed the man's arm, restraining him. Radge stopped cold. He looked down at Rowan's hand clenched tightly about his arm. 'I'd be movin' that hand if'n I was you, Sawbones.'

Uriah Coffin stepped between the two men. He had heard everything. 'You'll be settlin' this like we settle all disputes on this 'ere island.'

'Fight!' Billy Cake cheered. 'Fight! Fight! Fight!'

'Shirts off, lads, bare knuckles only. No weapons. Last man standin' is the victor.'

Rowan had suspected it would come to this. He was no stranger to bare-knuckle boxing; he had excelled at the sport at the Philadelphia College. He accepted the challenge. But Rowan hadn't even lifted his shirt above his head when he was felled blind by a right hook. The others gathered about in a cheering circle.

1814

Uriah Coffin leant over Rowan who threw his shirt aside and clambered groggily back to his feet. 'Sorry, Rowan,' the Maori said. 'There ain't no rules, neither.'

'No rules, no rules,' Billy Cake chanted. Captain Leblanc started a book to select the winner. 'Two guineas on Radge!' someone screamed out.

'A crown on Sawbones.'

Rowan assumed a boxer's stance, left foot before the right, knees bent, both fists balled and in position to defend his face and body. The second blow felt harder than the first. It glanced off Rowan's cheek but stung like a wasp.

Radge grinned.

He'd managed two punches. Overconfident, smug, he glanced at his mates. Rowan struck out—a lightning blow, smashing his opponent on the chin. Radge cursed, but instantly retaliated with four swift, ambidextrous blows. They all connected. Rowan faltered and nearly fell. *Stay on your feet, man!* he heard his Philadelphia instructor yell. *Stay on your feet!*

Rowan threw a well-aimed punch, but Radge sidestepped and Rowan's fist sizzled by Radge's cheek. It was time to fight dirty. Radge snatched Rowan's ear and, pulling his head downward, he elbow-punched Rowan in the face. Rowan felt his nose bleed. He could taste his own blood.

'A pound on Radge!' someone yelled over the cheering.

Radge's hand darted forward, catching Rowan in a *fishhook*, two fingers in the corner of Rowan's mouth. He pulled to tear the skin, but Rowan jerked his head and bit down, forcing Radge to release his hold.

So you like to play dirty... Rowan leapt forward, slamming the heel of his hand into his opponent's forehead. Radge's head snapped backwards and Rowan pounded his knuckles into Radge's throat. The man groaned in pain and dropped to his knees, gasping for air, his windpipe injured. Radge's head tipped forward and Rowan brought his knee up hard and fast, connecting with the man's nose. There followed a sickening crack and John Stuart Radge fell headfirst, unconscious, into a bed of kelp.

'Huzzah for Sawbones!' Billy Cake shouted.

Huzzah, huzzah, huzzah.

Chapter Nineteen

1815. Hobart Town,
population less than 5,000.

The prisoners were positioned along the deck, poked and prodded like cattle into straight lines by overseers from ashore, themselves ex-convicts with no compassion and a taste for authority. This was the first the disgraced sergeant Marcus Marriot and his fellow transportees had seen of Hobart Town. The town, with a population of around five thousand, looked orderly and neat enough. Beyond the township of lazy, smoky fires a large mountain dominated the landscape. Marcus had been told it was named after the great general Arthur Wellesley, the First Duke of Wellington.

Marcus stole a last look over his shoulder at the emptying hold, where he had been imprisoned the past 137 days, since sailing from Portsmouth. Van Diemen's Land might be a prison island, but anything would be better than life on board the barque *Indefatigable,* particularly under the captaincy of the iron-fisted Captain Alex Jack.

After standing on deck for three hours, they were herded down the gangplank and onto the Hobart Town dock, where blacksmiths waited with hammer and anvil to replace their shackles.

'"Old wives" some coves calls 'em,' the blacksmith cackled in good humour as he fettered Marcus. These ankle irons, known as basils, were connected with a short chain to prevent the wearer's bolting for the bushland. The more troublesome convicts were given even shorter chains, causing them to shuffle. They were then paraded before the muster master, Jacob Fletcher, an unpleasant old man with a surly and officious nature not aided by the grief his rotting teeth were causing his aching gums. Fletcher recorded the height, eye colour, hair colour and any anomalies—like warts, tattoos, birthmarks or moles—of each prisoner. They were now the property of Van Diemen's Land.

The ten-pound irons shackled to Marcus's ankles were painful enough, but the real suffering was to his pride—the humiliation as he was paraded along the wharf before the citizens of Hobart Town. The prisoners were marched less than half a mile from the Hunter Island wharves, up a wide street named after the governor, Lieutenant Governor Thomas Davey, and past government house to Murray Street, where the Hobart Jail awaited. The recently completed jail consisted of a small group of two-storey buildings surrounding an inner courtyard. A 20-foot-high brick wall guarded these buildings.

Marcus hobbled with novice difficulty in his new irons as he and the other prisoners were marched single-file up stone steps and through narrow, fifteen-foot-high iron doors. They passed through the turnkey's rooms and were assembled in the yard. Surrounding them, preventing all chance of escape, were the buildings of the judicial system of Great Britain: the guardhouses, wards, solitary cells, cookhouse, workshops, dining mess and lavatories.

1814

Here the men were made to strip naked and were given new slops—a prisoner's uniform of jacket, trousers, striped grey shirt, boots and a leather cap. The broad arrow symbol of the British Empire inked on the garments only added to their shame. These yellow and grey uniforms, the warders boasted, were of recent design, and were intended to humiliate the wearer by suggesting that he resembled a court jester.

Marcus failed to see the humour.

He was angry, and his anger festered.

Five thousand miles west of Hobart Town

Into the teeth of the tempest on the Indian Ocean...

The first squall slammed the *Magdalena's* starboard bow like skirmishing dragoons attacking the enemy's right flank. First Mate Robert Knight twisted to see the helmsman struggling with the wheel. 'Keep her steady, Bowen, steady into the waves!' Knight was nearly hoarse, shouting orders over the howling wind. 'The bitch has arrived!' he yelled, almost respectfully. He could tell that Bowen was tiring and should soon be relieved of duty.

But now this ... this bitch of a storm.

It would take two at the helm. He said nothing but gripped the wheel handles with all his strength and offered up a silent prayer. Darkness had already fallen on the *Magdalena* and the best the ship could do now was to steer into the waves on a nor'-east heading.

The men in the rigging worked frantically to shorten sail, for the threat of losing a mast was a reality, while diluted screams from the prisoners cast an eerie pall of uncertainty over the ship. Waves exploded over the deck, pouring through the hatches and down hawser holes, soaking the prisoners and their bedding and making the experience of the storm below deck as miserable as it was frightening for the crew on deck.

Third Mate Garre Skelton let the hatch slam behind him and stepped from the companionway amidships into pandemonium. The mutiny would have to wait. Facing east, he clamped the guide ropes, finding his footing as the bow rose on the white water of a mountainous wave. The *Magdalena* crested over the rise and raced down the other side. The ocean detonated beneath the keel. A shredded wave exploded across the deck while the bowsprit lanced deep into the next deluge of the raging, unforgiving sea.

There was no moon. The sky was black, and the only warning of the next wave was the luminescent white water atop the vertex of turbulence rushing at the ship.

Garre Skelton strained to see through the needling rain. He focussed on the main sail topgallant. It had shredded and was whipping in tatters. There would be no cutting it free -- not now, not until the storm eased, and that could be days away.

'We're shippin' a lot o' water below,' the third mate shouted at Knight as he climbed the quarterdeck.

'Lord help us, Mr. Skelton.'

'Lord help us, oright. I got two gangs on the pumps, but we'll need more.'

Without warning, they felt the ship go airborne. A brief unnatural steadiness. The men instinctively braced for impact. Instantly, the ship pounded the water, vibrating all the timbers. The raging seas washed up both port and starboard sides as *Magdalena* settled back into the water. The great Indian Ocean rolled across the decks from both sides, well above the helm. Knight and Bowen gripped the wheel as the retreating ocean dragged their legs from under them.

'Hold tight!' Knight screamed, but Skelton was less fortunate. Already unsteady on his feet, the withdrawing waist-deep water dragged him bodily, like a log on a rapid. Skelton slipped. He smashed his forehead into the stern gunwale, and darkness engulfed him.

In this state, Skelton had little chance of survival. Knight snatched a guide rope and pulled himself towards the man, but Skelton was swept over the stern rail and into the blackness of the vast and angry sea.

Bull Seal Island

Rowan was held in high esteem in the days that followed his defeat of Radge on Blubber Beach. He had proven his mettle, stood up for what he believed was right. Captain Leblanc also had a new respect for Rowan. He afforded him trust, and Rowan played on the man's approbation, demanding that the punishment trap be abandoned. To Rowan's surprise, Leblanc had the medieval contraption hauled away.

Rowan's opportunity to inspect Bone Beach finally arose, in the form of a full moon that illuminated the island in a whisper of soft light. He crept to the door of his hut and looked up. The moon was at its zenith—midnight or thereabouts. Rowan dressed quietly as Pollyanna snored loudly. He had grown fond of the aboriginal woman -- she was intelligent and dedicated. She was also the target of lustful advances by the sealers, so he and Pollyanna had made a pact—they would pose as intimate lovers. After the fight with Radge, the other men ignored Pollyanna; she was Sawbones's woman. And the sanctimonious hypocrites, Captain Amos Leblanc in particular, approved. ' 'Tis God's will,' he bellowed aloud, with a belly full of rum. 'God's will, I say. Tis not 'ealthy for a man's humours, not to lie with a woman.'

Rowan waited until he was certain it was safe and crept silently from his hut.   The dogs were sleeping off the kangaroo bones and seal offal that Rowan had fed them, along with a tincture of opium. He backed against the cliff face and waited, listening. Satan's Hole gushed and hissed. The pebbles under the arch tumbled rhythmically to the symphony of endless waves. All was peaceful on Bull Seal Island. Rowan pushed off. Suddenly a hand gripped his arm...

'Row-an. What you do?' It was Pollyanna. She stood before him, naked as the day she was born.

'Pollyanna! Go back to sleep.'

'Where you go Row-an?'

'I... ah... Pollyanna, there is something I must do.'

'Do?'

'Yes. I will be back before the sun rises.'

'Pollyanna come with Rowan...'

'No! No, Pollyanna. Go back to sleep. Say nothing to anyone. You understand?'

Pollyanna stood undecided a moment, and retreated to their shanty, as Rowan dissolved into the night.

The ocean off the north coast was a millpond -- not a breath of wind rippled its surface. Now familiar with the cliff track, Rowan jogged with confidence, pleased with his stamina. He had grown athletic and lean; the sea air on this island of plenty was serving him well.

At Bone Beach Rowan drove a driftwood shaft into the sand next to the first cairn. He hooked a small brass lantern on its branch, lighting it from a hemp fire created with flint and steel in a tinderbox. He looked back into the night. He could just make out the outline of the few remaining ship ribs, three hundred yards distant; the sound of the waves crashing in off the sea was comforting.

1814

Rowan dropped to his knees and dug with his hands. As he suspected, the shallow, sandy grave at Bone Beach was easy digging and it was not long before he exposed the first skeletal remains. It had been nearly three years since the ship had wrecked on the reef and nature had cleansed the putrid flesh, leaving leathery tissue under what little clothing remained. The first head was exposed—the head of a seaman, Rowan surmised. The skull stared back at him from its shallow grave, its jaw unhinged, with empty eye sockets wide, in a macabre plea for justice. Rowan worked swiftly, in silence. He exposed another three men in the same grave. They all appeared to have been stripped of most of their garments. However, Rowan reasoned, this could have been the work of the sea. Bodies washed ashore from storms were commonly stripped naked by Mother Nature. Clothing was also a valuable commodity to any island community and clearly of no worth to the dead.

Nonetheless, the scene was abhorrent. With a silent prayer Rowan was about to cover his tracks when he noticed something disturbing. One skeleton had had his finger severed; clearly this had been done to obtain a valuable ring. On closer inspection, the mouth of another was stuffed with the remains of a man's shirt. He had been choked to death.

An owl hooted. Rowan sat up. As far as he knew, there were no owls on Bull Seal Island.

Suddenly, he heard the snapping of twigs underfoot. Rowan wheeled about as a large figure stepped from the shadows -- Billy Cake!

Billy Cake stepped into the tight circle of light. He repeated the hoot of an owl. 'Rowan like looking at dead people?' he said dryly, peering into the grave with interest.

'B-Billy!'

'Why Rowan dig up dead people? Why Rowan at Bone Beach at night time when everyone sleeps? Why, Rowan, why?'

'Billy, I...'

'You make ghosts angry. Dead people don't like you digging here...'

'Billy, I just wanted to see how they died.'

'They drowned, Rowan.' Billy swung an arm around to the ship remains. 'Their ship, it smash on rocks. You know this. Cap'n Leblanc tell you already.' Billy grew more upset. Rowan hastily reburied the skeletons and went to him.

'Billy, I am a doctor. It is my duty to investigate such accidents.'

'Cap'n not be happy, Rowan diggin' here.'

Rowan took Billy by the shoulders. 'Billy. I need you to keep this a secret. No one else needs to know. Just you and me, all right? Our special secret.'

'Billy want laudanum.'

'But your toothache is better now.'

'Billy want laudanum.'

'Billy, laudanum is not good for you to have all the time. You will become addicted.'

'Billy want laudanum!' he shouted. 'Or I tell Cap'n you here at night time.'

Rowan sighed in resignation. 'All right, I will give you laudanum.' The simpleton's hooded eyes widened in victory. 'But not every day, Billy. You hear me? Not every day.'

'Come,' Billy clamped onto Rowan's arm. 'We get Billy laudanum now.'

Against Rowan's better judgement, he fed Billy Cake small doses of the opiate, weakened with the alcohol spirit ethanol, distilled from sugar fermentation and mixed with Madeira wine. It was sweet enough and potent enough without causing the full addiction of straight laudanum. Billy was happy, but Rowan agonised over the situation and prepared himself for questioning about his night on Bone Beach.

Some days later, Rowan awoke to loud voices outside his hut. Captain Leblanc was animated but cheerfully so. Pollyanna followed the captain inside. 'Yer awake, lad? If'n not, then wakey-wakey.' He poked Rowan with his whalebone swagger.

'What brings you to my cabin so early, Captain?'

'Get up. Up, up, up. Pollyanna's cookin' yer a big breakfast; splash some cold water on that dial o' yours, avail yourself at Satan's Hole and come with us.'

'Sealing?'

'Aye.' Leblanc towered over Rowan's cot, ebullient with haste. 'Yer been askin' the lads for particulars fer weeks now —where do we go, are they hard to slay, don't they dive into the ocean as we approach? Now yer can find out fa yerself. Up yer get, lad. Outta that cosy cot o' yours and yer comin' with us.'

A six-foot swell, in from the Indian Ocean, rolled beneath the keel. For Rowan it was invigorating to be back on the water. The two craft had a healthy tailwind, forcing their bows to dip into deep troughs, exploding in hissing spray, bow to stern. Rowan stood by Captain Leblanc at the helm of the sloop *Queen B*, while Cornelius Riddell helmed the *Jolly Mary* riding alongside, a hundred yards to port. Pollyanna and Beatrice sat together at the bow, honing the blades on fileting knives.

The mood on both vessels was cheerful enough. The harpooners kept busy, filing an edge onto their irons, the Negro Gabriel riding on the *Jolly Mary* and Uriah Coffin with his menacing geometric face tattoos on the *Queen B*. The other men were armed with clubs, vicious cudgels of hard wood with knots on their ends. Some men had fastened nails onto the knots. Joseph Scully noticed Rowan admiring his club, a bulbous-ended, naturally formed weapon with the root ball carved decoratively at one end. 'It's from the islands of Fiji,' he told Rowan. 'I traded a pair of boots for it. It's called a *Ula* war club.'

Captain Amos gave up trying to light his pipe in the wind and joined Rowan. 'I'm mighty pleased yer give Radge that beltin', lad,' he said of the beach fight. 'He's been takin' out his anger on all the women o' late, 'cepting, o' course, Queen B—'e wouldn't dare touch her.'

Rowan felt humbled. 'I was lucky, that's all. The fight could easily have gone the other way.'

'Luck, my arse. You know yer moves. He fought dirty an' yer knew how to settle it. Ya done good, lad. The bastard needed putting back in his box.' The captain tipped his head toward the southwest. 'There, lad.' Rowan looked off the starboard bow where a mile distant three rocky outcrops soared vertically, hundreds of feet above the seabed. 'Money Rock, The Guinea and The Bank o' England.'

'Is that what they're named?'

'Aye,' Leblanc laughed. 'Named by me and the lads. There's seals aplenty on them rocks and gold to be had, and the little devils aren't scared of us just yet, not completely, anyhow.'

'They're easy to kill, you say?'

'Aye. Trusting buggers.'

The uninhabitable rocks in the middle of the ocean had been perfect for seals, until the sealers discovered them. Some rock faces had wide ledges where the mammals bred their colonies.

'Thar she be, Rowan,' Leblanc said, as the sloop's sails were reefed. '"Bank o' England" we call this 'ere rock.' As they approached, the smell was horrendous. Some of the younger seals dived from the ledge and swam out to the boats, playfully diving beneath the hulls. They reminded Rowan of puppies with their pretty, cheeky faces.

Rowan had experience with the fur trade. He had assisted Silas, back in Baltimore, with the trade in pelts, but this kill would be a massacre, and nothing had prepared him for the carnage he would witness this day. The two sloops pulled alongside the rock-ledge shelf that was level with their decks. Gabriel and Uriah Coffin, with harpoons in hand, were the first to leap onto the natural platform. The women followed, ten in all. They stripped naked—Beatrice, Myunga and Pollyanna included—and washed themselves down in rock pools. Leblanc caught Rowan's attention.

'They're washin' the stink of humanity from their bodies,' the captain told Rowan. 'Them seals 'ave poor eyesight, but they can smell good.'

From where Rowan watched, he could see scars on Beatrice and Myunga's backs. They were subtle, but visible none the less. Then he noticed that the playful puppies had moved on. 'Where are the seals?'

'On the lee o' this rock. There's a whole colony waiting. They are lazy bastards and like nothin' more than to bask in the sun. If they knew we were here, they'd be off.'

The harpooners and the women, armed with long narrow clubs, stooped low and crept around the ledges to the seals on the other side. 'Come,' said Leblanc. 'This'll be an education for yer, Doctor Rowan.'

Rowan followed Leblanc to a covered position where they could observe the sealers at work. Uriah and Gabriel held back, harpoons at the ready, but it was the women that Rowan was fascinated to watch. They slid along the rock, imitating the seals. If a nearby seal craned its head and scratched itself with its flipper, the women mimicked it. 'The fat ones are the more convincin' to the seals,' Leblanc whispered to Rowan, referring to the native women.

Slowly the women inched forward, pushing their clubs before them. Four of them, Rowan noticed, were spread out along the water's edge. 'It's their job to separate them seals from an escape to the sea,' Leblanc told Rowan. 'Ideally, they herd 'em inland, where they can't see the water, but later, if'n there's no sharks about, they'll swim amongst the herd and rip their guts open with knives as the seals swim overhead.' These words brought a black-hearted smile to the man's lips. 'Watch, lad... watch now.'

When the women, who were coordinating their movements, were within clubbing range, they jumped to their feet, smashing the closest seal on the nose. If fate was kind, the seal would die instantly. The result was mass panic.

'Watch 'em, watch 'em!' yelled Leblanc now, waving his arms. He was animated, excited, enthralled by the kill. 'Them women'll get two seals apiece before the others take off.'

And he was right. Eight seals lay dead with their heads split open before the others realised what had happened. There followed a crush of confusion. The women at the shoreline clubbed any seals that headed their way. The others, in a cacophony of panicked barking, made for higher ground, where they became disorientated and were easy game for the harpooners.

Rowan was sickened. Leblanc laughed, a manic laugh fed by greed. And Rowan now realised he was witnessing the true Captain Amos Leblanc.

It was over in minutes. The dead and wounded lay in great pools of their own blood. Rowan watched the native women work on the pelts. The dead animal was flipped onto its back and the fins and tail restrained with rope. The seal was then sliced from under the chin, the full length of the body, to the tail. The skin was boned carefully off the ribs and the innards discarded before the backbone was removed. Once the animal was skinned, the pelt was slit with two cuts at one end where it could be threaded with rope and dragged to the sloops, as the pelts were also heavy with fat.

'Bull seals in the boats first. Come on, lads, yer know the drill. Bull seals first.' Leblanc turned to Rowan, trying to maintain a brave face. 'Them bull seals 'ave the most oil, see.' The captain pierced the tough skin of a large female with sharpened hooks and dragged the animal towards the sloops, where it slid easily in all the blood. Rowan was obliged to help. 'One seal yields five gallons o' oil, Rowan,' Leblanc said, as he dumped the carcass near the *Queen B* and rubbed his itchy nose, unaware that he bloodied his face. He caught his breath and watched the others for a moment. 'How many?' he asked Uriah.

'Forty-three, Cap'n, maybe a few more.' Uriah and Gabriel rolled a large bull seal carcass across the gangplank that had been prepared for the purpose.

'Them skins are worth up to fourteen shillin' each if'n I sell to a ship goin' to China,' Leblanc said. 'An' we'll take as many as we can carry back to Blubber Beach to extract the oil. Thart's another four shillin' a gallon.'

'What of the seals you can't load?' Rowan asked.

'Birds 'll eat 'em if'n the fish don't.'

All about the island the survivors, some wounded, thrashed about in a pathetic effort to find their young. Many pups, Rowan discovered later, died senselessly or were left to die, their mothers already taken. Some pups were dragged to high ground, where their mothers would come after them, only to be slaughtered. It was carnage on an industrial scale.

The sea around the ledge ran red with blood. For Rowan it was sickening, yet captivating at the same time. It was life, and now it was a part of his life. He looked on, bewildered at the speed of the men, and of the seals, and the chaos of the kill. He had been party to sea battles under the command of Joshua Barney and was accustomed to death and blood, but the plight of these helpless creatures disturbed him. Then he saw the first fin, the fin of one of the oceans most feared creatures. White death. A monstrous shark also found in the cooler waters off New England. Rowan had read that many grow beyond twenty feet, their jaws filled with three hundred teeth in many rows that could tear a man to shreds.

'Fearful monsters.' Captain Leblanc watched alongside Rowan as one huge shark glided effortlessly beneath the *Queen B* to take an injured female.

'They are indeed, Captain.'

'Deadly creatures... but thart's nature fer yer.'

With the seal colony on The Bank of England having been massacred, the *Jolly Mary* led the sail around the island to the lee side, a half mile distant, where another unsuspecting colony awaited on a separate rock. '"The Golden Guinea" we call this one, or "Guinea" fer short.' Leblanc was proud of the names he had bestowed upon these uninhabitable landmarks. Here, too, the cliffs soared hundreds of feet vertically from the seabed, and scores of gulls circled and dived in a feasting frenzy.

'Ahoy! Sail, Cap'n!' Edward Caleb yelled through cupped hands from the stern of the *Jolly Mary*.

Leblanc turned an ear toward Caleb. 'Did he say "sail"?'

'Aye, Cap'n.' Artilleryman Ned Talbot stood at the bow next to a one-pound swivel gun bolted to the gunwale. 'Shall I load, sar?'

'Aye. Just in case they're unfriendly.'

'What is she?' Leblanc called to Talbot.

'Three-master. She's at anchor.'

'Who would you expect to see here?' Rowan asked the captain.

'Dunno. A whaler, I'm hopin', since she be a three-master. There ain't no sealer in the strait with anything that size.'

1814

The Bull Seal sloops completed rounding the headland and the three-masted barque slipped into view. Immediately, on board the anchored ship, the starboard deck filled with crew, anxious to identify the two fast approaching sloops. Captain Leblanc cast an eye over the men; some were armed. He floated his spyglass over the stern nameplate. 'The *Eden* out of Sydney Town,' he muttered. 'A whaler.'

'Ahoy there,' a voice spilt from a speaking horn addressing the sealers on their approach. 'Identify yourselves, if'n yer please.'

'Captain Leblanc of the *Sea Rat* aboard our sealing sloops, *Queen B* and *Jolly Mary,* good sir. Permission to approach.'

With formalities and assurances exchanged, Captain Leblanc, Rowan and First Mate Elihu Smyth boarded the *Eden.*

'Cap'n Ryan O'May, lads.' The *Eden's* captain grinned warily, tipping back his head to study Leblanc through a pince-nez wedged on the bridge of his bulbous nose. The fiftyish Irishman was short, barely over five feet, but he had brawn on his side along with pluck, and he ruled the *Eden* with a firm hand. He brushed his shoulder-length grey hair aside with a mittened hand. 'Sorry about the welcomin' party,' O'May said, as his crewmembers re-sheathed knives and stowed a blunderbuss back in the arms locker, 'but yer can't be too careful in these waters.'

'Aye,' Leblanc agreed 'an' that yer can't.'

O'May, still wary, ran a keen eye over the sloops, their decks awash with fresh blood while native women trimmed fat from the pelts. The Bull Seal Islanders stood along the gunwales gripping the ratlines and studying the *Eden,* which they now realised was a crippled and vulnerable whaler.

'Sealers, huh?'

'Aye. An' you, sir, seem to 'ave a wee problem.' Leblanc watched the *Eden's* carpenter being lowered in a boatswain's chair off the stern with timber and tools to repair the rudder.

'Aye. We was hit by a damned squall out o' nowheres,' O'May said. 'We seen the gust approach but completely miscalculated its strength. It struck the ship three points off the weather quarter as the helmsman 'ere was putting her away to run before it.'

'Aye,' the helmsman nodded keenly, standing beside his captain with giant hands planted firmly on his hips.

'Within seconds, the ship rolled, with her yards almost in the water,' O'May said. 'Yards in the water, I tell yer.'

'Scared the shite out o' all aboard,' the helmsman groaned.

'But thankfully *Eden* soon came to the wind and righted. The squall roared down on us with repetitive thunderclaps directly overhead and stabs of lightning. Real fierce it were. But, fortunately for us, the violence was served up to us in the immediate gusts and soon dissipated—but not before it stove two of our boats, tore the roof off the galley and twisted the rudder.'

'Now, thart were bad luck, gentlemen,' Leblanc said. The lad on watch in Eagle's Nest on Bull Seal Island had warned Leblanc of the dark sky the afternoon before. That was one reason they had delayed sealing by a day. Leblanc fondled his rosary beads in view of all present like it was a confirmation of his devotion. 'But it sounds ter me like you can thank the dear Lord for deliverance to safe anchorage, Captain O'May. Eh?'

'Aye.' Captain O'May studied Leblanc a moment. Sealers in the strait were gaining a bad reputation. Many, he knew, were convict absconders, or 'bolters', as they were called by the authorities. Others were soldiers who had deserted or criminals evading the law. And they had been suspected of kidnapping native women and other piratical behaviour. O'May was also aware of an inquiry that was afoot in Sydney Town. An inquiry by Governor Macquarie into mooncussing, or the possibility of wreckers living amongst the barren unchartered islands. These were men who baited ships in bad weather by placing false lights on the rocks and beaches to cause shipwrecks. Then there was the problem of over culling the seal population.

'So, where is your base, Captain Leblanc?' O'May asked, eyeing Leblanc's rosary with suspicion. Leblanc sensed that the man offered the inquiry as a casual question, but noted that O'May avoided eye contact. There was something Leblanc did not trust about him. 'I mean, you mentioned your ship, was it the *Sea Rat?*' O'May continued.

'We 'ave a camp on the coast o' Van Diemen's Land,' Leblanc answered with equal cunning. 'Thart's where the *Sea Rat's* anchored sometimes. We use these 'ere sloops for speed, yer see.'

'Oh.'

'Aye. We co-'abit with the natives of the Northern tribe. We supply wallaby meat, seal meat an' hunting dogs and the men offer us the use of their women,' he lied.

'Oh, like Port Dalrymple?' O'May fished clumsily.

'Near there. Further west.'

'You find the Van Diemen natives amicable, Captain?'

'Aye, I do.'

'And the women, Captain?' O'May shot a lascivious glance at the topless women in the sloop and unwittingly smacked his lips. 'Yer find them amicable, taboot?'

'If'n yer mean do we share hammocks with 'em, Cap'n O'May, well, yes, we do. Black or white, we are all God's creatures.'

'God's creatures... Aye... quite. Yer a God-fearin' man, then?'

'Aye.' Leblanc swung his rosary and it hooked about his wrist. 'An' you, sir?'

'I respect our Good Lord, Captain, but I must confess the Sabbath has no importance to me.'

Leblanc had had enough. *This Cap'n O'May was a sneaky bastard and the sooner he could put a deep sea betwixt 'em the better.* 'Well, you tell thart to the Good Lord when yer see 'im at the Pearly Gates. Either thart or tell it ter Davy Jones. Now we ain't got time to stand 'ere chinwaggin' all day,' Leblanc said with a disparaging smirk. 'Good luck with yer vessel and yer whales an' good day to yer, sir.'

'Yes indeed.' O'May followed Leblanc, Smyth and Rowan to the Jacob's ladder dangling on the starboard side to the *Queen B*.

'Shove off, if'n yer please,' Captain Leblanc ordered Billy Cake, who had been pacing the deck with his captain away. Billy pushed away with an oar, and a jib sail was hauled up the line to capture enough breeze for the *Queen B* to re-join the *Jolly Mary* riding the swell two hundred yards away.

'I don't trust that bastard,' Leblanc said with his back to the *Eden* and well out of earshot. 'Don't trust 'im as deep as 'e would sink in a duck pond with a cannon chained 'round his friggin' neck.'

'I agree.'

'Aye. He'll be runnin' back to Sydney Cove with his report to the gov'nor, quick as a flash.'

'You told 'im about the *Sea Rat,* Cap'n?' Elihu Smyth said. 'Why'd yer do that?'

Leblanc was not one to be questioned. 'I didn't want 'im thinkin' we camped near, on account of us bein' in sloops.' Smyth didn't look convinced. 'An' mind yer manners, boy. Don't question the captain or I'll cut yer tongue out.'

'Maybe we should go back and do somethin', Cap'n.' Uriah Coffin ran a thumb gently over his harpoon head.

'Like what? Sink 'em? Kill 'em? We ain't pirates, Uriah. Jesus, man.'

'Then may I suggest something, Captain?' Rowan said.

'Fill yer boots, lad. Fire away. I'm all ears.'

'You need a defence,' Rowan warned bluntly.

'A defence? What like a fortress?' Leblanc scoffed.

'No...' Rowan chose his words carefully. 'Look, what you have created the past ten years...'

'Goin' on eleven now.'

'Eleven years, is unique. Mast Head Bluff is sheer genius. The whole island is cleverly camouflaged. No passing ship would give the island a second look, unless they saw smoke, and you have that covered with your round-the-clock lookout —it is brilliant.'

'So, why the defence?' Leblanc stroked his chin.

'One day... one day, I am certain, a ship will come calling. And God help us if it's the Royal Navy. You need some... how do I explain...? Ah... traps of some kind.'

'Like man traps?'

'Not exactly,' Rowan said, 'but a defence mechanism backed by training to defend against an attack.'

'An attack against the Royal Navy. Don't be daft.'

'Royal Navy, rival sealers, whalers—someone... You *will* get caught up with eventually.'

'But the Royal Navy?'

'Yes. You need to outsmart them.' Rowan was speaking from the heart. His thoughts were of the British redcoats— their arrogance, their bastardry, their ambition for supremacy over weaker nations. 'You need fortifications, traps to stall them and an evacuation... escape plan.'

Leblanc looked at Rowan a long moment, seriously studying the man. He looked over at Queen B, of whom he had grown fond, and thought of all he had created on Bull Seal Island.

'Yer said yer were with the Chesapeake Flotilla,' Leblanc finally said as their sloop cut alongside the *Jolly Mary*. 'I read of this in the London Gazette also. An' yer told me yer were in Washington when the British torched it?'

'Yes.'

Captain Leblanc broke into a positive chuckle. 'Then you shall be in charge of our defences, Doctor Rowan Craige, man of many talents. Come up with a plan an' together we'll —what did yer say?—*fortify* Bull Seal Island.' Immediately the toil of sealing demanded Leblanc's attention.

'Mr. Riddell, sir!' Leblanc called to the *Jolly Mary* helmsman.

'Aye.'

'Head ter The Guinea Rock—we've five hours o' good light left to us yet.'

'Aye.'

Rowan watched as their tillers turned and the afternoon breeze filled their jibs. The swell had eased somewhat, but clouds gathered before the sun, the sky had turned a dark ash and the sea about them an ominous grey.

On the lee and north sides of Guinea Rock, as the seal colony sanctuary had been named, the waters were reasonably calm. Only the eternal undulating swell off the Indian Ocean that rolled through Bass Strait slapped against the rock ledges, breaking into a million shards of white water before rolling back into the sea. Leblanc scanned the horizon with a trained eye. He was acutely aware of weather changes for the worse in Bass Strait.

The seals in the colony on the northern ledges were enjoying what little remained of the sporadic sun, unaware of the danger landing nearby. Leblanc pulled his scarf about his nose against the stink and looked to the sky. More heavy rain clouds had gathered, casting gloomy shadows across both rock and water. The sea turned from turquoise blue to deep green. Uriah Coffin, Gabriel and two sailors, with ropes about their waists, were the first onto the ledge. They pulled the sloops in bow to ledge, to allow the others to disembark with their clubs, knives, harpoons and ropes. Rowan was last ashore, jumping the four-foot gap to the landing only to slip on the sea moss on the wet ledge.

Gabriel clamped his shoulder. 'Be careful, mon, or yer go swimmin'.'

Rowan took a deep breath and watched the two helmsmen drift off shore and anchor against the changing tide. Guinea Rock was as bleak and as barren an outcrop as one would ever wish to walk upon—a jagged, pillar-shaped granite mass rising from the dark and menacing ocean.

Sickened once again by the slaughter, Rowan made the decision not to return on any more hunts. But feeling awkwardly obliged, he assisted the women in dragging the pelts from the colony back to the sloops. There the pelts were bundled on board in rope ties of seven in number, seven being the maximum weight to carry since the skins weighed an average of twenty to thirty pounds a piece.

'They are heavier than I thought,' Rowan said, making polite conversation with Queen B as the young native woman dragged a stack to the water's edge.

'You no like kill,' Queen B answered in fair English while she waited for Elihu Smyth to drift the bow of the *Jolly Mary* close to the sheer ledge.

'The kill? No.' Rowan was going to say something about being a doctor and the Hippocratic oath but realised how stupid that would sound to the mind of a Tasmanian aboriginal. For one thing, they were seals, not humans, and besides, how could he explain the meaning of 'Hippocratic'?

'Cap'n Amos say God put all creatures on earth for the use of all mans.'

'Do you believe in God, Beatrice?'

'Whitefella god good. Amos read Beatrice Bible at night time.'

'Well I'm happy for you...'

Beatrice slipped. Without warning, she expelled a sharp squeal and slid barefoot off the sea moss, plunging eight feet into the chilling sea.

'Beatrice!" Rowan cried out.

Beatrice surfaced, thrashing amongst the bloodied skins that had fallen with her. She gasped and coughed in the freezing dark waters. But blood seeped from a wound on her head. She struggled to stay afloat. Unconsciousness overwhelmed her...

'Shark!' someone screamed. Rowan wheeled about to the terrifying sight of a number of fins offshore. With so much slaughter about them, several sharks had gathered. The dorsal fin of the closest slid silently below the surface. It swam under the stern. Beatrice sank towards the seabed a hundred feet below. Rowan did not hesitate. He dived, slicing neatly into the sea between the sloop's bow and the rock face. Beatrice's head tipped backwards underwater. Her eyes opened, wide with fear.

But still she sank.

Rowan struck out, kicking with his feet, pushing himself harder and deeper: one fathom, one and a half...

He caught Beatrice under the shoulders, twisted his back to the rock face and kicked his feet hard for the surface. The shark swam the length of the sloop. Underwater visibility was clear for a hundred feet, but cloudy above from seal blood. Rowan struggled with the injured native. She had slumped, once more, into unconsciousness

Rowan broke the surface, snatching mouthfuls of air. He felt the shark slam against him, crushing him against the rock face, its head inches away, jaws wide, exposing terrifying teeth. Rowan saw its white belly pass by. He heard the jaws gnash around the bundle of skins. Its giant tail thrashed, throwing Rowan and Beatrice against the cliff. The shark shook its head violently, severing the skins, shredding them like parchment. At that moment, arms reached down from the sloop. Beatrice rose from the water, pulled free by several men. Rowan had never known such terror. He was slammed hard, choking on water, his gargled cries lost amidst the boiling seas. Sensing its mistake the shark turned in a tight circle and lunged at Rowan.

Rowan saw his life flash before him. He froze as the shark turned on its side, jaws wide, its eyes closed for the attack. Suddenly, frantic hands heaved him upwards. He rose up out of the water and the great white shark cruised beneath him...

Rowan was thrown carelessly to the deck by the very hands that had saved him. Everyone was in shock. Plucked from the jaws of death with inches to spare, Rowan felt his heart race. He tried to gather himself. Exhilaration surged through his veins. He wanted to scream 'huzzah!' but the faces staring down at him were distressed. No one cheered. Rowan raised himself on one elbow and turned about.

Beatrice!

She lay on the deck, bleeding profusely from a savage bite. Flesh was missing from her upper thigh and abdomen, with a portion of her bowel exposed. She was wide-eyed, dying peacefully in a puddle of her own blood. Pollyanna knelt by her side, distraught but silent. There was nothing anyone could do.

'Beatrice! Beatrice!' Leblanc was helped on board. He dropped to his knees, taking her hand and crying her name over and over. 'Do something!' Leblanc screamed at Rowan. 'For Chris' sake, do something!'

Rowan stood groggily. Beatrice's wounds were fatal. He had seen similar devastation from cannon ball injuries at sea. There was nothing he could do. Leblanc's terrified eyes strayed from Rowan back to his woman. Beatrice's eyes hooded over, her lifeblood pumped from her main arteries and onto the deck, pooling around her. Rowan felt useless—beyond useless. There was nothing anyone could do to save the woman from such a horrific wound.

The Bull Seal Islanders knew that also.

Beatrice expelled her last breath. Her head tipped to one side. Leblanc fell upon her, crying like a child. Rowan finally knelt next to the dead native and closed her eyes.

'Get away!' Leblanc shouted. 'Don't touch her!' he shouted, weeping.

Rowan felt powerful hands lift him back to his feet. It was Uriah Coffin. But the tattooed face of the warlike Maori reflected only compassion. Rowan's shirt had been ripped from him and he'd suffered abrasions from the sandpaper skin of the shark.

'Come,' the harpooner said quietly. 'She's gone. There was naught you could do. There was naught anyone could do.' Thrashing in the water drew the attention of those nearby ,as the shark contented itself with the bloodied skins floating on the surface. 'Yer did good, matey,' the Maori said. 'Yer a brave man for a sawbones.'

'Bastard!' Leblanc's sorrow turned to revenge. 'Bastard!' He leapt to his feet, wrenching the harpoon from Uriah's grip, and, raising the weapon over his head, he heaved it with all his strength at the frenzied shark. The iron spear pierced the surface, missing the great fish by inches before sinking to the seabed, hundreds of feet below. Sensing its own danger, the shark swam away.

'Bastard,' Leblanc said again, yet softly. He was drained of all energy.

The sail back to Bull Seal Island was a sombre affair. Pollyanna found a stretch of canvas and placed it over

Rowan's shoulders. She sat close to him to share her warmth. No one said a word. Captain Amos Leblanc slumped at the stern sheets, slipping into a dark mood, sobbing periodically, cursing the next, before uttering silent prayers over the canvas-covered body at his feet.

CHAPTER TWENTY

Sydney Cove

The governor of New South Wales, Major General Lachlan Macquarie, admired the portrait of himself hanging on his office wall. It was his favourite, amongst a few. It was also Mrs. Macquarie's most treasured portrait of her husband, painted by John Opie about eight years earlier. The general cut a fine figure in his military uniform with its red coat and gold braid. He had been in his late thirties when it had been done, and although he would turn forty-seven soon, he was still a handsome, lean-faced rooster, he thought: straight-backed, with the coiffure of a Roman orator, a subtle, knowing smile and large, dark, intelligent eyes.

Yes, intelligent, Macquarie reminded himself. This was another reason that this half Scottish, half Belgian sea captain of the barquentine *Sea Rat*—Leblanc, he believed the man called himself—would not slip through the fingers of Governor Macquarie of His Majesty's colonies in Australasia.

A sharp knock snatched the governor from his reverie and Mr. Bent, Macquarie's elderly head clerk, pushed the door open on a creaking hinge, another legacy of the infernal humidity of Britain's new territory.

'Captain Ryan O'May, of the whaler *Eden*, has arrived, sir,' Bent articulated in a slow drawl.

'Send him through, Joseph.'

Captain Ryan O'May shuffled into the governor's office and sniffed the air. Unbeknownst to him, it was Mrs. Macquarie's perfume he detected. The governor detected the essence of an unwashed body. He was not wrong. O'May was a seafarer who had little desire to waste precious silver on bathing and bottled fragrances.

'Yer Honour, 'ow nice it is to be makin' yer acquaintance at last,' O'May declared. The fifty-something captain—it was difficult to ascertain his age, what with his long, grey hair and matching, hirsute side burns—offered Macquarie a mittened hand. The governor exchanged niceties with the man and wished he had not, as the hand-knitted mitten felt waxy with grease.

'Please take a seat, sir,' Macquarie said.

O'May leant his whalebone and baleen walking stick, with its carved white bone handle of a Negro man's head—a souvenir from his less salubrious days as a captain on a slaver—against the cedar desk. He bent slightly to flick the swallowtails of his frock coat up his back and fell heavily into the horsehair upholstery of the office armchair. This action created a waft of body odours better left undiscussed in polite company. Lachlan Macquarie shuddered, pinching his lips. The governor then leant back in his own chair, positioning his torso at an angle to take advantage of the open window and its beneficial breezes.

'You wrote in your recent correspondence of a Captain Leblanc, Captain O'May,' the governor began.

'Aye. An' I have reason to believe the gentleman to be a scoundrel, Yer Honour—a mooncussing pirate and a wrecker, no less.' Captain O'May went on to recall his meeting with the sealers in Bass Strait. "E told me, Yer Honour, that 'e shared a camp with natives, West o' Port Dalrymple, 'e said, on Van Diemen Land's northern coast.'

'But you are of the opinion he fabricates this story?'

'Aye, sar. I got the strongest o' suspicions 'e an' his band o' ruffians was camped, permanent-like, on one o' Bass Strait's many unchartered rocks 'n islands.'

'And what gave you this intuition?'

'Twas the sniggerin' of 'is crew, Yer Honour. They was humoured by his dialogue, as if they knew the man was horse-shittin' me... if'n you'll forgive me language, sar.'

Macquarie disguised his contempt for this odorous sea captain, reminding himself that he could have expected nothing less. 'Our intelligence here in Sydney Town,' Macquarie stated, 'informs us that Americans from Nantucket and New Bedford have been using the Furneaux Islands for some years now. In fact, they have conducted commerce in this colony, trading scarce items otherwise unavailable to the better citizens of New South Wales.' Macquarie fiddled with a miniature brass cannon paperweight, while he considered his next words.

'Why, back in '98 there was one group of Americans attempting to rebuild a craft from the wreckage of the merchant ship *Sydney Cove,* on Cape Barren Island. Governor King sent the Royal Navy to stop them, of course, but peacefully, as we did not want further political conflict with America. So, as you can imagine, I must insist we have our facts straight.'

'Absolutely, Gov'nor.'

'So, this man engaged you aboard two sailing sloops. To me, that seems more suitable for shorter distances than the Van Diemen's Land coast.'

'Exactly. Ah, Gov'nor...' O'May shuffled in his chair and leant forward. 'With yer permission, sar, I enquired with your clerk, Mr. Bent, to fetch me a map o' the Strait. With that in mind, I think I can pinpoint an area where there is a yet-unchartered island. I feel the rogues are livin' on it.'

Joseph Bent crossed the office floor with an arthritic limp. He carried with him a scrolled admiralty chart of Bass Strait, drawn from the explorations of Captain Mathew Flinders and George Bass some fifteen years prior. Macquarie and O'May watched in silence as the clerk unfurled the parchment, weighting its stubborn corners with two inkpots, a chalk pounce and a pottery flask.

'Twas here in this area, Yer Honour, that I fear the merchant ship *Globe* was wrecked.' O'May placed a reverent, albeit soiled, finger precisely to the west of another inconspicuous island, yet to be named on the map.

Bull Seal Island.

Governor Macquarie hoped O'May was right. He had of late been at pains to discover the fate of two ships in Bass Strait. Both had disappeared without trace, neither having arrived at its destination of Sydney Cove. The *Globe* was a merchant vessel, assumed lost with all hands in 1811. The second ship was a French merchant trader, *La Marianne*, a French barque, lost last year. *La Marianne*, Macquarie had been informed, had been destined for the islands of Bali and then Java, where the French and the Dutch shared administration. However, *La Marianne* was to have delivered a cargo of medicines to Sydney Cove, en route. She had disappeared, and was assumed to have been lost with all hands.

'I have it on good advice, Governor, that Captain Leblanc sold barrel staves, 'ere in Sydney Town, near on two year ago -- eight pounds for a thousand staves, a bargain in any economy, Yer honour.'

'And you are implying, sir?'

O'May looked up from the chart, and, wiping wet lips on his mitten, he fixed his eyes on Macquarie's. 'I have it on good authority that the *Globe,* sar, had a cargo o' fifty thousand staves stored in 'er hold.'

Macquarie's brow furrowed. He looked to his clerk a moment. 'Mr. Bent, I believe we have cargo manifests of these two ships amongst our records. Fetch them, if you please.' The governor stood and peered sagely out the window and down at Sydney Cove, where a dozen ships were moored. 'If you are indeed correct, Captain O'May, then I am certain you are aware of the rewards posted for information relating to these vessels and their passengers?'

'Oh I assure you, Yer Honour, that my motivation was not gold'—O'May's eyes wandered anywhere, to avoid looking his superior in the eye as he lied through his teeth—''Tis my humanly duty to assist in the search for these lost souls, as is the charge o' any man, what 'appens to 'ave the correct knowledge.'

'Well said.' Macquarie knew an opportunist when he shared the room with one. 'So are you saying, sir, that you are prepared to forego said remunerations... the hundred guineas per vessel, that is?'

Macquarie watched the captain's goitre rise and fall as he swallowed hard. 'Oh! I... I... ah... I never said that, Yer Honour.'

An awkward silence was interrupted when Mr. Bent returned with the cargo manifests, which he had kept nearby, having anticipated the order.

'Thank you, Joseph.' Governor Macquarie eyeballed the tome while the clerk placed markers between the relevant pages. The governor then returned to the window, clamping his hands behind his back.

1814

'Will you be requiring anything else for the moment, sir?' Mr. Bent asked.

'Yes.'

'Sir?'

'The *Assault* has been readied for reconnaissance, has she not?' Macquarie inquired regarding the 38-gun frigate HMS *Assault,* anchored in the harbour.

'I do believe so, sir.'

'Then send a request for Lieutenant Greenwood to come to this office at his earliest convenience.'

Indian Ocean, on board the *Magdalena*

The three weeks following the storm had been uneventful. Garre Skelton, who had been washed overboard never to be seen again, was replaced by Ted Avery as ship's third mate. Ted was not the wisest choice for a replacement being pint-sized. He had an unfotunate dented brow, a receding chin, a brush moustache and hair parted in the middle, which ended up in curls over his forehead. However, to his credit, he was tenacious and dedicated.

Sally Fetter knew there was no replacement for Garre Skelton. The man had been a natural leader and ambitious. Sally had harboured high hopes of a new life of freedom in Madagascar with the ship's third mate. But with all hopes dashed, she grew increasingly depressed, delusional and frequently behaved violently toward her fellow prisoners. Now, over a month out of Cape Town, Sally Fetter expressed her misgivings to Betty Bryant and Elizabeth Eveleigh. Those two prisoners were friends, Sally knew, and she felt, unjustifiably, that a conspiracy was afoot against her.

Betty Bryant's pox appeared cured; if not cured, it had gone into hibernation with the aid of a salve prepared by the

Magdalena's surgeon—a paste of potassium iodide and small doses of mercury, applied over several weeks. Now, with the threat of the lash hanging over her head should she attempt to seduce more seamen, Betty was an easy target for the newly bestowed affections of Sally Fetter. Much to Elizabeth's irritation, Betty, under the spell of a manipulating rival, distanced herself from Elizabeth and became more and more enamoured of Sally. With time on her side, Sally Fetter planned a conspiracy of her own.

An hour before midnight, four men of the ship's armed guard stomped down the companionway. Under the supervision of Lieutenant Lane, they stormed the prisoners' accommodations, on the double. Two marines swung lanterns while two stripped the blankets from Elizabeth and the other women sharing her cot.

'What's this? What's going on?' one of the women said groggily, woken from a black dream. The women looked up, terrified, at the fixated faces of authority.

'You lot,' the lieutenant shouted at the women, 'out!' Elizabeth swung her legs over the side of the cot to the deck, but the lieutenant stabbed a finger at her, saying, 'You remain where you are.'

Elizabeth felt the chill of fear. 'W-what's happening?'

'Shut it. Do as I say, or you'll get a taste of the cat. Now disrobe.'

'What?'

'Are you deaf? I—said—disrobe.'

'No!'

'What?' Lieutenant Lane lacked diplomacy and an injured leg from a recent boating accident pained him. Intolerant to disobedience, he found that screaming out orders relieved his suffering. 'You want to disobey my order?'

'W-why?'

Elizabeth was immediately floored by an open hand. She dropped, ruddy cheeked, to her knees. Her eyes filled with tears—tears of pain, not self-pity. 'Take off your skirts,' Lane said coldly. 'I will not ask you again.'

Elizabeth stared at the man in horrified defiance. The women on the nearby cots were now all awake and Elizabeth looked beyond the lieutenant into a sea of stunned faces. There was no sign of support. Elizabeth became aware of Sally Fetter staring from the neighbouring cot. She wore a knowing smirk. *The bitch was actually smiling.* The soldiers with the lanterns fidgeted uncomfortably, lowering the light, affording some shadows for modesty.

'NOW!' The lieutenant raised his fist a second time. Elizabeth stepped back, however, she proceeded to unbutton her skirt. The officer lowered his hand, resting it on his sword hilt. 'That is more like it.' He leered victoriously at the other women, staring back from their cot benches.

Elizabeth untied the cords of her blouse and placed the garment neatly on the cot. She was aware of how her breasts had matured into womanhood over the past year. Now they lay bare for all to see, white, perfectly shaped breasts with pert nipples the colour of ripe raspberries. The soldiers shuffled. Some stole a sly glance. The lieutenant fixed his eyes on Elizabeth. His disdain was palpable.

'Mr. Morrison,' Lane said to the soldier next to him, without facing the man, 'search that blouse.' Morrison immediately explored the garment. He twisted to face his superior and shook his head. Lieutenant Lane nodded for Elizabeth to remove her skirts. The calico was heavy and stiff from being washed in seawater. Elizabeth felt beyond humiliated. When she hesitated, Lane's fingers twitched on his sword hilt, and he partially withdrew the weapon from its sheath, exposing some of the blade.

Elizabeth unbuckled a waist restraint. She paused, looking about her for support, but she was alone.

The officer's face reddened. 'I said…'

Elizabeth allowed the item of dress to fall about her ankles. Nearby were low gasps. The soldiers shifted, ogling. Elizabeth felt abused. Eyes of both sexes feasted on her nakedness. Eyes fixed on her mound of hazel curls while her chalk-white body shivered from the cold; Elizabeth cupped her hands over her mound of Venus.

'Step aside,' the lieutenant ordered. Elizabeth stepped out from the pile of petticoats and dress gathered around her ankles. Finally one of the women who shared Elizabeth's cot passed her a blanket. It was a brave move. Defiant. The act of kindness met with no rejection.

The soldier who searched the blouse ran experienced fingers through the creases of the dresses and petticoats. Almost immediately, he felt the hard object they sought. It had been worked into the hem. The guard manoeuvred the item free of its hiding place.

'Key, sar,' he said triumphantly. Lieutenant Lane returned a grim smile. He took the key, inspected it and then passed it to another soldier. 'You know what to do.'

'Aye, lieutenant.'

While the soldier hurried up the companionway, Lane ordered Elizabeth to re-dress. Moments later, the soldier returned with the key in his hand. 'It's the armoury key, all right, Lieutenant.'

The lieutenant rubbed his chin thoughtfully. 'Arrest her,' he finally ordered. 'Have her chained before the captain interviews her.'

Captain Cholmondeley had to stoop low to step into the dark recesses of the brig. After a late supper of roasted fowl—taken from the pens and killed especially for the officer's table this night—the proximity to the bilge, sloshing in the bowels of the ship beneath his feet, was particularly nauseating.

Elizabeth, fettered to the deck with 20-pound irons, cowered, pressed herself into a corner and hugged her knees to her chest. The ship's cell was cramped and the air stale with putrid humidity, while the lone lantern, just below the deck, flickered and crackled with the rising gases.

Captain Cholmondeley withdrew a scented handkerchief and placed it over his nose. As he did so, Elizabeth noted the man's gold ring. Other prisoners had mentioned the ring to her; it was worth five years' wages to a common servant. She had been told that the stone, an oval carnelian intaglio set in gold, was from ancient Roman times. It was a gift from the captain's wife.

'You say you do not know how a key to the ship's armoury came into your possession, hidden in the hem of your skirts?' Cholmondeley mumbled through his handkerchief.

Elizabeth raised her head slowly to look the man in the eye. She was aware that she looked a piteous sight. She had fallen as low as she could go. Surely, she could stoop no lower. Elizabeth's nose had run and she desperately wanted to wipe the mucus from her face, but her shackled wrists prevented her.

'Well?' the captain inquired again.

Elizabeth was in no mood to plead—she was stubbornly strong-willed—but *why*, she asked herself, *should she take any shite for Sally Fetter?*

'Twas Sally Fetter, sir. She was the one who had the key. She was the one who hid it on my person. She had it in for me, sir.'

'Sally Fetter?' the captain turned to one of the soldiers who had arrested Elizabeth. He was a skinny lad of eighteen, but still managed to fill the narrow cell doorway. 'This Sally Fetter? Do you know of her?'

'Yes, Captain. She occupies the cot next to this'un and it's common knowledge her and Miss Eveleigh here is not friends.'

'So,' the captain said to Elizabeth, 'pray tell me more.'

'Sally Fetter was in cahoots with Garre Skelton, your third mate... well, who was, that is, until his accident. They planned to rob the armoury and mutiny, taking this ship to Madagascar.'

'Madagascar! That sounds highly unlikely.' *But why else*, Cholmondeley considered, *would they want a key to the armoury?*

'I speak the truth, sir.'

'So where did this key come from? There is no key missing.'

'Garre Skelton got Samuel French drunk, Captain, and he borrowed Samuel's key while Samuel was sleepin' and made a copy of it in plaster. Then, when we were at Cape Town, he paid a visit to a locksmith and had a copy made.'

Cholmondeley was incredulous. *The industry of some people.* And the prisoner's story *was* believable. The captain thought hard. His port wine awaited, and the steward had promised steamed sultana pudding this night. He stepped back into the passageway where Lieutenant Lane waited.

'I must commend you, Lieutenant, for thwarting what could quite possibly have been a disaster,' he said quietly, 'but how did you hear of this conspiracy?'

'It were Sally Fetter, Captain. She told me she saw the act.'

'The act?'

'Aye, sir, the actions of Elizabeth Eveleigh in cahoots with Garre Skelton.'

'Damn their lies. Damn all of them. And Mr. Skelton? I find that story difficult to swallow.'

'I made enquiries, sir... about Mr. Skelton ashore in Cape Town. The lads said he were aloof.'

'Aloof?'

'He wasn't keen, like, to hang about with the lads in the taverns. He went off on his lone, like. They thought he were with a married woman, but Will Beaton saw him in the district of industries... the locksmiths, like.'

'Now the man's dead and cannot defend himself.'

'Aye, sir. Awful convenient for these here women.'

Captain Cholmondeley dabbed his nose one last time and stuffed the handkerchief back in his pocket. He craved soap and warm water after venturing so far below deck with the prisoners and vermin.

'I cannot be judge and jury, although I am the captain of this ship. That woman,' the captain said tipping his head to the brig door, 'is destined for New South Wales; she is a prisoner of the crown. We will see that this one and Sally Fetter are brought before the magistrates, upon arrival in Sydney Cove.'

'Yes, Captain.'

'But I do not want these women locked together or suffering failing health, incapable of facing justice. See that the carpenter builds two pens on the foredeck. Not too large, and not too small, either. They can languish out in the elements—give them time to consider their dastardly crime.'

Bull Seal Island

Sometimes in life one does not know what they have until it is lost, and Beatrice was Leblanc's big loss. The night they returned to Bull Seal Island after the shark attack, Leblanc held a funeral service for Beatrice. Although the service was read aloud from the Bible, he agreed to the aboriginal custom of cremating Beatrice's body over a pyre built on Forget Me Not Headland. Her ashes were then swept reverently into the ocean.

That night Pollyanna dragged a hipbath into the dwelling she shared with Rowan. A jar of French bath salts appeared from the captain's store. Rowan sank into the warm, perfumed water, soaking alone, with thoughts of Beatrice, the shark and his own destiny. Pollyanna, too, thought about her destiny. She poured Rowan a brandy, warming it in her cupped palms as Captain Leblanc had taught her. She then joined Rowan, sitting beside the tub. The brandy warmed Rowan's belly, as only a good brandy could. Pollyanna looked stunning in a long silk nightgown. The candles behind her shining through the material left little to the imagination. Easily visible were her long thin legs, wide hips, the hirsute mound of curly black hair between her thighs, and her pert breasts. Pollyanna was growing into a beautiful and mature woman. She knelt next to the tub and, soaping a sponge, began to wash Rowan's back. Rowan had grown fond of this native, but with the fondness of a sibling. Pollyanna, however, had fallen for this good-hearted whitefella. He was kind and caring, but she knew better than to suggest more than friendship. And, besides, she heard Rowan call out *her* name in his tormented sleep. Not Pollyanna's name, but *her* name... Jessica.

'You still love woman, Jessica,' Pollyanna said, in a whisper.

'Yes Pollyanna, I do.'

'But she has gone, Row-an, gone to spirit world.'

Rowan did not answer.

'Row-an?' she asked.

'Yes.'

'You leave this island soon, I think.'

'Maybe.'

'Then I come with you.'

Rowan sat upright in the tub. 'Pollyanna, I cannot take you with me. Where would you go?'

'Take me to my tribe. That all Pollyanna ask.'

Movement outside the cabin disturbed them. Rowan put a finger to her lips. 'We will see, Pollyanna,' he whispered back. 'We will see.'

Weeks passed, but Leblanc just grew morose. He blamed Rowan. He blamed God. He was inconsolable. Myunga moved out of his dwelling, as the very sight of her sickened the man.

Previously a moderate drinker, he was now frequently drunk and not pleasant company, ranting and raving, denouncing his religion. He burned his Bible and prayer books and tore pages from illustrated scriptures, scattering them across Satan's Hole. Eventually everyone avoided Leblanc—everyone except Billy Cake.

Rowan in particular kept his distance, as best as possible in the small community. Although he had made up his mind to escape the island when the first opportunity arose, Rowan busied himself, taking on the challenge of fortifying the island against an attack with serious verve. This challenge also gave him freedom to scour the island for suitable materials while wandering the cliffs alone or with Pollyanna. As the weeks passed he came to know the island like the back of his hand. He made several visits to the steep, rocky cove where the *Jolly Mary* and *Queen B* were moored in the bay. Amongst the stores collected from the *Globe* wreck were the frames of four dray wagons, disassembled for transport across the seas. They'd been made in Birmingham and had been destined to be reconstructed in the colonies, only to end up as shipwreck flotsam, stored in a remote cave on this desolate island. Rowan had the wagons carted, in their sections, to the top of the barren slope, well past Eagle's Nest lookout. Here, they were reassembled, with the aid of Henry Tuckerman the carpenter.

The drays were positioned in such a manner as to roll down the severely precipitous slope. Chocks of timber were wedged under the wheels to lock the carts in position. Finally, Rowan ordered their trays loaded with rocks large enough to be carried by one person. In this task, Rowan noted, the native women matched the strength of the men. It was laborious work, but should they have to evacuate Mast Head Bluff their escape route to the hidden sloops would take them up the 400-foot mountain and past the drays. And should they be pursued, the drays could be released, to career down the escarpment, creating a deadly avalanche for any who dared follow in their path.

Each day Leblanc slouched in a wicker chair, bottle in hand, and perched himself in position so as to watch Rowan's progress though his spyglass.

Descending from the mountain, Rowan jumped the wall to the village ledge, where Pollyanna passed him a tankard of fresh rainwater. Leblanc waited.

'So, where did you derive such cunning, Sawbones?' Leblanc asked Rowan with a cynical slur. Rowan drank his water greedily. 'Well?' Leblanc insisted.

'I worked alongside Commander Joshua Barney, remember?'

'Aye. Joshua Barney. The famous Commander, huh.' And Leblanc shouted to all in earshot. 'And Sawbones's best friend, taboot, eh?' Leblanc craned his neck over his shoulder to follow Rowan as he walked away. 'Then keep up the good work, Sawbones,' Leblanc called after Rowan in a deriding tone, 'an' pray we don't need it.'

CHAPTER TWENTY-ONE

Bull Seal Island

Over the following days, Rowan managed to get several cairns of rocks piled at Satan's Hole and another at the natural arched entrance that led to Mast Head Bluff from Seal Bay. They were built to simulate the landscape so as not to appear man-made. John Stuart Radge had worked the blacksmith workshop at the Hobart Town Jail before he absconded, so it was with his knowledge of ironwork that Rowan had brackets for the swivel cannon, normally fixed to the bows of the two sloops, built into the cairns. They were to be brought ashore after each hunt and mounted amongst the cairns, hidden, along with suitable amounts of black powder, flint and shrapnel. The powder and shrapnel—shards of glass and small jagged stones—were packed into stone jars with corks that had been waterproofed with wax. A third gun, a ship's carronade, was set up on the inside of the arched entrance, where it covered the main approach into the settlement.

'How much black powder do we have in store?' Rowan asked Leblanc's first mate, Elihu Smyth. Smyth had a new respect for Rowan since his attempt to save Beatrice.

'Two five-pound kegs.'

'That will not suffice.'

'I can fetch more when next in Sydney. Our next journey approaches.'

'Then buy more,' Rowan said, 'but not in one lot, for it may create suspicion. Send Uriah to purchase one keg, Radge another, and the next day *you* fetch a keg. You do not want to draw attention to purchasing more than seems reasonable for a sealer.'

'Aye. Yer a clever bastard,' Radge said, 'thart's for certain.'

'So what's the plan with the black powder?' Uriah Coffin asked with a mischievous smile. 'My guess is, it ain't jus' fer dem swivels.'

'No, Uriah,' Rowan answered, 'it is not. We are going to plant what are known as bombs.'

'Bombs, huh? Like explosions?'

'Exactly.' Rowan drew a rough map in the sand with a stick. 'We will plant them above the high-water mark, here'— he dragged the point through the sand—'and along Seal Bay, where any attacker would have to land. We'll fill carboys with powder and pebbles...'

'But them carboys are made o' glass.'

'Yes. And they are waterproof, you understand. You have several of them empty in the cave, I've noticed.'

'Aye. We drank the wine in 'em, years ago,' Uriah chuckled.

'We will fix the tops with flint, of which we have plenty.'

'Devil's blood!' Smyth shuddered. 'I wouldn't want ter be standing too close to one o' them when she blows.'

1814

Rowan had a moment to reflect on the carnage the bomb could possibly effect and a vision of Jessica's mutilated body passed before him. 'No,' he agreed coldly, 'Neither would I. To defend against an enemy on this island one must be resourceful. Who are our sharpest shooters?'

'Joseph Scully, by far,' Uriah said. ''E used to be a poacher, then 'e got nabbed. That's why 'e got transported.'

'An' I'm thinkin' Lutwidge ain't bad, neither. I seen him shoot a seal between the eyes, before 'e scared them others off with the noise.'

'Then these two men must be given muskets, balls and powder and allowed all the training we can give them,' Rowan said. 'We need marksmen. We will build sniper nests here and here'—Rowan speared the stick in the sand—'and we'll make them from dead trees, above the embankment over the bay. The Brown Bess has an accurate range of one hundred yards, so we will place the nests at 50. I've seen the redcoats in Maryland use them en masse at 50 yards. Frightening. But we will dig trenches here'—Rowan made his mark with the stick—'...and here and here, behind the sniper nests, for the marksmen will need cover, to make their escape over the ridge.'

'Clever,' Smyth said approvingly.

'If we have to evacuate'—Rowan waved his stick at the loaded drays balanced precariously up the hill slope in the distance—'then those drays, gentlemen, will see us safely over the ridge and to the sloops.'

'I seen me fellow Maoris dig spike pits,' Uriah Coffin contributed.

'Aye.' Skeffington Lutwidge shuddered. 'I heard 'bout them. Deep pits with sharpened spikes in the bottom, pointed skywards. Skewer any poor bastard what falls in.'

'Then we will dig those, also,' Rowan said, 'where the ground is easier to dig, at the base of the mountain. They will need to be camouflaged, but we will build them in such a way that we know their location without giving it away.'

'An' fall in the pits ourselves.' Smyth shuddered at the thought.

'We can drag blackberry bushes up from the gullies,' Lutwidge said. 'Replant them either side of the pits so attackers would pass between them.'

'Yes, that would work,' Rowan agreed, adding, 'and we will instruct everyone on the location of the hidden paths, so as to navigate around them.'

The sun set to the west earlier in the following months and Bull Seal Island harboured a menace about it. With the autumn months came huge seas. Air currents from the equator were displaced towards the South Pole, and with no landmass to act as a windbreak between the Indian Ocean and Bass Strait, the seas became unpredictable.

''Tis called the Roarin' Forties,' Joseph Scully told Rowan. A dozen men sat on the embankment above Mast Head Bluff, gazing north towards the great land of Australia, and watched the incessant waves explode ashore. They shared tobacco pipes and passed the rum around. The blowholes roared and hissed and a fine sea spray cast a mist over the shanties, creating an unwelcome dampness.

Billy Cake fussed with the evening meal; tonight was to be a communal affair, but with the wild weather most were reconsidering. Some of the women had already prepared food within their own shanties. Rowan watched Billy Cake's mood swings anxiously. More than three months had passed since Billy had caught Rowan exhuming shipwreck victims' bodies in the sand on the beach. Rowan had kept Billy in small amounts of laudanum and Billy had kept his word, but Rowan understood that the man was addicted, and that it would come to a head, sooner rather than later. With

Leblanc so bitter and unkempt, Rowan worried about the outcome. He knew he must escape, and soon.

'Sail ho!' Tommy's younger brother Eddy screeched at the gathering as he hurried barefooted from the lookout to fetch Leblanc; the captain, by all accounts, was still sleeping in his hut. 'Sail ho!'

Gabriel jumped to his feet and followed his son. The others clambered to higher ground for a better view.

'Where?' Edward Caleb cried out. 'Can yer see it?'

'Aye. North-west.' Ned Talbot stabbed a finger at a pinprick of white sail, only detectable because of a shaft of setting sun lighting its canvas. 'She be from the cape, headed to Port Jackson, fer sure.'

'Yer got better eyesight than me, Ned Talbot.'

Captain Leblanc scrambled clumsily up the hillside over the crumbling gravel, an oriental silk gown wrapped about his nakedness and otherwise wearing only boots. 'Where?' he demanded, raising his spyglass.

'There, Cap'n.' Elihu Smyth pointed to the horizon. Leblanc studied the ship for some time.

'What is she, Cap'n?'

'Can't tell yet, lads—four-master, I'm thinkin'.' Leblanc panned the eyeglass east. 'What I *can* tell yer, is she's got a battle ahead o' her. Look.'

The storm brewing on the eastern horizon had not gone unnoticed by the others; nor did the sudden interest in shipping and the camaraderie between the sealers go unnoticed by Rowan.

Billy Cake gave up on the communal fire and the men retired to their evening meals within their huts, but the community spirit was maintained and they split into smaller groups, feasting in their shanties, sharing company, wandering hut to hut in a festive move rarely seen of late. Rowan was finding that the merriment made a pleasant change when Billy Cake came to fetch him.

'Cap'n want Rowan.' Rowan looked bemused. Billy snatched Rowan's arm. 'Come. Cap'n want to drink with Rowan, sar.' Rowan had little choice, as Billy dragged him into the captain's dwelling.

Leblanc was jovial enough, social, even. 'Ah, Rowan.'

'Captain.'

Myunga, drinking with Pollyanna and the other women, passed Rowan a mug of rum. Leblanc was in high spirits, and although he was drinking, he was not intoxicated. He threw an arm around Rowan. 'You've been avoidin' me o' late, son.'

'Have I?' Rowan lied. 'It was not my intention.'

'Never mind. You've been busy with the fortifications and I commend yer for it.' Any further conversation was drowned out by frightful verse as the sealers sang "Leave Her Johnny, Leave Her." Henry Tuckerman proved a capable piano player whilst Skeffington Lutwidge made lively entertainment with his fiddle. The rum flowed. The cauldron of kangaroo stew simmered and there was baked damper aplenty and more.

Outside, the tempest howled ashore. It was no night to be at sea. Captain Leblanc dressed in his britches with wide belt and brass buckle, knee-high boots and laced calico blouse. He sang the ditties along with the rest. From time to time, Rowan watched young Tommy or Eddy weave amongst the revelry, wet to the bone, to relay updates on the storm, but above all to relay the progress of the mystery sail.

The hours passed. Captain Leblanc was in charge once more.

After the recent stress and strained relationships, Rowan found Leblanc's renewed friendship welcoming. The music played on and the festivities continued. Around the middle of the night, Rowan felt fatigue take control. He feared he had drunk too much rum and reprimanded himself. He was normally more guarded. Excusing himself, Rowan returned to his own cabin and collapsed into a deep sleep.

Indian Ocean entering Bass Strait, on board the *Magdalena*

The *Magdalena* was entering the fifth month of her voyage. The Indian Ocean was a vast and open mass of deep, unforgiving sea. Besides the islands of Amsterdam and Saint Paul, there was no landfall before the west coast of New Holland, six thousand miles from Cape Town. After passing east of Saint Paul Island, progress had been swift, and Captain Cholmondeley calculated that they had gained a week due to the strong winds from the south-west. But with the winds came tempestuous weather. Squalls became more frequent, and the closer they came to the southern reaches of New Holland's southern coastline, the dirtier the weather. Overcast days with constant rain ran into weeks, and it became more and more difficult to position the *Magdalena* with any accuracy.

'I can only make out our latitude at night, by the stars,' Captain Cholmondeley confided to First Mate Robert Knight, 'because there is no sign of the sun during daylight hours.' The first mate knew that the ship's chronometer also relied on the sun to plot exact longitude measurements..

Elizabeth and Sally Fetter were miserable wretches. Two cage pens had been built on the foredeck two yards apart, enclosed on all sides, yet open to the elements through their iron bars. More than three weeks had passed, and whilst Sally Fetter had flung constant abuse at Elizabeth, Elizabeth had ignored the antagonist and crouched in a corner, as far from the wind as possible. They were fed rations equal to those of the women prisoners' below and were allowed a blanket each, otherwise they remained miserable wretches, alone with their thoughts until they should be taken before the courts in Sydney Town.

Captain Winston Cholmondeley studied both chronometers in his cabin. They were reading somewhere between 41 degrees east and 39 degrees south, but he had managed a good observation of the sun the day before at noon. He was confident the *Magdalena* had entered Bass Strait, passing due east of the northernmost point of King Island. Here, the captain knew from his charts, the strait was 135 nautical miles wide. The swell had picked up substantially in the past few hours as dusk approached, and there was a density in the atmosphere. The temperature dropped dramatically. Captain Cholmondeley needed no prompting to go on deck.

The *Magdalena* was riding mounting waves, climbing twenty-foot swells with the wind behind her, and plunging down their other side, spearing her bowsprit into the trough of the next wave and exploding spray across the foredeck. The captain yanked the collar of his oilskins up around his neck and joined Robert Knight, his first mate, at the helm. Master's Mate Edward Browning manned the wheel. Both men were relieved to see their captain.

The wild weather was relentless as the *Magdalena* sailed into Bass Strait—a body of turbulent and relatively shallow water that manifested huge seas, especially during the gale-force winds blowing from north-west to south-west, like those tormenting the *Magdalena* this night. The wind on her beam had pushed her into a perilous 50-degree lean. The rains remained constant and this oppressive weather made it impossible for the captain to pinpoint their position to any degree of accuracy. It had been two weeks since they'd had a clear positioning.

'The barometer has fallen to its lowest this month—29.55 —while the temperature has risen only to 49 F,' Knight warned Captain Cholmondeley, 'alerting us to a major storm.' The captain squinted through the rain-drenched window of the binnacle cover. The compass headings were showing south-west to north, then spinning back to south-west again. Another bad omen.

'This weather, I believe, is early for this part of the world, sir,' the mate said. 'In August it is at its worst, I do believe. But look at this.' He waved a hand at the slurry ahead of them.

'Send more hands aloft,' the captain ordered, although the mainsail had already been reefed. 'Shorten more sail, Mr. Knight. Take in all the canvas. Just close-reefed topsails and reefed foresail.'

'Aye, sir.'

Browning barked the order at the boatswain, who'd been waiting nearby to receive it, and the wiry Devonshire seaman gave the order to the crew with piercing whistles that cut through the din of the ocean in a code only seamen understood. Gail-force winds were mounting, shrieking through the rigging.

'Keep her steady, dead east, Mr. Browning!' Overhead the sky was an ominous sharkskin grey, but what lay ahead was of greater concern. 'That's a major storm we're headed into!' The captain raised his voice so it was loud enough to be heard by the master's mate, but refrained from shouting so loudly as to concern the crew within earshot. Cholmondeley knew that a single black line represented most of the storms across the horizon; however, there was not just one storm front building, but two—two massive, boiling black walls, one north and one south, with only a narrow path between them as they converged. Forked lightning arced from the heavens into the ocean in terrifying flashes. The *Magdalena* dipped sharply into another trough—her carved figurehead of the biblical Mary Magdalene plunging beneath the huge wave—and all on deck were drenched again by the freezing grey waters around Bass Strait.

Bass Strait was what worried the captain most.

Had they been in the middle of the Indian Ocean, the captain would have been more confident. However, the shortcut between Van Diemen's Land and Australia, which reduced the voyage from England to Port Jackson by one week, had been in use only a decade or so. Much of this relatively shallow water with unpredictable currents was uncharted or, if charted, it had been hand copied from Admiralty maps by less than accurate copiers. Now they sailed into a storm as the sun deserted them.

'Keep that helm alee, Mr. Browning!'

'Aye, Cap'n!'

'Mr. Knight!'

'Aye, sir!'

'Make preparations! Secure the deck, furl the sails and have the stays ready on the main jib!' The captain wiped the spray from his face. He had weathered many a storm, but this was different. 'And tell cook to serve food early, before he douses the fires!'

While Knight delegated, the crew aloft went about securing the sails. All portable objects on deck were lashed down, including the two jolly boats, upturned amidships.

Captain Cholmondeley estimated the winds at fifty or sixty miles per hour, with gusts of eighty miles per hour. There was no predictable pattern to the waves. A dozen twenty-footers could be rolling beneath the keel when suddenly a set of sixty-foot waves would come from starboard bow or port bow without warning. *Magdalena's* entire bow could be ten feet clear of the ocean while sixty-foot waves were breaking overhead. It was terrifying.

Below decks was pandemonium. Although all hatches were closed, the ocean poured through the cracks. The prisoners were wet through on their bunks, their bedding soaked. They were miserable, sick and fearing for their lives.

Change of the watch. Three hours later.

Captain Cholmondeley had dined alone on cold cuts in the stateroom. His great and hairy fist pinioned a stemmed glass of Madeira to the swaying table while he stared off vaguely towards the barometer, swinging free on its gimbal. Ship's Surgeon Phineas Beckwith stepped over the threshold and through the stateroom door only to be caught off guard and slammed against the wall by a sudden swell. He had slumped into a chair and was looking at the captain with eyes framed by dark circles when the tempest threw him against the far wall. 'We lost another two, Captain'—the surgeon spoke of two more prisoners who had died of disease—'and Mary Thyme lost the infant that was born aboard three weeks past.'

Captain Cholmondeley sighed. What could he say? What could he do? He flicked a finger towards the wide-based decanter sliding across the table and the surgeon snatched its neck as it passed. Beckwith reached for a wine glass corralled in the centre of the table. 'It's not losing strength, is it?' he asked.

'No, Phineas, it is not. If anything, it is gaining in strength.' Captain Cholmondeley wanted to tell the surgeon he would normally seek deep water in this weather, but he did not know in which direction to turn, for he feared they were near land. 'Damn this cursed strait,' he said instead. 'As George Bass wrote in his Admiralty reports, there is no set quiet season in Bass Strait. It's a godforsaken and unpredictable stretch of ocean. God have mercy on us.'

The surgeon was less than impressed with his captain's skepticism. His life was in the man's hands. *Hell, the entire ship's company was in the man's hands.*

The storm persisted into the black of night. Finally, Cholmondeley struggled onto the deck. He had drunk more Madeira than usual, but he was of sound mind. Robert Knight, the first mate, had re-joined Mr. Irwin, the helmsman at the wheel.

'Captain,' the two men acknowledged Cholmondeley.

'It's getting' worse, Cap'n!' Knight yelled, through a mouthful of horizontal rain.

The captain gripped the binnacle. 'I agree, Mr. Knight!' he had to shout. 'I've sailed the East and the West Indies and this storm has the makings of a typhoon or hurricane. Heave to, if you please! You know what to do!'

'Aye, sir.' Knight agreed with his captain, it was wisest to heave to—turning the ship bow first into the wind—secure the helm and use sparse canvas, the idea being to avoid progress.

Elizabeth, trapped in her cage on deck, felt fear beyond the terror of entrapment, beyond the claustrophobia of her confinement. The water now surged through her prison. She was chilled to the bone, but her thoughts were for survival, not comfort. She looked to the seamen working the rigging and read fear on their faces—even these hardened sailors were scared for their lives.

The thought of the ship sinking plagued her. Going down with the ship was one thing, but being trapped in this wretched coop was just too much to endure. The winds lashed at the pen's timbers. Only a dozen small bolts held her box to the deck. Ten feet away was open sea... massive walls of undulating, eternal sea breaking over the deck and washing anything not tied down overboard.

Another wave crashed over her lockup. Elizabeth gripped the bars to steady herself from the retreating water, hoping, praying that the cage would break up enough for her to scurry belowdeck. Surely the marines would not begrudge her sanctuary in this hour of need. Elizabeth heard a guttural cry and glanced across at Sally Fetter's cage. The woman also clutched her iron bars, but she glared back at Elizabeth with demented, demonic black eyes of pure hatred. She seemed to have overcome her fears and channelled all emotion into loathing. Elizabeth held her gaze until yet another wave washed over them...

Bull Seal Island

Rowan awoke with a pounding headache. Something had woken him, a sound out of place over the racket of the storm outside. He felt about in the darkness. Pollyanna lay at his side, snoring from the rum they'd drunk earlier and blissfully unaware of the tempest. The woman had crawled into his cot after he was asleep. Immediately, he felt ill; he felt poisoned, his gut heaving. He rushed out into the gale and threw up. The howling, horizontal rain needling his face was sobering. Within moments Rowan was drenched. His stomach turned and he vomited once more. Why? he asked himself. Was it tainted food? Or the rum? But then he remembered feeling tired, exhausted, after eating. He recalled Lowanna, one of Uriah Coffin's women, passing him a beverage, a herbal she called it. It was bitter and he'd only drunk half of it, but now he remembered the weariness that had followed.

He had been drugged.

Why?

The foreign sound that woke him caught his attention—a distant sound, like the clanging of metal on metal, travelled with the wind, racing ashore off the wild ocean. The faint peal of a bell, maybe?

A ship's bell! The sound became more distinct—the distant, clanging sound of a bell over the howling tempest. Rowan gazed through the squall to the other huts. The wind was shifting direction and now the crater walls surrounding them protected most shanties. There were no lights burning. The communal fire was a darkened pit. Amongst the clamour of the raging storm, Mast Head Bluff seemed eerily deserted.

The bell clanged once more.

Rowan re-entered his hut. Pollyanna snored. He towelled himself down. With his head still thumping, he opened his medicine trunk and fished about in the light of a single candle for a jar of camphor. He rubbed some of the waxy paste into his forehead and felt some relief. Rowan dressed and threw a wet-weather sealskin jacket over his shoulders, pulled on seal-skin boots and pushed off along the ocean pathway.

It was dangerous going. Here on the cliff edges he was buffeted by the hurricane-force winds. Rowan used the pig-face to guide him. Passing above Blubber Beach, Rowan saw dark figures below, stumbling on the pebbles. Some carried lanterns with the lamp glass masked against the open sea. Another light caught Rowan's attention further ahead, on the headland towards Bone Beach. It was a subtle light, more of a flash, really. A signal?

Rowan climbed on, his journey perilous and painfully slow. He descended the gully on the lee side of the storm and ascended to the promontory, the western point of Bone Beach. Below, he made out a dozen or more figures, dark shapes lit sporadically by glints of escaped lantern light. Although it was pitch dark he could make out the whitewater surf crashing ashore. Rowan's eyes were searching the beach when he saw a brighter light, some half a mile distant. It appeared to be in the middle of the beach, half way between the shore and the cliff face. The light moved. It swayed gently side to side. Rowan concentrated. The light seemed to turn back towards him, drifting, swaying and returning along the beach towards the reef. Rowan heard the bell again. The clanging swept in from the raging sea. This time it was closer, approaching the shore, battling before the gale.

Then Rowan saw the dark black shape... *A ship!*

Rowan's jaw dropped. Although the storm was abating, his face was still pelted with rain. Through the mist and spray and blackness, Rowan made out a ship—the ship they had seen on the horizon, that distant speck from earlier in the evening. And now it drifted helplessly towards the reef.

'No!' Rowan screamed. But the single word was plucked from his lips, stolen by the wind. The approaching light on the beach grew faster, closer. Then Rowan recognised the shape of a donkey. One of the native women walked alongside the beast, her body lit in the undulating light beams from a lantern swinging to and fro on a long rod fastened vertically to the donkey's back.

Wreckers!

Rowan felt ill. His stomach knotted. He threw up once more. 'Bastards! No!' And again Rowan's words were whipped aside. The lantern, Rowan knew from the mooncussers in America, was a ploy used to attract a stricken ship towards land. The stricken ship thinking, fatally, that the swaying lantern was the stern light of another ship at sea.

On the quarterdeck of the *Magdalena*. 4 am.

Captain Cholmondeley had tried to catch some sleep, but rest was nearly impossible. Now the ship's bell pealed incessantly, its hollow brass case knelling unceasingly. The captain rose from his cot. Something was not sitting well in his thoughts.

The two helmsmen at the wheel were exhausted. They had fought the impossible, holding the *Magdalena* in a heave-to position for six hours, and now the faintest hint of dawn heralded ease from the tempest. Captain Cholmondeley gripped a safety line rigged between his quarters and the helm and pulled himself forward, clad awkwardly in his oilskins. First Mate Robert Knight and Second Mate Jack Phillips, standing by, showed signs of relief.

'What's with the bell, Mr. Knight?' The captain stood fast, with the rope in both hands.

'It has a mind of its own this night, sir.'

'Hmm,' the captain grunted. There was more pressing business afoot.

'The storm is losing muscle, Captain!' Knight called out.

'Aye, it appears so, Mr. Knight!' Cholmondeley cast an eye over the bow, and then turned to the stern, looking into the blackness of deep water. 'It will be light in an hour!' Cholmondeley estimated they were travelling at seven or eight knots when he suddenly caught a faint light well off in the distance. 'A light! Mr. Knight, did you see that? It appears we are not alone in this filthy night!'

'Yes, Captain. I've kept her off our bow for the past hour.'

'Oh?' Cholmondeley consulted the binnacle. 'It's running east by north also!'

'Aye!'

'Excellent, Mr. Knight!' The captain steadied himself on the binnacle as the ship lurched into yet another deep trough. 'Mr. Phillips!'

1814

'Sir!'

'Turn her into the wind and continue our course at east by north! Follow that light! And, Mr. Knight, see her run free with three close-reefed topsails and the reefed foresail!'

'Aye, sir!'

But the night was still black, the seas still large. Dawn was an hour away. The captain and mates watched with apprehension as the *Magdalena* turned into the wind and the topgallants filled with renewed life. Ahead, visibility was only a hundred yards, flagged by white water breaking at the peak of a wave.

'You've done well, gentlemen! Keep her steady...! Mr. Knight!'

'Captain!'

'Keep a sharp lookout, if you please!'

'Yes, sir!'

Barely had the captain's orders been swept away in a gust when a ghostly groan followed a violent shudder. The keel at the bow dragged across a reef, its timbers shredding on barbed and serrated boulders of picrite basalt, only scant feet below the surface. Both helmsmen were thrown across the deck, as was the captain.

'A reef!' someone screamed.

'Jesus Lord ... we've hit rocks!'

On the cliffs above Bone Beach the tearing of timbers and the screams of terrified humanity accosted Rowan on the winds. The ship struck the reef with frightening force, her keelson torn away from her hull, like the vertebrae of some large reptile. The masts cracked at their steps on impact, their lower yards crashing to the deck, crushing sailors and throwing others into the violent sea, but a more sickening sound reached Rowan from the beach below.

Cheering.

The screeches and hooting of crazed wreckers drunk on success and rum. They shouted and cheered, awaiting their prize as the stricken ship was shredded on the jagged reef, jettisoning its cargo into the tempestuous, frothing whirlpool. And the hapless victims who would die a horrendous death.

The *Magdalena* had jarred savagely, listing at twenty degrees while a neck-high sea washed across the deck, sweeping ten or a dozen men overboard. Captain Cholmondeley clawed at the binnacle to avoid being taken himself. He stood groggily, aided by the second mate. The *Magdalena* righted herself before another wall of water lifted the ship clear off the reef. She reeled forward. Knight rushed to the port gunwale but there was nothing he could do to save the men who'd gone overboard. Their screams vanished into eternity. The *Magdalena* tottered a hundred yards before again ploughing into submerged reef, ripping her belly open. Captain Cholmondeley caught a vague silhouette of land. 'An island! Jesus Lord, we have hit an island!'

Knight saw the speck of light once more... upon a stretch of beach. A lantern, no less.

'Dammed wreckers!' he roared, fury momentarily defeating fear, but the first mate's curse was drowned when the next massive wave washed him from the quarterdeck, tumbling him over the gunwale, and into the boiling sea.

Surviving crew scrambled onto the deck. There was nothing they could do to save the *Magdalena*. The sound of the screams from the imprisoned women belowdecks was gut-wrenching. It was panic and mayhem. The marines guarding the women were also panicked, and Elizabeth heard several shots being fired at point blank range. Shots fired into the terrified mob who were desperate to escape. But breaking free for the upper deck was impossible. The ship's companionway stairs to the prisoners' quarters had collapsed, trapping anyone not already on deck.

Elizabeth clung to the bars of her cage. She saw horror in Sally Fetter's eyes... horror wrestling with hatred. But they were both trapped, trapped like rats in their barred cages. Overhead, spas and huge rigging blocks weighing twenty pounds apiece hurtled towards the deck, killing outright anyone in their path; bodies were instantly swept overboard.

'Miss Elizabeth...!' The voice was shrill, barely audible over the pandemonium. 'Miss Elizabeth...'

Elizabeth stood unsteadily. Through the bars, looking into the storm, she saw Brinley Thurston, the fifteen-year-old seamen who had so generously smuggled her the suet pudding, struggling to advance against the tempest.

'Elizabeth!' he cried again, his face as white as his wind-whipped hair. But action was more urgent than words. The lad wrenched a belaying pin from the gunwale. He jammed it between the lock plate and the timbers of the cage. Elizabeth heard a weak wrenching sound. The lock appeared to shift.

'Oh, thank God,' Elizabeth barely heard her own voice.

The lad tugged at the lever. A bolt dropped to the deck. Then another. 'Nearly there...' The young seaman hooked his bare foot onto the bars for leverage. The iron plate buckled. Another bolt slipped from its chink. Teeth clenched, Brinley let out a determinate guttural groan. His face strained. Sweat pooled with the rain pouring off his body. At that instant the ship dragged over another reef. It listed violently. Brinley lost his grip, skidding on his backside to the gunwale. Elizabeth cried out his name as the *Magdalena* righted ten degrees and Brinley managed to snatch at a rope. Hand over hand he drew himself back towards the cage. The next mountain of water was as violent as it was unexpected. The ship listed so steeply, her yards were under water. Brinley Thurston somersaulted back along the deck. He crashed onto his belly, sliding backwards. His terrified eyes locked on Elizabeth's.

'Elizab...'

The deluge drowned Brinley's plea as the wave retreated, taking him with it—his young life lost to the savage sea.

Now that the ship was closer to shore, the wild breaking surf stormed across the deck. Elizabeth was terrified *and* sickened. The wash about her pen swept her up, throwing her against the rear wall. She scrambled back to attack the bars. But the one stubborn bolt held fast. Another wave exploded onto the ship. Elizabeth watched, helpless, as more seamen washed overboard, their bodies stripped naked, to be grated across the reef like cheese. Elizabeth slammed her shoulder against the door.

Suddenly overhead she heard a horrendous moan. Above the din of the tempest there came a shattering crack. Elizabeth jerked her head skyward. The main and foreword masts had snapped six feet above the deck and now careered towards Elizabeth's cage.

Elizabeth dived to the cage floor. She covered her head, fearing she would be crushed. The mizzen slammed into her lockup and she was tossed aside, winded but miraculously unhurt. Another wave rolled over the ship. To Elizabeth it seemed as if some great sea monster was devouring the *Magdalena*, piece by piece.

She rolled onto her back and blinked at the blackened sky overhead. Lightning sparked aloft. Rain pounded her face. Her cage had been broached and Elizabeth clambered up through the opening.

'Let me out... Elizabeth... please...' Sally Fetter was pushed up against her pen, her bare arms reaching through the bars, her clawing fingers reaching for Elizabeth. 'Elizabeth!' she screeched over the tumult. 'Help me... please! You have to help me! For mercy's sake! Please...'

Instinctively, Elizabeth wanted to save herself. Self-preservation had been the only thought on her mind.

'Elizabeth!' Elizabeth saw the belaying pin at her feet. Another wave rolled over her as she tried to ignore the screams of the women below. There was nothing she could do to help *them,* but one life she could possibly save—Sally Fetter's.

Elizabeth jammed the belaying pin between the sliding bolt and the lock plate. She wrenched hard and the latch came away, surprisingly, more easily than her own. Sally Fetter slammed her body against the bars and the door opened, knocking Elizabeth off her feet. The two women exchanged glances, both fearing for life itself. Another wave rolled up over the stern, lifting the ship thirty, forty feet into the air. The *Magdalena* moaned in its death throes... *The sea monster had yet to be sated.*

The ship came crashing down onto the reef. This time, her back was broken like that of a rabbit in a trap. The *Magdalena* split open, gaping holes spilling her guts into the raging sea. Elizabeth looked on as hundreds of women were swept through the shattered hull, stripped of their clothing by the turbulent seas, their bodies shredded across the jagged reef. The ship's bell finally tolled its last, fell from its cradle, bounced off timbers and tumbled into the sea.

Elizabeth had no idea how long she lay along the mainsail spar, her body tangled in rope, but the twenty-foot length of yardarm had saved her life. She remembered falling overboard, remembered hitting her head. She must have blacked out briefly, but somehow, miraculously she'd been entangled in rigging connected to an oak spar. All about her in the blackness were the screams of the damned, wretched screams for salvation clawing through the mayhem, reaching for the heavens...

Yet only their souls would prosper.

Continuous waves broke over the spar. What could only be bodies of the dead brushed beneath Elizabeth—all about was a cauldron of death and disaster. Suddenly a figure appeared. Outstretched arms, clawing fingers, a white face broke the surface... Sally Fetter.

The woman spat mouthfuls of water. She screamed something incoherent as a wave washed away her pleas. Fetter snatched at Elizabeth's leg. She clawed and scratched, her fingernails drawing blood. Instinctively, Elizabeth kicked back, but the woman gained purchase. The spar rolled, and Fetter pulled herself up Elizabeth's back. Elizabeth was losing her grip. She was inches from sliding back into the sea, her spar taken over by Sally Fetter, when she saw white water froth towards her. She hugged the spar as Fetter tore at her clothing. The wave hit. The spar rolled again. Sally Fetter lost her hold and slid beneath the surface. Seconds later, the spar rose on a new wave, grinding across the razor-sharp reef beneath her. Elizabeth heard a muffled scream but there was no sign of her adversary.

Another terrifying minute passed, then another dozen crushing waves. Elizabeth could hear the waves racing ashore now. Angry surf crashing onto the coast, where their energy would finally be spent...

The beach had to be close.

Another wave scooped her ten, fifteen feet into the air. The wave curled and Elizabeth was thrown clear of the spar. The wave exploded thirty feet from the shore and Elizabeth was slammed hard into the sand. She struggled to breathe as the mountain of water held her under, like a giant hand determined to drown her. Elizabeth was so close and yet so far. She felt the undertow drag her back to sea. Her lungs were bursting. Silently, she screamed for air. Something rolled with her, entangled about her.

A body!

The next vast wave pounded the shore. Elizabeth was tumbled afresh, but forced to the surface. She snatched a lungful of air and was immediately assaulted once more. But now she felt sand at her feet. Clawing at the beach with renewed energy and the will to survive, Elizabeth dragged her exhausted body against the flow that seemed so desperate to drag her back to the depths. The next wave detonated about her in a flurry of spray and foam, shoving her unceremoniously forward, tumbling her onto the beach.

Finally, Elizabeth was free. She dropped to her knees, dragging her semi-naked body to the high-tide mark, spewed up a bellyful of water and collapsed.

Elizabeth sensed she was not alone in this tragic night. There were others on the beach this early morning, but she cared not and collapsed into unconsciousness.

Rowan hid from sight, stunned. Although he had suspected this skulduggery, witnessing it sickened him to the bone. Nauseated, aghast, he looked on, a phantom voyeur amongst the gloom of a post-storm dawn. He crouched hidden near the cliff edge, revolted by the carnage he was witnessing on the beach. The lucky ones drowned. Others, unfortunate enough to float ashore on wreckage, some with horrific wounds, were smartly bludgeoned to death. No one survived. There would be no witnesses.

Witnesses! Rowan had no doubt about what would happen to him if he were caught, and a chill crept up his spine.

As a miserably bleak dawn chased away the remnants of the storm the Bull Seal Island wreckers started back towards camp. They struggled up the steep incline—the goat path from the beach—carting as much loot as they could carry. The storm might have subsided, but a fine soaking drizzle persisted. Rowan looked back along the coast to the Eagle's Nest mountain pinnacle. A heavy mist cloaked the mountaintop. He pushed back down the gully, hiding amongst ferns at the side of a spring now lively from the storm rains. He watched the parade pass, two hundred yards away. The wreckers were exhausted, marching single file. Weary, yet victorious. No one spoke. They would rest and return for more plunder later.

Captain Leblanc and Uriah Coffin were the last to appear on the cliff top. Uriah led the donkey, its alluring lantern still swaying back and forth on its shaft, the flame doused. Roped to both sides of the beast of burden Rowan saw two studded leather trunks. Passengers' private belongings, no doubt. He waited silently until they were out of sight and made his way down to Bone Beach.

1814

PART THREE
DESTINY

CHAPTER TWENTY-TWO

Bone Beach

Rowan dropped to his knees on the shoreline and wept. Half buried by seaweed and sand was the stern nameplate of the ship—gold writing on a glossy black background—*Magdalena, London.*

But far more poignant, far more sickening, was the body of an infant, a little girl. She lay naked and twisted, face down in the sand. Rowan struggled with the thought of his own lost child, stabbed in the womb by a murderous soldier. The two would have been about the same age.

What remained of the *Magdalena* was wedged firmly on the reef. It was now low tide, but ropes remained tied to her severed bow section where the wreckers had hauled the ship further ashore. Cargo was strewn along the beach, stowed well above the high-water line, to be retrieved later at the wreckers' convenience.

With Bone Beach's vertical cliffs facing north-west, the wreck site remained in the dawn shadows. The morning mist was in no haste to leave. Rowan's sight had adjusted to the light when something even more terrifying caught his eye. Amongst the ship timbers, spas, barrels, cargo and debris, he saw the bodies—dozens upon dozens of bodies—dumped where the waves had deserted them. As the light strengthened, Rowan made out the shapes of the dead, scattered along the beach as far as he could see. They were mostly women, mostly stripped of their clothing. But then he recognised soldiers, dragged beneath the waves by the weight of their water-soaked uniforms—dozens of soldiers, as well as the ship's crew—all casualties of a cruel sea and the greed of a few deplorable men. Rowan recognised the grey frocks of some of the women—a uniform...

A transport ship. Convicts. Women prisoners and their wee bairns. As if their lives had not been miserable enough, being transported like animals to a 'place beyond the seas'. Five months at sea, to end up drowned like rats.

Rowan felt immediately determined to drag the bodies above the high-water mark, but they were heavy, dead weight, laden with water, and there were just too many.

No sooner would he drag one corpse out of the foaming surf than another and another would appear. There were hundreds. It was futile. Rowan wiped the tears from his eyes and the rain from his face. He tried to focus and walked along the beach, stepping around and stepping over body after body. He was in shock. He yearned to walk and walk away, and never turn back.

Suddenly, he saw movement. Eighty or a hundred yards ahead, he saw movement. Someone was alive, he thought, but other bodies had appeared to live, also. Waves dumped them on the beach before dragging them back to the depths, their loose limbs swaying freely. Rowan hurried forward. The woman's head lifted. Rowan broke into a sprint and seagulls rose noisily to circle overhead like vultures.

'You're alive!' he cried out.

The survivor was young, younger than twenty, Rowan guessed. She had beautiful features, a fine body and white skin, but her hair was crudely cropped short. She wore a shredded uniform—another prisoner. The woman tried to raise herself up on her elbows. She vomited and vomited again. Rowan dropped to his knees before her. 'Thank the Lord, you are alive!' The woman tried to raise her face to look at Rowan, but collapsed through sheer exhaustion.

'Are you hurt?' he asked, casting a hurried eye over her many abrasions. Elizabeth tried to speak, but her words were croaky and faint. Rowan was brushing the sand from her face when a nearby wave peaked, curled and crashed ashore, sending a foaming flood over them both. The sea retreated and Elizabeth's body lifted with the undertow that was determined to drag her back to sea. Rowan grabbed her under the arms. He held her tight. 'Are you injured?'

'I—don't—think—so,' Elizabeth managed with a rasp, her throat raw from salt water.

'Can you move? Does anything feel broken?'

Elizabeth shook her head. Another wave surrounded them. Two feet deep, three feet. The undertow was powerful and Rowan felt himself tossed about.

'Hold tight.' Rowan dragged Elizabeth further up the beach. Although she was young and lean, she was still dead weight. He lowered her onto the sand beneath the cliff ledge and turned her on her side, where she vomited seawater once more. Mentally and physically drained, Rowan collapsed next to her.

For a long moment neither said a word. Elizabeth was traumatised, but forced herself to sit up, gathering her torn smock about her nearly naked body.

Wreckage was strewn along the foreshore for as far as Elizabeth could see. Then she caught her first sight of the cadavers. 'Oh no!'

Rowan jumped to his feet. Elizabeth crawled on her hands and knees towards the closest bodies. 'No! No... It cannot be...' Rowan helped Elizabeth to her feet and she steadied herself with an arm about his waist. Even in death, the faces were familiar. Elizabeth found her footing and limped from body to body. It was so surreal. She stumbled upon Captain Cholmondeley, at least Elizabeth thought this well proportioned carcass all twisted and distorted was the captain. His neck was broken and his head was skewed about, buried in the sand. Elizabeth took a handful of hair to shift his head and study the face. But seagulls had already plucked out his eyes, and bloodied, black orbs stared back. Suddenly Elizabeth remembered the large gold ring, the ancient Roman carnelian intaglio set into the gold—a gift from the captain's wife. The man's arm was trapped under his body. Elizabeth tried to roll the figure.

'What are you doing?' Rowan asked.

'Help me...'

'But what...'

'I think this is the captain. Help me roll him over. I'll know for certain if I see the ring he wore.'

Together they managed to turn him over. 'Jesus Lord!' Elizabeth covered her mouth.

'What?' But then Rowan, too, noticed the severed finger. The ring had been removed.

'Who would do such a thing... Who?'

'Wreckers,' Rowan said almost too softly for Elizabeth to hear.

'Wreckers!'

'Yes. You have been the victim of wreckers, moonlighters. Do you know... '

'I know what wreckers are.' Elizabeth backed away from Rowan. 'Who are you? I don't recognise you from the *Magdalena*.' Elizabeth's eyes darted about the beach, up the cliffs, along the headlands.

'My name is Rowan Craige... and you?'

'Where are we?'

'Bull Seal Island.'

'Where?'

'Bull Seal Island. Bass Strait.' Rowan lowered his voice. 'What is your name?'

'Are you a wrecker?' Elizabeth almost yelled.

'N-no. No... most certainly not.' Rowan had another approach. 'I am their prisoner. They have a camp a few miles from here.'

'We are on an island... and with wreckers?'

'Yes.'

'Jesus, no.' Elizabeth dropped to her knees. Tears filled her eyes.

'You are safe with me,' Rowan said rather lamely. 'What is your name?'

'Elizabeth ... Elizabeth Eveleigh. Are you Irish?'

'I-Irish? Ah... No... Why do you ask?'

'You sound Irish.'

'I am American.'

'American!' Elizabeth was not convinced. This entire situation was such a nightmare that she did not know what to believe. 'What are you doing here?'

'I told you. I am their prisoner. It is a long story.' Rowan gestured toward Elizabeth's grey frock. 'You were a prisoner yourself, were you not?'

'Y-yes.' Elizabeth was suddenly aware of her tattered and wet clothing clinging to her body. She felt exposed. She snatched at the clothing washed up onto the beach like so much kelp; a miscellany of garments was gathered at high water mark.

'Can you walk?' Rowan asked, looking away to allow Elizabeth some privacy to change her clothes. 'I mean, you have a limp.'

'I'm fine. Walk where?'

'We can't stay here.' Rowan's eyes narrowed and he studied the landscape along the skyline above Bone Beach. 'We must hide. They will return...'

'The wreckers?'

'Yes, the wreckers. And I am afraid to say, if we are caught...' Rowan's voice trailed away. 'Well, they will not set us free.' Rowan offered his hand, but Elizabeth pulled away abruptly. He searched about and found her a suitable length of driftwood to use as a staff. 'Here. Use this.'

'Where are you taking me?'

'Away from all this.' Rowan studied Elizabeth's feet briefly before returning to a nearby corpse with shoes intact. He removed them. 'Here,' he said, passing the shoes to Elizabeth, 'you'll need these.' Elizabeth said nothing. The shoes were tight but they fit. 'Good,' Rowan said. 'Now we need to climb the cliffs back to the headland and find somewhere to rest. I will tell you everything, for what I have to say will take some time and you will not want to believe any of it.'

To avoid being seen, Rowan pushed into the low bushland surrounding the gully. He led Elizabeth away from the track leading back to Mast Head Bluff. There was little breeze. The sun was rising, but it struggled behind dark clouds. A fine intermittent drizzle persisted and a stubborn fog cloaked the mountaintop, threatening to descend the slopes. Elizabeth was traumatised. She peppered Rowan with questions, but he recognised that the woman was in shock. He needed to find refuge—somewhere they could gather themselves. After a twenty-minute walk away from the wreck site, Rowan found shelter under a rocky overhang.

'We'll be safe here for the moment...'

'Talk to me,' Elizabeth pleaded. She was shaking. 'I need answers.'

'Please sit. I will tell you all I know.'

Elizabeth Eveleigh sat silently. She was stunned as Rowan told her his complete story, up to his learning of the existence of the sealers and, finally, the deliberate wrecking of the *Magdalena*. She said little, sitting on a rock shivering, hanging onto Rowan's every word. Finally, Rowan thought he had gained enough trust to sit at her side. Elizabeth flinched.

'I mean you no harm. Please... you are shivering.' Rowan placed an arm about her shoulder to share his warmth. Elizabeth sat stiffly, but the arm was comforting. Her muscles loosened and Rowan rubbed her back before holding her tight. The shivering stopped and Elizabeth felt tears welling for the first time since they'd left the beach. But Rowan saw strength in this young woman. In turn, he insisted that Elizabeth tell her story. He knew this would help alleviate her distress.

Elizabeth told Rowan about her ill-fated life, her unfortunate alliance with Uncle Theophilus and Auntie Tempess in Bristol, her time in Newgate, her trial, the prison hulks and the eventual tragic voyage on board the *Magdalena*.

'What are we to do?' Elizabeth finally asked.

'They will be back, and sooner rather than later,' Rowan said. 'They rest now at Mast Head Bluff. I need to return...'

'Return? But you...'

'I must, Elizabeth. I must get back and hope I have not been missed.'

'Don't leave me... You can't leave me.'

Rowan placed his hands on Elizabeth's shoulders and looked her in the eye. 'I will not leave you. I will not desert you. Please understand, Elizabeth, we are in this together. I will get you off this island.'

'How?'

'They have two sloops moored in a bay on the other side of the island.'

'Can you sail?'

'Yes, of course. Single-handed, if need be. I have a plan...'

'A plan?'

'Yes. There is a native woman, a Van Diemen's Land native, her name is Pollyanna. I have promised I would see her back to her tribe one day. She was kidnapped you see, as a young girl, and yearns to return to her tribe.'

'She was kidnapped?'

'Yes.'

'These people are animals.'

'I would not even endow the title of animal on them. I know now that they are plain evil.'

'Where is this native woman?'

'She resides with me at Mast Head Bluff.'

'Is she your lover?'

'No.' For the first time, Rowan laughed. 'I told you of Jessica, did I not?'

'Yes, but...'

'But nothing. I remain true to... to Jessica.'

The morning was proving bleak. The mantle of fog veiling the summit crept down the slopes like some mythical, amphibious creature to mask Eagle's Nest lookout and gather about Mast Head Bluff. Rowan stole ahead on reconnaissance. Not a lantern light shone nor was there a sound of anyone stirring. Even the hounds slept soundly.

Rowan led Elizabeth over the rocks on the shoreline. The tide was returning, limiting their access to Mast Head Bluff, but Rowan also knew this would be the high tide the wreckers were expecting to float the bow section of the *Magdalena* closer to shore. Soon it would be all hands on deck. Rowan stepped from the rocks onto the sand, where the tide approached rapidly, each wave leaving the beach in deeper and deeper water. Before long it would be over their heads, but Rowan knew of a shallow cave where Elizabeth could hide temporarily. The water was freezing, and now up to Rowan's knees. 'There'—he pointed to a small recess, a ledge within the cave—'hide in there; you will be safe. I will return to my bed and when they have all left for the wreck, I will come back for you.'

Captain Leblanc woke with a pounding head and groaned, slowly swinging his legs over the side of his bed. He had managed three hours of sleep. Immediately, the blood rushed from his head and the memories of the night's events returned. Billy Cake lay at his side, fully clothed where he had collapsed. Myunga lay asleep on the floor. Leblanc kicked Myunga awake. 'Fetch water,' he growled. Billy stirred, his eyes, red from laudanum, searching about like those of a startled lizard.

'Jesus, Billy. 'Twas a night and a half, eh, lad?'

'Billy sick. Billy need laudanum…'

'Laudanum?'

'Billy go to Sawbones for laudanum. Sawbones not in his bed.'

'Oh?'

'Billy see Sawbones at beach, digging up bodies.'

'He what?'

Leblanc was instantly alert. 'What are you sayin', Billy?'

Billy told the captain everything.

'Jesus Lord, Billy Cake. Why did yer not tell me sooner?' He stormed from his shanty. The village was stirring. Leblanc kicked Rowan's door open. 'Pollyanna!' he screamed in the native's ear as she slept, and dragged her out by her hair. Scully, Elihu, Radge and Tuckerman were the first to get to his side. 'The tide's comin' in, Cap'n,' Scully said. 'We'll have to move fast if'n we're to secure the ship.'

'Aye'—Leblanc threw Pollyanna to her knees—'Radge, Elihu. You know what to do with this bitch.' He looked at the others, gathering about in various states of undress. 'Get it together, you lot, we're headin' back to the beach. Now!'

Destiny had delayed Rowan by mere minutes. He waited with Elizabeth in the cave—something just did not feel right. He would have to trust that they were all sleeping off their night of debauchery, but what if he was caught returning? 'I'll be back shortly,' he said finally.

'Be careful.'

'That I will.'

Elizabeth watched Rowan drop back into the water and wade to the rocks, where he intended to spy on the settlement. Life had thrown Elizabeth some crooked dice and she had experienced humanity at his lowest, but she trusted this man—this ship's surgeon, Rowan Craige. He had a kind face and, besides, she had little choice. Her life was in this stranger's hands. Elizabeth pushed back into the narrow cave and sat, hugging her knees, and prayed.

Rowan crept about the headland near the blowhole. With each wave the water became deeper. Suddenly he heard a terrified whimper.

A cry.

'Pollyanna!'

Pollyanna was locked in the trap. The tide was almost covering her. She clawed at the top of the cage, barely keeping her mouth above the surface.

'Leblanc! You bastard!' Rowan swam to her.

'Ro-wan!' Pollyanna's eyes were wide with fear. Rowan unlatched the cage door and the woman swam free and into Rowan's arms. 'Captain mad!' she cried. 'He say Pollyanna help Rowan. He want Pollyanna dead.' The next wave lapped over them and the cage was lost beneath the surface. 'He want Rowan dead.'

'What does he know?' Rowan asked.

'He know Rowan see ship.' Pollyanna told Rowan how the captain had flown into a rage. She told of how the man had stood outside Rowan's shanty surrounded by all the sealers, searching the landscape with his spyglass. Pollyanna repeated Leblanc's angered words: 'He can't get far. And he'll pay for his insolence.'

'What'll yer do to him, Cap'n?' someone had asked.

'See that he keeps his gob shut, that's what I'll do.'

'Permanently?'

'Aye.'

'We must get away from here, Pollyanna. Can you help me with the *Jolly Mary*?'

'Ro-wan be captain... *Jolly Mary* captain?'

'I hope so, Pollyanna, our lives depend on it.'

'Pollyanna help Rowan sail to my tribe on big land.'

The next wave threatened to sweep them out into deep water. Shaking from the cold, the two were crawling back up the rocks, keeping their heads below the ledge, when Rowan stopped suddenly. 'Get down!' he hissed.

Sounds of excitement approached along the path above: dogs barking, women whooping, Philistine shouting and cheering. The camp was awake—high tide had returned and the plundering must continue.

Rowan threw his back hard against the rock wall. He drew Pollyanna close, putting a hand over her mouth. They waited. The rabble passed, only feet above their heads.

'We must hurry,' he whispered when he was certain the path was clear. 'But first we must fetch Elizabeth.'

'Elizabeth?' Pollyanna asked. 'Who Elizabeth?'

'Oh...' Rowan thought how to explain. 'One woman... from ship... she lives.'

'Woman lives?'

'Yes. She lived, after the ship wrecked.'

'Where this woman?'

'She waits. But first I must fetch dry clothes and medicine from the cabin.'

Rowan and Pollyanna hugged the rock ledge, crabbing parallel with the path in order to be hidden in the event of stragglers, but the camp was deserted. It appeared that no one was to miss out on the jollification. Only the eerie mist lingered behind.

'Wait here,' Rowan ordered Pollyanna. 'Keep watch.' He rushed across the ledge to his dwelling. Everything was where it should be. He collected his letters of introduction and the fifty pounds in Bank of England notes and gold remaining from the sale of the stallion in Boston. Then he packed a satchel with essential medicines, including a salve for Elizabeth's abrasions, and dry clothes. He hooked the kit over his shoulder and made for the door when something crashed onto his cabin roof.

Rowan froze.

Loosened shingles tumbled to the ground. Rowan snatched a bottle by the neck. Half full, it would pass for a club. Whoever had been on his roof leapt onto the path.

'Cap'n!' he heard young Tommy, the lookout, scream out, his voice shrill. 'Cap'n Leblanc!'

Rowan raised the bottle. He waited to be accosted. The lad was screaming at the top of his voice, but the sealers were well down the track.

'Cap'n. A ship!' Tommy broke into a sprint to catch the others.

A ship?

Rowan hurried from his cabin and dropped to the pebbled bay in front of the camp, where he could see through the arch to open water. As his vision adjusted, he could make out a square-rigged ship. It appeared from the mist like a sceptre of doom. A frigate.

A Royal Navy frigate.

Rowan was confused. He did not know which was worse.

Tommy caught up with the partying wreckers a quarter of a mile from the settlement. 'Ship, Cap'n! Ship!'—the boy was breathless—'It's Royal Navy!'

'Navy?'

'Aye, Cap'n, I'd bet me life on it.' Tommy passed his glass to Leblanc. Leblanc hiked fifty yards up the hillside. Everyone followed. The captain screwed his face up, clamping one eye shut in concentration. Slowly, through the distant mist and the fug of his hangover he focussed on the ship. 'Jesus Christ!' Leblanc cursed. 'Ryan O'May, yer Irish bastard!'

'Captain?'

'Ryan O'May o' the *Eden*, the bastard we seen making repairs on Guinea Rock when we was sealin'. He's notified the navy in Sydney Cove. I'll bet me balls on it. That ship's comin' right fer this island.' Leblanc steadied the glass on the approaching ship. 'I'm guessin' it's the HMS *Assault*, what was moored in Sydney Cove, last we were there. Christ Almighty!'

Lutwidge. 'That be a frigate, be it not?'

'Aye. Thirty-eight guns, if'n I remember correctly.'

'God help us.'

'What'll we do?'

'If'n they find the *Magdalena,* they'll hang us all.'

'Aye. An' right 'ere on Bull Seal Island. They won't take no prisoners.'

Leblanc ground his teeth, his eyes narrowed and the strain rippled his brow. He studied the distant ship through his spyglass for some time and then studied the clouds. The sky was still grey and moody and the air unseasonably still.

'We have the wind on our side, lads, or the lack of it, I should say. The ship struggles—you all know the drill. Get to yer stations.... You lot,' he shouted at the aboriginal women, 'return to camp! Douse all fires and then join the men, savvy? And heads down, all o' yer. They'll have the spyglass on us by now.'

Leblanc was proud of his mettle. He was a tough bastard and he had proved it over and over. Now his thoughts turned to his gold. He had salted away more than seven thousand pounds in guineas, escudos, Louies and notes on the Bank of England over the past twelve years. It was a small fortune and now he knew that retirement had come early. 'Billy,'— Leblanc's head swivelled about as he scanned his family of followers—'Billy Cake, where are yer, lad?'

''Ere, Cap'n, sar.'

'Come with me.'

As he'd expected, Rowan saw the wreckers return around the headland. 'Here they come,' he told Pollyanna. 'Head down.' The rabble passed along the narrow pathway overhead in single file. Their mood was now solemn, the wind knocked from their sails.

Rowan waited for them to pass and dropped back to the shoreline. Elizabeth waited on the ledge in the cave. The tide lapped about her feet. Pollyanna did not hesitate. She lowered herself into the water—now neck deep—and swam to Elizabeth. She said nothing but offered Elizabeth her hand. Elizabeth slipped into the icy water and together they joined Rowan.

'Here.' Rowan passed the women dry clothes. Pollyanna stripped naked and pulled a dry frock over her head. Trembling from the cold, Elizabeth looked at Rowan uneasily. He turned his back. Elizabeth stripped and dressed again.

'Pollyanna,' Rowan said quietly, 'this is Elizabeth.' The women exchanged disquieted nods. Races and worlds far apart, they shared a humble respect. 'Come,' Rowan said, 'we must hurry.' The women followed Rowan, climbing over rocks and out of sight of Mast Head Bluff. Once at a safe distance, they crossed the path leading east to Blubber Beach and started up the mountain slope. Now, from where they crouched, Rowan, Elizabeth and Pollyanna could make out the approaching sail more clearly. 'This changes everything,' Rowan said. 'I am certain it is the Royal Navy.'

'How can you tell?' Elizabeth asked.

'I can't, for certain, but the sight of it has them all spooked. If that is the Royal Navy, then I am a dead man and you, I am afraid, will end up back in irons.'

'What you do, Row-an?' Pollyanna asked.

'They are preparing to fight—to defend the island.'

'What do you mean "defend the island"?' Elizabeth looked horrified. 'Defend the island against the Navy?'

'Yes.'

'How?'

'Believe me, Elizabeth, this island has many surprises.' Rowan took a last glance at the ship. 'We have one factor in our favour. There is little wind this day. The ship is struggling to make progress.' Rowan craned his neck and looked up towards the mountaintop hundreds of feet above them. The low clouds and mist clung to the summit like an eerie shroud. 'We must climb over the mountain and hurry to the sloops before the Navy lands. Regardless of the island's defences, the Navy *will* land and the Navy *will* prevail at all cost. Come, quickly now.'

Pollyanna grabbed Rowan's wrist. 'Look!'

Rowan followed Pollyanna's eye. 'Jesus, no!' In the distance they watched two well-armed wreckers and four native women carrying clubs and climbing steadily towards the summit.

'Are they going to the sloops?' Elizabeth asked.

'No. They go to man the drays.'

'Drays?'

Rowan explained the rock-laden drays prepared to create an avalanche. 'Now we will have to go around the mountain.'

'We can still get to the sloops, can't we?'

'Yes. But we have much further to travel. We must move —now.'

Chapter Twenty-Three

Two hours later, Leblanc sat at the shoreline, studying the frigate drifting a mile out. There was little swell as the sea lapped the beaches and coves at full tide. There was little wind, and the fog blanketing the sea was tenacious, although not heavy. The vessel was under full sail, but the canvas hung limply. It was only a matter of time. He fondled his rosary between forefinger and thumb but gained little confidence from the religious artifact. He had burnt his cross with God the night the *Globe* had wrecked on the island over three years ago.

Damn them, he thought stubbornly. *Damn them all. Where was God when I struggled on the Isle o' Mull, or Falmouth? Where was God when the plague hit Bombay? And damn the navy.* Leblanc was angry with himself *and* God. He twisted the crucifix and the beads knotted, breaking the twine and scattering the small lava spheres at his feet.

'Damn!' Leblanc jumped to his feet. He tossed the crucifix aside. It was the perfect day for a scrap, but he knew this was the beginning of the end. There was no denying it.

Despite the threat, they had an escape plan in situ and Leblanc felt confident of a successful retreat. The *Sea Rat,* he knew, was doomed, trapped in Seal Bay. And he would have to sacrifice many of his flock of followers, but as long as he had a key crew to help him escape to the sloops, he would be safe.

'Cap'n!' a voice cried out.

'What?'

'Look!'

'Devil's blood!' Leblanc cursed. As he watched, four jolly boats were harnessed to the bow of the frigate and each craft filled with oarsman. 'They're goin' to row her in. Quick, lads. They'll be landin' in no time.'

The atmosphere about the camp was tense. Snipers Scully and Lutwidge were at their posts with their loaded carboys in position on the only approach. Six others had climbed to the summit with the native women and children to prepare the drays. The women carried baskets with powder and shot. It would be their job to reload. Leblanc, Riddell and Radge remained to engage the first assault at the entrance to Mast Head Bluff. Each man was armed to the teeth.

They waited in silence. No one was in the mood for chatter. A subtle breeze had picked up, sweeping the fog from the camp. However, this same breeze was strong enough for the frigate to approach the island with the aid of the rowers. Now, the four jolly boats, ten rowers apiece, towed the thirty-eight-gun warship through the headlands and into Seal Bay.

'They're anchoring' Tommy signalled from his lookout behind a cairn at Satan's Hole. But Leblanc needed no prompting. In the still of midmorning, all present heard the echoed splash of *HMS Assault's* anchors, followed rapidly by ropes and chain whipping through the hawser holes. The ship was positioned port side to the island. The gunports crashed open and loaded twenty-four-pound cannons were run out.

Leblanc's reverie of retirement on the Fijian Islands, or in Tahiti, maybe, had vanished. More urgent business was now at hand. From where they crouched, Leblanc's group could just make out the first group of marines boarding the *Sea Rat*, and finally declaring her deserted.

'This is it, lads. Heads down and wait yer orders.' Leblanc crouched behind a pile of rocks, camouflaging their only carronade, a smooth-bore ship's cannon cast in Scotland and designed to take ten-pound single shot. But Leblanc had canister for ammunition. These were homemade hardened leather cylinders packed with rock, broken glass, nails and foundry slag. Elihu Riddell knelt next to the gun, aimed at the arched entrance on the settlement side. He spat into his hat for good luck and teased the smouldering taper in his hand into a red glow.

They were ready.

Two of the jolly boats, ten well-armed men in each craft with an officer seated next to the helmsman in the sheets, dipped oars and rowed for the shore. They were determined men, well-armed with Brown Bess muskets with fixed bayonets. They gathered on the pebbled beach and immediately spread out. The approach to Mast Head Bluff was smartly identified. Two forward guard marines approached the arched cave. They advanced in silence. Through the natural arch, at the end of an open cavern, they saw buildings, huts...

The marines looked at each other amazed, then returned to the others.

'Sir, you have got to see this.'

'There's a whole settlement here, sir.'

'Any sign of life?'

'No, sir.'

'It could be an ambush.'

'The camp looks deserted, sir.'

'Then we will soon see.... Corporal?'

'Sir.'

'Take four men. Make certain the area's clear.'

'Yes, sir.' Five armed marines hurried up the embankment, along the pathway to the arched entrance. Their officer watched as their figures melted into the gloom of the cavern. Seconds passed... and then a terrifying explosion and a tongue of flame erupted from the cavern. Three men were torn apart, their shredded bodies flung from the entrance. The corporal ran screaming into the open, one arm dangling by skin. A fifth man, alive but badly wounded, lay where he fell.

'Re-load,' Leblanc hissed at Riddell, behind a cloak of smoke. He passed the man a canvas bag of black powder and a fresh canister, while Radge swabbed out the bore with a damp sponge in case of loitering sparks.

'Jesus Lord!' the Navy officer shouted. 'What was that?'

'That was a carronade!' someone yelled back. 'The bastards have artillery!'

'Someone help that man.' The delirious corporal collapsed on the beach. 'You!' the officer bawled at the second group. 'Get him back on the ship to the surgeon and tell the captain we need backup!' But already extra marines lined the port gunwale of HMS *Assault* as the other jolly boats were hastily deployed. 'You men, take cover!' the officer on the beach bawled out.

The second officer scrambled to higher ground. He extended a collapsible telescope. The cavern was obscured with smoke but he could make out a pile of rocks. 'Fortification for the cannon!' he muttered to himself. Immediately, a shot exploded and the bullet whispered by the officer's cheek. 'Snipers!' he yelled and hurried down the slope at the double, re-joining the others.

'They have a cannon,' he urgently informed his fellow officer. 'Watch for snipers. Keep low. Be vigilant.' An agreement was struck to send the second group of men further along the beach to the south, to climb the embankment and prepare a sortie over the crater wall protecting the settlement.

'You men, follow me!' one of the two sergeants ordered his crew.

Meanwhile, one jolly boat was pushed into the waves, bow first, manned by four crewmen and transporting the wounded, unconscious corporal. Although a hasty tourniquet of rope was tied at his shoulder, he was losing a lot of blood. Out on the bay the men of *HMS Assault* were already at action stations. More boats dropped over the side from davits, part of a well-drilled military procedure. Eight marines per boat including an officer, neat in their shakos, red coats, white britches and arms now beached on the double and jogged for cover in two lines across the pebbles.

Leblanc squinted through a clearing in the smoke. 'They're going for high ground.'

'Good'—Radge grinned—'and right into Scully's sights.'

'Aye.' Leblanc looked up the rise, over his shoulder. He couldn't see their sharpshooter, but he knew Scully lay waiting. 'It's over to you, Joseph,' he whispered.

Joseph Scully, three hundred yards up the barren mountain slope, fingered the good luck charm around his neck, the skull bone of a haddock. He could feel his heart beating—a continuous and fast thumping in his chest. He had been preparing for this very moment for weeks. Scully lay on his belly, hidden behind the trunk of a felled tree. He ran a keen eye down the barrel of his musket and sighted the glass carboy full of black powder and rocks. It was fifty yards away. It sat, nearly fully buried on the track, disguised with bracken. He had one shot at this—one shot only. Packed down the barrel of his musket was a lead ball, imbedded with iron filings. *All he had to do was hit the damned flint at the top of the carboy.*

Bobbing shakos appeared over the rise in the hillside. One second later, the soldiers appeared...

Heads, shoulders, chests.

Two close lines jogged up the embankment and onto the steep, gravelly mountain slope. Scully counted sixteen men. The goat track forced them close together. They approached the carboy at a trot, unaware of the danger.

Scully steadied his hand.

Confident bastards!

He took a deep breath and held it. He gently compressed the trigger. He waited for the first half dozen to pass the bracken, and fired!

The glass neck shattered. The ball skipped over the flint. Sparks flew and the two pounds of black powder detonated, along with handfuls of pebbles gathered off the beach. The result was devastating. Like canister shot exploding at close range, low shrapnel shredded legs. Others were lacerated with glass. Agonising screams reverberated about the mountain.

Scully reloaded. Thirty seconds. The officer closest to Scully screamed his command. 'There!' the officer shrieked. He staggered to his feet. 'There!' he cried, stabbing his sabre towards the felled tree. But he never heard Scully's next shot. The officer's forehead shattered like porcelain, spraying the wounded men next to him with flesh and blood.

Scully sprang to his feet, and in a crouch position turned and ran. As planned, he raced across the forty-five-degree incline of the steep mountainside. Underfoot, loose gravel avalanched down the slope. He drew level with the pinnacle and looked back. Some of the survivors were on their feet and in pursuit. A shot rang out. Then another. A ball whistled by his shoulder. There was no time to reload. Scully looked up the steep incline towards the stubborn fog. He saw Billy Cake and the others near the top and climbed hard, towards the loaded wagons and cover.

'Did you hear that?' Rowan was certain he'd heard cannon fire. Pollyanna nodded. ''Tis the carronade,' he said. Elizabeth was trying to think rationally. She had survived a shipwreck in a violent storm and wanted to live. *By God, did she want to live, to be healthy and grow old, even if it was in the godforsaken colonies.*

'Surely if we give ourselves up to the Navy, they will treat us with kindness,' Elizabeth said. 'Not like what they will do to these wretched sealers.'

'Have no doubt, Elizabeth Eveleigh, if you are captured you will be made to serve your sentence. For myself? Well, I don't fancy dangling at the end of a rope.' Rowan hefted himself up the mountainside using a branch the size of a shepherd's crook as a walking stick. Pollyanna took the lead. Elizabeth struggled with the terrain. She had been incarcerated so long that her muscles were in poor condition. Rowan took Elizabeth by the wrist and helped her over a ledge.

'Surely, what you did was an eye for an eye at a time of war,' Elizabeth persisted.

'"An eye for an eye,"' Rowan repeated, coughing a laugh. 'I am afraid the British do not accept an eye for an eye.'

Hobart Town

Time passed. Marcus had adapted to prison life. He adapted to the monotonous daily diet of a quarter pound of meat, half a pound of vegetables, one pound of bread, two ounces of flour, half an ounce of salt and—for his ablutions—half an ounce of soap. Monotonous, yes, but Marcus had to remind himself that he had not been fed much more as a soldier back in England. And after the months at sea, where the boiled meat, occasionally contaminated, came to the table tight with salt, causing constipation, and the biscuits full of weevil caused widespread dysentery and diarrhoea, well, he had little to complain about. But he continued to harbour his anger.

Marcus didn't make friends easily in the free world, and he certainly didn't make friends easily in servitude. He kept to himself, having made the calculated decision that he would be of good behaviour, eventually to be awarded lighter duties accompanied by a certain amount of freedom; would bide his time, and when the opportunity presented itself, he would bolt.

The months passed and the sawmills toned Marcus's body. Six mornings each week, Marcus and his chain gang walked the three miles west of Hobart Town to the foothills of Mount Wellington. The Sabbath was kept for services in the chapel, and half a day was allowed for the pursuit of personal interests within the prison system, like reading the scriptures.

Two main arterial roads led towards the mountain—Davey Street, and the one named after Governor Lachlan Macquarie in Sydney Town. They led to virgin bushland where springs cascaded down the slopes from the snow-capped peaks, supplying the settlement with clean, fresh water. Known as the Cascades, the area was undeveloped and not considered suitable for farming. Timber, however, was in huge demand, both for building and for fuel, and the Cascades had an abundance of it.

Marcus had fought his way to the position of top dog. Top dog was the title given to the sawyer operating the pitsaw at ground level, at the top of the pit. The man wielding the saw from the bottom of the ten-foot deep pit was titled bottom dog. The logs of wood were squared and then mounted on horizontal skids held in place by iron staples called timber dogs. A string dusted with chalk and pulled tight the full length of the timber was used to mark a straight line, and it took immense practise and skill to cut uniform boards. The words of the pit overseer on the first day were etched in Marcus's memory.

'Destroy a log while sawing it, eighteen lashes,' he had said. 'Come in under your daily quota, and you will be punished. Attempting to cheat the count, eighteen lashes. Cutting your sawing partner through neglect, eighteen lashes. Cussing, twelve lashes.'

At the end of the day, the men would shuffle the three miles back to the jail....

Wash. Eat. Shit. Sleep. And then do it all over, and over and over again.

Marcus lay in pitch darkness on his iron bed, on a canvas mattress filled with straw and horsehair. He pulled his one blanket up to his chin and locked his hands behind his head, staring at a ceiling he could not see. Dreams were for the fortunate. Marcus had nightmares, and these nightmares ate feverishly at his sanity as he lay in his lonely cell in total darkness, shivering with the cold, agitated and very, very angry.

Bull Seal Island

Leblanc whispered in Riddell's ear. 'Steady as she goes, Cornelius.' Minutes of deadly silence had followed their first assault. They waited. The tension mounted. Radge had reloaded the carronade and Riddell knelt by the cannon holding a smouldering taper. It was a chilly morning, yet beads of sweat trickled down his face. At the exterior entrance—on the Seal Bay side of the cavern—freshly landed troops gathered, determined to avenge their fallen comrades. But the soldiers were now nervous. Most of these men had been recruited to police the streets of Sydney Town, not fight in guerrilla warfare, not do battle with well-armed brigands.

On board *HMS Assault* Lieutenant Greenwood felt he had his hands tied. If only he had known these bastards were so well armed... He would have fired broadside after broadside at the island and brought the devils to their bloody knees. Now he had troops ashore—far too many. It would be butchery to fire the ship's cannons at this stage.

The officer on the shoreline felt apprehensive. 'Fix bayonets!' he ordered, with a sharp eye fixed on the arch. 'Keep to the walls, men, left and right. Keep hard to the cave walls. Forward, march.' The more experienced led the lines, one on each side of the cave.

Leblanc cupped both hands about the cascabel—the iron ball at the end of the cannon breech. The gun was heavy, weighing three hundred pounds. 'Give me a hand,' Leblanc told Radge. The gun shifted tightly on its homemade swivel. Leblanc brought the barrel to rest, aiming down the centre of the cavern. He knew that the canister of shrapnel would spread wide and do the most damage.

'They're comin',' Radge said anxiously. As they watched, moving shadows shifted about in the semi-darkness of the passageway.

'Fire when yer ready,' Leblanc said calmly.

Riddell hit the touchhole with his lighted taper. The powder flared, sending sparks into the breech, exploding the black powder. The canister burst from the breach, tore apart, and scattered the lethal debris far and wide. The charge was so powerful that the carronade kicked back violently. The cairn crumbled and the gun crashed to the ground.

Again, the screams of pain and distress reverberated from the cavern. Some attackers died. One man leading was decapitated whilst the closest victims bore the full force of splintering metal, rock and glass. *They were lambs to slaughter.*

'Time to say goodbye, my friends.' Leblanc cocked both his pistols, one in each hand, and led Riddell and Radge on the retreat back through their settlement. Return fire chased them, but with the cavern in pandemonium, the soldiers' shots flew wild.

The wreckers leapt from rock to rock and scrambled by Satan's Hole. A fearful gush of water surged through the blowhole and exploded, drenching the men with seawater.

Now the frigate spotted them.

Instantly, a single cannon fired from the ship. The ball sizzled high overhead. Leblanc knew the gunner was sighting his next shot, but they had no choice. They had to climb. The three men stumbled up the steep embankment. With the ground crumbling underfoot, gaining purchase was punishing. Leblanc's keen hearing caught the order as it echoed over the bay:

'Fire!'

He turned to face the ship at the moment the lone cannon retched smoke. The six-pound ball slammed into the ledge three yards away, on such a low trajectory that it skipped across the rocks, ploughing into the mountain in a geyser of dirt and rock. Leblanc looked back to Mast Head Bluff. The settlement was now swarming with redcoats. More were landing and hurrying up the far side of the mountain slope from Seal Bay. There was not a second to lose.

1814

Leblanc faced the first group of soldiers—six men climbing clumsily from the shelter of the crater. They were a hundred yards distant, but, like him, they were exposed. He fired both pistols. Riddell did the same. The soldiers dropped to the ground, giving Leblanc, Riddell and Radge precious seconds to continue scaling the mountain slope, their boots slipping and dislodging rocks. But these men were used to the terrain and they advanced swiftly in their ascent.

A third cannon shot echoed around the bay, but there was no time to look back. Leblanc heard the whistling shot approach and then a piercing scream. Cornelius Riddell fell back from where he had just climbed. The cannon ball had taken out a section of his gut. He writhed in agony, his lifeblood soaking into the mountain dust. There was nothing Leblanc or Radge could do.

'Help me!' Riddell screeched in his throws of death, 'Captain...'

Leblanc turned away and clawed on his hands and knees up the treacherously steep incline.

Musket shots rang out. All about them the ground spat shards of rock as musket balls peppered the mountain. With the redcoats in pursuit, the ship's cannon ceased firing. Leblanc and Radge jumped the goat path, following the coast. Shielded by dead tree trunks, they covered the first hundred yards, but there was a three-hundred-yard climb to the pinnacle. Leblanc heard the encouraging shouts from his mates at the summit, their whereabouts still masked by the thinning fog, but the sun was rising and the mist threatened to clear completely.

Uriah Coffin, Smyth, Caleb, Tuckerman, Talbot, Gabriel, Lutwidge and Scully watched while the women and children crouched on the lee side of the pinnacle. The fog about them was weakening but they could still only make out blurred shapes of red as the marines started up the slope. Uriah

Coffin threw back the latches on an armoury trunk. 'Shoot the bastards!' he yelled to the others. He rammed powder and ball down his own musket, steadied the barrel on a cart and fired at the nearest moving target. The redcoat dropped to the ground.

'Huzzah!' the Maori cheered. But the soldier rose again to his feet, only to advance once more. The others loaded and fired and loaded again...

The redcoats had no choice but to hit the ground. There was no cover. Some fired back, buying precious time to advance, but the defenders had the high ground. Leblanc took a hasty look behind him to assess the situation. He guessed there were a good thirty soldiers now following him. They were spread out in three lines, and, back at the beach, more soldiers and sailors were being ferried ashore from the frigate.

The firepower from their mates above gave the two Bull Seal Islanders the chance they desperately needed. This was, after all, a part of the plan. Although nearing exhaustion, Leblanc and Radge made it to the wagons. Both men were breathless, gulping the mountain air. But there was no time to rest.

'What of Cornelius?' Uriah Coffin asked of Riddell.

'What of' im?' Leblanc panted.

'Where's Riddell, Cap'n?'

'Dead!'

Leblanc briefly caught a dark side glance from the Maori, who was sickened by the captain's lack of sensitivity. Musket balls sizzled close by. Splinters of wood and iron spiralled through the air. 'They'll outflank us!' Leblanc shouted. He extended his spyglass and hunted through the lens. He noted that at least one man had fallen into the spike pits, but the that the remaining redcoats were now wary. They advanced anxiously through the blackberry bushes. Fires were starting

—the settlement was being torched—but there was no time for sentiment. Leblanc watched small skirmish parties inching east and west down on the shoreline. 'Shoot, shoot for Christ's sake!' he yelled at the lads.

A volley exploded around the captain as his men fired down the mountain. Leblanc's hearing suffered. He shook his head, fanning smoke before him, and raised the glass once more. 'Reload! Smartly, now!'

The next volley had soldiers scattering.

'Still they come,' Leblanc muttered. 'We gotta move fast, lads. We gotta get to them sloops.'

The wreckers awaited their order. The wagons were the ace up their sleeve. Leblanc made a mental roll call. He had ten men including himself, and thirteen natives, including their brats. Tommy and Eddy, the two half-caste tykes were already busy reloading the muskets.

Leblanc turned to the Negro harpooner. 'Gabriel.'

'Cap'n.'

'Get them women to the sloops'—Leblanc nodded to Tommy and Eddy—'an' take them brats with yer.'

'Aye.'

Leblanc's command did not denote chivalry. Rather, he saw the natives as expendable targets to confuse the soldiers —all the better for his escape. 'Where's Billy Cake?'

''E should be already at the sloops, Cap'n, like yer ordered, 'an' with the trunk.'

'Good.' Leblanc had settled his breathing. He felt suddenly calm. He stroked his chin and peered at the wary enemy framed between the wagon wheels. 'Come on up, yer bastards. That's it. Up yer come...'

Leblanc waited until Gabriel had gathered the natives together and started off down the west side of the mountain.

'Keep yer heads down, lads. Don't move a muscle. Let them bastards think we've scarpered. Let 'em march on up the slopes and then...'

Rowan, Elizabeth and Pollyanna had advanced around the waist of the mountain at a jog. Rowan and Pollyanna were fit, and with the help of the other two Elizabeth found a renewed energy, fortified by self-preservation and the possibility of freedom.

'We are near,' Rowan told Elizabeth. 'One mile, maybe less.' The sound of muffled musket shots circled the island on a stiffening breeze. The three looked at each other. 'Sounds closer than the last shots,' Rowan said in a tone that disguised his worst thoughts. 'Come.' He took Elizabeth by the hand. 'We must hurry.'

Leblanc collapsed his spyglass and slipped the scope into his pocket. He had seen enough. 'Stand by,' he said, almost softly. The fog had lifted steadily. Soon the wagons would be fully exposed. Leblanc watched the hints of movement behind rocks and ledges or wherever the redcoats had taken cover. The soldiers were regrouping, preparing to advance from three directions—directly forward and from the left and right flanks. A shako rose above a rocky incline, but Leblanc guessed the manoeuver was a ruse. From the hat's clumsy motion, he suspected that it was supported on the end of a musket barrel. The lack of fire worked. When all seemed clear, the shako's owner looked cautiously over the rise. *All was clear.*

More heads appeared. A dozen. Twenty. Three dozen. The redcoats spread out in a wide crescent and advanced guardedly on the strange wagons positioned at the summit, a hundred yards distant.

1814

'You ready?' Leblanc called along the line. The men nodded. Their consternation was palpable. They crouched at the wagon wheels in preparation for removing the chocks holding the tilting wagons in place.

'Ned, Lutwidge, Scully, Edward. Ready?'

There was electricity in the air. 'Aye, Cap'n, ready as we'll ever be.'

Four wagons, positioned in a fan configuration to cover one hundred and eighty degrees were piled high with rocks and on a relentlessly steep incline. Only stone chocks held them back. Gravity waited. It was a recipe for disaster.

The redcoats continued their climb, struggling breathlessly up the goddamned steep mountain of infertile wind-swept rock and weeds. The wreckers watched them advance. The nearest soldiers were now less than fifty yards away. They caught sight of the wreckers, but felt triumph. The soldiers could taste victory and grew increasingly confident, too damned confident. Some fired off shots.

'Look at the bastards. They think they have us,' Radge said, spoiling for a fight.

'Release the rocks,' Leblanc ordered.

Synchronised hammering pounded the stone wedges free. The result was instant. The wagons, weighing four to five tons apiece, trundled off down the precipitous mountainside, rolling out of the mist, slowly at first, before threatening to become a fatal rockslide.

The soldiers gazed curiously up the mountain towards the pinnacle. For the briefest of moments, it appeared that the top of the mountain was shifting. The wagons gained speed. They bounced over the rough terrain. Jouncing stones were flung up, each stone creating its own avalanche. The sound grew into a crescendo.

And then into a frightening rumble.

'Run!' someone screeched. But there was nowhere *to* run. The wagons thundered down the slopes. Faster and faster. Larger rocks were thrown free and the loose rocks chased after the wagons. There was no predicting their path. The renegade missiles spread out, rebounding off the terrain, gaining momentum like huge snowballs in an avalanche.

The first soldier was struck in the chest by a bouncing rock the size of a bread loaf. It punched him backwards, smashing ribs. He screamed in agony. But his screams were short-lived as the pursuing wagon crushed the man where he fell, along with eight others who were cowering helplessly. Heads cracked open. Limbs were torn from bodies. Another knot of soldiers stood in the path of a middle wagon. They rushed aside like panicked sheep, attempting to predict the wagon's trajectory. But the vehicle's front left wheel shattered, careening the wagon off course and mowing the soldiers down like a herd of goats. Another wagon hurtling down the mountain trampled two men on the periphery who were attempting to clamber to safety. The cries of all the men —their agonising shrieks of terror, pain and death—could be heard back in the bay.

'Dear god!' Henry Tuckerman cried, 'will yer look at that?'

The Bull Seal Islanders could not have imagined how successful Rowan's defence would be. The mountain slope was a battlefield of annihilation. Dozens lay dead or wounded. It was a pathetic and sickening sight.

''Move it, lads,' Leblanc ordered. 'We've gotta move fast. They'll regroup. There'll be comin' after us more than ever.'

Rowan, Elizabeth and Pollyanna caught their breath at the crest of a crumbling, desolate cliff. Here on the east coast of Bull Seal Island the wind had picked up. They would have to descend with care. Rowan stepped to the cliff edge and ran a keen eye over the landscape. Below them, in the sheltered bay, Leblanc's two sloops, the *Jolly Mary* and the *Queen B*, swung bow to shore on their stern moorings as the tide continued to creep in. Beyond the shelter of the bay, through the narrow headlands, Rowan was pleased to note white-peaked waves. A northerly was blowing, so he knew that they would have a strong wind to aid their escape to the northern coast of Van Diemen's Land, if they could take the *Jolly Mary*. Suddenly, freedom seemed a real possibility.

The hand-hewn path down the nearly vertical cliff face was as precarious as it was daunting. Rowan had climbed the path before, but recent heavy rains had washed sections away. Pollyanna insisted on leading. Rowan took Elizabeth's hand. 'Are you all right?' he asked.

'I'm not all that fond of heights,' Elizabeth replied. She had memories of being caught in bad weather on the estuary cliffs near Bristol and a chill shot up her spine. She closed her eyes briefly and took a deep breath.

'I am not in favour of heights, either, if am I to be honest,' Rowan said. The two watched Pollyanna negotiate the perilous track with the confidence of a mountain goat.

'Just take small steps,' Rowan offered. 'Don't look down. Do as I do.'

Elizabeth's face whitened. She hesitated, but when distant musket fire reminded her of their pursuers she began to take careful steps.

On one side, the precipitous cliff face rose a hundred and fifty feet from the rocks below to the cliff edge above. To the left of the narrow track was a vertical drop. Halfway down the wind changed direction, buffeting the climbers. Loose stones crumbled away underfoot, cascading down to the bay. Rowan felt Elizabeth sway. He squeezed her hand. 'Don't look down... Elizabeth, do you hear me?'

'Y-yes.'

'We're more than half way. Keep moving.'

You can do this, you can do this, Elizabeth said over and over to herself, her mind a foggy soup from the nightmare of the past dozen hours. She stared at the back of Rowan's head and, step by step, they descended.

Pollyanna stopped at the water's edge. She stood on a rocky shelf overlooking the sloops anchored to moorings thirty yards out. She shielded her eyes against the rising sun and studied the two sloops. Rowan and Elizabeth joined her.

'Where's the tender?' Rowan looked for the dinghy used to row out to the sloops, but Pollyanna just shrugged.

'What's wrong?' Elizabeth asked, as the blood flushed back into her cheeks. Pollyanna looked troubled.

'The tender is missing,' Rowan said, bewildered. 'It should be at the shore here, but it's missing.'

'Pollyanna swim,' Pollyanna said, and dived off the ledge into the chilling waters. Rowan and Elizabeth watched the sleek native glide underwater with the temerity of a seal. She surfaced and immediately broke into powerful, determined strokes, swimming towards the *Jolly Mary*. Moments later, she scaled the anchor line and boarded the sloop.

'Can you swim?' Rowan asked Elizabeth.

'I... I'm not certain if...' Elizabeth was a young lass from Wessex, where swimming was a rare pastime.

'It's not far. We'll jump together, all right? I'll hold your hand.'

Elizabeth peered over the rock ledge into the freezing water. Visions of the shipwreck returned: the screams of the dying, the terrified faces.

'J-jump?' Elizabeth hesitated.

'Feet first. All right?'

'I don't know...'

'Row-an!' Pollyanna cried out. She was pointing to the cliff top. 'Row-an... swim!'

An unsettling voice assaulted them from above. Rowan recognised the powerful Negro, Gabriel. Native women and their half-castes surrounded him, blackened silhouettes against the cliff-top skyline.

'Quickly, Elizabeth,' Rowan said. 'You must trust me.'

'Trust you?' It was not just the jump but the swim out that bothered Elizabeth. Barking wolfhounds pushed past Gabriel and started down the path. Gabriel followed as Hamish and Bones weaved down the path without fear. The natives gathered to watch. But instantly more menacing figures appeared...

The wreckers.

A shot rang out. The ball stung the ledge at Rowan's feet. Rowan snatched Elizabeth's wrist...

'Ready?'

The dogs rushed Rowan.

'Go!'

They jumped.

Elizabeth felt her body sink deep into the cold water. Rowan kept hold of her arm. He kicked away from the seawall and broke the surface three yards out. At the water's edge the frenzied hounds contemplated the jump. Still holding Elspeth's arm Jameson struckout with a powerful sidestroke for the Jolly Mary while the wolfhounds stalked them along the ledge.

More shots rang out from the cliff top, but they were poorly aimed. Rowan swam to the stern of the sloop, away from the shooters where Pollyanna helped them on board.

'The tender!' Rowan saw the tender drifting off to starboard. It had been out of sight from the shore. 'The boat Pollyanna... Why is the boat here?'

But there was no time for debating. Pollyanna shook her head and loosened the halyard, immediately hauling on the mainsail.

'Rowan Craige, yer traitor!' Leblanc's shout from the clifftop echoed around the amphitheatre of the bay. Another pistol shot rang out, expressing the captain's anger.

'Elizabeth,' Rowan yelled. 'Belowdeck... now!'

'Shoot true, yer bastards!' Leblanc screeched at his men. A volley of four shots resounded about the cliff walls. Lead balls punctured the *Jolly Mary's* deck. 'Yer goin' nowhere, Sawbones! I'll rip yer Yankee guts out!' The wreckers started down the cliff.

There was no time to weigh anchor. Rowan fire axed the anchor cable with one powerful swing and took the helm.

The winds buffeting the cliff face rebounded into the bay. *Jolly Mary's* jib stiffened with a sharp crack, the canvas filled and Rowan eased the sloop's nose toward the open sea. Realising he was a prime target, Rowan dropped to the deck, steering blind and using the steep, jagged headlands to guide himself. Pollyanna secured the mainsail halyard and took cover behind the companionway hatch just as a musket ball lodged in the cover.

Rowan glanced over his shoulder and saw that Leblanc was edging his way down the cliff. A dozen other figures followed as Navy Marines converged at the cliff top. They lined the edge of the precipice—a dozen or more. A shot rang out. One of the wreckers lost his footing and careered off the path. Rowan heard a short scream before the nauseating thud that sounded when the man slammed onto the rocks a hundred feet below. The soldiers threw rocks down from the top. More wreckers slipped and fell to their deaths.

Rowan kept the sloop steady by the helm as they approached the headlands. Suddenly an anxious voice rose from the companionway.

'Up. Up.'

Rowan lifted his head far enough to make out the simpleton.

'Billy!'

'Billy real angry now.' Billy Cake had the muzzle of a pistol pressed into Elizabeth's back. He pushed her before him, up onto the deck. Elizabeth looked more angry than scared. Back at the base of the cliff, the wreckers had spread out and a gun battle was in full swing.

'Billy!' Rowan cried out, 'leave her be, man! She is innocent. She has done nothing wrong!'

'Billy real angry.' Billy was tense, bordering on panic-stricken. 'Cap'n!' he squealed to the shore, but the gunfire drowned his cries. Pollyanna crouched behind the companionway hatch as musket fire sizzled by the sloop, some shot splintering the deck. 'Billy,' Rowan persisted, 'she has done you no harm.'

'Billy angry.'

A fresh breeze caught the mainsail and the sloop heaved fifteen degrees to starboard. The sunlight shifted and Rowan noted Pollyanna's shadow cast from the companionway and behind Billy as she prepared to strike.

'Turn boat back!' Billy yelled at Rowan. His voice was high pitched. 'Turn back! Turn back now, or I shoot woman!' He pressed the muzzle harder into Elizabeth's neck. Rowan could see the hammer pulled back. Billy was scared witless and could accidentally pull the trigger. 'Billy, no! Please!'

'Turn back, Sawbones!'

Just as Pollyanna sprang to her feet, Rowan heard a gunshot from the cliff top and the Navy marine's sniper fire slammed into the back of Billy's head. He knew nothing. The pounding lead threw him forward. Billy's pistol skittered across the deck and he tumbled overboard.

'Get down! Elizabeth!' Rowan screamed.

Elizabeth dropped to the deck. Pollyanna rolled onto her side just before a second and third shot shredded the timber right where she had lain.

Rowan held the helm steady. They were briskly approaching the entrance to the bay. It was a narrow gap but Rowan coaxed the sloop between the rocky outcrops with a measure of skill. Pollyanna was impressed.

Rowan took one last look over his shoulder as they left Bull Seal Island behind them. The gun battle continued. He thought he recognised Leblanc's distant figure climbing rocks to the south side of the bay, but he could not be certain. A fresh gust of wind hit the sail and the *Jolly Mary* listed perilously, but Rowan held her steady and tacked her southeast as the ocean's welcome swell rolled under the keel.

Pollyanna joined Rowan at the wheel. 'Good work, Pollyanna.'

Pollyanna smiled victoriously. 'Billy Cake bad whitefella. Now he fish tucker.' She laughed carelessly—or was it nervously? Rowan wondered.

Elizabeth steadied herself at the companionway, using the hem of her wet skirt to wipe Billy's blood from her neck and face. She rubbed vigorously; her eyes were wide. She was in shock.

'Take Elizabeth below deck,' Rowan told Pollyanna. 'See if you can find fresh clothes, and maybe some rum or brandy.'

Pollyanna turned to Elizabeth but immediately her attention was drawn back to Bull Seal Island, a mile southwest down the coast. The native's face darkened. 'Rowan. Look!'

The HMS *Assault* had passed through Forget Me Not headlands and was hauling full sail. The mainsails were already drawing the ship towards them with frightening determination.

'Damn!' Rowan's face was grim.

'Are they coming after us?' Elizabeth called through the wind.

'Damn right they are. Lookouts must have seen us. Christ! Why can't they just chase Leblanc and his cutthroats?'

Pollyanna swung one handed from the ratline. 'We go fast Row-an.'

'We'll see.' But Rowan felt a knot in his gut.

The thirty-eight-gun Royal Navy frigate left the island in her wake and under full sail she, too, listed heavily to starboard. With the northerly stretching all her canvas, Rowan thought she would look magnificent under ordinary circumstances.

But these were not ordinary circumstances.

At three quarters of a mile, a puff of smoke and flame spat from one of the *Assault's* bow chasers. The boom followed on the wind and the ten-pound cannon ball splashed into the sea, making a twelve-foot plume of water twenty yards ahead of the sloop.

'Oh, God!' Elizabeth bit her knuckle. 'Are they trying to sink us?'

'Not yet,' Rowan said as calmly as he could. 'That was a warning shot, for us to reef in the sail.'

Elizabeth looked terrified. Pollyanna knew Rowan a little better. The *Jolly Mary* dropped into a trough and ascended sharply, bow pointing skywards, to the sound of snapping canvas and hissing spray.

'And, are you?' Elizabeth cried out. 'I mean, are you going to reef sail?'

'What?' Rowan kept the sloop's nose aimed into the next wave. 'After all we've been through? Not likely.'

Rowan estimated the speed of each ship. The frigate was gaining on them. 'Hell's teeth,' he cussed, 'I'm not giving up that easy.'

Rowan tacked into the wind in a desperate attempt to gain knots, but, to add to their woes, the wind changed direction, slowing their progress. But what was inconvenient for the *Jolly Mary* was also inconvenient for the frigate. Stalemate.

The two craft struggled in unfavourable winds. Hours passed. Dusk approached and the *Assault* had not gained more than a tenth of a league.

Rowan looked to the west, as the sun was setting. He could lose the frigate in the dark, but had little knowledge of the islands. He was feared wrecking the sloop on rocks.

'Pollyanna.'

'Aye Ro-wan.'

'Night comes. Do you know these seas?'

'Pollyanna never fish night.'

Rowan looked at the southern horizon with reservations. The dark shapes of several islands were slowly being absorbed into the approaching night. Rowan knew that submerged rocks and remote seal colonies dotted the area. Bull Seal Island, however, was now a speck to the northwest.

'Look!' Elspeth shouted. They're turning about.'

Rowan looked over his shoulder. A mile distant, the square-rigged ship was tacking about. 'Pollyanna,' Rowan cried out, 'take the wheel.'

'Aye, Cap'n Row-an.' The aborigine's cheeky grin was infectious.

Rowan took the spyglass from the binnacle case. As he focussed on the frigate, a huge weight lifted from his shoulders. 'You're right. She's returning to Bull Seal.'

'May I see?'

Rowan handed Elizabeth the telescope. He watched her squint and fiddle, trying to adjust the focus. 'Here.' From behind, Rowan put an arm each side of Elizabeth and twisted the front piece. 'Tell me when you have a focal point.'

'Now!' Elizabeth said, delighted. They stood together a moment. Elizabeth concentrated on the ship. Rowan sensed

Elizabeth's scent through the salty dampness, her womanhood. For the first time in the past hectic hours, he was conscious of her beauty. Although Elizabeth's hair had been hacked short by the *Magdalena's* barber, it exposed her long thin neck, her dainty ears and her comely profile. Elizabeth was aware of Rowan's proximity. She wasn't certain why, but it thrilled her. She felt safe with this man. He wasn't like the others. Elizabeth held the glass on the frigate far longer than she'd intended. Rowan sensed the chemistry between them. Elizabeth was youthful but, now eighteen, she was a woman. And for the first time since losing Jessica, he felt attraction for another.

Guinea Rock was another half hour sail away. With only the bow spanker set, they had slowed significantly. Trusting Pollyanna's dead reckoning, Rowan sailed to the bleak, desolate and stinking rock, home to thousands of seals. Pollyanna jumped ashore on the lee side of the island and dragged a bow rope to high ground, where she anchored it to a large rock. They would have to sit out the night and set sail at first light. And Rowan was under no illusion. The HMS *Assault would* come searching for them.

They suffered the cold and wet. Pollyanna found an oversized frock coat, sailor's britches and several calico blouses in the clothes locker. She shared them out, but there were no blankets. There was nothing to eat or drink and they dared not light a lantern. It would be a long night.

'Why was Billy Cake hiding on board the *Jolly Mary,* anyhow?' Rowan asked Pollyanna in the dark.

'Billy Cake... Cap'n say Billy Cake fucked.' Pollyanna tapped herself on the head. Elizabeth spontaneously laughed at her vocabulary.

'But it makes no sense. Why would he hide on the sloop?'

'Maybe Billy Cake run away. Aye, Rowan... fucked in head an' runaway.' Pollyanna giggled and she heard Elizabeth half-supress another laugh. Although they could barely make out each other's faces, they exchanged smiles. Whitefella humour was not lost on Pollyanna's primitive background.

Rowan played along. 'Maybe you're right, Pollyanna.'

Silence again befell them. The night had turned still, and ice began to settle on the deck above. Only gentle swells splashed against the sloop, but their occasional thump against the hull conjured dark thoughts of sharks or revengeful bull seals. Soon Pollyanna snored in a fatigued sleep. Rowan could hear Elizabeth shivering in the dark, where they lay across the sails' locker.

'You asleep?' Rowan asked Elizabeth quietly.

Elizabeth's answer came on frosted breath. 'N-no.'

'It is going to be a cold night. I suggest we lie together for warmth.' Rowan's suggestion was practical and chivalrous. Elizabeth lay silent in the blackness for some time and Rowan felt an uncomfortable awkwardness. His intentions were gallant, not devious, and he felt his face redden.

Finally, Rowan heard Elizabeth shuffle along the boards, and she lay down next to him. 'Turnabout,' he said quietly, not wishing to disturb Pollyanna. Elizabeth obeyed. She turned her back to Rowan and he nestled his body close to hers. Elizabeth's' shivering moderated. Rowan stretched his arm over hers, dangling it before her and pulling her closer. 'If we have nothing else left this night, at least we can share our warmth.'

Elizabeth said nothing. She felt strangely comfortable, as for the first time in her miserable life she was experiencing genuine kindness. Rowan tucked a spare blouse under Elizabeth's head for a pillow. 'Goodnight,' he said.

Another thoughtful pause seemed to last forever, until finally Elizabeth said softly, 'Thank you.'

Rowan acknowledged by holding her even tighter. He fought sleep, lying awake while Elizabeth's breathing slowed.

Moments passed; he heard her rhythmic breathing, and finally he, too, drifted off into blissful, exhausted sleep.

Had the three escapees aboard the *Jolly Mary* but known, *HMS Assault* would sail directly for Sydney Cove two days later. There, Lieutenant Greenwood's first priority would be to dispatch a government cutter to George Town and Port Dalrymple in the north of Van Diemen's Land, and to Hobart Town in the south, in order to notify the respective authorities. This was the most ambitious attack on the Royal Navy since Napoleon, at least that is what the colonial newspapers would crow.

Lieutenant Greenwood and his men needed the two days to decimate Mast Head Bluff and gather evidence of the disasters that had befallen the *Magdalena* and the other ships. A shore party buried the dead. The marines lost fourteen lives in the tragedy, nine under the avalanche of rocks alone. The Navy killed three native women and eight of Leblanc's crew. Six wounded were captured and placed in irons under heavy guard. They would be returned to New South Wales to be hung as wreckers and pirates. The body of the Mongoloid, whom Lieutenant Greenway was told was named Billy Cake, had washed up in the small cove. The surviving natives with their offspring were put on board the sloop *Queen B* and given their freedom. Where they sailed to did not concern Lieutenant Greenway.

Surviving captive John Stuart Radge had no qualms about describing Rowan to his Royal Navy interrogators. 'Rowan Craige be his name. Ship surgeon from Maryland what murdered one o' yer own. Shot 'im in cold blood, 'e did.'

Captain Amos Leblanc, however, had eluded capture, and even more frustrating for Lieutenant Greenway was the fact that they never located his body.

CHAPTER TWENTY-FOUR

Days later.
North-east Van Diemen's Land.

The *Jolly Mary* sailed southeast from Guinea Rock on a strong tail wind for a full day. Pollyanna finally recognised the coastline and, eventually, the fires of her people, the North-east tribe on Van Diemen's Land. The homecoming of Gununa, for that was Pollyanna's tribal name, was as joyous as it was tearful, and Rowan and Elizabeth were accepted as her saviours. They settled into the ways of the natives. Elizabeth, being young, adapted without difficulty and was especially amazed at the range of food available on this seemingly godforsaken island. Daily, they dined on kangaroo, wallaby, possum, swan and duck, all dispatched with throwing sticks: long straight spears fashioned from tree branches, or clubs made from tree roots. Elizabeth was fascinated by Rowan's stories of survival. How on Bull Seal Island the women fetched the oily, migrating mutton-birds from their burrows and roasted them over the fire. Here, on the coast, the women caught young seals; they dived for crayfish and collected oysters. They made long, slender canoes from tree bark and paddled to offshore rocks to fetch their favourite delicacy, bird's eggs. Interestingly, Elizabeth noted that the only vegetables they consumed were plant roots.

Rowan had acquired an interest in anthropology on Bull Seal Island, where he had studied the ways of the natives, but here on Van Diemen's Land was an opportunity to study aborigines who were unsullied by the whitefellas' bad habits. He noted their bark canoe building and that all tribes were communal and had no sense of personal possessions, outside of the ownership of a club or woven basket. They had no religious beliefs, except the fear of evil spirits, and therefore avoided places believed to be haunted by such demons.

They were a happy people; however, the arrival of the whitefella and the taking of their land and food resources was making them resentful. Rowan learned that they were quick to take offence. Gununa told Rowan that marriage outside the tribe was accepted and that, interestingly, if a murder took place, the family of the deceased avenged it. The women cooked and maintained the camp, weaving baskets from bark fibres and threading necklaces of kangaroo sinew with small shells. The men knapped tools, for cutting or pounding, from flint and churt, another suitably hard rock. Animal bones were used in a variety of ways, ranging from drilling holes to needlework. They lived in the open, but Gununa told Rowan some tribes on the west and south coasts built huts of bark.

As for Pollyanna—Gununa—she was free. She was thrilled to be back with her people, although it took some time for them to accept her *whitefella* ways.

But as idyllic as life with Gununa's tribe was, it was not the life for the two *whitefellas,* Elizabeth and Rowan. As Gununa settled back into her previous life, she noticed that Rowan and Elizabeth became more and more restless. She watched Rowan's confidence amongst the tribe grow, but even more so, she watched his relationship with Elizabeth strengthen. Gununa saw them spend hours together, exchanging their stories, sometimes laughing, sometimes sad. And with a measure of sadness, Gununa knew they would leave, and soon.

Also, for Rowan and Elizabeth, being a part of this tribal family meant that they were never fully alone, and their friendship remained just that, but with the necessity for survival they had become inseparable, two *whitefellas* amongst a primitive tribe of sixty souls.

Then one evening, as they sat about the camp's huge fire, Gununa told Elizabeth and Rowan that the tribe was moving further east in the morning. Like the change of seasons, Gununa told them, the hunting had grown lean and it was time to seek food elsewhere. They were, after all, nomads.

Early the next morning, Gununa and several of the men from her tribe helped Rowan and Elizabeth drag the *Jolly Mary* from the inlet, where the sloop had been hidden for the past six weeks. They pushed it out beyond the breaking surf and then the men swam back to shore. Gununa dangled her feet in the water off the stern, while Elizabeth hauled the sail as she had been taught.

'Pollyanna sad,' Pollyanna said to Rowan at the wheel.

'I know, Pollyanna,' Rowan said, as the sail caught the breeze and the *Jolly Mary* pulled towards deep water. 'I will miss you.' As Rowan said this, he saw tears well in the native's eyes. He leant forward and kissed the aborigine gently on the forehead.

'I miss you Row-an... Pollyanna miss you.' Pollyanna sank from the stern and the surf washed the tears from her eyes. Rowan watched Pollyanna ride the surf to the beach, where she ran after her tribe and never turned back.

1814

The winds strengthened and Rowan and Elizabeth sailed through the day, not knowing exactly what their plans were. Rowan had suggested they sail to New Zealand, but then thought better of it. They would need more hands. 'Maybe,' he suggested, 'we will find like-minded souls along the coast.' But he knew anyone they found would be absconders or rogues wanted by the law.

Like him, Elizabeth had hardened to the outdoor life. They had become resilient, and both were happy barefoot. As he'd known this day was approaching, Rowan had trained Elizabeth in the rudiments of sailing and she took to it like a duck to water. 'Who would have guessed?' Rowan chuckled, as Elizabeth joined him at the helm with a gourd of water and pieces of cold roasted mutton bird.

'Guessed what?'

'The girl from Bristol, pirate queen.'

'Pirate Queen,' Elizabeth laughed, 'I like that.' For the first time in her life, Elizabeth felt alive.

As late afternoon approached they put into a sheltered bay. The bay looked safe enough, with a crescent shaped beach and a natural harbour of granite rock stacked by time at each end. There was little if any surf. Elizabeth stood at the bow, one foot hooked up on the gunwale, on lookout for rocks. As it was high tide Rowan planned to beach the sloop, anchor her to the sand, sleep on board and depart on the tide in the morning.

'How goes she?' Rowan called out.

'Six feet,' Elizabeth estimated. But the sloop was gliding ashore fast. 'Five feet, four... '

Without warning the *Jolly Mary's* bow soared skywards on a steep angle. The boat aquaplaned along a huge, smooth, hidden boulder. Elizabeth let out a squeal and was thrown head first into the water. Immediately, the *Jolly Mary* slid back onto the water, where she continued on slowly. Rowan saw Elizabeth floundering and was about to jump in, when she stood. The water was only up to her chest. 'Are you all right?'

'Y-yes,' she spluttered. 'I think so.'

Rowan loosened the halyard, reefing the sail. The *Jolly Mary* floated on until her keel harmlessly kissed the sand in a few feet of water, where she tipped slightly to port. They had stopped. Elizabeth climbed aboard, drenched once again, and they both laughed, an uncontrollable laugh. It felt so good to be alive.

'That's the last time I will ask you to do sounding,' Rowan managed to joke between breaths, looking back at the huge boulder, which was now clearly in view. 'I better check the hull.' Rowan disappeared down the companionway. Elizabeth followed. Below deck was a disarray of sail, rope and canvas. Leblanc's personal clothes trunk had spilled open, along with books and women's clothing that had been stored for Beatrice, no doubt.

'No damage,' Rowan was pleased to announce. 'All looks shipshape, Elizabeth Eveleigh...'

'What's that?' Elizabeth's smile turned to curiosity. In the dark recesses of the bow, where a berth had dislodged from the planking, they stared at dozens of shiny discs, button-sized and reflecting the low sunlight of late afternoon shining down the hatchway.

'No!' Rowan tripped across the decking, shoving empty kegs and bundles of seal skins aside. He mounted the incline to the berth. 'No! It's not possible...'

'What?'

'Devil's blood!' Rowan wrenched at planking loosened by the collision. Feverishly he pulled boards aside to reveal a small chest. 'Gold!' he screamed at Elizabeth.

'Gold?'

'It's Leblanc's gold! That's what Billy was doing on this sloop. Hiding this. They were to escape together.'

'The two of them?'

'Well, I'm thinking he would take others to work the sloop, of course. The remaining sealers had the use of *Queen B*. Why didn't Leblanc plan on taking the *Queen B*?' Rowan asked himself, and then answered himself aloud. 'Yes. It was once damaged, and ever after a slower craft.' Rowan tossed a handful of guineas at Elizabeth who scavenged them off the floor like a beggar snatching at pennies. Rowan hefted the chest onto the berth and gathered all the loose coins. 'Guineas and French 20-franc pieces mostly, by the look of it.' And amongst the gold were Bank of England five-pound and ten-pound notes. 'Mother Mary, son of Jesus...'

'Don't you mean Jesus, son of Mary?'

'I don't care what I mean. No wonder Leblanc was so angry. We could have taken the other sloop.' Rowan placed the heavy iron chest onto the sail locker and they both pored through the hoard. 'There must be thousands of pounds here.' Rowan raced back on deck and took in the surroundings, suddenly desperate to be certain they were alone. The beach and shoreline were deserted, without even the telltale smoke of native campfires to be seen.

To be certain, he took the spyglass and scoured the entire vista. When he was convinced they were alone, he returned to Elizabeth, who was lost for words, sitting on the locker, staring at the bullion. Never in all her wildest dreams had she imagined so much coin.

'Whose money is this?' Elizabeth eventually inquired.

'It's ours, Elizabeth...'

'No. I mean... who—owns—all—this?'

'You and I.'

'Impossible.'

'All right, so... strictly speaking... it's Leblanc's. It is his ill-gotten gains...'

'From... the wrecks he has caused? The dead people?'

'Mostly from selling skins and oil, I should imagine.' As Rowan said this, he knew it was only partly true. He had seen for himself the wealth the man had accumulated in his shanty on Bull Seal Island. Elizabeth was right about the source of much of the plunder.

'We must return it to its rightful owners.'

'Damn it, woman!'

Elizabeth shot Rowan a look of shock.

'Please forgive me... Look.' Rowan took Elizabeth's hands in his and looked into her eyes. 'If... and that is a big if... if this is from wrecked ships, we would never know who, where and how... now would we?' He did not sound too convincing. 'Most of it, in my opinion, was saved over the twelve years the man lived and worked the seal islands. If anything, most belongs to his crew... And a bunch of cutthroats they were. Now they'll all hang.' Rowan thought a moment and then threw in, for good measure: '...if they have not been disposed of already.'

'I–I don't know.'

'Well, to begin with, let us count it.' Rowan emptied the coins onto the listing sail locker and Elizabeth giggled as coins rained off the tilted edge and onto her lap, reminding her of her favourite folk story, the tale of Aladdin in the book *Arabian Nights*.

They counted the coin and notes twice and then calculated the total a third time, each time coming up with a different figure. 'Two thousand, nine hundred guineas, five hundred Louies, sixty-eight eight-escudo gold pieces and eighteen hundred pounds in Bank of England notes.' Elizabeth's grin was infectious.

1814

'Not a silver dollar in sight.' Rowan shook his head, trying to contemplate their good fortune. The sun had set and night was approaching when they realised how dark it had become below deck. 'We'd better secure all this in the secret cupboard before it's too dark. I don't want to light a lantern, in case we attract unwanted company.'

The night was still and the air balmy. They sat on the slanting deck, their backs against the gunwale, and dined on the remaining mutton birds in silence, each preoccupied with thoughts of sudden wealth. Elizabeth struggled with her conscience. Rowan read her thoughts.

'I have a proposal,' Rowan said thoughtfully.

'A proposal?'

'We are both felons in the eyes of the British Empire. You, Elizabeth, would be forced to complete your sentence. If I am ever caught, my punishment will be the rope. My proposal, as strange and dangerous as it may sound, is to sail to Launceston and establish ourselves as a brother and sister, of some means, who have ventured to the colonies to invest in agriculture—namely, sheep.'

'Sheep?' Elizabeth wanted to laugh.

'Leblanc gave me the idea some time ago. There is a Spanish sheep called the merino which takes kindly to the climate here in Van Diemen's Land. We would not be the first. Land grants are being given to settlers. It would be the perfect ruse, a disguise if you like. Masquerade as brother and sister, set up an estate and in a year or two, after we have turned Leblanc's gold into a legitimate profit, we could move on as legitimate gentry. What do you say, Mary Colchester?'

'Mary who?'

'Mary Colchester. It's your adopted name. I just thought of it.'

'You've really thought this through, haven't you?'

Rowan locked eyes with Elizabeth in the light of the rising moon. She had the most beautiful blue eyes and Rowan's thoughts returned to the night of their escape six weeks prior, when Elizabeth had allowed him to hug her for warmth. 'Well, what do you think?'

'Brother and sister?' Elizabeth questioned.

Rowan spoke without thought. 'Or we could masquerade as husband and wife.' The moment he said this he felt awkward. Elizabeth broke eye contact, but Rowan did not realize that she was blushing, not vexed. They sat in silence once more, listening to the sound of gentle waves lapping the shore twenty feet away, each once again alone with demons.

Launceston

The midday sun welcomed the *Jolly Mary* as she sailed past George Town and into Port Dalrymple at the mouth of the Tamar River. The settlements in this area consisted of groups of huts and cabins and little else. Rowan had been told by the sealers who occasionally traded here that these were pretty much lawless communities, predominantly composed of men, and not for the faint-hearted. The few soldiers stationed there were motley in attire, with many wearing kangaroo skins.

'Leblanc told me a Colonel William Patterson founded Launceston,' Rowan shared with Elizabeth, 'and he originally named it Patersonia.'

'Patersonia!' Elizabeth laughed. 'I do know there is a Launceston in Cornwall,' she added. 'It borders on the Tamar River that flows between Cornwall and Devon.'

Elizabeth stood beside Rowan at the helm, mentally pinching herself and inwardly affirming that this was actually happening to her, that it was not some dream to be cruelly woken from, only to find herself shackled to a cell wall. They had slept soundly—dreaming of a better future, dreaming of Aladdin, dreaming of sheep—and woken at first light. They caught some strange, bony flat-headed fish that lived at the bottom of the bay and then swam in the warmer shallows of the beach. Refreshed, they caught the high tide and set sail for deeper waters, forever watching for the Royal Navy.

Once they were underway, they fine-tuned Rowan's plan, and Elizabeth agreed to it. After all, they had few other options. To sail to New Zealand, they would need more crew. For now, the north end of this pioneer island would be as good a place as any to build a new identity. They would maintain a low profile. Maybe they could run a farm as brother and sister. They certainly were blessed with a fortune.

The morning transformed itself into a tranquil late afternoon, and the shallow-drafted *Jolly Mary* effortlessly pushed through the reeds and water plants of Launceston's marshland waterfront. It had been a six-hour sail and the two had had much to contemplate, including the fabricated histories of their masquerade. Shortly it would be dusk, and the sooner darkness fell on the decade-old settlement, the better, as far as the two travellers were concerned.

Together they studied Leblanc's charts. They had negotiated the shallow waters of the River Tamar and sailed east along the North Esk River that separated the village from the rural farmland on the north bank. Beyond the settlement, mapped on the charts, they saw an extensive plain that seemed to be made up of rich soil dotted with small swamps. This led to rising ground, which they could make out in the light of the setting sun. These hills terminated in verdant, tree-covered mountains.

The small township spread out before them, its shingled roofs framed by the gilded rays of a magnificent sunset.

From this position they could make out the village of Launceston, stretching from the North Esk River back to a place marked Cataract. Here, according to Leblanc's charts, a gorge was hidden in the western hills. The austerely named Tench—the name given to prisoners' barracks—was in the centre of the township. Nearby was the commandant's cottage, built by Port Dalrymple's founder, Colonel William Patterson. Next door was the government store, then the granary and, on the outskirts were the military barracks. Salted amongst these government buildings were the heart and soul of commerce: an inn or two, stores, mills, bakers, blacksmiths, sawyers, tanneries and lodgings. As Rowan had been told, it was no more than a pioneer settlement, like the frontier villages in North America.

Street lamps in the township on the south bank flickered to life. Homely fires were stoked for evening meals, accompanied by the alluring aroma of roasting meats and baking bread wafting towards them on a gentle southerly, coming off the unexplored highlands. The smell reminded Rowan and Elizabeth of their hunger—until they saw the sixty-ton brig *Lady Nelson* with its Royal Navy ensign hanging limply at the stern. The ship was anchored in the bay, but there appeared to be little life on board. As it happened, its commander, two mates and twelve seamen were ashore. The *Jolly Mary* drifted by the brig and, as inconspicuously as possible, they docked at the wooden esplanade.

Two other sloops and a fast, sleek government cutter shared the wharf. Thankfully, the sloops were being unloaded with barrels of grain. A dozen men were busy at the block and tackles, hoisting the heavy barrels from deck to bullock drays. All were pre-occupied with their set tasks. Rowan tied bow and stern ropes to bollards and met

Elizabeth below deck, where they dressed in respectable clothes from Leblanc's trunk.

'Are you ready for this?' Elizabeth asked nervously. Rowan looked a little uneasy. It now occurred to him that he had spent the best part of a year living a lawless life with brigands. He doubted his social skills. He looked at Elizabeth for a moment. She looked arresting in the clothes she had chosen and Rowan feared they would attract attention.

'You look beautiful,' Rowan said and took Elizabeth by the hands. She held his gaze a short while before answering with a brief thank you.

Elizabeth was scared... more afraid than she let on. 'I hope we are doing the right thing,' she whispered.

'So do I, sister Mary,' Rowan replied, attempting to put a little cheer into his voice 'so do I.'

Elizabeth sighed. The time had come. 'Do I look the part then, brother Henry?'

'Yes.'

Elizabeth forced a smile. 'You don't look too down at heel yourself, sir.'

Rowan looked at Elizabeth's hair. 'Is there a scarf amongst the clothes, a bonnet maybe?'

'A bonnet, yes.'

'Then you will need to cover your hair.' Elizabeth's hair was slowly growing back, and she had become accustomed to her short hair, as hacked by the ship's barber, but it was the tell-tale hairstyle of one of His Majesty's prisoners.

With her hair under a bonnet, Elizabeth's disguise was now complete. She hoisted her skirts above her ankles and headed for the companionway. Rowan re-checked his repairs to the secret cupboard. Leblanc's iron chest of specie was as safe as it could ever be. It was well hidden behind the false cladding, impossible to find unless one knew where to look. Leaving it there was certainly safer than carrying it with them through the streets of a pioneering township. Only Leblanc's trunk of clothes remained amidships, awaiting its removal on the morrow, when they had secured lodgings. Rowan took up Leblanc's carpetbag, packing it with immediate necessities along with ten pounds in gold, a pair of brass-barrelled pocket pistols and the necessary accoutrements. 'Ready?'

'Ready.'

'Then lead the way, Mary Colchester.'

PART FOUR

CHAPTER TWENTY- FIVE

A new life under the Union Jack

''Ere, miss, give ol' Bill yer mit an' I'll see yer safe on dry land.' The friendly face with the toothless smile belonged to a down-and-out opportunist standing on the dock. By all appearances he was a veteran of the wars with Napoleon, perhaps in his fifties, Elizabeth thought. He removed a tattered top hat in a gentlemanly manner, revealing sparse, greased hair combed close to his skull, and shuffled towards Elizabeth with a limp. He offered her his gnarly hand, covered with a woollen mitten. Before Elizabeth could protest, or, God forbid, prove herself independent and jump ashore unaided, Ol' Bill hoisted Elizabeth onto the dock where she ended up with all the elegance of a landed fish. Rowan appeared from the hatch and bolted the lock behind him. 'An' you, too, good sar,' the cove said. 'Maybe Bill can be o' service to you.'

'Thank you,' Rowan said, 'but I will manage.' Rowan slung the carpetbag over his shoulder and jumped ashore.

'Aye. Yer as nimble as one o' them Batavian monkeys, sar, if'n yer don't mind me sayin' so.'

'Thank you.' Rowan looked along the wharf into the darkness. The government cutter was unloaded and most of the workers had moved on. Except for Ol' Bill, they were alone.

'Say, what's that accent o' yours, sar, yer sound Scottish or somethin'.'

Rowan fidgeted a moment. He had forgotten that he had acquired a foreign accent. 'Maryland, America.'

'Well, I'll be. America, huh? Say, if'n yer need somethin', squire,' —he turned to Elizabeth—'miss... or is that "Mrs."?'

Elizabeth said, 'Miss.'

'Aye. Miss. If'n yer be wantin' somethin' done, Bill Malley's yer man.'

'Bill Malley,' Elizabeth replied, 'can you recommend a good inn close by?'

'Aye, miss. The County o' Cornwall Inn would be the best fer the likes o' such gentle folk.'

'Now, now, Mr. Malley,'—something about this vagabond put Elizabeth in a playful mood—'enough of that "gentle folk" business, if you please.'

'Sorry, miss. The Cornwall be the best o' two inns. They specialise in newspapers from over the seas,' he said, as if he thought the two new arrivals needed news. 'The innkeeper be a perfect gentleman 'imself. Does a most delicious kidney pudding and...'—Malley looked over at Rowan—''is ales are the finest in the colony. Nuthin' affectatious 'bout 'is ales, sar.'

Rowan always fancied himself a good judge of character. This man enjoyed good humour, although he was clearly on poor man's row. 'Say, sir... Mr. Malley...'

'Bill, sar. Call me Bill.'

'All right, then, Bill. How would you like to earn a guinea?'

'A guinea, sar!'

'Yes. A half guinea now and the other half in the morning.'

'Jayzus Lord!' Suddenly Bill remembered his company. 'Sorry, miss... I... ah... a guinea? How, sar?'

'Sleep on the *Jolly Mary* the night. There is a tarp at the helm for cover. Protect our vessel and I will give you another half guinea, first thing in the morning.'

'Done, sar. Goodness gracious me, sar. A guinea. Well, I never.'

The County of Cornwall Inn in Cameron Street, running parallel to and four streets away from the river, was a handsome brick and stone inn of two storeys boasting thirteen rooms. The rooms on the first floor facing the street had small latticework balconies, which also overlooked the main entrance where guests entered the parlour, the taproom or reception. Elizabeth noted that the left-hand wing, or parlour, was of an unusual pentagon shape. Tall, airy windows looked out from the ground floor whilst the upper level offered its view from horizontal windows. The right wing of the inn accommodated the taproom, which had its own entrance to separate the riff-raff from the better classes. The kitchen, dairy, scullery, barn and stables faced a courtyard at the rear.

'Good evening, good evening!' the Cornwall's innkeeper called out as he caught sight of the carpetbag and surmised he had guests. The older, rotund man would be lucky if deemed to reach five feet in height, and had a waxy, polished bald head circled by tight, curly silver hair, almost like a monk's tonsure. He was clean-shaven and wore an ankle-length apron tied half-way up his fat belly. 'Robert Ascough, innkeeper, at yer service.'

'Henry Colchester,' Rowan answered, then, hesitating briefly, introduced Elizabeth. 'Mary Colchester, my sister.' The falsified identities came naturally.

'Then I'll call yer Henry an' Mary, if yer don't mind me being so bold.'

'Not at all.' The friendly welcome had put Elizabeth at ease.

'Aye. We're most informal around here.' Ascough had a sudden thought. 'American, huh?'

There was no hiding the accent. 'Yes, sir—Maryland.'

'Aye, I knew it. We get Yankee whalers in here from time to time. Yer get to know accents after a while.' Ascough was less than subtle as he turned back to Elizabeth, his face wrinkled with uncertainty. Rowan read the man's puzzled expression. 'Our mother died when we were young,' he said, 'and my sister grew up in Bristol with our aunt, which is why we have different accents.'

'Oh, I see.'

'Yes, my father took me to sea when I was twelve,' Rowan continued. 'We were merchant traders across the Atlantic when my father was killed in an unfortunate accident. A shipping family in Baltimore adopted me. Then all this trouble betwixt our countries... and I was, well, trapped in America.'

'You have a quaint town here, Mr. Ascough,' Elizabeth said, steering the dialogue away from personal interrogation.

'Robert, Mary. Call me Robert. Quaint town, yer say? Well, I've never heard it called that before, but I'll take it as a compliment. Governor Macquarie visited Van Diemen's Land a few years back now, and ordered that George Town be named the capitol of the north end, but the settlers refused because o' the rich soil 'round here. And so this *quaint* village *is* the capitol. Now, yer be wantin' rooms, I am supposin'?'

'Yes.'

'Well I hope yer don't mind sharing, being siblin's an' all, cos I've only the one room remaining.'

Rowan didn't dare look at Elizabeth. As he was the older *brother,* it would be expected that he make the decision. 'That will be fine. We have been sharing below decks in our sloop and the thought of a comfortable bed on land will make up for any other inconveniences. Do you have a bath?'

'A bath!' the words shot from Elizabeth's lips without thought. She had an immediate apprehension. A vision. A vision of Rowan bathing in a room they shared.

The innkeeper hadn't noticed. 'Certainly. I will have the maid bring a tub and hot water to your room. However, it will be another florin on top o' the usual remuneration of a crown for the double room.'

'That will be fine. Thank you.'

'So, what brings you to North Side?' Ascough asked, North Side being the colloquial name for the north coast of Van Diemen's Land.

'Sheep,' Rowan said without hesitation, their history having been rehearsed as they sailed up the Tamar.

'Sheep?'

'Yes,' Elizabeth chimed in, beginning to enjoy the charade. 'We have, in the past, proven our mettle in the merchant trade and have money to invest. It is our intention to apply for a grant of land. In the meantime, we will rent a rural property already established and ship merino sheep from New South Wales.'

'I see.'

'The merino are already proving to be lucrative in that colony,' Rowan added.

'But they are a Spanish breed, the merino,' Robert said. 'And New South Wales is a warmer clime than is Diemen's Land.'

1814

'We have on good authority that the breed will thrive here, as well as they did in New South Wales.'

'Well good luck to yer both.'

Rowan felt wedged between two awkward options. The Cornwall's taproom was busy and he recognised some of the faces of the men who'd been unloading grain at the dock. He avoided making eye contact. It was not a situation he wanted to be in right now, especially as soldiers of the 46th Regiment of Foot were also arriving in numbers from the barracks. But Elizabeth was bathing and he'd told her to take her time, to wash away the sweat and tears, the salt of the sea, the fear. The past weeks had been restless, and their futures were still uncertain.

Rowan drank from his leather quart tankard of the innkeeper's brew, a brown ale heavy with malt and hops having a thick, creamy head. The brew filled his belly and the effects were instant. Soon, his thoughts returned to Elizabeth, especially the look of optimism in her eye as he'd locked their door behind him and stepped out into the passageway. Rowan envisioned her sitting in the hipbath—her white nakedness under her skirts cleansed in the perfumed water while she hugged her knees, pulled up to her bosom, and contemplated herself in his embrace.

Rowan sighed.

Rowan sensed a friendship he had not been aware of since escaping from America. He also felt a powerful sense of protection towards Elizabeth. Certainly Elizabeth Eveleigh was more than capable of looking after herself, but Rowan, too, had a sense that they would survive. He stared into his brew. *We will get through this together,* he was telling himself when his musing was disturbed by the innkeeper.

'Ah, Henry, here you are.' Robert Ascough was animated. He had removed his apron and now wore a waistcoat with a silver fob chain that dangled from a buttonhole down to his watch, which was lost in the folds of his left pocket. 'I've an acquaintance I would like you to meet,' Ascough announced.

Rowan looked at the young man accompanying the innkeeper. He was younger than Rowan—half a dozen years his junior, Rowan surmised. He was tall and slim with dark hair and a predominant, hooked nose. Despite the air of arrogance about him, he was striking in his dark green, double-breasted frock coat with its gilded buttons and short-fronted tailcoat worn over a plain white linen shirt. About his neck was tied a white linen neck cloth. He wore tight-fitting pantaloons and the latest fashionable hessian boots.

'Mathew Fawkner, this be Henry Colchester, the entrepreneur what I was tellin' you about,' Ascough stated, carrying out the introductions.

Mathew Fawkner returned Rowan's observation with a sharp eye. Rowan felt he was being evaluated by a young man of high society. There followed an awkward, albeit brief, silence. Fawkner drew in tobacco smoke from a long, thin cigar Rowan knew as a cheroot, finally exhaling and making no effort to direct his smoke elsewhere. 'Mr. Colchester,' he said as a nimbus of smoke swirled about them, 'Mr. Ascough here tells me you are looking for tenancy... a country estate, maybe.'

'Possibly,' Rowan said warily.

'Come,' the innkeeper said. 'I've cleared us a table and we can talk in private.' He snapped his fingers and the barkeep passed him a bottle of Madeira and three stemmed glasses; clearly, this had been pre-arranged. The three men sat at a high-backed booth table and Ascough poured the wine.

'Cheroot, Mr. Colchester?' Fawkner finally broke into a smile, sensing they had started on a negative foot. He flipped back the flap on a leather pouch.

'No, thank you, Mr. Fawkner. I do not indulge in tobacco.'

'You don't know what you're missing, sir. These are from Burma; my pa has interests there with the East India Company.'

'I see.' Now Rowan began to judge this opinionated and overindulged puppy. The cut in his tailored clothes bespoke Beau Brummel of London, the tone and attitude hinted at private tutoring in Europe.

'So, Mr. Colchester, how are you taking to the North Side so far?' Fawkner asked.

''Tis fine sir. I feel a connection to the island already.'

Fawkner lifted his wine glass. 'To good King George, gentlemen. Although I hear his health fails and George Augustus will be on the throne before the year's end.'

'King George,' the innkeeper cheered. Rowan shuffled. The situation was as problematic as it was vexatious. Saluting the enemy king put Rowan in a compromised position. He drank the wine in one gulp, angry at his own hypocrisy.

'What?' Fawkner said, 'no salute for the good king, sir? Ah, but you are American Robert informed me. Well, fear not, I shan't call the constabulary. I can understand your misgivings about raising a glass to King George.'

The innkeeper sensed Rowan's discomfort. 'As I told Mr. Fawkner here, you are an entrepreneur, looking to invest, are you not?'

'That is correct,' Rowan replied, relieved that the conversation had changed direction.

'Then, Mr. Fawkner, why don't yer tell Mr. Colchester of yer predicament.'

'Steady on, Robert. It is hardly a predicament.'

'Please excuse me, squire—I meant proposition.'

'Yes. That's it, proposition.' Fawkner filled his own glass, disregarding the others. 'I shan't beat about the bush,' he said. 'I am leaving this colony for a period. Off to Bombay, you see, and I have a fine estate to be maintained in my absence...'

'Beaumont Hall, Mr. Colchester,' Ascough said enthusiastically. ''Tis a handsome property of three hundred acres, not a day's ride south of here.'

'Oh—' Rowan was caught unawares. 'I... I don't know... it's all a little unforeseen, I mean my sister and I only arrived this evening.'

'Beaumont Hall is a modest dwelling, Mr. Fawkner,' the innkeeper persisted. 'Four bedrooms on the upper floor and a bathroom with running water.' Ascough looked to Fawkner for confirmation and then back to Rowan. 'Running water, sir. And on the ground level are a dining room, a sitting room, a gentleman's library and ladies' parlour, along with a kitchen, bakehouse scullery and dairy in houses surrounding a courtyard.'

Rowan had the impression that the innkeeper had been commissioned to dispose of the property. 'It sounds... well, wonderful, but...'

'Five hundred guineas per annum, not a penny more, not a penny less, on the proviso of it being maintained in perfect order. Two year lease, first three months in advance. What say you, sir?' Fawkner said smartly.

'F... five hundred, you say?' This outlay, should the estate be what the men said it was, seemed most reasonable to Rowan.

'Of course, outgoing expenses are yours, sir.'

'Of course.' Rowan tried not to show too much interest. 'And what might they be, approximately?'

'A thousand guineas per annum, give or take a few quid. You will have the employment of the housekeeper, Hannah Bevan, who is also an excellent cook; the chambermaid Annie Brown; Bessie the housemaid, who cleans and also looks after the dairy; a head gardener, Reginald; a shepherd; four farmhands; the gamekeeper, Charles Ratcliff; and two yard boys. They are accomplished and proficient in their stations, Mr. Colchester, and their remuneration is modest.'

'And presently incoming?' Rowan asked.

'The market gardens fetch in about five hundred guineas a year. The dairy is only a small affair, supplying locally, but there's another hundred there, and at the moment I run two hundred sheep, with an annual income of one pound a head. That's another two hundred pounds. Not in the black, I know, but the property is large enough to take another thousand sheep. Should you increase to that number, I will gladly reimburse you on my return.'

'And you will guarantee this in writing?'

'Absolutely. I am a man of my word.'

The innkeeper nodded enthusiastically.

Rowan could not believe his good fortune. He twisted the stem of his wine glass and gazed into its amber deliciousness in an intoxicating reverie. This could quite possibly be the answer to his and Elizabeth's problems. How onerous could it be playing the role of landowner and squire on a remote estate in a remote colony on a remote island? They could use Amos Leblanc's gold to procure tenancy of Beaumont Hall. Rowan could purchase merino sheep from New South Wales and, with the help of stockmen, they could manage the estate until such time as they had established their legitimate fortunes. Then, in two years' time, they could sail to the Orient to deal with the contacts Lucius Brown of Boston had told him of—letters for whom Rowan had safely in his satchel.

'If you are of a mind to, Mr. Colchester,' Fawkner said, 'you and your sister could ride with me to Beaumont Hall tomorrow. You could look over the property, explore the land, and stay as my guests for a day or two.' Then Fawkner added, as if in afterthought, to tempt Rowan, 'And, as I said, Mrs. Hannah Bevin, the housekeeper, is a damned fine cook. She will cook you her most delicious mutton pastry pie. What say you?'

'How would we get there? I mean, my sister does not ride, sir.'

'I will hire a chaise for her and for yourself. I am with my man servant, Mr. Gilbert Kelly. The two of us rode here, three days past.'

'I need to discuss this with Mary.'

'Certainly. But I return to the hall in the morning. I'll send Mr. Kelly for your answer at breakfast.'

Mathew Fawkner drained his third glass and stood, excusing himself. 'Now I must dine with Commandant McKenzie. Good night, gentlemen.'

Rowan and Robert Ascough watched Fawkner strut from the taproom, ever in the role of country gentleman. He stepped onto the street and donned his tall beaver hat, tapping it in position. Then, with his swagger stick tucked under one arm, he strolled towards Government House.

Rowan noted that Ascough's cheeks reddened from the wine. The innkeeper filled Rowan's glass with Madeira before topping his own and shuffling his backside along the bench closer to Rowan.

''E's got a gamblin' problem, Mr. Colchester,' Ascough said conspiratorially. 'That be why 'e needs to vacate Beaumont Hall for a spell. His creditors circle, sir, thart be why he is so hasty. 'Tis a grand property, sir, you mark my words. 'Tis worth twice what 'e asks... three times... but, as I said, 'e owes money in the colony and must leave. It's to his Pa in Burma he flees, not to Bombay.'

Rowan endeavoured to avoid sounding cynical when he said, 'I am compelled to ask you, Mr. Ascough...'

'Robert, sir.'

'Robert, then. I am compelled to ask you, what is in this for you?'

'Oh!' The innkeeper looked surprised. 'Is it that obvious?'

'Yes, Robert, it is.'

'He owes me money, Mr. Colchester. Nearly fifty quid. That's fifty quid I can ill afford to lose.'

Rowan knocked gently on the door of the bedroom he was to share with Elizabeth. Silence. He waited. Certain that Elizabeth had fallen asleep, he unlocked the door quietly and entered. The room was dark except for a fading candle that stood before a hinged vanity mirror on the dressing table. The curtains were only half drawn and some light filtered through the window from one of the street lamps. Eager to avoid disturbing Elizabeth, Rowan was silently locking the door when he caught her reflection in the mirror.

Elizabeth was sleeping soundly, spread across the double bed in fresh bloomers and a blouse taken from the carpetbag. She had barely covered herself with the blanket before collapsing. Rowan stared at her in silence for a moment. She had a fine physique, with long, thin legs and slender arms splayed across the bed. Rowan felt emotions he had not felt for a long time. While he stood enjoying the tranquillity, Elizabeth exhaled softly through full red lips; her breathing was even, her breasts rising and falling with each breath.

Suddenly, aware of his unintentional voyeurism, Rowan looked to the tub. The water was still warm and smelt fragrantly of lavender and other oils from the soap provided by the inn. He felt grimy, aware he was desperately in need of a bath himself. He removed his boots, peeled away the clothes he had worn for days, and slipped into the hipbath. His manly bulk raised the water level and he was careful not to overflow the tub. Rowan soaked a while; only his head poked above the waterline. He imagined Elizabeth naked in the tub. With the essential oils surrounding him he imagined that he could smell her womanhood. He sensed his own arousal. Elizabeth stirred, half beneath the blanket and half not. She did not wake, but rolled on the bed to face him, all the while sleeping. Her soft breathing resumed. Rowan felt guilty and quietly scrubbed—scrubbing away the grime and his culpable thoughts.

Rowan lifted himself from the hipbath and towelled his wet body. The bath had reinvigorated him. He felt fresh and alive, but, as hungry as he was now, he had no intention of returning to the parlour or taproom, where the sight of redcoats was all too common. He would have to wait for breakfast. Rowan stood naked for a moment in the shadows. He felt uninhibited for the first time since meeting Captain Leblanc in Sydney Cove, nearly a year earlier. He stepped past the bed, moving to the window, where he enjoyed the cool breeze on his nakedness. Elizabeth stirred. Rowan looked over his shoulder at her; she was now in a foetal position with her back to him. All was silent. Rowan considered his options. He would re-dress in the clean garments from his carpetbag but would sleep on the floor, using the bag for a pillow. After all, he was accustomed to sleeping rough. He dressed awkwardly in a dark corner and, finding a spare blanket, he made himself as comfortable as possible on the floor and drifted into the heaviest sleep he had had in months.

Elizabeth's rhythmic breathing had ceased. She lay quietly, now fully awake, facing the vanity mirror in which she had stared at Rowan's naked reflection. Her heartbeat had quickened as she'd feigned sleep and stolen glimpses of

Rowan's statuesque masculinity. Elizabeth had never seen a naked man before and her situation excited her. She felt flushed. Her mind raced with emotions foreign to her. Was this love? *Yes*—she smiled inwardly as she dozed off once more—*I think I am falling in love.*

Chapter Twenty-Six

The next morning.

The climb from the Launceston lowlands took the travellers up and over the moderately wooded Paterson's Plains and White Hills towards the inland wilds of northern Van Diemen's Land.

'So,' Rowan said to Elizabeth as their chaise wheels crunched over the gravel, 'Launceston's founder, Colonel Paterson, did, after all, have a grassland named in his honour.'

The going was arduous and slow. Fawkner rode a mount alongside his manservant, Gilbert Kelly, whose duties, Rowan guessed, included armed chaperone. The two men were armed with pistols, primed and ready with fresh flints; two Brown Bess muskets of military issue were also loaded and ready in the chaise.

'We can't be too careful, Mr. Colchester, Miss Colchester,' Gilbert Kelly had warned, as he inspected the primers in both pans of a twin-barrelled flintlock. 'Absconders can be desperate men.'

Rowan had had first-hand experience with absconders on Bull Seal Island, particularly John Stuart Radge, the blacksmith with whom he had the falling out. He took comfort in the fact that he had two pocket pistols from the *Jolly Mary* snug in his coat pockets.

'Then there's the natives,' Kelly added. 'Funny bastards... Excuse me, miss. Strange. Yer can't pick 'em. One minute they's friendly an' the next minute they'd throw a spear in yer back.'

Elizabeth and Rowan exchanged knowing smiles. Provocation was the whitefella's enemy, not the aborigines themselves. Rowan held Elizabeth's eye a moment. She looked extraordinarily beautiful in her new skirt and her blouse with its fashionable yard-long shawl in the style of a scarf. The new dark green bonnet and ankle-high boots complimented her beauty. They had knocked on the door of Richard Sherry the draper, milliner and importer of gentlefolk's attire in William's Street Lane, and paid the man half a guinea to open early. Now both wore clothes befitting gentry—not too ostentatious, but suitable for the charade ahead.

The ride was slow, the road but a track, and a rough one at that. They followed the South Esk River, passing near Collin's Hill, where, Fawkner told his guests, a military post had been in existence since 1811. They skirted an area of heavy bushland named Black Forest on the map, where red-eyed native hens watched their progress with inquisitive indifference. In the hills several big fires smoked.

'Natives,' Fawkner told them.

'Looks like they are burning off the land,' Elizabeth said.

'You know of these things?' Kelly was intrigued.

Elizabeth wanted to say she had lived with the indigenous of this island but instead said, "I have read some, Mr. Kelly. The natives burn the forests to clear the heavy bushland; this creates more pasture, which attracts kangaroo and emu.'

'Very good, ma'am, very good.'

While tossed from side to side in the chaise heading to the inland territory, Rowan had time to reflect on his first night in Launceston. Elizabeth had taken little convincing to visit Beaumont Hall. Where better to hide and bide time than a gentleman's mansion in the country? Money was not an issue, but privacy was. The entire scenario seemed like a dream. As promised, Fawkner had sent Gilbert Kelly to the County of Cornwall Inn. Kelly had been pleased to report back, that his master's contacts of the night before, Henry and Mary Colchester, were interested in inspecting the property. Rowan felt he could trust this Mathew Fawkner; he was, after all, an established settler in the colony and, besides, Rowan held an ace up his sleeve... the knowledge that the man was desperately in debt.

Another development occupied Rowan's thoughts: Elizabeth. Something played on his mind, as he lay awake on the floor of their bedchamber that morning—Elizabeth's gentle snores had been absent as he'd towelled his naked body dry the night before. And as they'd both brightened to the new day, Elizabeth had hinted that she was a light sleeper.

'And did you enjoy your bathing?' she smirked, with a cheeky smile.

'Pardon?'

'Your bathing, Rowan'—Elizabeth was almost giggling —'Did you take pleasure in your ablutions?'

'I... ah, yes. Why do you ask?'

'Oh, I was just curious, that is all.' Rowan was certain that he'd caught Elizabeth's eyes scrolling down his body. Had Elizabeth feigned sleep the night before? Was she a bit of a voyeur?

Beaumont House, forty miles southeast of Launceston, was everything Fawkner and Ascough had said it would be. *No, Rowan thought, it is more.* He had rubbed shoulders with the wealthy of Baltimore and Washington and had been a guest in many a mansion, and the thought of living in such a fine colonial home as Beaumont Hall had seemed impossible, until now.

The local kookaburra birds heralded their arrival as they rode down the hills towards Humphrey's Waterhole, the name by which the area had become known. Beaumont Hall sat in the centre of a clearing surrounded by a six-foot-high brick wall. Fortifications. Outside the wall, the paddocks and vegetable gardens were well manicured.

'Potatoes grow particularly well here, Mary,' Fawkner said, 'and I have a small orchard of apricots and apples that should bear fruit next year.'

Beyond the homestead was a small but imposing lake that was picture perfect. The whitewashed quarried sandstone and brick residence was perfectly symmetrical, with a central hallway and five main rooms on the first floor. Two giant chimneys serviced ten fireplaces.

'I was fortunate to have the use of convict labour,' Fawkner told his guests as they meandered slowly to take in the vista. 'You should keep that in mind, Henry. The government supply the labour and all you have to do is arrange accommodation and sustenance. It is a most viable situation.'

'How old is the homestead, Mr. Fawkner?' Elizabeth asked.

'Mathew, Miss Mary... please.'

'Mathew.'

'It was completed in '13. The upper floor has four bedrooms, with servants' quarters in the attic rooms. On the ground floor we have the dining room, the drawing room, gentlemen's library and a parlour for the ladies.' Fawkner flashed a smile at Elizabeth. 'Ah! There is even a fine stocked cellar, Henry, and, facing north, there is a sunroom conservatory overlooking Lake Fawkner.' The man chuckled. 'At least that's what I call it.' The landowner shot Elizabeth another cheeky smile. 'The perfect place to take tea, miss— the conservatory, that is.'

The two horsemen led the way through an open gate between two eight-foot-high brick balustrades. Rowan cantered after them in the chaise. 'You have fortifications here I see, Mathew.'

'Yes, 'tis but a precaution. As I said, absconders occasionally wander these parts and the natives have a habit of killing the odd sheep, or a duck on the pond. I scare them off with a blast from old Bess,' Fawkner said with the desultory casualness of a pioneer.

'By absconders, I guess you mean escaped convicts,' Elizabeth said.

'Yes, Mary,' Fawkner replied. 'One brute passed near here not so long ago, a Michael Howe. Ruthless cutthroat, and I mean that in the literal sense.'

'Oh?'

'Yes. It is customary, Mary, for captives' heads to be removed and taken to the governor for verification, so the captor can claim their reward.'

Elizabeth looked horrified. 'Is this the truth?'

'Yes, miss, and when one of Howe's gang members, John Whitehead, was shot and killed, Howe cut off his head and hid it in the bush, so pursuers could not claim their reward.'

'You said that he passed by here recently?' Rowan asked.

'Yes, but it is rumoured he has returned south, to the area near Hobart Town. We don't wish to alarm you, but one cannot be too careful. That goes for anywhere in the colony. Is that not correct, Gilbert?'

'Yes, sir.' Gilbert Kelly turned in his saddle to face the chaise. 'I heard it was Governor David Collins who came up with a quaint name for them.'

'Oh, and what is that, Mr. Kelly?' Elizabeth asked.

'"Bush rangers", he called them.'

'So you have never encountered any of these bush rangers at Beaumont Hall?' Elizabeth enquired.

Fawkner replied, 'No, thank God. There have been stories of late, though, I must add. Mad Jack Spanner has been seen south of here. He escaped from a work gang out of Hobart Town and has managed to get a gang of marauders together —seven in all, I believe.'

'The name "Spanner", is, of course, a sobriquet,' Kelly told the group. 'His real name is Jack Reynolds, but it is said the man is as nutty as a spanner.'

'Oh'—Elizabeth's interest had peaked—'and how is that, Mr. Kelly?'

Gilbert Kelly had picked Elizabeth out as a lass of a lower social background, more like himself. She certainly was not fully trained in the etiquette of gentle folk, although he couldn't quite put a finger on why he thought that. Her brother Henry, on the other hand, was different; Kelly was aware that the two had grown up worlds apart.

'Nutty as a spanner you were saying...?'

'Well, Miss Colchester,' Kelly began, "tis not a pleasant story I'd wish to repeat for a young lady of your upbringing.'

'Try me, Mr. Kelly.'

'Very well. It is said that when Mad Jack Spanner escaped, he met up with friendly natives in the hills behind a settlement north-west of Hobart Town called New Norfolk. But once he had their trust, he waited for the opportunity and took a native woman as mistress. When the *husband* intervened, Mad Jack killed the native, cut off his head and forced the woman to wear it around her neck on a rope, as a trophy.'

'Another cutthroat,' Rowan commented.

'That is indeed harsh, Mr. Kelly.'

'Aye, I did warn yer, miss.'

'Surely, it would not be difficult to apprehend these men.'

'On the contrary, Mary,' Mathew said, 'They are quite difficult to apprehend. They are like the highwaymen back home in England. They attack coaches and homesteads and steal guns as well as food and clothing, and then disappear back into the bushland, where they live in caves.'

'Hence the name "bush rangers",' Kelly added.

The young stable hands had been watching out for their master. The youngest, Pat, took the reins as Fawkner and Kelly dismounted. The older boy, thirteen-year-old Dan, whom Rowan guessed to be a half-caste native, made to assist Elizabeth in dismounting from the chaise, but she had dropped her guard and jumped from the buggy in a most un-lady like manner. Out of the right-hand door in the arched front doorway emerged a short, overweight woman in her sixties. She was draped in a flour-dusted apron and tottered unsteadily onto the veranda. 'Welcome home, Mr. Fawkner,' she enthused in a motherly fashion

'Thank you, Hannah.' Fawkner introduced his housekeeper and cook to his guests as Mrs. Hannah Bevin. 'There will be four for dinner this evening,' he said.

'Oh, I think I can manage that, sir,' the portly cook gushed in what Elizabeth recognised as an Essex accent.

Inside, a flagstone-lined hallway led to a double-storey portico, which was enclosed by walls at the centre of the homestead's façade. Two arched doorways on either side of the portico opened out onto the veranda, where slender cast-iron columns, suggesting the Egyptian influence so popular in Europe these days, held up the veranda's slate roof.

After inspecting her own room and skipping into Rowan's, Elizabeth hissed quietly in Rowan's ear, 'I love it, I love it!' She was beside herself with youthful excitement. Rowan felt the same. 'We must take it,' Elizabeth whispered. For the first time in her miserable life she was experiencing happiness beyond any dream. 'Oh, Rowan... we *must* take it.'

'Rowan put a finger to Elizabeth's lips. 'Shush... Elizabeth... be calm and collected—yes.'

'Yes, yes, of course. Calm and collected. Yes. Oh, Rowan, it's gorgeous—no, it's more than gorgeous.'

Rowan's heart melted. Elizabeth danced about the room, opening drawers and poking her nose into cupboards. Rowan desperately wanted to take her in his arms and tell her how he felt about her, for he was certain she harboured the same feelings for him.

Elizabeth rushed to the window, pushing back the drapes, and the afternoon sun fell about her body like limelight to a London stage diva. Rowan dashed to the door, closing it before Elizabeth's palpable enthusiasm could echo down the hallway. He went to stand behind Elizabeth at the window, where she was gaping through the glass panes at the tranquil view. He placed his hands on her shoulders. Elizabeth stood still.

'Oh, Rowan,' she whispered reverently, 'we must live here. Please, please... it's... it's everything I could ever dream of.' Elizabeth spun about. Immediately they were face to face. Rowan's hands fell from her shoulders, caressing her arms. Just inches apart, they gazed into each other's eyes. Elizabeth's breath smelt fresh from mint. Rowan's breathing hastened. He felt his heart accelerate. Elizabeth rested her hands on Rowan's hips. 'It's everything *we* could ever dream of,' she affirmed.

The words echoed in Rowan's thoughts. He felt light-headed. He felt so... so sanguine. He knew he was hopelessly in love. Rowan's hands tightened about Elizabeth's arms. They felt slender, but her muscles were toned. For the first time, their eyes exposed their true feelings for each other and any restraint finally abandoned them. They held each other tight, passion arcing through their bodies. Their lips touched.... A sharp knock at the door shattered the silence. Elizabeth pushed Rowan away and he stepped back.

'Y-yes,' Rowan said, his voice breaking.

The housekeeper's voice filtered through the cedar door. 'It is me, Mrs. Bevin, sir.'

'Oh... Yes?'

'Mr. Fawkner asked me to invite you and your sister to the conservatory for drinks before dinner, Mr. Colchester.'

The doors to the conservatory were propped open, allowing the country air to flow among the many exotic plants. The late sun shining through the glass panes of the conservatory created an equatorial humidity, especially as all the plants had recently been watered. Rowan ran a knowledgeable eye over the them. With his medical background, he recognised camomile, wormwood, dandelion, and tansy. If he had had a culinary eye, he might have identified rosemary, thyme, sage, parsley and mint.

'Ah, Henry, Miss Mary—welcome.' Fawkner sat at a marbled-topped garden table with iron legs. He stood to greet them while McDonald, the footman, placed a tray of decanters and crystal glasses on the table before them. 'Shall I pour, Mr. Fawkner?' the servant inquired.

'No. Leave it.' Fawkner said curtly, his eye on Elizabeth as he lit a cheroot with tinder. 'Do you enjoy gardening perchance, Mary?' Mary wanted to burst out laughing. Her background had hardly given her familiarity with the wealthy woman's pastime time of recreational gardening.

'No, actually,' she said, acutely aware that her manner might reveal her upbringing.

'More's the pity. I have quite the collection here: succulents, sago palm, jasmine, plumbago, Meyers lemons. I particularly enjoy the evergreen wall shrubs... those there.' He pointed to climbers with orange flowers.

'I must agree with you, Mr. Fawkner...'

'Now, now, Mary... Mathew. Please.'

'Mathew. But I grew up in a small home in Bristol. There was no room for gardens.'

'I see.' Fawkner, like Gilbert Kelly, suspected that Mary was socialising above her station. As middle class as she professed to be, she conveyed that subtle hint of a background in poverty. He turned to Rowan. 'Whisky?'

'Thank you. With just water.'

'And Mary, I know it is early in the evening, but can I tempt you in refreshment? A Madeira wine, perhaps?'

'Mary' was thirsty, but what she really craved was a quart of ale. 'A small one. Thank you.'

The landowner poured, drank, puffed his cheroot back to life and turned to face Rowan. 'So tell me, Henry, if you will excuse my boldness, are you a self-made man or were you fortunate like myself? Did inheritance seal your future?'

'I was a cotton and tobacco merchant in Maryland before investing in whaling for some time,' Rowan replied, feeling confident that he knew enough of the whaling industry to support the lie. 'Now I seek the quiet life in the colonies.'

'I see.'

Polite conversation followed. After refreshments, Mathew Fawkner gave the new arrivals a *Grand Tour,* as he insisted on calling it. As Rowan had expected, the property was more than they could have hoped for, and the terms of the contract were more than equitable from any businessman's point of view. However, being mindful, Rowan scrutinised the property for any faults. He could find none.

Elizabeth, on her part, kept pinching herself. *Is this really happening?* she kept thinking.

Over dinner, Mathew Fawkner revealed his true colours. Whisky was his devil and indeed it soon became apparent that the man's preference was for the peaty spirit of the Scottish Highlands, rather than the sumptuous leg of smoked ham, sliced thinly on a blue and white charger before them.

Elizabeth forked the meat onto her plate with cabbage, potatoes, carrots and parsnips. She was ravenous. Mrs. Bevin had done herself proud. Rowan watched Elizabeth furtively, smiling inwardly. They had both rushed a light breakfast and skipped the midday meal, and he, too, was famished.

Joining them at dinner was Gilbert Kelly, who, it now appeared, was more Fawkner's friend than manservant. He, too, enjoyed his whisky; however, Elizabeth was quick to notice, he was measured in its consumption. She had a feeling, though, that this was only on account of their company.

'So, where are you from?' Elizabeth asked Kelly, more in polite conversation than interest.

'Born in Ireland, but I grew up in London, Miss Colchester.'

'I thought as much.'

'Oh?'

'I mean, the London accent is so distinct to someone from Bristol,' Elizabeth said with all the airs and graces she could muster, while dolloping hot English mustard onto the side of her plate.

'I know what you mean, miss. So is your Bristol accent to me, what London's accent is to you.'

'London's a dreadful place.' Fawkner voiced his views boisterously. 'Simply dreadful. Have you ever been there, Henry, Mary?'

Elizabeth was quick to maintain their masquerade. 'We were born in Bristol.'

'So you were. Robert Ascough informed me. But you have never been to London... Henry?'

'No, I left England from Liverpool when I was twelve.'

'Ah, yes. Robert told me that, too.' Fawkner looked at his empty tumbler as if something was missing from the table setting. He frowned and poured four fingers of whisky into his own glass from a long-necked decanter that Elizabeth guessed was crystal. 'Take Wapping, in London, for example. One will meet Lascars, Moors, Chinese and Negroes at every step, and the air is heavy with the odour of cesspools and tidal sludge.'

'But you *are* partial to the inns, Mathew, you must concede,' Gilbert Kelly commented, emptying the decanter into his own glass.

'Inns!' Fawkner leant back in his chair and swallowed his whisky. 'Inns offering cheap lodging with rancid sheets or... or, God forbid, the Wapping alehouses and gin-shops catering to aroused sailors.'

'As I said, Mathew,'—Kelly allowed the hint of a smile— 'you enjoy the inns of Wapping.'

This conversation made Rowan nervous. He was determined to enjoy the meal and to retire to the relative safety of their bedchambers as soon as politeness allowed. He would discuss business on the morrow and leave for Launceston shortly after.

Fawkner plucked a dinner bell from the table and shook it impatiently. Footman McDonald appeared at the ready. 'Sir?'

'Where's Bessie?' Fawkner demanded, his demeanour haughty.

'I'll fetch her, sir.'

'Yes, do that.'

Bessie, the housemaid, was Elizabeth's age. She was petite, vivacious and fine-figured, with fair complexion and fair hair. She was also appeared to be uncomfortably presumptuous with her master. 'You asked for me, sir?'

'Yes, girl. Over here.' The maid stood close to Fawkner, who placed a hand on her back. Unwittingly, Bessie placed her hand on the man's shoulder. Gilbert Kelly rubbed his chin distractedly.

'Be a good lass and fill the decanter'—the landowner's hand dropped, caressing the girl's backside before pulling away—'and bring a bottle of Madeira for our guests.'

Rowan was about to refuse the wine, but thought better of it. He had only just started his meal and knew the cook had beaten egg whites and sugar into a baked meringue for a pudding. The meal would last some time, he told himself, and the wine could help pass it. Bessie hefted the heavy decanter from the centre of the table, leaning in Rowan's direction and making no effort to adjust her loose bodice, exposing white flesh and cleavage. In doing so, she managed to catch Rowan's eye, which she held a moment with uncomfortable familiarity. Rowan was no stranger to the habits of taproom barmaids, but he felt his face flush.

Fawkner and Kelly eventually piled their plates with food. It appeared to be a custom in this particular household for one to overindulge in spirits prior to eating dinner. The conversation involved the pasts of both host and guests. Rowan and Elizabeth had rehearsed their stories well, and although Fawkner fired one question after another, he did not appear to be interested in their answers—that suited the guests. With or without mouthfuls of food, Fawkner proceeded to monopolise the conversation. Inevitably, an intoxicated slur crept into his speech. 'So, how did you make your fortunes, Henry?'

Rowan decided it was best to humour the man. 'In cotton and tobacco. I was a merchant.' He wanted to add, "*remember*?"

'Oh, that's right, you told me that earlier. And a fisherman, eh?' Fawkner said, judging this comment with humour.

'Ah... whaling, actually.'

'Oh, yes. Big fish, eh?' he laughed and Elizabeth noticed that he kicked Kelly under the table. 'How about you, Miss Mary?' he asked Elizabeth, the moment she'd just swirled English mustard onto a slice of ham and placed it in her mouth.

'Pardon?' The word had barely escaped Elizabeth's lips when the oil in the mustard paste began to sting like a nettle. The fire attacked her sinuses and tears welled in her eyes. Elizabeth coughed and her hand shot up to her mouth where, in a most unladylike manner, she expelled the culprit into her serviette. Fawkner burst into laughter.

Rowan asked, 'Are you all right?'

'Yes,' Elizabeth retched. 'Yes... I'll be fine.' She wiped her mouth as well as the tears from her eyes.

'English mustard, eh?' Fawkner grinned. 'We grow the plant alongside the potatoes and it's a damned fiery brew. Excuse the language.' Elizabeth took her Madeira and finished the glass. 'That's the way,' Fawkner cheered, and proceeded to refill everyone's glass. *Bristol or not,* he thought to himself, *this lass ain't quite the lady she portrays.*

'You were saying, Mr. Fawkner... Mathew,' Elizabeth asked, red-faced from the incident.

'Oh... I was going to enquire, Miss Mary, if there is a suitor in your life. I mean, I was saying to Gilbert here earlier that a woman of such beauty must certainly have a suitor.'

Elizabeth feared there was an unsavoury motive behind this question. She felt vulnerable. All the while, Kelly sat staring, apparently deep within his own thoughts, his changing expressions seemingly the result of mood swings.

'What say you, Gilbert?' Fawkner sought his friend's support.

'Yes. Indeed.'

'Indeed what?'

'Indeed, Mathew... such an attractive lady one would expect to have a suitor.'

'No, there is no suitor,' Elisabeth said tactfully. 'My life is too busy for such indulgences.'

Bessie returned to clear the table for dessert, and Fawkner's eye followed the maid from the room as she departed. 'Why is it that women are expected to remain chaste,' he said as the door closed behind the maid, 'while it is expected for men to practise infidelity?' Rowan caught a flush on Elizabeth's face, but he knew it was from indignation rather than embarrassment. 'What I mean is, men have sexual appetites that should always be fulfilled, whether with a wife, mistress or whore.' Fawkner was enjoying his affront.

Elizabeth pushed her chair back noisily. 'I must bid you good night, gentlemen. Mathew, I'm afraid that mustard has quite spoiled my appetite.'

'But, Mary,' Fawkner said as the three men rose to their feet, 'Hannah has baked a meringue.'

'Then please apologise to her from me. I am exhausted from the day's journey.'

'Fine.' Fawkner sat heavily, with the churlish frown of a spoilt schoolboy. 'I bid you goodnight, Miss Colchester.'

Bessie had clearly been listening at the door. She caught Elizabeth at the bottom of the stairs. 'Lock your door, miss.' She spoke quietly, one eye scanning the dark hallway towards the dining room.

'Pardon?'

'I would lock your door, miss, if'n I was you.'

'Well I fully intend to, Bessie, but why do you tell me so?'

'On account o' Math—Mr. Fawkner's midnight wanderings, miss.'

'I guessed as much,' Elizabeth conceded, but avoided confiding too much to this troublesome maid. Elizabeth also suspected the girl of jealousy. 'I can assure you, Bessie, I do not find that rake in the least bit attractive.'

'Although I might add, miss, that Gilbert Kelly is sleeping under this roof tonight and on those occasions... well.'

'Well, what?'

'I don't know if'n I should say, Miss Colchester.'

Suddenly the long case clock in the hall chimed loudly, its bells heralding the hour for the entire household. Both women stood silently until after the ninth chime.

'Say what?' Elizabeth's curiosity had peaked. 'Let the cat out of the bag, Bessie. What are you implying?'

Just as Bessie was casting another glance down the ill-lit hallway the bell summoned her back to the dining room. 'He wants his merengue,' she said anxiously.

'What were you trying to tell me, Bessie?'

'Oh, gawd...' The maid had talked herself into a corner and this Mary Colchester was a determined woman who, she had discovered, might soon be her new mistress. 'Mr. Fawkner and Mr. Kelly have a habit of wandering in the night.'

'I see,' Elizabeth said. 'Why am I not surprised? And you, Bessie, does Mr. Fawkner visit your room in the middle of the night?'

Bessie blushed, but the bell peeled a second time. 'Goodnight, Miss Colchester,' the maid answered and hurried away.

Elizabeth changed into her night garments and lay on the bed. The stub of a candle crackled in its death throws while she lit another half burnt candle as its replacement. She could not sleep. As exhausted as she was, thoughts of her future clouded her mind. She was listening to the clock downstairs chime the half hour when there was a soft tapping on her door. She hurried across the room. 'Who is it?' she whispered.

''Tis me.' She recognised Rowan's voice immediately and unlocked the door.

'Are you all right?' he asked, genuinely concerned.

'Fine.' Elizabeth was guarded. 'Fine, thank you.' The two were standing in the open doorway in awkward silence, neither knowing quite what to do next, when drunken laughter from the dining room carried up the stairs. Elizabeth opened the door wide and Rowan stepped inside, closing it behind himself and turning the key.

'I wanted to apologise for putting you through that tonight,' Rowan said softly. 'The man is a rake and a braggart.'

Elizabeth's body was silhouetted by the candlelight,and Rowan could make out her nakedness beneath the silk nightshirt. Rowan's distracted eye did not go unnoticed and Elizabeth pulled her shawl over her shoulders. Rowan's face reddened, and he admonished himself for his lack of discretion, but Elizabeth felt strangely complimented. Gone were the feelings of repugnance usually brought on by oggling menfolk.

'Sorry.'

'Don't apologise,' she said. 'I've dealt with a lot worse men than him.'

'I meant... ah...' Rowan stumbled awkwardly. 'Yes, of course. I suppose you have.'

The candlelight cast faint shadows across Rowan's handsome features. Elizabeth felt her deep fondness for him return, but she was also guarded, questioning her feelings. *Was she truly falling in love with this man?* Memories of her molesting Uncle Theophilus, the groping hands of drunken men in Bristol taprooms, lewd innkeepers, and lecherous prison turnkeys haunted Elizabeth. The effects of the Madeira were wearing thin and she felt circumspect rather than carefree, afraid of once more letting down her guard and becoming a victim.

Again the awkward silence returned.

Rowan, too, was apprehensive, afraid that he would overstep the mark and Elizabeth would reject him as yet another libertine. Elizabeth stood motionless. Rowan fidgeted. He wanted to reach out and take hold of this woman, but he felt so damned awkward. The fear of rejection lingered. They stood close and Elizabeth caught Rowan's sweet breath with the scent of the meringue and wine. She *knew* this man held affection for *her*. There was no doubt in her mind. Elizabeth lowered her eyes, almost as if in submission. If he were to take her in his arms now, she decided, she would throw caution to the wind.

'Eliz...' Rowan's voice was inexplicably hoarse. 'Elizabeth... I...'

'What?' Elizabeth wanted to say yes.

Rowan desperately wanted to say he had fallen for her, but blurted instead, 'I told Mathew we would discuss business in the morning.'

'Oh.'

'And he agreed with me that it should be done over coffee, not whisky. He agreed with me, can you believe...?'

Elizabeth stepped forward, placing a finger on Rowan's lips. Her shawl fell from her shoulders, crumpling to the floor. 'Oh, Rowan,' Elizabeth said in a silken voice, 'I... I think you're...'

Clumsy footsteps stumbled outside Elizabeth's bedroom door. They heard muffled chuckles. There came a knock, and Rowan was certain it was on Elizabeth's door. Elizabeth heard her name whispered. It was sung rather than spoken.

'*MAY... ree...*'

Rowan snuffed the candle and the two stood motionless. A second knock was ignored. They waited. Finally some *shushing* outside the door was followed by unmanly giggles. A moment passed. The hallway fell silent. The long case clock downstairs chimed the quarter hour. A moment later, clumsy footsteps resumed and the creaking of floorboards denoted their withdrawal. Rowan heard the steps terminate at the end of the hall and he soundlessly opened Elizabeth's door half an inch. Elizabeth stood by and together they watched their host bid his manservant, Gilbert Kelly, a drunken goodnight as they adjourned to their rooms.

'It appears you have a suitor,' Rowan whispered in the gloom.

'It appears so. You had better leave.'

Rowan stepped quietly into the dark hallway. 'Goodnight,' he said almost silently.

'Goodnight.'

Elizabeth closed the door. Rowan waited, listening carefully. He heard a subtle snick as Elizabeth's key turned in the lock, then he retired to his own room.

Chapter Twenty- Seven

Beaumont Hall – weeks later

The contracted agreement to rent Beaumont Hall was concluded without a hitch. It was brokered by Charles Cruikshank of the Port Dalrymple lawyer's office of the same name, who walked with a vexing swagger and whom Elizabeth thought a boastful little man. An elderly clerk, Mr. Maurice Redding, represented The Bank of England; as Rowan and Elizabeth were to learn, there were no regional banks established in the young settlement of Launceston. The payment of a fee of twenty guineas to the bank ensured that no questions were asked about the gold. Fawkner would have to pay his commission to the broker out of his lease price, which remained at five hundred guineas per annum, fully furnished.

Mathew Fawkner and Gilbert Kelly sailed on the governor's cutter for Sydney Town the next day, the first leg of Mathew's journey to Burma to plead with his father, no doubt for finances. He took the footman McDonald with him.

As for the *Jolly Mary,* Elizabeth and Rowan learnt that river craft were in high demand. They also had no doubt that they might be in need of the sloop again. They renamed her

Lillie, and sought a lessee. The amicable old war veteran who had been looking after the *Lillie* while Elizabeth and Rowan were in Launceston, Bill Malley, knew of a man whose brother's friend had a sister and husband looking for just that type of craft. Ben and Gwen Thomas worked market gardens and needed to carry produce from Launceston to Port Dalrymple on a daily basis. Elizabeth and Rowan drew up a contract that the market gardeners could not refuse, with the condition that the *Lillie* be available at short notice should they require it.

The early days passed and Elizabeth and Rowan's masquerade continued for the sake of their new servants at Beaumont Hall. At first, Elizabeth struggled to lord it over her new staff. She was used to being subservient herself. Now the boot was well and truly on the other foot. Mrs. Hannah Bevan, the housekeeper and cook, took to her new mistress quite smartly, as did the chambermaid, Miss Annie Brown, the four gardeners, the two yard boys and old Reginald, the head gardener. The gamekeeper, Charles Ratcliff, she saw little of, as the man lived with his pregnant wife in a small cottage on the outskirts of the estate. But it was Bessie, the housemaid, whom Elizabeth felt she would have to watch. For one thing, the girl was a meddler and a gossip, a mischief-maker Elizabeth knew she needed to watch out for when in her company.

Although Elizabeth and Rowan's life on the country estate was idyllic in some respects, it was also weighted with frustrations. Their love for each other was palpable. Days turned to weeks and the two began to feel like prisoners in their own home. Elizabeth was acutely aware that Bessie shared the attic rooms with the other servants, and that the girl was a meddler and always attentive to household gossip, for which Elizabeth had no time.

Not a day passed that Elizabeth did not thank the Lord for her good fortune. She had never had much faith in the church, but she thanked the Lord all the same. Rowan saw Beaumont Hall as providing a refuge until he could establish a new identity, finally to re-surface in the Orient as a merchant, and eventually to return to the land he loved, America, as a self-made man. His affection for Elizabeth grew daily. The two went horseback riding or spent time alone in the conservatory or the library, but, as powerful as their love became, intimacy eluded them. They were constantly observed as brother and sister, and acting otherwise would be fraught with danger. Distractions however, were rare, and visitors in the lonely countryside were even rarer.

It happened on a Wednesday in autumn, when the fruit trees had already lost their leaves and the larger oaks and other deciduous trees were shedding theirs. Piles of rotting leaves mounted beneath the trees, to be scattered by the autumn winds, a sign that winter approached. Sunset at this time of the year created a landscape awash with golden light. The paddocks were lush and green and the sky sombre but clear. Elizabeth was watering a potted crimson red proteaceous in the conservatory. The only sounds were the chirping of birds flying back to their nests and the occasional mooing of the dairy cows. Then the barking of the cook's kelpie, Rags, disturbed the peace. Elizabeth watched the dog race up the front driveway to the main entrance, where Reginald the old gardener, was already opening the gates. Rowan joined Elizabeth in the glasshouse. 'We have a visitor,' he announced.

'So I believe.'

Together they walked to the veranda to watch the one-horse chaise ride up to the house. Two men were sitting on the front bench and an aboriginal man rode in the cart, his legs dangling over the tray. The older gentleman appeared to be average in height and had a receding hairline and grey-brown hair brushed back tightly to where it gathered in bunched curls. His mutton-chop side burns were worn fashionably, almost joining under the chin, and although outwardly serious, he appeared of gentle nature. The man holding the reins was ten years his junior, and looked like hired help. The bare-footed native, Elizabeth noticed, was neatly dressed, but in ill-fitting clothes.

'Good day to you, sir.' The older man offered a smile.

'And a good day to you, sir,' said Rowan. Not being a man to mince words, Rowan asked, 'And what brings you all the way out into Van Diemen's wilderness?'

'Joseph Lycett, sir,' the older man said. 'And these are my travelling companion Roger Dumfries and our native guide Jarli, although everyone calls him Charlie. I am a landscape painter and we travel the countryside of Van Diemen's Land in an artistic quest.'

'Oh.'

'Yes, sir. I have been commissioned to prepare lithographs of Hobart Town, Launceston and their environs by none other than Major General Lachlan Macquarie, governor in chief to the colonies.'

'How interesting,' Elizabeth said.

Rowan introduced himself and Elizabeth. Lycett dismounted and shook Rowan's hand and Rowan noted how soft the artist's hands were, like those of a bookkeeper, not calloused like his assistant's.

'Hobart Town and Launceston, you say, Mr. Lycett,' Elizabeth said, 'then you are a long way from your intended destinations.'

'Yes, Miss Colchester, you are most observant. You see, I must confess I also have a fascination for the native peoples of this foreign land, and in particular I wish to sketch the Van Diemen's Land natives in their natural habitat.'

'You may find them scarce about here,' Rowan said.

Lycett turned to Jarli. 'That, sir, is why I have Jarli here, my native guide and a liaison between myself and the indigenous peoples of this land.'

'You must come inside for refreshment,' Elizabeth insisted, 'and Jarli, too.'

'Why, thank you, but Jarli will stay with the cart, Miss Colchester,' Lycett said, 'to guard the trunks.' Lycett alluded to four round-topped, brass-studded trunks on the cart. 'That is all my work, Miss Colchester. Albums and albums, hours and hours' of work in the field. Not to mention my stock of paper, paints, inks, brushes, etcetera, etcetera.'

Rowan ordered Pat, the older yard boy, to stable the horse and chaise, and gave orders to fetch Jarli refreshment from the kitchen.

Bessie served tea, along with Mrs. Bevan's wattle-seed cake, in the conservatory, where Joseph Lycett admired the plants, in particular one with crimson petals. 'Beautiful. This is a Van Diemen's Land wild flower, is it not?—the Waratah.'

'Yes.' Elizabeth was impressed.

'Being an artist I have an interest in plants and animals, as well as in the natives.'

'Do you share this interest, Mr. Dumfries?' Elizabeth asked Lycett's travelling companion.

'Yes, of course. But I cannot draw, let alone paint. Mr. Lycett here hired me to hunt and set up camp and to keep an eye out for trouble.'

'And Jarli?'

'He is our interpreter and guide. I fear that without him, we could attract mischief from the natives. One cannot be too careful in this land.'

'Then you must "set up camp" here tonight.' Elizabeth looked to Rowan who readily agreed. 'I'll have rooms prepared for you.'

'Oh, you are too kind Miss...'

'Mary,' Elizabeth insisted. 'And my brother, Henry.'

'Mary, you are too kind. It was our intention to ask if we could sleep in your stables.'

'Nonsense. And you must join us for dinner. It is not every day we have such interesting company.'

Over a satisfying dinner of stewed mutton with onions, currants and pepper and a fine dessert of prunes steeped in claret and sugar, artist Joseph Lycett told of his plans to eventually return to England and publish his work.

'How terribly interesting,' Elizabeth said.

'I have commissions to complete for various government officials. Governor Macquarie, for one, wants detailed paintings of both Hobart Town and Launceston; but in so doing, I am also collecting renditions of the natives to be redrawn and published as lithographs in London.'

'Published!'

'Yes, back home there is a hunger for information regarding the colonies.'

'Speaking of which, do you have any news from Sydney Town?'

'To be quite honest, Sydney Town offers little of interest to me. It is a cauldron of misery for most.' Joseph Lycett looked at his prunes and played with the cream jug, contemplating putting extra cream on his dessert. Unbeknownst to Elizabeth and Rowan, in truth back in 1811 Joseph Lycett had been transported as a felon convicted of forgery at Salop Assizes, for which he was sentenced to fourteen years' transportation. He'd been caught again in Sydney Town in 1815 for forging five-shilling banknotes, drawn on the postmaster. Elizabeth had more in common with their visitor than she could possibly have guessed. But good fortune followed Joseph Lycett to Newcastle, a prison for secondary offenders. There, he'd been finally given a pardon by the commandant, Captain James Wallis, for public services rendered through his talent for design and art.

in answer to Rowan's enquiry Roger Dumfries said, 'There *was* some excitement in Sydney Town a few months back'—he looked over at Lycett—'when some of the men, those wreckers, were brought to justice from the sealing islands in Bass Strait.'

'Yes,' Lycett concurred. 'You must have heard of the tragedy that befell the transport ship *Magdalena*.'

Elizabeth felt her face flush. 'Oh, yes...'—she feigned a nodding acquaintance with the matter—'Henry... We heard about that. Terrible business.'

'Yes, well'—Lycett picked up the conversation—'the Royal Navy captured the malefactors and brought some of them back to Sydney Town for trial. They were publicly executed, which created quite the sensation.'

'Yes,' Dumfries cut in. 'About two months since.'

'We did not hear the full story,' Rowan said. 'Pray tell.'

'Well, many of the scoundrels were killed on the island...'

'Bull Seal Island it was named in the gazette,' Dumfries said.

'Yes. Bull Seal. 'Twas an unchartered island, named by these criminals themselves.' Lycett finally decided on an extra dollop of clotted cream. 'Many were killed trying to escape. Seven, however, were captured and brought to justice. There were several native women on the island with them, along with their illegitimate offspring, but they were left to fend for themselves.'

'And the *Magdalena?*' Elizabeth asked, her voice almost breaking.

'No survivors, I'm afraid. Hundreds died, and for what? Greed.'

Rowan and Elizabeth felt a measure of relief until Dumfries added, 'Disturbingly, they never caught the ringleader…'

'Oh.'

'Yes, a man with a French name.'

Dumfries said, 'Leblanc.'

'Yes, that is it, Leblanc.'

Elizabeth felt a cold shiver run up her spine. She didn't dare look at Rowan, who asked, as indifferently as he could, 'Do they know what happened to him?'

'No, unfortunately,' Lycett said. 'He escaped, apparently. The rumours were that he escaped with a ship's surgeon, of all people, and a native woman, on a sloop hidden in a remote bay.'

'Yes. One of your compatriates, I believe,' Dumfries said nonchalantly, spooning a mouthful of prunes. 'A renegade American.'

'Oh!' Rowan clumsily dolloped cream on his dessert.

'We watched the navy sail the murderous scoundrel's ship into Sydney Cove,' Dumfries added. 'Escorted by the *HMS Assault*—it was, a prize for the lieutenant responsible for the capture of the criminals.'

'The *Sea Rat,*' Lycett announced.

'A fine ship it be, too.'

'You *are* American, are you not Henry?' Lycett asked.

'Yes.'

'Not all Americans are renegades, Mr. Lycett,' Elizabeth said haughtily.

'My apologies, Miss Colchester. It was not my intention to offend.'

'Of course not.'

'There are many American seamen here in the colonies,' Elizabeth said casually. 'Mostly whalers, I believe. My brother and I were born in Bristol and Henry here went to sea when he was twelve. Papa died and, thanks to our uncle, Henry was brought up in Baltimore.'

If Lycett was suspicious, he certainly did not show it. 'How interesting.'

'I should warn you, gentlemen'—Rowan looked Lycett directly in the eye and switched subjects with skill—'you must be aware of absconders as well as unruly natives in these parts.'

'Well, I did apply for soldiers from Launceston to accompany me,' Lycett said, 'but Commandant McKenzie refused—said he had none to spare. That is why I hired Roger here. And Jarli, of course, can advise me on the cultural and ceremonial aspects when we encounter tribes.'

Rowan and Elizabeth shared a stolen moment in Rowan's room once the household were asleep. 'Do you think he suspects anything?' Elizabeth whispered.

'No. No, I don't. Why should he? I think we handled that quite well.'

'So Leblanc escaped.'

'Apparently.' Rowan smiled at the irony.

'But where would he go? Did he hide on the *Queen B*?'

'I doubt it. That would be the first place they'd search—I know!'

'What?'

'Leblanc hid in a cave. There were many caves around that coast. Some you can only swim to and they are hidden—at high tide, especially. My guess is that he had prepared for this day and told no one.'

Rags the kelpie woke the household early, barking at the guests as they prepared to hike into the bushland, where Joseph Lycett was keen to catch the dawn light. For four days he used Beaumont Hall as his base, venturing off into the wilderness. Each evening, as Elizabeth and Rowan's hospitality was repeated, they shared stimulating conversation, but the subject of Bull Seal Island and its tragedies was never mentioned again.

Upon his return, Joseph Lycett would treat his hosts to an exhibition of his day's renderings. Jarli proved a valuable asset, he told them, in particular on their last day trip, when they encountered two separate tribes early one evening. They had come together for a corroboree and a tooth evulsion ceremony, Jarli had informed his master. Elizabeth and Rowan were aware of the native ceremony where a particular tooth was deliberately knocked out to denote which tribe the recipient was from.

'Interestingly,' Dumfries told Elizabeth, 'the first governor, Governor Phillip, who landed at Botany Bay in '88, had a missing front tooth and the first aborigines he encountered took this as a sign of his tribe.'

'Really?'

'Yes, really.'

Elizabeth found Lycett's drawings superbly detailed. The man was an efficient and fast-working artist. His work was prolific; he had albums packed with drawings and detailed notes. He would sit and sketch Rowan's and Elizabeth's portraits with remarkable skill while they casually dined.

After breakfast on the fifth morning they bid their farewells in the library. Joseph Lycett thanked his hosts profusely. "I feel I have made friends for life,' he said.

'Please feel free to visit anytime, Joseph,' Elizabeth said, 'should you ever again venture to Van Diemen's Land.'

'Thank you. You are both too kind, but I doubt I will ever return. I have a small gift for you.' Lycett held out a silk handkerchief containing a small parcel. ''Tis not much, but it is something that gave me a lot of pleasure—a remuneration, if you like, for your excellent hospitality.'

Blushing slightly, Elizabeth took the parcel and unwrapped it. 'Painted on cow bone to simulate ivory,' Lycett said proudly, 'compliments of your excellent cook, Mrs. Bevan.'

Elizabeth held the two miniature portraits before her, one of Rowan and one of herself. They were oval and framed in black lacquered pine.

'They are... so beautiful, so lifelike,' Rowan commented. Elizabeth had never had her portrait painted before. 'Thank you so much,' she said, and meant it, then placed the portraits on their small easels and onto the mantle.

'He is certainly gifted,' Rowan said as they waved farewell to their guests. 'I have a feeling the man will make a success of himself.'

Bessie shared the attic rooms with the other servants, a circumstance that could not be altered, giving rise to awkwardness between Elizabeth and Rowan. They stole moments of togetherness when alone in one bedroom or the other, but intimacy eluded them. Their situation was becoming untenable, with the servants being under the same roof. Elizabeth was acutely aware that Bessie was a meddler, and always attentive to household gossip.

CHAPTER TWENTY-EIGHT

Some weeks after the departure of Joseph Lycett, Hannah Bevan, the old cook, told Elizabeth in the kitchen one afternoon, 'I think your brother's taken a shine to our Bessie.'

'What!' Elizabeth shot back with unmasked belligerence.

'Oh!' Hannah sucked in a quick breath, pursing her lips. She realised she had said too much already and hovered distractedly over a pot of boiling custard, thrusting a wooden spoon into the bubbling cauldron of sugar and milk and stirring frantically.

'What do you mean?' Elizabeth demanded.

'Sorry, miss, I didn't mean to surprise you, like.'

Elizabeth's eyes narrowed, but she curbed her anger in time. 'Tell me, Hannah,' she said in a manner that was now more calculated, 'what do you mean by that comment?'

'Ah...' The cook's face reddened. She looked about nervously, to be certain her colleagues were not within earshot, especially Bessie. 'I meant no harm, Miss Mary, it's just the way Bessie talks, that's all, the things she says...'

'Like what?'

'Oh... ah... Mr. Colchester might compliment Bessie on her hair, for example.'

'Her hair?'

'Yes, miss.'

'Has he made any advances towards Bessie?' Elizabeth asked, as casually as she could. 'Advances that maybe I should know about?'

'Oh, no, miss.' The cook was adamant.

'Then kindly cease with this tittle-tattle. There is one thing I will not abide in my household, Hannah, and it's idle gossip.'

Elizabeth marched from the kitchen; she stormed through the house and down the hallway, throwing open the library door unannounced. The room was empty. 'Henry!' Elizabeth called out. No answer. A stray butterfly fluttered about Rowan's desk before retreating back to the garden through the open French doors and drawing Elizabeth onto the veranda. Reginald, the head gardener, was nearby, trimming roses and lost in his own world. He stiffened upon Elizabeth's approach.

'Reginald.'

'Good morning, ma'am. Beautiful day.' The spring morning was indeed beautiful.

'Have you seen my brother?'

'Why, yes, Miss Mary.' Reginald arched his tired back and Elizabeth noticed beads of sweat drizzle down the old man's cheeks. 'He went off to the dairy with Miss Bessie.'

Elizabeth's stomach was too knotted to answer. Trying not to appear concerned, she skirted the homestead towards the outhouses and, avoiding the kitchen, she proceeded directly to the dairy. The door was open. Elizabeth entered, anxious about what she might encounter.

'Mary,' Rowan said cheerfully, 'is everything all right? What hastens you?'

Elizabeth curbed her anger. Bessie stood next to Rowan, pouring freshly collected milk from a leather bucket into a stone churn.

'What are you doing?'

'What am I doing?" Rowan asked, incredulous.

'Yes. Why are you here in the dairy?' Elizabeth asked, glaring at Bessie.

'Oh.' Rowan was pre-occupied and the question seemed so irrelevant. 'I'm discussing cheesemaking with Bessie, here.'

'Cheesemaking?'

'Well, you have said yourself that you miss a good strong cheddar.' Elizabeth stepped back—she felt suddenly foolish. 'I am instructing Bessie on how we can process our own cheese. We can purchase rennet to separate the curds from the whey. I watched Jessica's mother make cheese in Baltimore and we have the perfect climate here to mature it.' Rowan gestured to the sterilised, whitewashed walls of the dairy, a prerequisite for any such process.

Elizabeth looked to Bessie, who seemed blindly innocent. 'Please leave us,' she ordered the maid. Bessie covered the churn with clean muslin and hurried away.

Rowan stepped forward with a concerned frown. 'What is it?' he asked. 'What bothers you so?'

'Did you compliment Bessie on her hair?'

Rowan coughed a disbelieving laugh. 'Are you serious?'

'Well, did you?'

'God forbid. With whom have you been conferring?'

'Yes or no? Did you compliment that... that girl, on her hair?'

'Yes!' Rowan said flatly. Defiantly. 'She has dry and unruly hair. She complained to me one morning and I instructed her on the merits of bandomine.'

'Bandomine?'

'Yes, it's a glutinous pomade for the hair...'

'I know what bandomine is,' Elizabeth snapped. 'But why would you...? Oh, it doesn't matter.'

Rowan stepped forward, taking Elizabeth by her wrists. Clearly she was jealous. 'Elizabeth,' he said quietly, 'I am a doctor. I have studied such things.'

Elizabeth mellowed. She felt deceived. 'It's that cook, Mrs. Bevan. She told me you had taken a fancy to Bessie.'

'Ha!' Rowan's laugh seemed heartless, but he understood the problem immediately. 'Elizabeth, Elizabeth'—before he realised it, Rowan had drawn her close, pulling his body against Elizabeth's with his hands on her hips—'the girl is smitten, yes. I can see that. *She* has taken a fancy to me. I am single, remember. Henry Colchester the settler, living alone with his sister, Mary.'

Elizabeth looked up into Rowan's eyes. They were so understanding, so kind. 'I feel so foolish,' she said. Instinctively, she placed her hands on his wrists.

'I would never encourage *anything* like that,' Rowan said of Bessie's flirting. He so wanted to say, 'I love *you*, only *you*, Elizabeth Eveleigh.' They stared into each other's eyes for what seemed to be all of time. What was holding back their true feelings? What was the barrier between them? Rowan would never forget Jessica, his first love, but she had passed and he had an entire life ahead of him. 'Elizabeth,' he said in a whisper. She could smell his fresh sweat. 'Elizabeth... I... only have eyes for you.' Elizabeth raised herself on her toes, leaning forward. Her lips parted. She closed her eyes. Their lips met, and he threw his arms about her squeezing with such passion that he feared he would do her harm. Elizabeth returned his love—their ardour would last an eternity, he was sure of it!

'Master! Master!' Reginald's voice carried across the courtyard. The gardener sounded panicked. 'Master! Mr.

Colchester, sir!' he cried out. Elizabeth and Rowan untangled themselves and hurried from the dairy.

'What is it, Reginald?' But the loud report from a musket heralded danger.

'My God, what was that?' Elizabeth shouted.

'Gunshot!' Rowan exclaimed.

'Absconders, miss,' Reginald explained

'No!'

'Aye. There be half a dozen or more.'

A second shot reverberated about the courtyard. Rowan spun toward Elizabeth. 'Get to the cellar. You know the drill.' And, indeed, Elizabeth and Rowan had discussed exactly what they would do in such a situation. Elizabeth reached out and Rowan took her hand and squeezed it tightly. To Reginald, the action appeared to denote brotherly and sisterly concern. Elizabeth knew better. Their eyes bade farewell. Elizabeth hurried by the kitchen, lifted the exterior yard hatch to the cellar and silently descended.

Rowan took a deep breath. He looked at Reginald, who was sweating profusely. 'Deep breath in, Reginald, deep breath. We give them what they want and they'll go away.' Reginald's eyes were filled with fear. He wasn't so certain it would be that easy. 'Go and see to Hannah and Bessie,' Rowan ordered. 'Take them and hide... I'll handle this!'

Another gunshot and Rowan heard a window shatter. 'Come on out. There's no point hidin'.' The voice was an angry drawl. Thirteen-year-old Dan appeared from the side of the house, pitchfork in hand.

'What are you doing?' Rowan hissed urgently, disbelieving the boy's courage.

'I'll tell 'em ter bugger orf, sir.'

'Good Lord, lad, they'll kill you. Run and fetch Charles,' Rowan said, referring to the gamekeeper at his forest cottage near the river.

'But…'

'But nothing. Do as I say. And tell him to be discreet.'

Rowan waited and watched the boy slip away before stepping from behind a wall buttress.

'I'm here!' Rowan called out. 'There's no point in shooting out my windows.'

'Get here. Put yer hands out where I can see 'em.' The aggressor was average height but looked taller wearing a shabby top hat. He was of solid build, with the calloused hands of a convict. He sat on a brown mare with a shaggy mane, and was leaning forward, resting his hand on the saddle horn. In his right hand he clenched a hefty flintlock. 'Yer hear me? I said put yer hands out where I can see 'em.'

'I heard you.' Rowan splayed his arms wide and stepped forward.

'Oh, got a hero 'ere 'ave we?'

Rowan didn't answer. He cast an eye over the others. There were four on their mounts. All were armed, either with pistols or long muskets. One, a particularly ugly man, with all his upper front teeth missing, held a burning torch, its head fouling the air as the flames crackled on the tarred rags. He wore a pinstriped cotton shirt stained with what looked to be dry blood. All the men were unshaven and dishevelled. They smelt like the stables. Two other horses whinnied restlessly beside the mounted men and Rowan guessed that their riders were in the homestead.

'You the squire?'

'Yes.'

'So, hero, what's yer real name?' The bushranger's eyes were constantly on alert, darting this way and that, like a rock lizard expecting an ambush.

'Henry Colchester.'

The Lizard ran a finger between his lip and lower teeth where chewing tobacco had caught. 'You American, ain't yer?'

'Maryland.'

'Ooh! Maryland! Well, well.' The lizard looked at his comrades for an ovation.

A squeal came from the house. 'Lookee what I found!' One man pushed a terrified Bessie before him, out through the front door and onto the veranda. 'Tasty little bit o' skirt for yer, Jack.'

Jack! Rowan's stomach twisted. Surely, this must be Mad Jack Spanner. The Lizard's keen eye caught Rowan's flinch. 'You've heard o' me, then?' he said with a sour smile and spat a glob of chewing tobacco at Rowan's feet. Rowan didn't dare answer. 'Mad Jack Spanner. Aye. Thart's me. Now who else is hidin' in that lovely house o' yours?'

Rowan remained silent, quietly seething.

Jack Spanner turned to the man wielding the flaming torch. 'Burn the firkin' house to the ground,' he commanded coldly. The horseman dug his spurs into his mount and the horse broke into a short trot.

'No!' Rowan shouted.

The torchbearer anticipated the call and stopped.

'Well, then?' Jack Spanner said, one hand raised to the torchbearer.

'Bessie!' Rowan called over his shoulder to the maid, 'Fetch the others.' Bessie stood frozen. Tears streamed down her cheeks. 'Bessie. Now. Please.' Bessie and her entrapper disappeared back into the house, while the other missing man dragged young Pat, the yard boy, through a side gate leading from the gardens.

'Bring 'em inside,' Jack Spanner ordered. The gang dismounted. 'McFerrin,' he ordered the torch man, 'stay 'ere and watch the gate an' keep that flame burnin'. Savvy?'

'Aye.'

Mad Jack Spanner buried the muzzle of his pistol in the top of Rowan's back. With the hammer cocked and Spanner's finger twitching on the trigger, Rowan felt suddenly vulnerable. 'Move it,' Spanner spat. 'An' don't try nuthin' or I'll shoot yer in the spine.'

They gathered in the library: Ben, Jarred, Matt, Evans. One man—Sage, Jack called him—had no trouble finding Reginald in the scullery, where the old gardener hid behind troughs, praying loudly. Annie Brown, the chambermaid, was dragged out of her attic room by the oldest in the gang, a Welshman they called Evans, and, shortly afterward, two of the farm hands were corralled.

'Who's missin'?' Jack Spanner narrowed his eyes at Rowan.

Rowan was defiant. 'We're all here.'

'Shite, yer are.' Jack Spanner jammed Rowan's face against the wall, cheek to the panel. He buried the pistol barrel harder into Rowan's spine. 'I said... who's missin'?'

'I told you!' Rowan was angry, his tone recalcitrant. Mad Jack cracked Rowan's head hard against the wall. 'Now answer the bloody question.'

'I have only recently taken up this life in the country,' Rowan said valiantly.

'"I've only just taken up this life in the country,"' Spanner mimicked, mocking Rowan in an effeminate voice. 'So what?'

Rowan ignored the taunt. 'I travelled from America to take up sheep farming. I live alone. I have not had the time to appoint all positions. We are all here... Ask the others.' Mad Jack Spanner took hold of Rowan's hair, twisted his head violently and cracked the pistol grip hard against Rowan's head. Rowan felt light headed and Mad Jack forced him backwards, where Rowan fell into an armchair. Immediately, a bloodied welt appeared on Rowan's head.

'I'll only ask yer once more. Where are the others?"

'You hard at hearing?' Rowan said obstinately, making to retaliate. 'I travelled from America to take up sheep farming...'

'Hold 'im back!' Spanner yelled to Matt, at his side. The oaf stepped behind the chair, pinioning Rowan with an arm about his throat.

'I live alone,' Rowan persisted obstinately. 'I...'

Spanner's face flared with anger. Rowan locked eyes with Mad Jack who balled his knuckles, punching Rowan in the jaw. Rowan drew strength from Commander Joshua Barney at Chesapeake, defying the British. He had witnessed violent battles at sea. He had beheld violent battles on land. And he sure as hell was not going to let this animal defeat him. Blood trickled from the corner of Rowan's mouth. 'Is that the best you've got?' he almost laughed.

'Why, you Yankee shite.' The next punch packed twice the pounding of the first. Rowan fixed eyes with the bushranger. Spanner glared back, his manic grin gone, to be replaced with a scowl of vengeful anger. 'What are yer lookin' at?' Mad Jack shouted. Rowan's heroics were unnerving the man.

'What am I looking at?' Rowan spat blood. 'I'm looking at an escaped felon who likes to intimidate the helpless, who bashes his opponents when they can't fight back.' Rowan shook his shoulders violently, but Matt had them secured. 'I'm looking at a criminal who needs the protection of other self-minded brigands—a man too afraid to make it alone. Why, I'd wager you beat women and children.'

There was truth to this, Spanner knew. The bushranger was unnerved by Rowan's unexpected heroics and he felt compelled to shoot the man in the face without delay.

But that would only turn the bastard squire into a bloody martyr.

'He's telling the truth,' one of the farmhands blurted, and immediately wished he hadn't.

'He's what!' Jack roared back.

'About others in the house, sir. He tells the truth.'

This welcome interruption gave Spanner some face—an excuse to turn away from Rowan. He twisted to face the young man. 'Is he, now? An' you are?'

'Michael, sir. Michael O'Bourne. Yard boy.'

'Yard boy, huh? Tellin' the truth, is 'e?' Mad Jack looked to the old gardener, Reginald, a man in his sixties and quite defenceless. 'Is 'e tellin' the truth?' Mad Jack pressed the muzzle into Reginald's forehead. The gardener promptly wet his britches. But, to the old man's credit, he nodded his head.

'Oh Jayzus,' Jarred said, ''e's pissed his britches.' The men laughed as Reginald stood shaking in a puddle of his own mess.

Mad Jack Spanner looked carefully into the eyes of the remaining captives before turning to two of the gang. 'Matt, Ben... search the house. You know what to look for— jewellery, silver, gold. Jarret,'—he turned to a twenty-year-old redhead—'food, grog, anythin' easy to carry. Move it.' The absconder now paid attention to the two young women. 'What's yer name?' he asked the chambermaid.

'Annie, sir.'

'"Sir"—I like that.' As he stepped close to Annie, she wanted to retch at his foul breath. 'How would you like me to be your sir?' Jack Spanner cupped the girls groin with gnarly fingers, taking a handful of her womanhood. Annie let out a whimper and he ran his tongue the full length of her cheek. Rowan made to jump to his feet but a second blow from the butt of a long-armed musket landed him back in his chair. Knowing his back was guarded, Mad Jack Spanner moved on to Bessie. Tears were spilling down her cheeks. Mad Jack pushed Bessie against the wall and worked his fingers into her privates. The other two grinned on lasciviously, anticipating their own pleasure.

'Please…' Bessie pleaded.

'Please wha'? Please please me, sir?' Spanner chuckled at his game. His arousal was primed, his muzzle loaded. He hadn't smelt the scented fear of a woman about to be violated for weeks.

'For God's sake, man,' Rowan yelled, 'do you not have any decency?' Another musket butt slammed into Rowan's chest. He collapsed back again, winded and angry. Mad Jack lifted Bessie's skirts, nestling his own body against hers. Pushing, thrusting in a frenzied attempt to position himself. He pinned her arms to the wall and lifted himself on his toes, shoving, groaning, frantically disrobing…

'Jack!' Matt and Ben re-entered the library. 'Jack!'

'Jesus! What?'

'There's a cook missin', cos there's stuff cookin' in the kitchen an' there sure ain't no cook amongst this lot.'

'Damn and firk!' Mad Jack Spanner threw Bessie aside. 'Do I always have to do everything meself?' He tidied his britches.

'Where's yer cook?' he spat at Rowan, slouched in the armchair.

'Gone to get help,' Rowan spat back, and was rewarded with another closed fist to the jaw.

'Watch 'em.' Mad Jack stormed out of the library and into the hallway, a loaded pistol in each hand. He headed for the kitchen. Matt and Ben followed. Mad Jack stepped from the rear door onto the courtyard, marching to the out-house kitchen. He was furious. He would find this cook and shoot her bastard master, Henry Colchester, dead before the cook's very eyes.

'Where are yer?' he yelled, bounding up the steps into the kitchen. Matt rushed in behind him. 'See, there's stuff cookin',' Matt pointed to the stove...

But the stove was clear.

'Well?' Mad Jack Spanner yelled in Matt's face. 'Well?'

'There was a pot cookin' on there a minute ago.'

'Oh, yeah!' Mad Jack turned to leave when Hannah met him face on. She had the pot of bubbling custard held high. and tipped the steaming, sugary, flour-thickened brew over the man's head like boiling tar. He squealed a piercing screech of blinding pain as the custard coated his face, poured into his eyes, and down his arms. He instantly dropped to his knees in excruciating pain. His skin blistered and he fell to the ground, unconscious.

Matt raised his flintlock to shoot Hannah, but she quickly swung the the iron saucepan, staving in the man's skull. His body crumbled back down the kitchen steps. Ben heard the commotion and leapt from the back door, panicked. He fired a loose shot. The ball chiselled the brickwork directly next to Hannah. The cook made to escape but Ben rushed her, throwing her violently against the wall. He drew a hunting knife from his belt, raised the blade and made to plunge... At that very moment Elizabeth lifted her head from the cellar hatch, aimed and fired, her ounce of lead splintering Ben's elbow.

Ben's squeals of agony chased the sound of the gunshot to the library, where the two remaining bushrangers deserted their posts. Jarred, rummaging through the upstairs bedrooms, bounded back down the stairs. Rowan staggered to his feet. He was disorientated and groggy but resolute. Enraged, Elizabeth slammed back the hatch and rose from the cellar, shouldering a second loaded Brown Bess. With the stock pressed into her shoulder she stepped through the backdoor, oscillating the barrel down the hallway, searching for a target, as Sage and the Welshman, Evans, charged her. Elizabeth had Sage in her sights. She thumbed back the hammer.

Eight feet, six... but Elizabeth was no killer. She lowered the barrel and fired.

Sage cried out, shot in the thigh. Through a blanket of smoke, Elizabeth watched the man fall. Evans, behind him, tripped and tumbled. Evans rolled to one side. He raised his pistol at Elizabeth, but she was shoved unceremoniously aside. Ratcliff, the gamekeeper, stepped into the hallway, kicking out at Evans. His pistol skipped across the floorboards. Not a man to waste ammunition, Ratcliff rammed his shotgun stock into Evan's face. There was no dodging the heavy walnut butt, and with a jaw full of shattered teeth, Evans crashed back to the flagstones.

At that same moment Jarred leapt down the bottom treads of the staircase. Reginald, fired by adrenalin and humiliated anger, charged from the library, armed with the fire-poker. He stabbed the iron between the banisters and Jarred tripped, crashing to the floor headfirst, his head twisted at a sickening angle, while gold coins spun and scattered about the floorboards.

Rowan threw open his desk drawer, taking out both travelling pistols, always kept loaded. He lurched clumsily to the French window and stepped onto the veranda, just as the torch-wielding McFerrin mounted the front steps.

'Back!' Rowan yelled at the man. 'Back, I say!' The man stood dumbfounded, trying to ascertain what had gone so horribly wrong in such a short time. He looked at his flame, deciding whether he should throw it into the house and run. 'I'll not warn you again,' Rowan said more calmly. 'Back away.' McFerrin studied the two small pistols aimed at his chest. Death knocked at his door. He backed away from the veranda and threw the torch onto the front lawn.

Immediately Elizabeth appeared on the veranda, while the others, led by the gamekeeper, took charge of the wounded prisoners. Rowan's face was swollen, his eyes red and inflated. Blood ran down his shirt, but he could not have been happier. Elizabeth ran into his arms and they embraced. 'I love you,' she whispered in his bloodied ear. 'I love you, Rowan Craige.'

'And I you, Elizabeth Eveleigh.'

CHAPTER TWENTY- NINE

Hobart Town

Marcus Marriot found it easy to prey on the weak and vulnerable. It came naturally to the man, and his baby-faced good looks easily deceived the gullible.

Fate cast its shadow over the disgraced soldier at the sawmill one autumn morning, providing an advantage that began with tragedy. A splinter that twitched from the axe blade as he worked speared Marcus in the right eye. The pain was immediate and excruciating, so painful, in fact, that Marcus slipped in and out of consciousness, and with great difficulty, he was taken by cart to the prison infirmary. The inch-green pine sliver had pierced the cornea and there was no choice but to remove the eye. Throughout this trauma Marcus was thankfully unconscious.

Four days passed before the matron, Mrs. Hyacinth Wharton, gave Marcus the news. Hyacinth was a motherly, jolly-natured, kind soul in her late fifties, the wife of reverent and conservative Reverend George Wharton of the prison chapel. He was seventy-three.

After an initial period of concern, Marcus healed quickly, convalescing in the infirmary, where his charm was not wasted on the good matron. The untenanted eye socket, where once a healthy orb had resided, was stitched over, and the dead skin blackened into a leathery anomaly. Marcus hated his new appearance, his baby face distorted by the ugly scar, but Matron Wharton, with all the care in the world, tailored a leather eye patch to hide the abnormality.

With his health repaired, Marcus realised he would be back in the chain gang sooner rather than later. He volunteered for duties in the infirmary, emptying nightsoil buckets, cleaning the floors, washing bandages and cremating the odd limb that had been amputated for one reason or another. He was dedicated, to the extent of debating bible stories with the matron. For the matron's part, she saw redemption. This prisoner had turned the corner and looked to the Good Lord for forgiveness.

With this in mind, the prison warden granted the matron's request for an assistant in the infirmary from amongst the prisoners. Marcus Marriot threw his energy into the new position. For him, this was the first real step towards his escape.

During the first week of summer, a stone wall caved in on a construction site on Hunter Island, where a new wharf was being constructed to connect the tiny island and its isthmus to Sullivan's Cove proper. Marcus and three other stretcher-bearers were hastened to the scene of disaster.

'One man's dead,' the overseer told Marcus, 'buried under that lot.' He nodded to where a ten-foot wall of sandstone had toppled over. 'There's three wounded, two bad, over there with the surgeon.'

Twenty feet away the surgeon of a recently docked transport ship, which had fortunately been in the vicinity at the time, was being assisted by other seamen in attending the injured. 'He'll want them taken to the infirmary, I should imagine,' the overseer said, noting the stretchers.

Marcus and the other bearers pushed a path through the onlookers. 'Stretcher bearers!' he yelled over the babble. 'Move aside.' Blood pooled about the ground at their feet and Marcus was nauseated at the unmistakable metallic odour of fresh human gore, but a more familiar smell caught his senses—rum. The surgeon was clearly inebriated. The casualty lay in shock, while his leg bled profusely from where his crushed fibula pierced the skin, half severing his leg. The man's eyes were wide and staring up at the heavens. He was bleeding to death. Marcus had positioned himself for a better look at this useless surgeon when anger overcame him. The surgeon was no other than Superintendent Surgeon Hugh Llewellyn, from the convict transport ship *Indefatigable*. Llewellyn fumbled clumsily with the leg of the dying man. The surgeon's assistant, more a barber than doctor, arrived, carrying a case of surgical instruments. The patient's face whitened.

Marcus whipped the rope from around his waist, securing his britches. 'Move it!' he said, outraged by the surgeon's conduct. He dropped to his knees, tying a tight tourniquet about the man's lower thigh, directly above the crushed leg. The bleeding slowed considerably. Marcus looked the surgeon in the eye. 'Well, you know what to do!' he shouted, 'Do it!'

Llewellyn was clearly panicked. He gaped at Marcus, incredulous. The man had lost his nerve. Llewellyn's assistant withdrew an amputation saw from its case. 'Hold him down,' he told Marcus while Llewellyn stood and then backed away. 'Bite on this,' the assistant continued, shoving a wooden gag in the injured man's mouth. The man clamped down and groaned, gritting his teeth, anticipating the inevitable.

The razor-sharp knife cleanly severed through flesh to the bone. With more blood welling about the cut, the assistant did not hesitate with the saw. Not much more than a minute later, the shattered limb fell free from the patient. Boiling tar was brought from the building site and painted onto the open wound to cauterise the exposed flesh. The patient fainted, but Marcus knew that he now had a fifty/fifty chance of survival, against the odds of certain death, had the amputation not taken place.

'Get him and the others on the stretchers,' Marcus told the other bearers. Marcus stood, nervous sweat pouring down his face and the arch of his back. He focussed his good eye along the dock, to where Surgeon Hugh Llewellyn had made himself scarce, avoiding prying eyes. Marcus watched the man uncork a spirit flask and greedily gulp down rum.

'Marcus, we need 'elp,' one of the prison stretcher-bearers called, beckoning him. 'We're a man short, like.'

Marcus turned to his companions. 'Take him,' he said, inclining his head to the amputee. 'Now, like. There's a good man.' Marcus looked at the others. 'I'll be with yer in a moment. I've business to attend to.'

They watched Marcus approach the intoxicated surgeon. Llewellyn looked over his shoulder at Marcus. Clearly he had not recognised him from his last voyage, over a year before, and now Marcus wore an eye patch.

'What do you want?' Llewellyn demanded angrily of Marcus.

'You're a disgrace...' Marcus seethed as the memories of the lashings he'd received on board the transport ship *Indefatigable* flooded back vividly. He could feel the cat on his back once more: the terror, the pain, the smirk upon the surgeon's face, red from the juice of the poppy. 'You're a disgrace to yer profession.'

'Excuse me?'

'You heard me.' Marcus approached, gritting his teeth, his fists balled, the sweat rolling from his brow and stinging his eye.

'Do you know who I am?' Llewellyn demanded, his voice breaking.

'Aye. Yer Hugh Firkin' Llewellyn. A piece o' shite if'n I ever met one. An' now I'm goin' ter expose yer for the drunkard yer are. That man would have died. 'E still might die—bastard!'

The surgeon took another swig before punching the cork back into the flask with the heel of his hand. 'Do I know you?' he demanded, the fire in the rum peppering his courage.

'Aye. Marcus Marriot o' the *Indefatigable*.'

Llewellyn looked beyond Marcus to the departing sightseers, only to take courage from two constables who had come to restore order at the building site.

'Yes,'—Llewellyn slipped the flask into his pocket—'I remember you now. You cried like a girl when they whipped you...'

'What?' Marcus could not believe what he was hearing. 'What?' he said, unaware that his voice was high.

'I said, you cried like a girl,' the surgeon reiterated in a high-pitched, effeminate voice, mocking Marcus, and then turned his back to walk away. Marcus pounced. He managed a cowardly punch to the back of the man's head and then several others. Llewellyn dropped to his knees, suffering a short blackout. Marcus was pent up with anger, wound up like a clock spring. He did not hold back. His right knee jerked upwards, connecting with Llewellyn's mouth. The surgeon spat a bloodied glob from a loosened tooth as Marcus threw a third punch, a haymaster, slamming into the side of the man's head. Llewellyn threw back his head to plead with Marcus, only to be pounded in the face, before the constables arrived. It took both constables and two of

1814

Marcus's colleagues to wrench Marcus away from the surgeon.

'Oh, you will pay for this, Marcus Marriot.' Llewellyn spat the words in a slurry of blood and saliva, his eyes swelling and bruised. He suspected a broken nose. 'You hear me? You will pay for this.'

Beaumont Hall. Late 1816.

The affront on Beaumont Hall brought about an unexpected bond between the servants and their masters, Henry and Mary Colchester. It had brought them all closer together, exposing their strengths and their weaknesses, but mostly strengths. Old Reginald, in particular, felt he had redeemed himself. The felon known as Jarred, whom he had tripped on the stair, died later that day from a broken neck. Reginald felt no remorse. He had served as carpenter's mate on HMS *Orion*, and been present at the Battle of Aboukir in '98, when the French attacked. He'd lost two fingers that day, seen death close up, and nearly been deafened, and he still suffered from anxiety and shock. Jarred had been the first to intimidate him when his bladder failed, so, no, Reginald felt no remorse.

Bessie, however, became withdrawn. As the others moulded into more of a contented family, Bessie became insolent, and was frequently chastised for disobedience.

Directly after their attackers' defeat and capture, Elizabeth had wrapped Rowan's chest in bandages. He had at least two cracked ribs. With some difficulty, Rowan then administered medical attention to the wounded gang members: one had a cracked skull, two had bullet wounds and one a smashed jaw. Mad Jack Spanner died from his burns and, Rowan suspected, heart failure. Only the torchbearer, McFerrin, had survived unscathed. All the while, Reginald stood guard in the cellar where the ruffians were imprisoned, sighting down the barrel of his thirty-year-old blunderbuss loaded with rusty boot tacks.

For Rowan and Elizabeth to draw attention to themselves by delivering the captive bushrangers to the Launceston watch house in person would be a fool's errand. Besides, Rowan was in no shape to travel. So it transpired that the morning after the attack Rowan put Charles Ratcliff, the gamekeeper, in charge of transporting the five surviving gang members and the two cadavers to Launceston on the farm bullock dray. They were securely bound and well guarded by two well-armed farm hands.

It was with grave fear s that Rowan and Elizabeth listened to their servants' excited voices on their return, three days later, relaying what had happened in the township. 'We were feted as heroes,' the farm hands prattled in animated excitement.

'Mad Jack Spanner's body was displayed on a gibbet in the town square,' one said.

'Aye. An' his face was all blistery. Turned black, it did. It were an awful sight. Yer should have heard the children squeal.'

'But the commandant wishes to thank you personally,' the gamekeeper told Elizabeth and Rowan.

'That's out of the question.'

'But why?'

Elizabeth shot the man a sharp look.

The gamekeeper suddenly remembered his place. 'Please forgive me, miss, but it is such an honour.' He looked to Rowan, whose face was puffy and sore. 'You are perceived as heroes.'

'Mr. Colchester is in no shape to travel,' Elizabeth insisted.

'Besides, Rowan added, 'I look like I have been bare-knuckle boxing.'

'I understand, Miss Mary, Mr. Colchester, but you will be cured soon. All shipshape, as they say, and then you will be able to travel. Commandant McKenzie was most insistent.'

'Commandant McKenzie has been stationed in Sydney Cove for some time, I have been told,' Rowan told Elizabeth when they were alone. 'God knows what information he holds. It is a possibility that my description, made by the condemned wreckers, has been well documented. We would face this man at our peril.'

Months passed without further disruption of their everyday duties. Life was idyllic, although Rowan and Elizabeth's love for each other frustrated their daily activities. The masquerade of brother and sister could never be undone, and should their true relationship be revealed, it would bring instant suspicion upon them. However, rare moments of passion were purloined. Rowan bought Elizabeth a mare and taught her to ride. This pastime let them venture to remote locations, usually by the river, where they could share rare moments of passion. Other trysts were stolen in the middle of the night, with the utmost care and discretion.

Rowan learnt what he could about rearing merino sheep, but contented himself with the flock in hand. He spent hours with the gamekeeper and the farm hands, considering the merits of buying in the merinos. He discussed raising cattle with Elizabeth but, again, he knew nothing about livestock. Their stratagem continued. A year had passed. They had celebrated a Christmas and an Easter there. The seasons changed, which was one thing Elizabeth found endearing about her adopted home.   The weather was similar to

England's, with four distinct seasons: spring, summer, autumn, winter.

Rowan contented himself with the fact that they still had two thirds of Leblanc's fortune intact. When the time came to leave, they would prepare books to back their wealth, to make it legitimate, and then they could voyage to the Orient and invest, both in business and in a new life as husband and wife. As the months passed, Rowan became more and more impatient.

'How would you feel about going to sea?' Rowan asked Elizabeth over breakfast one morning when they were alone.

'How would I feel? Terrified. How would you expect me to feel?'

'Fair enough.'

'Why do you ask?'

Rowan walked to the serving trolley and poured himself another cup of tea. When he was assured no one was within earshot he said, 'I am becoming restless, Elizabeth. I am not certain I can continue this... this lie, much longer.'

Elizabeth moved to the window, looking out at old Reginald attending the wild orchids he had had such success with. Elizabeth loved her new life. The only thing she could possibly want would be to expose their true relationship, to be Mr. and Mrs. Craige. But the deceit had gone on for too long. Maybe the move *would* solve their problem. Rowan joined Elizabeth at the French windows. They watched Reginald for a moment.

'"Pink fingers", he calls them,' Elizabeth said.

'Pardon?'

'Reginald's orchids. He calls them pink fingers. He is so pleased with them and so proud.'

'Oh.' Rowan so wanted to hold Elizabeth, share the warmth of the morning sun with her, share her with the world. But he reigned in the temptation. 'I've been thinking more and more of pursuing the life of a merchant. I understand the sea, I am a mariner and I know enough about trading. I have contacts in the Orient. To be honest with you, Elizabeth, I would be safer away from here. We both would.'

'I knew it could not last for ever.' Elizabeth turned to face Rowan; she ached to take *him* in *her* arms, but there was always one or another servant within sight. 'When did you have in mind?'

'I am of the opinion that we should wait no more than another half year.'

'Half year!' Elizabeth sighed.

'I know, Elizabeth. It pains me also. In the meantime it's Henry and Mary Colchester, huh?' With Reginald's back turned, Rowan kissed Elizabeth affectionately on the forehead. 'Come to my room tonight,' he whispered, and stepped out onto the veranda.

CHAPTER THIRTY

1817. Early winter.

It was a cold and damp Saturday afternoon and almost dusk when Rowan went to call, as pre-arranged, at his gamekeeper's cottage. The dwelling, a four-room stone, wattle and daub, shingle-roofed cottage, sat by the river near a forest on the Beaumont Hall Estate. It was an idyllic setting, reminding Rowan of Maryland. They were to hunt kangaroo. Ratcliff was a man of similar age and stature to Rowan, and Rowan had grown to enjoy his company and intelligent rhetoric. But as Rowan approached the house on horseback, a spare horse in tow, he heard a fearful row from within. His horse whinnied. The raised voices went silent.

'Mr. Colchester, sir,'—Ratcliff appeared at the door looking red-faced, embarrassed—'I wasn't expectin' yer for a whiles, yet.'

'Sorry, Charles, I hope I am not disturbing anything.'

'No, sir, just me and the wife airing our differences. I'll get me coat and gun right away.'

Rowan made idle conversation when they were clear of the property. 'Your wife is with child, is she not?'

'Aye. She only got a week to go. She's getting' a trifle cranky, thart's all.'

'Oh, I did not realise. You should be with her, then. From tomorrow, you must stay at home until the bairn is born.'

'It's all right, sar, her sister's arriving soon with her own brats. She'll be lookin' after her.'

Ahead of them on a common track, they came across Jefferson Mendel. Mendel was a shepherd and neighbour they knew as a reclusive and private man. He managed a horse and two-wheel cart covered with a canvas tarp, and was a giant of a man, as tall as any full-grown stallion. He wore long straight black hair parted in the middle and tied back in a ponytail. His face was large and oval, his brow sizeable, his nose huge, and his full-length wiry beard cascaded to his breast. Mendel was usually seen wearing his favourite frockcoat, black, with a black blouse, black britches, knee-high black boots and immense, calloused hands protruding from the cuffs of his black coat. But it was his eyes that people mistrusted. Small, close together and intense, they betrayed a devious mind. If Jefferson Mendel had been seen shirtless, the observer would have noted a ten-inch scar under his left arm, running down to his belly, where he'd been slashed by a whore whom he'd cheated out of a crown in a brothel in Cape Town a decade earlier.

Mendel was a shepherd, employed by Mr. Samuel Burns and his wife Audrey, whose estate bordered on Beaumont Hall's property. Their homestead was three miles to the west. Mendel's hut, a modest three-roomed dwelling, was by the river, where he tended to the Burns' four hundred sheep and was left pretty much to his own devices.

'Mr. Mendel!' Rowan called out to the shepherd a hundred yards distant, and slapped his horse on the rump, getting into a canter. The shepherd turned, startled at meeting anyone in this remote area. He immediately stopped and dived beneath the tarp, only to reappear as the two riders steadied their mounts at his side.

'Henry Colchester, Mr. Mendel,' Rowan said, a little hesitant as he suspected that the man had a gun beneath the canvas. 'And this is my gamekeeper, Mr....'

'I know who yer are.' Rowan was close enough to smell the rum on the man's breath. 'What-d'ya want?' he demanded, as low growls warned of the two huge hunting dogs under the wagon.

'Well, I don't mean to be a bother, sir,' Rowan answered in a friendly enough manner, one eye on the largest dog, a mangy, reddish-brown mongrel with only one eye and a drooling snarl, baring all its teeth, 'but I was considering rearing merinos on my land and I thought... well, having just bumped into you, so to speak, that you might be willing to come to Beaumont Hall some time... as my guest, of course, and I could... well... ask you a hundred questions.'

Rowan's horse whinnied—something was spooking the creature and it clearly wasn't the dogs. The gamekeeper, too, felt a strain from his mount and he circled the cart, only to unsettle the shepherd.

'I'm busy,' Mendel grumbled and gave his horse a lick of the whip. The cart trundled on.

'Well, thank you for your time, Mr. Mendel,' Rowan called out, over the sound of creaking cartwheels grinding on gravel. 'If you change your mind, you know where I live.'

'Rude bastard.' Charles Ratcliff bit his lip and spat dry skin off to one side.

'Yes,' Rowan conceded. 'He's a strange man.'

'I've never liked the bastard, sir, or them bastard dogs. Especially that one-eyed monster. I reckon he's a deviant one, that one.'

'Deviant? The dog?'

'No, Mr. Colchester, the bloody shepherd.'

1814

Hobart Town

Thirty days in solitary confinement would break the toughest of men, but Marcus Marriot was not the toughest of men. He sat in one corner, staring blankly, staring off into blackness, as his cell was windowless and soundproof. The faintest arrow of light filtered through a crack in the door; otherwise, it was dark. Dark, cold, silent and tormenting.

Marcus mulled over the thought of mutilating himself. But he was a coward. He took on a fancy that his bladder was continuously full, that it was impossible to empty. He stood over his night bucket for hours, trying to expel more fluid, but it simply wasn't happening. At other times he saw the demons, usually from the corner of his eye, but like all his tormenting ghosts, they vanished the moment he spun about to face them.

Marcus would rather have been flogged. *Fifty lashes* he considered. *A hundred. Two hundred.* Anything was better than solitary confinement, not knowing the time of day or the amount of time served. He subsisted on bread and water —nothing else. The bed was a hammock supported by leather straps fastened to each end of the cold, miserable stone walls. Marcus paced the six-foot-wide cell like a caged animal, walking its nine-foot length in four steps and then returning. After an hour he climbed into his hammock, but lay awake. Then, finally, after what must have been hours, he wept himself into a tortured sleep.

At the end of thirty days Marcus was returned to timber cutting, however, not at the Cascades Mill but to recently opened shipyards on the River Derwent foreshore at Battery Hill. Back in irons, back as top dog, sawing timber for shipbuilding—his only saving grace, keeping him from the bottom dog position, was the fact that Marcus had lost an eye. Bottom dog sawyers frequently caught sawdust in their eyes—some went blind. It was this fact that saved Marcus.

As time passed, Marcus found that he had a genuine interest in shipbuilding. His attentive curiosity, combined with good behaviour, caught the attention of Wight Fairfowl, master shipwright at the Battery Hill shipyard. Fairfowl was an old man with brawny, bare arms exhibiting fading tattoos, now misshapen on aging, weathered skin. Fairfowl was himself a pardoned transportee from Norfolk Island with a kindly nature, a full silver beard and an unruly grey mane tied back in a ponytail. Over the months that passed, Marcus Marriot's interest and concerned efforts earned him respect from the shipbuilder, and he was finally given a position to train as a shipwright's carpenter. Rehabilitation, the authorities thought, was finally succeeding.

But the threat of Marriot's past was forever near. The threat of being returned to servitude for stepping out of line was constantly haunting Marriot, especially when an easterly breeze sent the stink of human decay from the gibbets—two hundred yards away on Secheron Point—gusting by the shipyard.

North End, Van Diemen's Land

Settlement by the Europeans on the island of Van Diemen's Land was approaching its twentieth year. Now, for the past handful of years, more and more emancipated convicts had moved inland, away from the bad memories of their imprisoned pasts. They built small huts with vegetable gardens and chicken pens on plots of granted land along the riverbanks and in the wild foothills of this ancient, untamed land. But life was tough. Kangaroos ate their crops; the ferocious devil cats and wild tiger dogs stole their chickens and other livestock. In response, the settlers killed off the native animals, which were livestock for the aborigines, who in return speared the whitefella's sheep. For this, the intruders murdered the indigenous peoples of the land. It was tit for tat—there was no law and order in the wilderness. Resentment brewed. Dotted on the finer pastoral lands of lush fertile soil near the major rivers, and enjoying great vistas, were the gentry's estates, the likes of Beaumont Hall.

'I am worried about Charles,' Rowan said of his gamekeeper, Charles Ratcliff. Rowan lay on his bed, drained from their lovemaking. They lay together naked, skin on skin, with Rowan behind Elizabeth, like two spoons in a cutlery drawer. With an arm across her perky breasts, he stroked Elizabeth's silky hazel hair. It had grown long once more, since having been hacked short on the hulk in the Thames. Elizabeth loved it when Rowan played with her hair. She had fallen for this kind and thoughtful man—an alliance she could never have imagined over a year earlier.

'Elizabeth, did you hear me? I am worried about Charles.'

Elizabeth knew exactly where this conversation was headed. Their gamekeeper had lost his wife and child in a tortured childbirth, in which the baby had been breach. Mrs. Ratcliff had bled to death. 'Yes, my love. I feel for him, too,' Elizabeth said. 'But what can we do?'

'He's become morose, living in that cottage alone. It is not healthy for a man's mind.'

'He needs time.'

'We must start thinking about what we are going to do in the future, also.'

Elizabeth broke free from their embrace and wriggled about to face her man. 'But I love it here. You love it here; we are so happy.'

'True, my love. But this is a British colony and we are both fugitives. Besides, we are only tenants. It cannot last forever.' Rowan had not broached the subject of becoming a merchant and purchasing a ship since their earlier discussion, but Elizabeth knew it was never far from his thoughts. Rowan propped himself up on one elbow so as to look clearly into Elizabeth's large blue eyes. 'And sneaking about our own home to snatch moments of intimacy is not... well... not an ideal situation.'

That was true. Elizabeth and Rowan had stolen their first moments together only months earlier, and it would not be too long before they were caught out. Incest! Just the thought of being accused of such an abhorrent crime sickened Elizabeth. A spitting candlewick on the bedside table finally extinguished, replaced by the soft light from a half moon filtering across the bed. 'I had better return to my own room,' Elizabeth said, stifling a yawn.

Rowan tugged at the scrunched bedding, pulling the blankets to cover them both as the room's chill suddenly became apparent. 'In a moment,' Rowan said. 'I just want to hold you a little longer.' And then fatigue overcame them both.

Bessie found that invention came easily to her. Invention, that is, as in fabricating the truth. Some one hour's ride north of Beaumont Hall, a small unit of soldiers were stationed at Glen Esk, a military post commissioned to guard against bushrangers and the increasing threat of marauding aborigines. It was also a military post one unavoidably encountered should one wish to travel on the northern road. The camp was under the command of Corporal Adney Zachariah, a veteran of Napoleon's last battle, lost to the First Duke of Wellington, Arthur Wellesley, in the Netherlands.

Corporal Zachariah had learnt of Henry Colchester's achievements in capturing the Spanner Gang and had made a visit to Beaumont Hall to thank the man in person, on behalf, he claimed, of Commandant McKenzie. But his motives had seemed ambiguous.

For Bessie it seemed as if cupid's arrow had struck a bullseye from the moment they met in the hallway of Beaumont Hall. Without Rowan and Elizabeth's permission or knowledge, Bessie's trysts with the young soldier were becoming more and more frequent. Their regular rendezvous was a few miles north, at a newly opened inn called The Stockman, a disreputable place with a taproom, kitchen, scullery and stables and three small bedchambers on the upper floor. It was built, essentially, for the increasing coach traffic from Hobart Town.

Bessie was smitten. However, this veteran of Waterloo was no more than a handsome and strapping rake with a lust for using naïve women.

'Brother and sister they be, Mary an' Henry Colchester,' Bessie told her lover as they sat up in the inn bed like an old married couple. 'From Bristol.'

'Yet he has a foreign accent.' Corporal Zachariah drew on a churchwarden clay pipe packed with Virginia tobacco. 'Maryland, you said?'

'Yes. 'E were taken to sea as a young man and growed up in America.'

The exhaled smoke seeped from the soldier's mouth and nostrils. 'Cos I don't like them Americans,' he said. 'Warmongers, the lot o' them.' He faced Bessie. 'I lost a brother in America. Fightin' the bloody Yankees, 'e were. Shot in a skirmish along the Potomac River.'

'I'm sorry to hear that.' Bessie happened to look out the window. 'Lord!' she burst out. The half-moon was low in the sky. 'Oh, dear Lord, I better scamper or the sun 'll be up.'

'Fridee, then?' Zachariah reminded Bessie as she dressed. 'Wha'?'

'I rented this 'ere room fer Fridee, so see yer then, huh?'

The corporal sent Bessie away with a frail hug. He watched her hurry away along the riverside road leading south, snipped the inn's back door latch and retired to his bed.

Elizabeth was certain she'd heard a noise downstairs. She awoke startled and sat bolt upright.

'What is it?' Rowan whispered, waking groggily.

'I thought I heard someone downstairs.' Together they listened in silence. Nothing. Rowan crossed the floor and unlocked his door. He opened it a crack and peered out. *All clear*. He shrugged nonchalantly. Elizabeth quickly dressed in her nightdress and joined him. They shared a final embrace. Elizabeth stepped out into the dark hallway. And froze.

In the pitch dark, she could hear the creaking of the treads as someone ascended the stairs towards her. Elizabeth, disorientated from her sudden awakening, called out without thinking, 'Who's there?' The footsteps ceased. 'Who's there, I say?'

''Tis only me, Miss Mary.'

'Bessie?'

'Aye, miss.'

Suddenly Elizabeth's voice broke. 'W-what are you doing?'

'I was thirsty, miss. I went to fetch a glass o' milk.' Rowan's room filled with soft candlelight as Rowan lit a fresh candle and joined Elizabeth on the landing. 'Sorry to wake you, Mr. Colchester, but I couldn't sleep and...' immediately Bessie had questions of her own -- questions she certainly could not ask. Mr. Colchester was topless, and what was Miss Mary doing, anyway, standing outside his door in the early morning? 'I... ah... I just went to the dairy and took a glass of milk—just the one, sir.' Bessie looked afraid—was *she* also hiding something?

'You are dressed, Bessie,' Elizabeth observed.

'Pardon me, miss?'

'You are fully clothed.'

'Oh… Aye. On account, I didn't want to go outside in my nightgown, miss.'

Rowan suspected this to be a lie, but he and Elizabeth harboured a more dangerous lie. 'That's all right, Bessie,' he said, 'now go back to bed.'

Suspicions lingered. Gossip spread. The mood of the servants towards Rowan and Elizabeth changed. It was a subtle change, but they now felt observed, judged, vilified. And above all, they felt spied upon. The two daren't even show the affection of brother and sister. They were continuously on guard, and could only conceive of future liaisons in the distant future.

Some weeks later, Rowan sat in silence, reading the Hobart Town Gazette. He had been enjoying breakfast when a public notice advertising the sale of a whaling vessel caught his attention:

To be sold
The Lucy.
Due to the untimely death of Captain Smith of New Bedford, this two-decked, three-masted, 27-sail square-rigged whale ship the Lucy, *is to be sold. The* Lucy *is 250 tons, 95 feet, maximum breadth 25 feet, depth 12, in the hold. Built from oak and pine with cedar fit out. For sale, complete with 5,000 feet of rigging, 5 anchors, anchor cables, complete cordage of halyards, sheets and tack. All articles essential for the trade of whaling: tripods, barrels etc., etc. Price 3,000*

guineas. Situated in Kangaroo Bluff. For particulars call at the offices of shipping agent Adam Bolten, Collins Street, Hobart Town, or agent's representative living aboard said vessel.

Rowan read the article twice and checked the date at the top of the page. The gazette was only a fortnight old. 'I must leave for Hobart Town immediately,' Rowan told Elizabeth when they were enjoying a rare moment alone in the conservatory. Elizabeth stood before a hanging basket of pansies. She looked across at Rowan, nonplussed; his face was tight with thought. 'You *are* serious,' she said plucking dead flowers from their stalks.

'Here. Read this.' Rowan marched across the flagstones and presented Elizabeth with the paper. With the sombre mood in the household Rowan had again broached the subject of his merchant ambitions, detailing sailing to Shanghai and Canton in the Orient, as well as Manilla, Malacca, Batavia and maybe even Madras. The possibility of riches was a warming thought for Elizabeth, but the thought of a life at sea unnerved her.

''Tis an opportunity not to be missed,' Rowan said excitedly. 'What are your thoughts?'

'I... I don't know. Ah... it is all so sudden.'

'Sudden!' Rowan dropped his voice to a whisper. 'Elizabeth. This is what we have been waiting for. You knew —we both knew—we could not hide here indefinitely. We have the capital. We can sail away and start a new life, away from the threat of being caught up with in Van Diemen's Land. We have lived under the nose of tyranny too long already.' Rowan took the gazette from Elizabeth, putting it aside and, being certain they were alone, he took her hands in his. 'We owe this to ourselves. There's a fortune to be made. What say you, Elizabeth Eveleigh?'

'Rowan, I… I…'

'Say yes, my love. Just say yes.'

Elizabeth's eyes welled with a mixture of happiness and trepidation. 'Rowan.'

'Yes?'

'I am with child!'

For Rowan, the news that Elizabeth was with child was both thrilling and terrifying. It was estimated that the unborn was eight weeks old and, they both agreed, in a few weeks Elizabeth would have problems concealing her pregnancy from the household. Elizabeth eventually agreed. If they could secure the vessel and a crew, Rowan could pursue the course of a merchant.

'What of our lease with Mr. Fawkner?' Elizabeth questioned. 'I mean, we don't want reprisal from a broken contract to add to our woes.'

'We will fulfil the contract. Pay the sum owed and explain we… ah…'—Rowan paced the conservatory, thinking of a ruse—'We will say an uncle died and left us a large estate in Bristol and that we must return to England.'

Elizabeth was impressed. 'Perfect.'

'We have more than enough in Leblanc's chest to purchase the ship, make moderate structural changes to convert her from a whaler to a cargo vessel and, I estimate, we would have near enough to two thousand pounds to purchase our first cargo.'

'Which would be…?'

'Wool. We purchase as much as we can possibly afford and sail directly to Canton. We deal with the East India Company only, sell the wool, buy up ceramics, tea and textiles and sail that to Calcutta.'

The very thought of such exotic locations excited Elizabeth, but her excitement was short-lived. Rowan immediately looked pensive—worried, even. 'What is it? ' Elizabeth asked. 'What bothers you so?''

'Well, it means riding to Hobart Town.'

Elizabeth was only too aware of the dangers. 'Yes, but no one knows your true identity—surely.'

'The officers of the Royal Navy have long memories, their reach is infamous, and they are relentless and unforgiving.' Rowan stood and folded the gazette into his pocket. 'I'm going to see Charles.'

'Oh?'

'He's been to Hobart Town. He knows the layout. He can advise me.' Rowan had another thought. 'Maybe he could ride with me.'

'That's the most sensible idea yet,' Elizabeth agreed.

The sky was overcast and, for the first time, Rowan thought the gamekeeper's cottage, its surrounding forest and the nearby river all looked gloomy. There was no smoke escaping from the cottage chimney. Rowan dismounted at the front of the dwelling and called out. No answer. He thumped on the door. No response. Fearing the worst, Rowan walked to the back of the dwelling.

Rowan called out, 'Charles!'

The gamekeeper was kneeling at his wife's grave, a pathetic mound of earth with a simple wooden cross. Directly parallel was an even more pathetic mound of earth, much smaller.

'Charles.'

Charles remained on his knees, his back to Rowan. 'Molly...' Charles muttered incoherently, his wretched voice breaking. 'We was goin' to call the wee one Molly,' he told Rowan.

The gamekeeper suddenly remembered his station and stood to acknowledge his governor. 'Forgive me, sar... it's just that I...'

'Forget it, man.' Rowan felt the pall of sadness press down on his own shoulders. Charles Ratcliff was a mess, and his eyes were red from tears, with blackened bags of skin beneath them, making the man appear ten years older. He seemed unaware that mucus had set on his upper lip. His breath was foul, with hints of rum. He smelt unwashed and his clothes were soiled. Rowan put an arm about the man's shoulder. 'Come inside, Charles. I could use a cup of tea, if you have some.'

Rowan started a fire and boiled a pot of water while Ratcliff washed and changed. It seemed the presence of his master had cheered the man somewhat. It had been weeks since he had lost his family and now Rowan felt guilt for not having kept a closer eye on the man.

Aware of how he had let himself go, Charles Ratcliff tidied the kitchen table, clearing away rum bottles and scraps of stale food while Rowan sought to steer the conversation in a positive direction.

'Charles, I believe you once told me that you lived in Hobart Town.'

'Only for a short while, sir. Bloody awful place, if'n you'll excuse me language.'

'Why, exactly?'

'Many parts is dangerous, even in daylight hours. It's a town full o' criminals, and the freed ones do little to mend their evil ways.'

'Oh?'

'Burglars have a field day, fist fights in the street are common, especially after the inns close at nine hours in the evenin'. The law is mostly run by ex-convicts—javelin men, they's called. Corrupt bastards. Anyone with a bit of clobber's gotta be careful in the streets, cos muggings are all too common. Even wives are traded...'

'You jest!'

'Nay, sar. I've heard o' men with their ticket o' leave, tradin' their wives for a keg o' rum.' The gamekeeper looked Rowan in the eye. 'Why do yer ask about 'Obart Town, Mr. Colchester?'

Rowan cupped his hands about his tin mug of sweet black tea and stared into the dark amber a moment, uncertain of how much to tell the man. 'Because I have to pay the town a visit,' he finally sighed.

'Oh. May I enquire why, sar, if'n it ain't too bold?'

Rowan had given this very question a lot of thought on his ride to the cottage. He liked the gamekeeper and wanted to help the man, especially now in his time of need. 'Have you any experience as a seaman, Charles?'

'Nay. I sailed to Port Jackson as a foot soldier, but was discharged on account o' me affliction. But you know this, sar.'

'Yes, of course.' Rowan knew that Charles Ratcliff suffered from swamp fever picked up in India and periodically had fits of shaking and the chills.

'Why do yer ask?'

Rowan took a moment. This would be a great test of his servant's loyalty. 'Because I wish to inspect a ship, Charles.'

'A ship!'

'Yes. It is a whaler put up for sale. The owner, you see, has passed away and his wife wishes to dispose of the vessel. I intend to convert her to a cargo ship and become a merchant.'

'Heavens above, Mr. Colchester. You—a merchant, sar. Well, I never.'

'Look Charles, I tell you this in confidence. I wish to keep the whole venture a secret.'

'Absolutely, sar. You can trust me completely.'

'Then I would like you to accompany me to Hobart Town.'

'When, sar?'

'Day after tomorrow.'

There was no established road to Hobart Town, so, at the recommendation of Charles, who was an acquaintance of the mailman, Adam Toombs, they set off on the seven-day trek with the mail. The going was tough and on foot. A mule called George was burdened with the mail while Charles' mangy, cantankerous mule carried the supplies. Toombs appreciated the company but bid them farewell at a crossing on the River Derwent called Austin's Ferry, sixteen miles north of Hobart Town. Rowan and Charles continued on through Coal River Valley, finally sighting Hobart Town across the wide expanse of the river at Kangaroo Bluff. They sat on the foreshore, soaking their blistered feet in the salty water, staring out across the River Derwent at Hobart Town, about two miles distant. To their right, moored in the middle of Kangaroo Bay, was the whale ship *Lucy*.

'What do you think, Charles?'

'I know little about ships, Master Henry, but she looks sturdy enough.'

'That's what I was thinking. Let's eat some vittles, then I will find a ferryman to take me to her.'

They ate a late lunch in silence, sharing the remains of a kangaroo steamer they had boiled the night before, eating it with Mrs. Hannah Bevan's relish pickles and the last of their apples.

The agent's crippled watchman, Richard Hawley, limped to the starboard gunwale and watched the small tender, with its gentleman passenger sitting on the stern sheets, row towards the whaler. He had chewed another fingernail and now nervously gnawed at the quick. The responsibility of looking after the *Lucy* was wearing him down, and to make matters worse, he'd drunk the last of his gin the night before.

'Who goes there?' he shouted down.

'Mr. Henry Colchester, sir,' Rowan called back. 'Come to inspect the *Lucy*.

'Come aboard, sir.'

'Wait here, if you please,' Rowan told the ferryman and clambered up the Jacob's ladder.

'Richard Hawley, squire.' The caretaker introduced himself with a weak hand, half hidden in a woollen mitten. 'Welcome aboard.'

Rowan noted that the man's hair was long and knotted, his personal hygiene was lacking, and he pulled awkward faces as he moved—on account of being painfully crippled, Rowan surmised. He was sixty if he was a day.

'Yer want to inspect her, I imagine.'

'Yes, Mr. Hawley. But please do not trouble yourself. I am quite able to show myself about.'

'Fine, sir.' The cripple looked pleased with this decision, for Rowan noticed the man had made himself accommodations amidships, between tripods, under a makeshift shelter and he doubted that the invalid had been belowdeck in weeks. 'You take yer time. Fill yer boots, sir.'

Rowan was pleased with what he saw. There was no sign of rot. The hold was vast, especially as Captain Smith's wife had disposed of the oil barrels.

Shipping Agent Adam Bolten of Collins Street, Hobart Town, was notified of Rowan's interest and met him on board the whaler the next morning. Mr. Bolten was a contented and jovial soul with a generous girth about the waistline from fine dining. He had pristine teeth, the result of attentive dental care, and proudly displayed them as he smiled and joked. His dress bespoke success in his chosen profession and he liked what he saw in this American entrepreneur. A deal was soon struck, and the agent could not have been a happier fellow.

'You camp, sir?' Bolten sucked in a breath at Rowan's admission that he was camped by the foreshore. 'Why do you not partake of Hobart Town's hospitality?' he asked, stabbing a bone swagger at the distant settlement smoking across the water.

'I prefer the solace of Van Diemen's Land's outdoors, Mr. Bolten,' Rowan fabricated. 'I have no interest in social niceties.'

'Oh, well, I was going to suggest that you and your manservant enjoy rooms at my humble abode in Davey Street for the night.' Mr. Bolten had another thought. ''Tis a pity, as I have guests this evening, whom you would most likely care to meet.'

'And who might that be, sir?'

'A seafarer like yourself, Captain James Kelly. He circumnavigated this island in an open boat two months past. Fearless character, a little rough around the edges, but an excellent raconteur at the dinner table.'

'Thank you, sir. My apologies, but I must decline your offer. Now, you have your advance payment.' Rowan alluded to the necessary exchange of one hundred guineas which he had brought along. He had carefully folded the receipts into his saddlebag. 'And, frankly, I am keen to return to my sister at Beaumont Hall. But I thank you all the same, sir.'

'Quite. I understand.'

The hours alone had haunted gamekeeper Charles Ratcliff. He sat staring into the campfire as Rowan approached their campsite. He appeared not to be aware that his master approached.

'Charles, Charles… are you all right?'

The man looked up from where he sat on a flat rock. His eyes were reddened once more, black circles of misery. 'No, sar, I ain't. I'm not too certain I can go on no more.'

'Don't talk like that, man. Hell's teeth, you have a lifetime before you. Things will heal in time.'

'Yer think so?' The gamekeeper words were soft and slow and laced with doubt.

Rowan felt knots of sadness tighten in his own stomach. 'Come along. We have a long hike ahead and when we return, I want you to move into Beaumont Hall.'

If any insidious whispers regarding his masters, Henry and Mary, had reached the gamekeeper's ears he certainly did not acknowledge the fact. He had refused Rowan's offer and insisted on remaining in his cottage, whilst his master's words, *things will heal in time,* played daily in his tormented mind.

Rowan and Elizabeth stole rare moments of passion, their love for each other cemented in the knowledge they would, soon, be able to live as man and wife. Elizabeth giggled and Rowan cuffed her mouth before her mirth woke the household. They gazed into each other's eyes a moment, intoxicated with their joy. Finally Elizabeth pinioned Rowan's wrists above his head, spreading herself wide as she silently mounted his manhood. That night it had rained hard, the heavy downpour cascading by their window from a damaged drain. But maintenance was the last thing on their minds as they lay side by side once more, physically spent, and fell into a deep sleep.

Nine weeks passed before Rowan made his second visit to Hobart Town, this time as a passenger on a coastal trader, *The Sparrow,* sailing down the east coast of Van Diemen's land transporting barley and other grains to the settlement's capitol. Rowan hid two thousand, nine hundred guineas in the false bottom of his travelling satchel. On arrival at Waterman's Dock in Sullivan's Cove, Rowan hired a hansom cab. Although the distance was but a short walk to the offices of Mr. Adam Bolten in Collins Street, there would be less chance of public exposure. Here the transaction was completed for the purchase of the whale ship *Lucy*. It was agreed that the vessel would be relocated off Battery Hill, where it would await conversion into a merchant ship and all necessary repairs there at the slip yards.

Finally, some weeks later, Rowan received a letter inviting him to the shipyard to witness the launch of the recently completed government vessel *The Reprisal*. The invitation was a mark of good faith, meant to show off the yard's craftsmanship; it also represented an opportunity to discuss his plans for *Lucy*. The date was set for three weeks in the future.

Chapter Thirty-One

Hobart Town. Battery Hill Shipyards.

Shipwright Wight Fairfowl saw potential in Marcus Marriot from the time Marcus started as a shipwright's carpenter. He saw shades of himself in Marcus—he was a pardoned prisoner who had found direction in life, at last. And Fairfowl was determined to teach Marcus everything he knew. He saw Marcus as his successor. Marcus was an apt learner.

The local blue gum was a sturdy, long and straight tree, perfect for a ship's keel. So long and straight, Marcus learnt, that a keel could be hewn from one tree. This keel rested on blocks the length of the ship. Transoms and futtocks were made from naturally curved branches. Marcus learnt the art of scarfing, where pieces of the frame were joined. Once the keel was in place, the apron and stem were joined at the bow and the sternpost and stern transoms were fit into place at the stern. Marcus now supervised the deck timbers' fitting. He watched as frames of futtocks were constructed on the ground and raised into position to build the hull, held in place with horizontal ribbands running the length of the ship. These ribbands were propped with long log cribbing, wedged on forty-degree angles into the shipyard floor, and holding the entire structure steady. At both bow and stern, Marcus saw that great tree trunks were lashed together like an A-frame, towering well above the upper deck line. These sheers, as Fairfowl explained to Marcus, were used with block and tackle for the heavy lifting. An inner keelson was now fitted above the floor timbers in line with the keel. Once all this was in place, Marcus and the other carpenters started the laborious layering of the framework with outside and inside planking. Months later, after laying the decks, Huon pine masts were erected into their shoes. Now it was time to fit-out the ship.

This fifty-five-ton government-commissioned schooner was the third vessel built at the Battery Hill shipyards, and launching the *Reprisal* had gone smoothly. It was a proud moment for Marcus, Wight Fairfowl and all the fitters, sail makers, and rope makers, as well as for the myriad of tradesmen involved in shipbuilding. Marcus helped the carpenters hammer loose the cribbing, allowing the ship to settle onto launchways erected under the hull. The launchways now bore the full weight. Gravity undertook the rest. The ship rolled, stern first, down rails lubricated with tallow and whale oil, to splash into the River Derwent.

'Huzzah! Huzzah!' the yard workers roared.

Rowan watched from the perimeter of the slip, on the west embankment. He chose to keep a low profile, as a small delegation from the soldiers' barracks was present to witness the launch and conduct a short traditional ceremony, including the smashing of a champagne bottle over the bow.

It was late morning and the sun shone directly into Rowan's eyes, creating a galaxy of sparkling diamonds on the surface of the wide River Derwent. It reminded Rowan of the Patuxent River back home in Maryland. He had travelled to Hobart Town especially to watch the launch and was impressed with what he had seen. The *Reprisal* was a handsome ship. She looked hardy and robust and had fine lines, but his *Marybeth* would be much larger.

Lucy, the two-hundred-and-fifty-ton whaler from New Bedford—previously moored at Kangaroo Bluff on the eastern shore of the River Derwent—was now anchored offshore at Battery Hill.

Shipwright Wight Fairfowl tightened the band on his unruly ponytail and waved Rowan into a spare chair in his crowded, untidy yet organised office. 'The bill of lading from Adam Bolten's agents is in order, Mr. Colchester,' he said.

Rowan sat down. 'I am pleased to hear that, Mr. Fairfowl. The broker has his guineas and you have my *Lucy* moored yonder, I see.' Rowan gestured out the office window to his property, which was at anchor a hundred yards offshore. 'Speaking of which, sir, my sister, who is also my business partner, and I, have chosen to rename her *Marybeth.*'

'*Marybeth!*' The old shipwright grinned. 'And a lovely name it is, Mr. Colchester. Would that be your sister's name, sir?'

'Well, yes and no,' Rowan answered with some irony and a smile to himself. 'Mary being my sister's name and Elizabeth being the name of her unborn, should the child be a girl. Her husband, you must understand, was taken suddenly, I'm afraid. Disease of the heart.'

'Oh, how awful. Very well, then. *Marybeth* she be.' The old man leant back in his chair with his hands cupped behind his head a moment. He stretched. Rowan heard joints crack. '*Marybeth*, aye, I like that,' the shipwright reiterated. 'We had better celebrate. Drink, sir?' Rowan followed the shipwright's eye to a cabinet where an assortment of bottlenecks jutted out from shipbuilding drafting charts. 'I have whisky, gin and ah... more whisky.'

'Whisky it is, then, Mr. Fairfowl.'

1814

'Wight, sir. Now we are drinking mateys, yer best call me Wight.'

'Wight. Call me Henry.'

The next two hours were intense. Rowan knew exactly what kind of vessel he wanted the *Lucy* transformed into. The three-masted, square-rigged whaler would have to be stripped of its main deck, fire hearths and blubber tripods. All necessities of the whaling industry would have to be replaced with the requirements of a merchant cargo vessel. The tween decks would have to be maximised for cargos of wool, rum, rice, sugar, tobacco and textiles from Bengal, Rowan told the shipwright. 'We will be taking bails of opium from Bombay and Calcutta to Shanghai and Canton...'

'I've heard them Chinese are difficult to deal with, lad.' Wight's eyes were bright with Rowan's adventure and his nose red from the whisky.

'Yes. That is why we will be dealing with the East India Company in China and not the Chinese.'

'Good advice, Henry.'

'From China I will fill her hold with tea, silk and ceramics to trade in Europe, so I need that hull to be watertight.'

'Aye.'

'Speaking of which, I would like her hull coppered.'

'Now that, Henry, is something we cannot do in Van Diemen's Land. That can only be done in England.' Mr. Fairfowl stroked his long beard. 'Trustin' you'll be sailin' her to England in trade.' Rowan nodded a lie. 'And you will be required to register her with Lloyds, while yer there.'

'Hmm.'

'Now, a crew, Henry'—Wight leant over, filling Rowan's pewter measure with another four fingers of whisky—'you'll be wantin' a crew. Yer ain't no captain, I can see that.'

'You are a perceptive man, Wight. Yes. I will be wanting a captain.'

The old man sniffed crudely and wiped his nose along his sleeve. 'I may be able to help yer there. I happens to know fer a fact, the ship's mate off'n the *Lucy* remains in 'Obart Town. 'E is yet to leave the colony. I heard 'e were lookin' for a position on another whaler. '

'First mate?'

'Aye. One step a-ways from cap'n, in my book. Frederick Jaxon be 'is name, like. Some o' the Yankee crew are still 'ere, too, so I hear.' They all be lodging' at the 'Ope and Anchor, near Hunter Island.'

'How long do you think these alterations to my ship will take?'

'Well I hate ter say this, but I have the governor's launch to complete.' Wight jerked his head out the window to the second slip, where a single-mast cutter was nearing completion. 'Yer can see she is nearly ready to be fitted out. One month, I'd say. Then your *Marybeth*... say two months. That'd mean three months, Henry.' The old man looked at his empty mug and then at the governor's launch. He needed to be out in the yard cracking the whip. He pushed the mug aside and stood, stretching his back, as a knocking thumped on his door. 'Aye. Enter.'

Marcus Marriot entered the office. 'Ah, Mr. Marriot. What is it?'

'The modified capstan for the *Reprisal*'s ready for your inspection, Mr. Fairfowl.'

'Very good, Marcus. I'll be down shortly.' The old shipwright thought briefly. 'Ah... Marcus.'

'Sir.'

'This gentleman be Mr. Colchester. It is he who owns the *Lucy*, our next assignment.'

'Very good, sir.' Marcus gave Rowan a cursory glance with his one eye. 'Nice to make yer acquaintance, Mr. Colchester. Fear not, we will do a fine job on 'er.'

'No doubt. I have a lot of faith in your master here.'

'Three months, Henry,' Fairfowl said when they were alone once more. 'You come back here in three months and the *Marybeth* will be shipshape.'

Rowan found Frederick Jaxon at the Hope and Anchor tavern. The innkeeper's young son fetched the ship's mate from his lodgings and ushered him downstairs to the parlour. Rowan flicked the young tyke a halfpenny and he rushed out the door to the confectioner's.

'I'll wage a bet that lad's always in a mad rush,' Rowan said to his guest, his grin chasing the boy out the door. He turned to greet the ship's mate, who was a head taller than Rowan, a tall man with a lean but strong-looking body. A beaver fur top hat gave the man an appearance of unnatural gauntness.

'What can I do for you, Mr. Colchester?' Jaxon asked after introductions. Rowan explained his situation. He needed a captain and Jaxon had been recommended.

'So my question to you, sir, is... are you up for captaincy? To captain a merchant around the Orient?' Rowan asked.

'I'd be a fool if'n I said no, sar. Aye.' The man grinned from ear to ear.

Rowan liked what he saw and Frederick warmed to Rowan. It was also fortuitous to Frederick that this shipowner, Mr. Henry Colchester, was an American.

'And is it your intention to sail *Marybeth* to America?'

'Eventually. Definitely.'

'Then count me in, sar.'

Over a meal of rabbit stew, cabbage and dumplings, Rowan divulged his plan. The men exchanged stories and learned they had much more in common than they'd realised.

'Crew, sar—what have you in mind?' Jaxon finally asked.

'Well, I'll be drawing on your expertise there, Mr. Jaxon. How many should we require?'

'Well, the rule of thumb is ten men required for every hundred tons' burden. So we'll need about twenty-five. Then we'll need a second mate, a carpenter who understands cooperage, and a cook.' Frederick picked up a ribcage and was about to suck at the gravy on the bones when he added, 'Preferably, a *good* cook.'

Late 1817. Beaumont Hall.

Elizabeth's baby grew steadily in her belly. By all accounts, she estimated she was twenty-five weeks into her pregnancy but her girth was not totally blatant. Not yet, at least. Elizabeth took to wearing larger frocks and dresses and discreetly complained to Hannah and the other servants, 'It seems it does not matter what I eat these days, I gain weight.' But this situation was not sustainable and the deceit grew more burdensome daily.

Shortly after breakfast one Sunday morning, Rowan and Charles pored over maritime charts and maps of the Orient. Elizabeth, meanwhile, honed her reading skills on the pages of a leather-bound book, *Cornwall and Devonshire Illustrated*, which had been left behind, with dozens of others, by their landlord. Elizabeth was reading silently, articulating the words in her mind like a learning child, when old Reginald threw open the library door without knocking.

'Natives, miss... Natives, sir!'

'What?' Rowan was taken aback by the sudden intrusion.

'There must be a dozen of 'em. They got spears an' clubs. I don't like the look of their behaviour, sir.'

'Where?'

'At the gates.'

Rowan and Elizabeth were comfortable around the Van Diemen natives, but they had heard dreadful stories of murders lately, of both blacks *and* whites. Charles, the gamekeeper had misgivings. The situation between the original owners of the land and the *whitefella intruders* was dire, to say the least. Elizabeth and Rowan approached cautiously to meet the group, thirteen in all, who were standing or squatting in a tight group just inside the gateposts, alert and aware that they could be imprisoned if they did not take care. Elizabeth guessed they represented two families: four grown men, five women of childbearing age and four older children. Presumably, the elderly and the very young waited in the bushland nearby.

To the Englishman the most striking feature of these natives was the men's curly hair, forming tight ringlets spiralling down to their shoulders. The women chose to crop their hair, using primitive stone tools. The men plastered their hair with a mixture of ground red ochre and animal fat, making it resemble a hat rather than a hair. Hairstyles aside, Rowan noted a similarity in appearance to the African Negro slaves in America, except the skin of these people was reddish brown rather than nearly black. On average, the aborigine's height was shorter than that of the whitefella, men being just over five feet and the women just under. They were lean, with long thin legs, but physically strong and well built.

'Wait here,' Rowan said, turning to Elizabeth, who stood directly behind him, only to watch Reginald hurry after them, carrying his ancient blunderbuss. 'Devil's blood, man, stop!' he shouted at the gardener. 'Stop I say!'

'But, master, these savages are armed!'

Rowan turned back toward the natives. They all now stood, stiffened in defensive positions, and Rowan noted their straight throwing sticks and clubs made from tree roots. He put the palms of both hands in the air in a sign of submission.

'It is all right,' he said in a low, amiable tone. They would not comprehend the language but he thought the gesture was clear.

'Reginald,' Rowan muttered over his shoulder while facing the group.

'Sir.'

'Back away with that gun, man... now!'

The old gardener backtracked, keeping a sharp eye on the aborigines. 'I 'ope yer know what yer doing, sir,' he grumbled.

So do I, Rowan thought to himself. He scanned the aboriginals' faces, hoping he might recognise one or two from the northeast tribe. Nothing. The natives relaxed once more, chatting amongst themselves in a primitive language Rowan could not imagine understanding. Elizabeth joined him.

'Wait here,' he ordered. 'I'll do this.'

'I don't think so,' Elizabeth said stubbornly, and stepped ahead of Rowan with her hands out before her, as Rowan had. 'Friends,' she said, in a warm assuring voice. Immediately, other natives filed through the gate, chatting gaily, more older children, women and young men. Elizabeth stopped in her tracks. Her mouth opened in astonishment.

'Pollyanna!' she cried out.

Pollyanna was equally surprised. Their old friend pushed the warrior men aside to embrace Elizabeth. 'Bloody blackfella! Blackfella bastards come before Pollyanna!' she cried. Elizabeth sighed with relief. It was good to see their old companion once more. 'Pollyanna, tell *blackfellas* wait at trees.' Pollyanna pointed to a stand of gum trees near the potato paddock, where Elizabeth now saw another twenty aborigines squatting on the ground, some digging the young potatoes from the soil. 'Row-an!' Pollyanna hurried to Rowan and threw her arms about his neck. 'Row-an!' Pollyanna looked open-mouthed at Beaumont Hall. 'Ro-wan... Elizabeth, camp in big whitefella hut?' she asked, waving a hand at the homestead.

'Yes, Pollyanna.' Rowan was relieved to see Pollyanna amongst these natives. 'This is not your family?' he asked.

'My tribe far away. This Mannamargenna tribe.'

Rowan and Elizabeth knew the Mannamargenna people to be from the northeast, as well. These natives all lacked the same tooth from their bottom left jaw. Tooth evulsion. Rowan remembered Joseph Lycett informing him that the deliberate knocking out of teeth was an adult ritual denoting what tribe you were from.

'Why are you here, Pollyanna, so far from your lands?'

Pollyanna's eyes welled with sadness. She went on to explain, as best she could, how white men, hunters, had attacked the Mannamargenna camp, the cycle of three moons earlier. She told how two men and a young boy were killed with guns and the mother of one, Pollyanna's friend, was stabbed in the stomach. A child was taken, kidnapped, a young girl ten years old named Lowanna. 'Pollyanna help Mannamargenna tribe to find Lowanna.'

Horrified, Elizabeth consoled Pollyanna. Rowan heard footsteps approach from the homestead. The gamekeeper stood protectively nearby and Rowan noted that the man had a pair of flintlocks secured behind his britches' belt. They were less than subtly hidden by his frockcoat.

'Steady as she goes, Charles,' Rowan said softly out of the corner of his mouth while forcing a warm smile.

'Aye, sir, just thought it best I join yer.'

'This not first time whitefella take children,' Pollyanna continued between sobs.

'I understand, Pollyanna,' Rowan said. 'But why are you here on this land, so far from the sea?'

'You know this savage?' Ratcliff looked confused.

'She is not a savage, Charles.'

'But... you know her?'

'It is a long story, which I will tell you one evening, over a Madeira or two.' Rowan turned back to Pollyanna. 'Why are you here?'

'Mannamargenna tribe, meet Waddamanna tribe,' Pollyanna went on. 'Waddamanna tribe, them from Big River, one blackfella Waddamanna mans... name Jarli... he help whitefella make... writing on paper...' Pollyanna mimed painting and drawing.

'Painting?'

'Aye, Row-an... pain-tin'.'

'Did you say Jarli?' Elizabeth asked.

'Aye. Blackfella fren with whitefella, like me and you.'

'That's the native interpreter who was with Joseph Lycett.'

Rowan nodded silently.

'Jarli, he say they seen whitefella with young blackfella girl...'

'Here, inland, so far from the sea?'

'Aye. This man big, big ugly firka. Old whitefella. Big beard. Big nose on big face. An' he like black. Black coat. Black britches. Black boots. Waddamanna tribe say he live on big river near here. He live with big huntin' dogs, one ugly firka, like whitefella. Ugly firka dog with one eye.'

Rowan wheeled about to his gamekeeper. 'That's Isaiah Mendel.'

'The Burns's shepherd?'

'Exactly.'

'Then we must help these people,' Elizabeth said 'Immediately.'

1814

Rowan caught the young yard boys spying clumsily from behind the stable door. 'Pat,' he called out. The older boy, Dan, an aboriginal half-caste, shoved Pat in the back and the twelve-year-old stumbled into the open. 'You, too, Dan—out you come.'

'Sar,' Dan said sheepishly, standing next to his fellow yard hand.

'Prepare our mounts. Smartly, now. And prepare the trap as well.'

'Yessar.'

'I'll fetch arms,' Rowan told Elizabeth.

'I'm coming, too.'

'No... ' Rowan wanted to say, *you are with child*, but he read the look of determination in Elizabeth's eyes.

'Pollyanna,' Elizabeth told her friend, 'gather four of your best warriors. Tell the Mannamargenna to rest here.' Elizabeth pointed to the front lawn where shade under fruit trees awaited. Hannah, Bessie and Annie now watched, incredulous, on the veranda. 'Hannah,' Elizabeth ordered.

'Yes, Miss Mary?'

'See these people are fed.'

'Fed, miss?'

'Yes. We have plenty of milk. Give them what is stocked in the dairy. Make plenty of damper. There is much jam in the larder, I noticed. We have barley and peas—make a soup.'

'Soup! Yes, Miss Mary...'

'And ginger beer, Hannah. I think these people would like ginger beer. But no ale, you understand.'

'Certainly, miss.'

Reginald, the gardener, had listened from the veranda. 'I'm comin' too, Miss Mary.'

'No, Reginald.'

'No? But...'

'We need you here, Reginald.'

The gardener looked to Rowan for confirmation. 'Miss Colchester's right, Reginald. We need you here. And keep that great antique cannon of yours nearby, but not on show. You hear me?'

'For the savages, Mr. Colchester?'

'These natives will give you no grief, Reginald. But you are the man of the house in our absence. All right?'

'Yes, sar.'

Charles Ratcliff returned with his own two-barrelled Springfield shotgun converted from flintlock to the new percussion hammer. About his waist were his copper flask of powder and a leather horn of buckshot. 'I'm ready.'

Rowan felt less at risk with the gamekeeper at his side. Elizabeth had changed into riding britches and threw one of Rowan's coats over her shoulders, hiding the bump in her belly. As boyish as she looked, Rowan could only see beauty.

'Ready?' he asked, although in truth he had reservations about Elizabeth joining them.

'Ready, Pollyanna....' Elizabeth offered Pollyanna her hand and she mounted the horse as Elizabeth's pillion. While Dan and Pat brought the horse and open carriage from the stables, Elizabeth told Pollyanna to order her well-armed warriors onto the back.

They rode southwest for an hour, Elizabeth and Pollyanna leading Rowan and Charles, with the armed natives dangling legs over the sides of the cart and enjoying the unique experience, chattering and grinning like schoolboys.

'Mr. Colchester... Henry,' Charles said to Rowan as they negotiated the track running alongside the fast flowing river.

'Yes, Charles?'

'This 'ere Pollyanna—you are previously acquainted?'

'Yes, Charles, and, like I said, it is a long story and I shall tell you one day.'

'But she called yer Row-an did she not?'

Rowan felt his face redden. He and Elizabeth had been so careful with their charade and this was the first time their cover had been broached. 'Tis an aboriginal word, Charles. I do not know its meaning, but, yes, I concede, it does sound a little like an English name.'

Charles Ratcliff was a man of the land, a gamekeeper on an estate, but he was an educated man, and he was not buying Rowan's explanation. 'So is Elizabeth another aboriginal word?'

Rowan reined his horse to a sudden halt. 'Devil's blood, man, what are you implying?'

Now it was the gamekeeper whose face reddened. 'I meant no insult, sir. It's just that... well, it came as awful strange, Mr. Colchester.'

'Tis nothing, Charles. Nothing. You hear me?'

'Yessar.'

'The woman is a native struggling with our language. Nothing more.'

The river widened considerably, forming a natural shallow ford—no more than three feet deep—before narrowing and strengthening once more into a deep and fast-flowing river. They crossed to the south side and continued three miles, finally encountering the Burns's estate sheep, grazing contentedly. Another ten minutes' ride and Mendel's wattle and daub hut came into view. It was positioned high on the south bank. Here the river was thirty yards across and a good ten feet deep and, as recently snows had melted on the mountains, the water swept by swiftly. From here, the shepherd enjoyed a clear view of the more than four hundred fat and contented sheep in his care.

Rowan ordered their party to dismount two hundred yards from the shepherd's cottage, where they were hidden by a gully and a copse of myrtle and beech trees. Charles Ratcliff secured the horses. Pollyanna briefed her warriors.

'Wait here.' Rowan took his spyglass from the saddlebag and he and Elizabeth climbed to the crest in the gully. The scene was idyllic. Smoke escaped lazily from a stone chimney in a thatched roofed. Eucalyptus trees bordered a clearing that spanned from the cottage to the river. A tall leatherwood eucalyptus stood next to the cabin, its upper branches alive with black yellow-tailed cockatoos. Any fragrance from the leatherwood tree was swept aside by the cloying stink of death—the stink of curing animal skins nailed to the outside walls of the cottage.

Elizabeth saw the shepherd first. 'Down!' The shepherd's head appeared from what seemed to be a pit next to the cottage. They all dropped from view. 'Did you see him?'

'Not really.' Rowan was not certain exactly what he had seen. 'Did he see you?'

Elizabeth had no answer. She shrugged. Taking the spyglass, she crept further along the ridge. Warily, she peered over the crest. Nothing. 'He must be in the cottage,' she mouthed quietly.

Rowan joined her. 'Are you certain?"

'Not really. His head appeared from a hole—a pit, maybe.'

Rowan took the glass. 'Where, exactly?'

'Off to the right of the cottage. There's a mound of earth next to it.'

Rowan brought the lens to focus.

'I'm certain I saw a head rise in the grass,' Elizabeth said quietly. 'From a hole.'

Rowan studied the land. 'You're right. I can make out what looks like a trapdoor.'

'To an underground pit, maybe?'

'Maybe... Dear God.'

'What?'

1814

'Are you thinking what I am thinking?'

'Only one way to find out.'

Rowan and Elizabeth backtracked down the embankment into the gully. 'Where are your men?' Rowan asked Pollyanna.

'Go bush,' Pollyanna said matter-of-fact.

'We said stay to here,' Elizabeth said, angrily.

'Blackfellas go bush near hut. Blackfellas mad bastards.'

'Charles?' Elizabeth chided their gamekeeper.

'I tried to stop 'em, Miss Mary, but they were determined devils.'

Rowan squeezed Elizabeth's arm. 'We'd better move fast.'

Ratcliff hooked his shotgun over his shoulder. 'What's the plan?'

'The man appears to be alone,' Rowan explained. 'This should not be too difficult.'

'Does not the man keep dogs?' Elizabeth asked.

'Hell's teeth!' Rowan had forgotten about the dogs. 'They must be on the far side of the cabin. But we're downwind, because we can smell the skins.'

'Then I suggest yer leave the dogs ter me, Mr. Colchester, on account I got the two-barrelled shotgun.'

'I agree. The shot will spread and you'll have a better chance.' Rowan checked that his brass-barrelled traveller's pistols were primed in the pan before returning them to his coat pockets. The military-issue Brown Bess musket was loaded with powder and a one-ounce lead ball packed down the breech. 'Spread out,' he ordered. 'Mary'—he faced Elizabeth—'it's best you stay here with Pollyanna.'

'I don't think so, *Henry*.' Elizabeth shook her head, annoyed that Rowan would even suggest such a thing. 'I want to see justice as much as anyone.' Elizabeth looked at Pollyanna. The native returned a look of bemusement.

Mary? Henry?

Elizabeth ignored her.

'If you are joining us, then you had better take this,' Rowan handed Elizabeth one of his pocket pistols. He wasn't comfortable exposing Elizabeth to danger, but the woman was so determined...

'Stay close to me,' Rowan told Elizabeth. They crawled along the riverbank under cover of a small rise that dropped sharply into the rushing water. Rowan alluded to Elizabeth's belly. 'Take care. You carry precious cargo, remember?'

They waited a moment, fifty yards south-east by the river, watching Pollyanna disappear into thick scrub in search of her kin. Their gamekeeper circled in a wide arc to the west. He would use the cover of the gum trees south of the hut, attracting the dogs to him, and dispatching them. The shotgun would also be the signal for Rowan, Elizabeth and the natives to move in.

Elizabeth and Rowan negotiated a narrow path, an animal track, running parallel to the boiling, rushing river. They kept low. 'Keep your head down,' Rowan whispered. 'We're nearly... ' Barking, angry dogs severed the tranquility. Ratcliff's gun discharged. A painful yelp followed. Immediately, the sky above filled with a flock of cockatoos, deserting their lookout and regrouping mid-air with a high-pitched and raucous wail.

'Hell's teeth!'

Rowan clambered up the nearly vertical riverbank. Elizabeth followed. Neither saw the vicious hunting dog. It leapt at Rowan with such ferocity that both man and beast were thrown into the careering river. Instantly submerged, Rowan's first sensation was the freezing cold of this racing mountain river. Then he felt snags and tree roots claw at his legs. He foundered, lips pinched, lungs screaming for air. He tumbled in the rapidly flowing waters. He felt his frock coat torn from his body. He felt the wild dog spill by. Rowan had no idea how far he had travelled before he managed to break the surface. He seized lungful's of air—fresh, sweet mountain air. He was now midstream, where the riverbank was at its fastest.

Rowan!

Rowan heard the faint call of his name, but he had no control. Suddenly, terrifyingly, drowning seemed a reality. Rowan rolled awkwardly onto his back. The water was deep and turbulent. He was dragged downriver with the speed of a galloping horse. Suddenly, Rowan felt his feet slam into rocks. But his body was numb from the cold.

Was the water shallower here?

Ahead, the landscape changed. Highlands dropped to lowlands. Rapids approached. Whitewater.

Rowan!

Twenty seconds earlier Elizabeth had risen over the embankment behind Rowan. She caught a blur in her peripheral vision—the blurred shape of a wild hound. She heard Rowan gasp, winded, and then the loud splash. In the second it took her to turn back to the river, Rowan was underwater and moving away swiftly. It all happened so fast. A living nightmare. Instinctively, Elizabeth screamed his name.

Rowan!

Elizabeth heard the second shotgun barrel discharge. Yelling followed. Shouting. Cursing. But her priority was Rowan. Elizabeth raced back to her mount and galloped south, following the river.

The river narrowed at the rapids, channelling into a higher speed. Rowan slammed into boulders. He was bruised and battered... but alive.

Rowan clawed at the rocks. He was only in waist-deep water, but the pressure was immense. The rocks were too smooth to grip. He felt himself tugged back into deep water, colliding with more boulders, thrown head over heels and tumbling. He was forced into a whirlpool, a rapid vortex created by the rocks and currents. He was trapped.

The flicker of hope vanished. Rowan was circling in an intractable vortex. The water was once again over his head. The vortex sped him faster towards the centre. Rowan felt his body being tugged beneath the surface. Choking, he had a flash of his past... *Maryland, Jessica, Elizabeth, his unborn child...*

Suddenly Rowan was thrown aside, ejected like unwanted flotsam. Nearly senseless, he floated to the calmer eddies of a small inlet, where he felt rocks beneath his feet. He clawed his way ashore. Waist deep—knee deep—finally he collapsed onto a smooth, pebbled cove. Exhausted, he dragged himself onto the embankment of button grass and heath. Calm overcame his thoughts. *He was alive!*

The river continued its eternal flow, racing by only feet away, and now, strangely, making hardly a sound. Scarlet-breasted robins flew in and out of the tall grass, curious about this strange creature lying face down before them, breathing heavily, happy to be once again in the land of the living. Suddenly, the birds darted away.

Inches away, a deep growl was accompanied by bursts of angry barking.

Rowan pushed himself up on his hands to face the one-eyed Irish wolfhound. It was so close. Dripping wet. Rowan could smell its putrid breath as viscous drool dripped from its clenched jaw. The dog sensed Rowan's fear. It lowered its head and inched forward. The lips rolled back in a display of canine teeth, sharp incisors for shredding and jaws for crushing. Rowan lowered his eyes in a submissive gesture. He thought of diving back into the river. But the dog had judged its adversary—it was time to kill.

The animal lunged forward...

1814

The explosion of a pistol at such close range was as terrifying as the attack. The small lead ball punched a neat hole in the side of the hound's head. Rowan heard a piercing yelp. He threw himself sideways and the dog somersaulted into the water, to be picked up by the current and dragged, once more into the madness of the racing river. Rowan rolled onto his back. He looked up, focussing on a woman's figure standing over him. The sun, directly behind her, silhouetted her slender body, an unidentified deva.

'Elizabeth,' he said rather feebly, 'is it truly you?'

'Why, is there another?' Elizabeth answered, bemused. 'Are you injured?'

Rowan stood shakily. Besides a slight limp and a dozen bruises, he had fared well, considering. 'Wh... where did you come from?'

'We do not have the luxury of time at this moment. We must make haste back to the shepherd's hut.'

Rowan noticed that Elizabeth was still holding the small pistol. 'No!' he blurted.

'What is it?'

'I lost the Brown Bess and the other pocket pistol.'

'You are alive. Is that not enough?' A distant gunshot saw Rowan straighten. He winced in pain. 'Can you ride?' Elizabeth asked, urgently.

'Yes. How far did I travel?'

'A good mile, I should imagine.'

Two hundred yards from the hut Pollyanna met up with Elizabeth and Rowan, who were riding twin. 'Row-an!' she cried out. 'Pollyanna thought river take you.' The native rushed to meet them. Rowan slid awkwardly from the saddle, unarmed, less his coat and wet through. He took Pollyanna by both hands. 'What's happening, Pollyanna? We heard gunshots.'

'Whitefella bastard dead, Row-an. Lowanna, she here. She one hurt little girl.' Pollyanna looked distracted for a moment, but immediately brightened. 'She hurt, but she good. Come see.'

'Where is Mr. Ratcliff? Is he all right?'

'Whitefella friend?'

'Yes.'

'Come see... Come.' Pollyanna dragged Rowan by the hand. Elizabeth, more guarded, followed on her horse.

Gamekeeper Ratcliff stood red-faced at the entrance to the shepherd's hut. The second dog lay dead at his feet. 'Oh, thank the good Lord yer alive, sar. I feared the worst.' Ratcliff's greeting was overshadowed by the natives. Already the horse and trap was half loaded with sacks of flour, potatoes, rice and dried peas ransacked by three of the aboriginal men. 'I could not stop 'em, Mr. Colchester. They's vengeful blighters, bent on ransackin' the hut.'

'Do not worry, Charles, they have earned it.'

'You're wounded, Charles.' Elizabeth noticed blood escaping from beneath a rag tied tightly about the gamekeepers wrist.

'Aye. The mongrel bit me,' he spat, and hoed a foot into the dog's carcass.

'Is it bad?'

'No, miss. I'll live.'

'The little girl?'

'We found her where you said.' Ratcliff pointed to a small rectangular pit, some six feet deep, eight feet in length and three feet wide. Next to the pit was a mound of grass-covered dirt. A hatch door, also sewn with grass, had been slid aside from where it had hidden the child's prison. Elizabeth joined Rowan and they peered into the open ditch.

'It's no bigger than a grave.' Elizabeth wiped back a tear.

'Bastard!' Rowan swore. He kicked the pile of dirt next to the pit. 'He'd planned this for some time; it's covered in grass. Bastard!'

Elizabeth stepped back from the pit. 'Where's the girl?'

'She's fine, Miss Mary,' the gamekeeper said.

'Where is she?'

'She be with one o' the native men. I believe he is 'er uncle.' Ratcliff nodded to a clearing behind the hut. Lowanna was in the arms of one of the native men. He squatted before her, holding her close, consoling the terrified child. Elizabeth knew there was little she could do. She wanted to hurry to her, hug her, take her home and spoil her, but she knew there was nothing, other than time, that could heal the little girl's wounds.

Rowan read Elizabeth's mind. 'She's in safe hands now. There is nought we can do.'

Elizabeth felt the slightest of kicks in her belly and her eyes welled with emotion. 'How could anyone be so cruel?' Elizabeth's tears turned to anger. There was one last chore. 'Where is this animal?'

'Jefferson Mendel is dead, miss,' Charles Ratcliff said.

'Where is he?'

'Beggin' yer pardon, miss, but you'd not want to be seein' 'im.'

'Where—is—he?'

Ratcliff sighed and rose, leading the way between a thicket of trees and bushes to another clearing. Rowan anticipated an unpleasant sight. He hurried to Elizabeth's side. Elizabeth gasped, sucking in a breath. Thirty feet away, the large body of the shepherd was trussed to a gum tree, his grotesque, sagging corpse dangling loosely from its bloodstained tree trunk. The shepherd had been stripped naked. Elizabeth noticed the penis was missing. The man had been penetrated by three bloodied holes—one through the belly, one though the neck and one through the heart. Where the spears had been retrieved, there were now clusters of flies.

'Native justice,' Rowan said almost inaudibly. 'Justice has been done.'

'Justice?' Elizabeth was disgusted. But not disgusted with the native punishment. 'Death was too lenient for that... that animal.'

'Animals aren't that cruel, miss,' Ratcliff said solemnly. 'If'n you'll forgive me sayin'.'

Rowan severed the ropes binding the corpse to the tree and Mendel's body collapsed in a lump of death beside the tree trunk. Tonight, Rowan knew, the little black devil cats of Van Diemen's Land would make short work of the carcass. 'Charles.'

'Yes, Mr. Colchester.'

'Ride on over to the Burns's homestead and notify them of their loss. Kindly explain the situation in detail. They have sheep here to attend to.'

'What will I tell them, sir...? I mean...'—the gamekeeper looked in the direction of the hut—'Well, relationships with the settlers and the Van Diemen natives 'as been strained o' late. Will the Burnses believe the story? About the kidnappin', that is?'

'Tell them the truth.'

'And if they are in doubt'—Elizabeth was still reeling in disgust—'tell them to visit Henry and me at Beaumont Hall.'

The smell of acrid smoke and the sound of crackling timber and bark drew them back to the shepherd's hut. The fire caught quickly. The shepherd's dwelling would soon be nothing but glowing ash. Pollyanna and the native men were delighted. They had their little girl safe and a cartload of food as some compensation.

1814

That night at the Beaumont Hall Estate, the natives celebrated. A huge bonfire lit the landscape while the men danced a corroboree. From this day on, they had a new story to tell—the story of the little girl saved with the help of whitefellas.

The Beaumont Hall servants watched in awed silence. Two sheep were killed and Elizabeth and Rowan helped Hannah prepare and roast the meat over the campfire, where they celebrated late into the night.

In the morning, Pollyanna made her way to the homestead to say her farewells. Elizabeth and Rowan knew that, this time, it would be their final goodbye.

'Row-an be good to baby,' Pollyanna said, in parting.

'Pollyanna?' Rowan questioned. Shocked at her revelation.

'Elizabeth carry Row-an baby. Pollyanna know.' Pollyanna hugged them both, a whitefella hug, and for the last time, she turned and walked away.

Rowan and Elizabeth watched in silence as the Mannamargenna tribe hiked slowly north. One of the last to depart was Lowanna's uncle. The ten-year-old victim of an evil mind was propped up on her uncle's shoulders. She turned to take one last look at the whitefellas who had saved her life, and smiled. It was difficult to smile. But that smile meant everything to Elizabeth and Rowan.

'What are we to do?' Elizabeth arched her back. Her belly was growing heavy.

For once, Rowan was lost for words. 'I really don't know.' He turned about to Elizabeth and with sincerity in his eye, he thanked her.

'Thank me? For what? Carrying your child?'

'For that, yes, but thank you for saving my life.'

'The dog!' Elizabeth shrugged.

'If the river didn't kill me, that damned animal would have.'

Elizabeth could relate to the near drowning experience but said humbly, 'Then we share that experience, along with everything else.'

They gazed into each other's eyes, throwing caution to the wind. Their love for each other was profound. Rowan looked over his shoulder, back towards the homestead. 'We must take care,' he whispered, as he caught the slightest movement behind a curtain in the drawing room.

Elizabeth came up with a plan before Rowan did. It was as bold as it was simple and they agreed that they would explain to the servants as soon as the time felt right. However, good intensions are often thwarted and it was Hannah who finally asked Elizabeth, less than a week later.

'You're with child, are you not?'

Elizabeth froze. Hannah had caught Elizabeth totally unawares, while sitting in the drawing room. Hannah held her mistress's eye. Elizabeth was speechless. Panicked, she instinctively looked about to be certain no other servants were within earshot. Hannah broke into a motherly smile, almost a gush. 'Come, come, Mary'—Hannah placed a gentle hand on Elizabeth's arm—'I might be an old cook, but I am not stupid, miss, if you'll pardon me boldness.'

Elizabeth jerked her arm free. 'What in heaven's name are you suggesting, Hannah?' she said weakly, searching for words that just were not there.

'Your action just now confirmed my suspicions.' An awkward pause followed, when Hannah added. 'Yer secret's safe with me, miss. I'm guessin' yer past half term. Yer cannot be hiding that bump much longer.'

'Who else is of the same opinion, Hannah?' Elizabeth finally said. It was more a query than a confession.

'No one's said nuthin' to me, like. The men folk 'round 'ere are blind to such events, but Bessie, miss, well she's hinted at yer belly to me, like, and Annie mentioned to me, on more than one occasion—yer bleedin' cycle appears to have stopped. Yer not using rags, miss.'

Elizabeth felt herself blush—a deep red blush, like a beacon of guilt. Merely the thought that the servants suspected them of incest was abhorrent.

Hannah went on. 'And I seen the way master Henry looks at yer.'

'What? No Hannah! You have it all wrong.'

'Come, now, Miss Mary. Tis lovely to see how yer big brother cares.'

'Oh.'

'He is a good man, miss. It's about time he married, I'm thinkin'. If'n yer don't mind me sayin' so.'

'Ah... no, Hannah.' Elizabeth watched Dan and Pat out the window in the yard, where they groomed the pony and the mares in the sun. The animals loved the attention, with the short-toothed comb massaging their backs to remove dirt and grime. The horses seemed so free, but Elizabeth suddenly felt the weight of the world on her shoulders.

'I'll fetch Henry.' Elizabeth turned for the door.

'No, miss!' Now Hannah panicked. 'Your secret's safe with me. I'll say nought...'

'Please, Hannah,' Elizabeth said, 'I want you to fetch everybody, Dan and Pat included.'

'But I...'

'That's an order, Hannah.' Elizabeth was back in control. The time had come, and she felt a weight lift from her. Elizabeth went directly to Rowan. It was time to put their rehearsed plan into action.

The women—Hannah, Bessie and Annie—stood to one side of the drawing room. Their acting skills were minimal and it was clear they had a hint of what was to come. Dan and Pat managed to roust two of the farmhands, while Reginald fidgeted, standing behind an armchair for cover, concerned at having exposed his holey socks, having left his boots on the veranda. Rowan and Elizabeth soon joined them. The missing servants would have to hear the news second-hand.

'Well, thank you for your time,' Rowan began a little awkwardly, 'but Mary and I have something to tell you all. Firstly, I want to say...'

'I am with child,' Elizabeth interrupted. She couldn't delay any longer. Rowan looked to the floor and scratched at an eyebrow.

'I was engaged to be married,' Elizabeth continued. 'I promised my hand in marriage to a gentleman whose name I will not mention here. As a matter-of-fact I will never speak his name again. We met in London two years past and he proposed to me then. But I left for the colonies to rendezvous with my brother Henry, and this man, whose name will never again pass my lips, eventually followed me to Van Diemen's Land. We met again in Launceston six months ago and I visited him several times. We were to marry. I was in love and I trusted him, but I was a fool.' This admission was shock enough, but then Elizabeth dealt her coup de grace. 'Yes, I was indiscreet with this man and now carry his child.'

The males in the room stood dumbfounded. They had not had the slightest clue. Hannah continued to blush while Bessie and Annie exchanged knowing smiles.

'So, now you know.' Rowan raised his chin, once more the master.

'What 'appened, miss?' Bessie asked. 'If yer don't mind me askin'.'

'I was used,' Elizabeth answered with a convincing bitterness. 'The oldest ruse in the world. He met another, and vacated the colony, leaving me in this condition.' Elizabeth put her arm through Rowan's. 'It is for that reason my brother and I wished to keep this business to ourselves. But clearly'—and Elizabeth gestured to her growing belly —'this is an impossible task. I hope you will forgive us for not being more forward earlier, but I expect you all to be discreet.'

'Of course, miss.' All agreed. Congratulations were in order. It was only Bessie who had her doubts of her masters' sincerity.

Months later, Charles Ratcliff's depression still festered. His heart ached for his lost wife and child. He grew gaunt. His mood swings became more intense—one moment he was agitated, then confused and anxious. He complained of insomnia and headaches. He had occasional spells of good cheer but, more often, long periods of depression. To Rowan's chagrin, the gamekeeper refused to move into Beaumont Hall where he could have kept an eye on the man. But even more vexing for Rowan the surgeon, was the fact that he had not diagnosed the rabies contracted from the dog bite during the Mendel siege.

With Hannah complaining of an empty larder—as only one kangaroo hung in the cellar—Rowan thought Charles could use the distraction of a hunt. He saddled his horse and rode to the gamekeeper's cottage.

The day was warm, the sun bright and the door to the cottage was wide open. 'Charles!' Rowan called out. As Rowan dismounted and approached the house he was accosted by three native dirt devils bolting from inside.

'Christ!' Rowan dodged the escaping animals. 'Charles!' Rowan warily entered, not wanting to encounter more of the loathsome carnivores. Inside, the shutters were drawn and the kitchen dark, but there was a familiar smell—the metallic stink of blood. Rowan caught sight of a figure in a chair by the burnt-out fire. 'Charles?' Rowan's eyes adjusted to the light. 'Jesus, no!'

Charles Ratcliff's body lay, thrown back in a kitchen chair; his shotgun lay on the floor. His body was stiffly arched as if he looked to the ceiling, but Rowan suddenly realised that his face and upper head were mostly missing. The head where depression and paranoia had festered was now an empty, bloodied vessel. The man had taken his own life with the muzzle of the gun in his mouth. Although the body felt cold, Rowan estimated the time of death at no more than a couple of hours before his arrival, as there was still brain matter about the mantelpiece, and congealing had barely set in. The devils had had time to gnaw at the corpse's ankles, but little more.

By letter Rowan alerted the authorities in Launceston of yet another death at the cottage, and saw that Charles Ratcliff's body was interred next to that of his wife and child. He and Elizabeth paid for a local blacksmith to build an iron rail about the triple gravesite and a sandstone headstone was erected. It simply read;

The Ratcliff family.
Rest in Peace.

Chapter Thirty-Two

Hobart Town. Sandy Bay. Sandwich Islander Inn.

The humping was good. No, it was better than good. The humping was great. Marcus *bloody Casanova* Marriot thought himself the best plougher in Hobart Town. Barkeep Paislee Fleur of the Sandwich Islander Inn thought otherwise, but the thirty-eight-year-old wasn't the shiniest shilling in the strongbox and this shipwright's assistant with his ticket of leave would be as good a catch as she could hope for. That is, if she could lure him into nuptials. *But he was a wary, slippery bastard under all that charm.*

With his employment as shipwright's assistant Marcus was finally in a position to take lodgings a mile and a half from the shipyard in Sandy Bay—two hundred yards from the Sandwich Islander Inn. At two shillings and sixpence a week, it was one bedroom—of four—tacked onto a hovel, over the rivulet that ran into Sandy Bay. The felled logs used for a crossing fifty yards further up the rivulet often trapped flotsam in heavy rain, and so the hovel was liable to flood. The wattle and daub was draughty and the shingles leaked when it rained, but not in Marcus's room, mind; the roof over his head was fine, and that was all he cared about.

Mrs. Effie, who owned the property, was kindly. She was a battler whose husband had died of snakebite several years earlier. At seventy-three, she was stooped, bearded and toothless, relying for support on her lodgers, all of whom were emancipated felons. They would share her kitchen and open fire for an evening meal, usually soup and damper, sitting at a table made from discarded timbers, on chairs made with skill by her deceased husband, that is, bushman-style, from tree branches. Outside, a dozen chickens scrounged an existence along with a rooster, who ruled the yard. A tethered goat supplied milk.

For Marcus, the gaps in the walls had a positive. As his room backed onto the kitchen, he could spy on the old lady. He watched where she squirrelled her savings in a hole in the dirt floor by the fire; a flat stone beneath the wicker basket of kindling covered her cache.

'Mr. Marriot... Marcus.' Mrs. Effie tapped on his bedroom door. 'Marcus.'

'Yes, Mrs. Effie.'

'Your rent is overdue. It's been two weeks now,' she said weakly, her voice breaking from the confrontation she so disliked.

'Sorry, Mrs. Effie. Tis this day I get me remuneration. I will settle with you this very evening.'

'See that you do, Marcus.' Marcus did not open his door. He sat on the end of his cot and silently mouthed her next words, as he was rehearsed in their repetition. 'I am a poor widow. I have debts of my own, you know.'

Marcus placed his eye over one of the small openings in the wall and watched the old lady throw her shawl over her shoulders and hook her basket of eggs over her arm. She was off to the soldier's barracks to sell them. He was alone; the cottage was empty. He went to the door and watched Mrs. Effie negotiate the log bridge. When he was certain the coast was clear he moved the wicker basket aside and lifted the rock. Inside was a cracked salt jar used to store the widow's coins. There must be four pounds or more, he thought, but there was no time to count them. For now he would take two florins; they wouldn't be missed. He thought to himself, *I'll take the bloody lot when I leave.*

Beaumont Hall

Beaumont Hall's gamekeeper, Charles Ratcliff, rested in peace. Unfortunately however, months of peace were soon broken for the Colchesters. Elizabeth watched from her bedroom window as the handsome soldier in a red coat with gold braid and brass buttons, white britches and knee-high black leather boots summoned the gardener to unfasten the main gate. After a short conversation, the old man lifted the iron latch and swung the gate open, allowing the corporal and three other mounted soldiers to enter the homestead. Elizabeth felt a chill. Amicable greetings were absent and she feared this visit was official.

Elizabeth almost let a slip of the tongue betray her:

'Ro... Henry...' She hurried as fast as her rounded belly would allow to join Rowan in the library. Rowan stood peering out the window, masked behind the drape. 'Yes, Mary,' Rowan said, quietly, 'I see them.'

The brass doorknocker reverberated down the hallway. It did not sound friendly.

'What do you think they want?'

'That's the young corporal who represented the commandant when we received accolades for the capture of the Spanner gang,' Rowan said, more confident than Elizabeth.

'Yes, but now what?'

They heard Bessie's voice as she opened the door.

'Come.' Rowan placed a hand on Elizabeth's shoulder. 'Let us go see what they want.'

Bessie could barely hide her fear that her liaisons with Corporal Adney Zachariah were about to be exposed. 'Why are you here?' she hissed through clenched teeth at the soldier as he pushed past her.

'Fear not,' he whispered, 'I'm here to see your master.'

'Corporal Zachariah,'—Rowan marched along the hall, one arm outstretched—'how nice to see you again.'

'Mr. Colchester,' the soldier acknowledged, briefly shaking Rowan's hand. 'Miss Colchester.' Interestingly, the soldier paid no attention to Elizabeth's condition. It was neither a surprise nor of interest.

'And what brings you back to Beaumont Hall on such a fine morning?'

'May we speak in private, sir?' the corporal asked, eyeing Bessie briefly once more, as she now blushed a darker shade of red.

'Certainly.' Rowan led the way to the library. Elizabeth followed defiantly.

''I'll be brief, Mr. Colchester,' Zachariah said, as the library door closed behind them. 'We have had a complaint from a Mr. George Mendel.'

'Mendel!' Elizabeth gasped. 'As in the Burns's shepherd, Jefferson Mendel?'

'We both know he's deceased, miss,' the corporal said caustically, causing the hairs to prickle on the back of Elizabeth's neck.

'Well?'

'Well, Mr. Mendel, the shepherd, had a cousin, George Mendel, who only recently heard of his cousin's demise in your company, sir.'

'Only recently? Months have passed since.'

'He has been residing in Sydney Town. He returned, not long ago, and the magistrates' court have placed the investigation into this man's death squarely on my shoulders, as my outpost is the closest to the Beaumont and Burns's estates.'

'I see.' Rowan remained calm.

Elizabeth bristled. 'That man was a child kidnapper. He was justly speared by the natives, relatives of the kidnapped child.'

'I understand, miss. All the same, George Mendel has exhumed his cousin's body and...'

'He what?'

'Mr. Burns, the shepherd's master, buried Mendel at the base of the tree where he was murdered. George exhumed Jefferson's body to find answers. He says his cousin had three musket ball holes in his body -- one in the neck, one in the belly and one through the heart.'

'They were spear holes, Corporal.'

'Not according to George Mendel.'

'We saw it with our own eyes.' Elizabeth was irritated. 'And the spears were retracted after his death.'

'Can you prove that, miss? I mean, for a start, where *are* these... natives?'

'You know as well as we that the Van Diemen natives are nomads. They could be anywhere by now.'

Corporal Zachariah smelled guilt. Bessie had told him there was more to these *gentry* than they let on. They were hiding something; he just knew it. *And as for Mary Colchester, sweet little titbit that she was, she hadn't been born a lady—not a true lady.* 'Where's your gun sir?' he asked Rowan.

'My gun?'

'Yes. The Brown Bess I saw on my first visit here.'

'Why, it's lost.'

'Lost? How?'

'I was attacked by one of Mendel's hunting dogs. I fell in the river and lost the musket. I nearly drowned.'

'You—lost—your—gun?'

'That's what I said.'

'How convenient.'

'I beg your pardon?'

Zachariah realised this caustic comment had overstepped his thin authority.

'Mr. Ratcliff, your gamekeeper—he accompanied you, I believe. He was witness to this most unusual event.'

'Mr. Ratcliff is no longer with us,' Elizabeth said in a tone between sorrow and anger.

'Oh, left your employ, or was his employment....'— Zachariah chose his word carefully—'...terminated.'

'The man is dead... *Corporal.*' Rowan emphasised the soldier's minor rank.

'Dead!'

'Self-murder,' Rowan said. 'The man suffered depression from the loss of his family and I suspect he suffered rabies from a dog bite at the Mendel hut.'

'Self-murder—how?'

'He shot himself.'

'So the natives that you say murdered Mr. Mendel have wandered away into the wilderness, the suspected murder weapon is lost in the river and your only witness is dead...' The corporal wanted to add "how convenient", but held his breath.

'I am a witness to Mr. Mendel's demise.' Elizabeth was now angry.

'Fine, miss.'

'It is Miss Colchester,' Elizabeth spat.

'Sorry, Miss Colchester, but as a close relative of Mr. Colchester, the magistrate will most likely not allow you to testify.'

'Magistrate! What are you saying?'

'There will be a travelling magistrate in Launceston in a week. George Mendel has made a serious allegation, and as he is a clerk at Government House... Well...'

'George Mendel is in the employ of the commandant?'

Corporal Zachariah realised he had revealed more than he should have. 'Well, yes,' he said cautiously. Elizabeth and Rowan exchanged frustrated looks. 'Therefore, Mr. Henry Colchester, Miss Mary Colchester, you are requested to present yourselves to the magistrate for an inquiry, Thursday one week hence, 10 am of the morning, at the Launceston watch house.'

Rowan's fist clenched. He felt his blood boil. 'Are we being accused of murder?'

'Not exactly. As I said, there are questions to be answered and you have been summoned.' The corporal took a vellum document and thrust it towards Rowan. 'Here is the summons, signed by Commandant McKenzie.' Rowan snatched the warrant.

'Look,' the corporal went on, 'this is as uncomfortable for me as it is for you. I'm just doing my duty.'

Elizabeth said nothing. She walked awkwardly to the door and opened it. 'Good day to you, Corporal,' she said with undisguised venom.

Government House. Sydney Cove.

From the north, the searing southern hemisphere sun drenched the government house veranda. Governor Lachlan Macquarie sat under a sail shade and looked across the cove to where HMS *Assault* was anchored in front of the Dawes Point Fort. Studying the ship a moment, Macquarie's thoughts turned to Captain Amos Leblanc, who had eluded capture in Bass Strait. This was unfinished business, and unfinished business irritated him. In front of the governor, on a campaign trestle, was a leather portfolio of paintings and sketches left behind by the emancipated artist, Joseph Lycett. He had recently delivered the artworks to the governor for his perusal and pleasure. The man was prolific, the variety astounding and his talent unquestionable. The renderings of Sydney Town and Hobart Town in particular were vibrant and *alive* with detail. Macquarie was impressed.

The governor sipped a ginger beer and cast an eye over Mrs. Macquarie in the garden. She was seventeen years his junior, but the woman was a champion companion. He'd met the Scotswoman, a distant cousin, near Edinburgh, where the two had fallen in love and married in 1807, Macquarie's first wife having died in India. Elizabeth Henrietta Macquarie was twenty-nine and he forty-six. The Macquarie's son, four-year-old Lachlan, played nearby, trampling honeysuckle bushes, much to the chagrin of the gardeners.

The governor looked at his wife and sighed. He loved everything about her and indulged her every wish. He loved his wife's reddish brown hair, tied back in a chignon, with tight curls springing over her brow. She had a long thin face with a pleasantly curved but pointed nose, small, thin lips and well-shaped ears. Today she wore her favourite ankle-length Indian muslin dress with its flat bias-cut bodice. Mrs. Macquarie chatted to one of the gardeners, apparently about the difficult soil. The short, stocky ticket-of-leave man was bent low over a vegetable garden, plucking at handfuls of dirt, allowing it to run through his fingers like dust, while shaking his head.

The governor smiled, enjoying this peaceful reverie, when Mr. Bent, his elderly secretary, limped onto the veranda. 'Lieutenant Crabbe has arrived, sir,' he said in his unmistakable lazy drawl.

'Thank you. Send him out here to the veranda, if you please.'

Governor Macquarie had a moment to reflect. As Crabbe was the newly appointed lieutenant in charge of HMS *Assault's* military guard, he had summoned the man to government house to discuss another search for the fugitive, Amos Leblanc. Leblanc was a mass murderer of innocent people and must, at all costs, be brought to justice. And Macquarie had a powerful feeling the man was still in hiding on the islands. A man that resilient, he thought, could survive anywhere.

Lieutenant Ernest Crabbe had been a veteran of New Orleans and other battles in North America before volunteering for the southern colonies in the 48th Regiment of Foot. He stepped onto the boards of the veranda and approached the governor, who sat with his back to the soldier. The veranda floorboards squeaked and splintered planks creaked, heralding his arrival.

'No assassin could creep up on me here,' Macquarie said, in a jovial mood, apparently studying something before him. 'The thirty-year-old building bricks are falling out of the walls, as the sea-shell mortar is poor quality, ants are overrunning the household and now those boards creak worse than a sinking ship. What do you say, Lieutenant?'

'Aye, sir. I would say it's time the New South Wales governor built a new Government House.'

'That is my plan, Lieutenant. That is my plan.' Macquarie whirled about effortlessly to face Crabbe. It was then that the lieutenant realised—the chair on which the governor sat had only one leg. The lieutenant's mouth dropped open.

'Wonderful invention, what?' the governor said, noticing his reaction.

'Aye, it is that, sir.'

'Invented by Thomas Jefferson, no less. Those Americans are good for some things... apparently.' Lieutenant Crabbe stepped forward to study the engineering of a chair that swivelled.

'You know who Thomas Jefferson is?' Macquarie asked.

'Aye, sir. American president before Madison.'

'Well done.'

'I fought in the American war in 1812, sir.'

'Oh, so you did.' Macquarie pushed the chair back. 'Take the weight off your feet. Feel free to remove your coat. Would you like refreshment? Ginger beer?'

'Thank you.'

Macquarie poured a glass of the effervescent cordial from a stone bottle into a stemmed glass and pushed the refreshment across the trestle. 'It is damned hot, is it not? It would be winter back in England. Everything is the opposite here—the trees are a greyer shade of green, the weather sunnier—even in winter—and the birds are noisier.' Macquarie cast an eye over his favourite Lycett painting of Sydney Cove on top of the portfolio. 'And the light... it is so crystal clear.'

'I agree, sir.'

'That is one reason Mr. Lycett enjoys painting here in the colonies. The light, he told me, is so different from that of England.'

1814

Lieutenant Crabbe had met Joseph Lycett on his last visit to Government House and knew of the governor's commission. 'Are these his drawings, sir?'

'Yes—take a look. I must say, the man is better than the last artists we used.'

The soldier enjoyed art, and had even dallied in paint and brush, but, alas, art was not to be his forte. Lycett's portfolio was huge—hundreds of watercolours, oils and sketches in pencil and charcoal. The coloured landscapes of Sydney Town and Hobart Town were particularly well done. Then there was a myriad of portrait sketches. Some complete, some painted and others similar to sketched portraits done hastily in an inn for a threepence...

'Who is this, sir?' the soldier suddenly asked, holding up a preliminary sketch of Rowan.

'I would not know. Is there a name on the back?'

Crabbe flipped over the eight-by-six-inch portrait and there was, indeed, an artist's reference in a scrawled script. 'It looks like it says 'Henry Colchester', Governor!'

'Yes?'

'I know of this man. He is a villain—a murderer—a wanted felon.'

'No!'

'Aye, sir. He murdered one of ours in Washington, a soldier of the 44th East Essex Regiment of Foot.'

'Washington! Surely not?'

'That is him, sir. Look.' The lieutenant stabbed a finger at the mark sketched on Rowan's neck. 'That is a scar. See. I would swear on my life it is him.'

'But he...'

'I was there, sir. He shot our man in cold blood. I *was* there.'

Governor Macquarie rose from his swivel chair and marched to the front door, calling down the hallway to Mr.

Bent. The old man poked his head out from the dining room, where he was taking his lunch.

'Sir?' Bent called back, plucking a large serviette from where it was tucked into his collar.

'Fetch Mr. Lycett immediately, Mr. Bent. Immediately, now.'

'Mr. Lycett?'

'Yes, man. The artist Joseph Lycett. Tell him I wish to see him, at the double.'

1814

PART FIVE

CHAPTER THIRTY-THREE

In a world of injustice, true love prevails.

Six days after Corporal Adney Zachariah left Beaumont Hall to return to his barracks, Elizabeth and Rowan packed the pony trap. They packed the bare necessities. No more, for fear of attracting suspicion from the servants. Despite having grown fond of their domestics, there was no room for error. For their ostensible ride to Launceston to meet the magistrate, they took a small amount of clothing, having smuggled personal items into the trap the previous night. Rowan wedged the carpetbag of remaining gold and bank notes under the rider's trunk. They rode to the hills south of Launceston, where Rowan paid a messenger to find Ben and Gwen Thomas, the market gardeners and lessees of the *Jolly Mary*—renamed *Lillie*—on the Tamar. The rendezvous was set. Later the next day, they skirted the settlement of Launceston, continuing on to rural lands near Legana on the west coast of the River Tamar. There they took possession of the *Lillie*.

At dawn the following day, they set sail for Hobart Town. Rowan felt freedom, being on the water once more. Elizabeth propped herself on sail bags and watched Rowan with differing emotions. She was more in love with him than ever and she knew he felt the same. They had left Beaumont Hall in their wake—Elizabeth knew in her heart that their time had come to move on. Now the random kicks in her belly were becoming more and more prevalent. *Yes, it was time to move on, in more ways than one.*

The Tamar's early morning breeze was sparse and their progress slow. Like an omen of mixed fortunes, the Tamar Valley mist followed the little sloop north for some time, but as they neared the mouth of the river giving out onto Bass Strait the fog lifted, the sail snapped and cracked, and the little craft tacked onto the ocean with a lively northerly behind her—Rowan followed the compass east.

The *Lillie* had enjoyed a clear run south, down the east coast of Van Diemen's Land. It was only after sailing around Tasman's Peninsula into Storm Bay towards the River Derwent estuary that they encountered rough weather.

Here, in these vast waters, Elizabeth counted no less than five whalers and all, it seemed, were successfully plying their trade. Rowan gave them a wide berth. The last thing he wanted was for the *Lillie* to be stoved in by an angry whale.

'Here.' Rowan passed Elizabeth the spyglass. Two whalers were anchored close to shore, butchering an adult sperm whale, which was roped securely to their port hulls.

'What are they doing?'

'Cutting and trying.' Rowan explained how the blubber was cut into huge cubes and rendered in boiling cauldrons on the deck. 'It is usually done ashore, but the catch is plentiful, I see, and so they are staying at sea.' Elizabeth caught sight of a ship's longboat skipping across the surface at an impossible speed. She tried to focus and follow the action through the glass. Rowan watched the action also. 'They have a whale harpooned. That is called "the Nantucket sleigh ride". See, the whale tries to escape them but the harpoon is buried deep in the monster's back.'

'How exciting.'

'Yes. But the creature will dive, sooner rather than later. That's when it really gets thrilling. I call it more dangerous than exciting.'

Elizabeth watched another whale being hauled to the mother ship and suddenly felt pity for the graceful mammal. 'All this killing and for what, for their oil?'

Six hours later, as Rowan tacked towards the prison settlement, he became aware of the same unease he'd felt on his first visit to Hobart Town. It *was*, after all, a colony of prisoners. A colony of misery and, although he trusted their waterproof identities, Elizabeth was with child—his child—rendering confrontation with the law far more dangerous than otherwise. Elizabeth sensed Rowan's trepidation. His smiles of confidence had been replaced with a serious awareness.

It was early evening and darkness descended as they approached Sullivan's Cove, where Rowan sailed west into the bay of a sandy beach, a headland before the township, avoiding the harbourmaster's lookout. Here, two brigs and a cutter were tethered obediently to moorings in the bay. Rowan reefed *Lillie's* mainsail and coasted by the *Marybeth*, under the power of a single jib.

There was no disguising the return of Rowan's smile. 'Well?'

'Well, what?'

Rowan nodded to the stern plate as they drifted by.

Elizabeth made out one word in the shadows of the approaching night: *Marybeth*. 'Oh, Rowan, *Marybeth!*'

Rowan's smile grew into an infectious grin. 'Well? What do you think?'

1814

In truth, Elizabeth did not know what to think. Rowan had described the ship to her in some detail: the 250-ton, three-masted brig, once an American whaler. The ship had been stripped of its whaling accoutrements, from the tripods and their hearths on deck to the hull platform for dissecting the whales. The stern cabins were enlarged and the crew quarters made more comfortable without compromising cargo space. The ship had also been given a good airing and a thorough scrub belowdecks with honing stones and vinegar, to rid it of the atmosphere of death—not a simple task. But now the reality had struck Elizabeth. She was as nervous as she was excited.

'Ahoy, there!' Wight Fairfowl, the shipwright, was doing his rounds before locking the yard down for the night. Normally it was the duty of the night watchman, but he was nowhere to be seen this evening, and so Fairfowl had completed the duty. 'Ahoy!' he called to the *Lillie*. 'Cast away now. You're trespassing.'

Rowan recognised the stooped back and ponytail in the shadows. 'Mr. Fairfowl, is that you, sir?'

'Aye. And who be you sir?'

'Tis Henry Colchester.' Rowan allowed the *Lillie* to edge along the jetty and the shipwright snatched the mooring rope offered, lassoing a bollard.

'Well, I'll be blowed. I got yer correspondence, sir, but wasn't expectin' yer for days yet.'

'Yes, well, we are ahead of schedule.'

'And this be yer sister, sir?' Fairfowl watched Elizabeth stand with some difficulty. 'Oh!' was all he managed to say, staring at Elizabeth's belly.

Wight Fairfowl was the most gracious host, insisting on sharing a hot supper of mutton and potatoes. The old shipwright was smitten with Elizabeth and listened to their stories, whether true or false. Elizabeth explained how she'd lost her husband to illness and now enjoyed her brother's support. Fairfowl listened in awe, his nose red from whisky and his cheeks ruby, as they shared tales of adventure and laughter.

That night, Elizabeth and Rowan slept soundly on board the *Lillie*, only to be woken at sunup by loud cussing and lewd seafaring language. Elizabeth pushed the hatch aside to be greeted by the *Marybeth*, their *Marybeth*, towering over the Lillie. The ship was being docked at a separate wharf next to the shipyard, in preparation for their voyage.

Chapter Thirty-Four

Spring 1817.
Hobart Town. Sullivan's Cove.

HMS *Assault's* anchors plunged into the River Derwent, crashing forty feet to the riverbed in an explosion of fine silt. Lieutenant Ernest Crabbe on the quarterdeck shielded his eyes from the late afternoon sun and gazed at the young settlement of Hobart Town. This assignment, to arrest the American murderer Rowan Craige, was his first visit to the southernmost colony, and he hoped the sight of His Majesty's frigate would not attract too much attention, as it had in Launceston, where half the town had greeted them. Crabbe harked back to that visit, seven days earlier, when they'd discovered that their prey had flown the coup, and he prayed that this time he would have better luck.

Crabbe was anxious—Hobart Town was a long shot. There was no evidence that the fugitives had travelled south, no witnesses to the fact. However, he surmised, if they did not escape Launceston or George Town by sea, where else could they depart from the penal island, other than from Hobart Town?

The lieutenant waited while a midshipman piped the ship, his whistle notifying the crew that their commander was going ashore. The signal echoed about the still waters of Sullivan's Cove, a distinct and inescapable sign that His Majesty's Royal Navy was in the harbour, and Crabbe made a quick calculation before stepping to the Jacob's ladder. He counted sixteen ships moored nearby. *Sixteen!* He would have his work cut out.

Battery Hill Shipyards

The *Marybeth* sat low in the water with her cargo of four hundred hogsheads of fine-grade whale oil in the hold, ready to be shipped to Calcutta. Rowan had several dozen bails of merino wool aboard also, but it was the oil that he trusted would be more lucrative. Already living below deck were five of the original twenty-five American crew from the *Lucy*. Rowan had given them permission to move on board, where the whalers were preparing for their new duties as seamen on a merchant trader.

Elizabeth and Rowan had taken a woollen rug, along with a stone bottle of sassafras ale—a non-alcoholic brew of sassafras, sarsaparilla, wintergreen and ginger—to high ground at the shipyard, where they could admire the *Marybeth*, take refreshment and talk in private.

'When will I meet this Captain Jaxon?' Elizabeth asked, taking pleasure in the commanding view of the slipways and the River Derwent.

'Captain Jaxon has been visiting whalers down south,' Rowan said, referring to the bay whalers with their sporadic camps along the coastal waters. 'He is scouting for crewmembers, and I am expecting him to return this evening.'

Rowan enjoyed a renewed confidence. He felt optimistic about their future and now experienced a joy he had not felt since he had heard the news of his wife Jessica being with child in Maryland, back in '13. Elizabeth's belly was at full bloom and Rowan estimated they had no more than a fortnight before their child entered this world.

A delivery cart caught their attention, trundling lazily down the pathway towards the slips, and Elizabeth recognised it as belonging to Montgomery, the grocer. 'Our preserves have arrived,' she said. 'We had better meet him.' Rowan helped Elizabeth to her feet and they made their way alongside the perimeter stonewall to the shipyards.

'Elizabeth,'—Rowan took Elizabeth by the wrist—'wait a moment.' Elizabeth turned to face her man. He appeared awkward—anxious, even.

'What is it?'

'I... ah...' Rowan looked ill at ease.

'Rowan, are you all right?'

'Will you marry me?' Rowan uttered suddenly. It was as if the words were conjured from thin air. Elizabeth took respite against the stone wall. She was utterly astonished, taken aback. Their lives had been so tumultuous of late, and she had not entertained the thought of marriage. Yet, masquerading as brother and sister had taken its toll. But now, with her tell-tale belly, scandal entered the equation and they would be wise to pose as man and wife, once at sea.

'You mean to pose as man and wife?'

'No—not pose. We should actually marry.'

'Rowan... you must not feel obligated... to marry, that is. I mean, we...'

'Elizabeth,' Rowan persisted, 'I love you. Will you marry me?'

'I... I...'

'Yes or no?'

'Yes'—Elizabeth stood up straight and threw her arms about Rowan's shoulders—'of course I will marry you.'

Rowan sighed with relief. 'Dear God, I thought you were going to say no. I *do* love you, Elizabeth.'

'And I you, Rowan Craige.' They hugged awkwardly, with Elizabeth's belly so large and firm, and shared a laugh at their folly.

Marcus Marriot stepped out from behind a stone archway. He had heard everything. 'Well, well, well. Ain't this sweet?'

'What?' Rowan was aghast that this shipyard employee, a ticket-of-leave man, no less, had been spying on them.

'"*I love you, Elizabeth,*"' Marriot mimicked in a high voice, his one good eye cold and black.

Rowan stepped forward. 'Why, you insolent...'

'Sergeant Marriot?' Elizabeth stepped between them. Suddenly she felt faint and reached out to support herself against the wall.

Rowan's jaw dropped. 'You know this man?'

Marriot intervened. 'She surely does, lover boy.'

Rowan's face reddened. He raised his fists but Marriot stepped aside. 'Oh I wouldn't be doin' thart... It's Rowan, ain't it?'

Elizabeth's breathing grew heavy. 'Leave him, Rowan.'

'Yes. You listen to yer little doxy there ... *Row... an.*'

'Damn your eyes.' Rowan threw a punch but Marriot was fast. He ducked, drawing a large knife from a sheath at his side.

'Rowan!' Elizabeth screamed. 'Please.'

'Who the hell do you think you are?' Rowan yelled at the assailant and stepped in front of Elizabeth, pushing her behind him.

'*Who the hell do I think I am?*' Marriot taunted, the point of his blade oscillating before him. Rowan's eyes darted about. This man had chosen his ambush well. Although they could see down the embankment and into the slips, the workers below could not see them. 'I'm yer new passenger,' Marriot grinned.

'What?'

'You 'eard me. I'm yer new passenger. The man what you'll be takin' with yer to the Orient. And in luxury, too, I might add.' Marriot was enjoying his goading. *He* was in charge now. *He was the man.* 'Tell yer lover 'ere how we met, Elizabeth bloody Eveleigh.'

Elizabeth fought back tears of anger. 'How... how did you end up here?' She asked quietly, trying to slow her breathing for the baby's sake.

'I got done, didn't I? Transported fer a pissy silver spoon. Done me time an' ended up 'ere at the slips with me ticket, buildin' your flamin' getaway ship. Now wha' are the chances o' that, eh?'

'Rowan was totally stunned. 'So you *do* know this man?'

Elizabeth felt her face flush. 'Yes, I know this blaggard. He was the sergeant who arrested me in Bristol. He was the wastrel who saw me sent to prison.'

'Blaggard? Wastrel? I'd go easy on the insults, Elizabeth Eveleigh. I've only got to open me trap, scream out "Escapee!" and the guards'll take yer back ter the cells.'

'You wouldn't.'

'Try me.'

Rowan tried diplomacy. 'What exactly do you want?'

'I don't know about you, matey,' Marriot tipped his head to one side and cast a lascivious eye over Elizabeth. 'Why, you could be an absconder, too, for all I care. Henry Colchester, my arse. But I can 'ave yer precious *wife* arrested. An' I see she's with child. Hmm.'

'What do you want?'

'Like I said, I'm yer passenger. I keep me trap shut and you take me to the Orient. Who knows?—I might make a good sailor.'

Rowan exchanged serious glances with Elizabeth. 'Leave us a moment, will you?' he asked Marriot.

'Fill yer boots. Go ahead an' have yer chinwag. But I'll be watchin' yer every move. Remember, I know yer history, Elizabeth Eveleigh.' Marriot obliged them with half a dozen paces.

Elizabeth spoke to Rowan in an urgent whisper. 'What will we do?'

'Do?' Rowan looked over Elizabeth's shoulder at Marriot playing with the knife blade. 'What will we do? We do not have much choice.'

'You cannot be seriously thinking of taking him with us! It would be aiding and abetting an absconder, for one thing.'

'He has a ticket. Fairfowl told me.'

'Yes, but not a full pardon.'

'Elizabeth'—Rowan took her by both arms—'I love you. I love you more than anything. You carry my child. I cannot allow anything to happen to you. Nothing. You understand? We will take him with us and deal with him later.'

Rowan kept Elizabeth behind him. He stepped forward once more and said in a quiet voice. 'We leave with the first tide, Marriot, on Sunday.'

'I know thart.'

'You are to ship on board after the midnight bell,' Rowan continued. 'You are to tell no one. Do you understand?' Marcus Marriot was almost surprised at how easily his threat had been accepted. 'I said—do you understand?'

'Aye, I understand.' Marriot met Rowan half way. He reached out with the knife, allowing its needlepoint to caress Rowan's chest. 'An' you take note, Row-an, you will not let me down. You or yer doxy...' Rowan's eye twitched. 'Or I will cut all three o' yer... you, then yer doxy and then yer wee bairn.'

Rowan did not flinch. He stood fast. 'Listen to me and listen good,' Rowan began, 'if you so much as...'

'Save it, hero. I'll only cut yer if'n yer betray me.' Marriot sheathed the blade. ''Til midnight, then, on Saterdee.' He made to walk back through the archway but then had a thought. 'Oh,' he said, looking over his shoulder, 'I gotta ask yer Elizabeth Eveleigh. Did any other doxies survive the wreck o' the *Magdalena*? It was the *Magdalena,* were it not?' Elizabeth ignored the question. 'Well o' course it were. I 'eard about it not long after it 'appened. Ship lost, huh? All hands drowned, so they thought. And now yer wash up before Sergeant Marriot once more. How convenient.'

'What are we going to do?' Elizabeth asked, once they were alone.

'Strangle the little sod.' Rowan wanted to laugh out loud at his suggestion, but the situation was too serious. 'Seriously. I would like to see him drown.'

'We are not killers, Rowan.'

'No,' Rowan sighed, 'we are not killers, but I agree with you now—we cannot take him with us. Not to the Orient.'

'Well?'

Rowan was pained for answers. 'Even if we tried to smuggle him out, I hear that redcoats search all ships leaving Hobart Town, looking for absconders. He would be the death of us.'

'Then we sail early,' Elizabeth said, 'ahead of schedule.'

Rowan agreed. 'But we will need a ruse to distract him. We need to find out where he lives, for a start.'

'He is permitted in the inns, is he not? I mean, he has a ticket of leave.'

'You mean...'

'Get the man drunk Saturday night.'

'It might work.'

'We have few options. I will wager a bet the man has a penchant for drink.'

'Oh?'

'I caught a hint of whisky on his breath.'

'Yes, well, I would not put it beyond the man's capabilities to steal a dram from Mr. Fairfowl's whisky bottle, now and again.'

The following days went swiftly; all the while, Rowan and Elizabeth maintained their false identities. Captain Jaxon had secured a full crew of twenty-three men. Sixteen were *Lucy's* familiar crew—Americans who had been working the docks since the whaler'd been sold from under them, months earlier. Jaxon had also secured the services of a Mauritian cook, whom Elizabeth was keen to meet.

Elizabeth and Rowan moved into their cabin and shared their first meal with Captain Jaxon, who took an immediate liking to Elizabeth. In Elizabeth the fatherly man saw his own daughter back in Bedford, although his Sarah was only fifteen. The Mauritian cook, Auberon, a self-proclaimed Creole, soon permeated the galley with aromas from his private spice box. The first meal for his masters was of fish he himself had caught off the dock, pan-fried with turmeric, garlic, mustard, ginger and onion, making Elizabeth nervous about its reception in her system, but the baby seemed to enjoy the change.

Elizabeth had planned well for her journey. She had a taste for decorating and soon settled into their stern cabin. For a surprise gift on Rowan's birthday she had purchased a mahogany apothecary chest, fully stocked. A captain of the marines had sold it to her, selling up to return to England, after a decade's service to King and country. Elizabeth also purchased a three-drawer oak chest with brass-bound edges and flush-fitted handles, along with a sailor's chest with rope handles that would double as her sewing and embroidery workbench. The soldier also parted with many items of crystal, silverware and dining china at a reasonable price, and his wife separated herself from a washstand with vanity mirror for one guinea.

Elizabeth and Rowan would, however, have to share bunk accommodations. These were fixtures already in place, as was the seat of ease installed in the cabin by the deceased whaling captain and his wife, so as not to have to share the head at the bow with a watchful crew.

Rowan removed the last of the crates from the *Jolly Mary* and brought them into their cabin, leaving Leblanc's cache where he felt it was safer for the moment, in situ in its secret cupboard. He supervised the remaining cargo; he had managed another hundred barrels of prime spermaceti at the extremely low price of eight shillings a gallon. This, too, was packed into the hold in an orderly way.

All the while, Marcus went about his business at the shipyards, observing the *Marybeth*'s every move.

Captain Frederick Jaxon moved onboard. Jaxon's accommodation was in an annexed cabin between a newly-fitted stateroom and Rowan and Elizabeth's cabin, recently built by the shipyard as part of the *Marybeth*'s improvements.

'I've managed to purchase some charts,' Jaxon told Rowan as he straightened out dog-ears on the well-used maps. The two men sat at the long, narrow table in the long and narrow stateroom, sampling a bottle of the captain's private stock of burgundy wine, recently purchased from wine merchants in the township. 'But,' Jaxon continued. 'My guess is that we will be afforded a better selection of charts in Sydney Town.' Rowan agreed, but clearly he had something else on his mind. 'Mr. Colchester, you look troubled.'

'Frederick,' Rowan took the liberty of refilling their glasses, 'we need to talk.'

Elizabeth unwrapped their portraits by artist Joseph Lycett and was admiring the artwork when Rowan stepped back into their cabin. 'Lovely, aren't they?' she commented. Rowan nodded vaguely. Elizabeth knew Rowan had been meeting with their captain, and although Rowan looked serious, he was not noticeably worried.

'Well?' Elizabeth asked quietly, as only thin panelling separated the cabins.

'Jaxon's a good man. I trust him and he *is* an American with a dislike of the English. Especially, I am pleased to announce, of Marcus Marriot.'

'Oh?'

'Yes. Jaxon has had many a run-in with the man, throughout the *Marybeth*'s rebuild. Our arrogant friend is not a well-liked man.' Elizabeth suddenly winced as a sharp kick in her belly reminded her that her time was near. 'Are you all right?'

'Yes. It's getting close. I just know it.'

Rowan expelled a deep sigh. He took Elizabeth in his arms and hugged her gently before dropping to his knees with an ear to her belly. 'Stay there another two weeks, little one,' he said to the unborn child. Rowan looked up into Elizabeth's large blue eyes. She seemed to grow more beautiful daily. But Elizabeth read an ill-concealed look of uncertainty on Rowan's face.

'Are you all right?'

'Yes.' Rowan jumped to his feet. 'Why?'

'You look worried. You are a doctor, remember? A surgeon. I could not be in better hands.'

'Yes, you've got that right.' Rowan made himself busy unpacking to avoid further eye contact. In truth, he was a ship's surgeon, apt at amputating limbs, but he had never delivered a baby before.

'So, when do we leave?'

'Tomorrow.'

Elizabeth caught her profile in the vanity mirror and felt nothing but love for the mystery bundle that grew inside her. But it was difficult to defeat her apprehension regarding the uncertainties involved in escaping this prison island. 'Tomorrow comes as a surprise.'

'And a surprise for Marriot, also.'

'I thought we had days. But you are right, of course.'

'The sooner we sail from here, the better.'

'How much, exactly, did you confide in our good Captain Jaxon?'

'As you and I discussed, I told Jaxon the truth... well, mostly the truth. I told him about Marriot in Bristol and that he was blackmailing you...'

'Oh, God. What did he say?'

'He was disgusted. Jaxon is American. "We are fellow Yankees," he told me. He is for emancipation and against slavery and he sees that what the English do here in Van Diemen's Land is nothing but an excuse for slavery. He was horrified that such a kind and beautiful person as yourself could be returned to prison, especially with child, and especially for a crime for which you are not guilty.' Elizabeth looked culpable. 'Well, he need not know the full truth,' Rowan whispered softly.

'Can we trust him?'

'Absolutely. I even offered him one hundred guineas, but he refused... refused downright... He felt insulted, in fact. I consider Frederick Jaxon a friend.'

The Battery Hill Shipyards.

Early evening.

Captain Frederick Jaxon waited silently in the shadows of Napoleon Lane at the top of the embankment behind the shipyards. The paddocks behind him were dark and deserted and the only sounds were of distant revelry at an inn somewhere on the point. He harboured feelings of restlessness about his reckless plan, but a sense of adventure also played on the American captain's mind. He stepped back into the concealing gloom of blackberry bushes and waited for Marcus Marriot to pass by.

The shipyard worker's workday had finished and Jaxon knew the man to be a creature of habit. Marriot would head directly to the Sandwich Islander, an inn in Sandy Bay, which Jaxon and Rowan had discovered that Marriott visited most nights, before retiring to his lodgings. Jaxon armed himself with Rowan's remaining pocket pistol. Sandy Bay was not a safe place, especially after Norfolk Island's prisoners were relocated there, following the closure of that penal settlement in the Pacific.

Footsteps approached. Jaxon peered between the brambles and recognised Marriot's lean, brawny figure passing through the moonbeams, casting an ominous glow over the lane.

'Mr. Marriot,' Jaxon said, stepping out from the shadows, feigning an incidental meeting. Marriot was at first defensive. His hand went for his dagger.

'Captain Jaxon!' Marriot's hand was smartly redirected to his boater, in respect for the older man. He was a head shorter than the lanky American with his beaver-skin pipe stack top hat.

'Your day's toil complete?' Jaxon asked in a friendly manner.

'Aye, sir.'

'I take it you are imbibing at the Islander this fine evening?'

Marriot turned his head slightly to accommodate his one good eye and scrutinise the captain. 'Aye, sir.' Marriot had seen the captain at the Sandwich Islander only the day before.

'I'm walking that way... about to imbibe at the good inn myself... to meet a friend, you see. Care if I walk with you?'

Marriot's face brightened; after all, it was not every day a sea captain took interest in Marcus Marriot. 'Certainly, sir.'

'Tell me, Mr. Marriot,' Jaxon asked, as the two men negotiated the reeds above the high-water mark along the esplanade 'besides your voyage to Van Diemen's Land, have you any experience as a seaman?'

'Not really, Captain.' Marriot was alert to their surroundings, as they walked through the night. To their right, the lanterns of the fishermen's shanties threw eerie shadows, and Marriot knew the esplanade was not the safest of places to walk alone. If it was not the fishermen one had to watch for over a shoulder, it was the fiercely defensive smugglers. Marriot knew that kegs of rum, thrown overboard from incoming ships, were dragged ashore on this very beach and carted up the same path to the inn. 'Have I had experience as a seaman?' Marriot said quietly. 'Why do you ask?'

'Well, you are to embark with me on the *Marybeth* to go to the Orient, are you not?'

Marriot stopped dead in his tracks, gripping the captain's arm. 'Who told yer this?'

'Why, Mr. Colchester, of course—your benefactor, sir.'

'My what?'

'Your benefactor. You need not be humble with me, Mr. Marriot. I know how you saved his sister Mary's life. Mr. Colchester told me everything, and how he is forever in your debt. And now you sail with us on the morrow. "It is the least thing I can do to help Mr. Marriot," Mr. Colchester told me.'

'Well I never... never thought 'ed tell yer, like.'

'Do not bother yourself, Mr. Marriot—your secret is safe with me.'

'My secret?'

Captain Jaxon looked about them as if he was about to divulge a government secret. 'You are a ticket man, are you not, the holder of a ticket of leave? You do not have a pardon, sir, so we must maintain the utmost discretion if you are to leave this dreadful place behind you.'

'Oh, yes, Captain Jaxon. Yes, sir.' Marriot's warped mind was overjoyed at this unexpected deception.

Aye... well, then, Elizabeth Eveleigh, ya secret's safe with me... for the present, he told himself, silently.

Rowan had watched the two dark figures stroll over the rise in Napoleon Lane and descend the steep hill leading to the esplanade before approaching Sandy Bay, and he knew they had a half-mile walk inland to the Sandwich Islander Inn at the crescent of the beach. So far, so good.

It was time to roust the crew under orders of the second mate, Mr. Luke Northeast. Northeast had also been promoted, from the position of third mate on the whaler *Lucy,* and only he, besides Jaxon, had an inkling of the plan afoot. Rowan and Elizabeth had met most of the crew in the preceding days and they'd liked what they'd seen. They were, after all, mostly American and a camaraderie bound them together on this godforsaken island. The crew had also languished in Hobart Town after their Yankee whaling captain died and most had made ends meet with dock work. But now... now, at last, they would feel the swell of freedom below their feet once more.

'How many are on board at the moment?' Elizabeth asked Rowan, back in their cabin.

'Five,' Rowan answered, looking over at the apothecary chest. 'Mr. Northwest has left for their lodgings. I told the man to be certain the crew returns to the ship in small groups over several hours, so as not to attract attention.' Rowan plucked the small opium bottle from the chest and held it to the lantern to ascertain how much remained, hoping he had given Jaxon enough laudanum for their plan. He sighed in silent prayer.

'It will be fine.' Elizabeth placed her hands on Rowan's shoulders. '*We* will be fine. Do not worry so.' But, in truth, Elizabeth feared for their safety. Rowan shook the bottle. 'I tripled the measure.'

'That is more than enough, is it not?'

'Enough to make him sleep till morning, yes, Elizabeth. If, that is, he does not taste it first.'

'He drinks the Indian overproof rum—you said so yourself. And you added a little treacle to disguise the tartness.'

'Yes,'—Rowan sighed again heavily—'that I did. We are in the hands of Providence and those of Captain Jaxon now.'

Captain Jaxon looked about the Sandwich Islander taproom. It was a small and grubby pit-sawn timber knock-up with a low beam ceiling, filled with smoke, foul odour and reprobates. The innkeeper at the counter offered the sea captain a sour nod of greeting before Jaxon made a show of looking about the inn for someone in particular. Jaxon made a point of shaking his head in disappointment. He turned to Marriot, whose sixpence spun on the counter as he showed signs of familiarity with the barkeep, a rather unattractive woman whom, Jaxon thought, had the head of a terrier.

'It appears the man I was supposed to meet this night has not shown,' Jaxon told Marriot. 'Would *you* care to join me?'

'Aye. Aye, I would Captain.' Marcus Marriot could already smell the coin within the loose purse strings of this friendly Yankee.

'Then save your sixpence, man, and we can share a bottle.' Jaxon flicked a silver crown at the barkeep. She snatched the coin mid-air like a toad might tongue a fly. 'A bottle of Indian, miss.' Jaxon smiled. The smile was not returned.

'You seem rather forward with the barkeep,' the captain said as the woman's back was turned.

'Aye. Yer could say that.' Marriot gave the captain the lascivious grin of a young stud who might boast of his conquests in public. 'Paisley Fleur she be. I ploughed 'er only this mornin'.' Marriot grinned, running his tongue over his bottom lip, and winked at Jaxon as if he was waiting for a congratulatory slap on the back. The captain humoured Marriot with an approving smile.

They sat at a booth by the fire, where Jaxon beguiled Marriot with tales of his travels, for Captain Frederick Jaxon was a man of the world. Marriot proved an attentive audience, captivated by the captain's tales of his travels from the Hudson River to Canton, some true, but many fabricated. It was an hour before Jaxon's target finally stepped outside to relieve himself. Ensconced in the darkness of the taproom and surrounded by drunkards, Captain Jaxon made certain no one was watching. It was a simple task. The coast was clear. Jaxon poured the phial of Rowan's strengthened laudanum into Marriot's tankard and sat back, staring into the fire.

The nightwatchman, old Jack Brown, sat on a wobbly chair outside his watchman's cottage at the slip yard. He filled his clay pipe, packing the Virginia tight with his tamper —carved to look like a lady's leg, from whale bone—before lighting the baccy with burning kindling plucked from his brazier. The night was clear and still, with the full moon spilling down the River Derwent as far as the eye could see. Brown enjoyed his pipe and thought of imbibing in a nip of rum to warm his cockles when he saw a distant figure skulk about in the darkness at the wharf. The figure was up to no good, he was certain. As he watched, the shape dissolved into the blackness, where the newly renovated *Marybeth* was docked. Jack, who had been given a full pardon the year before 'and by the way, never missed a trick,' studied the figure a moment before identifying Marcus Marriot, the ticket of leave convict who worked at the yard.

What are you up to, yer sneaky bastard? Jack muttered to himself. Jack had never liked Marcus Marriot. He was a stuck up bastard and, although he could not prove it, he was certain the man had stolen his tobacco the week before. He also suspected Marriot of stealing tools to sell on the black market, but he couldn't prove that, either.

Maybe tonight's me chance, the nightwatchman thought, and he took that swig of his rum anyhow, for he would need it. Jack was no spring chicken; he was in his sixties his mates guessed, but he didn't know exactly. He'd never known his mother, either. But this Marcus Marriot was a tough little bugger, ex-soldier and prisoner toughened at the sawpits.

Jack stepped back into his cottage to collect his musket and cosh. He would have to investigate. It was his responsibility, after all—what he was paid ten shillings a week for. Jack extinguished his pipe and started down the embankment to the wharf, where he saw *Marybeth's* stern cabin lantern burning brightly. The new owners of the renovated brig were on board, that he knew. Jack had met them days earlier and liked the young siblings.

It was still early when Rowan and Elizabeth heard the first light footsteps crossing the deck aft, over their cabin.

'They return already,' Elizabeth said, pulling a shawl over her shoulders. She lit a second lantern with a taper, resting it on the sanity cabinet and opened Rowan's fob watch. ''Tis just past the hour of nine.'

As the steps came from aft, Rowan suspected they belonged to the captain. A brief silence was interrupted by the steps approaching their cabin door from along the narrow passageway.

'Jaxon!' Rowan called out in a hushed voice. 'Frederick?' No answer. Rowan hurried to the door, throwing it open. 'Jesus!' Rowan stared down the muzzle of a loaded musket.

Marcus Marriot said nothing.

The hammer was cocked while his finger tickled the trigger. Marriot twitched the muzzle, only inches from Rowan's face. 'Move,' Marriot said, 'slowly.' Rowan stepped back into the cabin. Marriot followed, kicking the cabin door shut behind him with the back of his boot.

'What do you think you're doing?' Rowan demanded.

'Not too smart, are we Row-an?' The one-eyed tormentor enjoyed articulating Rowan's name. The nearest lantern underlit the assailant's face, making him appear a demon in some cheap pantomime. 'Think yerself a clever bastard, huh?' Marriot's anger was palpable.

'What are you talking about?'

'This!' Marriot screamed out. He heaved the empty opium vial at Elizabeth. The glass bounced off her arm, shattering against the cabin wall. They recognised it immediately. 'Tried to drug me... *your* Cap'n Jaxon.'

Elizabeth and Rowan were speechless.

'Oh... cat got yer tongue, eh?'

'Where's Captain Jaxon?' Elizabeth asked, managing to remain equitable.

'Asleep. Asleep in a bloody ditch somewheres, I'm thinkin'.'

1814

Rowan tried to remain calm, plotting his next move. 'What do you mean "asleep"?'

'Oh, don't act all high and firkin' mighty with me, Rowan. I swapped drinks, didn't I? The stupid bastard drank the lot. Good trick putting treacle in it... more's the pity, cos it tasted oright at first. That is, until me mate Paislee Fleur, barkeep at the Islander, said she saw 'im spike me drink when I was takin' a piss... So when the cap'n wasn't lookin', a doxy changed 'em tankards around. Yer won't be seein' 'im no time soon.'

'You lie.'

'Oh, do I?' Marriot became indignant at the suggestion. 'Stand next to yer whore.' Marriot waved the musket at Elizabeth, and Rowan stepped between them. Marriot bowed his head under a low beam...

And Elizabeth saw her chance. She threw her shawl over the nearest lantern. The cabin darkened. Marcus stepped back to take aim, but Rowan threw a punch. The gun discharged in a deafening explosion within the confined space. With the bullet buried in a beam, Marriot swung the pistol like a club. But his swing was wild and connected with Rowan's shoulder. Rowan leapt forward. Marriot sidestepped, unsheathing his knife. He lunged at Elizabeth, the blade puncturing her chest below the sternum. The knife fell. Elizabeth gasped and clutching her bloodied belly, she fell to her knees.

'No!' Rowan screamed. 'No!' He rushed to Elizabeth's side. Marriot saw the blood and panicked. He unhooked the ceiling lantern and hurried onto the deck, unarmed. Nightwatchman Jack Brown had seen and heard everything, standing on the dock, watching through the stern windows. He was horrified. Aghast, he knew he had to react smartly. Jack followed the swaying lantern light amidships. Marcus Marriot was back on deck.

'Stand fast, yer mongrel!' Jack levelled his musket at Marriot on the gangway. Marriot turned and ran. Jack fired, but the ball whistled by Marriot's ear as he disappeared from sight.

'Elizabeth!' Rowan used his neckerchief to staunch her bleeding.

'I'll be fine.' Elizabeth pushed Rowan away. 'You must get to him.'

'Elizabeth... you're hurt.'

'I'll be fine. Go.'

'But Elizabeth...'

'Damn it, Rowan, you must catch him before he goes to a magistrate.'

'I'll be right back.' Rowan ran along the passage and onto the main deck. He spun about to the gangway.

Nothing.

The nightwatchman's head appeared over the gunwale. He aimed his musket at Rowan.

'Tis me, Jack!' Rowan shouted. 'Henry Colchester.'

Jack was visibly shaking. 'I saw the bastard. 'Twas Marcus Marriot.'

'Where did he go?' But before Jack could answer, Rowan saw lantern light shifting the shadows on the companionway below. Rowan scuttled after Marriot, dropping the seven feet to the orlop deck. Beyond the nearest bulkhead, the lantern pitched black shapes in scattered directions.

'You're going nowhere, Marriot!' Rowan raged.

Nothing but the sound of panicked steps.

Rowan rushed after the dancing flame. It descended further, towards the hold. Lantern light silhouetted the bails of wool, shifting shapes around the barrels of oil. Rowan trod warily while all about him were moving shadows, conjured demons and sinister visions. Suddenly Marriot stopped at the hatchway to the lower companionway, his legs spread apart and the lantern swinging in one hand as he faced Rowan. Rowan was twelve feet away. 'You can't get out of here, Marriot.'

Marriot's voice was breaking. His body shook. 'Neither will you, or yer bitch with child.'

Rowan stepped forward slowly, desperately calculating his next move.

'You're trapped, Marriot.' Marriot held the lantern high. Rowan was beyond reasoning. He took another step forward. Suddenly Marriot heaved the lantern down the companionway and into the main hold below. The glass shattered. The oil spilt and the flames spread on contact.

'No!'

The result was immediate. The fire swept over the straw packing. The greasy casks ignited instantly. There would be no stopping the conflagration. Rowan attacked. Marriot tried evasive action. But Rowan rammed him, tackling him with such force that both men somersaulted down into the hold. Marriot's body cushioned Rowan's fall. The man was winded, but powerful. Marriot twisted, rolling on top of Rowan, pinning him to the deck and punched... once... twice.

The nearest barrels burst, oil pouring from their bungholes. Flames licked after the spillage. The fire spread wildly. The heat was horrendous. Marriot managed a third strike before Rowan's knee jerked into his groin, but Marriot had twice the strength. He pinioned Rowan's throat with both hands and started to choke him.

Flames now encircled them. They would be trapped and burnt alive in seconds. Marriot's grip tightened and Rowan felt consciousness slipping away. Marriot leant in close for the kill. Rowan smelt his hatred. He struggled to breath; he wrenched one hand free and rammed his finger into Marriot's good eye. The result was instant. Marriot was blinded and the pain was agonizing. He released his grip in order to tear Rowan's hand from his face. Marriot's guard was down and Rowan managed to roll from under him, while Marriot groped about blindly.

Rowan clambered awkwardly up the companionway, now taken by the flames. As he hit the orlop deck, a loud explosion threw him across the boards. The steps behind him collapsed. Rowan did not look back. He crawled on his hands and knees through smoke and flames, finally collapsing on the main deck.

'Mr. Colchester!' Jack Brown yelled from the gangway over the blazing timbers. 'Hurry, sir!'

'Elizabeth!' Rowan cried out coughing for breath.

'Who, sir?'

Elizabeth. I must get to Elizabeth.

The fire belowdeck had taken hold. It was completely out of control. Flames reached up from the bows of the ship, gasping for oxygen before storming between the decks. The night sky filled with sparks and smoke, as if at some crazy Guy Fawkes celebration. Rowan stood awkwardly. He watched, horrified, as the flames, fuelled by thousands of gallons of whale oil, combusted on the deck below, and raced towards the stern cabins.

Elizabeth!

Rowan stumbled across the quarterdeck, shouldering the buckled door open. Stepping into the smoke-filled passageway he called Elizabeth's name. There was no answer. He felt his way along the panelled walls, blinded by the smoke until the flames pursued him, lighting the way.

Elizabeth lay where she had been stabbed, lying in a pool of her own blood. A pall of thick black smoke hovered above her.

'Elizabeth!'

Elizabeth's eyes were hooded. She bled profusely. Rowan scooped his arms beneath her. She hooked her arms weakly about his neck.

'Hang on!' Rowan hefted Elizabeth from the cabin floor. He became aware of shouting from the dock. Rowan heard cabin windows popping with the heat, only to let in fresh air, fuelling the fire. Rowan turned to their only escape—the passageway. Hooking one boot about the door, he jerked it towards him. But the renewed air supply created a firestorm. Flames swirled about them as in a wood-fired oven, feeding on the wooden panels, the furnishing and the bedding. With Elizabeth almost unconscious in his arms, Rowan wheeled about on the spot. Where there was no fire there was smoke. Choking acrid, black smoke.

Rowan was weakening. He battled to breathe. He struggled to hold Elizabeth. They were trapped!

Rowan fell back against the cabin wall, exhausted. Never had he thought he would die like this...

Then Rowan heard the shattering of glass. The remaining cabin windows were broken, one by one. A face appeared, then another, and another. 'Mr. Colchester!' a man's voice yelled over the splintering and shattering of ship's timbers.

'Here, sir! Over here!'

Through the smoke, Rowan saw salvation. Members of his crew had smashed the windows. They frantically ran planks from the dock into the cabin.

'Hurry, sir!'

But the blaze leapt ahead, rushing the windows, greedy for air. Window glass melted as more frames burst across the ceiling. They moved through to the upper deck and assailed the superstructure, devouring the masts and the rigging. Rowan made one last ditch effort. He rushed the open window. Hands groped for Elizabeth and she was lifted through the scalding framework to safety. Other strong arms caught Rowan, and he was dragged unceremoniously out through the broken windows and onto a plank, where they were both helped to safety away from the burning ship.

'Elizabeth!' Rowan knelt beside Elizabeth who was lying on the grass. She was weak, but another man had already wrapped the wound.

'The bleeding's stopped Mr. Colchester.' It was Auberon, the Mauritian cook. 'She's lucky, sir; it is only a flesh wound.' The giant Creole looked at Rowan and started slapping Rowan on the head. 'Yer on fire, Mr. Colchester.' It was then Rowan smelt the stink of his own singed hair.

'Over here, you lot!' Jack Brown screamed for help. Auberon joined the crew, and while some axed the mooring ropes, others used oars and poles to shove the burning ship out on the retreating tide before the dock became engulfed. Already the sail and rope makers' sheds lining the dock area were blistering.

Elizabeth's lungs filled with the fresh night air. She finally looked up at Rowan as the night sky all about lit up like day. "*Marybeth*?' Elizabeth was more upset about losing their ship than her own situation.

'Elizabeth.'

'I'm fine... *Marybeth*?'

Rowan shook his head. 'Lost.'

A shrill and panicked voice grabbed everybody's attention. 'There's someone still on the ship!'

Marriot's blackened face appeared. As the ship drifted away from the wharf, the eye of the ill-fated man stared back from a break in the timbers near the waterline. Marriot was alive, trapped in the hold with the raging fire. He tore at the planking like a crazed man, shredding his fingernails and tearing the skin from his fingers, but the opening was only large enough for his head.

'Help!' he screamed—an agonising, piercing scream. 'H-help me! For God's sake help me!'

The handful of crew stood about in horrified silence, the heat from the intense fire forcing everyone back. There was nothing anyone could do to save the man. Rowan joined the gathering on the dock. He drew as close as he dared, shielding his face with his arm. As he watched, Marriot caught his eye. Marriot was trying to speak when his body caught fire. His smoking hands with peeling skin clawed at the opening in a futile attempt for freedom, while his face blistered into flames. Marriot expelled a final screech, like some wild animal, and then faded into the smoke and fire. For those present, the terror in Marriot's black eye would haunt many in their nightmares for years.

'Marines are comin'.'

They all turned. The gates to the shipyard were forced open and dozens of onlookers from the neighbourhood hurried down the path. But more disturbing for Rowan was the sight of uniformed marines, gathering at the top of the embankment. Lit by the fire, a dozen soldiers could be seen regrouping. For Rowan, it was the burning of Washington all over. Like silhouetted toy soldiers in their red coats with white britches and shakos, they fixed bayonets on the end of their long muskets and prepared for the order to march quickstep in two lines towards the unfolding disaster. Lieutenant Crabbe pushed through the ranks. He surveyed the scene and could not believe what he was witnessing.

'Please tell me that is not the *Marybeth*,' he told the sergeant of the guard, now beside him drifting a spyglass over the ship. It had been less than an hour since his informant had told him that a merchant ship named the *Marybeth* was preparing to sail from this very wharf. More importantly, it was owned by an American who fit Rowan Craige's description. The sergeant could just make out enough of the stern plate to confirm the worst.

'I'm sorry to say it, Lieutenant, but that burning wreck *is* the *Marybeth*.'

'Hell's teeth. Rally these men at the double.'

Rowan smelt trouble. 'Sir, Mr. Brown.'

'Jack, sir,' the nightwatchman said. 'Call me Jack.'

'Jack. I am forever in your debt,' Rowan said with haste. 'But I need to ask you one more favour.'

'Anything, Mr. Colchester.'

'My sister and I are still on board the ship.'

'Sir? But...'

'Please, I beg of you. Tell anyone who asks that we both perished in the fire.'

Jack looked to the roaring flames. The heat was intense. They would all have to move further back. The nightwatchman caught a glimpse of the soldiers scrambling down the embankment.

'By chance, when yer say "if'n anyone asks", do yer, per chance, mean them soldiers, Mr. Colchester.'

'Yes... please.'

The nightwatchman's eyes sparkled mischievously in the fiery light. 'I owe them bastards nuthin'. It'll be me pleasure, sir. Best be off with yer, then.'

'Thank you. You are a kind gentleman. And pass the message on to the others. I know they will understand.'

Rowan called to two of his American crewmembers waiting to help nearby. 'You two.'

'Aye, sir.'

'Follow me. Get Miss Colchester belowdeck on the sloop.' Rowan gestureded to the *Lillie,* tied up at the wharf thirty yards away. 'Hurry, now.'

1814

With the sail and rope sheds masking their escape, Rowan hurried the thirty yards east along the shoreline, where he leapt aboard the *Lillie*. The two crewmembers hefted Elizabeth on board, securing her below. Rowan hoisted the mainsail and the fresh breeze, drawn by the fire, billowed out the canvas.

'Go, go…. Take her out. Fast as you can, lads.' The men were apt sailors. One took the helm while the other secured the ropes. *Lillie* tugged at her moorings. Jack Brown snatched an axe and hacked the ropes.

'Go!' The watchman yelled, looking over his shoulder for trouble. 'Make haste, lads, fer gaud's sake.'

The *Lillie's* sail filled into a magnificent crescent and immediately pulled away the sloop from the shore, and she was swallowed by darkness—all eyes were on the fire.

Lieutenant Crabbe leading the marines through the slip yard drew his sabre and pulled his coat over his head for protection against the heat. He ran along the wharf by the burning ship and singled out Jack Brown.

'You!'

'Sar.'

'Who are you?'

'Night watchman for the yard, sar.'

'Where's the owner of this ship?'

'Ship, sar?'

'That burning ship, man!' the lieutenant screamed impatiently.

'Why he's…' Jack Brown shook his head. He knew he would have to be convincing. He overreacted to the horror he had witnessed. His bottom lip quivered.

'Well? Speak, damn you.'

'Oh, sar… oh dearie me, sar…, 'twas an awful sight—a sight I never want to witness ever again.'

'What?'

'Awful. The screamin', the cries fer 'elp, sar. Cries no one could do nuthin' about.'

'For Christ's sake, man, what are you talking about?'

'The owners of that vessel, sar.'

'Well?'

'They's on board, Lieutenant.'

Lieutenant Crabbe strained to peer into the flames of a once fine vessel being reduced to ashes. 'They were on board? They did not escape?'

'No, sar. That's what I'm tryin' to tell yer. The screams... I'll never forget them.'

Jack Brown took his hat from his head and, with the utmost respect, said, 'We did everything to try an' save 'em, sar. Everythin' possible. But them flames, sar. Well, yer can see fer yourself.'

There was little anyone could do but watch the *Marybeth* burn to the waterline. Lieutenant Crabbe sat with his men on the embankment. He was angry with himself. He had failed Governor Macquarie—so close, yet so far.

Jack Brown was proud of himself. He was one up on the constabulary that had seen him hard done by in the past. From his cottage he and the American crewmembers watched the dying flames, as the burnt out hull settled on the riverbed. Here, the gathering became a celebration of sorts. 'There will be an inquiry,' Jack Brown told them. 'They'll be questioning witnesses,' he said. 'But they'll find nought. The owners of the Marybeth lost their lives in a disastrous accident. Agreed?'

They all agreed. And the rum was passed around.

CHAPTER THIRTY-FIVE

The *Lillie* sailed the Derwent estuary along the path to freedom, led by a full, round moon. The water about them sparkled like jewels spilt across the surface. Less than an hour after their escape, the sound of a newborn echoed across the water. The baby was two weeks premature, the birth brought forward by trauma, but Elizabeth was in good hands. Rowan's textbook delivery—his first—made for a successful birth, and six-pound Pollyanna took her first breaths in the hold of the escaping sloop.

'Pollyanna,' Elizabeth held the baby to her bosom. She was beautiful, angelic. Rowan wrapped his coat about mother and child.

'Where are we headed?' Elizabeth finally asked, when Pollyanna slept soundly.

'The lads know of a Yankee whaling station on an island called Bruny,' Rowan said of the two *Marybeth* crewmembers who had helped them escape. 'They know some of the men. We'll be safe there until we find a ship to sail home.'

'Home?'

'America, of course.'

Elizabeth's eyes filled with tears: the trauma, the emotions, the stress. 'Are you all right?' Rowan asked.

'Oh, Rowan. We've lost everything we had so carefully saved.' Rowan laughed. Elizabeth grew annoyed. 'What are you laughing for? It's serious ...'

'We have each other, Elizabeth, do we not? And a healthy daughter?'

'Yes, but...'

'Do not stress so.' Rowan placed a finger on Elizabeth's lips, then leant in to kiss her. When he thought he could tease her no longer, Rowan picked up a small crow bar and wedged the boards free from Captain Leblanc's hidden cupboard in the bow. He pulled the old worn carpetbag free and, prising the clip open, he presented it to Elizabeth. 'As the French would say, "*Voilà!*" Golden guineas, escudos and Louies stared back. 'I thought it safest to leave the bag here until we were about to sail. Rowan knelt closer to his sleeping daughter and whispered in her ear, 'Happy birthday, Pollyanna, our little darling.'

THE END

EPILOGUE

Nightwatchman Jack Brown was more than surprised when the man he knew as Captain Jaxon called him aside at the shipyard one day, two weeks later. 'I'm sorry I missed all the action,' Jaxon told old Jack. Of course, Jack knew that the captain had been away with the demons the night of the great escape, unconscious with Madam Laudanum, drugged by Marcus Marriot, no less. The two men looked to the *Marybeth's* blackened remains above the water line as a work crew sawed at her timbers, to clear the river channel where she'd sunk. A moment passed in silence and then Jaxon finally handed the nightwatchman an envelope. 'What's this?' Jack asked.

'Open it.'

Jack tore the paper and stood gobsmacked. For the first time in his life, he held a hundred pounds in his hand—five twenty-pound notes. Enclosed with the money was a note. It simply read, 'Thank you!' and was signed, 'H.'

Jack Brown looked at the American sea captain. 'From Henry Colchester, huh?'

'Aye. He wanted you to know how much he appreciated what you did for him.'

'Oh, it was nuthin'. I'd lie to those bastards anytime. Can I ask where he is and if'n his sister is in good health?'

'Yes you can, Jack. Miss Mary is fine and she had a baby girl. And by now... well...' Jaxon looked down the estuary. 'They'd be in New Zealand, I should imagine.'

'New Zealand. Well, I never. And you, sir. What will you do?'

'I'll find a ship to captain soon, Jack. Soon, I hope.'

Elizabeth, Rowan and baby Pollyanna sailed for America on the *Plymouth*, a fully laden whaler returning to New Bedford. They arrived in March 1818 and immediately married. Rowan never did manage to travel to the Orient, but with the money they'd acquired they bought a merchant store in New York specialising in apothecaries and homewares and eventually gained a reputation for having the best stock of toys in America. As Pollyanna matured she showed an interest in medicine and was pressured by many to become a nurse. But with determined parents like Rowan and Elizabeth, she studied medicine and became the first female doctor in America. She would die a wealthy woman in 1902. Rowan's life was taken unexpectedly by yellow fever in 1838, when he was only fifty-two, but Elizabeth Craige—née Eveleigh—lived to read of the Cessation of Transportation in Tasmania in 1853, to witness President Abraham Lincoln's Emancipation Proclamation and his eventual assassination in 1863, and, at last, the abolishment of slavery in 1865. Elizabeth died of old age in 1879 at the age of eighty-four.

Captain Amos Leblanc stepped from the hidden cave to see HMS *Assault* in full sail on the horizon, heading north to Sydney Town. He was the sole survivor of his clan on Bull Seal Island. The British Marines took much evidence of the wrecking activities back with them and torched the rest. Leblanc became a Robinson Crusoe, living on shellfish and fresh water; there was not much else left behind. At the end of his first week, he ventured to the beach where the

Magdalena had been wrecked and was astounded to find a survivor, who had hidden when the marines scoured the beach. Sally Fetter told the captain how she had survived, washed overboard from her pen on the deck. Leblanc told Sally how he had survived a similar disaster, a fabrication she readily believed. The two lived in a cave for some months; however, one morning sealers saw their campfire and came ashore. Unfortunately for Leblanc, he was recognised by one of the men—Albert Cook, a man he had cheated in Port Dalrymple three years earlier. Cook stabbed Leblanc and sailed away with Sally Fetter. She never made it to Madagascar, but found her pirate heaven in Bass Strait. She lived to tell her story, but died of the pox in 1821 on Flinders Island, Bass Strait.

Have no doubt, Van Diemen's Land and the Bass Strait islands in the first decades of settlement were lawless, violent and dreadful places. The cold, dark actions of the sealers, absconders, deserters, and corrupt officials were as heinous as the crimes of the vilest pirates and buccaneers who'd sailed the seas in the centuries before them.

While it is difficult to imagine, the earliest convicts brought to Sullivan's Cove had no accommodations—not even tents. (Sullivan's Cove was named after John Sullivan, the undersecretary at the Colonial Office in London.) These first Van Diemen's Land settlers were required to make do the best they could. As famine threatened the remote colony, some prisoners were given muskets and ammunition and sent into the bush for two or three days at a time, to hunt. Most returned. Some became more and more proficient as hunters, spending longer and longer in the wilderness, learning the layout of the land: where there was fresh water, where there were caves to hide in, and eventually they did not return. Many of these men became bushrangers, some better natured, but most ruthless.

The colony's early years were rife with corruption, desolation and depravity. The streets of Hobart Town and its environs early in the 1800s were dangerous places, even in daylight. Many crimes went unsolved or unpunished. Backyard inns of wattle and daub, selling rum, gin or ale, were run by prostitutes working for the officers.

There is no concrete evidence that wreckers or moonlighters operated in Bass Strait. Such criminals were, however, a menace in Cornwall and Devon, although descendants will deny this fact. The truth is, occasionally falsified lights were lit to misguide ships onto rocks during stormy nights. The more common problem for the excise men was the hoards from nearby villages who descended the cliffs from the coastal villages to pillage the flotsam and jetsam washing ashore amongst the wreckage.

For the sake of a good yarn, I brought Launceston's development forward one decade. Prior to 1820, it was a frontier shanty town.

About The Author

Craig Godfrey

Craig Godfrey was born in Hobart in 1952 and traveled extensively, which has given him many of the experiences and escapades he so enjoys putting into print. These include working in the early 70s as a chef for a restaurant owned by figures from Sydney's criminal underbelly, and cooking in Darwin when cyclone Tracy destroyed the city.

After decades in the hospitality industry—and nearly forty years after opening the Drunken Admiral Seafood Restaurant—Craig decided to hang up his apron and leave family at the helm in order to indulge in his other passion: writing fiction. And with Tasmania's fascinating past he has plenty to write about.

Craig loves nothing more than to weave adventure, mystery and mayhem together, incorporating colourful characters from all walks of life. He has published eighteen previous titles, and is currently writing the seventh book in a series called *Shadow Hunter*, in which Caspian Hunter travels to Van Diemen's Land from Birmingham in 1855 to take a position as second in charge of Hobart Town's fledgling police department. His adventures around the waterfront inns are boundless.

The chef of a Hobart waterfront restaurant called the Hook, Line and Sinker is the protagonist of a series set in modern times. He and his partner, the assistant curator of the Tasmanian Museum, continuously find themselves in trouble, whether it be solving the disappearance of rare art works on Tasmania's west coast, caught in hang-glider dog fights over the Caribbean Sea, finding their way out of the myriad of tunnels under the battlefields of Flanders, or being imprisoned by antiquity thieves in Venice. Number five in the series has recently been completed. Other action-adventure novels are set in 1830s Van Diemen's Land, the Tasmanian wilderness of the 1940s, and during a murder investigation in Sydney and Darwin in 1974.

In the 1990s Craig independently shot two feature films: a murder mystery set in Southern Tasmania, which aired on television, and a splatter comedy still available online. He wrote, produced and directed both.

Craig's life has been busy and interesting, to say the least.

BELLERAPHON'S

CHAMPION

BY

JOHN DANIELSKI

Deep within each man, lies the secret knowledge of whether he is a stalwart or a coward. Three years an un-blooded Royal Marine, 1st Lieutenant Thomas Pennywhistle will finally "meet the lion," protecting HMS Bellerophon at the Battle of Trafalgar.

Not only will Pennywhistle be responsible for the lives of 72 marines aboard Bellerophon but their direction will fall entirely on his shoulders since his fellow Marine officers consist of a boy, a card shark, and a dying consumptive. If he has what it takes to command, it will take everything he's got.

In the course of battle, he will encounter marvels and terrors; from valiant foes to women performing miracles, from the skill of acrobats to the luck of the ship's cat, from a dead man still full of fight to a coward who has none. He and his marines will meet enemy élan will with trained volleys and disciplined bayonets. Most of all, he will meet himself; discovering just how dark his true nature really is.

Europe will be changed forever by Trafalgar, and so will Pennywhistle.

PENMORE PRESS
www.penmorepress.com

The Captain's Nephew

by

Philip K.Allan

After a century of war, revolutions, and Imperial conquests, 1790s Europe is still embroiled in a battle for control of the sea and colonies. Tall ships navigate familiar and foreign waters, and ambitious young men without rank or status seek their futures in Naval commands. First Lieutenant Alexander Clay of HMS Agrius is self-made, clever, and ready for the new age. But the old world, dominated by patronage, retains a tight hold on advancement. Though Clay has proven himself many times over, Captain Percy Follett is determined to promote his own nephew.

Before Clay finds a way to receive due credit for his exploits, he'll first need to survive them. Ill-conceived expeditions ashore, hunts for privateers in treacherous fog, and a desperate chase across the Atlantic are only some of the challenges he faces. He must endeavor to bring his ship and crew through a series of adventures stretching from the bleak coast of Flanders to the warm waters of the Caribbean. Only then might high society recognize his achievements —and allow him to ask for the hand of Lydia Browning, the woman who loves him regardless of his station.

PENMORE PRESS
www.penmorepress.com

Taken to The Grave

BY

Craig Godfrey

This adventure continues....

Nineteenth Century Van Demonian sleuth, Caspian Hunter, is a colonial lawman deeply immersed in the life and crimes of Hobart Town, where convicts transported from Mother England form a majority of the population. Caspian and his decidedly unconventional associates are sworn to uphold the law where lawlessness is almost a way of life.

The fledgling colony includes newly pardoned convicts – 'ticket of leave men' – on a sort of parole. Misfits and unsavoury characters come this remote outpost of the British Empire to get as far away as possible from whatever lives they seek to leave behind.

But by the middle of the century, free settlers are arriving in ever greater numbers from Britain. Hobart Town is blessed with one of the world's most beautiful deep-water harbours, so it also attracts sailors and whalers. And it is rapidly becoming prosperous. There are inns aplenty, and a growing number of enterprising ladies are skilled in the arts of making sailors, whalers, gentlemen and even lawmen briefly happier and certainly poorer. This is Caspian's town.

A murder most foul committed with the most blunt of instruments, a hot flat iron, leads Caspian to the prison hell of Port Arthur, traveling on a railway man-powered by convict slaves, and an illicit liaison with a British Army officer's wife. The motive for murder: a diamond worth a king's ransom, hidden in a most incongruous place.

PENMORE PRESS
www.penmorepress.com

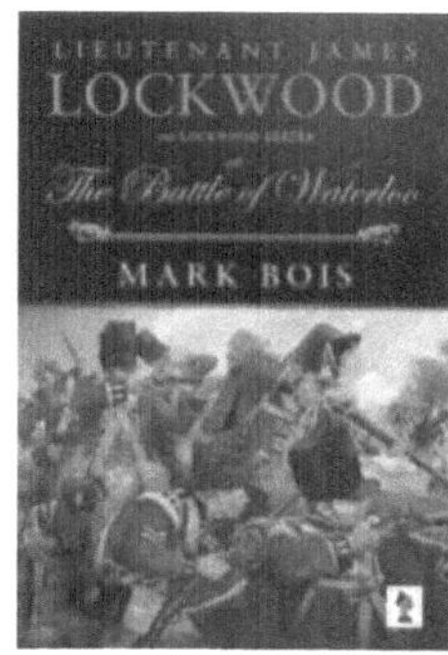

Lieutenant James Lockwood

By

Mark Bois

"Captain Barr desperately wanted to kill Lieutenant Lockwood. He thought constantly of doing so, though he had long since given up any consideration of a formal duel. Lockwood, after all, was a good shot and a fine swordsman; a knife in the back would do. And then Barr dreamt of going back to Ireland, and of taking Brigid Lockwood for his own."

So begins the story of Lieutenant James Lockwood, his wife Brigid, and his deadly rivalry – professional and romantic – with Charles Barr. Lockwood and Barr hold each other's honor hostage, at a time when a man's honor meant more than his life. But can a man as treacherous as Charles Barr be trusted to keep secret the disgrace that could irrevocably ruin Lockwood and his family?

Against a backdrop of famine and uprising in Ireland, and the war between Napoleon and Wellington, showing the famous Inniskilling Regiment in historically accurate detail, here is a romance for the ages, and for all time.

"... Bois' meticulous research and command of historical detail makes this novel a must read. He sets the standard for research and understanding... and the audience will demand more novels from this new author. Historical fiction welcomes Mark Bois with open arms." – Lt. Col. Brad Luebbert, US Army

PENMORE PRESS
www.penmorepress.com

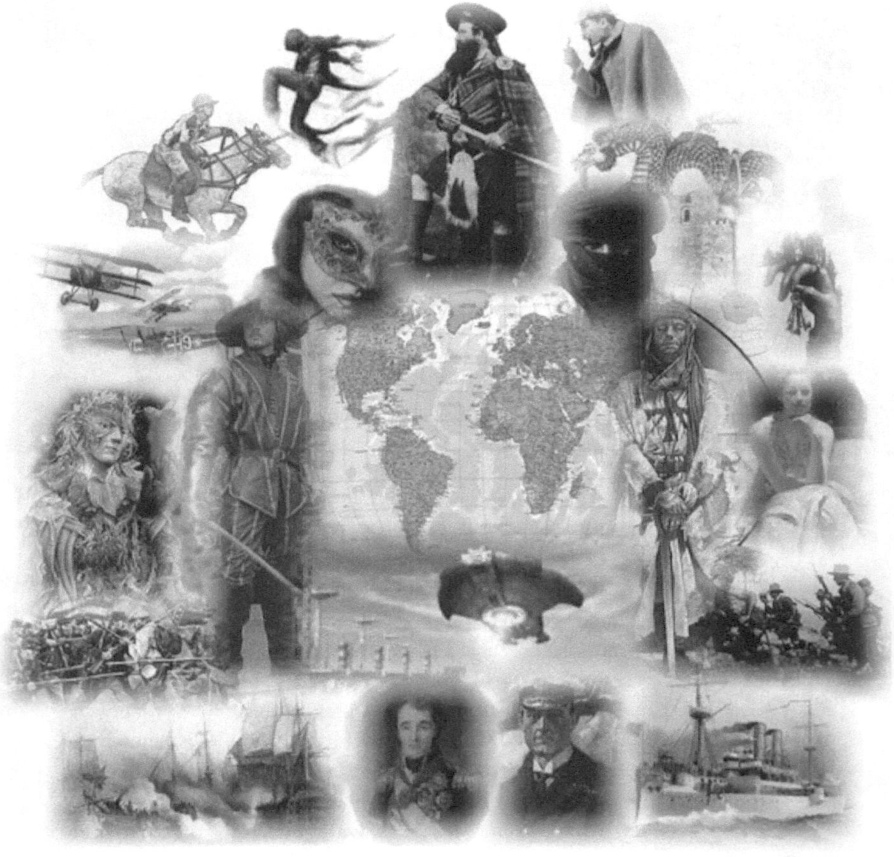

Penmore Press

Challenging, Intriguing, Adventurous, Historical and Imaginative

www.penmorepress.com